Bertolt Brecht

HIS LIFE, HIS ART
AND HIS TIMES

By Frederic Ewen

THE PRESTIGE OF SCHILLER IN ENGLAND

THE POETRY AND PROSE OF HEINRICH HEINE

BIBLIOGRAPHY OF EIGHTEENTH-CENTURY ENGLISH LITERATURE

*

with David Ewen

MUSICAL VIENNA

*

with Phoebe Brand and John Randolph
dramatic adaptations of

JAMES JOYCE'S A PORTRAIT OF THE ARTIST AS A YOUNG MAN

THOMAS MANN'S THE MAGIC MOUNTAIN

Bertolt BRECHT

HIS LIFE, HIS ART AND HIS TIMES

by Frederic Ewen, 1899 –

The Citadel Press

NEW YORK

FIRST EDITION

Copyright © 1967 by Frederic Ewen

Published by Citadel Press, Inc., 222 Park Avenue South,
New York, N. Y. 10003. Published simultaneously in
Canada by George J. McLeod Limited, 73 Bathurst St.,
Toronto 2B, Ontario. Manufactured in the United States
of America by The Haddon Craftsmen, Inc., Scranton, Pa.

Library of Congress catalog card number: 67-25655

PICTURE CREDITS:

Bertolt Brecht Archiv; Berliner Ensemble; Vera Tenschert;
Percy Paukschta; Willy Saeger; Martha Swope; Culver Pictures,
Inc.; Repertory Theatre of Lincoln Center, Leonard Baskin.

For Miriam, Petra, and Joel

Contents

9

CONTENTS

List of Illustrations

Acknowledgments

The author wishes to thank the publishers and authors listed below for permission to quote from copyright materials:

SUHRKAMP VERLAG and STEFAN BRECHT: Bertolt Brecht, *Gedichte*; *Prosa*; *Schriften zum Theater*; *Stücke*; *Versuche*; *Materialen*; *Dreigroschenbuch*. Copyright © 1949, 1953, 1955, 1957, 1959, 1960, 1961, 1964 by Suhrkamp Verlag, Frankfurt am Main; copyright © 1965 by Stefan S. Brecht.

ALFRED A. KNOPF, Inc.: Thomas Mann, *Last Essays,* translated by R. and C. Winston and T. J. Stern. Copyright Alfred A. Knopf, Inc. New York, 1959.
Arthur Waley, *Translations from the Chinese*. Copyright Alfred A. Knopf, Inc., New York, 1941.
Arthur Waley. *The No-Plays of Japan*. Copyright Alfred A. Knopf, Inc., New York, 1922.

VERLAG DER ARCHE, Zürich: H. O. Münsterer, *Bert Brecht: Gespräche und Erinnerungen*. Erinnerungen aus den Jahren 1917-22 mit Photos, Briefen und Faksimiles. Copyright Verlag der Arche Peter Schifferli, Zurich, 1963.

CLAASSEN VERLAG, Hamburg: Heinrich Mann, *Essays*. Copyright Claassen Verlag, Hamburg, 1960.

COLLOQUIUM VERLAG, Berlin: Willy Haas: *Bert Brecht*: Köpfe des Jahrhunderts, Band 7. Copyright Colloquium Verlag, Berlin, 1958.

VERLAG KURT DESCH, München: Arnolt Bronnen, *Tage mit Bertolt Brecht*. Copyright Kurt Desch Verlag, München, Wien, Basel, 1960.

DOUBLEDAY & COMPANY, INC., New York: *Rudyard Kipling's Verse*: Definitive Edition. Copyright Doubleday & Company, Inc., New York, 1954.

Europe. Janvier-Fevrier 1957, XXXV année.

S. Fischer Verlag, Frankfurt am Main: Thomas Mann, *Betrachtungen eines Unpolitischen.* Zwölfbändige Thomas-Mann Ausgabe, Band XII. Copyright S. Fischer Verlag, 1960.

Thomas Mann, *Buddenbrooks.* Copyright by S. Fischer Verlag, Berlin, 1922.

Walter Rathenau, *Gesammelte Schriften*, Band I. Copyright S. Fischer Verlag, 1918.

Franz Werfel, *Gedichte aus den Jahren 1908-1945.* Copyright 1946 by Bermann-Fischer Verlag, Stockholm.

Hugo von Hofmannsthal. *Gesammelte Werke in Einzelausgaben: Lustspiele IV.* Copyright 1956 S. Fischer Verlag, G.m.b. H. Frankfurt am Main.

The Hudson Review, Vol. XV, No. 2, Summer 1962. Norman Holland, "Shakespearean Tragedy and the Three Ways of Psychoanalytic Criticism." Copyright 1962 by the Hudson Review, Inc.

Insel Verlag, Frankfurt am Main: Rainer Maria Rilke, *Briefe aus Muzot: 1929 bis 1926.* Copyright Insel Verlag, Leipzig, 1936.

Rainer Maria Rilke, *Gesammelte Gedichte.* Copyright Insel Verlag, Frankfurt am Main, 1962.

Rainer Maria Rilke, *Tagebücher aus der Frühzeit.* Copyright Insel Verlag, 1942.

Sidney Kaufman, 14 Fairways Close, Forest Hills 75, New York. Ernst Toller, *Prosa, Briefe, Dramen, Gedichte.* Copyright, Sidney Kaufman, 1961.

Kindler Verlag, München: Alfred Kantorowicz, *Deutsches Aagebuch.* 2 Bände. Copyright, Kindler Verlag, München, 1961.

Fritz Kortner, *Aller Tage Abend.* Copyright, Kindler Verlag, München, 1959.

Albert Langen Georg Müller Verlag GMBH München: Frank Wedekind, *Prosa, Dramen, Verse.* Copyright Albert Langen Georg Müller Verlag, München.

Limes Verlag, Wiesbaden: Gottfried Benn, *Gesammelte Werke,* 3 Bände. Copyright, Limes Verlag, Wiesbaden, 1958-1960.

Paul List Verlag KG, München: Ludwig Marcuse, *Mein zwanzigstes Jahrhundert.* Copyright 1960, Paul List Verlag, München.

W. W. NORTON & COMPANY, INC., SIGMUND FREUD COPYRIGHTS, LTD.,
MR. JAMES STRACHEY, and THE HOGARTH PRESS, LTD: Standard Edition,
The Complete Psychological Works of Sigmund Freud. Vol. XXI.

VERLAG OPRECHT, Zurich: Alfred Polgar, *Handbuch des Kritikers.* Copyright 1938, Verlag Oprecht, Zurich.

ROWOHLT VERLAG GMBH Reinbek bei Hamburg: *Arnolt Bronnen, gibt zu Protokoll.* Copyright 1954, Rowohlt Verlag, Reinbek by Hamburg.
Erwin Piscator. *Das politische Theater,* Copyright 1963, Rowohlt Verlag, Reinbek bei Hamburg.
Kurt Tucholsky, *Gesammelte Werke.* 3 Bände. Copyright 1960-1961 Rowohlt Verlag, Reinbek be Hamburg.

R. PIPER & CO. VERLAG, München: Walter Muschg, *Von Trakl zu Brecht.* Copyright Piper Verlag, München, 1961.

SACHSE & POHL VERLAG GMBH, Göttingen: Fritz Sternberg, *Der Dichter und die Ratio.* Erinnerungen an Bertolt Brecht. (Schriften zur Literatur. Herausgegeben von Reinhold Grimm. Band 2.) Copyright 1963, Sachse & Pohl Verlag.

VERLAG LAMBERT SCHNEIDER GMBH Heidelberg: Rudolf Frank, *Spielzeit meines Lebens.* Copyright 1960, Verlag Lambert Schneider.

JOSEF STOCKER AG. Luzern: Hugo Ball, *Flucht aus der Zeit.* Copyright 1946, Josef Stocker AG.

FREDERICK UNGAR PUBLISHING CO. INC., New York: Erich Fromm, *Marx's Concept of Man.* Copyright 1961, Frederick Ungar Publishing Co., Inc.

FRITZ VON UNRUH, Diez/Lahn: *Vor der Entscheidung.* (1919).

THE VIKING PRESS INC., New York: Lion Feuchtwanger, *Success.* Translated by Edwin and Willa Muir. Copyright 1930, 1958 by The Viking Press, Inc.

THE KENYON REVIEW, Vol. XXI, (1959). Ernst Bornemann, "Credo Quia Absurdum—Epitaph for Bertolt Brecht."

WALTER VERLAG, Freiburg/Br, Alfred Döblin, *Die drei Sprünge des Wang-lun.* Copyright Walter Verlag, 1960.

Preface

The present work was undertaken with the object of presenting Brecht as a poet, playwright, theoretician of the drama, story-teller, and thinker, and set him against the background of German and world history, of which he was so very much a part. It is based upon an examination of unpublished materials in the Brecht Archives in East Berlin, as well as published works by and about Brecht, and observation of the work of the Berliner Ensemble in rehearsal and performance. I have received help from many sources. First and foremost, from Dr. Helene Weigel, Director of the Berliner Ensemble, and the Brecht Estate, who permitted me the use of the rich resources of the Brecht Archives, and made me welcome at the Ensemble; from Frau Elisabeth Hauptmann; from Werner Hecht, Dramaturg of the Ensemble; from Frau Vera Tenschert and Percy Paukschta of its photographic department; from Fräulein Lise Kiel and other members of the Archive staff. Equally great is my debt to the Arbeitskreis zur Pflege der deutschen Kultur und Sprache of the DDR, and its representatives, Frau Erika Ohde, Frau Wanda Bloch, and Dr. Bruno Langner, for their gracious hospitality and assistance. The following have also been very helpful, directly and indirectly, and I wish to thank them: Lee Baxandall, Dr. Annette T. Rubinstein, Dr. Alberta Szalita, George Tabori; and the Directors of the Master Institute, Mrs. Nettie S. Horch and Mrs. Oriole Farb. I am grateful to the Directors of the Columbia University Libraries, and of the New York Public Library for the use of their valuable collections. The officers and staff of The Citadel Press have been most cooperative. My wife, Miriam Gideon, has through her patience and encouragement made an agreeable task doubly agreeable. I have

profited from the writings of Eric Bentley, Martin Esslin, Helge
Hultberg, Werner Mittenzwei, Ernst Schumacher, and John Willett
(among others), and I acknowledge my thanks to them. It is a
source of profound sorrow to me that Erwin Piscator and Charles
Humboldt are no longer here to see the finished book, and receive
my thanks. Let this work be a partial tribute to their memory.

FREDERIC EWEN

New York City
June 1967

NOTE

Unless otherwise indicated, all translations
in the following pages are by Frederic Ewen.

Prologue

THE WORLD AROUND BRECHT

Did you know him? He wore
A gray coat to make himself smaller.
For he fought, the mover, for equality.
When a giant rises to fight for equality,
Yes, he would make us all giant-like.
PETER HACKS, "Brecht"

Chausseestrasse, in the eastern sector of Berlin, is today one of the
relicts of pre-war Germany. Though repaired and rehabilitated, it
still preserves some of the shopworn antiquity of an older day. Its
historic continuity with the past is underlined by the Dorotheen
Cemetery, which makes a sober, though not depressing frame for
the building at Number 125. Here, not long after their return from
exile, Brecht lived with his family. They occupied the rear of
the house, approached through an open court. The upper story was
used by Brecht as his workrooms; the lower as the family's living
quarters. From the windows of his study Brecht loved to look out
on the cemetery where his favorite philosopher, Hegel, lay buried,
and where he himself was to be laid to rest in August, 1956.

Up to the end of his life and his final illness, when he was in the
city and there was work to be done at the theatre, Brecht would
get into his old car, and make his way to the Theater am Schiffbauerdamm—the theatre of the Berliner Ensemble. The distance is
very short, but Brecht hated to walk.

This was his and Helene Weigel's theatre. It had been rebuilt
for them exactly as it was before the war, more than a quarter of
a century ago, when Brecht celebrated his first world-wide triumph
with *The Three Penny Opera*.

Let us follow him into the theatre in this, his last year, 1956. There are many students there, to watch the rehearsal. Here too, Brecht will greet associates of former days: his lifelong friend and co-director, Erich Engel; his collaborator Elisabeth Hauptmann; and many others who were present in the twenties. And now, as the auditorium darkens, and the actors begin speaking—one wonders: How often did Brecht go over in his mind the long and devious journey that, beginning in Augsburg, his birthplace, has brought him back to Berlin, the scene of his first great successes—a journey that physically spanned continents, but morally, spiritually, and artistically provided experiences of sorrow and joy, victory and defeat, that for depth could not be measured in years?

How distinctly are two divergent periods of history symbolized here! The theatre building on the Schiffbauerdamm speaks of an old, bygone time. What is now being uttered on its stage is of a new time, a new world. There on the stage is Ernst Busch, as Galileo, instructing his young student about the meaning of a "new age," and the significance of the "new science," proclaiming a changed and changeable world. To Brecht, sitting in the theatre, Augsburg must have seemed very far away, indeed. . . .

I

The City and the Land

Ich führe euch herrlichen Zeiten entgegen.

I lead you toward glorious times.

KAISER WILHELM II

Augsburg, the South German city named after Emperor Augustus Caesar, is even today an impressive monument to the past. A pedestrian beginning his walk at the old Roman gate called "das rote Tor" soon finds himself retracing a formidable segment of history. On the expansive Maximilianstrasse, Augsburg's principal thoroughfare, he will be treading in the wake of the Roman legions as they moved on to their futile campaigns against the Germanic tribes. Here too, centuries later, was the riot, bustle and many-tongued Babel of the Crusaders eastward bound for Oriental booty and the redemption of the Savior's grave from the infidel. Framing the magnificent street, stand, at one end, the beautiful St. Ulrich's Church, and, at the other, the ancient cathedral, with its unequalled stained glass windows, probably the oldest in Europe.

Midway on the spacious avenue, the traveler would pass the palatial Fuggerhaus and be made aware that this was the city of the great banker and trader family of the Renaissance, as well as of the builders of the first workers' community housing, the Fuggerei. The Fuggers of Augsburg were the creditors of the mightiest kings, emperors and popes.

Two magnificent Renaissance edifices also crown this street: the

25

Perlach Tower and the City Hall. Turn to the right at the Perlach, and a few squares beyond you come upon a small alleyway called Auf dem Rain. Here, at Number Seven, Bertolt Brecht was born, on February 10, 1898.

Today Augsburg is a provincial suburb of Munich. Not so in other days. As a Free City it saw and took part in many of the most violent struggles that swept across the land. In the thirteenth century it witnessed an uprising of burghers and artisans against the ruling absolutism of the bishops; some years later it saw an equally violent uprising of artisans against the burgher aristocracy. Even bloodier conflicts took place during the Protestant revolt, and during the repression of the Anabaptists. It was here that the most important Protestant statement of belief was formulated in 1530—the Augsburg Confession.

As an industrial and commerical city, Augsburg won distinction, aside from its banking enterprises, for textiles, the dye industry, paper manufacture. It was to the Haindl paper factory that the elder Brecht migrated from the Black Forest, eventually rising to the position of factory manager.

This is a city of many waterways, canals, one of them flowing right past the Brecht home. This was the cradle and background of the early Bertolt Brecht.

Ten years before Bertolt Brecht was born, Wilhelm II ascended the throne of Germany. He inherited from his grandfather, Wilhelm I, and from the "Iron Chancellor," Otto von Bismarck, a unified Germany—a Germany which was soon to assert for herself a predominance in European and world politics. He was also to inherit one of the most efficient armies in the world. In the course of his thirty years' reign he was destined to see Germany rise to a position of foremost importance in the economic and political life of the world, and take her place among the great imperialist powers. He was also destined to see her go down—and along with her, the monarchial system—to utter destruction in 1918.

The unprecedented growth economically, industrially, and technologically of the country found its counterpart in the growth of the working classes, and the amazing expansion of the German Socialist movement. By 1914 it could count on the support of almost one-third of the German population, and became the largest single party in the Reichstag.

Bismarckian policy proved phenomenally successful. It made a profound impression on the German mentality. Though in theory Prussianism might be deplored and even mistrusted, it was thoroughly respected. Efficiency and reverence for authority were the watchwords of practically every segment of society, bulwarked as that was by the social stratification, the almost hierarchical separation of classes and professions, by the official bureaucracy, the army, the government élite, the Prussian Junkers, the nobility, and the intellectual elements in the universities. A form of "divine right" penetrated down from the Emperor to the lowest strata of society—generating that curious amalgam of subalternism and authoritarianism, sentimentality and hard-headed efficiency, submissiveness and explosiveness that was to mark German life for decades to come.

With pride Wilhelm II could boast: "Our Lord God would not have taken such pains with our German Fatherland if He did not have still greater things in store for us."

But Germany was also abetted by terrestrial forces. A nation that had already coined such philosophical terms as "Weltanschauung" and "Weltschmerz" to describe metaphysical states of mind and heart, soon also found such terms as "Weltmacht" and "Weltpolitik"—world-power and world-politics—to fit the new and more practical adventures, such as seeking a "place in the sun" alongside of the older imperialist powers.

Such was the German nation and the German people—a nation and people thrust into the vortex of twentieth-century history and competition with the burden of an eighteenth-century mentality, and without the saving grace and schooling of a bourgeois-democratic revolution.

Yes, German history can flatter itself on a movement which no people on the historical horizon has demonstrated before or will repeat. We have shared the Restoration of modern nations, without sharing in their revolutions. We were restored, in the first place, because other nations dared undertake a revolution, and secondly, because other nations suffered a counter-revolution. The first time, because our masters were afraid, and the second time, because they were not afraid. We, with our shepherds at the head, found ourselves only once in the company of freedom—on the day she was buried.[1]

How would such a nation fare?

II

The Life of the Mind

The German soul has passages and galleries in it; there are caves, hiding places, and dungeons in it; its disorder has much of the charm of the mysterious; the German is well acquainted with the by-paths to chaos.

FRIEDRICH NIETZSCHE

Culturally, too, Germany's entrance into the twentieth century represented a sharp break with the past. Around 1900, Germans were still looking back to a late neo-Romanticism. They were attached to such poets as Eduard Mörike and Theodor Storm; composers like Robert Schumann; and artists like Spitzweg and Richter. Not that there were no literary figures of distinction and talent present, novelists such as Wilhelm Raabe, Theodor Fontane, and Gottfried Keller; poets such as Detlev von Liliencron and Richard Dehmel. But who outside of Germany had heard of them? And even in Germany itself?

And now, suddenly, the barriers of provincialism crashed. The small-townishness—the idyllic isolation of hamlet and ducal city—began to give way before the onrush of the new technology and Prussian efficiency. The life of the intellect, whether scientific, literary or philosophical, now began to be harnessed to the interests of the new powers, or, in some instances, in opposition to them. Time could no longer be told, as in Kant's Koenigsberg, by that philosopher's regular after-dinner rambles. Universities, institutes,—

whether archaeological, physical, or metaphysical—were drawn on to subserve the wider interests of a new world-power. What Heinrich Heine had predicted was coming to pass: natural philosophers were taking their cosmic views down from the clouds and transforming them into practical, worldly realities.

From the outside, major cultural impulses invaded the land. From Russia, from the Scandinavian countries, from England, France and America, new nurturing elements, favored by the time, found a ready soil. The writings of Tolstoy and Dostoyevski; of Ibsen and Strindberg; of Zola and the French Symbolists; of Bernard Shaw and Walt Whitman; the art of the French Impressionists and post-Impressionists—all these breached the walls of the past, uprooted traditions, and stimulated to new creativeness. Undreamt-of horizons seemed to open, and undreamt-of problems loomed.

Infinite appeared the promises of the future. Of the beginning of the new century Gerhart Hauptmann wrote:

At the basis of our existence and life at that time was faith. We believed in the irresistible progress of humanity. We believed in the triumph of science and therefore in the ultimate unveiling of nature. The triumph of truth, we believed, would put an end to the chimaeras and phantoms of religious delusions. Before long, we believed, the self-destruction of mankind in war would have become a chapter of past history. We believed in the victory of fraternity. . . . Above all, we believed in ourselves.[2]

Could any German be blamed, if, say, in the year 1914, looking back upon the preceding thirty-five years, he gloated over the catalogue of distinguished names that marked the achievements of his country in so many fields: in science, medicine, history, political economy, archaeology, and letters? Names like Georg Cantor, Heinrich Hertz, Wilhelm Ostwald, Max Planck, Albert Einstein, Paul Ehrlich, Robert Koch, Leopold von Ranke, Theodor Mommsen, Julius Wellhausen, Karl Lamprecht, Karl Kautsky, Max Weber, Franz Mehring?

Here we have, then, the German Reich: A stratified society, capitalist and monarchial at the same time; absolutist and hierarchical; managed by a highly efficient bureaucratic administration—a society exhibiting unparalleled growth and expansion within a short span of time. Naturally, it would be subject to major tensions and stresses. In a bourgeois-democratic state such tensions find their outlet in political activity and in the participation of a more or less alert electorate. However, the bulk of the German population was politically immature. Germany had not, as we have seen, participated in any bourgeois-liberal revolution. Her intelligentsia tended on the whole to be apolitical. That night-cap paternalism which Heine so beautifully described as prevalent before the Napoleonic era, had changed its headgear, perhaps, but not its methods or manner. It still prevailed, but in a more expanded and efficient form. Parliament was turned into a debating society. Decisions and policies were handed down from "above," like Bismarck's "socialism." Social reforms and social legislation—among the most advanced of any country in Europe—were "granted" to the German people.

Nor is it to be wondered at that a good portion of the population—especially the intellectuals—looked with decided suspicion and distrust, if not disdain, upon ideas of Western democracy as practised in France and the United States. Such certainly were the sentiments of Thomas Mann up to the end of the First World War. Such were the sentiments of the philosopher who perhaps more than any other figure, captured the minds and hearts of the intelligentsia—Friedrich Nietzsche.

The mental atmosphere of a nation is not easy to describe or define precisely. But there can be little doubt that the impact of Nietzsche's ideas stamped the period with a special character. Poets, novelists, playwrights—artists of essentially divergent schools or persuasions—testify to his overwhelming influence at certain periods of their lives, though a number of them might come eventually to repudiate him. Thus, Thomas Mann recalled the shock which his world experienced in 1889, when "word spread of Nietzsche's mental breakdown."

Upon this soul [Mann wrote], the deepest, coldest solitude, the solitude of the criminal, was imposed. Here was a mind by origin profoundly respectful, shaped to revere pious traditions; and just such a mind fate chose to drag by the hair, as it were, into a posture of wild and drunken truculence, of rebellion against all reverence. This mind was compelled to violate its own nature, to become the mouthpiece and advocate of blatant brute force, of the callous conscience of Evil itself.[3]

His brother, Heinrich Mann, wrote in 1939:

[Nietzsche's] work is terrifying. It has become a threat, instead of sweeping us along as it did years ago. *Then* he seemed to be justifying our own selves.[4]

For in the closing decades of the nineteenth, and even more potently in the opening decades of the twentieth century, Nietzsche affected the Wilhelminian generation with the explosive force of the world-shaker.

"I am not a man," he said. "I am dynamite."

He acted thus not only on the conservative elements, and on reactionary ones, but also on those that thought of themselves as liberal, even revolutionary. That dualism served many camps. For the disaffected bourgeois, no longer fully at ease with the new bureaucratic, mechanized state, he represented the unremitting and pitiless enemy of German smugness, nationalism, philistinism, cant, and conformity. He was the avenging angel warring against the *status quo,* the heroic nihilist of subversion. To the energetic pan-German, hungry for "Lebensraum," he preached execration of German "slave morality," exposed the "bad conscience" and "potential pessimism" of the German bourgeois; anathematized democracy, and proclaimed the new religion of brute strength and pagan affirmation. He called for a "will to power," even to war. "You say a good cause justifies even a war? I say to you a good war is one that justifies all causes." An effete Judaeo-Christian morality must be replaced by a new paganism embodied in the "blond beast," the Nordic superman.

To the more radically minded he appealed with the audacious insults he hurled at German barbarism, Prussianism, industry, capitalism, the machine and its product, modern man—that nondescript egalitarian, whether bourgeois or proletarian—that faceless, eviscerated nothing.

In Richard Wagner, Nietzsche imagined he had found the fortunate musical and dramatic apotheosis of his dream; in the composer's Siegfrieds, Wotans, and Valhallas the embodiment of that imperial paganism that could be a counterpoise to the decadent Judaeo-Christian ideal then in vogue. So, like the twin eagles of the Imperial Reich, Nietzsche and Wagner hover over the German abyss. How symbolic and right, too, that the newly awakened German imperialism should find its counterpoint in the musical and dramatic imperialism of Wagner! That combination of supreme genius and charlatan, magician and vulgarian, political revolutionary and arch-conservative, who roused the German nation with the horn-calls of Siegfried, and sang its Götterdämmerung with the ruin of Wotan and Valhalla!

It is from these two, Nietzsche and Wagner, that an entire generation of artists, poets, and thinkers drew nourishment. They served, in fact, to aggravate and re-enforce the two characteristic psychic tendencies of the German artistic mentality from the time of the Sturm und Drang to the First World War—"Zerrissenheit," self-division, and "Innerlichkeit," inwardness.

How do the principal poets of the Wilhelminian era reflect the mentality of the period? Let us look at three poets, by common consent regarded as pre-eminent: Stefan George, Gottfried Benn, and Rainer Maria Rilke.

In Stefan George, the Nietzschean new order finds its most characteristic and its strongest poetic embodiment. Laureate and high priest of a German Symbolist cénacle, he modeled his pagan tabernacle on that of Mallarmé, whose exclusive Paris gatherings he had attended at one time. Since there were no German Verlaines, Rimbauds, Debussys, and Valérys available, George had to be content with devout but somewhat mediocre adherents. His finely chiselled verse—for George was a supremely gifted poet—glorified a neo-paganism, an aestheticism, and an artistic asceticism. He elevated the poet to the rank of "vates"—prophet and leader at the same time. With these notions he combined a consecration of the flesh, "Vergöttung des Leibes," and an incarnation of divinity, "Verleibung des Gottes." This pagan god-quest took many non-ascetic and deviant erotic forms, such as the physical adoration of a young boy, whom he called Maximin, who, fortunately for a god, died young, and to whom he dedicated some exquisite poems. Pagan "cruelty" is hymned and Heliogabalus adored. A "Third Humanism"—millennial successor to that of the Renaissance and of Goethe —is proclaimed. Like Nietzsche, George called for a new "leader,"— a "new man"—and in lieu of the ideal, compromised with substitutes such as General von Hindenburg. He prophesied the coming of the "only One, who will shatter our chains, and bring order out of disorder, and be master again, and plant the new Reich." Disciples in years to come saw in these verses anticipations of the Messiah— Adolf Hitler. George's prominence as a poet, and his ideas, encouraged the Nazis to woo him as their poet-laureate. George was at first attracted to them; then repelled by their crassness and vulgarity, he withdrew to Switzerland, where he died in 1933.

No such qualms stood in the path of Gottfried Benn. He found his way straight from a Wilhelminian "heroic" nihilism, to the somewhat less heroic nihilism of Hitler. In an age in which "Kultur" was said to epitomize the German mentality, he represents "Kulturmüdigkeit"—cultural weariness, and disgust with civilization. For Benn, reason and logic are disintegrative elements of modern life. Consciousness is the only reality. There is no material, external reality. "There is the human consciousness . . . constantly reforming and forming the world," but "life is not meant to gain possession of knowledge. Man is not meant to struggle for an explanation of the material world." The only criterion by which to "assess the great mind of man," i. e., of the white nations, is in "the degree of ineradicable nihilism" they exhibit. The highest state of being is represented by a sinking back into the "natural," the "primitive," the "primal." In one of his most quoted poems he pleads:

Oh, that we were our first ancestors, a lump of slime in a warm swamp! Life and death, birth and conception would then glide from our dumb juices. An alga, a leaf, or a sandhill formed by the wind, and bottom-heavy, a moth's head, or a seagull's wing—these would already be too much, and given over to suffering.[5]

A practising physician all his life long, he brought to poetry the "aesthetics of the repellent," the horror, slime, and ulcerous sores of the operating room, translated into life itself. An early volume of poems is significantly entitled *Morgue*. Benn's hatred and disgust for life were to be intensified by the First World War, and were reflected in his chants of a cloacal humanity—"Man—the crown of creation—the swine—and Man." He combined stylistic virtuosity and a mastery of the vocabulary of science unequalled by any of his contemporaries. He fused Nietzsche, the macabre elements of Baudelaire, and the anti-rationalism that ran like some mysterious underground stream throughout German thought. Intellectual man is a "brain-gorged carrion," his self-awareness a primal curse. Oh, to sink back into amoebic, protozoic nothingness! "No more forehead!" he cries. "I want to be lived!" His quest for Nirvana, which he names Ithaca, at other times Sparta and Alexandria, was not to be satisfied until he heard the call of blood and soil, and could bury his weary head in the bosom of National Socialism. Having proved his racial purity, he was awarded a post in the cultural ministry, and a place in the Prussian Academy of Letters. ("If the Chinese invaded Germany," Kurt Tucholsky said of him, "he would grow a pigtail.") But soon he too found himself *persona non grata,* even among the amoebic Herrenvolk, and retreated into a convenient "inner emigration." After the Nazi collapse, he was awarded by the West Germans the Georg Büchner prize in 1951—a piece of crowning irony, for the prize was named after one of the most courageous and revolutionary writers of the nineteenth century!

Among these searchers for a "homeland" away from the unsettling chaos of Wilhelminian Germany, few spoke with such beauty and pathos as Rainer Maria Rilke. He died in 1926, but it is doubtful if his quest for a home would have led him to the same haven as that of George and Benn. Unlike them, he never turned to brutality and dehumanization as an outlet. He emigrated spiritually into himself and shut out the outside world. "Nowhere is the world," he wrote, "but within." The distortions he suffered psychically as a child through the perverted fixation of a mother who strove to convert him into a girl are only a part of that estrangement he felt and expressed throughout his life. He was most completely at home between "day and dream," and his poetry has just that texture—a frieze, a two-dimensional projection—the lost third dimension being that of living human beings. His refuge is in art—and in that he is in the age-old tradition of the German Romantics and post-Romantics; it is a refuge both into art and through art. In an age in which the meaning of God and angels had become attenuated, his poetry is a constant prayer for a solipsistic salvation. The tempered "Weltschmerz" of modern man is fused with the lyricism of the French Symbolists, Rodin, and the mysticism of old Spain and Russia.

But he remained to the end the homeless poet—fatherless too. "Ich habe kein Vaterhaus," he wrote, "und habe keins verloren." "I have no paternal house, and have lost none." Neither does he have ancestors.

His ear was attuned to every other sound of nature—animate and inanimate—but not to the sound of man.

But that life which is denied him among men, he finds in a mystical union with God, whom, in his poetic arrogance, he even appropriates as a son, and whom he addresses with all the audacious majesty of another Creator. In fact, he dares affirm the supremacy of the poet's creation over that of the Lord God himself.

For painters paint their pictures only so that you may receive back Nature imperishable, which you have made to perish.[6]

And then, "Was wirst du tun, Gott, wenn ich sterbe?" "What will you do God, if I die?" "I am your pitcher," he continues, "What if I break? I am your drink—what if I spoil? I am your raiment and your vocation, and when I am gone . . . my meaning is gone. What will you do, God? I am afraid."[7]

He was obsessed by "Einsamkeitsfanatismus," this "fanaticism of loneliness." He rejects love and being beloved as an unbearable burden, and yet glorifies love in the abstract. He is terrified of life, of cities, of factories, of the degradation and misery he sees around him. In 1915 he wrote: "How is it possible to live, when the very elements of life are unintelligible to us? When we are everlastingly inadequate in love, uncertain in resolve, and incapable in the presence of death, how is it possible to exist?"[8]

He is led to conclude: "Wer spricht von Siegen? Überstehn ist alles." "Who speaks of victories? Endurance is all." For him there was no "redemption from chaos"—whether in the pagan gods of George or in Benn's retreat into the protozoa. At most Rilke had to be content with a "truce with the anonymous powers on the other side,"[9] the powers of nothingness. So that almost naturally Death becomes the process of "ripening" within us:

> For we are naught but chalice and the leaf,
> The great Death each has within him.
> This is the fruit, around which all revolves.[10]

If there is a savior, it is the artist. He is the "transfigurer of existence."

"The artist is eternity projected into the times ahead."[11]

If by its very nature poetry tends to be homophonic—personal; the novel, on the other hand, is compelled to a polyphony; in other words, to be more communal, more social. Its late development in Germany is itself a mark of the disruptions and discontinuities within the German community. As a force in European (and later, world literature), it comes into its own in the twentieth century. As a reflection of the temper of the times the German novel may perhaps be best studied in the contrasting work of two brothers, Heinrich and Thomas Mann.

It is not to be marveled at that both writers (Heinrich being Thomas' senior by four years) began writing under the tutelage of Goethe and Friedrich Nietzsche. Both succeeded in establishing the modern German "social" novel. In addition to Nietzsche and Goethe, Heinrich Mann also fell under the influence of Balzac, Flaubert, Gabriele d'Annunzio, and the French aesthetes and symbolists. Thomas Mann was a disciple of Schopenhauer, Wagner, Tolstoy and Freud. He was to remain under these early influences for many years, while his brother was to break with his first allegiances, and turn to Rousseau, Voltaire, Zola, and Anatole France— a shift that eventually led to radical differences with Thomas Mann.

For already as far back as 1907 Heinrich Mann bade adieu to the enchanting gospel of the strong man and the hedonist: d'Annunzio's amoral *condottiere* and Nietzsche's "blond beast." With the novel *Zwischen den Rassen* (*Between the Races*) he began turning a critical eye on his own country and his times. With particular care he now examined the new German bourgeoisie, staff and stay of Wilhelm's Reich, as well as the bureaucracy and the ruling classes. To this subject he devoted his most ambitious trilogy *Das Kaiserreich* (*The Empire*), of which the first volume *Der Untertan* (*The Subject*) was completed on the eve of the First World War.

It may be asserted that no German novelist before him had presented so pitiless, truthful, and vivid a depiction of the "new" man. He is Dietrich Hessling—an unscrupulous, hard, self-seeking German bourgeois who rises by devious means to a position of high importance and power within the commercial and political life of his town. He models himself outwardly on Kaiser Wilhelm, even to the bristling mustache, fortifies himself with a wealthy wife, and becomes the small tyrant of his community. He sees himself, in fact, as a miniature Kaiser, "draped in imperial purple." Of another man he says, "Real patriotic feeling is incompatible with ears like that. I always suspected him." To a political opponent he boasts, "Blood and iron are still the most effective of remedies. Might before right." He ends up in a drunken brawl with the cry, "I will smash!" After attempting a particularly shady business coup in conjunction with a Junker, he remarks to his sisters: "You can see what it is like when two honorable people do business. It doesn't happen too often in the business world today. There are too many Jews." This is the new bourgeois, whom Gustave Flaubert had portrayed as M. Homais in *Madame Bovary*. In Heinrich Mann he becomes, in the succeeding volumes of the trilogy, a manufacturer of armaments, whose chicanery is well masked by patriotism. He is the model citizen who dedicates a town monument to Kaiser Wilhelm I (having cashed in considerably on it), and who addresses the assembled crowd:

Rendered efficient to an amazing degree, full of the highest moral strength for positive action, and in our shining armor, we are the terror of all enemies who in their envy threaten us, as we are the élite among nations, having attained, for the first time, a German master culture, which will never be surpassed by any people, no matter who.[12]

Such, at least in part, is the picture we obtain of the era: its militarism, chauvinism, anti-Semitism, authoritarianism, arrogance, corruption, Junkertum and anti-liberalism.

In his own political and social ideas, Heinrich Mann diverged more and more from his brother. The differences reached their apogee with the publication of *Geist und Tat* (*Spirit and Deed*), a manifesto in which Heinrich Mann called upon writers and other intellectuals to abandon their "apoliticalization"—their self-indulgence in private griefs and problems—and adjured them to follow in the lead of the great Frenchmen: Voltaire, as in his championship of Calas; Zola, in his defense of Dreyfus; and such libertarians as Victor Hugo and Anatole France. What must have appeared as most shocking to Thomas Mann, as well as many other Germans, was Heinrich Mann's appeal to his people to abandon once and for all their great hero-poet and apostle of humanism, Goethe.

His work, his name, his memory have changed nothing in Germany, have erased not a single act of barbarism, cleared not even an inch of ground toward a better future. At Goethe's obsequies there was not a single Calas present. . . .[13]

Yes, Heinrich Mann admitted, Germany and the Germans have ever been proud masters of thought. But to what end? "We cling to lies and injustices, as if we feared there were an abyss stretching right behind Truth." He derided the monarchy, "that master-state of organization; this school of animosity," that has subordinated individual man; and he castigated the intellectuals who served the ruling caste as guilty of treason against the Spirit. "For Spirit is not conservative. It grants no privileges. It dismembers. It is egalitarian; and across the ruins of hundreds of strongholds it presses on toward a realization of truth and justice, and their fulfilment, even unto death."[13]

And in one of his most impressive later essays, written in 1915, and dedicated to Emile Zola, Heinrich Mann prophesied the collapse of the German Empire.

Nothing could have seemed farther from or more abhorrent to Thomas Mann than these sentiments. For, writing in 1907, he had defined the artist as the "enemy" of society—useless to the state, "refractory," "classless," something of nature's child in his aloofness and amoralism.[14] In his eyes, writers like his brother were nothing but "Zivilisationsliteraten,"—that it, cultural belle-lettrists, not artists, for the "Literat" imposes upon himself a high moral purpose that takes the form of *action*. But action is foreign to the true artist.

In a series of essays, *Betrachtungen eines Unpolitischen* (*Reflections of a Non-Political*), written after the outbreak of the First World War and concluded on the day a truce was declared between Germany and Russia, Thomas Mann set forth his views of the nature of the German mind. This was in answer to his brother's appeals. "Either you are political, or you are not," Thomas Mann wrote. "If you are, then you must be a democrat." But so far as Germans are concerned, "politics is foreign to their nature. . . . I confess that I am convinced that the German people can never love political democracy, for the simple reason that it can never love politics, and that the much decried 'authoritarian state' is and will remain in reality a much more suitable and rightful political system for the German people, and is actually what the German people want."[15]

Coming from the most prominent novelist of the nation, and at a time when it was undergoing its most severe crisis, in which its fate was to be decided, these words could not but carry weight. They were the expressions of a man who was not blind to the inadequacies of Germany's polity or her social system. In 1901, he had at the astonishingly young age of twenty-five produced a major novel, *Buddenbrooks,* in some ways probably the most perfect of his longer works. It was also to be the first contemporary German novel to penetrate beyond its country's borders and take its place among the literary masterpieces of the century. Themes and ideas that were to preoccupy its author for decades to come were here announced and developed with unparalleled mastery: the decay of an ancient upper-burgher sturdy morality in its conflict with the newer, unscrupulous, arrogant amoralism of the rising commercial and industrial bourgeoisie; the role of the artist within that society, and the relationship between art and disease; the moral "ambiguity" of the artist and its threat to a stable society. Death, disease, the ethos of resignation—how these hover over this and subsequent works! *Buddenbrooks* is the chronicle of a patrician North German family of the nineteenth century through four generations, from 1835 to 1875. It ends with the extinction of that branch. It stands under the shadow of Schopenhauer and Wagner, and in a lesser measure, of Tolstoy. Pessimism and music haunt its pages. Decay and art! This is the novel of the end of an age, and Death is salvation.

No one who has read *Buddenbrooks* can ever forget the scene in which one of the last scions of the revered family, Thomas Buddenbrook, comes upon Schopenhauer's *The World as Will and Idea*

at a moment of profound depression and despair, when the fortunes
of the family, as well as its moral fibre, are declining. Thomas Buddenbrook opens the book to a chapter "On Death and Its Relation
to our Personal Immortality," and obtains a saving revelation:

> What was that? he asked himself as he entered the house, mounted
> the steps and sat down at the dinner table with his family. . . . What
> happened to me? What have I been witness to? What is it that was
> said to me, Thomas Buddenbrook? . . . Can I bear it? I don't know
> what it was . . . I only know that it was too much, too much for my
> poor burgher-brain.[16]

What was that revelation? It was that death was not to be feared.
"Death was a joy, so deep in fact, that it could be gauged only in
such moments of grace as this."[17] Thus he pronounces the end of
an age, the end of a family, the end of a long tradition, fittingly
consummated in the death of little Hanno, the last of the clan, this
delicate child of nature—musician and "outsider."

Disease stalks Thomas Mann's stories like some avenging angel.
The crippled characters—whether crippled morally, physically, or
spiritually, or tainted by being artists—can offer but very meagre
resistance to a ruthless and self-confident bourgeoisie. Where Heinrich Mann had found a joyful satisfaction in contemplating the
leavening effect of the artist upon his environment, and had anticipated a marriage of art and human progress (as, for example, in
Die kleine Stadt), his brother saw nothing but an unremitting and
inescapable war between the artist and the community. The "new,
hard, practical sense" of this harsh, vigorous competitive society has
driven into the grave "a generation of feeling."

Though severely schematic, and like all schemata only partially
true, the choice of the two Manns to reflect the dialectical opposition
within the German mind and the German novel of the Wilhelminian
period can be supported by reference to such works as the Austrian
Robert Musil's monumental torso, The Man Without Qualities, and
Hermann Hesse's early novels, with their pictures of isolation, terror,
anxiety, and autonomous fantasy.

Theatre is, by its very nature, conflict. It is conflict set forth and stated through the utterances and actions of characters who live out their lives and deeds vividly in our presence. For this reason it is of all the arts the one that comes closest to giving us an "imitation" of life.

It is within the theatre, and in drama, that Germans found that outlet for their agitations, discontents, and hopes that seemed denied them in real life. The theatre, not the ballot-box or even political parties, represented the true arena of social activity for them. So it had been since the eighteenth century when Lessing sounded the call to battle of the Enlightenment in *Emilia Galotti* and *Nathan the Wise,* and brought modern middle-class drama into being. So it was when on the eve of the French Revolution Schiller wrote *The Robbers* and Goethe *Goetz von Berlichingen,* in the war on medieval feudalism. The tensions and agitations of 1815, the German "War of Liberation" and its aftermath, found voices in Heinrich von Kleist, Christian Grabbe, and Georg Büchner. Even the blight that followed the collapse of the Revolution of 1848 could not completely undo the theatre, and drama spoke out through Friedrich Hebbel and the Austrian Franz Grillparzer.

The theatrical renaissance that swept over Europe toward the end of the nineteenth century derived its impetus from the great Scandinavians, the Norwegian Ibsen and the Swede Strindberg. It resulted in the establishment of "free" theatres in England, France, and finally in Germany. In Berlin, Otto Brahm founded the "Freie Bühne," which opened in September, 1889, with Ibsen's *Ghosts.* Its program echoed that of Zola and of Antoine's *Théâtre Libre*—that is, "Naturalism." It was radical in that it did not shy from delving deep into nature's and society's backyards and cellars—the lower depths—to show how human beings are shaped by nature's laws, the laws of heredity and environment. Derided by Kaiser Wilhelm II as "sewer culture,"[18] it throve for a generation. It impressed itself on a number of gifted writers, and particularly on the playwright whom the Freie Bühne could claim as its discovery—Gerhart

Hauptmann. In 1889 it produced his *Vor Sonnenaufgang (Before Sunrise)*, a crude but powerful study of the degeneration of a family (as in Zola, hereditary alcoholism plays an important part), set in a Silesian mining district, and spiced with half-apprehended genetics and bits of socialism—nonetheless a startling attack on traditional morality. But it was the production of *The Weavers* in 1893 by the same organization that established Hauptmann as the voice of the new theatrical movement. Despite obstacles placed before this play by the governmental authorities, it was finally produced. Set once more in his native Silesia, this chronicle play records the revolt of Silesian weavers in 1844, the theme also of one of Heinrich Heine's most celebrated poems. Hauptmann's drama may be said to be the first modern proletarian masterpiece of our period. The protagonists are the collective masses of weavers in their frustrated attempt to struggle against the starvation and misery imposed by the masters. The unprecedented vitality of background, characters and speech (the Silesian dialect) makes it even today one of the most moving of such depictions.

The remarkable fact about the Freie Bühne was that it had come into being through the efforts of the Socialist and working class forces within German society. This was even truer of its rival, the "Volksbühne," which was supported by a membership making small contributions. It was designed to come closer to the immediate interests of the proletariat, and though its repertory was far from revolutionary, it concentrated on such works as came closest to its needs: Schiller's *Robbers* and *Cabal and Love,* Ibsen's *Pillars of Society,* Zola's *Thérèse Raquin.* Both theatrical groups drew audiences of astonishing size, enthusiasm and understanding. Ibsen, who was present at some of the performances, was overcome. "What an audience!" he exclaimed. "For the first time," the critic Julius Bab wrote, "since the days of the Greeks, a theatre has been founded in a natural way, through organization by the people."[19] Despite incessant badgering by the police, the people's theatrical movement prospered, so that at the outbreak of the First World War, both

institutions numbered approximately seventy thousand members—a
figure unprecedented in theatrical history.

Though many of the German cities had possessed successful theatrical groups, it was Berlin that became the theatrical center of the
country. One might venture to say that nowhere else in the Western world was it possible to enjoy such a rich and varied dramatic
fare as was being offered here, at the turn of the century. Max
Reinhardt was already active as producer and director. In the
numerous theatres of the city it was then possible to see within a
short space of time the plays of Hauptmann, Hofmannsthal,
Wedekind, Strindberg, Schnitzler, Shaw, Gogol, Molière, Shakespeare, Sophocles, Tolstoy, and Grillparzer. The admission charges
were unusually low. Though the plays presented were not revolutionary, such playwrights as Bernard Shaw, Anton Chekhov, and
Maxim Gorki supplied considerable social protest. Native playwrights were less bold. The censorship was severe, and overtly
proletarian plays of revolutionary character were prohibited. But all
the more violent were the manifestations of anti-bourgeois sentiments.

Aside from Gerhart Hauptmann's, the sharpest indictments of
contemporary society came from Frank Wedekind and Carl Sternheim. Of Wedekind we shall come to speak later in these pages,
in connection with Brecht. Carl Sternheim is the theatrical counterpart of Heinrich Mann. Like the novelist, he turns his pungent,
sometimes malicious wit upon the petty bourgeois. A trilogy, entitled *Aus dem bürgerlichen Leben* (*Scenes from Bourgeois Life*)
depicts the new "heroism" of the German middle class. Beginning
with *Die Hose* (*The Bloomers*) in 1911, continuing with *Der Snob,*
in 1914, and concluding with *1913,* Sternheim traces the family
fortunes of the Maskes. The father, Maske, is at the start, a petty
civil servant, but his son attains not only a fortune, but also a title
—"Freiherr von Buchow." The most celebrated of Sternheim's
comedies, *The Bloomers,* hilarious as well as heartless, recounts how
Theodore Maske's pretty wife loses her bloomers on a critical day

—just when Emperor Wilhelm II is parading through the streets of Berlin. This contretemps at first forebodes for poor Maske nothing but disgrace and possible loss of his job—nothing less than the destruction of his little world. But the gods who care for the petty bourgeois are kind. Disaster turns to good fortune, as prospective lodgers besiege his quarters in search of the vacant room he has advertised. Maske ends up with a handsome profit (to which his wife is not at all averse), and after adding up the sums he has received, and assured now of a secure future, he declares himself ready for a baby!

Such are Sternheim's "heroes." In their smugness, self-assurance, and brutal self-seeking one senses the character of an era on the eve of an explosion. When one of his figures remarks, "We are ripe," the expression falls upon the ear ominously.

The insurgency manifested in the theatre of this period found its parallel in the other arts: painting, sculpture, music. The dominant impulses came from France and Italy in the pictorial arts; from Russia and Vienna in music. In the turbulent artistic circles of Munich, Berlin, and Dresden, impressionism, expressionism, cubism, futurism, surrealism all vied for supremacy—and sometimes lived side by side. The establishment of "Die Brücke" group in Dresden initiated the artistic revolt in Germany. The names associated with that movement were soon to achieve world celebrity: Ernst Ludwig Kirchner, Erich Heckel, Emil Nolde. In Berlin, Herwarth Walden founded a periodical and an art gallery, both named "Der Sturm," to exhibit futurists "without politics." The cubism of Guillaume Apollinaire and Max Jacob soon became domesticated here too. Oskar Kokoschka arrived in Berlin in 1910, and in 1911 Vassili Kandinsky, Franz Marc, Paul Klee, and Alexander Kubin formed the "Blaue Reiter" group, and began exhibiting in Munich. On the political left, futurism found expression in Franz Pfempfert's journal, *Die Aktion.*

Munich, already the seat of the most advanced and courageous of satirical journals, *Simplicissimus,* became an international art center. French Fauvists, Spanish and French cubists, and German futurists rubbed shoulders here. Slogans and apocalyptic manifestoes clashed and resounded. Creativity overflowed bounds: Ernst Barlach the sculptor wrote brilliant short stories and expressionist plays; Oskar Kokoschka fashioned dramas of "absurdity"; Arnold Schoenberg composed music, wrote poetry, and painted pictures. Anti-bourgeois invectives, like the Italian Marinetti's "Let us make the ugly in literature! We want to sing the love of danger!" immediately re-echoed in the German heart.

No less sharp and remarkable was the revolution in music. The extent of the decade's transformation may be gauged by the work of Arnold Schoenberg, as he proceeded from the post-romanticism of Richard Strauss at the beginning of the century as in *Verklärte Nacht* to the atonality and "Sprechstimme" of *Pierrot Lunaire* in 1912.

All this storm and turmoil, however, must have seemed like some minor barbaric yelp to the generality of Kaiser Wilhelm's subjects as they prepared to celebrate the twenty-fifth anniversary of his accession in 1913. Amid Hosannahs to Emperor, prosperity, peace, and national greatness, there were a few discordant voices sounding dark premonitions. The political scientist and industrialist, Walther Rathenau, saw shadows rising, and warned of "insolence gone mad."[20] Frank Wedekind, playwright and poet, wrote toward the end of 1913:

> And yet I think: Before a year is gone,
> This graveyard peace will end. And evil signs
> Portend a war—whose equal none has seen,
> Since earth's beginnings.
>
> And yet fate hangs as by a single hair,
> Not fathomed by even the wisest.
> How shall we find this world once more—
> If we do find her—in the coming year?[21]

And with an equally acute sense of prophecy, Carl Hauptmann, Gerhart Hauptmann's brother, composed a play, *Krieg: Ein Te Deum* (*War: A Te Deum*), a nightmare vision in which the various imperial powers in the guise of beasts and birds of prey dispute for the possession of the earth, and fill it with cripples. The author might have been pleased had he foreseen that not long thereafter his book would fall into the hands of a young gymnasium student named Bertolt Brecht.

III

World War I and Its Aftermath

> Remember that the German people are chosen
> of God. On me, the German Emperor, the
> spirit of God has descended. I am His weapon,
> His sword, and His vice-regent.

KAISER WILHELM II

On June 28, 1914, the Austrian Archduke Francis Ferdinand was
assassinated in the Bosnian city of Sarajevo by a Serb nationalist.
On August 1 Germany declared war on Russia.

A war fever unlike anything witnessed before swept through
the nation. In political circles a "Burgfrieden"—a political truce—
was declared; anti-war sentiment was drowned out, war credits
jubilantly voted by the Reichstag, with only Karl Liebknecht and
Otto Rühle opposing them. The hope for a lightning war envisaged
in the celebrated Schlieffen plan, which was to crush France and
then England, was soon blighted. The opposing armies became
locked in frightful combat that offered no immediate decision.
Events far beyond the calculation of the involved generals began to
play a determining part in the ultimate destinies. Russian Czar
Nicolai was overthrown by his own people in March, 1917. In
April, America entered the war on the side of the Allies. Within
the Reich itself, the prolongation of the war, the effects of the
blockade began to be reflected in a general discontent, especially
among the working classes. In January 1918 numerous strikes broke
out. In August the intiative on the military front passed to the side
of the Allies, and the German collapse began. Mutinies spread

throughout the armed forces. Germany was in the throes of a revolution. A general strike swept Berlin. The Kaiser was forced to abdicate, and Friedrich Ebert became chancellor. On November 10, 1918, a general assembly of workers and soldiers councils elected a republican government headed by the majority Socialists.

Great occasions thrust great responsibilities upon the leaders of the people. It seemed now that the momentum of revolution would carry the entire nation with it. Never had a time been more propitious for radical changes. The feudal landed aristocracy, no less than the large industrialists, were powerless. Radical changes were called for, and would have laid the basis for a firm German democracy. As it turned out, the leaders of the German Social Democratic movement were not able to rise to these critical opportunities and occasions. Weighted down by a traditionally paternalistic and patriarchal structure of the party, essentially conservative and hesitant, they looked with amazement, suspicion, and finally with dread upon the newly formed workers' councils. They were scarcely aware of how the country had broken down. They opened themselves to tragic mistakes, such as leaving the old army intact, and retaining the old army leadership; and even turning to them in order to quell the insurgency of the workers. Thus in January, 1919, the uprising of Berlin workers was crushed; and on the fifteenth of that month Karl Liebknecht and Rosa Luxemburg were apprehended and shamefully murdered. In Bavaria, the abortive revolutionary government of Kurt Eisner was quickly suppressed, and Eisner himself assassinated in February, 1919. Rightist elements pursued their advantage, murdering not only those of the left, but liberals like Walther Rathenau, as well. The equivocal role of President Ebert in these suppressions has been a subject of acrimonious debate since, but there is no doubt that his ties to the army were close. Even the moderate *Manchester Guardian* was forced to comment that it seemed as if Germany was "now under the control of the same elements which applauded and carried on the war."[1]

With the left temporarily out of the way, the path was opened for the rightists and nationalists to prepare the grave for the infant Weimar Republic. A number of attempted "putsches" were but the preliminary and experimental skirmishes—the Kapp Putsch of 1920, which forced President Ebert into virtual flight; the abortive Munich Brauhaus Putsch of 1923, in which General Ludendorff and Adolf Hitler played major roles.

In January, 1923, the German mark stood at 4/10,000 of its original value. One and a half million workers were unemployed. The middle classes found themselves suddenly expropriated—and not by Socialists but by the bourgeois state itself. Faced by the danger of a total collapse and unpredictable political and social upheavals, American capital moved in, and in association with that of the Allies, succeeded in temporarily stabilizing the German economy with the Dawes Plan.

Part One

BERTOLT BRECHT IN GERMANY
1898-1933

I

The Beginnings:
Augsburg and Munich 1898-1920

> I came to the cities in times of disorder,
> When hunger reigned.
> I came among men in times of revolt,
> And I revolted with them.
> And so my time passed
> That was granted me here on earth.
>
> BRECHT, "An die Nachgeborenen"

Bertolt Brecht was born in Augsburg, Auf dem Rain, Number
Seven, on February 10, 1898. He was baptized as Eugen Berthold
Friedrich Brecht. Both parents came from Achern, in the Black
Forest where the family's tobacco shop, presided over by Bertolt's
cousin, still exists. His father, Berthold, found employment in the
Haindl paper factory in Augsburg, and eventually, in 1914, became its
director. He was Catholic by birth, and had been living in Augsburg
since 1893. His mother, Sophie Brezing, was Protestant, and young
Bertolt was brought up in her faith. A younger brother, Walther,
continued in his father's profession, and is now professor of paper
technology in Darmstadt.

The household was a good bourgeois one.

> I grew up the son
> Of well-to-do people. My parents
> Tied a collar around me, and brought me up
> In the habits of being waited on
> And instructed me in the art of commanding.[1]

55

Arnolt Bronnen, who lived with the Brecht family for a short while after Brecht's mother died in 1920, describes the widower as crotchety, demanding, and authoritarian. Brecht was always remarkably reticent about his personal feelings, and there is little expression in his writings of any deep relationship with his father. The only evidence that the situation in the Brecht household was more than tolerable lies in the fact that Brecht never composed an anti-father play, as Bronnen, Hasenclever, and many other German writers of the time did.

His mother is mentioned occasionally. Once she reproves him for loose language, and the son notes in a poem, "Why do they print so much about Truth in the Catechism, when you can't even say what *is*?"[2] When she died, on May 1, 1920, he mourned her in two poems (unpublished during his lifetime). "Why," he asks, "don't we say the important things to people while they're still alive?"[3]

> When she was gone, they buried her.
> Flowers grow, butterflies play above her grave.
> She, who was so light, she scarcely pressed the ground,
> How much pain was needed, to make her so light![4]

When Bertolt Brecht was still very young, the family entered upon some measure of prosperity, and they removed to the more spacious factory-sponsored housing in the Bleichstrasse, No. 2. Both his birthplace and this house are still intact and preserve something of the quiet serenity and Gemütlichkeit of those earlier days.

In this new home, as Brecht was to describe it, there was an "avenue of chestnut trees along the old city moat; on the other side lay the ramparts with the remains of the one-time city walls. Swans swam in the pond-like waters. The chestnuts shed their yellow leaves."[5]

Four years of elementary school were followed by entrance into the Realgymnasium (destroyed during the Second World War). Young Eugen Berthold seems to have derived little benefit from his education here.

Elementary school, [he wrote later to the critic and friend Herbert Jhering] bored me for four years. During my nine years of being "preserved" at the Augsburg Realgymnasium, I did not suceed in educating my teachers. My tendency toward indolence and independence was constantly fostered by them. At the university I attended courses in medicine and learned to play the guitar. During my stay at the gymnasium I contracted a heart condition as a result of my indulgence in sports, which opened the way for me into the mysteries of metaphysics.[6]

The young boy's curiosity no doubt drew him to places where there was more excitement and life than at school, and others, perhaps less reputable, like the red-light district not far from the Cathedral, in the notorious Hasengasse.[7] More respectable and no less exciting were the annual *Herbstplärrer,* the autumn barkers' fairs, with their

booths on the "little drill ground," with the music of many merry-go-rounds, and "panoramas" that displayed crude pictures of historical events, like "The Shooting of the Anarchist Ferrer at Madrid" or "Nero Surveys the Fire of Rome" or "The Bavarian Lions storm the defenses of Düppel," or "The Flight of Charles the Bold at the Battle of Murten." I remember the horse of Charles the Bold. It had enormous frightened eyes, as though it felt the horror of the historical situation.[8]

This was, of course, better than school. In the Realgymnasium, Brecht recalled many years later:

Our best teacher was a huge, amazingly ugly man, who in his younger days had aspired to a professorship, but had failed in the attempt. This disappointment brought all his latent powers to fruition. He liked to surprise us with examinations, and exclaimed with ecstasy when we did not know the answers. He made himself almost more obnoxious because he had the habit of retiring two or three times during the lesson behind the blackboard and fishing out of his coat-pocket a piece of unwrapped cheese, which he proceeded to crunch while he was instructing us. He taught us chemistry, but it would not have mattered if it had been knitting. . . . We did not learn chemistry from him, but we did learn how to avenge ourselves. Once every year, the school commissioner came, allegedly to see how we were getting along, but we all knew actually to find out how we were being taught. Once, when he came, we used the occasion to "break" our teacher. We did not respond to a single question, and sat there like idiots. This time the man did not exhibit delight in our failure. He developed the jaundice, was laid up for a time, and on his return was never the same cheese-crumbler he had once been.[9]

The other teachers, who year after year repeated the same "quantity" of knowledge with mechanical dullness, sublimated their suppressed domestic and personal troubles in the classroom, and instructed their pupils "in all forms of fraudulent behavior."[10]

When it came to duping a severe instructor, Brecht was no mean practitioner himself, as when he discovered that the best way of raising a low grade on an otherwise deficient French composition (graded in accordance with number of errors), was not to try to erase the red markings, but actually to add to them under the correct formulations, thus embarrassing the teacher and compelling him to revise the grade![11]

Brecht was sixteen years old when Germany declared war on Russia on August 1, 1914. Like so many millions of his countrymen, he became feverishly patriotic. He had already begun to write poetry, and with some of his productions he now approached the Augsburg newspaper, the *Neueste Nachrichten*. Almost thirty-five years later, one of its editors, Wilhelm Brüstle, recalled how he had "discovered Brecht":

In the first years of the First World War—probably around 1915—I was then an editor of an Augsburg newspaper—a young gymnasium student came to me—he might have been in the fifth form—and brought me his first poems. They had something to do with the war. They were marked by a compressed, almost intoxicating rhythm, not only completely free of the conventional and epigonal—but so full-blooded that they brought a new note into German poetry—something of the kind Baudelaire had brought to French poetry. . . . Brecht was greatly encouraged by my reception . . . , and the publication of his poems. He was a timid, retiring young man, who spoke only when he was wound up. . . . Politically, he was inclined to the left. I learned from one of his professors that he was near being expelled from school for writing an anti-war essay during the war; but this teacher saved him by persuading his colleagues that this was a case of a "student's head turned by the war" . . . [Brecht] discharged something of an electric current.[12]

Some allowance must here be made for a blurred perspective and chronological confusion. Brecht was not, in 1915, much "inclined to the left," as we shall soon see. But on the whole, this is an accurate picture of him. Actually, during the first year of the war, he was an unalloyed patriot. The poems he wrote were by no means remarkable, and Brüstle is undoubtedly thinking of one or two later ones. But they are not unworthy of so young a boy. He signed them "Berthold Eugen." "Der Freiwillige," which appeared in the newspaper in 1914, recounts the experiences of a volunteer who finds that now that he is a German soldier, the bystanders, who had not addressed a word to him because his son had misbehaved, throw him a rose.[13] "A Modern Legend" is more sober, and describes the contrasting behavior of victor and vanquished—the rejoicing on one side and the wailing on the other as the casualty reports come in. Then there is quiet. "Only the mothers wept, there as here."[14] Other poems still glory in the brave soldier. "German songs, German flags," Brecht exclaims, "will wave over your head, soldier."[15] A note of doubt creeps into "The Ensign." A soldier writes his mother that he can no longer take the war; but three days later he is dead, having led a heroic charge.[16] In "Der belgische Acker" ("The Belgian Field") he celebrates German soldiers as they plow and seed Belgian fields, "digging from cemeteries fields of bread."[17]

But suddenly, amidst much pedestrian verse, the fifteen-year-old Brecht reveals the unmistakable gift of the true poet. The poem "The Burning Tree" first appeared in the Gymnasium publication.

> Through the evening's hazy, ruddy mist
> We saw the red, steeply mounting flames,
> Swelling and beating toward the dark sky.
> In the fields, in sultry silence,
> A burning tree
> Crackled.
>
> Rigid, fear-numbed branches stretch
> Black and wildly ringed
> By mad rain of sparks.

Through mist the fiery torrent flames.
Eerily mad, withered leaves dance,
Jubilant, free, to char the ancient tree trunk,
In mockery.

But grand and silent, lighting up the night,
Like some old warrior, weary, worn to death,
Yet royal in his straits,
Stood the burning tree.

And suddenly he raised his stiff, black branches.
And sky-high shoots the purple flame,
An instant stands he upright against the black sky—
Then midst the cavorting of sparks,
The tree-trunk crashes.[18]

Already he exhibits that passion for a strutting, dashing Americanism that was to be with him for many years. The "Song of the Railroad Gang of Fort Donald" was written in 1916, and anticipates his later style:

The men of Fort Donald—heigh-ho!
They journeyed upstream—to woods soulless and eternal.
But the rains came one day, and the woods turned to seas,
And they stood knee-high in the waters.
And morning will never come, they said,
And we will drown before dawn, they said.
And wordless they listened to the Erie wind.[19]

His war spirit seems to have waned at about this time. He read Carl Hauptmann's *Krieg* not long after its publication, but even in this anti-war play he saw only "Heldenmut"—heroic courage and self-sacrifice. But there is no doubt that he soon got himself into hot water over a pacifist essay, with its theme that "it is not *dulce et decorum pro patria mori*." Only blockheads, he stated, could think of death lightly. He was saved through the intercession of his teacher, the Benedictine Romuald Sauer of St. Stephen's.[20]

Brecht matriculated at the medical faculty of the University of Munich in 1917, but he was soon drafted into the army and transferred to an Augsburg military hospital as a medical orderly. Whatever war spirit still survived within him was forever crushed out in the horrifying experiences to which he was now subjected. This is the way he described his feelings many years later to the Russian writer Serge Tretyakov, his description no doubt romantically heightened by time's distance:

As a very young boy I was mobilized, and served in a hospital. I dressed wounds, applied iodine, gave enemas and blood-transfusions. Should a doctor have said to me, "Brecht, amputate this leg," I would have replied, "At your command, Excellency!" and would have amputated the leg. Had someone said to me, "Brecht, make a trepanning!", I would have opened a man's skull and messed with his brain. I saw with my own eyes how they patched up people post-haste so as to ship them back to the front as soon as possible.[21]

It is out of these experiences that the true poet was born. At about this time he composed what is probably one of his best-known poems, "Die Legende vom toten Soldaten," "The Legend of the Dead Soldier," which was not only to make him famous but also to place him on Hitler's blacklist of 1923. Here Brecht already exhibits a mastery of the ballad-metre and of satire. Here he shows himself the true descendant of Heinrich Heine.

> Und als der Krieg im fünften Lenz
> Keinen Ausblick auf Frieden bot
> Da zog der Soldat seine Konsequenz
> Und starb den Heldentod.

> And when the war had lasted five springs,
> And of peace there wasn't even a breath,
> The soldier saw what it was all about,
> And he died a hero's death.[22]

But the Kaiser could not be satisfied with so premature a demise, and at his command a commission draws the dead man from his grave, hangs two nurses and his half-naked wife about his neck and declares him once more fit for duty. With the snarl of military bands as accompaniment, and with the help of two orderlies and a priest with incense, the soldier is marched through town and village amid general jubilation, once more to go to his hero's death.

> And since the soldier stinks a mile,
> A priest limps on before,
> Waving an incense burner over him,
> So he should stink no more.

The revolutionary upheavals at the end of 1918 and at the beginning of 1919 in Bavaria, though they no doubt affected Brecht, did not as yet deepen his political understanding. In later years he tended to predate his political maturation. Thus, in 1955, when he went to Moscow to accept the Stalin Prize, he gave a somewhat heightened account of his reactions at the time.

I was 19 years old, when I heard of your great Revolution. I was twenty when I saw the reflection of that great fire in my own homeland. I was a medical orderly in an Augsburg hospital. The barracks as well as the hospital became empty. The old city was suddenly filled with new men, coming in large processions from the suburbs, and filled with a liveliness such as the streets of the well-to-do, of the officials, and tradesmen, had not known before. For a few days working-class women spoke at the swiftly improvised councils, scolding the young workers wearing army togs, and the factories obeyed the orders of the workers. Only a few days, but what days! Everywhere fighters, yet at the same time peaceful people, people who were building.[23]

Acually, his understanding of the political situation of 1919-1920, was, to say the least, scanty. He gave a more accurate picture of his sentiments in the *Berlin Film-Kurier* of November 9, 1928:

At that time I was a member of the soldiers council in an Augsburg hospital, and I became one at the pressing exhortations of some friends, who insisted they had a deep interest in that matter. (As it turned out later on, I was in no position to change the state so as to make it beneficial to them.) We all suffered from a lack of political convictions; and I particularly from a lack of capacity for enthusiasm. I got a pile of work to do. The plan of the High Command of the army to send me to war had failed the year before. Favored by fortune, I understood how to inhibit my military education, and after six months I had not even mastered the military salute, and I was considered too sloppy even in those slack times. . . . In short, I was hardly different from the preponderant majority of the other soldiers, who, of course, had had enough of the war, but were unprepared to think politically. I do not recall this situation with pleasure today.[24]

What actually happened in those crucial, brutal days, in the midst of the uprisings in Munich and the establishment of the short-lived soviet government in Bavaria, no doubt unsettled Brecht. As he told Tretyakov:

In 1919 Leviné raised the banner of soviet power in nearby Munich. Augsburg reacted in the purple glow and reflected glory of Munich. The hospital was the only military unit in Augsburg. It elected me to the Augsburg revolutionary committee . . . We did not have a single red guardsman. We did not have time to issue a single decree, or to nationalize a bank, or close a church. Two days later a military patrol of General Epp's troops—the "pacifier"—swept into the city. A member of the revolutionary committee hid in my room till he could escape. Then Bavaria disappeared into the past.[25]

There were upheavals in Augsburg on the occasion of a demonstration against the murder of Kurt Eisner on February 22, 1919, that took a toll of six killed and almost forty arrested and convicted. Brecht no doubt shared the horror at these outrages, as he had done at the murder of Rosa Luxemburg and Karl Liebknecht in January.

He returned to his studies at the Ludwig Maximilian University in Munich. But these became more and more desultory, as his interests shifted from medicine to general science, and from science to literature. He was probably most interested in the seminar on the drama conducted by Dr. Arthur Kutscher, Frank Wedekind's fervent apostle and future biographer.

However, Munich was more than merely a university town. The magnificent city by the Isar River gloried in being the Paris of the south and the Florence of the north. And with some justice. Though politically conservative, nationalist, and after the revolutionary upheavals, more reactionary than ever, it was yet the meeting ground of the most advanced literary and artistic figures of

Germany. Thomas Mann and his brother Heinrich had settled here. This was the city of Frank Wedekind, and also the home of the boldest, frankest of satirical journals, *Simplicissimus,* to which the most talented writers and artists of the time contributed. At the Café Stefanie one could meet painters, poets, playwrights, journalists —such men of letters as Arnold Zweig, the novelist, Johannes Becher, expressionist poet turned Communist, Lion Feuchtwanger, already a literary success, destined to play a providential part in Brecht's life, and, on occasions, the legendary Frank Wedekind himself.

Brecht would commute between Munich and Augsburg; for in his native city, and in the attic of his paternal home he could find that freedom from distraction which enabled him to write. Here, his only indulgence consisted in visits to the movies.

He had begun writing dramatic criticism for the Augsburg *Tageszeitung* in 1918, and for the left-wing Augsburg *Volkswille* in 1919. With his mother's death in 1920, his ties with Augsburg—certainly with his family—were practically severed. He removed to Munich, where he settled in the Akademiestrasse 15.

Life here proved far from unpleasant. True, this was the cradle of National Socialism, and its manifestations were already all too evident. Anti-Semitism was rampant. Bavarian separatism was in the air. But to compensate for these unpleasantnesses, there were the theatres, the opera, the art exhibitions, and not least, so far as Brecht was concerned, the political cabaret, the so-called "Überbrettl," and its "Bänkelsang" or "Moritat"—those frank, sharp, biting, unsparing ballads and songs, modeled on the French cabaret chanson, often barbed with political satire. The most celebrated of the Munich cabarets was that of the Elf Scharfrichter ("The Eleven Executioners"), in which outstanding poets like Richard Dehmel, Detlev von Liliencron, and Otto Julius Bierbaum recited their own verses. At the Münchner Kammerspiele, in the Maximilianstrasse, was to be found the most advanced theatrical company of the city, headed since 1913 by the enterprising Otto Falckenberg. Falckenberg was very soon to discover Brecht.

Brecht in the Munich Lachkeller
with Karl Valentin, 1919-1920

Brecht, 1927

Brecht, 1927

"Bertolt Brecht" by Leonard Baskin

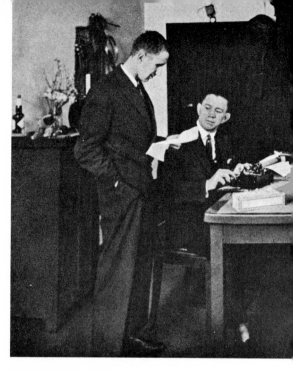

Brecht and the boxer
Samson-Körner

Kurt Weill
in the Twenties

Brecht liked to sing. He liked to accompany himself on the guitar, to settings of his own making. He liked to recite his own poems in a strident voice. At heart he was a minstrel. He very soon found himself a member of a troupe of entertainers in the Lachkeller, the "Laughing Cellar." This was a group led by Karl Valentin. We can still see young Brecht, in a contemporary photograph, with his clarinet, cap slung down over his brow (already a characteristic Brecht mannerism), sitting alongside Liesl Karlstadt, who often played the "straight man" to Valentin, who is shown standing in front.

Karl Valentin! Today his is a name almost totally unknown; but to his contemporaries he was a legend. He has been called the "metaphysical clown." Consensus has it that he was inimitable (like Charlie Chaplin). His skits, monologues, songs, comic interludes, performed in the local dialects, with mime and gesture conveying even more than words, were to become proverbial. He composed his own sketches, recited his own poems, and joined to himself a skillful band of associates. He most frequently took the part of the "little man," the "kleine Seele"—a sort of Chaplinesque character, whom the critic Walter Benjamin was aptly to describe as the "cudgeled hero," and who appealed to Brecht with imperishable force. A number of sketches Brecht wrote in the twenties testify to the direct influence of Valentin; but even more profoundly Brecht was impressed by Valentin's mimetic art, that which Brecht was to call the "gestus"—the totality of the imitations of the "unheroic heroes" of the sketches. They were the Schweyks in embryo.

Brecht never forgot Valentin, nor the debt he owed him. Later he described the "deadly-serious" way in which Valentin operated through the confusion and noises of the tavern, so that "one immediately had the feeling: this man will not make jokes. He is himself a joke."[26]

We have another unforgettable portrait of Valentin in Lion Feuchtwanger's novel *Success*. He is called Hierl,

the melancholy clown [who] was always trying to solve absurd problems by a lugubrious pseudo-logic. Asked, for example, why he wore a pair of spectacles without glasses, he would reply that surely it was better than nothing.[27]

In one of his most celebrated skits, he was an orchestra violinist.

He was crudely painted, his bottle-nose woefully white and two red spots on his cheeks, and he could not be said to sit on his rickety chair, he clung to it like a fly; he had enormous shoes on and his lean shanks were cleverly twisted round the leg of his chair. It was supposed to be an orchestra rehearsal. Hierl played the violin at first, but he had also taken on the kettledrum, since the drummer wasn't there . . . , and the conductor's tie was coming undone, one ought to tell him . . .[28]

Such was Karl Valentin, a sharp contrast to the writer who was to exercise perhaps the profoundest effect on Brecht, Frank Wedekind. Brecht could hardly have gotten to know Wedekind, for he died on March 9, 1918, but he must have seen him on occasion. He knew Wedekind's poems and plays, and he shared Wedekind's passion for declaiming and singing (if singing it may be called) his own poems.

One of the earliest of Brecht's prose pieces is dedicated to the memory of Wedekind.

Last Saturday [Brecht wrote] we sat on the banks of the Lech in Augsburg, under a star-spangled sky, and sang his songs, accompanying them with guitar. We sang the song of Franziska, about the blind boy, and a dance song. . . .

His vitality was the best thing about him. Whether it was an auditorium he was entering, where there were hundreds of noisy students, or a room, or the stage, with his peculiar gait, his sharply-cut, iron cranium, tilted forward—somewhat awkward and disturbing—everything suddenly became still. . . . A few weeks ago he sang in the Bonbonnière with his guitar—those songs—with a brittle voice, somewhat monotonous and untrained. Never has a singer so moved and inspired. . . . He did not seem a mortal. . . . He belonged with Tolstoy and Strindberg among the great educators of the new Europe. His greatest work was his personality.[29]

But Brecht was not the only one to feel the sway of Wedekind. It is not too much to say that in some respects his was one of the most powerful influences in German literature at the beginning of the century. He was the bête noire of the German bourgeoisie, its scourge and terror. His earliest succès-de-scandale, *Frühlingser-wachen* (*Spring's Awakening*), in 1891, outraged the moral sensibilities of society and its policemen, and failed of production until many years later. A "sex-tragedy" of ignorant adolescence, it thrust upon society the responsibility for its hypocritical treatment and destruction of young people. How much more shocking even than the frank presentation of a sexual relationship was the appearance in that play of a young corpse, with his own head under his arm! This was Expressionism with a vengeance . . .

Wedekind was to outrage his fellow Germans up to the end of his life. His plays and poems are filled with social buccaneers, swindlers, amoral castigators of polite society. They are all avenging Wedekinds, who in turn were to be scourged and decapitated by that very society!

Actor, poet, playwright, minstrel (like Brecht, he composed his own accompaniments), Wedekind had a passion for circuses, zoos, and cabarets. A storm-ridden genius, he poured vials of vitriol and wrath upon convention and upon his Germany. One of his satirical poems in *Simplicissimus* (to which he contributed frequently) was directed against the Kaiser himself, and brought upon him the charge of lèse-majesté and a prison sentence. The world of Kaiser Wilhelm II was to him a zoo, through which man wandered, in reality an animal—savage, bestial, poisonous. Yet he was full of compassion, and in his poems there is genuine feeling for the downtrodden. For he was the son of a Francophile and Americanophile father, a liberal who had lived in the United States and imbibed some of the free traditions of republicanism and democracy. In Wedekind's plays, the capitalist world of Wilhelminian Germany is turned into a grotesquerie and monstrosity. In *The Earth-Spirit* and *Pandora's Box* (his most notorious, if not most celebrated plays) he changed the biblical character of Lilith into Lulu, the demonic vampire, the terroristic élan-vitale, the satanic demi-urge, symbol

and embodiment of that elemental force of sex which Wedekind
regarded as the absolute "Ding-an-sich"—a transcendent, irresistible,
irrepressible power. It was as if Zola's Nana, that incarnation of
Paris, the courtesan, were turned into a natural force, the erotic
"Will" of Schopenhauer, as natural and naive as Nature herself,
and equally shameless and inexorable. She was "das wahre Tier,"
"das wilde schöne Tier," ("the true beast, the wild beautiful beast"),
the Earth-Spirit.

"Morality," Wedekind once said, "is the best business in the
world," and "sin is the mythological term for bad business."[30] Unlike
Ibsen, whom he detested, he did not ascribe to his characters a
pre-history of "guilt." There is only one guilt, the guilt of living
in this world, and "sin" is the sin against the Holy Ghost of Life
itself, that is, the Flesh. Nature wars with ossified custom—the decayed order of the world. Dead custom has today deromanticized
everything, so that even Mephistopheles is nothing but an insurance
agent.[31] Strindberg's horror at the world and existence becomes in
Wedekind a kind of mad exultation at the triumph of instinct.
Working-class audiences interpreted his plays as onslaughts on
capitalist society, as the unmasking of a dying order, and the irrepressible Lulu as the incarnation of that force that was eventually
to destroy it.

Frank Wedekind was himself someting of a wild animal, fero-
cious and untamed. An intellectual giant with a physical deformity
(he limped), he was an astonishing sight as he stood on the stage
and recited his poems in a cracked voice. To Brecht, little as he
knew him in person, Wedekind came to represent not the past but
the present and the future of the world. For Brecht, too, was
haunted by the animal nature of man, and the savage combat for
survival; and he found Wedekind's grotesque, merciless, fierce but
marvelously disciplined language, with its touches of racy vernacular, models he could easily identify with and follow.

Brecht, at this time, was like his own literary creation, Baal, insatiable. His powers of absorption were unlimited. What he ab-

sorbed he used, or was to use. Later he would be charged with plagiarism—an accusation he would admit and dismiss with his usual sang-froid. Whether it was from the present or the past, he could take generously. If Valentin and Wedekind stood for the present, to which he was drawn, the French *poètes-maudits*—the "damned" poets Arthur Rimbaud, Paul Verlaine, Charles Baudelaire —attracted him no less. He knew little French; and his knowledge of other foreign languages was, to say the least, to remain elementary. But at this moment, the Bohemianism, the nihilism, the Satanism, the rebellion of these poets found ready response within himself. He understood their raptures and hatreds when they proclaimed the terror and magic of cities, when they damned the bourgeoisie, when they exulted in their carrion-lusts and loves, when they preached the night. For even through the German translations they came close to him, in their superb music, in their immaculate precision of words, in their images. Rimbaud and Verlaine drew him particularly—their tragi-comic relationship, their hunger for life, their passions. In Rimbaud's defiance of civilization, in his exaltation of the savage, Brecht saw reflections of himself and his needs. Rimbaud's beautiful "Bateau ivre" and his *Une saison en enfer* ("The Drunken Boat" and *A Season in Hell*) imprinted themselves upon him indelibly.

To another bohemian of a more distant age he was drawn with equal passion. François Villon, fifteenth-century poet-martyr, scholar, vagabond, lover of cities, of brothels, of people, of dingy corners of his land, poet of the insulted and the strayed—what a fit companion to the French *poètes-maudits* of a later generation! German poets, Klabund, Wedekind, Morgenstern, had already translated his "Testaments"—and Brecht must have felt like another Villon, standing between two ages.

To Villon, Brecht dedicated a number of poems, among them a sonnet:

> François Villon was poor people's child,
> His cradle was rocked by cool spring winds,

In his young days—amid snow and wind,
Only the sky above him was truly fair.
François Villon who never a bed could find,
Found soon enough that he loved the wind.
Heaven's sweet guerdon never beckoned him,
And constables soon broke his heart's great pride,
And yet he too was God's own son,
Through wind and rain, he is gone—long, ago.
And all his reward—the martyr's block.

François Villon died when he fled this prison
Before they caught him on the road, his last ruse.
But still his shameless soul lives on and on,
Long as a song—that can never die.
But when he stretched, and then gave up his ghost,
He found too late indeed, such stretching pleased him most.[32]

Brecht's *Three Penny Opera* was to be filled with lines and reminiscences of Villon, which, as we shall see, unkind critics were not slow in pointing out.

Of all the German writers of the past, there was one to whom he felt most akin: Georg Büchner, stormy petrel of the early nineteenth century. The "marvelous boy" died at the age of twenty-three in 1837. His plays had almost completely disappeared from men's memory, until restored by an accidental discovery of a manuscript in the third quarter of the nineteenth century. Gradually, one of Germany's major literary geniuses was resurrected. Two of his plays were destined to fill a decisive role in shaping the post-war German drama: *Wozzeck*, forerunner of the modern expressionistic theatre, was revived at the Berlin Lessing-Theater in 1913, to be followed by Max Reinhardt's productions of this and another masterpiece, *Dantons Tod (Danton's Death)*. Like Brecht, Büchner had been a medical student; but in addition, he was also a most original scientist and a brilliant zoologist. In his philosophical outlook he was a materialist, and in his politics a revolutionary, though he died despairing of Germany's future. His revolutionary political ideas he expressed with fervor in *Der hessische Landbote* (*The Hessian Courier*) in which he framed his own declaration of the rights of man for Germany. Its motto read, "Frieden den Hütten! Krieg den Palästen!" "Peace to the huts! War on the palaces!" "Our young people," he wrote, "are reproached with using force. But are we not now living in a condition of force?"[33]

In the tragedy *Wozzeck,* Büchner created the first German proletarian play. In *Danton's Tod* he anticipated the modern "epic" theatre. Aside from his revolutionary appeal, Büchner opened for Brecht many new resources: linguistically, the broken speech patterns, the so-called "Nebeneinanderreden"—the way his characters have of speaking "past" one another; the skilful manipulation of a strong, racy dialect. In dramatic structure, Büchner was to reenforce Brecht's preference for the loose, Elizabethan episodic chronicle play. There were other points of sympathy too. They both saw a close relationship between "food and morality"—Büchner particularized the former as potatoes! Equally interesting is the preference of both playwrights for the "passive" hero—Büchner in the character of Wozzeck, and Brecht, soon, in the character of Andreas Kragler, in *Drums in the Night* and elsewhere.[34]

II

The Heaven of the Expressionists

Niemand weint bitterlich, man lacht, man
   lacht,
he, he, die Schädelstätte Abendland—
beschädigte Crescencen, Wermuthsterne—
Die Orgie 1920.

No one weeps bitterly; they laugh, they laugh,
He, he, Golgothan Occident—
Damaged crescent moons—wormwood stars—
Orgy 1920.

GOTTFRIED BENN, "Prolog—1920"

"Gedanken sind frei" ("Thoughts are free")—so goes the old German song. In the hectic and harrowing years of 1918 to 1923, a dismembered society—hungry, unemployed, politically convulsed and confused, repressed in its potential for external activity—turns its eyes inward. As never before "Zerrissenheit" and "Innerlichkeit" mark the creative artistic response of these years. Where the body seems chained to the earth, the mind soars. So it had been before in the time of Schiller and Goethe, when art appeared to be the refuge and realization of ideals apparently unattainable on earth. Now chaos mingles with apocalypse, street-fighting with chiliastic visions. The despairing eyes turn eastward toward Russia, where the hopes of mankind rest upon the building of a new social order. Or they turn to the Germanic past, with the dream of resuscitating the Holy Roman Empire. Or they turn upward, toward the sky.

Or they merely turn downward, to rest in inaction, or flounder in sardonic cynicism, undirected defiance and rebellion.

Brecht was a child of this age, and shared both its chaos and its wilder hopes. Around him in Germany, as rarely before, he saw a restless artistic activity, thrusting in innumerable directions. There is, at first sight, something bizarre, if not macabre, in the contemplation of the various schools—dadaists, futurists, surrealists, and many other "ists"—meeting over tables at the Café Grössenwahn in Berlin, to take only one example, arguing, shouting, planning world-shaking changes, against the background of a downward-spiralling German mark, a skyrocketing American dollar, and the prospect of a menu of turnips and rolls and ersatz coffee—and, toward early morning, the dreary return to an ice-cold lodging. "Épater le bourgeois"—shocking the bourgeoisie—(and themselves too!) became their favorite pastime. Dadaists provoked with their shameless absurdities, such as the poet Hülsenbeck's "Die Kühe sitzen auf Telegraphenstangen und spielen Schach. . . ." "The cows sit on telegraph poles and play chess." Dadaist and futurist magazines which badgered the government were born and quickly died, or were suppressed and prosecuted. Such was the fate of *Pleite* (*Bankruptcy*), in which the gifted Georg Grosz published his savage caricatures of the contemporary German Bürger. We can still see him in a photograph of those days, along with his fellow painter John Heartfield, proclaiming the glories of constructivist art and carrying a sign: "Die Kunst ist tot—Es lebe die Maschinenkunst Tatlins" ("Art is dead—Long live the machine art of Tatlin"), which served as advertisement for the first Berlin Dada exhibition of 1920. (Vladimir Tatlin was the celebrated Russian representative of the "Constructivist" school of art.)

Futurists and dadaists dreamt that art would somehow bring about a new "revolution" of man, with other than political or social weapons. Thus, one of the founders of Dada, Hugo Ball, relates an incident which took place in Zurich (Dada's cradle) in 1916. Around him gathered such figures as Hans Arp, Tristan Tzara,

Hülsenbeck; and their scandalizing performances were given at the Cabaret Voltaire in the staid Swiss city.

Strange coincidence! [Ball writes]. While we were having our Cabaret in Zurich, Spiegelgasse 1, there lived directly across from us, in the same Spiegelgasse, Number 6, if I am not mistaken, Herr Ulianov-Lenin. Every evening he must surely have heard our music-making and our tirades —I don't know whether with pleasure and profit. And while we were opening our gallery in the Bahnhofstrasse, the Russians journeyed to St. Petersburg, in order to set the revolution on its feet. Is Dadaism something of a mark and gesture of a counter-play to Bolshevism? Does it oppose to the destruction and thorough casting-up of accounts the utterly Don Quixotic, unpurposeful, incomprehensible side of the world? It will be interesting to observe what happens there and here.[1]

It would, indeed, be interesting to know what Lenin really thought of such a perpetration, seriously recited to an entranced crowd at the cabaret by its author, Hugo Ball, himself:

'Gadji, beri bimba . . . .' (etc., ad infinitum), declaimed, as the author states, "langsam und feierlich" ("slowly and solemnly").[2] For Dada was bent on a campaign to "destroy language as a social organ."[3]

But the literary and artistic movement which probably most graphically reflects the delirium of the years between 1918 and 1923 is Expressionism. It is not easy to define, for it has many faces, and its bosom is broad enough to embrace divergent, often contradictory, offspring. Expressionism has been defined as the "intellectual revolt against the bourgeoisie that is on the verge of suicide," and expressionists as "prisoners of an unfree age," in which they "affirm absolute freedom."[4]

Theodor Däubler, archpriest of expressionism, announced in 1919: "Unsere Zeit hat ein grosses Vorhaben: einen neuen Ausbruch der Seele! Das Ich schafft die Welt!" ("Our times have a grand design: a new eruption of the soul! The I creates the world!")[5]

Into the boiling cauldron of expressionism are poured ingredients from Darwin, Freud, Marx, Hegel, Zola, Ibsen, Wedekind, and Strindberg. But despite this ragoût character, it does have a central element: the Absolute Ego. Consciousness and the "I" are the creators of the universe, and truth lies in the "colonization of the in-ward." Subjective idealism is once more rehabilitated and enthroned; the battle-cries of German Romanticism and Novalis' dictum, "Nach innen geht der geheimnisvolle Weg" ("The secret path threads its way to that which is within us") are re-echoed with explosive fervor.

As the self-proclaimed creators, and hence the masters, of reality, the expressionists insisted that the "sense of the object must be rooted out." The expressionist's "whole dimension becomes vision. He does not look, he sees . . . The chain of facts no longer exists: factories, sickness, whores, shrieks, hunger. What exists at this moment is the vision of them."[6]

If the "I" is the creative center, then Man is the object of the expressionists' address. Already as far back as 1910, Franz Werfel, one of the most gifted of their poets, had cried out, "O Mensch!"

> My only wish, O Man, is to be kind to you!
> Whether Negro, or acrobat, or still at your mother's breast,
>
> Soldier, or aviator, patient and courageous. . . .
>
> Thus I belong to you, and to all.
> Do not, I beg of you, resist me!
> O that it might some time soon come to pass
> That brothers, we embrace as brothers![7]

Such addresses echo Baudelaire, probably Walt Whitman too. With that appeal to "O Mensch!" is conjoined the heart's cry: "Wandlung!"—Change! Transformation! For expressionism is also revolution by incantation. The ego of the poet thrusts itself forward, opens its heart and exposes its passionate, if somewhat vague, love of humanity—generalized humanity, humanity in the abstract. Declamation instigates rebellion. Prospero's magic wand and books are suddenly resurrected to effect unpredictable changes in man.

Expressionism is autobiography of the soul. Its sources are as complex as its nature: German Romanticism, Novalis' dream and night world; Goethe's *Faust*. Its more modern roots are to be sought for in such figures as Strindberg, Wedekind and Freud. Strindberg had broken the mould of the naturalistic drama (of which he had been an outstanding exponent), and had turned toward the drama of the "soul," in the *Dream Play* and, even more notably, in *Toward Damascus*. In the latter he had charted his personal journey toward salvation—his own *via crucis*—through symbol, nightmare, vision, finally to reach the Nirvana of resignation. No less significant for the German expressionists was that whole tradition of the "unconscious" that threads its way from Schopenhauer to Sigmund Freud. The irrational, the unconscious, the repressed, the dream-world, all these are fused in the dramatic work of the expressionists. Discontinuity—with its own internal logic, the stream of consciousness—internal dialogue, kaleidoscope, dissociation, break-up of time and space sequences are utilized to give a picture and history of the soul. Inner reality is laid bare through symbol; character becomes abstracted, because conceived as universal. Man is capitalized, as Brother, Sister, Mother, Poet, Prophet, Warrior . . .

In the roll call of the pictorial arts, the reputations of few of the expressionists have survived to this day, but there were great names among them: Max Beckmann and Georg Grosz, to mention only two. In the theatre, where they were even more vocal and numerous, though many of them are today forgotten, their influence has been profound: One need only name them to realize the extent of the movement: Walter Hasenclever, Fritz von Unruh, Reinhard Goering, Ernst Toller, Franz Werfel, Georg Kaiser, Hanns Johst, Arnolt Bronnen . . . , and, though not part of them, but in many ways related, the young Bertolt Brecht.

Two seemingly contradictory elements predominate in literary expressionism: passivism and activism. In Franz Werfel expressionism is chiliastic and, at times, pessimistic; in Ernst Toller it is humanitarian and revolutionary.

But its central core is rebellion: Rebellion of youth against age, son against father, pupil against teacher, the new against the old. "Jugendkultur" and "Jugendautonomie"—"youth culture" and "youth autonomy"—become the battle-cries. That violence which was inhibited in the political arena now storms through bedroom, father's study, the classroom. The paternalism of fist and glove, the discipline of the army, the celebrated "Kadavergehorsam und Wachtparade"—obedience of the carcass and of parade grounds—are assaulted with unprecedented vigor and frankness. Parricide runs like a ghoulish strain through plays and stories, from what is taken as the first German expressionist drama, Reinhard Sorge's *Der Bettler (The Beggar)*, 1912, to its most rabid successor, Arnolt Bronnen's *Vatermord (Parricide)*, 1920. Walter Hasenclever's *Der Sohn (The Son)*, 1914, speaks filial rebellion and defiance in the name of "community," crying out, "Death to all fathers who contemn us."

The war against our fathers is the very same as the vengeance carried out against princes a hundred years ago. Then crowned heads enslaved, oppressed, and ground down their subjects. . . . Today it is we who chant the Marseillaise.[8]

There are, of course, other than parricidal notes to be found in the expressionist drama. The prematurely deceased poet, Ludwig Rubiner, called for an active participation in what he called "living," and pleaded for an end to the lethargy that seemed to have overtaken the artists. In *Der Mensch in der Mitte (The Man in the Center)* (1917) he pleads for an end to the irresponsibility of the writer and poet, and against the traditional and impotent culture of the day he advances these slogans:

We are against music—for an awakening toward community;
We are against the poem—for a call to love,
We are against the novel—for a pathway to life,
We are against the drama—for a pathway to action.[9]

He asks for man to become the "center" of the universe. In the aftermath of the failed revolution, he adjured the "little men" now no longer "little":

Wir sind nicht mehr die Kleinen . . .

We are no longer the little men. We have climbed from darkness to light, comrades of all people on earth.[10]

But most of all, the expressionist playwright is haunted by the problems of war and peace. The issues are broader than in the parricidal plays; and the participants and the backgrounds more real. The pacifistic strain, the passionate appeal to human beings to rediscover their humanity, marks a number of conversions, such as that of Fritz von Unruh, scion of an aristocratic soldier family, who had solemnized his patriotic fervor in the play *Offiziere,* and had on the eve of the war, recanted. *Vor der Entscheidung (Before the Decision)* is a play that presents a fighting soldier on the field of battle with two alternatives seen in a vision: in one, the Romantic playwright Heinrich von Kleist, expounder and extoller of Prussian patriotism, appears; in the other, Shakespeare, spokesman for man. Shakespeare appeals to the soldier:

> Was heute Sieg in lauten Hymnen preist. . . .

> That which loud hymns today proclaim as victory,
> Is not the soul's true sanctuary.
> O, enter now upon the solemn war for peace:
> With justice in your sword, and kindness in your heart.[11]

In a similar vein, Walter Hasenclever used the ancient classical figure of Antigone to make her the protagonist of peace.

The most eloquent poetic voice, however, came from behind the walls of a prison, where Ernst Toller sat, condemned to five years' confinement for his participation in the Bavarian Revolution.

He had some time before his conviction written a drama, *Die Wandlung (Transfiguration),* the symbolic transformation of the Jewish artist Friedrich from a soldier in colonial wars to an apostle of peace and revolution. In thirteen scenes, many of them grotesque and bitter, macabre and horrifying, Toller takes his protagonist through various experiences, from patriotic to disenchanting ones; until, having destroyed a nationalistic statue he had been sculpting and having left home forever, he faces an assembled populace in front of a church, and hurls his passionate addresses at them:

Now brothers I call to you: March! March! toward the light of day!
Go to those in power and proclaim to them with thundering organ

voices that their power is but a sham. Go to the soldiers, and say to them: Beat your swords into plowshares! Go to the rich and show them their hearts, how they have been turned to offal. But be kind to them, for they too are poor, erring souls. But smash the citadels with laughter, yes, smash the citadels, for they are made of slag—dried-out slag. March, march in the light of day. Brothers, raise your martyred hands,—let fiery joy resound. Let it stride through our free land! Revolution![12]

The play was produced in the Tribüne of Berlin, in 1919, with Fritz Kortner in the part of Friedrich. In the succeeding drama, *Massemensch* (*Man and the Masses*), written in prison, the pacifistic Utopian strain dominates. The protagonist is a Woman who pleads against violence by whomever committed. She is overruled and arrested by the counter-revolutionary forces. But in her last conversation with the "Nameless One," the leader of the revolutionary group, she says:

> I would be betraying the masses
> Were I to ask one life of a man.
> The doer may offer his own life.
> Hear: no man may kill another
> In the name of a cause.
> Unholy the cause that asks this.
> Whoever asks human blood for his own sake
> Is Moloch:
> State was Moloch.
> The masses were Moloch.

Yet, in the face of death, when a priest attempts to persuade her to prayer, and affirms that "man is evil from his very birth," she insists:

> Man *wishes* to be good. . . .
> For even when he does evil
> he mantles it in good . . .
> I believe!
> I believe![13]

Less humanistic and revolutionary than Ernst Toller, Georg Kaiser ran the gamut from a pre-war pacifism in the drama, *Die Bürger von Calais* (*The Burghers of Calais*) to post-war messianism, pessimism, and even nihilism. He is the author of probably the most celebrated of expressionist plays, *From Morn to Midnight,* a twelve-hour chronicle of the life of an absconding bank clerk, which mirrors the hopeless night of the German petty-bourgeois, no less than of Germany's world. Kaiser's depths of utter despair are exposed in the trilogy *Gas,* which carries a billionaire, his son, and grandson through fantastic inner and outer journeys, and culminates in the shattering of a Utopian dream of a return to the primal soil, when the workers whom the grandson has been trying to transform, refuse to abandon the factories, even though they are manufacturing lethal war materials. The world ends in one final explosive war.

Such were the passageways to salvation offered by expressionist playwrights and poets. There were other voices too, less apocalyptic, less feverishly ethereal, to counter the chiliasm of the expressionists. Thomas Mann's *The Magic Mountain,* published in 1924, counseled a descent from the regions of sickness and death into the valleys of decision—unfortunately, in this case, into participation in the world war. Käthe Kollwitz's graphic and superb designs brought the urgent social realities of these years with overwhelming directness and vigor. Russian theatrical groups, visiting Berlin and other cities, presented new views of man and society. In Berlin, Erwin Piscator was revolutionizing the theatre. Johannes Becher fused poetic expressionism with Communism. From prison, Erich Mühsam was sending his proletarian poems to hearten flagging spirits.

Bertolt Brecht, too, had to come to terms with the chaos of the times, before he could transcend it.

III

Brecht's Chorales of Chaos and Doom

Ich gesteh' es: ich
Habe keine Hoffnung. . . .

I admit it—I
Have no hope.
The blind speak of a way out. I
See.

When all the errors are expended,
The last companion sitting opposite us
Will be Nothingness.

BRECHT, "Der Nachgeborene"

In Brecht is reflected the chaos of these years. In his poems of
1918 to 1926, the pent-up rebellion of an entire generation finds
utterance. The anarch, the nihilist, and the cynic; the alienated, the
lost, all speak through him. He is the laureate of the transitory and
the doomed.

In contrast to the fuliginous and impassioned apostrophes of the
"O Mensch!" expressionists, Brecht wears an air of brutal detachment and calculated coldness. He is suspicious of rhetoric, as he is
of pathos or over-emotionalism. Moving invocations to mankind
leave him stone-cold.

When he finally collected the poems of these years and published
them, first in the limited edition of the *Taschenpostille*, and then,
in 1927, in the *Hauspostille*, he fixed the age and himself consum-
mately as the "lost generation"—as the finale of an era.

In composing the poems, he made tributaries of the German folk song and ballad, of the classical ode, the religious hymn and chorale, no less than of Kipling, Villon, Rimbaud, and American folklore.

His revulsion from sentimentality—though not entirely from sentiment—takes the form of deliberate and brutal obscenity, almost a call to debauchery—sex, cigars, alcohol, opium. But it also represents a challenge to smug and solid bourgeois morality. The poems are composed against the background of hunger, misery, and near-despair. The exaltations of decay, these celebrations of putrescence are the bitter antidotes to sweetness and light. They are tentative and groping searches for a way out of chaos. Are they pose, truth, or, as one critic called them, "synthetic debauchery"?[1]

At times Brecht's nihilism calls to mind *The Waste Land* of T. S. Eliot, a product of the same generation. There is the same cold and calculated detachment, and parallel verbal and poetic virtuosity. But what a difference between them! Eliot's *Waste Land* is an arid inferno, populated by mannikins, long lost to any heroism of either feeling or action. Brecht's world is also an inferno, but peopled by human beings. In Eliot there is no trace of feeling for man, except the urge to eviscerate him. In Brecht the waifs and strays, the betrayed and rejected find a place of sympathy. Eliot sees Nothingness in Nothingness; Brecht sees the victims of Nothingness.

How different, too, is Brecht's celebration of the "I" from that of the expressionists:

Ich, Bertolt Brecht, bin aus den schwarzen Wäldern

I, Bertolt Brecht, come from the black forests.

He declares himself at home in the asphalt cities, where he is provided with such modern "deathbed sacraments" as newspapers, tobacco, and whiskey. He "stinks" like all other human beings. As for women, he likes them well enough, but he's "not the kind on whom they can rely." Nature is disrobed of romanticism, for the trees "piss" and the birds are "vermin" in the morning light. His

own sleep is "restless." But that is all as it should be, for everything
is passing away. Of these immovable cities, he says, which we have
built, what will remain? The wind. And after us? Nothing worth
mentioning.

> In the coming earthquakes, it is to be hoped
> I won't let bitterness quench my cigar.[2]

The traditional ballad measure he uses in his poem, "Concerning
poor B. B.," staggers us in its simplicity; yet it is so thoroughly
sophisticated, it can afford to speak naively. Its tone is so destructive,
it can afford to colonize its crude obscenities and domesticate them.

Brecht is haunted by the passing of things. He wanders through
cities and reflects:

> Underneath them, the drains.
> Within them nothing; above them—smoke.
> We were within them. We have relished nothing.
> We vanished quickly. And so will they.[3]

Within him is loneliness, as he wanders along the asphalt streets.
He feels as if his insides were "papered with cold sayings."[4] Nature
he sees symbolized by a tree ravaged by vultures, who tear its
immortality to pieces.[5] Where in all this creation is God?

> Deep in the dark shadows the hungry are dying,
> You—show them bread, and let them die.
> You—are enthroned invisible, eternal,
> Radiant, and cruel above your eternal plan. . . .
>
> Many say that you are not—and it were better so.
> But how can that not be—that can so deceive?[6]

A number of poems that Brecht had written during those years
he kept from the *Hauspostille*. They were not to be published until
after his death. They are brutally frank and personal self-de-
pictions. He calls himself "Bidi." Bidi is lazy, "conceited to the burst-
ing point," his mouth is agape, he smokes, reads the papers, drinks,
plays billiards, "scratches his balls"; he is as "cold as a dog. . . . , and
without a bit of human feeling."[7]

"Ach, wir sind einander fremd," he mourns. "Alas, we are total
strangers to one another."[8] Naturally, he is more than casual about

love. How quickly one forgets! Sometimes phantoms of the past rise up, especially at night:

> Aber nachts zuweilen wenn ihr mich trinken seht . . .

> But at night, sometimes, when you see me drinking,
> I see her face, pale in the wind, strong, turned
> Toward me, and I bend before the wind. . . .[9]

A photograph of a woman is inscribed, "pure, objective, malicious." And he wishes "they'd write these words on my tombstone . . . One rests more comfortably under words like these."[10]

Love between man and woman, involving a basic and deep relationship, is foreign to him. If it appears, as it does on rare occasions, it is in surroundings and circumstances sordidly cruel and explosive. In such instances, it is the woman that is the active agent, frequently enslaving herself to the man. Love of one man for another, however, is depicted more tenderly, and appears to be more deeply felt. Lovemaking with a woman is cynically dismissed: "You can't compare it with a cigar."[11]

The flow and transitoriness of life and nature are symbolized for Brecht in the flowing of waters. Drowning . . . passing into nothingness . . . animate life changing into the inanimate . . . decomposition . . . Ophelia—these are ever-present themes. His friend, Arnold Bronnen, speculated about the lure of these waters in Brecht's early life:

Just behind the house (in Bleichstrasse 2), lay a pond with blackish waters. Iridescence of bubbles coquetting. Doubtless they inspired the young boy Brecht to write his poems of the water corpses.[12]

A no less immediate source was undoubtedly the poetry of Arthur Rimbaud, whose unforgettable "Bateau ivre" with its haunting lines:

> Comme je descendais des fleuves impassible,
> Je me sentis plus guidé par les haleurs. . . .

and

> . . . où, flottaison blême
> Et ravie, un noyé pensif parfois descend,"

untranslatable for its sounds, "As I descended the impassive rivers, I no longer felt guided by haulers," "Where, flotsam, pallid and entranced, a dreaming drowned man goes down . . . ,"[13] turns, under Brecht's magic, into

> Durch die klaren Wasser schwimmend vieler Meere
> Löst ich schaukelnd mich von Ziel und Schwere.
> Mit den Haien ziehend unter rotem Mond.[14]

This is Brecht's ballad of the ship, "Das Schiff": "Through the clear waters swimming of many an ocean, swaying, I freed myself of weight and goal, floating with the sharks, under a red moon." The boat gives itself over to the waters and to eventual decay, until it gradually becomes a resting place for seagulls and algae; and fishermen seeing it, look with amazement as it floats down, no longer recognizable, so full of algae, the moon, and death.

For human beings, too, there is forgetfulness in the water: It is pleasurable to turn into vegetation in the pallid afternoons, or to be driven downstream, doing nothing, "just like the Lord, when he swims in the streams in the evening."[15]

These are indeed chorales of quiet doom, whose entire text is written into the "Ballad of the Many Boats," song of the lonely seafarer in a rotting boat, who, accompanied by a school of sharks, sails his way to ultimate destruction, singing a farewell to his bloodthirsty convoy:

> And then one evening in the month of October,
> After a day spent without song,
> They saw him at the stern, and they heard him say:
> And what does he say: "Tomorrow is doom."[16]

But Brecht can also lay aside his resigned quietism, and chide the Almighty with His indifference to man's plight, the plight of the wretches here on earth. His troubled feeling about his fellow men he can encase in moving poems, such as those he wrote about Christmas, which brought upon him the attention of the government authorities on suspicion of blasphemy. They are among the most unexpected, and most moving of Brecht's verses. One of them is entitled "Mary":

> Die Nacht ihrer ersten Geburt war
> Kalt gewesen. . . .

> The night of her first birth was cold,
> In latter years, however,
> She forgot it altogether—
> The pitiful, frosty rafters
> The smoking fireplace
> And the throes of afterbirth
> And above all the bitter shame
> Of not being alone,
> Which is the poor man's birthright.
> That is why in after years
> This became a feast-day for all to attend.
> Stilled was the rude shepherds' talk.
> History later turned them into kings.[17]

And in "A Christmas Legend," he makes the poor speak:

> Tonight is Holy Night and we
> Poor ones sit in ice-cold room
> The wind howls here, and outside too.
> Come sweet Jesus, and give heed.
> Tonight we are in bitter need. . . .

> Come, dear wind, no longer roam,
> For you too have no home . . ."[18]

Many of these poems and ballads Brecht would sing and recite to whoever was willing to listen, in the manner of his own creature, Baal. Peter Suhrkamp, lifelong friend, admirer, and later Brecht's publisher, recalls his first meeting with the German minstrel:

My personal relationship with Brecht begins at a country tavern in the early winter of 1919. There I met, besides draymen, a student who sang ballads to the accompaniment of a guitar, among them the "Chorale of Baal." In this way I first got to know his poems.[19]

Upon the publication of the *Hauspostille* in 1927, Brecht was immediately recognized as *the* poetical genius, whether to be hailed or reviled as such. The title of the book was deliberately ironical and blasphemous: *A Household Book of Devotions*. Hostile critics labeled it "The Devil's Breviary." It is divided into five sections of "Lessons": Rogations, spiritual exercises, chronicles, Mahagonny songs, and a calendar of the departed. In an acidulous "guide" to the poems, Brecht enumerates the occasions appropriate for the use of each of the sections, such as times when "Nature is unruly," or "when one becomes aware of one's flesh and one's presumption."

Such was Brecht's counterpart to the Protestant book of piety. Brecht's book is also touched with compassion and profound feeling. Here is to be found the balladry of the poor: the story of sixteen-year-old Apfelböck, who kills his father and his mother (a true Augsburg incident); and the ballad of Marie Farrar, who did away with her illegitimate child after trying to abort it. Here is Brecht's plea (after Villon):

> For you—I pray you—do not be irate.
> For every human creature is in need of human aid.[20]

As parodist, Brecht has scarcely been surpassed. The seventeenth-century religious poet Neander had composed a great hymn:

> Lobet den Herrn den mächtigen König der Ehren. . . .

> Praise ye the Lord, the mighty King of Glory,
> O my beloved Soul, that is my desire.
> Come gather together with psaltery and harp,
> Wake, oh wake, and let us hymn His praises. . . .

In Brecht's hand, this becomes the celebrated "Great Chorale of Thanksgiving":

> Lobet die Nacht und die Finsternis, die euch umfangen. . . .

> Praise ye the night and the darkness that enfold you.
> Come gather together.
> Look up to the heavens:
> Already day is done. . . .

This is a stark glorification of oblivion. Man in his life and passing is no different from the beasts in the field. Brecht sings: "Praise that Heaven has forgotten you! Praise the cold, the darkness, and decay! Praise death."[21]

He takes one of the most famous German lyrics, Goethe's "Wanderers Nachtlied"—"Über allen Gipfeln ist Ruh' "—and turns it into his "Liturgy of the Breath," a bitter denunciation of indifference to poverty, hunger and death![22]

His hatred of war finds expression in "The Legend of the Dead Soldier," as well as in "The Ballad of the Woman and the Soldier," in which the young soldier, unheedful of the woman's warning, insists on going to war and finds his end there.[23]

His bitterness de-romanticizes the failed German Revolution of 1918-1919. "The Song of the Red Army Soldier" (which was dropped from all subsequent editions of the *Hauspostille*) describes the march of Red soldiers, hopeful of that freedom for which they had been fighting—"oft watching the red sky, they held it for the red of dawn." But time passes, and "if heaven were to come for them now, it would have to do without them."[24]

Brecht's hidden "heartbreak house" is here, none the less. The human cast-off, thrown into the grave or into the "dirt-yellow" sea, has had in him "more than you know." For every one of us, no matter who, has his own impenetrable secret that he carries with him into "tomorrow's doom."

Hauspostille won the acclaim of the most discerning critics of the day. Julius Bab wrote, "This Bertolt Brecht is a poet. . . . Few in any time have possessed his musical mastery of the German language.[25] And Kurt Tucholsky: "He and Gottfried Benn appear to me to be the greatest lyrical talents living in Germany today."[26] They caught the new, the different note. As one later critic summarized it, "In place of intoxication, pathos, and magic Brecht offers sobriety, irony. In place of verbal filigrees—unadorned and aggressive morality."[27]

Brecht had the capacity of making lasting friendships. His Augsburg circle included his school-fellows, among them Caspar Neher, the artist who was to design the scenic sets for many of Brecht's plays; Georg Pfanzelt, the "Orge" of his poems and plays; Otto

Müllereisert; and H. O. Münsterer (who was to write a touching reminiscence of those Augsburg days, and who was to sign Brecht's death certificate). He now added new friendships made in Munich: Carola Neher, wife of the poet Klabund; Peter Suhrkamp; Johannes Becher, the poet; Karl Valentin, many actors, and, not least, Lion Feuchtwanger.

Feuchtwanger was already then an established man of letters. He proved to be not only one of Brecht's most enlightened and sympathetic critics, as well as valuable collaborator, but also a mentor and teacher—in fact, one of "his very few teachers." "Through him," Brecht is reported to have said, "I learned which aesthetic rules I was inclined to break. He was as knowledgeable as he was great-hearted."[28] Feuchtwanger was thirty-five years old when young Brecht began showing him his writings, toward the end of 1918. Brecht was "thin, ill-shaven, unkempt," as Feuchtwanger describes him in those days; speaking his heavy Suabian dialect, and with pocketfuls of manuscripts. Among these was a play entitled *Spartacus,* which Brecht told Feuchtwanger was written expressly to make money. Feuchtwanger read the play, recognized an extraordinary talent, chided the author on his pretended money-appetite, and received an almost violent reply. "He had indeed written this play for the sake of money only, but he had another play, which was really good, and he would bring it along. . . . It was called *Baal.*"[29]

Brecht then seemed a strange figure, with his "long, narrow skull, high cheekbones, deep-set eyes, black hair growing down on his brow."[29] This figure impressed itself on Feuchtwanger in other ways too, for he was to appear as a character, Kaspar Pröckl, in a subsequent novel, *Success,* in 1930. Here he is an engineer (Brecht was always interested in mechanics), living in Munich, at a time (this is the early twenties) of violent personal and political intrigues, on the eve of the aborted Hitler putsch of 1923, a time of inflation, starvation, demagogic attacks on Jews, Catholics, and Socialists. Here is Kaspar Pröckl: "Lean, sullen . . ., badly shaven . . . Leather jacket and cap. . . . The young engineer, unversed in social amenities,

had thought out a theory of how to deal with other people; he
always spoke to them about their interests, never about his own, or
about general matters."[30] He is seen more adversely through the
eyes of the capitalist Herr von Reindl:

The way he had his hair growing low down on his forehead betrayed
a kind of naive coquetry. It was a queer thing that he should be so
popular with women. . . . The man literally reeked of sweat, like
soldiers on the march. . . . , and he smelled unmistakably of revolution. Obviously it must be his vulgar ballads that fascinated them. Whenever he sang them in his roaring voice, the women were swept out
of themselves.[31]

And somewhat more dispassionately by the author of the novel:

He planted himself in the middle of the room, and with open effrontery
in a horribly shrill voice began to deliver his ballads to the thwanging
of the banjo, pronouncing his words with unmistakably broad accent.
But the ballads dealt with everyday happenings in the life of the ordinary
man, from the point of view of the large town, as they had never been
seen before. . . . Pröckl . . . . kept his burning deep-set eyes fixed
unwaveringly upon [Reindl], and yelled his indecent, proletarian verses
straight into that well-groomed, solid face.[32]

Not too exaggerated a portrait of Brecht of that time! He had the
capacity to attract, and the women who were drawn to him remained
loyal to him, even after his close relationship with them had been
broken off. An early love affair with a beautiful girl in Augsburg
had already produced a little boy.[33] In the eyes of his Augsburg
companions he was even then something of a legend. Münsterer
recalls nostalgically how Brecht and his friends sat by the river
Lech in Augsburg.

We sat on the ground, Bert, Otto Müller and I. The sky is high up,
wide and gorgeously blue, slowly turning orange, and finally violet.
Below us, the glass-like, white-spumed river and far away the dark
silhouette of the city with its towers and gables. The grass is wet with
dew. Brecht sang.[34]

Thus they sat, dreaming of the Ganges. Now and then Brecht

would begin writing.[35] Between 1919 and 1921 he was dramatic critic for the radical Augsburg newspaper *Volkswille,* organ of the Independent Socialist Party. With his brash, frank, uncompromising comments he succeeded in making many enemies. His scathing remarks about the quality of the municipal theatre, his demand for a socially and culturally responsible repertoire and production brought down the wrath of the personnel of the Stadttheater. He retorted with customary aplomb. He charged the theatre with lack of imagination, poor use of its actors, parsimony, inadequacy of technical equipment, and, above all opportunism and timidity of its artistic managers. He paid tribute to one of the directors, Hermann Merz, who was soon to be forced out, and praised occasional performances by the artists. He was merciless toward "kitsch" like *Alt Heidelberg,* which he calls "that swinish piece of trash."[36] He had not as yet become rabidly unconventional. He still regarded Hauptmann's *Rose Bernd* as praiseworthy and found in that tragedy "our own misery depicted. This is a revolutionary piece."[37] But already he judged classical plays in the light of the present time. Speaking of a performance of Schiller's *Don Carlos,* he added: "I have always been fond of *Don Carlos,* the Lord knows. But these last few days I have been reading Upton Sinclair's *The Jungle,* the story of a worker who dies of starvation in the stockyards of Chicago. . . . This fellow catches a glimpse of freedom for a moment, and then gets beaten up with rubber truncheons. His freedom, I know, has little to do with that of Carlos, but I can't take Carlos' bondage very seriously any longer. . . . By all means go and see *Don Carlos. . . .* but when you have the chance, read Sinclair's *Jungle.*"[38]

Brecht's sense of concreteness rebelled at the expressionist theatre. Toller's *Wandlung* he regarded as a "poeticized newspaper. . . . , with flat visions, almost immediately forgotten. Thin cosmos. Man seen as object, proclamation, instead of as Man. Abstracted man."[39] The playwright he respected most at this time was Georg Kaiser.

"Where," he asks, "is the political comedy of significant dimensions? The foundations of our bourgeois society have scarcely been touched. Wide areas of human interests lie fallow. The imagination of these people is frozen. Invention seems to be exhausted. Why, they don't even have enough ingenuity to invent new neckties."[40]

Other, even more experienced, critics shared Brecht's disaffection with the contemporary theatre. Herbert Jhering describes his depressed feelings after witnessing a revival of Racine's *Phèdre* in Schiller's adaptation, and not long thereafter, on a fateful night in November, 1918 (the time of the revolutionary uprisings), Reinhardt's production of *The Merchant of Venice:*

> It was this shadowy evening that fortified me in the conviction that the impressionistic refinements of Reinhardt had outlived their day; that this empty exhibition of technical knowledge and skill could no longer be of use to the theatre.[41]

What, he asks, have these productions to do with the shattering events taking place outside the theatre?

Was Brecht ready to take up such a challenge? He felt sure he was. Münsterer reports Brecht's boast in 1917: "I can write. I can write plays better than those of Hebbel, wilder than those of Wedekind."[42] To judge from his earliest dramatic efforts at the Gymnasium, such as *Die Bibel,* published in the school periodical (an old Dutch Protestant believer voluntarily accepts death rather than give up his faith), he had a long way to go.[43] But his progress was swift. Ready or not, he was pitting himself with two plays against the major playwrights of his day—against Fritz von Unruh, Reinhard Goering, and Walter Hasenclever, with their pacifistic statements; against Franz Werfel and Carl Zuckmayer, with their post-Romanticism, their Faustian and Ahasuerian soarings; against expressionists like Toller, Georg Kaiser, and young Friedrich Wolf; against such rehabilitators of a grand Germanic past and proponents of a new folk-community and "leader king" as Hanns Johst.

He was always fired to original work by another man's efforts. His first dramatic attempt of consequence, *Baal,* was directly inspired by a play of Hanns Johst's, *Der Einsame (The Lonely One).*

Hanns Johst was a talented young writer who found the transition from individual nihilism to Nazism very easy. In due time he composed the laureate drama of Hitlerism, *Schlageter,* and ended up as a Nazi cultural leader and president of the Reichschriftskammer (the Reich Chamber of Literature). In his younger days he had steeped himself in the Romantic past of Germany, and exhibited a strong chauvinist strain. Brecht found him and his work thoroughly antipathetic. While he was attending Arthur Kutscher's seminar in Munich, he openly derided one of Johst's novels, *Der Anfang* (as well as Reinhard Goering's play *Die Seeschlacht*), much to the angry amazement and displeasure of the professor, who returned the compliment by announcing that Brecht himself did not show the least signs of literary talent, and who was he to behave like that?[44]

Johst's play of *The Lonely One* is an exaltation of an unfortunate and unhappy poet of the Romantic school, Christian Grabbe (1801-1836), a contemporary and enemy of Heinrich Heine, and a playwright of considerable talents and considerable antipathies. Grabbe was profoundly nationalistic and anti-Semitic. He lived a miserable life and died insane. Since the days of the German classicists, the glorification of the "Ich-poet" as the embodiment of prophecy, leadership, and wisdom had been a favorite theme for writers. The vocation of the poet was acclaimed as the crown of life, and his wretched fate only a symptom of the world's blindness and cruelty. In a more hectic and mechanized era, this poet-regenerator of the world sometimes becomes quite violent, as in Sorge's *Der Bettler,* where in the pursuit of his somewhat vague poetic mission he, The Poet (always kept abstract), kills his crazy father and his sick mother. Johst's Grabbe pursues his unhappy poetic vocation in less gory, but no less individualistic ways. In a number of forceful episodic scenes he is shown composing a vast Napoleonic drama in his attic, while his pregnant mistress is dying of a miscarriage. The poet is brokenhearted. In a tavern he outrages his friends, jubilantly proclaims the grandeur and individuality of the poet,

denigrates Jews, and Heine in particular. Thereafter, irresistible to
sensitive womanhood, he wins his friend Eckhard's betrothed (for
poetry transcends all, as she tells her rejected lover). Another of his
seduced girls throws herself into a river. Grabbe's fortunes, never
high, decline. Utterly reviled by the smug citizenry, he starves, and
finally is seen dying in his attic, while an impatient landlady waits
for his demise so as to admit the new tenant. As he is passing out,
a group of friends come to serenade him to the music of Beethoven.
Johst subtitled the play, *Menschenuntergang* (*The Downfall of
Man*). It was produced in the Munich Kammerspiele, in March,
1918.

Johst's *Der Einsame* was the fuse that fired Brecht's first important dramatic effort. He was always at his best when he could
weave variations, in his own unashamed manner, around an arche-
type; in this case one he could counter. The image of the poet as
Johst depicted him, in his typical "Schwärmerei"—so idealistic, so
given over to the call of the spirit, filled with such rhetoric—lent
itself in Brecht's hands to being "turned upside down." Not that
Brecht did not himself share some of Grabbe's anarchic attitudes, or
for that matter, his horror of the bourgeois! But he revolted against
that "Sehnsucht," that yearning for the infinite and the impossible
that had always characterized this aspect of Romanticism. Brecht
too was going to write an *Untergang,* the débacle of a poet, but it
would be a glorification of defeat, written not so as to scale heaven,
but to absorb the earth, with all that is elemental, earthy, and obscene
in it.

Of the three versions of the play which are extant (the third
one completed as late as 1926), the first draft of 1918 is filled with
autobiographic reminiscences—Baal is an anarchic drama critic for
a respectable paper, who outrages with his reviews (like Brecht
himself); like his prototype in the Johst play, he has a badgering
mother who adjures him to respectability. Both of these episodes
disappear in the 1919 version, which Brecht published. Here, Baal
is truly an "Einsamer"—the lonely one.

For *Baal* is Brecht's individual poems turned into a dramatic psalm of a return to Nature, to its primal algae and weeds, to its animal existence. If there is an eternity, it is in absorbing the "Now." Baal moves through a world of living people, working men, bourgeois, thieves, harlots, the declassed, the male and female lovers, a world of instinctual and primitive desires and passions—hunger, thirst, the flesh, sex, in which the human being is aware almost without thinking that on the morrow he too will be a piece of the earth, of the tree, of the plant, or of the animal—to decay, decompose, and then revivify a new cycle of existence. Baal is the poet of natural thriftlessness, wasting not only himself but other people as well, consuming, consuming, and never satisfied. He sings to people, but not for profit; for there is no material profit that's worth a brass farthing.

Augsburg is writ large in this play, as in his poems—the river Lech, the inns, taverns, meadows, the woods. He had composed the play as he walked along the moats close to home, writing on a sheet of typewriting paper folded in four. "I put together word-mixtures as if I were mixing drinks—whole scenes in sensuously felt words of well-defined material and color quality."[45] Named for the Phoenician deity of nature (by the Israelites abhorred for his sensual abominations), Baal, the poet, moves through twenty-one kaleidoscopic scenes, an animal-man ravenous for experience, taking it where he can, fearless of life as he is of death, poet-laureate of crass animalism, of a cloacal, cosmic nihilism. A scatological psalm sets the tone of the play. To Johst's romanticism, Brecht opposes naturalism. To Johst's high ethic of spiritual striving, Brecht opposes the ethic of natural man: "a better sort of animal." In his fecal and erotic anti-humanism, in his defiance of an accepted world morality. Baal practises only what the bourgeois world likes to keep hidden. This play is, as Muschg well names it, "der Mythus des Fleisches," "the mythos of the flesh."[46]

In many incidents and scenes Brecht parallels (though he also parodies) Johst—in the seductions of girls, in the suicides, in the

homosexual affair with Ekart (the names are alike in both plays);
in the way the principal characters of both plays sacrifice friendship
to their whims or passions.

But Brecht's is a hymnal to dissolution. "Putrefaction," Baal says
at one point, "is creeping up. . . . Worms are singing and praising
one another."[47] The ballad he composes for his drowned mistress,
in momentary contrition, tells that "God gradually forgot her—
first her face, then her hands, and at the very last, her hair. She
became carrion in the waters, along with other carrion."[48] This is a
poem of hungry oblivion, of a world which "in mild light . . . appears as the excrement of the Lord." It is a paean to the outsider: "O
you, who have been driven both from heaven and hell—you murderers, whom great ill has befallen, why did you not stay in your
mothers' wombs where it was quiet, and one slept, and *was?*"[49]
Baal's death is, like his life, that of an animal. He dies abandoned,
in a woodsmen's hut, alone, as he had really been all his life long.

Brecht claimed for Baal an actual prototype in the character of a
certain Josef K. of Augsburg, who perpetrated a number of shady
acts, seduced women, murdered a friend, but was a man endowed
with a most magnetic personality. In all probability the relationship
between Verlaine and Rimbaud colored that between Baal and Ekart.
The language of Brecht's play is often that of Rimbaud's *Illumin-
ations* and *A Season in Hell*. Expressionism is parodied through the
declamation of poems of Johannes Becher and Georg Heym; and
the musical romanticism of Johst and his Beethoven cult is set off
through the mordant use of themes from *Tristan und Isolde,* sardon-
ically underscoring Baal's de-romanticized loves.

Brecht revolutionized poetic language. He domesticated its
brutality, tamed its cloacal aspect. Such speech as was found in *Baal*
had not been heard on the German stage before. Here was the
popular idiom of the marketplaces and the fairs, caught directly
"from the mouth" of the speakers, but fused with the language of
Luther's Bible, and fitted into the broken patterns learned from
Büchner—but all unmistakably Brecht. The poem that Peter Suhr-

Brecht, Hanns Eisler, and Slatan
Dudow at work on *Kuhle Wampe*

Arnolt Bronnen

ABOVE: Brecht and Caspar Neher, Zurich, 1947

FACING PAGE:
(Top) Erwin Piscator
(Bottom) Brecht and Martin-Andersen Nexö in
Sweden, 1938

OVERLEAF:
Brecht in 1953

kamp reports having heard from Brecht's own lips, to guitar accompaniment, was the "Chorale of the Great Baal":

> Als im weissen Mutterschosse aufwuchs Baal
> War der Himmel schon so gross und still und fahl
> Jung und nackt und ungeheuer wundersam
> Wie ihn Baal dann liebte, als Baal kam.

> When Baal grew up in his mother's white womb,
> The sky was so vast and still, and weird,
> Young and naked, and hugely strange,
> The way Baal loved it—when Baal appeared. . . .

> Toward the fat vultures above Baal blinks,
> Waiting among the stars for the carrion that is Baal.
> Often Baal shams death, and if the vulture's fooled,
> Baal dines on vulture, in the quiet evening meal. . . .

> And when in the dark lap of the world Baal is sucked down,
> What's that to Baal? He has had his share.
> So much of the world has Baal beneath his lids,
> That even in death, he has skies to spare.[50]

Adroit cloacism reaches its apogee in Orge's chorale of the outhouse:

> Of all the places that on earth he loved,
> It was not the grassy seat on parents' grave,
> Nor priest's confessional, nor bed of whores,
> Not laps soft, white and fat, such as men crave:

> Orge said to me, of places known to man,
> The loveliest far on earth is the can.[51]

And by contrast, the noble and moving lines in a later scene, the beautiful "Death in the Woods":

> Und ein Mann starb im ewigen Wald
> Wo ihn Sturm und Strom umbrauste. . . .

> And a man died in the everlasting woods,
> With storms and floods around him,
> Died like a beast, scratching into roots,
> Looked up at tree-tops—where in the woods,
> Storms raged and raged around him.[52]

This was the play that probably nestled in Brecht's pocket when he came to visit Feuchtwanger. It was not destined to be produced until the other play, *Spartacus,* eventually renamed *Trommeln in der Nacht* (*Drums in the Night*) came on the boards.

Baal was the play that the critic Alfred Kerr (Brecht's life-long enemy) called, with a great measure of justice, "chaos with possibilities." Many, many years later, when Brecht came to reissue his collected works, he revalued this play in the light of his subsequent Marxism. He agreed that it might now occasion various difficulties to those not schooled in dialectical thought. These might see in it nothing but a glorification of naked selfhood. But actually, Brecht states, we have here the "Ego" set in opposition to a world that does not recognize a usable productiveness, only an exploitable one. "Baal's art of living shares the fate of all arts under capitalism: it is warred upon. Baal is asocial, but in an asocial society."[53]

IV

Berlin 1921-1922:
"Drums in the Night"

> Can you get rid of the army or of the good
> Lord? Can you get rid of all the pain and
> suffering man has taught the Devil? No. You
> can't get rid of it, but you can drink whiskey.
>
> BRECHT, *Drums in the Night*

Berlin was the city of theatres, and to Berlin Brecht was drawn. Here were experimental playwrights and directors. Here were the influential critics like Alfred Kerr, Julius Bab, and Herbert Jhering. Here were artistic directors like Max Reinhardt, Leopold Jessner, Felix Holländer, Erwin Piscator, Erich Engel, and the most celebrated actors and actresses of the day: Alexander Moissi, Albert Bassermann, Agnes Straub, Werner Krauss, Alexander Granach, Emil Jannings, Emanuel Reicher, and many others. Berlin was also a city of social upsurge, with a large working-class population. And drab and unimpressive as might be its architecture, it was still a dynamic cultural center.

From 1921 on Brecht had made frequent trips to Berlin. Finally, in 1924, he decided to settle there. In a city in which a great portion of the population still lived wretchedly and had little to eat, Brecht too went hungry. He knew the meaning of the extra penny saved from a trolley ride; or the extra roll garnered in a coffee shop. But that was the way many writers and artists lived in those days, and handouts were not disdained. He was himself not without some theatrical experience. In Munich he had already filled the

post of "Dramaturg"—theatrical poet, reviser, reader—at the Kammerspiele under Otto Falckenberg.

In Berlin, too, Brecht made himself at home, and gathered new
friends. Early in 1922, at the house of the writer Otto Zarek, Arnolt
Bronnen, a young playwright already famed as a thunderbird of
expressionism, but not yet the political Proteus he was destined to
show himself, caught his first sight of Brecht:

Somewhere someone had put aside the stub of a moist cigar, had taken
up a guitar . . . . and in a harsh, strident voice had begun to intone a
song:
     "She was so white, and came from heaven above,
     Perhaps the plum trees still may be blooming. . . ."
I looked at the singer: a young man, twenty-four years old, with a
lean, dry, bristly, sallow face; piercing eyes, and short dark bristling
hair that fell over his forehead in two curls. . . . A cheap pair of steel-
rimmed glasses hung loosely from remarkably shapely ears across the
bridge of his sharp and narrow nose. His mouth was extremely delicate,
and seemed to be dreaming the dreams that eyes dream. I, the newcomer, had the feeling of recognition. In that small, insignificant man
beats the heart of our times. . . . Give me that man as a friend, I
prayed . . . [My host, Otto Zarek] took me by the hand and led me
toward the singer. "Yes, Arnolt Bronnen," he said, "that is Bert Brecht."[1]

This was the beginning of Brecht's long association with Bronnen,
a man whose career was to take him from his expressionist revolt of
the twenties, and the adoration of Nietzsche and Stefan George,
straight into the arms of Hitler and an influential post under National Socialism, then into anti-Nazi resistance, and into Communism.

How did women look at Brecht? Here is a contemporary description of him by Lotte Eisner:

A tall, young man—shy and proud at the same time—with that shyness
that the good bourgeois mistakes for arrogance. Lean—almost emaciated
—somewhat bent over—he seemed to float in his clothes that appeared
too large for him. He had brusque, ungainly movements, somewhat
like those of a hungry puppy. What impressed me most about him was
his beautiful hands, with their long sensitive fingers, and his strange

eyes, deep and penetrating at the same time. His forehead, underneath a fringe of hair, ruffled and uneven, was smooth. He was already sporting that eternal cap, common to the underworld, pushed forward on his skull, and a jacket of shabby leather, and an enormous cigar. He showed himself to be like his poetry. A fierce cynicism, touched by a comedian's melancholy, at first sight disconcerted many people. He loved to show himself as hard, and made many enemies by his uncompromising spirit. However, he was capable of great charm, and could attract when he wanted to. He had written, "In me you have a man on whom you can't count"—but for certain of us he was a friend on whom we could count without reservations.[2]

The gifted playwright and novelist Marieluise Fleisser knew him intimately in those early years, and in a very recent autobiographical short story, *Avantgarde,* has given us a more ambiguous and complex, though no doubt a very authentic and graphic picture of young Brecht. Here he emerges as a kind of Baal, at once fatally attractive and repellent, frighteningly single-minded, insatiable for experience, and already surrounded by that aura of untouchability—that mythical detachment that masked the inner disruptive storms. A bird of passage, he quickened, enkindled, unhinged, and changed those women who were bold enough to venture an attachment.

There were less friendly eyes that saw him in a different light. Writing from recollection, the journalist Willy Haas recalls meeting Brecht in the Berlin streets, dressed in his old leather jacket ("like some secret commissar of a mysterious Moscow propaganda agency"), but underneath that jacket, Haas was sure, "Brecht wore a very expensive silk shirt, that only people with sizable incomes could afford." His head was shaved like that of "a convict in Sing Sing, or an army recruit;—and that steel-rimmed pair of glasses! But there was also something about him of the headmaster of a school dictating 'banalities', in a hard, slow, somewhat affected voice."[3] Obviously, Herr Haas did not like Brecht.

Be that as it may, Brecht's first years in Berlin were not surrounded by prosperity. As a matter of fact, in the spring of 1922, he was so run-down he had to be confined in the Charité Hospital.

"I was undernourished," he told Herbert Jhering, "and Arnolt Bronnen's earnings as a clerk could not support both of us. After seeing the light of day for twenty-four years, I am nothing but skin and bones."[4]

Bronnen and Brecht became the closest of friends, and planned a number of collaborations and joint enterprises. Brecht insisted that he was the only one competent to direct the impending production of Bronnen's *Vatermord,* at the Deutsches Theater in Berlin. As remarked above, parricide, incest, and "personal freedom" are the principal themes of this cyclonic tragedy. Cast in the play were two outstanding stars: Heinrich George and Agnes Straub. Young Brecht respected neither reputations nor theatrical traditions; but his iconoclasm was not always welcomed. Troubles came speedily. Bronnen describes one of the scenes:

There in the full bloom of her expressionist style stood the mighty actress Agnes Straub, and there stood the actor Heinrich George, and here was the thin, scarcely fullgrown Augsburger, and he was telling them in dry, precise tones that everything they were doing was tommyrot. There were terrible explosions. Seeler [the producer] wrung his hands and hurried to my side. . . . I sat next to Brecht in the dark, empty auditorium, and shuddered, as up there on the stage, George who was nearing the height of his fame, spoke my words. Brecht tore the actor and actress apart with predictable results. George hurled the script as far as the fifteenth row of the orchestra, and Straub rushed off in a huff, and in tears. Brecht congratulated me with a sarcasm which always concealed his triumph. "With those people there you couldn't have done it anyway."[5]

As it was, Berthold Viertel took over, and though the opening had to be deferred, the play was finally produced. It proved to be sensationally successful. Perhaps some insight into the temper of that hectic time can be gained from the few final words of Bronnen's *Vatermord.* The son has just murdered his father and slept with his mother. The mother, Frau Fessel, calls to him, "Come to me, oh, oh, oh, come to me." And Walter, the son, responds:

I've had enough of you.
I've had enough of everything.

> Go, bury your husband. You are old.
> But I am young.
> I do not know you.
> I am free.
> No one stands before me. No one at my side.
> No one above me.
> My father dead.
> Heavens! I leap toward you. I fly!
> How it presses on, trembles, groans, moans.
> Must up!
> Swells, gushes, bursts, flies.
> Must up! must up!
> I ——
> I bloom ——[6]

But undeterred by this episode, Bronnen and Brecht went on planning a movie. Again differences arose, and Bronnen went his own amicable way. Yet it would have been a real experience to witness *Vatermord* under Brecht's direction!

Brecht's life did not lack excitement of its own. He had fallen in love with Marianne Zoff, sister of one of his writer friends. At the same time, *Trommeln in der Nacht* (*Drums in the Night*) was about to be produced at the Munich Kammerspiele.

To assure himself of at least one friendly reviewer, Brecht asked Herbert Jhering, who had already mentioned Brecht favorably, to come to Munich. Jhering was the influential critic of the Berlin *Börsen-Courier*. Brecht wrote:

I know what I am asking of you, but for me very much depends on it. Ever since Berlin has stopped taking chances on anything new, it's become damned hard to get decent reviews when one needs them most.[7]

Jhering consented. And so opening night came around. Hans Otto Münsterer, close friend of Brecht's, describes the evening:

Friday, September 29. . . . The theatre sold out. We were all very nervous. The curtain was long in rising. An excited Brecht whispered that the Berlin critics had arrived, above all, Jhering. All the Brechts were there: the father, brother Walter, housekeeper Röckert and Bie [one of Brecht's sweethearts]. I was taken for Brecht's brother. . . . Then at last, the curtains parted, and evil fortune took its course. . . .

Good rehearsal, bad opening—that's an old theatrical superstition, and it seemed to be realized. Everything that had gone well in rehearsal that afternoon, now fell apart. Yet the play had great success, due exclusively to its elemental power and Brecht's language—a speech one had not heard on the German stage for years. There were to be two more days of waiting and worrying, for the reviews were not to appear until Monday.[8]

Herbert Jhering did not disappoint the young dramatist. In one of those reviews that every starting playwright dreams of, the critic of the *Börsen-Courier* hailed Brecht in unambiguous enthusiasm:

The twenty-four-year-old poet Brecht has changed the literary physiognomy of Germany overnight. With Bert Brecht a new tone, a new melody, a new vision has come into our time. . . . His figures are phosphorescent. . . . He experiences chaos and disintegration physically. . . . He lets the naked human being speak, but in a language we have not heard in years. And with the very first words of the play we become aware: *Tragedy has begun.* Not since the days of Wedekind have we had such soul-storming experience.[9]

And,

Otto Falckenberg and the Munich Little Theater . . . have done more for the German drama with this production of Bert Brecht than has Berlin in recent days with all its theatres put together.[10]

Julius Bab, no less influential, spoke of "a thrilling, and soaring energy . . . A raw cry from a blood-veiled throat."[11]

The great dissenter Alfred Kerr of the *Berliner Zeitung,* who had privately spoken of *Baal* as "chaos with possibilities" (Brecht had sent him a copy of that play), now thought that *Trommeln* showed "obvious talent, but is hardly an independent piece of work, despite its natural freshness"—not so independent as Toller's plays, only a sort of Georg Kaiser. "Brecht must remain a hope."[12]

Whatever the criticisms, Brecht had attracted wide attention and had become a celebrity. His sudden and astonishing rise to fame at this moment is well illustrated by an anecdote related by Jhering. Felix Holländer, general manager and artistic director of Reinhardt's

Deutsches Theater, phoned one day: "Herr Jhering, you must get me Brecht, the only genius I know living today." When Brecht met Holländer, the latter, without even stopping to greet him, said, "Herr Brecht, from now on at the Deutsches Theater the Brecht premières will be what those of Hauptmann were before," and he immediately accepted Brecht's first plays: *Baal* and *Trommeln*. Unfortunately, Jhering continues, during the rehearsals there occurred, as was to be anticipated, some stormy to-dos between Brecht and Holländer over *Trommeln*, which Falckenberg was directing. Later, when Holländer was appointed critic of the *Achtuhr Abendblatt*, he became one of Brecht's most dedicated antagonists, second only to Kerr.[13]

There could no be doubt that the Munich production, with the magnificent figure of Erwin Faber as Andreas Kragler, had shocked, caused wonder, admiration, and uneasiness. *Trommeln in der Nacht* is a "Heimkehrer" drama (Brecht called it a comedy)—a play of a returning soldier. Hundreds of such plays were to be written after 1914, from Toller's *Wandlung* and *Hinkemann* after the first World War to Wolfgang Borchert's *Draussen vor der Tür* after the second.

Brecht's play is set against a background of revolution—the Spartacus uprising in Berlin. Its protagonist is the soldier, Andreas Kragler, home from Africa after a four years' absence, reportedly dead. He finds on his return to Berlin that his betrothed, Anna Balicke, has in the meantime been promised to a well-to-do war profiteer, and is pregnant by him. A thin, sickly specter, Kragler follows the couple and Anna's parents to the Picadilly Bar in the city, where the betrothal is to be celebrated. Outside, the Spartacists have already taken to arms, and the sound of gunfire punctuates the eerie drama of personal relationships. The nightmarish quality is heightened as the ghost-like figure of Kragler appears at the festivities and encounters the coarseness and brutality of Anna's betrothed, Murk, and the crass opportunism and cold-bloodedness of her father. This is the way the betrothed addresses the soldier: "What do you want? You're nothing but a corpse! Why, you already stink to high heaven! [Holds his nose.] Do you want to be canonized just because you swallowed some African sun? I've been working too. I slaved till my blood flowed right down into my boots. Look at my hands. . . ." Cynically, he offers to buy Kragler's boots. "They belong in the military museum. I offer you forty marks for them."[14] And Anna's father:

Yes, the sun was hot, eh? Well, that's Africa for you. It's all in the geography books. You were a hero? It'll all be written up in the history books. But in the bookkeeper's ledger there's nothing. That's why the hero must go back to Africa once more. Period. Waiter, take that thing out of here. . . .[15]

Kragler lifts Murk off the floor, high up into the air, and pushes him out of the room. "Come to me, Anna," he says.

He wanted to buy my boots. . . . The sleet bored into my skin, so that it's turned red, and cracks in the sun. My pack is empty and I don't have a red cent in all the world. I want you. I'm not beautiful.[16]

Outside shots echo and re-echo, accompanied by the singing of the *Internationale*. Balicke, the father, reacts at once:

Spartacus! Your friends, Herr Andreas Kragler! Your dark companions. Your comrades. They're roaring through the newspaper district, reeking of fire and murder. Beasts. Beasts. Beasts. If anyone asks, Why beasts? You eat human flesh, and you must be crushed.[17]

The humane waiter objects to this sort of vituperation. Replying to another character, he says: "Why it concerns me? The stars are hurled from their courses, when meanness leaves a human being cold."[18]

What follows is a weird "Ride of the Valkyries," as the various characters stagger through the streets of the city: Anna in search of Kragler, who is now in flight. Desperate, he hears the firing, and asks himself, "Perhaps they need me there?" but he does not go. Instead he stumbles into a bar with the prostitute Marie, and listens to the tavern keeper as the latter sings the "Ballad of the Dead Soldier."

Kragler's despair is heightened by drink: ". . . There is no longer time for injustice. The world is too old for better times to come, and whiskey is cheaper and the heavens are all rented out, my dear ones.[19] But when he meets Anna, he still wants her, his "bride, the whore." And he will not join the Spartacists: "Every man is best off in his own skin. . . . I'm a swine, and the swine's going home . . . Tomorrow morning the crying will be over, and I'll be lying in my bed, and I'll replenish the race, so that I won't die out. Don't stare so romantically, you skinflints . . . Cutthroats . . . [Drums] Blood-thirsty cowards . . ." And the stage directions conclude: "His laughter is choked; he staggers, hurls the drum at the moon, which is really a lantern, and drum and moon topple into the river, which has no water in it."[20]

This *was* different theatre. How different may be gathered from a comment by Alfred Kantorowicz, who notes that in *Trommeln* there are no "O Mensch!" apostrophes, no horrifying outcries, no pleas for self-transcendence ("Ausser-sich-sein"), no wild despairs, no father-son conflict, no formulae—nothing but the starkest realism and reality, no pat answers and no wish-fulfillments.[21]

No other Heimkehrer drama had spoken like Brecht's. This was, to stretch Kerr's simile, chaos embodied. Chaos taking form. In *Trommeln* Brecht reveals a striking affinity to Büchner's *Wozzeck,* written almost a hundred years before. Büchner's character, a soldier, Wozzeck, like Brecht's Kragler, reflects the hopeless pathos and desperation of the little man deprived of his self-respect, and incapable of self-expression. Wozzeck is poor, deranged, insulted, yet endowed with something of a natural, instinctive, pithy wisdom. Wozzeck is the "cudgeled hero," who has no choices: he is subjected to "scientific" investigations by the army doctor; he is sermonized and misunderstood by a cliché-ridden captain, deceived by his mistress, and then driven to kill both her and (in one version) himself. He is a social fatality. But Andreas has one marked advantage over Wozzeck. He does have a choice. And he chooses survival. The world in and of revolution means nothing to him. He cannot transcend his petty bourgeois dream. He is the embodiment of that chaos and disenchantment that followed the collapse of the 1918 Revolution. He is Brecht's chaos as well. But he is chaos defined. How close the affinities are between Brecht and Büchner can be felt time and again, when listening to the latter's Wozzeck:

Yes, Captain, I don't have a great deal of goodness. . . . You see, we— the common sort—we don't have goodness, all we've got is nature. But if I was a gentleman, and had a hat and a watch and a monocle— and could talk high-class and fancy, I'd want to be good. It must be very nice to be good, but I'm only a poor sort of a fellow.[22]

The pithy, homely idiom of Büchner is there in Brecht too, mastered and perfected.

He had already begun to "de-romanticize"—that is, to practice that "estrangement" which was to become a fundamental part of his dramatic theory. The stage settings of the Munich production provided for screens that merely suggested rooms, behind which loomed, "childish-like," a sketched Berlin, with an illuminated moon that glowed now and then. In the auditorium, placards proclaimed to the public: "Every Man Is Best in His Own Skin," and "Don't Stare So Romantically."

The Berlin performance caused Brecht much worry and displeasure in anticipation. He was unhappy with Otto Falckenberg; he had a secret desire to take over the direction himself. He stayed away from rehearsals as much as possible, for whenever he appeared there was bound to be "Krach," as the Berliners amusedly anticipated—that is, an undue ruffling of sensitive feathers. Finally, on December 20, 1922, the play opened at the Deutsches Theater. The cast was a notable one, including Alexander Granach, Blandine Ebinger, Paul Graetz, Heinrich George. But the performance failed to satisfy both Brecht and Jhering. From Munich, Brecht wrote a mournful note to his critic friend:

Holländer has ruined my "Trommeln." The man has a black heart in his breast. The good Lord will judge him. That'll be quite unpleasant for him. But I too will sit in judgment on him—and that'll be even more unpleasant.[23]

Through Jhering's influence, the much coveted Kleist Prize, be-stowed on the most promising young playwright, was awarded to Brecht for the year 1922.

As in the case of *Baal,* when Brecht came to republish this work in his collected plays in 1954, he expressed a number of reservations. Speaking of *Trommeln* he said:

Only the consideration that literature belongs to history, and that the latter must not be falsified, no less than the feeling that my present views and capacities would be worthless without a knowledge of my earlier ones—provided that there has been an improvement—prevented me from mounting a small auto-da-fé. Furthermore, suppression is not enough. The False must be rectified.[24]

As a result of these reservations, Brecht undertook a number of changes in *Trommeln,* with the object of supplying a more "posi-tive" note. The tavern-keeper Glubb was now given a nephew, "a young worker, who participates in and falls in the November up-rising." However, the changes in the text, though numerous, were not far-reaching or profound enough to alter the essence of the play. It is still a play of the early 1920's. Brecht himself was aware of this:

Apparently my understanding at that time was not sufficiently deep to grasp the profound seriousness of the uprising of the winter of 1918-1919, but only sufficed to realize the lack of seriousness on the part of my unruly hero in his participation in the rising. The initiators of the struggle were the proletarians, but Kragler was the beneficiary. They needed no personal loss to justify their rebelling. Kragler could be indemnified. They were prepared to share jointly in his cause; but he sacrificed theirs. They were the tragic figures, he the comic one. I did not succeed in showing the spectator the Revolution otherwise than through the eyes of the "hero," Kragler, and he saw it as something romantic. The technique of "Estrangement" was not yet at my com-mand.[24]

A curious, though macabre, postcript to *Trommeln,* dating back to 1919, is furnished by Lion Feuchtwanger.

The manuscript of *Spartacus* [as *Drums in the Night* was then known] subjected me to an unpleasant experience. In the spring of the year [1919] a regime of soviets was established in Munich. It lasted only a very short time, and then the city was invested by White Guards. The homes of intellectuals were searched. Soldiers with drawn pistols and hand-grenades entered my home, forced me to open my desk. The very first thing that fell into their hands was the manuscript of *Spartacus*. In those days people were treated none too ceremoniously in Munich; bullets were easily discharged, and the number of victims ran into many hundreds. The matter of the Ms. of *Spartacus* would have gone badly with me, if among the soldiers there had not been present a number of students from Düsseldorf, who had seen some plays of mine, and had read some of my books, and so understood that *Spartacus* was not intended as revolutionary propoganda material.[25]

V

"In the Jungle of Cities"

Fourmillante cité, cité pleine de rêves,
Où le spectre, en plein jour, raccroche le
passant!

O swarming city, city full of dreams,
Where the ghost accosts the passerby in broad
daylight!

BAUDELAIRE, "Les Sept Vieillards"

In den Asphaltstädten bin ich daheim.

In the asphalt cities I am at home.

BRECHT, "Vom armen B. B."

Even if the Berlin production of *Trommeln* was not the success he
had anticipated, Brecht was still the talk of the town. His busy
mind was already astir with fresh plans—films, stories, adaptations,
and, of course, new poems and plays. The movie project with Bronnen had been abandoned by Brecht, but in his own right he began
an adaptation of Selma Lagerlöf's famous novel *Gösta Berling,* of
which he only completed two acts. He was still hopeful of directing
another of Bronnen's plays, *Verrat.* History attracted him too, and he
was on the lookout for new materials for a historical play. For in his
mind was already born the intention of "de-mystifying" traditional
heroes and heroism, and of rehabilitating forgotten and often "unheroic" figures. He was drawn to Rome rather than Greece, and he
asked Bronnen to find him materials relating to Hannibal, who had
already been made the subject of a play by Christian Grabbe.

Max Reinhardt had asked Brecht to adapt this play for production at the Grosses Schauspielhaus in Berlin. It was to be one of the highly "operatic" and "monumental" spectacles dear to Reinhardt, designed with a gigantic figure of Moloch in the background. Brecht was filled with a hope that he would be entrusted with its direction. The plans fell through, but a few fragmentary sketches of Brecht's treatment of the Hannibal theme throw an interesting light on his view of that historical figure, and on his methods of procedure. "One of the most remarkable men of history," he writes about him. "Known to us only through the eyes of his enemies, the Romans. . . . I believe he was of the native race of Negroes. Roman historians know of no man whose hatred of Rome was so great. And yet this man Hannibal behaved like any ordinary workingman." (Brecht was always an admirer of good craftsmanship.) "His life between battles was devoted to technical experiments which he tested in battles (somewhat like Rockefeller between business deals in oil)." Brecht also remarks on Hannibal's capacity of keeping a popular idea before his people for thirty years."[1] These are the beginnings of his historical interests and revaluations, which were to continue to the end of his life, when he was to write a chronicle novel about Julius Caesar.

Personal affairs also occupied him. Marianne Zoff was expecting a child by him, so they were married, and settled in modest quarters in the Akademiestrasse in Munich. The closely-knit trio consisting of Caspar Neher, Bronnen, and Brecht throve on projects and expectations. They were continually in a ferment of ideas and plans.

Brecht had been working on two new plays, *Im Dickicht der Städte* (*In the Jungle of Cities*) and an adaptation of Christopher Marlowe's *Edward II*. *Trommeln* and *Baal* had already been contracted for and were awaiting production. *Edward II,* on which Brecht was collaborating with Lion Feuchtwanger, was now in the hands of Heinz Lippmann, the Dramaturg of the Berlin Staatstheater.

Munich was at that time teeming with hopeful and disorderly

Brownshirts, preparing a "putsch." Anti-Semitic excesses were becoming more and more frequent, and though not a Jew, Brecht did not like what was happening. To Bronnen he expressed himself about that sort of "excrement," and Hitler's "cavalcades of dismal sons of bitches," in letters as amusing as they are obscene, but which Marianne thought so "wonderful," she begged Bronnen to save them, for some day she hoped to make a "great deal of money out of them."[2]

And so 1923 came along, with its new events: the birth of Hanne, and the prospect of *Dickicht,* to open on May 9, at the Prinzregententheater in Munich.[3]

"Dear Arnolt," Brecht wrote to his friend Bronnen, "Wednesday *Dickicht* première. . . . You must come without fail."[3] Bronnen, who was then at spiritual odds with himself, did not come. Perhaps less noble sentiments prevented him. The new play only achieved moderate approbation. Erich Engel had directed it; Caspar Neher had designed the scenery; and Otto Wernicke and Erwin Faber had taken the principal roles of Shlink and Garga respectively.

The play had at first been titled *Im Dickicht,* or *Garga,* and was finally renamed *Im Dickicht der Städte.* It is Brecht's first "American" play, for its background is Chicago.

Post-war Germany had constructed out of America a fabulous, visionary domain, partly concocted out of reality, mostly built on fantasy. The reality had, of course, been the presence of American troops in Europe, the occupation of German territory, the collapse of President Wilson's dream of a new world and a new Europe, and, not least, the ever-present lure of the American dollar seen as a sort of radiant vision against the background of the nightmarish collapse of the mark. There were also reminiscences of the past, the "American dream" brought to Europe by Walt Whitman; the American West and the Indian, celebrated by Fenimore Cooper and domesticated by Karl May; the grand adventures of the open prairies, buffaloes, cowboys, and not least, the lure of the great American cities with their "Wolkenkratzer"—their skyscrapers.

Brecht himself had been singing America:

Hallo, wir wollen mit Amerika sprechen . . . .

Hello! we want to speak with America
Across the Atlantic waters with the great cities
Of America. Hello!
We asked ourselves, in what language shall we speak
So that we may be understood.
But now we have singers in common
Who can be understood here and in America
And everywhere else in the world. . . .

The machines sing. . . .[4]

In those hectic, hysterical days, when Germany was a land that felt enclosed and prison-like, the appeal of "open spaces" was supplemented by the wonder aroused by skyscrapers, the fury and battle of the prize-ring, American boxers, six-day bicycle races, American lingo, American jazz, and Negro spirituals. Nor was Germany alone enthralled by this American invasion. All of Europe was captivated. Add also the "terror" and awe inspired by the American's cavernous, tortuous, labyrinthine cities, with their inexhaustible potentialities for mystery, crime, and adventure. So, in German eyes, appeared New York, Chicago, and San Francisco.

What ambivalences cities contained within themselves! Did it really matter very much whether it was Chicago or London, New York or Berlin? The city was a symbol. From the time of the Romantics and the Industrial Revolution this twofold feeling toward the city had become evident: attraction and repulsion. While Wordsworth and Coleridge fled to the Lake Country to escape the city, Charles Lamb was writing his encomiums of London. William Blake bewailed its "dark Satanic mills." The city was at once a vast hospital, a canker,[5] and an object of frightful fascination. Thus Baudelaire, Verlaine, and Rimbaud were drawn to their mistress, Paris, with her horrors, lusts, mysteries, which only reflected their own souls' depths of horror and passion; and Zola's Nana is none other than that opulent and sinful, but imperial courtesan, Paris herself. On the other hand, Walt Whitman had chanted the beauties and wonders of Manhattan and Brooklyn; but the later American novelists, Frank Norris and Upton Sinclair, had seen the great American cities differently. Upton Sinclair's *The Jungle* seemed to stand as the embodiment of Chicago. For the Berliners, who had no beautiful Paris to chant (Berlin was admittedly ugly), it was natural to superimpose Walt Whitman on Upton Sinclair in images of confusion, in which racial groups, nationalities, classes mingled and fought, explored new territories, built skyscrapers, formed gangster bands, but altogether stood for adventure and expansion: filled stockyards and constructed railroads—gateways opening on infinite wildernesses and possibilities! America meant all these, and also Charlie Chaplin, plenty of money, food, energy, and what the Germans did not least envy: America meant the future!

What mattered then a little distortion, when so much was real? Brecht wrote:

> I hear it said:
> He speaks of America,
> And doesn't understand a thing about it.
> Why, he wasn't even there!
> But believe me:
> They understand me very well when I speak of America.
> The best thing about America is
> That we understand it.[6]

This was the America which Brecht called "our familiar, unmistakable boyhood friend."[7]

In the Jungle of Cities is set in Chicago in the year 1912.

You are observing [Brecht wrote in a prefatory note to the play] the inexplicable boxing match between two men, and you are witnessing the downfall of a family which had come out of the savannas into the jungle of the great city. Do not wrack your brain about the motives of this match, but concentrate on the human stakes involved, objectively judge the style of the antagonists, and fix your whole interest on the finish.[8]

This is one of Brecht's strangest and in some ways most perplexing plays. Superficially, we are dealing with a "metaphysical" boxing match, watched dispassionately by both spectator and Brecht, in which, unfortunately, the stakes are high: the lives and fortunes both of the contestants and their associates. Actually, it is not Chicago that is involved, but Berlin; and the so-called "boxing match" is really a drama of loneliness, and a struggle to reach communication, even if only by means of battle, in a world that is detached, and defies communication. The principal antagonists in this puzzling play are a well-to-do but diseased Malayan lumber merchant, the middle-aged Shlink; and George Garga, a poor, young man, employed as a clerk in C. Mayne's lending library. Between these two takes place a sharp contest for the "possession of the soul." Shlink offers to buy Garga's opinion of a book; Garga refuses. Even after Shlink uses all possible resources at his disposal to win Garga over, the latter remains immovable. Though Shlink turns over his own successful lumber business to Garga, impoverishes himself, and with the assistance of his underworld associates, the Worm and the Baboon, prostitutes both Garga's sister and his girl friend, he is helpless. Garga, in turn, fights back by involving Shlink in a shady deal which will send him to jail, heaps coals upon him, by going to jail in Shlink's place, and then exposes Shlink as having seduced and raped the two girls, thus almost making sure that Shlink will be lynched. In the end, the two opponents face each other as a mob is wildly approaching to lynch Shlink. They face each other "exposed" in their "loneliness." Shlink commits suicide, and Garga, heir to what has been left, sets fire to the business, and goes off to New York, as to some other "jungle" in quest of his "freedom."

What are the elements that make up this drama, and what is its meaning? Remove the setting from Chicago, and what we have is once more the chaos that is Germany, and Berlin as its "jungle." But the actual jungle is life itself; the disintegration of the family of Garga is the disintegration that Brecht had already voiced in *Baal* and in *Trommeln*. What is the nature of the "freedom" that Garga is defending against the incessant assaults of Shlink? It is his personal detachment, his refusal to be possessed, actually to participate. Not that there is no attachment or attraction. As a matter of fact, here, as in *Baal,* the homosexual element is very powerful. Verlaine and Rimbaud are here once more. For Brecht, such relationships seem to have had a special fascination at this time. In an engrossing short story, "Bargan Lets It Be," written at about the same period, he describes the downfall of Bargan, a highly skilled and successful buccaneer, who cannot resist the lure of and his attachment to a degenerate associate, for whose sake he welcomes his own ruin and destruction.[9]

Garga then, in Brecht's play, stands for survival, Shlink for attachment, in a world in which the only possibility lies in loneliness; and contact is unattainable even in a fight. Garga can survive only as an isolated human being; this is his "freedom." And the price for it (willingly accepted) is his alienation both from persons and property. He is another anarch, in an anarchic society. Actually, the contest Shlink and Garga are engaged in is less a fierce boxing match than a deadly chess game, in which the opponents play with human pawns. Human beings are "things," "commodities," *used* at the will of the contestants. Thus, Shlink debauches Marie, Garga's sister (who is in love with Shlink) as well as Garga's sweetheart Jane; while Garga himself in the deadly battle against Shlink plays the part of the pander. The dehumanized, abstract character of the sporting arena reflects the dehumanized world outside as Brecht saw it, as well as its dehumanized contestants. The very concept of "freedom" is a dehumanized, detached one. It has little to do with the family or the community.

But is that sort of "freedom" attainable? Even Garga knows otherwise:

No . . . We are not free. It begins with coffee in the morning, and with a beating if you act the fool; and a mother's tears salt the children's food, and her sweat washes their shirts, and you are secured till Doomsday, and the roots of it dig deep into your heart. And when you are grown up and want to do something with your own skin and hair, then you get paid, initiated, stamped, sold at a high price, and you don't even have the freedom to go to the dogs.[10]

For the commonplace, workaday world and its toiling members, Garga has nothing but contempt. But where find freedom from that? Is New York the wilderness that will satisfy that search? Brecht had in mind Rimbaud, who went off on his hazardous and anarchic adventure into Africa, to become a slave-dealer.

Rimbaud had written:

Je reviendrai, avec de membres de fer, le peau sombre, l'oeil furieux. . . .[11]

which in Brecht's translation becomes literally,

I will go there [to New York], and I will come back with limbs of iron, dark of skin, and fury in my eyes.[12]

Rimbaud had written:

Le combat spirituel est aussi brutal que le bataille d'hommes.[13]

The spiritual battle is as brutal as the battle between men.

In Brecht, Shlink says to Garga at the end:

You did not understand it at all. You wanted my end, but I wanted the battle; not the physical, but the spiritual.

To which Garga replies:

Now you see that the spiritual is nothing. It is not important to be the stronger, but the living one. I can't win over you. I can only trample on you.[14]

We know from his poetry of that time that Brecht liked to think of himself as dispassionate and detached. Likewise, he imagined that in looking on life he was looking on a sport. One of his great objects of admiration at this time was the middleweight champion Samson-Körner, whose biography he was planning to write, and with whom he was frequently photographed. Garga is given to frequent quotations from Rimbaud, using the latter's whiplashes against contemporary society, and glorifications of primitivism and savagery. For the title of his play, Brecht undoubtedly went to Upton Sinclair's novel *The Jungle,* which was to serve him in good stead in the future, too.

A very serious debt, however, is that to the Danish novelist, H. V. Jensen, whose *Hjulet* (*The Wheel*), published in 1905, made a very profound impression on Brecht. Jensen worshipped America as the newborn embodiment of his mystical Teutonic ideal; and he saw in Chicago, in the West, and in American industry and technology a realization of the *Edda*. In *The Wheel* he depicts another "metaphysical" struggle taking place in Chicago, at the beginning of the century, between two human beings, bent on personal domination, with an explicitly homosexual tone. The strange combat takes place between a writer, Winnifred Lee, and Joseph Evanston, a charlatan preacher—a criminal, but the possessor of a magnetic personality—who openly declares his love for Lee, and is at the end murdered by him. Its resemblance to the themes of *Bargan* and *Im Dickicht* needs no further elaboration. The difference lies in the conception of Chicago. For Brecht it was a "jungle," for Jensen a "wheel" that turns industry, commerce, machinery, and creates wealth.

Jensen describes the "metaphysical struggle" between the two opponents:

And herewith began the battle between two men—two altogether different nervous systems, a battle that was relentless and could only end with the destruction of one of the combatants, because it was carried on by one of them blindly and with all the strength of elementary appetite, and for the other meant nothing less than life itself.[15]

Bronnen suggests that certain personal elements may have entered into Brecht's treatment of Garga and Shlink. Was Brecht, Bronnen asks, bringing into *Dickicht* his own "embryology, the genealogical history of the Brecht family"?[16] Was Garga Brecht? And was Shlink's language the sovereign, resilient speech of Feuchtwanger?[17] According to Bronnen, Brecht himself was inclined to give differing interpretations of the play at different times. Brecht was not accustomed to being probed, and if his "motiveless action" in *Dickicht* did not offer sufficient clues to what he was thinking about the world at large, then it was too bad.

The Munich production of May 9, 1923, directed by Erich Engel, with the scenery of Caspar Neher, and the subsequent one at the Deutsches Theater in Berlin, on October 29, 1924, with Fritz Kortner in the role of Shlink, aroused mixed feelings among the critics.

Herbert Jhering was almost alone in his unreserved appreciation. He insisted that Brecht had now mastered the "dramatic complex" in interrelating living characters with one another. "Garga lives only through Shlink, and Shlink through Garga."[18] He assailed current theatrical taste that only approved the conventional and philistine, and fought the unconventional and original.[19] In a way, he put his finger on the very nerve of the play, in declaring that it truly reflected the spirit of the times, when battle-lines were being drawn up not so much on the political, as on the cultural and moral field. In this drama, he stated, "human beings drain each other like vampires; in it, good deeds destroy . . . . and swamps exude light."[20]

Julius Bab was more reserved, but no less penetrating. He was especially struck by the unforgetttable effect of the "stone jungles" of the city, in which one could not differentiate inner rooms from streets, and in which it seemed as if the sky and air were themselves of stone, all "a wilderness, in which man is wolf to man." This might have been a great play, he continues. For "this man Brecht has the true chaos within him. But so long as his dangerous friends persuade him that chaos has value for itself, and constitutes a goal in itself, he will never give birth to dancing stars."[21]

Brecht was winning respect and admiration from his professional contemporaries as is shown in the actions of Fritz Kortner, then already acknowledged as an outstanding actor. He had been reciting Brecht's poems publicly, among them the ever-popular "Legend of the Dead Soldier." When the opportunity arose to take part in Brecht's Dickicht, he accepted it eagerly and turned down a most flattering offer by Max Reinhardt to act in Shaw's St. Joan. "Brecht," he said, "was at that time thoroughly reviled by the press, except for Herbert Jhering. He fascinated me. It was my own free will, rather than any sense of duty, that prompted me to come over to

his side. Working with the director Engel, and with the poet himself, who took an active part in all the rehearsals, and in consulta-
tion with us would often rewrite entire scenes, preserved me from
that smugness that attends success. New vistas opened before me."[22]
And now, at long last, Brecht was to achieve a performance of
his firstling, *Baal.* But not in Berlin. Berlin was not venturesome
enough, Leipzig was. The approaching première of an already
notorious play by the *bête-noire* of the German drama stirred both
excitement and thrill, not lessened by the rumors of a possible public
scandal.

The public was not to be disappointed.

Friend, foe, and neutral gathered on the evening of December 8,
1923 at the Altes Theater in Leipzig. The performance was suddenly interrupted after the actor Lothar Körner had recited one of
the most moving passages of the play, by someone shouting, "What's
this poem all about?" But there was an ovation at the end. Herbert
Jhering exulted: "Leipzig has dared to do, with limited resources,
what Berlin could have carried off with triumph."[23] But at the
command of the mayor of Leipzig the play had to be withdrawn
from the theater's repertory. He apparently agreed with a critic who
had called the play a "mudbath."[24]

But other productions followed, in Munich, then in Berlin. In
the latter, at the Deutsches Theater, on February 14, 1926, Brecht
himself directed along with Oskar Homolka, who also acted the
part of Baal. The playwright Hanns Henny Jahn gives us a vivid,
contemporary description of what took place in Berlin:

Some time—I believe it was after Orge's Song: "The sweetest place on
earth . . .", the tumult broke loose. . . . Whistles, cat-calls, cries, applause. . . . The actress swung herself on to the top of the piano, and
belabored the keys with her feet, and sang, "Allons enfants de la patrie!"
I thought panic would break out. But it was confined only to the noise.
. . . Suddenly there was a death-like silence, and a voice from the gallery
broke in, "You're not really shocked! You're doing it only to—", followed by the slapping of a face. Applause. More applause. And then
the play went on.[25]

Baal also moved on to Vienna. That that city by the Danube should want to produce the play was indeed a sign that the world had changed. Vienna was, and always had been, the most conservative cultural city of Europe. Even more startling was the fact that Austria's foremost poet, Hugo von Hofmannsthal—that most gifted and epigonal romantic—should have been willing to write a prologue to *Baal* and produce the play.

This prologue, "Das Theater des Neuen—eine Ankündigung" ("Theater of the New—A Proclamation") is a fascinating piece of work. It utilizes the participating actors, speaking in their own person (Oskar Homolka among them) to discuss the significance of *Baal* for the modern theatre. When one of the actors in astonishment asks whether this is a historical play, being entitled *Baal,* and whether it will be understood, Homolka replies:

This is the mythos of Existence, the elemental configuration of our Being. Man today penetrates into everything, imbibes all that is alive, in order in the end to return to earth. . . . The poet we are presenting today does not talk. . . . He is a poet of a chaotic time . . . , a goal-seeking visionary.

To which the other actor, Egon Friedell, adds that our time wishes to be redeemed from individuality, that European individuality, which "has been digging its own grave."[26] That is what Brecht was representing.

This is Hofmannsthal's tribute to Brecht. But it is no less a tribute to the enterprising spirit of Hofmannsthal himself.

As for the scandals, we may be sure Brecht relished every moment of riot connected with his plays. He could even poke fun at himself. In one of his shorter farces, he has the following conversation:

YOUNG MAN. Have you . . . seen the piece, called "Baal" in the theatre?
MAN. Yes, I have. It's a filthy thing.
YOUNG MAN. But there's something powerful about it.
MAN. Well, then it's a powerful piece of filth. And that is worse than a weak piece. If a man has talent for the beastly, does that excuse him? It just doesn't belong in such a play.
FATHER. With these modern playwrights, family life has been dragged in the mud. And that's the best we Germans can boast of![27]

VI

"Edward the Second"
and the Cult of the Heroic

The world is going under. What's an oath?
I'll give you absolution.

BRECHT, *Eduard der Zweite*

The cult of the heroic, popularized in the nineteenth century by
Thomas Carlyle and his "heroes and hero-worship," had never died
out in Germany, though it had been severely flawed. The "heroic"
had been compromised in the tarnished figures of Kaiser Wilhelm
II, General von Hindenburg, and the other military leaders, not to
mention Ludendorff; though in the eyes of the extreme nationalists
their glory remained intact.

But for the generality of Germans there was urgent need of
replacements. The early twenties of the new century engaged in a
search for historical characters who might restore the lustre of
heroism to a somewhat threadbare present. Writers turned to the
figures of Napoleon, Martin Luther, Maximilian of Habsburg. Walter Hasenclever made Napoleon an architect of a Pan-Europe; Fritz
von Unruh turned him into a scion of the Enlightenment; the
dramatist Blume made him a pacifist. Franz Werfel changed Maximilian into a mild and democratic ruler of a barbarous Mexico;
Hanns Johst glorified Luther as a German liberator at the expense
of a reviled Anabaptist, Thomas Münzer, whom he called a mangy
dog. And at his great theatre in Berlin, Max Reinhardt was staging

Bernard Shaw's *St. Joan,* and bringing to life another great historic figure.

Now Brecht was deeply interested in the historical drama. He was, as we have seen, working on an adaptation of the Hannibal theme, no doubt stimulated by the revival of Grabbe's *Hannibal* in 1918. He was drawn to the drama of the Elizabethans, because in structure and language they seemed to come closest to that which he himself had been aiming at. As Dramaturg of the Munich Kammerspiele he was also responsible for the staging of at least one of Shakespeare's plays. *Macbeth,* which was being considered, was fortunately beyond his capacities at that time, and he was wise in turning his eyes elsewhere. He lighted upon Christopher Marlowe's tragedy, *The Troublesome Reign and Lamentable Death of Edward II.* Lion Feuchtwanger offered to help. This was certainly at the moment a much safer venture than a well-known tragedy by Shakespeare.

There might also have been other reasons for the appeal of Marlowe's play and of its author. Here was another *poète maudit,* fit company for Brecht's other idols, like Rimbaud and Villon, a suspected freethinker, if not a heretic, a bohemian, possibly also touched by the underworld, and dead at an early age. The theme of Marlowe's tragedy had its points of attraction too. Here was an unnatural relationship between a king and an underling, bringing with it a tragic ending. King Edward and Piers Gaveston paralleled the relationship of Bargan and Croze, as well as of Garga and Shlink, not to mention Baal and Ekart.

Brecht had always reacted against the strict or "closed" form of the classical play, with its act structure, its climaxes and resolutions. The "open" form of the chronicle play, with its freedom of movement, its discontinuity, its changes of scene—in other words, its "epic" character as he was to call it—suited his own particular needs and style.

Once again Brecht retired from the hubbub of Munich to Augsburg's quiet, and came back from it bringing Feuchtwanger pages of new verses. Feuchtwanger criticized and corrected, very often transforming smooth lines into "stumbling" ones. Nevertheless, this was a daring thing to undertake at a time when such directors as Jessner had achieved notoriety and success with a stylized *Richard III*, and Berthold Viertel with his *Richard II*, in the manner of the Russian Tairov and the Kamerny Theatre. Anyone who exposed himself with an adaptation ran afoul of the kind of response Feuchtwanger wittily describes:

> I, for instance, sometimes make
> adaptations. Some call them "free renderings"—
> and that is true. I take old matter
> and make a new piece. And underneath
> the title I put the name of the dead poet,—
> someone very famous, of course, but totally unknown,
>
> and place before the name of the dead poet
> the little word "after."
> Then some people say, "He's full of reverence."
> Others, "He hasn't got any respect at all."
> And what's amiss in the work,
> they attribute to me,
> and what's good, they ascribe to the dead poet,
> who, as you know, is very famous, and totally unknown,
> and about whom no one really knows
> whether he's the author or perhaps only the adapter.[1]

Christopher Marlowe's *Edward II* was probably written around 1592, and is that dramatist's most finished play and, fortunately, also the best preserved one. It chronicles the events of the English king's life from 1307 to 1330—that is, from the time of the return of his male paramour Gaveston to his death. It describes the unhappy wars of the barons and the other feudal lords, secular and spiritual, their unmitigated hatred of the "upstart churl" Gaveston, his murder, and finally, the forced abdication of the king, his torture and persecution at the hands of the queen's lover Mortimer, and his eventual murder in prison. The play ends with the queen's banishment and the execution of Mortimer, at the behest of the young King Edward III.

In Marlowe's tragedy, which hinges entirely on the fateful and fatal attachment of king and paramour, the role of Gaveston is heightened by his "Italianate" proclivities; that is, as Elizabethan Englishmen conceived them: corruption and effeminacy, debauchery and delight in voluptuousness and Italian masks of satyrs dancing "with their goat-feet an antic hay." For the Lords and high churchmen he is a "night-grown mushroom" of vulgar extraction. The people of England as such do not appear in the play, neither soldiers nor peasants, nor citizens, except as silent participants or onlookers, or victims of the bloodthirsty struggles. For Marlowe they had no true existence. There are drums only to sound forth the appearance of Kings, Lords, and Cardinals. The play has beauty, however. Its characterizations and action have momentum and precision; the language is rich. The scenes of the imprisonment and murder of the King were not to be equalled—except by only one contemporary of Marlowe's.

What Brecht and Feuchtwanger did to Marlowe's play throws an interesting light on both of the adapters. In its final shape *Leben Eduard des Zweiten von England* is predominantly Brecht's work. The movement is hastened; it is swifter, the language tauter. As might have been expected, the political and social elements are emphasized, as they are not in the original. Interjected scenes bring in the populace of London, to express its bitterness toward the King and his male "whore." A typical Brechtian street-ballad laments the wastefulness and oppressions practised by king and paramour:

> Eddy's whore has a beard on his chest,
> Pray for us, pray for us.
> So the war gainst Scotland has had to rest,
> Pray for us, ora pro nobis.

> The Peer of Cornwall has gold in his hose,
> Pray for us, pray for us,
> So Pat has no arm, and O'Nelly no nose,
> Pray for us, etc.

> Eddy is busy delousing his "bride,"
> Pray for us, etc.

And Johnny croaks in the swamps of Bannockbride,
Pray for us, etc.[2]

In place of Marlowe's opulence, Brecht introduced a terseness
and economy of language and plot that make it possible for him
to pinpoint the moral chaos of the times, where betrayal follows
betrayal, perjury perjury, all at the hands of nobles, churchmen, and
kings. Marlowe's two Mortimers, father and son, are contracted
into one, an elder statesman, scholar, cynic, philosopher, who in
counseling the banishment of Gaveston to Parliament speaks a
typical Brechtian idiom. He draws an analogy with the Trojan War:

But were not most agreement
Inhuman, and human ear not stopped up—
What mattered if Helen were a whore,
Or grandame of sound progeny?
Troy would still be standing, four times
The size of our own London—Hector not
Dismembered, shamed, his privates maimed,
And dodd'ring Priam's ancient head not
Dog-beslavered;
And a race of warriors in their prime
Not undone.
Quod erat demonstrandum. Of course,
We should not then have had the *Iliad*.[3]

Only one betrayal is condoned, that committed by the lowly Baldock
against the King. Baldock is a scholar and poor, and he falters in
the face of his want. Brecht, with the idiom of the Bible in his head,
fashions the scene after another, more world-shaking, betrayal:

The Bible teaches us how it's to be done:
When your men come with chain and bonds,
I will say to the King: Dear Liege,
Be calm; here is a handkerchief.
And he to whom I give it is the King.[4]

And as the King looks at his betrayer, Baldock weeps:

My mother in Ireland is in want of bread.
Mylord, you will forgive me.[5]

"Calculation thrives" in all quarters, but the poor populace is the loser. The Church, no less than the nobility, becomes partner in this drama of double-dealing.

Here is the Archbishop of Winchester, speaking to Mortimer: "The Church was with whom God was."

"And with whom was God?" Mortimer asks.

"With him who was victorious, Mortimer," is the answer.[6]

Unlike Marlowe's, Brecht's King Edward, toward the end of his life, while he is in prison, recalls his own misdeeds, his inordinate exactions from the poor, his treatment of the Queen.

In words and tone reminiscent of Brecht's chorales of darkness, the King says:

> Praise lack, praise torture,
> Praise the darkness . . .[7]

Brecht dispenses with Marlowe's wonderful rhetorical lengths, his pregnant similes, his lushness of language. He pointedly employs crudity, and a rhythmic pace that is "stumbling," so as to mirror the pace and havoc of the times. Deliberate inversions in grammatical structure startle and arrest the ear. Thus Gaveston describes his state as he is fleeing:

Since sounding of drums, the swamps swallowing horse and catapult— my mother's son's head is all distraught. Do not pant! Are all now drowned and done for? And only noise now—suspended between heaven and earth? I'll run no more.[8]

In the original:

> Seit diese Trommeln waren, der Sumpf ersäufend
> Katapult und Pferde, ist wohl verrückt
> Meiner Mutter Sohn Kopf. Keuch nicht! . . .

Brecht directed the play, which was produced at the Munich Kammerspiele on March 18, 1924, with Erwin Faber and Oskar Homolka in the principal roles, and with scenic designs by Caspar Neher. Of the nature of Brecht's talents as stage director we have the first full contemporary account from Bernhard Reich, who took over the post of general manager of the theatre in the fall of 1923.

He describes Brecht's quiet, but deceptive, manner of speaking. "He made assertions, forming them in a paradoxical manner." But he was a determined man, and did not meet objections, says Reich, "he shaved them away." The twenty-five-year-old "novice" made demands of the older and established actors that were "astonishing and unheard of" at that time. Such things as precise attention to the minutest details of eating, drinking, duelling, which the traditional artists were wont to treat cavalierly, became in Brecht's direction moments of importance and evidences of great skill. Details were worked out for hours, for Brecht insisted on the audience's understanding what was taking place on the stage. In typical fashion, Brecht changed the scripts in the light of practice, sometimes to the dismay of the actors who were to memorize them.

As the dress rehearsal drew nearer and nearer, Brecht became more and more active; from the auditorium he handed the actors whole sheaves of new text. If one of the actors grumbled, Brecht would look at him with unconcealed and honest amazement, so that the actor quickly took the new text and prepared to memorize it.

Brecht insisted on very primitive, simple stage sets. Despite differences, there can be no doubt that those who worked with him respected him and his methods. Here was a true theatre man. "We derived great pleasure from this production," Reich continues, "for here sentimentality and rhetoric had almost been transcended."[9]

It was this meticulous procedure of Brecht's that was to draw to him in this and subsequent performances of *Edward the Second* such actors as Erwin Faber, Oskar Homolka, Agnes Straub, Werner Krauss, Ernst Deutsch, Heinrich George, Alexander Granach, and Elisabeth Bergner.

Brecht was already developing some elements of the theory of "estrangement" ("Verfremdung"), at least in the staging of that play. Thus, Edward's plight in prison was accentuated by the way he scraped the last morsel of food from his wooden bowl, and the way the wide-meshed fence that separated audience from prison rattled whenever the King brushed against it. The background was formed by tall London houses, with numerous window casements, that flew open and revealed the populace chanting the derisive ballad against the King and his "whore," suggesting, one writer comments, "an oncoming revolution." At one point, Brecht felt dissatisfied with the performance of the soldiers, and asked, "How do soldiers behave?", to which Karl Valentin, who was present, replied, "They are scared." Whereupon Brecht had each soldier whiten his face, and thus immediately created the atmosphere he was looking for.[10]

Julius Bab reacted to this "estrangement" unfavorably, commenting that despite the effect of terror achieved, he sensed Brecht standing on the sidelines—"the fair-barker Brecht . . . . with his invisible pointer."[11]

Herbert Jhering caught an even more important intention of Brecht's, that of the "de-heroization" of royalty: At a time when heroism had become questionable,

Brecht substituted for the concept of greatness that of *distance*. . . . He did not reduce the human being. Nor did he atomize him. He "removed" him . . . This production in Munich was the turning point of the classical theatre.[12]

Thus Brecht had converted Marlowe's tragedy into ironic demystification.

Though Munich was offering him and his plays productions Berlin had not been willing to risk, life in that city was becoming far from supportable. Brecht's marriage had proved unhappy, and was on the point of breaking up. Brownshirt excesses in Munich were becoming more and more numerous and virulent. At that time Brecht invented the term "Mahagonny." It came to him as he watched the processions of brown-shirted petty-bourgeois, those wooden figures, with their decorated and hole-ridden banners. In that summer of 1923 "Mahagonny" signified for him the philistine's Utopia, that cynical, stupid coffee-house state which was brewing, out of anarchy and alcohol, the most dangerous witches' potion for Europe. "Should Mahagonny come, I go," Brecht said in farewell.[13] Bronnen, who reports this, also adds that within himself, he, Bronnen, felt a strong attraction for that sort of brew. Later on, in fact, he succumbed to it.

Feuchtwanger and Arnold Zweig were no less concerned about the approaching menace, and kept warning Brecht. Bronnen and Brecht attended one of Hitler's mass meetings and listened to the future Führer. Brecht remarked, "He has the advantages of a man who knows the theatre from the galleries."[14]

In November, 1923, the abortive beerhall "putsch" took place, was temporarily suppressed, and Hitler was sentenced to imprisonment. Brecht had been placed on Hitler's blacklist, a candidate for liquidation, should the counter-revolution succeed.

So Berlin looked like a more comfortable place in which to live and work. He had been invited by Reinhardt's Deutsches Theater to become co-Dramaturg alongside of Carl Zuckmayer. Toward the end of 1924 he settled in Berlin in the Spichernstrasse.

"One had to climb five stories," Bernhard Reich wrote, "and balance oneself on a break-neck staircase, push open a massive iron door, walk through a wide corridor to reach his garret. From the large windows one could look down on Berlin. This ocean of roofs Brecht kept constantly in view, as he planned the conquest of the capital." For Brecht saw himself as some sort of captain of a band of faithful souls who would win adherents and believers for him all over the land.[15]

He was already at work on a new comedy, *Mann ist Mann*. Comedy was his medium. He had not gone to school with Karl Valentin in vain. He was hoping that a number of comic sketches he had been composing since 1919 would now, in the light of his growing reputation, also reach the stage. These short farces, in the manner of the French *sotie,* or dramatized *fabliaux,* were music-hall productions, full of slapstick and biting humor, and of a folk-character. Of these the most amusing is *Die Kleinbürgerhochzeit* (*The Petty Bourgeois Wedding*), a satirical take-off of a wedding-party, in which the break-up of good feelings of the guests is paralleled by the gradual collapse of the new furniture the bridegroom had constructed all by himself. The father is a hopeless bore, the bride is already pregnant, a wedding guest flirts with the bride, the couple quarrels, and the lights go out, and in the dark, the last piece of furniture is heard collapsing.[16]

A more subtle piece is the skit, *Lux in Tenebris*. It is also more typically Brechtian. The background is the red-light district, probably the one Brecht knew from his gymnasium days. The principal character, a touter, Paduk, sets up an "educational" tent-exhibit directly opposite a brothel, and presents the dire effects of venereal disease—for a price, of course. His placard reads: "Let there be light! People be enlightened!" Paduk also lectures and has numerous clients, among them a chaplain accompanied by seventy-three members of his association. The madam of the brothel, Frau Rogge, is naturally outraged by the competition, especially since Paduk had been one of her clients and had been thrown out of her house. In a cogent speech she persuades her competitor that his best interests lie in joining with her, for his customers come only once, but hers . . . . Furthermore, if her enterprise goes to pot, what would happen to his? The economic argument Paduk finds irrefutable, and he capitulates.

The other short farces are also amusing: *The Beggar, or the Dead Dog, He Drives out a Devil* and *The Catch*, the last two being somewhat bawdy.[17]

Bernhard Reich, who was preparing Alexandre Dumas' *Camille* for the theatre (Elisabeth Bergner was to play Marguerite), was distressed by the extremely sentimental ending of the play, and came to Brecht for help. Brecht was to rewrite the last act. In typical fashion he proceeded to unmask the bourgeois romanticism of the death scene: Marguerite was not to die in blessed certainty of being loved, but miserably and wretchedly disenchanted. Horrified by this threat to box-office receipts, Bergner rejected the new version.[18]

But Brecht's major occupation was *Mann ist Mann*. In characteristic fashion he was always sharing his plans and ideas with friends.

Reich recalls how after reading to him a few sketches of the play, Brecht asked, "Will the comedy attract an audience?" Reich replied, "No." Brecht decided to make changes more in keeping (as he thought) with popular taste, and a few days later showed the results to Reich. To the amusement of both of them, it turned out that Brecht had not made any really significant alterations. "We laughed," Reich reports, "heartily over the failure of the attempt to compromise. Brecht could only write as he had to write."[19]

VII

The Surrender of Identity:
"Man Is Man"

GUILLEMIN. And what are you working on now?

BRECHT. On a comedy called *Man is Man*. It concerns the technical dismantling and reassembling of a human being into another kind for a particular purpose.

Interview with Bernard Guillemin, in "Die Literarische Welt," July 30, 1926.

What "man has made of man" has been the theme of literature from times immemorial, and Robert Burns' "A man's a man for a' that" has sung its revolutionary refrain around the world. Brecht is concerned with probing "what man makes of man" and "what man can be made into" in our present society and times. It will be a while before he finally turns to the theme of "what man *should* make of man."

He had been living with the question of what man can be changed into as a subject for a play since 1921. Then he already anticipated the later figure of Galy Gay, who first appears under the name of "Galgei":

The subject of "Galgei" has something barbarous about it. It is a picture of a lump of flesh . . . who, because he lacks center, endures every sort of change, just as water flows into every sort of vessel. The barbarous and shameless triumph of a senseless life, that grows rankly in any direction, utilizes every format, suffers from no sort of reservations. Here lives the ass, who has been willed to live on as a pig. The question is, Is he really living? The answer: He is being lived.[1]

Besides exotic America, Rudyard Kipling's India also served as a magnet for the roving imagination of the Germans. A strange fantasy, pieced together from the *Barrack-Room Ballads* and the brilliant short stories and novels, spiced with some knowledge of British imperialism, and sifted through a generous imagination that cared little for accuracy, brought forth a never-never land. Such is the background of Brecht's *Mann ist Mann*.

The place is Kilkoa, India. Galy Gay, a poor Irish dock-porter, sets out one day to buy fish for himself and his wife, and on the way is befriended by three British Tommies, who, having lost their fourth companion, must at all costs find a replacement. For their comrade, Jip by name, along with whom they had tried to break into a pagoda, had lost part of his hair in the adventure, and could not be seen without the risk of being charged with the crime. The unhappy Jip, left behind, is caught by the pagoda's bonze, and is "converted" by the latter into a "god," to mislead the true believers. At the same time a curious and fascinating process is set afoot to convert Galy Gay into Jip, a process he only too willingly submits to, in anticipation of profit, even to the extent of denying his own wife. Further to ensnare him and bind him to them, his companions beguile him into selling a fake elephant (made of materials belonging to the army), charge him with the swindle, sentence him to a mock execution, and bring him to the point where, having denied his past and his name, he even pronounces a funeral oration over the presumptive body of his former self. So thorough is the transformation of Galy Gay into soldier Jip, that he becomes an efficient battle-machine, and singlehandedly overcomes the fortress of El-Dschur. When the true Jip finally returns, he is unrecognized, and is turned into Galy Gay!

Was this play intended by Brecht as some sort of anti-romantic counterblast to the expressionist's "Wandlung"—grand transfigura-

tion of man into Man? We do not know. But it is remarkable that
for the first time in Brecht's writings the element of *change* begins
to play a part. Man *is* changeable. Unfortunately, the changeability
is a negative one. Galy is pliant putty in the hands of external forces
that do with him what they will. Before, Brecht had been asking
us to sit back (preferably with cigar in mouth), and watch, as at a
wrestling or boxing match, the futile conflict of human beings, and
their striving for contact in a world without form and void, an
unchanging chaos. But now he is asking us (also with cigar) to
scan a figure of a man (Galy Gay) as he allows himself wittingly
to be changed into anything society wishes. Though in the other
plays he had already suggested the social interplay of forces (for
example, the "cash-nexus" with which Shlink attempts to bind
Garga to himself is obvious), the social forces that play upon Galy
Gay in *Mann ist Mann* become more clearly defined. Martin Esslin
is right in pointing out that this represents a transition from Brecht's
early "anarchic nihilism" to a tentative form of "social awareness
and didacticism."[2]

Such awareness is limited; the depiction of "change" is one-sided;
and Brecht's understanding of the social context within which the
change takes place is narrow. This is Brecht's transitional stage.

For the first time, too, in any of his plays, Brecht addresses the
audience directly in his own name. The canteen proprietress, Widow
Begbick, steps forward and announces the theme of the play to the
spectators.

> Herr Bertolt Brecht behauptet: Mann ist Mann.
> Und das ist etwas, was jeder behaupten kann.

"Mr. Bertolt Brecht," she says, "asserts Man is Man. And that is
something everyone can assert." What Mr. Brecht is proving is that
one can do anything one wishes with a Man. This evening will
show how a man is being reconstructed like an auto. More than
that: one can even turn him into a butcher. But it is not only Galy
Gay that is changeable, everything in this world is, the ground you
stand on, and man of course, too.[3]

If Galy Gay will be exhibited as the passive object of change, Widow Begbick will be its philosophical analyst and advocate. She may not be aware (though of course Mr. Brecht was) that she was voicing the sentiments of an ancient Greek philosopher, Heraclitus of Ephesus, when he said:

You cannot step twice into the same rivers, for fresh waters are ever flowing in upon you.[4]

Her song of mutability states that

> No matter how often you look at the river,
> Lazily flowing, you never see the same waters,
> Not a drop ever returns, to flow again,
> Not a drop returns to its source,[5]

and wisely counsels not to "cling to the wave that breaks at your feet," for new waters will ever break against them so long as you stand in the stream.[6] For she is one of Brecht's apostles of survival with its bitter lesson: Change! Her own man is dead, but even at that, she has come far since then. For man is like a machine: he can be taken apart, and put together. He is a thing on an assembly line.

Mr. Brecht, she had said before, had warned that life on this earth is a dangerous thing. And the most dangerous possession is "individuality." Galy Gay will be buried as the last individual. He will even pronounce the death sentence of his own individuality—and what does it really matter? "Twixt Yes and No the difference is not so great."[7] For man in any form is a "usable thing" . . . "the one I or the other I"—it's a toss-up. Especially if, as he says, he is most comfortable in his "new flesh."

There is a secondary episode, in which Sergeant Fairchild, nicknamed Bloody Five (he has coldbloodedly and deliberately murdered five Hindus) is so deeply attached to his own personality, which alternates between severe bouts of cruelty and equally severe bouts of sensuality, that to preserve it intact, he castrates himself. Again, personality is a dangerous possession! Galy Gay cries out to him, "Do nothing for the sake of your name! A name is something unsure—you can't build upon that." When the mutilation has taken place, Galy Gay muses: "That's lucky for me. Now I see to what a pass stubbornness can bring one, what a bloody mess it can turn out to be for a man who is always dissatisfied with himself and makes such a to-do over a mere name."[8] In the opinion of Uria, one of the other soldiers, Galy's capacity for change is a proof of vitality. And Galy supports that view when at the end he remarks: "I would have been happier if they had named me Nobody-at-all, instead of Galy Gay."[9]

Thus, Brecht has foreshadowed the alienation of the machine-made man, and social conformism. The will to be metamorphosed into nonentity arouses in him, at this time, a mixture of admiration and contempt. How wonderful is man! Throw him into a pond, says Brecht, and he grows webbed fingers.[10]

For this phenomenon of transmutation which had just taken place, the soldier Jesse instructs the Widow Begbick, is a "historic" one. Technology has taken over, he says. "In the vise of the workbench, or on the conveyor belt, the great man and the little man all are alike when looked at from the point of view of size." And he concludes that everything has been shown to be relative by modern science. "Table, bench, water, shoehorn . . . You, Widow Begbick, and I, we're relative."[11]

And as for "reconstructing" a man, what tool can be more efficient than the military? Galy Gay is a "natural" as a thorough war-engine. Does it matter what war is being fought, or against whom?

When they need cotton, it's Tibet; and when they need wool, it's Pamir. . . . We haven't as yet been told which country we are to invade. But it looks more and more like Tibet.[12]

Such is Brecht's India, viewed with Kipling's glasses. Tommy Atkins, Fuzzy Wuzzy, Danny Deever have been turned into Uria, Jip, Polly and Jesse. Like Kipling's soldiery, they chant the praises of grog in Widow Begbick's canteen, where you can drink "for twenty years," from "Singapore to Cooch Behar." From Kipling

too Brecht learned to warn the Tommies about being caught
thieving, to work in pairs when, as Kipling says, they're " 'acking
round a gilded Burma god" with his eyes of precious stones.
Brecht's friend, the novelist Alfred Döblin, supplied another incident for this play. The novel, *Die drei Sprünge des Wang-lun*
(*The Three Leaps of Wang-lun*) appeared in 1915. The story is
that of Wang-lun from the province of Hai-ling, son of a fisherman,
who is converted from rogue and thief to leader of a mass movement to liberate Chinese society peacefully, but is in the end defeated
and falls under the attack of the enemy.

An early episode of the book tells how Wang-lun broke into a
temple of the musicians' god, to steal the contributions of the faithful, which he finds concealed in the statue of the god.

But as he made to descend on the stool, he felt that someone was holding
him by his pigtail, actually, that this beautifully coiled pigtail was stuck
fast to the roof and wall of the room. He groped with his free left hand
up and down, and behind, and he felt a thick, tar-like mass. With
difficulty he freed his hand. . . . Painfully, and with great loss of hair,
he wrenched his pigtail loose from the messy, sticky stuff. Softly cursing
the bonze, he sneaked out into the street.[13]

It is a similar loss of hair that proves the undoing of the British
Tommy, Jip, and the beginning of Galy Gay's transmogrification
into Jip.

Anachronisms and wilful inconsistences abound in Brecht's play.
But does it really matter that Queen Victoria is still alive in 1925,
and Chinese worshippers betake themselves to Tibetan temples?
Delhi, Kilkoa, Berlin, New York—what is the difference? This is
an apologue on the transformability of man in an age of machines.
The reader of today can supply his own footnotes, whether the
mechanisms of change be the computer, "subliminal" advertising,
or other pressures and bribes. That man can also be transformed
into an animal—and Galy Gay becomes that too—needs no comment
at this point in history. When Galy Gay shrieks, "Jesse, Uria, Polly,
the battle is beginning, and already I feel I want to bury my teeth

in the neck of the enemy,"[14] we can merely shudder in recognition. If we wish something less sinister, we need only recall Charlie Chaplin's transformations in *Modern Times*.

Along with *Mann ist Mann,* and as a sort of *entr'acte* to be played "during the intermission in the foyer of the theatre," Brecht composed *The Baby Elephant,* a farce, almost surrealist in character, and no doubt indebted to Karl Valentin and the Bavarian folk-comedy. Critics have seen in it touches of Pirandello,[15] and amateur psychoanalysts have detected reflections of Brecht's subconscious.[16]

The interlude enunciates one of Brecht's favorite recommendations for good theatre, that is, smoking, drinking, and betting during the performance—in other words, beerhall and sporting-arena activities. Interchanges take place between the audience (in the interlude they are soldiers) and the actors who impersonate the Mother of the Baby Elephant, the Baby Elephant, the Moon, and a banana tree. The baby elephant is accused of murdering his own mother. Galy Gay, the elephant cub, claims he broke a milk jug on a rock, not on her head. This farcical horse-play, now and then interrupted by the rowdy soldiery, proceeds to prove the murder by compelling the cub to pull the mother from a chalk circle as evidence that he is not her son. (Brecht here anticipates his own later *Caucasian Chalk Circle.*) It all ends in a song, and Galy Gay's challenging a soldier to a boxing match.

> Oh, how jolly was Uganda
> Seven cents a chair on the veranda,
> And oh, the poker game with the good old Tiger . . .[17]

The farce is, in fact, an embryonic manifestation of the principle of "estrangement," with the use of outsiders as objective and "disinterested" observers and judges of the proceedings.

To come back to *Mann ist Mann.* Transitional as it is in Brecht's history, it marks an important and necessary step in his development. The "I," long celebrated from the time of the Romantics to the time of Walt Whitman and the Expressionists, is dead. Personality and individuality have become fictions. Yet the "collective" is as fraudulent as the "individual," for it cheats both the actors and those acted on. Galy's soldier companions are no different from Galy himself. The imperialist army is a collective too—a collective of destruction. There is a near-pathos that is horrifying in Galy Gay's ultimate refusal to look into the coffin, where his own body is presumably lying. *A fortiori,* how can other men, better instructed and informed, bear to look at themselves, in their own mental and moral coffins?

Yet in *Mann ist Mann* we encounter the element of change. Baal, Kragler, Garga, none of these underwent significant changes. Galy Gay does. Though the changes exemplify the unheroic "heroism" of our times, for they are passionless, false, opportunistic, yet in Brecht they reflect the very image of bourgeois society (down to the workers) who have become faceless, nameless—mere "identification cards," which may even be interchangeable. Galy disowns not only himself, but everything and everyone around him.

The first production of *Mann ist Mann* took place in the Landestheater at Darmstadt on September 26, 1926, under the direction of Jakob Geis, and with stage designs by Caspar Neher. It was not a success. The critic Bernhard Diebold saw in the title of the play a Bolshevik slogan and in the play itself a confused mass of comedy and pathos, with very little that was truly modern in a work by "this very modern playwright."[18]

Lion Feuchtwanger wrote a fervently appreciative review in *Die Weltbühne,* pointing to the play's mastery of improbability and the marvelous "inner logic" of the transformation of Galy Gay. He was particularly carried away by the funeral oration delivered over the dead body of Galy Gay by Galy himself, and he could think of "no scene written by a contemporary that could even approach it in grandeur of its grotesquely tragic invention and basic conception."[19]

Herbert Jhering thought that in this play Brecht was the first German playwright "who neither celebrates the mechanism of the machine, nor attacks it, but takes it for granted, and thereby transcends it."[20]

With *Mann ist Mann* we are already on the highroad toward Brecht's new theatre. The lyrical portions are sharply separated from the main plot—a sort of "caesura in the regularity of the principal action."[21] The use of interim titles; the "estrangement" produced in the audience as it watches the sale of a mock elephant ("estranged" in seeing this as the counterpart of so much "business" carried on in the outside world); and the shocks which Galy Gay's transformation undoubtedly effect—these are preliminaries to the "epic" theatre.

VIII

In Quest of Identity:
The Road to the Epic Theatre

When years ago, studying the goings-on on the Chicago
    wheat exchange
I suddenly understood how the world's wheat was ad-
    ministered.
Yet, at the same time, failed to understand—and put
    down the book,
I saw at once:
You've hit upon something bad. . . .

There was no bitterness in me, nor was I terrified
By the injustice—only I thought and I thought—
That's not the way. No, not the way *they're* doing it. . . .

These people, I saw, lived from the harm
They do to others, instead of the good.
A situation that can only continue to exist
Through crime; bad for most human beings.
So every achievement of reason,
Invention and discovery
Must lead to ever greater misery.

Such and the like were my thoughts at that moment,
Far removed from anger or lamentation,
As I put down the book describing
The wheat market and the exchanges of Chicago. . . .
Great pain and discontent were in store for me.
           BRECHT, "Als ich vor Jahren"

For Germany, as well as for Brecht, the years between 1923 and
1930 were to be both crucial and instructive. Politically and eco-

nomically the country was entering upon a period of outward
"equilibrium." The mark was stabilized, and international tensions
appeared measurably abated with the signing of various pacts, such
as that of Locarno; and the paramount economic and political influence of American capital seemed indisputable. The crisis over
reparations was momentarily lifted and the threat of civil war dis-
pelled. These were menacing realities as the mark continued to fall,
and the French were marching into the Ruhr; while sabotage, bloody
collisions, Bavarian separatism, and agitation against what was
called the "Jewish Republic of Weimar" threatened another convulsion.[1] The "Ninth of November" putsch of 1923 on the part of
Hitler and his adherents had failed. Now it appeared that the evil
years were done with—years of unemployment, starvation, and the
dole, during which, as one cynic remarked, the only overtime work
was done by government presses turning out paper currency. Speculation and inflation, however, while impoverishing the masses of the
people, proved a Godsend to such enterprises as those of Hugo
Stinnes, who managed to build up the "most spectacular fortune and
the most amazing trust in post-war Germany. From iron and steel,
he branched out into shipping, transportation, lumber, hotels, paper,
newspapers, and politics."[2]

The economic and social catastrophe that appeared imminent was
averted by the fortunate intervention of American capital, which
through the Dawes Plan of 1924 and the Young Plan of 1929 sought
to settle the matter of reparations, and with huge loans succeeded in
raising the fallen country, so that, in a short time, it rose to be one of
the industrial giants of the world. Who in the years before 1933 was
not acquainted with the names and the power of Siemens, Hapag,
Vereinigte Stahlwerke, or IG Farben?

But no such good fortunes attended the general population, which
found itself increasingly pauperized and unemployed. The political
scene remained confused. The parties on the left were riven apart
by the Trotzky-Stalin split in the Soviet Union, with its repercussions in the German Communist movement. In 1925, President

Friedrich Ebert died, and was succeeded by General von Hindenburg. Some time before, Adolf Hitler had left the comparative comfort of his Landshut prison, and returned to political activity. Assisted by Gregor Strasser, General von Epp, and Josef Goebbels, he proceeded to establish the National Socialist Party. Its first ventures politically were nugatory. In the elections of 1928, the new party polled only 800,000 votes. Other wings of the extreme right, the National Party, Alfred Hugenberg's Pan-German League, and Franz Seldte's Stahlhelm were in the process of consolidating their anti-Weimar opposition, raising bloody cries against the Dawes and Young Plans and the Versailles Treaty. Yet, in spite of inner dissensions, both Socialists and Communists made significant gains in 1928, and accounted for about 40% of the total national vote.

In art and literature, the wild, young days of expressionism, with its cosmic humanitarianism, were over. A new realism, which wanted nothing of Dada or of expressionism's "O Mensch!" ecstasy, now took possession. It called itself Neue Sachlichkeit ("New Objectivism") and its goal was the presentation of the historical present, its mode of expression the document, and its tutelary divinity America. The watchwords were Taylorian efficiency, Watsonian behaviorism, functionalism, jazz, machinery and technology, boom, Lindbergh, and, above all, American pragmatism.

We leaned to America [Hans A. Joachim wrote]. America represented the "good idea"; it was the land of the future. It was at home with itself, and had been for a decade now. We were too young to know it, yet we loved it.[3]

The "Ding-an-sich" for this "New Objectivism" was the triumph of modern technology. Its theatrical correlative was the writing of the "Zeitstück," the timely piece, such as the hunt for oil in the world markets, poison gas, war, peace, class justice, abortion, capital punishment, bourgeois morality. The theatre became filled with these "Zeitstücke," the equivalents of the later documentaries.[4]

The cry was "Utility above all."

On the part of the playwrights who had already achieved prominence there took place a serious dispersion of interest, once expressionism went out of style. Franz Werfel and Carl Zuckmayer retreated into romanticism or religious mysticism; Georg Kaiser and Walter Hasenclever contented themselves with frothy boulevard successes; Hanns Johst, Reinhold Goering, and Arnolt Bronnen turned toward the political right, and became increasingly nationalist, chauvinist, and reactionary. Toller, Piscator, Brecht, and Friedrich Wolf became more and more closely identified with the left.

The theatre continued to be the exciting arena of the cultural life of the day. The impact of the Soviet Union was particularly strong. The visits of the Moscow Art Theatre, under the direction of Constantin Stanislavski, left their profound mark on the German theatre. But for the younger generation, it was Stanislavski's associate, Vsevolod Meyerhold, who fascinated with the newer Soviet theatrical techniques. Meyerhold saw in the Russian Revolution an unprecedented opportunity for the renewal of the theatre and a break with the Stanislavski tradition. He advocated the principle of "biomechanics," that is, translating dramatic emotion into typical "gestus"; the abolition of individual characterization, and the emphasis on the "class-kernel" of the dramatic presentation. In some ways he anticipated Brecht in desiring the spectator never for a moment to forget that he was in the theatre, in contradistinction to Stanislavski, who wanted the spectator to forget that he was in the theatre.[5] Meyerhold also laid a great deal of emphasis on the popular theatre and the local Russian folk-drama. His "constructivist" stage set the audience immediately into the theatre, dispensed with curtains, utilized movable stage sets, and attempted to create a "symphony of motion," using the audience as "co-creators of the drama."[6] "Our artist," Meyerhold said, "must throw away the paintbrush, and compasses; he must take in hand hammer and axe in order to reshape the stage in the image of our technical century."[7]

Important too for the new theatre of Europe were the theories of Platon Kerzhenev, who advocated a thorough break with the bourgeois theatre of Stanislavski and Chekhov, and the creation of a proletarian "mass" theatre, "under the open sky."[8] Another very gifted innovator of the Russian theatre, Alexander Tairov (referred to in Germany at this time as the Russian Jessner), brought with him what he called "three-dimensionality", "simultaneity," and "constructivism." He utilized cubes, squares, pyramids, levels and inclines, with backdrops in colors. His "synthetic actor" had to be master of many arts. Tairov modeled himself on the theatre of India and the Italian *commedia dell'arte*.

Under the influence of the Soviets, theatrical groups were organized by the working classes in Germany, the so-called "agit-prop" movement (agitation and propaganda). In the Soviet Union they and the "prolet-cult" associations were used to bring the message of the Revolution and Communism to all sections of the nation and were particularly influential because so great a part of the population was still illiterate. The German counterparts took over the form and even the names of these groups, calling themselves variously Red Shirts, Blue Shirts, and Red Rockets. With their "living newspapers" and their theatrical "mock-trials of the reactionary bourgeoisie" they represented a seething ferment in that convulsive era.

Their mass-pageants, such as *Spartakus* or *Der arme Konrad,* engaged between a thousand and two thousand participants, and were performed before close to fifty thousand spectators. Between 1928 and 1930 it is reported there were over three hundred such groups in Germany, with a membership of almost four thousand. They were not always blessed with the greatest talent; but the "Tendenztheater" (theatre with tendency) was a useful medium, since it could readily be transported to any place, and could perform its satirical skits, reviews, declamations, and mass chants in streets, factories, and beer halls. Alongside of them there were the more expert professional agit-prop associations, of which one, inspired by Erwin Piscator and called Die junge Volksbühne, became celebrated for its high artistic standards and its productions, often written by well-known playwrights.

Such were some of the influences that in part bore upon the

German theatre of this era. Nor must one overlook the impact of
the Moscow Art Theatre and Stanislavski in bringing with them
that exceptional group of artists who made of the plays of Chekhov
or Gorki symphonies of movement, word, and setting. The motion
picture too played a significant part at this time: whether that of
the Russian Eisenstein or of Charlie Chaplin. In one way or another these impulses helped shape the imagination of one of the
most creative and revolutionary personalities of the German theatre
—Erwin Piscator, originator of the "epic" theatre, associate of many
of the most gifted artists of the nineteen-twenties, and not least,
notable for the profound influence he exercised in determining the
career and theories of Bertolt Brecht.

In an interesting exchange in 1947, Brecht and Piscator pay each
other compliments. Brecht wrote to Piscator:

Let me state for the record that among the people who "made" the
theatre during these twenty years no one was so close to me as you.

And Piscator countered:

I believe, for my part, that no writer came closer to the conception I had
of the theatre than you.[9]

Undoubtedly they were both right.

Five years older than Bertolt Brecht, Erwin Piscator was descended from an old German Protestant family. Like so many of
his contemporaries, he underwent a radical transformation during
the First World War, going through the stages of initial enthusiasm
at its outbreak—then the bitter army experiences, total disenchantment, and finally conversion to the cause of revolution.

My history [he wrote] begins on the 4th of August 1914. What is the
thing called "personal development"? No one develops himself "personally." Something else "develops" him. Before this twenty-year-old
youth stood the War. Fate. He made every other schoolmaster super-
fluous.[10]

He returned from the army a convinced Communist and joined

the Spartacus League. His first independent theatrical effort was *Das Tribunal*, which he established at Königsberg during 1919-1920, and for which he planned, but did not realize, a production of Ernst Toller's *Wandlung*. The enterprise lasted only one season, and Piscator moved to Berlin, where the atmosphere (even among the dadaists) was charged with revolution. Here he found the traditional political theatre of the Volksbühne, harking back to the nineties of the preceding century, with a continuous history if not of political, at least of literary radicalism, and boasting a huge supporting membership. The time was ripe for new ventures and new blood. Even Max Reinhardt had become aware of the need for change, and had encouraged the establishment of "Das junge Deutschland" in 1917, a theatrical group that made the war and its consequences the immediate concern of its repertory.

With his friend Hermann Schüller, Piscator founded in 1919 the "Proletarisches Theater," the "stage of the revolutionary workingman," and announced in the first of its programs:

Comrades! The soul of the Revolution, the soul of the approaching society of the classless and communal culture represent our revolutionary feelings. The Proletarian Theatre wishes to ignite this feeling and help keep it alive. The experiences awakened in us by socialist art fortify us in our consciousness of the seriousness and the greatness of the historical mission of our class.[11]

"We banned the word 'Art' completely from our program," Piscator reports. "Our pieces were incitements with which we wished to engage in living history, and 'act' politics."[12]

The Communists reacted ambivalently toward Piscator's project, not yet being sure in which direction he was tending, and somewhat suspicious of the somewhat high-sounding and ambitious claims to make the theater a means of transforming the workers into a "revolutionary force." Young prophet that he was, Piscator in his zeal tended to overestimate the influence of the theatre. But in the course of the years, both the attitude of the Communist Party and the vastness of Piscator's claims underwent marked changes.

Fortunately, the Volksbühne, in need of new talent no less than new vigor, invited Piscator to take over in 1924 the direction of a play by Alfons Paquet, *Fahnen* (*Flags*), which no other director was willing to touch. The play dealt with the Chicago Haymarket trials of 1886, which resulted from the so-called Haymarket Square riot of that year, in which amidst a demonstration by workers for the eight-hour day, a bomb exploded and killed and wounded a number of people. In the subsequent hysteria, eight anarchists were convicted, and four of them hanged. The play was very powerful; there was no single hero. This was a "dramatic" novel. And for the first time it was announced programmatically as "epic" drama. This was used to describe a new theatrical form in which the main action of the play was broken into by narrative and explanatory devices, such as film, projections, addresses to the audience. The films depicted labor leaders, financial moguls, police functionaries, etc. Intermittent titles flashed explanatory texts or other information between scenes, on each side of the stage. The cast consisted of fifty-six characters.

Alfred Döblin, himself a proponent and practitioner of the "epic" novel, saw the profound meaning of these innovations.

Paquet has consciously dramatized the anarchist upheaval in Chicago in such a way that the resulting image remains poised between narrative and drama. . . . Tendentious plays will always have this inclination toward the dramatic novel, and their authors are moved epically, not lyrically. . . . I would say that this borderland is a very fertile one, and will be sought out by those who have something to say and to show, and who are no longer at ease with the petrified form of our drama. . . . In the novel-drama of the age of Aeschylus, there was still the native soil of drama. It can become such once again.[13]

Piscator's theatre was "mobile"; he could move it wherever he wanted, wherever there was a place or an audience.

It is out of three principal elements, then, that Piscator developed his special style: the political, the "epic," and the technical. "Fluidity, simultaneity, and cinematic cuttting to the topical, historical, factual material . . . was now beginning to invade the arts."[14]

It was theatre with a "message," which in Piscator's eyes was to be directed simply and concretely, like a "manifesto by Lenin," at a new audience and a new "hero."

Can anyone seriously maintain [Piscator asked] that in the face of this monstrous convulsion, from which no one can exclude himself, the image of Man, his feelings, his interrelations still remain eternal, absolute, and unchanged by time? . . . This period, that through its social and economic necessities has deprived the individual of "humanness," without replacing it with the humanness of a new society, has raised a new hero on the pedestal—HIMSELF. No longer is the individual with his private, personal fate the heroic factor of the new drama, but Time itself, the fate of the masses has become such. . . . Not his [man's] relation to himself, nor his relation to God, but his relation to society now stands at the center. Where he appears, his calling and rank appear alongside of him. Wherever he enters upon a conflict, whether this be moral, spiritual, or instinctual, it is a conflict with society. If Antiquity placed him centrally in relation to Fate, the Middle Ages in relation to God, Rationalism to the forces of emotion . . . , then the present time cannot view him otherwise than in his relation to society and social problems—i.e., as a political being.[15]

It is needless, perhaps, to say that at a time when even a mild political play like Schiller's *Wilhelm Tell* became the occasion of rioting and rowdyism, Piscator's efforts would create a stir. For the Communist Party's campaign for the Reichstag elections of 1924, Piscator prepared a most provocative and exciting revue, *Revue Roter Rummel,* which he romantically conceived of as a "possibility for direct action." The concourse of spectators was immense. We have an eyewitness description of the event:

When we arrived, hundreds were already in the streets, demanding admission, but in vain. Workingmen fought for places. In the hall, crowds, the air stuffy enough to make one faint. Music . . . Lights out . . . Silence . . . In the auditorium two men are squabbling. The audience is alarmed. The disputants advance to the center of the hall. The stage lights go on and the disputants appear in front of the curtain. Two working people discuss their situation. Man in top hat arrives. A bourgeois. He has his opinions, and invites the contestants to spend an evening with him . . . Curtain up . . . Kurfürstendamm. Doorman with gold braids; war-crippled veterans, beggars. Haunch, paunch, and jowl. Swastika. The beggar is thrown out by the porter. Workers demolish the establishment. Audience takes part, whistling, howling, demonstrating. Excitement . . . Unforgettable.[16]

Of course, these revues proved as costly as they were sensational. Piscator, undeterred, followed with another one, *Trotz alledem* (*Despite All*) (words spoken by Karl Liebknecht), a monster presentation that traced the history of revolutions from the outbreak of the World War to the murder of Rosa Luxemburg and Karl Liebknecht. For the first time, film was organically integrated into the staging; documentaries derived from the national archives, authentic photos of the war were shown against a gigantic stage set, consisting of what Piscator called a "Praktikabel"—terraces, inclines, stairways, platforms on revolving planes. Everything was there: speeches, essays, newspaper reports, addresses, flyers, photos, films of war and revolution, historical personalities, Liebknecht and Luxemburg among them—all this at the huge Grosses Schauspielhaus that Max Reinhardt had built expressly for classical drama! Once more the audience was drawn in as actors, film melted into stage, and the amazed reviewer of the conservative *Frankfurter Zeitung* gasped, as a Reichstag war session was re-enacted before his eyes; and now he saw Karl Liebknecht speaking, and a soldier heckling him, who the very next moment was standing on the street, distributing leaflets and making speeches against the war.

He is arrested, and as the crowd stands by, and sees him taken away, and does nothing, the audience in the theatre roared its dismay and self-accusation.[17]

Piscator was not one to shy away from scandals. His radical transformation of Schiller's *Räuber* provoked a storm of protest. But even that was exceeded with the 1927 production of a play by Ehm Welk, *Gewitter über Gottland* (*Storm over Gothland*), a historical drama of the Hanseatic period, which Piscator brought up to date, so that one of the characters appeared in the mask of Lenin, and the play ended, as one hostile critic reported, with the "Soviet star rising in full lustre on the stage." Alfred Kerr, strangely enough, came to Piscator's defense, but the administration of the Volksbühne became alarmed and had a film depicting the Russian Revolution, withdrawn. The matter even reached the floor of the Prussian Diet. The journalists had a holiday: "There, in the Volksbühne, we see the organization of the Bolshevik stormtroopers."[18]

The expenses for such ventures proved gigantic, and Piscator's vast experiments might have collapsed totally had not a bourgeois Maecenas appeared in the person of the wealthy husband of Tilla Durieux, the actress, and offered to underwrite a new theatre, to be designed by Walter Gropius. This never materialized, but in the meantime Piscator moved to the Theater am Nollendorfplatz. Here between the years 1927 and 1930 he reached the peak of his achievements. With a cast of actors of unequalled excellence, such as Durieux, Helene Weigel, Paul Graetz, Ernst Deutsch, Ernst Busch, Alexander Granach, Max Pallenberg, he succeeded in establishing a collective of working forces such as had fallen to the lot of few directors. Writers and artists joined him, among them Brecht, Georg Grosz, and John Heartfield. This great period of Piscator's theatre included notable productions, such as Ernst Toller's *Hoppla! wir leben,* with which the theatre opened its season on September 3, 1927. This was followed by Alexei Tolstoy's *Rasputin,* Leo Lania's *Konjunktur,* and the most brilliant production of them all, Jaroslav Hašek's *The Good Soldier Schweik. Rasputin* provoked legal suits which involved the former Kaiser Wilhelm and a Russian financier. Piscator lost the cases in court, and parts of the play had to be altered. Georg Grosz's sardonic drawings for *Schweik* brought on him the criminal charge of blasphemy, and *Konjunktur* was attacked both on the right and on the left, and it too had to be changed, at the last moment.

Piscator was fortunate in that his writing collective included along with Leo Lania and Felix Gasbarra, Bertolt Brecht. Emergencies arose frequently, as can be imagined, and they had to be met head-on. Thus, the adaptation of Hašek's novel, *Schweik,* which had been prepared by Max Brod and Hans Reimann was found to be unacceptable, and Brecht and the others set to work to create a new one. This proved to be the most lasting and certainly the most important of all of Piscator's efforts. Here was a subject particularly appealing to Brecht. As for Piscator, for him too this was the chance of a lifetime. The "unheroic" hero of the Austrian army, Schweik, who in his naive, fumbling, shrewdly inept ways exposes both wars and armies, but who, however, succeeds in "moving" history, was enticing. Georg Grosz designed the sketches. Piscator introduced two conveyor belts (treadmills) running in opposite directions. "For the first time," he said, "an actor could perform his entire role on the stage, riding, walking, running." To round out the meaning of the play, the collaborators devised an ingenious and original scene in heaven, in which Schweik was to confront the authorities up above, as he had on earth. A procession of cripples (real ones) was to appear on the stage, to the accompaniment of the Austrian military "Radetzky" march. But this idea was too gruesome even for Piscator, and was abandoned. Trick films, puppets, masks—Grosz's trenchant pen was at its best—and with the inimitable Max Pallenberg in the principal role, Piscator had triumphed!

How the collaborators worked is illustrated by an amusing incident. The play *Konjunktur,* which dealt with imperalist machinations in cornering the oil market, involved a lady Soviet agent, and brought down criticism from the left. Just before opening, it proved necessary to undertake revisions. Piscator tells the rest:

Outside, day was dawning, the day on which we were to open. Wan, sleepless faces, unwashed, unshaven, totally exhausted after three weeks of uninterrupted work. . . . We stood before the finished task, which, however, we could not bring before the footlights. It was the severest test our nerves had ever encountered in all our theatrical experience. The only person who was unruffled, and even cheerful—the eternal cigar in his mouth, leather cap pulled menacingly over his brow—was our old friend Bert Brecht. He thought it possible to change the function of the principal female character overnight, and offered to do so with Lania and Gasbarra. . . . It was five in the morning. . . . Beautiful spring day. . . . We drove to my apartment and by the afternoon the new version of the "Barsin" character was ready.[19]

The attractive agent actually turned out to be an agent for a South American complot!

The double-edged Damocles sword of expense and scandal hung perilously over Piscator's head. Each production proved costlier than the one before. Piscator had a passion for complicated machinery. Yet he held on for a short while longer. But disturbances provoked by the right opposition became more numerous and disruptive, and soon the theatre went down, in the midst of a world economic crisis, in 1930.

Ideologically, Piscator had set out to serve the cause of the revolutionary left, strengthen the class-consciousness of the proletarian audiences, and using both classical and new material, project it in terms of the social and economic needs of the times. His theatrical form, the "epic," was to be simple, direct, anti-expressionist, and the techniques the most modern. In acting, too, he developed a "hard, unequivocal, unsentimental" style[20] at odds with the traditionally emotional, declamatory manner prevailing in most of the other theatres. He organized a theatre "collective"—including even the audience—and obtained the cooperation, frequently entirely voluntary, of an extraordinary group of actors, writers, and artists. A membership of five to six thousand enabled his theatre to survive for a time. But he had to rely on bourgeois capital to sustain the magnitude of his experiments, and that support was vacillating. The working class audience came, but it was in no position to finance such an expensive theatre. For all that, Piscator had brought to the stage the excitement of a social experiment in which an audience could participate, and feel itself a part of historic events, and experience instruction and pleasure at the same time.

This excitement was shared by the actors themselves. Tilla Durieux, one of Piscator's principal performers, recalled many years later how, at a performance of *Rasputin,* in which she acted the Czarina, a background film suddenly flashed Red soldiers marching.

She was stunned. "Imagine," she thought, "what it must have been like for the audience."

Brecht remained grateful to Piscator to the end of his life, and paid him innumerable tributes in his writings.

The experiments of Piscator [Brecht wrote] at once produced a thorough-going chaos in the theatre. Just as they turned the stage into a machine-shop, so they turned the auditorium into a meeting-hall. For Piscator theatre was a parliament, and the audience a legislative body. Before this body were visibly set the great public questions that demanded decisions. In place of speeches by delegates, concerning certain untenable conditions, we had an artistic reproduction of such conditions. The stage set itself the task of prodding the audience—the parliament—. . . . into making political decisions. Piscator's stage did not forego approbation, but it was more eager to arouse discussion. It did not aim only to provide a spectator with an experience, but wanted to wrest from him practical conclusions, make him take hold of life itself, and actively participate in living.[21]

Such was Piscator's "total theatre."

It is not too much to say that his association with Piscator was one of the decisive factors in Brecht's development. But it was only one of his many activities in those years. He was interested in the boxing arena. In one of his poems he chronicled the great prize-fighters of history from Bob Fitzsimmons to Jack Dempsey.[22] He was contemplating a biography of the boxer Samson-Körner. His ideal theatre, as we have seen, still resembled the boxing ring, with its cigar-smoking spectators. He was becoming aware of jazz, which he confessed had finally reconciled him to music!

A writer very much in the public eye, he was invited in 1926 to act as a judge in a poetry contest conducted by the *Literarische Welt,* carrying considerable monetary prizes. Brecht created a scandal by rejecting all of the close to five hundred entries by around four hundred competitors, as full of "sentimentality, insincerity, and un-worldliness," and instead suggesting a "poem" by an unknown non-competitor be given the prize. This was a concoction entitled "He, he, the Iron Man" (the original title is in English) by a certain

Hannes Küpper, a crude piece of nonsense, a tribute to Reggie McNamara, the six-day bicycle racer. It runs something like this (no translation can possibly spoil the poem!):

> There's a legend abroad
> That his arms, legs and hands
> Are made of wrought iron. . . .
>
> He, he, the Iron Man. . . .
>
> And even if all is legend,
> One thing is sure—
> He's a miracle man—this Reggie McNamara!
> He, he! the Iron Man.[23]

Even more infuriating than this recommendation, was Brecht's explanatory comment on the submitted poems. He confessed his low opinion of the lyrical work of Rilke ("otherwise a very good man"), of Stefan George and Franz Werfel, whom the contributors were all imitating.

These young contestants, Brecht said, are

quiet, refined, gentle, dreamy creatures—the sensitive sector of a decayed bourgeoisie, with whom I want to have no truck.[24]

He was, of course, slapped down, notably by the critic Rudolf Borchardt, in the *Deutsche Allgemeine Zeitung,* who resented Brecht's diatribe against George, and who attacked Brecht as "un-talented" and accused him of "dismal rowdiness."[25]

In the midst of such minor turmoils, Brecht was supervising productions of *Mann ist Mann* and *Baal,* working with Piscator, writing journalistic essays and short stories, attending sporting events, preparing a collection of his poems for publication, reading, studying extensively, and engaging in disputes. He came to his friend Bronnen's aid when the critic Alfred Kerr (the dislike was reciprocal) wrote an unfavorable review of Bronnen's *Katalaunische Schlacht* (which Kerr had not troubled to attend). Bronnen's play was, to tell the truth, pretty terrible. One of his horror scenes exhibited a group of dead soldiers in a dug-out. Brecht, however, was also paying Kerr back on his own account for that critic's remarks

about his early plays: "Noise without content. Explosiveness for its
own sake." Brecht's squib, à la Horace, is hardly a Horatian gem,
but it hits hard:

> When someone insists on writing, he is happy
> If only he has a subject.
> When the Suez Canal was being built,
> A certain character became famous
> Because he was against it . . .
>
> When railroads were young,
> Post-chaise owners derided them,
> Saying, "They have no tails, They don't eat oats.
> Anyway you can't view the scenery at leisure,
> And when did you ever see a locomotive defecate?"
> And the better they spoke,
> The greater orators they seemed . . .[26]

Another bit of mild scurrility was occasioned when Brecht, Bronnen, and Alfred Döblin were invited to Dresden to the ceremonial
première of Verdi's *La Forza del Destino,* for which Franz Werfel
had written a new text. Arrived there, they found themselves neglected, and in a joint poem they derided their ungracious hosts,
turning the River Elbe into Alibe, Dresden into Alibi, and Franz
Werfel, (in German Würfel means dice) into the Latin Alea.

> They invited three gods
> To Alibi on the River Alibe
> And made grand promises
> Of 150 hecatombs for each of them,
> And honors—as many as they craved.
> But when they arrived,
> There was only the rain to greet them . . .[27]

So when they came to the festival hall, they could only find accommodations in the coat-room, with its rain-soaked garments; and
when they went to "gather the crumbs" from the table of Alea, lo,
there were none to be gathered.[27]

Nothing could soothe their bruised feelings, not even a belated
apology and a specially arranged program. at which they were asked

to read from their own works. Brecht avenged himself by reading the mildly amusing, but certainly somewhat obscure, squib.

Amidst these minor excitements, there was the greater one of the publication of *Hauspostille* in 1927 (it had appeared privately as *Taschenpostille* the previous year), and the acclaim and reprobation with which it was greeted, and on both of which he thrived. He was writing stories and sketches, chiefly, he claimed, to make money, and one of these, *Die Bestie,* really won him a prize of three thousand marks. His circle of friends and admirers was growing. It now included Elisabeth Hauptmann, his amanuensis, collaborator, counsellor, and, what was also important, his translator from the English; the painter Georg Grosz; Piscator; the composers Paul Hindemith, Kurt Weill, and Hanns Eisler; and social scientists like Fritz Sternberg and Karl Korsch. And he kept his good old friends from the Augsburg and Munich days.

Lotte Eisner describes him as he directed a rehearsal:

From my seat in the orchestra I could follow his patient and ardent manner. How he balanced the value of every sentence, adapting gesture to it, shaping the counterpoint of facial or bodily expression, modulating at one and the same time the bearing and diction of his interpreters.

She hears him reading aloud from Luther's Bible:

. . . savoring the sentences of that powerful epic hammered out by the hand of Martin Luther—then noting the turns of phrasing that pleased him, and putting them down in his little notebook. He did the same with German proverbs, whose down-to-earth qualities he loved, as well as their pithy wisdom.[28]

He was becoming prosperous, though one could scarcely tell it from his outward appearance. Publishers were now after him.

In his immediate personal life an important change had taken place. On November 21, 1927, Marianne Zoff and Brecht were divorced. The following year he married Helene Weigel, whom he had met when she appeared in one of Bronnen's plays some time before. By one of those strange coincidences that make life interesting, she had not long before made her first great impression as

an actress in a play by Hanns Johst, the writer who had been the
direct "inspiration" of *Baal*. [29]

Some time around 1926 Brecht began a serious study of political
science and economics. In October, 1926, he writes to Elisabeth
Hauptmann: "I am eight feet deep in *Das Kapital*. I must know
exactly . . ."[30] He began to attend courses in Marxism at the Karl
Marx Arbeiterschule, as well as lectures by Karl Korsch, the future
biographer of Marx. He engaged Korsch in many coffee-house discussions on the Alexanderplatz—discussions they were to continue
personally and by letter until the day of Brecht's death. Brecht was
beginning to project his new interests onto his plays. He was planning a comedy on the inflation. He was rewriting *Mann ist Mann*
(Frau Hauptmann believes for the seventh time); he read Sherwood
Anderson's *Poor White*, and was thinking of a play on Dan Drew
and the Erie Railroad. America haunted him. He had visions of a
whole series of plays around the theme of "the influx of humanity
into the Great Cities," to show and explain the rise of capitalism.
Actually, he began working on a play called *Joe Fleischhacker* (*Joe
Butcher*), set in Chicago, and dealing with the wheat market. In
preparation for this work, he called upon Elisabeth Hauptmann for
assistance.

We gathered [she recalls] the technical materials. I myself made in-
quiries of several specialists as well as of the exchange in Breslau and
Vienna, and at the end Brecht himself began to study political economy.
He asserted that the machinations of the money market were quite
impenetrable—he would have to find out how matters really stood, so
far as the theories of money were concerned.

And she adds a very significant note, showing how closely Brecht's
economic studies were bound up with his aesthetic theories, even
as early as 1926:

Before, however, making what for him were important discoveries in
that field, he recognized that the current dramatic forms were not suited
to reflecting such modern processes as the world distribution of wheat
or the life-story of our times—in a word, all human actions of consequence. "These questions," Brecht said, "are not dramatic in our sense

of the word, and if they are transported into literature, are no longer true, and drama is no longer drama. When we become aware that our world no longer fits into drama, then drama no longer fits into our world."[31]

And in a note dated March 23, 1926, she wrote:

Brecht finds the formula for the "epic" theatre—the play from memory, (gestures, attitudes to be cited), and in his writing now works entirely in this direction. Thus what he calls "scenes that show" have come into being.[31]

In reality the road to the Epic Theatre was to be a slow and devious one; and even when fully mapped out and constructed, it was to be subjected to many crucial alterations. For Brecht never regarded either his plays or his theoretical statementts as final. He believed in change. He considered all his efforts as "Versuche"—experiments.

But his speculations on theatre and drama, as well as society, became more concrete, and more clearly directed toward a goal. On the one hand, he continued his sharp criticism of the contemporary theatre. "The old theatre," he wrote, "no longer has a physiognomy. . . . A theatre without contact with the public is no theatre."[32] He found it hard to understand why older people even attended theatrical performances at all! As for the younger generation, they simply had no reason to go. For the older generation there was, at least, the left-over memories, with their quota of erotic pleasures.[33] As for Brecht, give him the sports arena any time. Here the public knows "exactly why they buy tickets of admission; and what it is that is being offered them."[34] They get "fun," "sport," "ease." Germans, he noted, were particularly inured to boredom and the absence of humor.[35] "One lone cigar-smoking individual at a performance of Shakespeare would bring about the downfall of all of western art. . . . I would gladly see a public smoking at a performance— particularly for the sake of the actors. It would be impossible, I believe, for an actor to perform in an unnatural, convulsive, and antiquated manner in the presence of a smoker in the pit."[36]

"The sociologist is the man for us," he exclaims. We need him,

for the sociologist knows that there are situations that are no longer amenable to improvement. Such is the case of the older theatre. The aesthete thinks otherwise. But the sociologist is immune to the "charms" of the older plays merely because they happen to be "beautiful," though they have in fact long outlived their usefulness. The downfall of the older theatre can only be postponed; it cannot be avoided. A new theatre—the epic theatre—corresponds to the new social situation prevailing at this time, but will be understood only by those who understand the new situation.[37]

These ideas occurred in an exchange of letters between Brecht and the sociologist Fritz Sternberg, where the question was raised whether it wasn't time to "liquidate the old aesthetics." Brecht believed it was futile to try to modernize or revise the classics, such as Shakespeare or the ancients. The great Shakespearean dramas, the basis of the modern theatre, he believed, were no longer workable. They belonged to another age, and "were succeeded by three hundred years in which the individual developed into a capitalist, and they will be transcended, not by that which comes after capitalism, but by capitalism itself."[38] In a radio broadcast preceding his and Alfred Braun's adaptation of *Macbeth,* on October 24, 1927, Brecht pointed to the particular relation that existed between the play, its author, and the latter's times. How, he asks, are we to understand the "unlogic," "the wild arbitrariness," the indifference to scenic organization and lack of center in Shakespeare's plays? And he answers that Shakespeare was in close touch with his period. In the "disconnectedness of his scenes one recognizes the disconnectedness of human fate." Nothing, he goes on, is more foolish than to try to produce Shakespeare as if he were writing "clearly." Shakespeare was by nature "unclear." Brecht saw in Shakespeare a practitioner of the "epic" style; and only the presentation of Shakespeare in the "epic" style could restore him to life.[39]

Brecht envisages a reckless Shakespeare composing *Hamlet* (somewhat in the manner of Brecht himself). He imagines a moment when the composition of the piece is stalled, to the despair of Shakespeare's fellow writers and actors. "William," as Brecht calls him, is instructed to refurbish an "old, crude piece, with a theme of the 'cleansing of the Augean stables by a youth'." Originally, Brecht continues, the part was intended for a fat, asthmatic actor who had created the role of Richard III. "And so William brought with him a brief scene which he had composed at home. . . . and the asthmatic was saved." This was the scene (which Germans with their beautiful logic omit) in which Hamlet encounters Fortinbras marching past with an army, and suddenly understands that war need have no motivation to be truly bloody. "And he sees it just at the right moment too—that is, a half-hour before the audience is ready to break up and leave the theatre."[40]

Like Piscator, Brecht insists that the theatre of the individual is *passé*. For in modern society the individual, *qua* individual has disappeared, and the theatre displaying the individual (and Brecht includes his own) has proved a depressing experience to audiences. "It doesn't matter whether it is *Oedipus,* or *Othello,* or *Drums in the Night.*" In a radio broadcast from Cologne, in which Fritz Sternberg and Herbert Jhering took part, Brecht considered Shakespeare's treatment of individuality. "Shakespeare," Brecht stated, "propels his great individuals through four acts"—Lear, Othello, Macbeth—away from human relationships to family or state, out into "the heath," where they are left all alone, in their grandeur and their downfall. They are driven by passions, whose end-goal is "the great human experience."[41] Sternberg is in agreement: Shakespeare's is the drama of individualism, in an age of disappearing individualism. In the declining stages of capitalism the individual as an indivisible and uninterchangeable entity vanishes, and the collective becomes the determinant factor. The three interlocutors then agree that there is need for a new drama to reflect this new "collective" man; and Jhering adds that that is to be found in Brecht's "epic" theatre. Brecht accepts the tribute, in turn paying some of it back to his predecessors, Bronnen, and Georg Kaiser, as well as the Naturalists.[42]

He might here have added the name of Bernard Shaw, to whom

along with other writers he extends homage on the Irishman's seventieth birthday. In some ways Shaw was kin to him, as he states in an "Ovation for Shaw." Brecht admires the "terrorism" of Shaw's humor, and his joy in "disconcerting our customary associations." Here is an anticipation of Brecht's own theory of "estrangement." He delights in Shaw's world, which is one of "opinions." "The fate of his characters is their opinions." He admires Shaw's razor-edged reasoning, which cuts through all mystifications, down to the very core of the social realities.[43]

Already Brecht's reading of those he was to call the "classics"—Marx, Engels, and Lenin—began to show in his writings and his theorizing. He demands a closer examination of how drama is rooted in the "substructure of society," i.e., the social milieu. He asks for a theatre that would create the "ideological superstructure" for the "effective and real rearrangement of our present mode of existence."[44]

His own customary associations too were being disrupted and disconcerted. He began looking at his own plays from the new point of view.

When I read *Das Kapital* of Marx, I understood my own pieces. It will be obvious that I desire a wide diffusion of this book. I did not of course discover that I had unconsciously written a whole batch of Marxist plays; but this Karl Marx was the only spectator of my pieces I have ever seen. For to a man with such interests, these pieces must have been of interest, not because of their intelligence, but because of his. They would represent illustrative material for him.[45]

And actually, with these new tools, he re-examines *Mann ist Mann* and the problem of "change." In an introduction to a broadcast of that play in April, 1927, he again speaks of the need for a new theatre that corresponds to the "new type of man" existing today. The "old type," he says, is on its way out—the type that allowed itself to be changed by the machine. The new type, however, "will change the machine, and no matter how he will look, above all else, he will look like a human being."[46] That his ideas are still in a turbid state of confusion is indicated by his discussion of the figure of his Galy Gay, "perhaps a forerunner of the type I have been speaking about." For despite the fact that Galy Gay cannot say no, he is no weakling, as most people might imagine. On the contrary, he is the "strongest," when he has ceased to be a private individual, by virtue of being a part of the "mass."[47] Though what sort of mass, and what the actions of this mass are, Brecht still leaves quite unsettled!

He was, however, utilizing his new knowledge to sharpen his view of tragedy, current and past. Reexamining such works as Hauptmann's *Rose Bernd* and *The Weavers,* he concluded that the situations presented there could no longer be termed truly tragic in our day (in one case a seduction, and in the other the revolt of the weavers), since they were amenable to civilizing corrections. Their subject matter becomes antiquated as history and conditions change. On the other hand, Brecht asks, how can one depict serious contemporary situations, say, the struggle for wheat or oil, on the traditional stage, within "grand forms of drama?"

The answer is, you cannot. The new subjects demand new forms.

IX

The Social Zoo:
"The Three Penny Opera"

No more of this, I pray you. Give him food
and a home.
Once you have covered his nakedness, dignity
will come of itself.

FRIEDRICH SCHILLER, "The Dignity of Man"

Erst kommt das Fressen, dann kommt die
Moral.

First comes the belly, then morality.

BRECHT, *The Three Penny Opera*

Das Theater am Schiffbauerdamm, on one of Berlin's many canals, and just off the populous Friedrichstrasse, stands today as it stood in the fall of 1928. It has been completely restored after the Second World War, and has all its gargoyles, nymphs, cupids, and that studded fantastic gilt, all the way up to the angel-starred ceiling, and retains its quaint antiquity. It has almost eight hundred seats. In 1928 it had fallen into disuse, and an enterprising actor, Ernst Robert Aufricht, had undertaken to revive it. Looking around for a hopeful opening presentation, he lighted upon Brecht. Such was the origin of one of Berlin's greatest theatrical successes, *Die Dreigroschenoper* (*The Three Penny Opera*), which opened on the evening of August 31, 1928, with music by Kurt Weill and scenic designs by Caspar Neher. The director was Erich Engel.

There was nothing to indicate such a potential triumph. On the contrary, as Lotte Lenya tells us, all signs pointed to the reverse. A series of fatalities, disaffections, and prima-donna imbecilities had all Berlin on edge, and Aufricht on the point of collapse. The actress Carola Neher was forced to rush off to the bedside of her dying husband, Klabund, in Davos; Helene Weigel developed an attack of appendicitis; Rosa Valetti, a noted cabaret singer, suddenly became outraged by the alleged obscenities in the songs she was to sing; Lotte Lenya's name had been accidentally omitted from the printed program, infuriating her usually placid husband, Kurt Weill. An expectant audience, ever alert for and wishful of a scandal, watched the opening night. The house darkened. On the stage, before the curtain, appeared a street-singer, with hand-organ, to grind out a Moritat (on the morrow all of Berlin was to whistle it), and the audience listened and waited. In the second scene of the play, which took place in a stable, Mackie Messer (Mackie the Knife) and Tiger Brown, the police chief, and former Indian army crony of Mackie's, join in singing the "Cannon Song."

An unprecedented and incredible storm broke loose. The audience was in an uproar. From that moment nothing could go wrong. The audience was with us—it was beside itself. We could trust neither eye nor ear.

Thus Lotte Lenya describes the première.[1] She herself had taken the part of the prostitute Jenny, and overnight became a celebrity, as did many of the others in the cast, as well as Brecht and Weill. And Aufricht rejoiced, happy and rich.

The initial inspiration for *The Three Penny Opera* came to Brecht from Elisabeth Hauptmann, who called his attention to a revival that had taken place some years before in London. John Gay's eighteenth-century ballad-opera, *The Beggars' Opera,* with tunes arranged by Johann Christian Pepusch, had scored an extraordinary triumph there. Nigel Playfair had brought it back to the Lyric Theatre in 1920, and it ran for almost two years. Frau Hauptmann translated the English text, and Brecht set to work on his own version. Of course, the old tunes, beautifully set by Pepusch, would not serve his purpose. Kurt Weill, one of the *enfants terribles* of atonal music, a pupil of Ferruccio Busoni, had already set a few of Brecht's songs, and took as readily to Brecht's text, as Brecht had taken to Gay's.

History, we are told, does not repeat itself. And a British wit has added that it's historians who repeat each other. But historic parallels do occur. To wit: the one between Brecht's and Gay's operas. At the beginning of the eighteenth century, John Gay, one of the lesser, but by no means puny, luminaries of the English Augustan age, a friend of Swift, Pope, and the other "wits" of the era, was inspired to try his hand at a parody of the then all too fashionable and prissy pastorals, already on their long overdue death-beds. He had travestied them in a series of poems, but now the contemporary vogue of the Italian opera, and the prestige and fame of Handel, gave him additional impetus for a new effort. He set out to create a Newgate pastoral—that is, a pastoral built around the Newgate prison, with its rogues, thieves and harlots, and surround it with all the accoutrements and artificiality of the formal opera, at the same time spoofing its aristocratic trappings, Gay was a brilliant satirist, and a man with an eye on the main chance. He turned his guns on contemporary society, especially its upper strata. He was also venting his pique at the Court, having failed to secure a well-paying sinecure. But his principal target was Robert Walpole, the prime minister.

This was an age of and for satire. On the throne of England sat not the nefarious and oppressive Stuarts, but respectable "bourgeois" Hanoverian monarchs. Two revolutions had seen to that. A new age had dawned. Tradesman and wife strutted with pride, alongside of courtier and courtesan. Money, trade, profit were in the air as never before. A recent speculation, the South Sea Bubble, had brought ruin and fortune to many. Robert Walpole was accused of a cynical saying that every man had his price, and current machinations at Court and in the City, manipulations of parliamentary votes and boroughs and offices, turned that saying into an all too manifest truism.

What more natural than that the "roguery" of the outside world find a place in letters too? The Spanish "picaresque" narratives, realistic stories of rogues and vagabonds which were the precursors of modern realistic fiction, had already become domesticated in England. Society's waifs and strays—adventurers, premature bohemians, pickpockets as much by necessity as by choice and profession, wandering students—had attracted and terrified, excited sympathy and distrust. They represented, when depicted in story, an acrid antidote to the sweetly nauseating heroes and heroines of the pastoral romances then currently read in high and low society, and they soon found an English master stylist who was to give England classical rogues, male and female. This was Daniel Defoe. Gay could look to Defoe, but he could also watch models closer at hand in Newgate; read the chronicles of thievery and murder in the Newgate Calendar; observe London in the marvelous realistic drawings of William Hogarth; and in real life, take his cue from the notorious highwaymen of the day, such as Jonathan Wild. As for analogues in other quarters, they too were at hand.

The Beggar's Opera by John Gay opened in the Theatre in Lincoln's Inn Fields on January 29, 1728. It ran for ninety-four consecutive performances before June 19. It made, so the common saying went, Gay rich, and Rich gay. Rich was the producer.

The story of Mr. Peachum, the fence for thieves, and the revenge he takes on highwayman Macheath for marrying his daughter; the way in which he snares his hated son-in-law and finally brings about his hanging, gave Gay the opportunity of unmasking contemporary society. Tongues began to wag, and identify the characters of the play. Was Peachum meant for Robert Walpole? And Mrs. Peachum for some equally elevated prototype? And Macheath? He was certainly much more than the notorious highwayman and cutthroat Jack Shepard or Jonathan Wild! Resemblances between the play's characters and the gallants who gambled, fought, wrangled, and sometimes even killed; lived on advantageous marriages, or squandered paternal estates were too clearly suggested to be missed.

The "acquisitive society," which was already here, offered Gay the opportunity of depicting the money-market not only in goods but also in persons. Peachum reviles his daughter for having secretly married Macheath, principally because she has thus forfeited her usefulness as "bait."

My daughter to me should be like a court lady to a minister of state, a key to the whole gang.[2]

Once married, however, she must utilize her advantage. She must fast become a widow and heiress. The business Peachum is conducting down "below," he remarks, is carried on with as much fineness of duplicity as up "above," except that it is, perhaps, more honorable in his hands.

Macheath asks, "Why are laws levelled at us? Are we more dishonest than the rest of mankind? What we win, gentlemen, is our own by law of arms, and the right of conquest."[3] Betrayal is so rampant all over the world that even in his gang there is no more trust to be found than elsewhere, and like "great statesmen" his men encourage those who betray their friends. The predatory nature of human behavior finds its apt commentator in jailer Lockit, who remarks that "lions, wolves, and vultures don't live together in herds, droves or flocks. Of all animals of prey, man is the only sociable one. Everyone of us preys upon his neighbor, and yet we herd together."[4]

But since this is a spoof of the absurdities of the opera, its conclusion must not be tragic. And so the Beggar Narrator agrees to another ending than the hanging of Macheath.

Your objection, sir, is very just and is easily removed. For you must allow that in this kind of drama 'tis no matter how absurdly things are brought about. So . . . let the prisoner be brought back to his wives in triumph.[5]

It is two hundred years after the first production of Gay's *Beggar's Opera,* and we are in Berlin, in 1928, back at the Theater am Schiffbauerdamm. The hurdy-gurdy man has just sung his ballad of the

Shark, that is, Mackie Messer, Mackie the Knife, or Macheath—that
Don Juan of the underworld, highwayman, lover, gentleman and
thief. No one catches him at the scene of the crime, but he is there
none the less. The curtains part, and we are in the establishment of
Jonathan Jeremiah Peachum, haberdasher and outfitter extraordinary
to beggars, thieves, panhandlers; an exceptional man of business,
who makes his profits out of human pity and human misery. How
fitting that he begin his day with a morning chorale—a hymn—
(had not Brecht himself written a whole household book of such
devotions?):

> Awake, you maggoty Christian!
> Get on with your life of crime!
> Show yourself the true villain you are,
> The Lord will repay you in time.
>
> Sell your brother, you pox-ridden knave,
> Barter your own wife away,
> The Lord—is he nothing but words?
> He'll requite you on Judgment Day!
>
> Wach auf, du verrotteter Christ!
> Mach dich an dein sündiges Leben![6]

This morning, however, he is in a bad mood, for his daughter Polly
has fallen in love with Mackie the Knife, and plans to "marry"
him. He is properly outraged by the very idea of marriage, which
is a "filthy business." But in the meantime, deep in Soho, a stable is
undergoing miraculous transformation as Mackie's associates bring
in appropriate furnishings variously purloined for the wedding of
Mackie and Polly. Distinguished guests are awaited: Pastor Kim-
ball and Tiger Brown, police chief of London. Back at home, there
is the devil to pay. "If you are so immoral as to marry," Peachum
shouts at Polly, "need it have been a horse thief or a highwayman?"
With the assistance of the adroit Mrs. Peachum, he plans to entrap
Mackie, using none other than Mackie's friend, police chief Tiger
Brown, thus leaving Polly a well-to-do widow. The ethic of betrayal is enunciated by Mr. and Mrs. Peachum in the ballad con-

cerning the "uncertainty of the human lot"—in which Peachum, "with Bible in hand," first proclaims the right of man to happiness. Unfortunately this and his other good impulses of goodness in man are frustrated, for the "circumstances just aren't so." When there isn't enough for two, your own brother will kick you in the teeth. And who wouldn't rather be loyal and true? In which sentiments Polly joins. "The world is poor, and man is bad."[7]

Mackie, who cannot resist his fleshly urges, must seek his regular "refreshment" in the brothel of "Turnbridge," and is betrayed to the police by his favorite whore, Jenny, but not before they have both sung a duet, the "Ballad of the Pimp," describing the happy household of pimp and whore, to the rhythm of the then-popular tango!

> It was so lovely, in that half-year,
> In the brothel, where we two kept house . . .

Mackie escapes the jail through the connivance of Lucy, the jailer's daughter, another of his conquests, to the rage and consternation of Peachum. But Mackie's escape is short-lived, for his flesh is weak! And now he will really be hanged. The populace flocks to view the execution, as Mackie makes his final address:

Ladies and gentlemen: You see before you the vanishing representative of a vanishing class. We petty middle-class professionals, who work with honest jimmies on the cash-boxes of the small shopkeepers, are being pushed out by the large enterprises backed by the banks. What is a bank robbery compared to the founding of a bank? What is the murder of a man next to the employment of a man? Fellow citizens, I herewith bid you adieu. . . . Some of you have been very close to me. That Jenny should have betrayed me amazes me. It is clear proof that the world never changes. . . . Very well then, I fall.[8]

And he follows with the ballad, in the style of François Villon, begging forgiveness of all:

> Ihr Menschenbrüder, die ihr nach uns lebt. . . .
>
> Oh, fellow-man, who after us survive,
> Shut not your heart against us sinners,
> Nor laugh when on gallows high you see us hanging. . . .

He forgives men and women, thieves, whores, and pimps—all but those dogs, the police! However, just at the moment of the hanging, Peachum steps forward, and, in the manner of Gay's beggar-narrator, announces that the public will now see "that at least in the opera mercy prevails over law," and that consequently the mounted emissary of Royalty is approaching—and sure enough, he comes. It is Tiger Brown himself, bringing Mackie the Queen's pardon, a title of nobility, and a pension of ten thousand pounds! Saved! "How nice and peaceful our lives could be," Mrs. Peachum reflects, "if only a royal messenger kept on arriving." Peachum adds, addressing the actors:

I beg everyone to remain in his place, and sing the chorale of the poorest of the poor, whose hard life you have today shown, for in reality their end is always bad. The mounted messengers of the King come only rarely, and he who gets kicked only kicks in return. Hence, don't be too hard on injustice.

> Do not revile injustice, for it soon
> Perishes of cold, for it is cold.
> Remember life's frost, and darkness too,
> In this vale of sorrows and tears untold.[9]

The Three Penny Opera is indeed a "chorale of the poorest of the poor," expressed both cynically, bitterly; sometimes sadly and movingly. Among the themes that intertwine, one is central—that stated by Mackie the Knife:

> You gentlemen who teach us to live uprightly,
> And eschew deeds of vice and of sin,
> First give us something to fill our bellies,
> Then you can talk—then you can pitch in.
>
> Show us first how a wretched oaf,
> Can get his share of the world's great loaf.

For what does man live on? Cheating, robbing, flaying his fellows—and only by forgetting that he is a man.

> Das eine wisset ein für allemal
> Wie ihr es immer dreht und wie ihr's immer schiebt
> Erst kommt das Fressen, dann kommt die Moral.

"First comes the belly, then morality"—a line all Berlin was to repeat for years to come.

> So gentlemen, enough of all this fooling,
> Man only lives from evil-doing.[10]

Another equally bitter song of the play, that of the "Pirate Jenny," voices the savage resentment of the downtrodden barroom slavey and her dream of the coming of a "ship with eight sails and fifty cannons," whose crew would put all her persecutors to the knife, and take her on board and away.

The audience filed out that night, humming, whistling the memorable tune of Mackie the Knife—the Moritat of the shark with its sharp teeth, which are visible, and of Mackie's knife, which is invisible:

> Und der Haifisch, der hat Zähne
> Und die trägt er im Gesicht
> Und Macheath, der hat ein Messer
> Doch das Messer sieht man nicht.

—a tune that neither Brecht nor Weill, the composer, could have foreseen would travel around the world.

What had those first-night spectators really made of this work? Was it spoof? Serious? Opera? Or just another "Schlager" ("hit"), to be added to the season's other hits, filled with the customary "Kitsch" ("corn"), like the current *Es liegt in der Luft* with the inimitable Marlene Dietrich; or Max Reinhardt's slick success, *Victoria*? For the *Dreigroschenoper* was a smash hit. It ran on and on, for more than a thousand performances. Critical opinion ranged all the way from celebration to gutter denunciation. On the political right, it was condemned as "class-conscious Bolshevism" and "bolshevist madness."

No doubt, however, that it had enough for everybody. For part of the audience it was a vicarious and daring excursion into the lower depths of crime and prostitution; for another part it offered the delights of cynicism and scurrility, brilliantly set in words and music. The excoriation of humanity was general enough not to touch anyone in particular. Each spectator could turn his pharisaic eye on his neighbor and mutter, *De te fabula!* Peachum's invocations to mercy and pity could be accepted with little discomfort. And who could refrain from nodding agreement, when he proclaimed the "inadequacy of human exertions"?

> Der Mensch lebt durch den Kopf
> Der Kopf reicht ihm nicht aus. . . .
>
> Man lives by his head,
> But this head won't suffice.
> Try it and see, how with your head,
> You'll barely nourish lice.
>
> Yes, just to live this life,
> Man isn't sharp enough,
> He never seems to see
> That it's all deceit and bluff.[11]

Did they draw a parallel between their own lives, outside the theatre, and what they had just witnessed on the stage? Peachum's business dealings that made use of piety and human pity as sources of income; his and Mackie's collaboration with the police; the reciprocal betrayals—did not all these convey to the audience an indictment of its bourgeois morality? Did they not see in Mackie, the "gentleman," a replica of the more respectable gentlemen with whom they associated, and whose enterprises though grander, were equally shady?

If they did not see all these things, the fault was not entirely theirs. How could they be sure that the songs and sentiments expressed in the play were not Brecht's, but those reflecting the bourgeois society in which they were living? For actually, there are two Brechts within the *Three Penny Opera,* and they overlap. There is the sky-storming nihilist, laureate of the asphalt jungle; and there is the initiate into Marxism, who was attempting to parallel the lesser duplicities and betrayals, the thievery of the netherworld with the more seemingly respectable but crasser and more thoroughgoing iniquities and corruption of the upper world. But could Mackie be taken seriously as the exemplar of the contemporary "expropriating" bourgeois? And what social content could be assigned to the injunction "not to be too harsh on injustice, because it will perish of itself"? There was nothing here to revolt any listener, except one already socially aware that injustice *can* be done away with.

Brecht himself became conscious of the ambiguities in this work, and in subsequent annotations tried to clear the air by insisting on the close analogy between the character of Macheath and the modern bourgeois. He instructed the actor to represent the highwayman as "a bourgeois phenomenon," with the bourgeois' regular, almost pedantically meticulous social habits, such as visiting certain "Turnbridge coffee-houses."

Actors must therefore avoid presenting these bandits as a mob of sad-looking individuals, with red bandanas, who inhabit various honky-tonks, and whom no respectable citizen would stand a drink. They are, of course, settled persons, even portly, and without exception quite affable, outside of their professional engagements.[12]

Yet, despite inconsistencies and ambiguities, the *Three Penny Opera* represents a long step forward from *Baal* and *Drums in the Night*. Few works of this time so clearly mirror certain aspects of the twenties. Its acid irony, and parody of operatic sentimentality and make-believe are in keeping with the anti-sentimentalist demands of the period. Brecht had replaced the traditional and frequently meaningless operatic libretto with one that was easily accessible, highly poetic, yet realistic and contemporary in setting. He had also tried to achieve a "critical distancing" on the part of the audience, to replace the customary "primacy of feeling." He was employing a number of devices (later to be subsumed under "estrangement") such as establishing a deliberate dichotomy between words and music—brilliantly realized by Kurt Weill; separating the various elements of the play, such as action and song; utilizing projections of placards with biblical and other mottoes; direct addresses to the audience; and, not least, revolutionizing the character of the musical settings. The spectators were never left in doubt that they were in a theatre. Yet there was the traditional tie to and attraction of the old Singspiel of Mozart and the Viennese folk-comedy, of the cabaret, and the French vaudeville.

As the savage world of *In the Jungle of Cities* was presided over by the spirit of Arthur Rimbaud, so the lower regions of the *Three Penny Opera* stood in the shadow of François Villon. Brecht was a generous taker, and into this opera he wove many strands of Villon's poetry, in the translations of K. L. Ammer. It was not long before Alfred Kerr spied the "plagiarisms." In the *Berliner Tageblatt* of September 1, 1928, following the performance, he was remarkably laudatory. He called this a "magnificent evening," and the play a pioneer drama. He loved the Moritat ballads. Kerr was unusually perspicacious in raising the question whether in comparison with Gay's ballad-opera, Brecht had not sacrificed the specific weapon of social criticism, and denied himself "home thrusts at the burning present." Had not Brecht diluted his thesis with a "vaguely-ethical content"?[13] But upon the publication of the *Songs der Dreigroschenoper* in 1929, Kerr raised a hue and cry of plagiarism, charging piracy not only of Ammer's Villon, but of Kipling too. Scandal was nothing new in Brecht's life, and he replied with typical effrontery, in *Die schöne Literatur* of July, 1929:

A Berlin newspaper has remarked, somewhat belatedly, but remarked none the less, that in the Kiepenheuer edition of the *Songs of the Three Penny Opera*, the name of the German translator is missing underneath the name of Villon, although of the 625 verses only 25 are identical with the excellent translation by Ammer. I declare in all honesty that I forgot to mention the name of Ammer. And this, in turn, I explain by my fundamental laxity in the matter of intellectual property.[14]

A subsequent comment enlarged upon the thesis of "plagiarism" and dubbed such accusations favorite pastimes of the bourgeoisie, which is always worried about "property." He called to mind the generosity with which Shakespeare covered "what was spoken on the stage with his name." After all, he added, it was the grand line of the drama that counted and that never could be borrowed.[15]

Ironically enough, the scandal revived interest in Ammer's version, which had appeared in 1908, and was now republished with a prefatory sonnet by Brecht:

> Here you see on perishable sheets
> His Testament—once again—in reprint new,
> In which he scatters ordure to those he knew.
> Will such as want their share now answer, "Here!"

For the price of a few cigars, you can now buy these bitter drops, so let everyone take whatever he can use. "You may be sure I've taken my share too."[16]

Unexpectedly, Brecht now found a new champion as a result of this little to-do. Karl Kraus, already celebrated as one of the most gifted and virulent satirists of the age, editor of the provocative Viennese journal *Die Fackel* (mostly written singlehandedly), and long a bitter enemy of Alfred Kerr, replied to "Kerr's Disclosures." In his little finger, Kraus wrote, "with which he took some twenty-five verses of Ammer's translation of Villon, this fellow Brecht has more originality than that man Kerr who is stalking him."[17]

But, of course, there were plenty of jibes at Brecht, such as the one by the humorist Kurt Tucholsky:

> Who wrote that piece?
> It's by Bertolt Brecht.
> Well, who wrote that piece?[18]

Had Brecht been acquainted with Kipling's quatrain, he might well have used it to close the incident:

> When 'Omer smote 'is bloomin' lyre,
> He'd 'eard men sing by land and sea:
> An' what he thought 'e might require,
> 'E went an' took—the same as me![19]

Herbert Jhering extolled the play in the *Börsen-Courier* of September 1. The work, he wrote,

proclaims a new world, in which the frontiers of tragedy and humor are eradicated. This is a triumph of the open form. . . . Brecht has torn language, and Weill music from their isolation. Once more we listen to speech on the stage that is neither literary, nor shop-worn; and music that no longer works with thread-bare harmonies and rhythms.

The Three Penny Opera brought fame to such newcomers as Lotte Lenya and additional celebrity to such others as Erich Ponto, Kurt Gerron, Roma Bahn, Ernst Busch, Carola Neher, Rosa Valetti, Hermann Thimig. The success of Berlin was duplicated in Munich, Leipzig, Prague, and Riga, not without some abuse and denigration. So far as Brecht was concerned, *he* was a success. For the first time he was really making money. But he did not, for all that, change his habits, or his unprepossessing outfit, which he would wear even at Soviet state receptions, where, as his friend Wieland Herzfelde reports, he would argue continuously—about the theatre![20]

Brecht's *Dreigroschenoper* and Kurt Weill's musical score represented a critique not only of society but of drama itself, and the opera in particular. "Thus was created a new genre," Weill wrote. Brecht's literary work, as we have already seen, had always been bound up with music in one way or another. His musical taste was Brechtian—that is, extreme, one-sided, even bizarre. His own poems and songs he used to accompany with original settings on the guitar. There was this "popular" strain in him, that never left him. But he had original views on the relation of music to text, and these impressed themselves on composers with whom he collaborated, no matter what their previous training or background. That he was able to attract to himself such gifted figures as Kurt Weill, Hanns Eisler, Paul Hindemith, and Paul Dessau, and in most instances find with them a common ground of objectives and intentions, speaks volumes for the immediacy and persuasiveness of his aesthetic theories and convictions. For his associates were, for the most part, representatives of the more advanced schools of music.

The musical life of the twenties was open to new impulses and movements, and in this respect too the decade was to prove one of the most creative and inspiring of the century. Here, as elsewhere,

America played a central role, bringing jazz, Negro spirituals, and its technological achievements. Brecht found no common ground with those composers who were practitioners of the new tonal systems, and with such works as Schoenberg's *Pierrot Lunaire* or Alban Berg's *Wozzeck*. But he was open to the American musical influences, and closer to those composers who had absorbed the American idiom. The French had already paved the way there: Cocteau was serving up libretti in the American style. Milhaud composed a Negro jazz ballet, *La création du monde*. The Russian Igor Stravinsky used American jazz in his *Histoire du soldat* in 1918; and the Austrian Ernst Křenek did the same in *Jonny spielt auf* in 1927. George Gershwin's *Rhapsody in Blue* (1924) captivated all of Europe.

Under the influence of Paul Hindemith and Heinrich Burkard, festivals of new music were established at Donaueschingen in 1921, in which German as well as foreign composers participated. The same influences prevailed at Baden-Baden, which succeeded Donaueschingen. It was here that the first joint effort of Brecht and Weill, the Singspiel *Mahagonny* (known as *Das kleine Mahagonny*) was performed in 1927.

That many of these productions proved as ephemeral as they sometimes were sensational does not detract from their general importance and influence. They served to bring together "high-brow" and "low-brow," they experimented with new techniques such as those of the film and radio, and had a strong "popular" appeal, in the best sense of the word, in introducing "Gebrauchsmusik" (utilitarian or functional music) as well as "Gemeinschaftsmusik" (communal music), particularly under the leadership of Paul Hindemith. Compositions were written for and performed by special, often amateur, groups, of varying ages and aptitudes, with texts (when needed). Thus learning and performing were combined.

Such is the origin of the Lehrstück, or didactic piece, that Brecht was to make his own individual province in years to come.

Kurt Weill was aware of the social implications of this movement, as well as of the importance of his participation in Brecht's work.

In a period of mounting sophistication [he wrote] jazz appeared as the most healthy, the strongest artistic expression, which, by virtue of its folk origin, immediately became an international folk music, exercising the widest influence.[21]

He remarked that *The Three Penny Opera*, a realization of the new genre, had come at the right time both from the point of view of creators and public. The aristocratic origin and nature of the opera, he said in another connection, made it inconceivable to transport it to the theatrical stage. Brecht's and his work represented a return to a primitive "original"; the music was written so as to be sung by actors, that is, laymen. Thus, a new genre came into being.[22]

Brecht, too, commented some years later on the revolutionary character of this work, as a successful demonstration of the "epic" theatre.

This represented the first application of theatrical music in accordance with the new point of view. Its most striking innovation consisted in the strict separation of the musical from the other elements. This could be seen at once, in that the small orchestra was visibly installed on the stage. For the singing of the songs a change of lighting was arranged, and the orchestra illuminated, and on the screen in the background appeared the projected titles of individual numbers, such as the "Song of the Inadequacy of Human Endeavors." . . . The actors changed their positions before each number . . . . So that the music, because it deported itself in a purely emotional manner, and did not scorn the customary narcotic appeals, cooperated fully in the unmasking of bourgeois ideology.[23]

What Brecht is speaking about is "Verfremdung," "estrangement," produced by contrasting the seemingly conventional, but brilliantly original, music of Weill with the shocking, unconventional, almost brutal character of dialogue and lyrics—so as to startle the audience and provoke them to thinking.

X

The Mahagonny Paradise, 1930

> We need no hurricanes,
> And we need no typhoons,
> For all the frightful things they do,
> That we can do too.
>
> BRECHT, *Mahagonny*

A historian, writing about the period between 1927 and 1931 might have noted the following interesting occurrences:

In October, 1927, President Hindenburg of Germany was presented with an estate, Neudeck, the gift of a group of grateful Junkers and industrialists. The following August, 1928, Foreign Minister Stresemann went to Paris to sign the Kellogg Pact, renouncing war. In Paris jubilant cries filled the streets: "Vive Stresemann! Vive la paix!" At the same time, as everyone seemed to know, but no one wished to say, Germany was secretly rearming. When, in April, 1929, the liberal organ, *Die Weltbühne,* exposed the secret air rearmament of the country, which had been proceeding illegally since 1921, its editor, Carl Ossietzky, and the writer Walter Kreiser were sentenced by a Leipzig court for "divulging military secrets and high treason." According to the British General J. H. Morgan, the Allied governments and their control commission probably knew all about these proceedings, but were willing to close their eyes to them.[1]

In 1929, May Day demonstrations were prohibited by the Socialist government. Berlin workers were "ordered to disperse," and the police opened fire, killing twenty-five and severely injuring thirty-six.[2] On May 4, 1929, Prussian Police President Zoergiebel, a Socialist, issued decrees against the inhabitants of the working-class district of Berlin: "Between 9 P.M. and 4 A.M. all traffic in the streets mentioned below is prohibited. . . . During the day no person is allowed to linger in the said districts and streets, or on balconies, at corners, or in entrances."[3] The *Hamburger Nachrichten* wrote: "We may remind our readers of the words of Napoleon that each rebel killed means 100,000 citizens saved. If instead of several arrests and only a few killed, the proportion had been reversed, the middle classes could have confidence in the present Government." The "present" government consisted of Reich Chancellor Hermann Mueller, Reich Minister Severing, Prussian Premier Otto Braun, and Prussian Minister of the Interior Grzesinski—all Socialists.

In the elections of May, 1928, the Socialists and Communists together controlled over two hundred seats, the National Socialists fifty-four.

Following is a report of a conversation between Foreign Minister Aristide Briand of France and Foreign Minister Gustave Stresemann, of Germany, in August, 1928:

BRIAND. What disquiets me are the national organizations in Germany. What is all this business with the Stahlhelm?

STRESEMANN. . . . . From the military point of view they mean nothing . . . Nor must the Stahlhelm be conceived as a reactionary organization. . . . Men want color, joy, and movement; hence the Stahlhelm.

BRIAND. That is just how I conceived matters. A man naturally enjoys putting a steel-helmet on his head and behaving as though he were still a mighty warrior. I don't attach serious importance to all this.[4]

In October, 1929, the Wall Street crash took place. Its consequences were to become evident very soon.

In March, 1930, Heinrich Brüning became Chancellor and, addressing the Reichstag, said: "Ladies and Gentlemen, please do not try to connect me in any way with November 9 [1918]. . . . Let me finish. Where was I on November 9th? . . . . Gentlemen, I was with the troops at the head of the Winterfeld Group formed to overthrow the Revolution."[5]

The Reichstag elections of September 14, 1930, showed the following results:

Socialists:	143 seats
Communists:	107 seats
National Socialists:	77 seats.

The National Socialists polled six and a half million votes. The *Völkischer Beobachter* of October 16, 1930, wrote:

The Reichstag shall resolve: The entire property of the banking and the Bourse magnates of Eastern Jews and other foreigners . . . . shall be confiscated for the benefit of the German people without compensation. . . . All large banks, including the so-called Reichsbank, to become the property of the State without delay.[6]

In January 1931 there were 4,765,000 unemployed in Germany.

We may be sure that Brecht watched these events with great concern. Fritz Sternberg, the sociologist, now a close friend of Brecht's, though politically far from agreeing with him, reports that as, in the year 1930, the situation grew more and more grave, and the tensions increased, Brecht became alarmed. Sternberg writes:

He had asked me to give him a few pamphlets with the writings of Marx and Engels. One day he told me that he had acquired five copies each of the *Communist Manifesto*, Engels' *Road to Socialism*, other Marxist texts, among them one of mine—and had them all placed on a shelf. Brecht was then so well known that many young playwrights came to him for advice or to ask his opinion of their plays. He told me that he invited each of them in and then pointing to the shelf asked them whether they were acquainted with the particular piece of writing there. If the young writer said, "No" (which was always the case), Brecht replied, "Take these as a present. If, after reading them, you still believe that your play stands up, then come to me again."[7]

Sternberg was present with Brecht, as they both witnessed the clashes that took place between workers and police on May 1, 1929. Again, Sternberg reports:

From my window [in the Koblanckstrasse]—I lived on the third floor —we could see them [workers and police] clearly. Brecht, too, stood at the window. . . . He saw how the police dispersed and pursued the demonstrators. So far as we knew, they were unarmed. But the police did fire again and again. At first we thought they were only warning shots. But soon we saw a number of the demonstrators falling and then being carried off on stretchers. So far as I can recall there were twenty dead in Berlin. When Brecht heard the shooting, and saw that human beings were being killed, he turned white, as I have never seen him before. . . . I believe it was this experience that was not least in-fluential in bringing him closer and closer to the Communists. . . . Later we drove in an auto through Berlin. . . . The police were unusually courteous toward us, since we had a car, and as one of them remarked, since we didn't belong to the "rabble." That workingmen who were demonstrating on May 1 should be termed "rabble" by the police was something Brecht was never to forget. Even ten years later, when we were both emigrants, he would recall that incident.[8]

Following the success of the *Dreigroschenoper,* Brecht hoped for another hit, and with Elisabeth Hauptmann's collaboration con-trived a venture named *Happy End* (using the English title). The play was destined to have neither happy beginning nor happy end. The new "Singspiel" was taken off the boards almost immediately after its première in September, 1929, and with more than adequate justification. Elisabeth Hauptmann said[9] that it was she who first drew Brecht's attention to the dramatic possibilities of the Salvation Army as another subject on an American theme. At any rate, the notion of combining the underworld of the *Dreigroschenoper* with the supraterrestrial ministrations of the Salvation Army proved at-tractive. Kurt Weill was drawn in too, to set the songs, and with a cast that included Carola Neher, Helene Weigel, Oskar Homolka, Peter Lorre, and Kurt Gerron, this promised another success. The unhappy farrago was announced allegedly as an "adaptation" of an American story by one "Dorothy Lane."

Once again we are in Chicago. In Bill Cracker's Ballhaus the crooks foregather under the generalship of the "woman in gray," otherwise known as the "Fly", to plan a bank robbery. Into this den of theatrical American iniquity steps Halleluiah Lillian of the Salvation Army to convert the sinners; but in a moment of forgetfulness imbibes three whiskeys and sings a provocative "Sailor Song" (which loses her her job). She manages to convert Bill Cracker in due time. Need one go on to tell how the "Fly" rediscovers her long absconded husband (formerly police chief!)? Add a spice of murder; and conclude with a general rehabilitation of criminals, a sermon by the "Fly" (memories of Macheath!) that the two-bit crook is a thing of the past, for the big boys have taken over; round it out with a chorale, with illuminated pictures of Salvation Army "saints" like St. Ford, St. Morgan, and St. Rockefeller, intoned as a Hosanna to millionaires:

> Give to the rich ones, riches. Hosanna!
> And virtue give them too, Hosanna!
> To him who hath, give more, Hosanna!
> Give him the country; the city too . . . ,[10]

and you get some idea of this impossible play!!

Were it not for the brilliant songs of Kurt Weill, the whole thing might well be forgotten: The "Bilbao Song" that celebrates Bill's Ballhaus (for a dollar you get all the noise and pleasure you want); the "Song of Surabaya Johnny" with its deliberate barrel-organ banality (American style?): "You've got no heart, Surabaya Johnny, I love you so,"[11] and Lillian's scandalous "Sailor Song" (à la "Mandalay"). "Ho, ho," she sings mockingly, "now we go to Burma," where there are unlimited prospects of good things, where we don't need God or respectability. And she concludes with the dire warning of storm and sinking ship, and "the end to big talk," as "with gaping mouth you'll stand before the throne of God" and "babble Pater Nosters":

> Yes, the sea is blue, so blue so blue
> And everything takes its course,
> But when it's all over, you can't begin anew . . .[12]

Much more promising, though existing only in fragments, was a play to be called *The Downfall of the Egoist, Johann Fatzer.*[13] It was actually intended for Piscator's theatre and announced by

him for production during the 1929-1930 season, along with another
of Brecht's unrealized plays, *Aus nichts wird nichts*.[14] The *Fatzer*
fragments suggest that Brecht might have been planning a counterpart to *Drums in the Night,* and treating a problem that was to
occupy him more and more urgently in the years to come—the
transformation of an individualist into a social being. Johann Fatzer
and three war comrades, members of a tank corps, have deserted
the army toward the end of the war, and Fatzer wanders about
the city of Mühlheim in search of provisions for his comrades and
himself. Fatzer looks for signs of war fatigue and discontent, if
not rebellion, but finds none. As a matter of fact, women waiting
in a queue for bread, berate him as an alarmist and provocateur. It
is not clear what the final intention of the piece was to be, but the
few powerful poetic and dramatic sections suggest that the "egoist"
Fatzer apparently jeopardized the safety of his comrades-in-hiding
through his behavior and exposure in the city, and must justify himself (in tones reminiscent of Kragler):

The air and the streets are for all, aren't they?—To listen to human
voices, to see faces, freely to mingle in the stream of human beings—
you can't keep me from that![15]

Overcome by loneliness, he "rises in the middle of the night and
goes out into the streets and shouts: 'Hey, where are you all? Here
I am, Fatzer. I can't stand it any longer. Isn't there someone who
will shoot me? I am shit!' "[15] A moving chorus that appeals to
Fatzer suggests that Fatzer will find his way to the community and
so change the world around him. But first he must "touch bottom".

> The victim cannot escape
> Wisdom.
> Hold tight and sink.
> Be afraid!
> But sink. On the bottom
> You will find instruction.
> You who have too often been the one to be asked,
> Now take a portion of the priceless instruction of
> the masses.

> Take up your new post.
> Statesman. You are done for.
> But the state is not yet finished.
> Allow us to alter it according to life's needs.
> Agree: we are statesmen too, statesman. . . .
> The state has need of you no more,
> Turn it over to us.

Another chorus chants: "Injustice is human; but more human still is the war against injustice."[16]

And now amidst all this activity, successful and unsuccessful, scandal broke upon Brecht. He became involved in a court proceeding.

In the fall of 1929, the Nero-Film Company, struck by the popular appeal of the *Three Penny Opera,* decided to film it, and engaged Brecht and Weill to do the screenplay, with the assistance of Slatan Dudow, Caspar Neher, and Leo Lania. G. W. Pabst was to direct it. The following summer Brecht submitted his story outline, which, it turned out, was too strong both for Pabst and his employers. For Brecht had moved away considerably from the social attitudes he had expressed in the *Three Penny Opera,* and felt dissatisfied with many of his formulations in that work. He had drawn closer to the Communists, and now he wished to clear up some of the misinterpretations which had arisen from the ambiguous social views expressed there. The motion picture script, which he entitled *Die Beule* (*The Welt*), was substantially different from the original opera. Now Macheath turns from being a petty burglar into a banker, in which enterprise he is eventually joined by Peachum. Before the merger, however, warfare between the two had taken an unhappy turn, as one of Peachum's underlings is beaten up and is given a welt on his head when he tries to interfere with Macheath's henchmen, who are pilfering the furnishings for Macheath's and Polly's wedding. Peachum vows revenge, and the welt becomes the symbolic standard of battle and of Macheath's villainy. Other incidents include Peachum's mobilization of all his beggar hordes in an effort to disrupt the Coronation Procession in London, only to find that

the forces he has unloosed, which are also joined by the truly poor
and beggared of London, threaten to overwhelm the entire status
quo. One of the most vivid portions of the story represents a dream
of Police Chief Tiger Brown in which he sees wave upon wave of
the derelict and disinherited sweeping over the city and destroying
it. Another brilliant incident depicts the appropriation of a bank by
Macheath and his forces, who step from a stolen auto, and as they
mount the stairway are suddenly transformed into well-groomed
and established executives.

The supersession of thief by banker is celebrated in a song: If
you can't inherit money, you must get it another way; and for that
bonds are better than either gun or knife. The old Moritat of Mackie
the Knife and the shark now shows a variant: Mackie sits in the
bank, while in Hyde Park sits the bankrupt whom Mackie has
ruined.

"Prove he's done it, if you can."[17]

The basic social theme of the film is underscored in the concluding song:

> Denn die einen sind im Dunkeln
> Und die andern sind im Licht
> Und man siehet die im Lichte
> Die im Dunkeln sieht man nicht
>
> There are those sit where the sun shines,
> And the others sit in the dark.
> Those in the sunlight you see clearly,
> But the others . . . you never mark,

sung to the tune of the Shark Moritat—but how different now!

Such a radical transformation—the shifting of the original setting
of the criminal underworld into the higher realms of the banker
and the capitalist—could scarcely expect to be greeted with joy by
the producers of the fiilm. Here a generalized indictment of society
had been particularized. They proposed changes that displeased both
Brecht and Weill, who initiated court action to bar further shooting of the film. Brecht lost the case, largely because he had failed to

work seriously on the screen version and could not be easily reached for consultations. The hearing took place on October 17 and 20, 1930, and set all Berlin on its ears. Eventually Brecht accepted a sizable settlement, declined to appeal, and the film was produced as written by Bela Balázs, and directed by Pabst. It proved eminently successful, and for all its attenuated form, it is an unusually powerful indictment. Brecht profited from the experience, for aside from the financial balm, it also led him to think more seriously about the writer's relation to industry in general and the film industry in particular.

Of course, there were jibes and witticisms directed at him. The Frankfurt journalist Ludwig Marcuse wrote a squib entitled "Brecht is Brecht," and in the manner of *Mann ist Mann* told how Brecht came out of Augsburg into the wilderness of Berlin. "Herr Brecht of Augsburg proposes, and Marxism disposes. . . . In this picture you will be shown how Herr Brecht of Augsburg is again reconstructed and reassembled. . . . Such is the outcome of Brecht's campaign for purity of art against the dirtiness of industry: a campaign which was concluded with Brecht's waiver of an appeal in return for a compensation of 21,000 marks."[18]

Unlike many of his contemporaries, Brecht was fascinated by the technological advances in what we today call "communication." Film and radio interested him particularly, not only because of their scientific aspect, but principally because they offered such direct and swift means for diffusing ideas. He wrote a long essay on the relation of the writer to the film industry, touched off by his recent experience. Far from being, as one of Brecht's critics asserts, "long and pretentious,"[19] the essay, "Der Dreigroschenprozess. Ein soziologisches Experiment," was in fact an acute and valuable analysis of the capitalist nature of film production, consumption, and of the consumer—all problems valid in any day.

"The Three Penny Opera Case" is introduced by a brief motto: "In contradictions lie our hopes." It enlarges upon the exciting potential of the film medium for the writer. To disparage it, as many writers do, is to deprive them of an extraordinary opportunity and apparatus, as well as a means of their own education. To say that "art can do without the cinema," that the writer who does not like it can stay away from it, is nonsense and damaging not only to the writer, by precluding him from the use of a wonderful new tool; but also to the film, by depriving it of the special talents of the writer.[20]

Brecht was not speaking *in vacuo*. In many ways the film came close to his own conception of the "epic" theatre. For one, it seemed to him that it brought with it emancipation from the incubus of "psychologism." It laid bare external reality by means of action and not through "introspective psychology." Film, in Brecht's eyes, dispenses with "empathy and mimesis"—the human being is seen as "object" in his behavioral activity. Thus, the "introspective psychology of the bourgeois is smashed." Social behavior is made visible as "reflexes."[21]

If he could not create the film he wanted out of the *Dreigroschenoper*, Brecht decided he would at least write a novel based on it. He could not then know that the result, the *Dreigroschenroman*, would not see the light of day until he himself was no longer in Germany.

On March 9, 1930 *Der Aufstieg und Fall der Stadt Mahagonny* (*The Rise and Fall of the City Mahagonny*) by Brecht and Weill opened in Leipzig. The critic Alfred Polgar was present, and describes its reception:

Right next to me, the following took place: The lady on my left was overcome by a heart-spasm and wanted to get out—and only the warning that this might prove a historic occasion kept her from leaving. The ancient Saxon on my right embraced his wife's knees and was overcome. A man behind me muttered to himself, "I'm only waiting for Brecht to turn up," and licked his chops. Readiness is all . . . . Finally, *levée en masse* of the malcontents—but they in turn were discomfited by thunderous applause. There were very impressive episodes: A dignified gentleman with a parboiled blowzy face had taken out a bunch of keys, and launched a valiant assault on the epic theatre . . . The tone he produced had in it something implacable, so that it cut right into one's innards. It must have been the key to his money-box. . . . His wife did not abandon him in this decisive hour. A hefty Valkyrie, "Hoio—o! Hoio—o!", with a bun on top, and a blue dress with yellow flounces below. She shoved two thick fingers into her mouth, screwed up her eyes, blew up her cheeks, and outshrilled the key to the money-box. . . . It was the first experiment of Brecht's epic theatre, and the scandal which was unloosed already portended the approaching break-up of the country.[22]

Mahagonny was, to paraphrase Oscar Wilde, the mirror Brecht and Weill were holding up to the bourgeois Caliban, and Caliban was not pleased. *Mahagonny* was society—the Weimar Republic, with its anarchy—a society that did not as yet realize how near it was to a precipice. The impact of the world economic crisis was just beginning to be felt; but there could be no mistaking the meaning of the increased aggressiveness of the nationalists and National Socialists; nor of the secret militarization of the rightists; nor of the weakness of the Weimar regime in the face of these threats. The population was bewildered, especially the working classes, in the face of the innumerable parliamentary crises, changes of government, and most disturbing, the frequent resort by Hindenburg and Brüning to government by decree. Dissensions on the left—the inability of Communists and Socialists to form a common front in the face of mounting unemployment and patent disaster, undermined faith in leadership. Scandal after scandal in high places, involving even officials of the Weimar regime, and several prominent Social Democrats (the notorious "Sklarek" affair) made for cynicism. That large industrialists and financiers were openly supporting the National Socialists was taken for granted.[23]

Mahagonny said, "Everything is permitted." The question was, to whom?

The Rise and Fall of the City Mahagonny was the outgrowth of an earlier, much briefer, *Little Mahagonny,* a Singspiel, produced at the Deutsche Kammermusik in Baden-Baden on July 17, 1927, with the score of Kurt Weill. This was really a short skit, which opened with a pistol-shot, and in outline embodied the fuller conception to be developed in *Mahagonny,* and contained six Mahagonny Songs which had appeared in 1927 in *Hauspostille,* with original tunes by Brecht.

In its final version, *The Rise and Fall of Mahagonny* brings on the scene four unsavory characters who have constables breathing down their necks. Among them is our old friend Leokadya Begbick (of *Mann ist Mann*). They are all on their way to the American gold fields "out West," and now have decided to halt and found a city of joy, Mahagonny, the "net" city with which to capture the gold that flows in from the West and from Alaska. In this city of happiness there will be "gin, whiskey, girls, and boys." Peace and harmony will reign, for in the world outside there is "nothing which one can hold on to."[24] In the wake of the arrival of these characters and the founding of the miracle city, with its hotel, "At the Sign of the Rich Man," come the "girls." And with them comes Jenny who sings, in English, the "Alabama Song."

> Oh, show me the way to the next whiskey bar. . . .
> Oh, moon of Alabama
> We now must say good-bye . . . ,

which she follows with "show me the way to the next pretty boy," as well as "to the next little dollar."

Sure enough, customers arrive—among them four lumberjacks from Alaska, with pockets full of money, singing, "Let's go to Mahagonny," where in addition to other amenities, "we'll be cured of civ-civ-civilization." But they soon discover that it is not all heaven. Paul Ackerman, one of the lumberjacks, finds life not too pleasant here. Something is missing. There are, in fact, too many "Thou shalt nots," and he would have left, had not a hurricane suddenly arisen that threatens the extinction of the region. While the others chant a chorale of fearlessness and reassurance ("Stand up and have no fear, brothers"), Paul laughs, and rejoices:

> See, that's the way the world goes:
> Peace and harmony, that's all lies . . .

He compares hurricanes and typhoons to human beings intent on having fun, and Mrs. Begbick joins in:

> The hurricane is bad,
> Typhoons are worse,
> But worst of all—is Man.[25]

Paul Ackermann then proclaims the universal doctrine for Mahagonny: "Everything is permitted," the morality of *laissez-faire*. The hurricane miraculously spares Mahagonny, and now the new gospel is put into practice, with its four principal tenets, announced by the chorus:

> First, remember, comes your belly,
> Then the whoring act,
> And don't forget there's boxing
> And guzzling—per contract.
> And best of all, one precept's true:
> 'tever you wish, that you can do.[26]

They proceed t.   : practice: Jacob the glutton eats himself dead; the others proceed to "love"; Joe is killed in a boxing match with Trinity-Moses; and Paul makes love to Jenny. The duet between them is one of the most beautiful lyrics Brecht ever wrote, or Weill ever set to music:

> Jenny: Sieh jene Kraniche in grossem Bogen!
> Paul: Die Wolken, welche ihnen beigegeben
> Jenny: Zogen mit ihnen schon, als sie entflogen
> Paul: Aus einem Leben in ein andres Leben . . .
>
> See those cranes in great arcs swinging,
> The clouds beneath them now have drawn alongside,
> Moving with them, as if leaving one life,
> They enter another. Thus, as they drift,
> At the same height, and equal too in swiftness,
> As if mere chance had brought them together.
>
> That cloud and crane should in their flight be sharing
> The lovely sky which they so swiftly course,

That neither linger in his flight nor tarry,
And nothing see but how the gentle wind
Makes heave the other like a wave that brushes
Both, as flying side by side they lie—

So into nothingness may the wind convey them,
If neither of them changes, wanes, disperses,
So long will nothing touch them—wound them,
So long they'll drift from all those places
Where rains may threaten, or shots re-echo.

So under sun and moon's indifferent changes,
Merged, they fly, each a portion of the other.
Where to? Nowhere. From whom fleeing? From all.
How long together? One brief while. And parting when?
Soon. Such is for lovers love. Brief stay.[27]

(Was Brecht echoing in his own way the equally beautiful
poem of the nineteenth-century poet Nikolaus Lenau, "Liebe und
Vermählung," which begins, "Sieh dort den Berg mit seinem
Wiesenhange"?)

But Mahagonny has one shortcoming. It requires money. This is
what Paul Ackermann discovers very soon after he has squandered
his all and can no longer pay his bills. He must be tried by a court,
"not worse than other courts"—

because of lack of money
which is the greatest of crimes
in the world.[28]

Paul is condemned to death, and when he pleads with Mrs. Begbick,
"Don't you know there is a God?", she replies with a request to the
others to perform the play of God who came to Mahagonny, "in the
midst of whiskey." God said to the topers: "You drink like sponges
year in, year out, and you waste my grain. Now the day of reckoning
has come. You're all going to Hell. So, put out your cigars, and off
to Hell with you." But the men of Mahagonny say, "No. You can't
drag us to Hell, because we're there already."

Paul Ackermann is executed, and the final scene is introduced by
the legend:

In the ever-intensified confusion, the rising cost of living, sharpened animosities of all against all, there take place in the last weeks of the net-city demonstrations of those who have not yet been disposed of and have learned nothing, in the name of their ideal.

In the background one can see the city of Mahagonny in flames, as the demonstrators pass before our eyes, carrying such placards as:

For higher prices. For the war of all against all. For chaos in our cities. For the continuance of the age of gold. For private property. For the equitable distribution of other-worldly goods. For the inequitable distribution of worldly goods. . . .[29]

"We're in Hell already." Such is Brecht's picture of society—an inferno of parasites, where men are worse than typhoons; where everything can be bought if you have the money; where the gospel reads:

> On the bed you have made you must lie,
> There's no one to trouble about you.
> If there are kicks to be given—I'll give them,
> And if there's someone to be kicked—it'll be you.[30]

This play was a provocation and was sensed as such by the bourgeois audience that responded articulately from its "bad conscience." They felt as if they were being attacked "by the united proletarians of all lands."[31] The bourgeois heaven was being torn apart by sacrilegious hands, and its inner emptiness exposed. Gone was the feeling of good cheer that had greeted the *Three Penny Opera,* which could be taken as a jest. *Mahagonny* meant business.

By the time it was produced in Berlin, in December, 1931, the historical picture had changed, the crisis had sharpened profoundly, and the anarchy depicted on the stage could not but seem an exact replica of what was happening in the world outside.

During the second performance, assembled Nazis created such an uproar that a hundred of them had to be ejected from the theatre. They foregathered with others on the Opernplatz, and shouted, "Deutschland erwache!", "Germany, awake!"

Mahagonny is Brecht's last "bourgeois" testament. Uncompromising though it is in its sardonic unmasking of the cash-nexus of society and its effect on human lives, it stops short of actually revealing the *process* of such destructiveness or the forces involved in such a process. There is no true conflict. Paul Ackermann must go down to defeat (and be executed) without ever coming to understand the forces that are destroying him. The "lessons" he and his companions have learned have come to them not as a result of their perception of the true nature of social relationships (such as they are), but because of a typhoon. Once more anarchy comes face to face with anarchy. Paul attempts to withdraw from a general world anarchy into a personal one. He is doomed. Once more abstract man is seen as the volcanic destructive force, superior even to natural forces—irresistible and incomprehensible. The fact that the proletarian lumberjacks are made the mouthpieces of the ethos of exploitation and small parasitic organisms like the Begbicks and the Joes its instruments only adds to the confusion.

But despite these inadequacies, *Mahagonny* remains a masterpiece. It represents Brecht and Weill at their most original in this period. It is less derivative in its source material. Its canvas is broader and more complex. The American background is, of course, mere fantasy. Mahagonny is Germany. Mahagonny is the world of capitalism. Weill's score serves to underline the unreality of a very real situation. Traditional folk and jazz elements deritualize the essentially serious elements of Brecht's play. This is in reality a capitalist "black mass," an acid dethronement of solemnity. Thus, at the end, Ackermann's earthly possessions are brought in on a linen cushion: his watch, revolver, checkbook, and shirt, and the chorus intones, "Oh, moon of Alabama." Earlier, when in his heyday Paul had proclaimed the gospel of "Thou may'st," stage directions note that all present "rise, and bare their heads," while outside is heard the sacred chant, "Do not be dismayed."

Thus Brecht epitomized the world of Weimar. Himself, now standing on the threshold of a new continent, he could look upon what was behind him to see, as he himself was to describe it, "how the great deluge swept over the bourgeois world. First there is still some land visible, soon turning to puddles and sounds—and then far and wide the black waters, with islets, which quickly crumble."[32] He had participated in that deluge-swept world, first as an onlooker of doom, praising "the coldness, the darkness, and decay"; gorging himself on the beautiful chaos; a Kragler rushing away from the call of battle to gratify the flesh; and he had come finally to consummate his testament to the night in the *Hauspostille*. Thereafter, with a new compass in hand, he began steering the unsteady skiff of the self, guiding it past reefs, still uncertain, but goal-bound. He had begun to see that chaos was society, and that society was men and women, whether socially bound or dissevered, moved by forces that were controllable by human beings. The skiff he was maneuvering would find its way, provided he understood the winds and the waters, and knew how to handle the boat. With surer grasp now, in 1930, he was steering toward land.

XI

The Recovery of Identity:
The Epic Theatre

It was not through Marx that you came to recognize the decline of the drama. It was not through Marx that you came to speak of the epic theatre. For, let us put it quite gently, Epic Theatre, that is you, dear Herr Brecht.

FRITZ STERNBERG TO BRECHT, 1927

To think, or write, or produce a play also means: to transform society, to transform the state, to subject ideologies to close scrutiny.

BRECHT, 1931

I

With the completion of *The Rise and Fall of the City Mahagonny* Brecht had reached a stage in his development where he was ready to crystallize the theory of the epic theatre. Since he had always regarded himself as an "experimenter," and his works as "efforts" or "experiments," he continued in the years to come to refine, alter, and modify many of his concepts. But the fundamental principles of the epic theatre were to remain essentially the same. When the term "epic" proved unsatisfactory, Brecht changed it to "dialectic." But it is "epic" theatre that has remained associated with Brecht's name, and though there were before him, and were

199

to be after him, many practitioners of this type of theatre, consensus
has made that form Brech's own domain.

To avoid confusion, it may therefore be useful at the very outset
to set forth as precisely as we can the fundamental and basic nature
of Brecht's epic theatre that differentiates it from similar efforts by
others that sometimes pass by that name.

Brecht's epic theories are constituted of the fusion of two principal
elements, the formal and the ideological. For Brecht they were inseparable and a discussion of one without the other unthinkable.
Some of the formal or technical elements have already been mentioned in these pages, particularly in connection with the theatre
of Erwin Piscator.[1] These will be reconsidered in the light of their
relation to the ideological element.

Brecht's epic theory presupposes a general theory, a Weltanschauung, in this case Marxism, which by him is fused with the
various elements that constitute theatre: audience, performers, form
and content of the play, staging, music. In all of these respects
Brecht's epic theatre demands not a renovation of the older element
or elements, but a total change.

Few practising playwrights have given so much thought and
effort and time to theorizing about their craft and its product, the
theatre. Names that come to mind immediately are those of Lessing,
Hebbel, Schiller, Strindberg, Shaw, and Corneille. He is the only
modern who has composed an "organum" of the drama that can
be set alongside those of Aristotle and Hegel. Brecht began theorizing about the theatre almost as soon as he began writing at all;
and inchoate and scattered as his earlier remarks may have been,
they prove that between his practice as a playwright and his theorizing about drama there was never that gap which certain critics have
been only too eager to explore and expand.

Brecht took his theory seriously. What Piscator and others had
already indicated, he was capable of realizing practically by virtue
of his numerous talents: for he was a poet, a playwright, a stage
director, of the first rank; and to a lesser extent, a musician; and,

as we hope will appear from subsequent discussion, a thinker. But his thinking embraced not only what was happening on the stage, but also that which took place in the audience, and beyond that, that which was taking place in the world outside the theatre.

Nohing seems so far-fetched (to put it gently) as to imagine, as some writers do, that Brecht invented his theory to suit or justify a poetic or dramatic practice which was either faulty, or did not seem to conform to tradition. Such for example is the boast of a theatrical director, Rudolf Frank, who recalls (after a lapse of many years) having spoken to Brecht after a performance of *Edward II*:

You [Brecht] have something more original to contribute than that which corresponds to rules. You know that they will chalk up against your plays the fact that you have broken the rules; until you have suc-ceeded in bracing them with a new theory of your own. Invent a theory, dear Brecht! When Germans get a theory, they swallow everything else.[2]

Brecht viewed theatre as an entity, not the least important ele-ment of which was constituted by the audience. He believed it nec-essary to develop the art of the spectator, no less than that of the writer or actor. He regarded the audience as a "producer," and its share in the theatre as of great importance. To transform the theatre, therefore, meant also to transform the audience. What was needed was to make that audience "productive" and to end its role of being "putty" at the mercies of what Brecht called the "culinary" theatre—that is, a theatre that served up or "dished out" its fare to be savored, tasted, gobbled up, consumed—or, to change the figure, an audience that would have its palate tickled, titillated and satis-fied, then go home, smacking its lips.

How did Brecht see the contemporary audience as it really was in his day?

Rushing out of the subway stations, eager to be turned into putty at the hands of magicians—grown men, tried and tested in the struggle for existence, scurry to the box-office. There they check their hats, and along with those, their customary habits, their normal attitudes of everyday life. Once outside the cloak-room, they take their seats with the bearing of kings.[3]

He is here speaking of the operatic audience, but it is obvious that he is thinking of the theatre as a whole. Let us, with Brecht, follow this audience to a performance, say, of a Wagner opera.

Let us go into one of these theatres and observe the effect which it has on the spectators. When we look around, we see somewhat motionless figures in a peculiar state: They seem to be tensing their muscles strenuously, unless they are enervated and exhausted. They scarcely communicate with one another—their association here is like that of sleepers—but sleepers who dream incessantly. . . . True, their eyes are open, but they see not—they stare. They hear not—but listen. They look at the stage entranced, with an expression like that of the Middle Ages—the ages of witches and clerics. Seeing and hearing are activities, and can be pleasurable ones. But these people seem relieved of all activity and like men to whom something is being done.[4]

"To whom something is being done." Since this notion is crucial to the understanding of Brecht's general theory of drama, let us carry this visit to the opera a step farther, and observe a hypothetical spectator at a specific opera of Wagner's, *Tristan und Isolde*. Let us catch him as he is watching the magnificent second act. He sees before him the ramparts of a medieval castle, shrouded in darkness. Two figures are conjured out of the dark (and the medieval romantic past), two lovers, Tristan and Isolde, locked in an unfortunate but irresistible and forbidden love. The night is sinking, bringing with it what the lovers wish (and sing) for—"the loss of consciousness," i.e., of the reality of the outside world, from which still come the shrouded and ever-distancing notes of the horns of King Mark's, the husband's, hunting party. Metaphysical eroticism superimposes itself upon the physical, as the sensuously rapturous music rises and falls at magician Wagner's command. He has cast his spell-woven net, and our spectator sits (along with the hundreds of others) rapt, joined vicariously in the passion of the lovers:

> O sink hernieder
> Nacht der Liebe,
> gib Vergessen
> dass ich lebe . . .

> Oh descend upon us
> Night of love,
> Make me forget
> That I live . . .

The night does descend, but it is passing, and the lovers must hurry. The song and music sweep on until we hear the Liebestod—the love death:

> Ewig einig
> ohne End
> Ohne Bangen . . .
>
> Ever one
> never severed
> never waking
> past all pain . . .[5]

So vicariously too our spectator dies a love death. When it is all over, he goes home, sensuous appetite stilled—"all passion spent"—filled with a vague Schopenhauerian pessimism distilled into a Wagnerian earthly love and death, darkness and renunciation.

He has yielded, wittingly or unwittingly, to the theatre of "illusion," that has deliberately placed him in a trance. He has been overpowered, and, as a contemporary and successful playwright recently expressed it:

There is something attractively violent in this, so that [he] may truly surrender, think along, and feel along.[6]

To achieve such an effect at its utmost, it is of course necessary to employ a whole apparatus of highly technical devices, psychological as well as physical. Richard Wagner, long in advance of Madison Avenue, carefully projected just such "subliminal" techniques. For that purpose he designed his own theatre and called for a "mystic gulf" in which the orchestra would be concealed and which would also establish a spatial distance between audience and stage, "dividing the real from the ideal," and giving the effect that the dramatic personages were "magnified into superhuman proportions." The "tableau," as Wagner put it, "retreats from the spectator, as in a dream" . . . .

Meanwhile the music, as it comes forth like a spirit voice from the "mystic gulf," or like the vapor rising from the sacred bosom of the Earth beneath the tripod of the Pythia, induces in him that spiritualized state of clairvoyance wherein the scenic representation becomes the perfect image of real life.[7]

No one could have set forth more lucidly the direct contrary of what Brecht desired of *his* spectator. Brecht does not deny that the illusions the opera offers have a serious social function. For, he believes, its intoxicants are indispensable to today's audiences. It is in this atmosphere that the human being has the opportunity of feeling himself "human" once more, coming as he does from an outside world where "his collective rational functions have been for a long time now thoroughly squeezed out, down to the level of anxious distrust, selfish calculation, and the capitalizing on his fellow man."[8] What is rare for him, Brecht cites Sigmund Freud in support of his claim. Life, Freud stated, was too hard for man to support and entailed too many pains, disappointments, so that man cannot do without "palliative remedies":

There are [Freud continues] perhaps three such measures: powerful deflections, which cause us to make light of our misery; substitutive satisfactions, which diminish it; and intoxicating substances, which make us insensitive to it. . . . The substitutive satisfactions, as offered by art, are illusions in contrast with reality, but they are none the less psychically effective, thanks to the role which phantasy has assumed in mental life.[9]

The service rendered by intoxicating media in the struggle for happiness and in keeping misery at a distance is so highly prized as a benefit that individuals and peoples alike have given them an established place in the economics of their libido. We owe to such media not merely the immediate yield of pleasure, but also a greatly desired degree of independence from the external world. . . . As is well known, it is precisely this property of intoxicants which also determines their danger and their injuriousness. They are responsible, in certain circumstances, for the useless waste of a large quota of energy which might have been employed for the improvement of the human lot.[10]

So far as the theatre is concerned, it doesn't, of course, matter whether the "intoxicant" is offered in the form of music by Richard Wagner or Richard Strauss, or in the form of classical drama. For Brecht insists that

The all-important thing in these theatres, so far as the spectators are concerned, is that they are enabled to swap a contradictory world for a harmonious one, a world they scarcely know for one they can dream about.[11]

The traditional drama (not to mention its debased analogues) can offer such intoxicants through its rhetorical, declamatory, and highly emotional style (Germans call it "Pathos"), its sententiousness, the unreality of its plot and setting, so that the spectator identifies with the individual fate of the hero, with the distant scene, and is brought to the point where the "burden of existence" is temporarily lifted from his shoulders. In Brecht's eyes, a contemporary audience at a conventional spectacle is "taken out of itself," worn down through suggestion, and given an image of the world as a fixed and unalterable entity, which must be taken for granted. Additionally, the spectator is infused with the notion that thought determines being. Pent-up feelings are thus "liberated"—the world has been made "visible" to him, but not "transparent." He has been enabled to *see it,* but not *through it.*[12]

And the spectator of this kind of theatre reflects: "Yes, I have felt that. That's the way I am. That's only natural. That'll always stay that way. This man's sufferings affect me deeply, because he has no way out. That's great art: everything is self-evident. I weep with him who weeps, and I laugh with him who laughs."[13]

Though these reflections of Brecht are scattered throughout his writings of this and later periods, they are sufficiently characteristic of his central and basic thinking at this stage, around 1930, to suggest that his theory was being fully organized then, though not completely to be set forth in his *Brief Organon* until some years later. Thus he is voicing a long-standing sentiment, when, while in exile, he addresses actors of a conventional theatre in the following lines:

> For many, the theatre is the abode
> where dreams are created. You, players,
> sellers of drugs, in your darkened houses,
> people are changed into kings and perform
> heroic deeds in safety. In rapture
> over themselves, or seized with pity
> they sit in happy distraction, forgetting
> the toils of daily life. Runaways.
> . . . . Of course, should someone come in,
> his ears still full of the roar of the city,
> himself still sober, he would scarcely recognize
> there, up on the stage, the world he has just left.
> And leaving your house, he would scarcely know
> the world—now no longer king, but lowly man—
> he'd scarcely find himself at home in real life.[14]

What sort of spectator, what sort of audience, then, is Brecht in search of? First of all, he states, the theatre of today fails to understand that it is dealing with "a public of a scientific age."[15] In the face of such an audience, the "sole piety" is to value its intelligence as highly as possible. "I appeal," he says, "to the judgment of human beings."[16] This kind of spectator would bring to the theatre his thinking mechanism and keep it awake. He would come as an *observer* and *critic* of the action that is taking place; he would, so to speak, "stand outside" it. Instead of allowing his feelings to be churned up, and his activity dissipated, he would be provoked— to decisions. In other words, he would also become a "producer," so that "less takes place *in* him, but more *with* him."[17]

An audience that is at home in science and sport can combine both in coming to the theatre. Its symbols are the radio towers, the giant chimneys and conveyors of the Ruhr region, and the stadia and sport palaces of the cities.[18]

Let us now look into the mind of this hypothetical spectator of the new kind of theater. Unlike our other spectator, this one would now reflect as follows:

"I hadn't thought of that. That's not the way it should be. That's very strange . . . , almost unbelievable. That must stop! The sufferings of that man affect me deeply, because there is a way out for him. This is great art—nothing here is self-evident. I laugh at the one who is weeping, and weep at the one who is laughing."[19]

In a later poem he gives us a "final" picture of his kind of spectator:

> Recently I found my spectator.
> On a dusty street
> He held a power-drill in his fist.
> For a brief moment he looked up. And I quickly
> Pitched my theatre between the houses. He
> Looked up expectantly.
> In the bar
> I found him again. He stood at the counter
> Sweat-stained; he was drinking, in his hand
> A sandwich. Quickly I pitched my theater. He
> Looked up amazed.
> Today
> Luck was with me again.
> In front of the railway depot
> I saw him jostled by rifle-butts
> Amid drum-beats—being hustled into war.
> Right there, in the middle of the crowd,
> I pitched my theater. Over his shoulder
> He looked back toward me:—
> And nodded.[20]

Of course, Brecht is not speaking only about his audience, but also about the kind of theatre this audience would "nod" to.

2

What kind of theatre? The creation of this new kind of theatre, in Brecht's words, was a revolutionary act. It was to be a radical theatre, that is, it would go to the root of things. It presupposed, therefore, not only a new aesthetic of the theatre and a new kind of drama, but also an examination of the very basis of these forms and institutions, society itself.

His own artistic activity had now gone through two major phases. The first was marked by a strong anti-bourgeois revolt—under cover of nihilism, individualism, and cynicism, not excluding, however, compassion for the "ignorant armies" of waifs and strays of society, neglected and overlooked and humiliated by it. The second phase exhibits a closer study of the social nexus, behind these phenomena; it shows a greater awareness of the impact of capitalism and money on the world. In general in this phase, Brecht "interprets" or "describes" the world of Weimar, without as yet indicating how it might be changed. As in the first phase man is viewed as man's enemy—wolf to his brother—and the world a ruthless, unchanging battleground of unsatisfied appetites, so in the second phase, that includes *The Three Penny Opera* and *Mahagonny,* man's struggle becomes a struggle for survival, closely bound up with the lack of and need for money and its quest. Here anarchy and partial social understanding stand side by side.

With the 1930's begins the third phase of Brecht's career, in which he succeeds in synthesizing his political and social views—his Marxist studies—with his views of the nature and function of drama and the theatre. He makes practical application of Marxism in his life as well.

This fusion of Marxism, theatre, and life has given a number of Brecht's judges uneasy moments. Literary critics who would recoil in horror at the notion that one could give an intelligent account of T. S. Eliot without reference to his early nihilism and then his later turn toward Anglo-Catholicism, royalism, anti-Semitism (all of these magnanimously dissolved in the generalized "love" of the later poems and plays); or, to take greater names, John Milton, without reference to his Puritanism and anti-royalism; or Dante, without accounting for his relationship to Roman Catholicism and his dream of Empire (one could continue *ad inf.*), critics such as these display a virginal prudery when they approach Brecht's Marxism, as some sort of unbecoming, deviant obscenity, some derangement of the mind of an otherwise gifted—and, but for that, an acceptable—literary talent, if not genius. Armed with unofficial passports into his unconscious, they dwell on potential or latent or overt "masochism," "sadism," "Aesopism," "displacements," or whatever else the prolific vocabulary of modern psychiatry offers them to cover up their own projections. Thus the journalist Willy Haas, for example, attributed Brecht's conversion to Communism to the Amazon craftiness of his wife, Helene Weigel. Another critic, an American, suggests (perhaps in the light of current academic experience) that Brecht's conversion and convictions were accommodations to the demands of his employers who would give him what he wanted—above all, a theatre. Let us, mindful of Virgil's words to Dante, simply repeat with the former: "Non ragionam di lor, ma guarda e passa." ("Let us not speak of them, but look and pass.")

The world-view which underlies Brecht's epic theatre, and which he openly adopts, is Marxist. Marxism posits the existence of a material universe, outside of, independent of, but accessible to man's consciousness, knowledge, and activity, and amenable to his influence. It affirms the primacy of matter. It affirms the *primacy of reality*. This real world, animate and inanimate, is in constant process of change. Change is fundamental. Such changes as occur do so not unilinearly, but often in curves, leaps, or in explosive ways. To understand the world, then, it must be conceived as reflecting *process* and *change*. These occur *dialectically,* that is, as a result of conflict or struggle. Man is a part of this world; he is a part of the social structure of the existing society; and he in turn reflects its character and movemens. His consciousness, too, is a reflection of the society in which he lives, and it too is a determinant factor in playing an effective role in changing both the world around him and himself. It becomes such a factor through "conscious living." This means activity upon the world resulting from a conscious understanding of the world process, change, and the possibility of change. The goal of such "conscious living" is freedom, that is, the achievement of a fully integrated, rich, individual

personality, through the realization of man's creative potential. Such
freedom, however, is not attainable without a conscious understanding of the physical and social laws which control nature and society
and govern the universe. Through an understanding and mastery
of these laws man is enabled to *utilize* them, to turn from being
"slave" to them to being their master. This is what is meant by
emerging from the Kingdom of Necessity into the Kingdom of
Freedom. But he cannot do this alone. For just as human consciousness is the highest manifestation of "matter in motion," so
society too is a manifestation of these movements and conflicts
among men. The history of man is a history of his relation to nature
and the material elements of life: the way he makes his "living,"
how he relates to production and the productive forces of nature
and society—the means of production, their ownership, and the
labor that makes such production possible. History is the epitome
of these processes of change which have taken place in the fundamental relations of production, hence a reflection of the "class-
structure" of society from immemorial times, through feudalism,
capitalism, and on to socialism.

Religion, philosophy, ethics, law, art, and literature are the
superstructures upon this material, economic base. They mirror that
substructure, and the nature of society at a particular epoch in history. But changes in the superstructure do not necessarily take place
immediately or even directly in relation to changes in the substructure. Having, so to speak, "lives" of their own, they play a
part in determining the course of history, though not a primary
one, for they can at times abet, at other times retard the tide of
progress or change; they can aid or obstruct the "reform of consciousness." But progress is ultimately determined by that sector
of society which is most class-conscious and revolutionary—the
bourgeoisie at one time; today and tomorrow the working classes.

This is what Brecht believed. This is also what determined his
attitude toward the theatre. Paraphrasing the celebrated words of
Marx about the function of philosophy in our day, Brecht held that

the theatre was the concern of philosophers, "at least such philosophers who sought not only to interpret the world, but also to
change it."[21]

From now on, Brecht's concern with the theatre will be to use
it not only to interpret the world, but also to change it.

3

To what extent then was the theatre of today capable of fulfilling
this high demand? Was it possible to utilize the old theatre to
reflect the world in its true character: The world in process of
change? Human character in process of change? The human being,
who, as Hegel put it, stands in the "constant process of dissolution
and generation"?[22]

For all men are agreed that today the "discontinuity" of personality is a fact. Whether this "discontinuity" takes the form of "aliena-
ion," "self-division," discord between the "id," the "ego," and the
"super-ego," or between the "unconscious" or "subconscious" and the
"conscious," thinkers of all schools are united in their assertion that
the contradictions between human aspirations and goals and their
fulfillment within our social system have become sharpened to the
point of explosion. All are agreed that there is a dismemberment
and a need for "reintegration." How this latter is to be achieved is
a matter of hard and often harsh dispute. Solutions differ in their
"metaphysic" no less than in their therapeutic cures, both depending
upon their presuppositions concerning the nature of the universe,
the nature of nature; whether they posit a variable, or an eternal
constant; whether that in turn is Oedipal or the Jungian collective
"unconscious"; whether the trouble lies solely within the human
being or outside, or both; or, perhaps in the "stars."

Brecht wrote:

Today, when the human being must be understood as the "sum-total
of all social relations," the epic form is the only one which can embrace
these processes, and which can provide the drama with material for a

comprehensive picture of the world. So too Man—Man in the flesh—is only to be comprehended through the processes in which and in the course of which he exists.[23]

He had, of course, been concerned with "changing" man for some years. In *Mann ist Mann* he had shown the dismantling of a human personality and its reconstruction as an altogether new one. The operation was, so to speak, a one-sided one. Galy Gay, the human object, was acted on without ever himself becoming more than a passive recipient of the action. There was no conflict. The dialectical element was absent.

The epic theatre of Brecht comes into full being when the "dialectical" element makes its appearance. This is what will differentiate it fundamentally from its predecessors and its "epic" contemporaries and successors. For as early as 1930, Brecht had begun to substitute "dialectic" for "epic." And on the analogy of Francis Bacon's *Novum Organum,* as well as the new mathematics (non-Euclidean geometry), Brecht set about constructing the *Brief Organon,* a counterpoise to Aristotle's *Poetics,* calling his own a "non-Aristotelian" poetics—a new poetics for a new world, a new theory of the drama. "Art follows Reality," Brecht wrote.[24]

And just as Karl Marx had asked, in reference to the relationship of Greek mythology and Greek art:

Is the view of nature and of social relations which shaped the Greek imagination and Greek art possible in the age of automatic machinery, and railways, and locomotives, and electric telegraphs? Where does Vulcan come in against Roberts & Co.; Jupiter, as against the lightning rod; and Hermes, against the Crédit Mobilier. . . . What becomes of the Goddess Fame by the side of Printing House Square?[25]

so too Brecht asks: How is it possible to speak of money in the iambic pentameter?

The rate of exchange of the mark, the day before yesterday quoted at 50 to the dollar, now stands at a hundred, and tomorrow may stand even higher. . . . Petroleum resists the five-act structure, the catastrophes of today do not take a straight line, but run in cyclical crises. The "heroes" change with the individual phases, are interchangeable, etc. The graph of human actions is complicated by miscarriages. Fate is no longer a unitary power; rather there are fields of force with counter-vailing currents; power-groups reveal movements not only against each other, but also within themselves.[26]

The old theatre built its materials out of the presuppositions of "eternities," on the basis of the "typical." But how "typical" will our successors regard these so-called "eternals"?

In what sense, then, was Brecht constructing a "non-Aristotelian" poetic? He was directing his attention (and attack) chiefly on three fundamental elements: catharsis, empathy, and mimesis. The first two specifically connect with tragedy; the last with poetry in general. From Aristotle, Brecht took the term "epic" to define the narrative form in which, according to Aristotle, it is possible to describe "a number of simultaneous incidents," and which are not bound by the organic structure of tragedy as to unities, nor in terms of plot complication, rising action, crisis, and resolution. Brecht had already used the term "epic" for theatrical works in the twenties.

But Brecht does not confine himself exclusively to Aristotle in discussing the nature of the "epic" theatre.

For us [Brecht wrote], that is of the greatest social interest which Aristotle sets as the goal of tragedy, namely Catharsis, the cleansing of the spectator of fear and pity through an imitation of incidents arousing these emotions. This catharsis takes place on the basis of a special psychic act, that is Empathy, of the spectator with the individuals whose actions are being imitated by the performers. We designate such a dramaturgy as Aristotelian, if it is producing such an empathy, whether or not it follows or does not follow the rules advocated by Aristotle. The special psychic act of Empathy is produced in various times in altogether various ways.[27]

Actually, Brecht was concerned not so much with disputing Aristotle on tragedy, as the interpretations to which Aristotle has been subjected by his successive commentators and the practitioners of drama.

What had Aristotle actually said about tragedy?

A tragedy . . . is the imitation of an action that is serious, and also, as having magnitude, complete in itself; in language with pleasurable accessories, each kind brought in separately in the parts of the work; in a dramatic, not in a narrative form; with incidents arousing pity and fear, wherewith to accomplish its catharsis of such emotions.[28]

(The curious reader interested in comparing the various renderings of this passage by other translators, will find marked disagreements. Rivers of ink have flown in an effort to explain the meaning of Aristotle's terms.)

Most crucial of all discussions has been that around "catharsis." It is this matter that Brecht is primarily concerned with in redefining the nature of drama. It is probable that Aristotle himself thought of catharsis in medical terms—at least this is the way he discusses it in relation to the purgative effect of music. The comment is made in his work on *Politics* that certain forms of music serve to restore affected persons from sickness (for example from a "frenzy")—"as though they had found healing and purgation . . . , and their souls [are] lightened and delighted." And this, according to Aristotle, also includes those who are "influenced by pity and fear."[29]

For Brecht, catharsis is bound up with the more modern term and concept of "empathy." "Empathy" (Einfühlung) was coined by nineteenth century German aestheticians to define the projection of the recipient of a work of art into it—his identification with it. In drama it is identification with the feelings of actors and their actions on the stage, a merging of the onlooker with the performer and the character he is re-enacting. The notion of empathy was suggested by Aristotle in discussing the nature of the poetic experience:

For the most persuasive poets are those who have the same natures as their characters and enter into their sufferings; he who feels distress represents distress; he who feels anger represents anger most genuinely.[30]

This was given its most popular formulation by Horace, with his famous dictum that "if you would have me weep, you must first of all feel grief yourself."[31]

To produce this kind of identification, the playwright, according to tradition, arouses in the spectator the feelings of "pity" and "fear," of which the latter is purged in witnessing the tragedy.

In trying to come to grips with the problem of "catharsis"—hence with the very nature of tragedy itself—Brecht was touching on one of the most sensitive spots in all dramatic history and theory. He was actually setting the stage for an assault on the very stronghold of the aesthetics of the drama. What is the nature of tragedy and of "catharsis," which it is intended to awaken? What sort of "world-order" (or "disorder") do these presuppose? What is this purging-away or cleansing of feelings that takes place? Why does it, or why should it, take place? Must it take place if the proper effect of a drama is to be achieved? What is this "equilibrium" of the passions that Goethe speaks of as necessary to all dramatic works, this "reconciliation" of pity and fear?[32]

As a Marxist, Brecht would also ask: In what way are the traditional practices and interpretations of "catharsis" themselves the products and reflections of a particular historic period and its Weltanschauung? To what extent may such interpretations be considered (Aristotle's included) "absolutes" or "variables"?

In approaching so complex and controversial a subject, it may be useful to glance at three representative and dominant (non-Marxian) views of tragedy and catharsis: those of Schopenhauer, Hegel, and contemporary psychoanalysis.

For Schopenhauer, the edifying power of tragedy, and its catharsis, consist in persuading the spectator of the need for resignation in the world that is ruled by irrational forces (Schopenhauer's "Will") and an acceptance of suffering as in the nature of the universe—an "awakening in us of the knowledge that the world, that life cannot satisfy us thoroughly and consequently is not worthy of our attachment."[33] Hence, he counsels a reconciliation with the universe as it is. Life is tragedy.

For Hegel, one of the profoundest thinkers on the subject, "tragic resolution" exhibits the fact that "Eternal Justice is operative . . .

under a mode whereby it restores the ethical substance and unity in and along with the downfall of the individual which disturbs its repose." Once more the "rationality of destiny" has been shown. Hegel's Eternal Reason is triumphant, for "Fate drives personality back upon its limits, and shatters it when it has grown overween-ing." Contradictions are "annulled"; the tragic character awakens our "fear" as we contemplate "the might of violated morality," and "pity" as we contemplate the consequences of his own act.[34]

Once again, the spectator's emotional attitude is tranquilized. He is reconciled to an "eternal and just world order."

The contemporary psychoanalyst is also deeply concerned with the problem of tragedy, catharsis, and the pleasures derived from viewing the tragic action. To quote only one representative:

A tragedy acts out two wishes: the first is the child's wish to rebel against the authority of his parents (which the tragedy projects as fate, God, or the social order). The second wish is . . . the wish to be pun-ished for the rebellion. Thus the audience at a tragedy feels fear for its own audacity in rebelling and pity for its own suffering for that rebellion. . . . In other words, catharsis in a psychoanalytic sense, means mastering both the fears of childhood and the adult's pity for the individual (himself) suffering those fears.[35]

Similarly, another view of tragedy allies it with the "monomyth" of the "hero with a thousand faces," whose encounters with hostile forces are finally consummated in symbolic or actual expiations and "resurrections." Here the spectator's "catharsis" is precipitated by the upsurge within him of archetypal recollections "buried in the innermost layers of the group consciousness."[35a]

Taking then these various (and fairly representative) views of tragedy and catharsis, we are in a position to summarize their essential similarities. What is common to all of them is the affirmation of some "absolute" which underlies the tragic view: the "Will," "Eternal Justice, or Reason," and an "Oedipal" or some other "infantile" entity. Catharsis, in one way or another, brings about a state of satisfied equilibrium. Or, to put it more bluntly, it

results in an acceptance of the world-order as it manifests itself and
works out its designs in the characters on the stage. The feelings
of the spectator, now also vicariously involved in these actions and
their outcome, are "purged" out of him.

Brecht subjects all these views and elements to a social analysis.
He turns his microscope even upon this very problem of "feeling."
Just as the theatre needs to bathe its audience in an "illusion" on
the stage to make them forget the world outside, as we have already
seen, it also has a compelling need to exploit their feelings. The
stronger the sense of decay or disintegration in a particular historic
period, the more urgent the demand for an "overflow" of feelings,
to conceal the true state of affairs, and divert from social actions
or reactions. Human feelings are as historically conditioned as
other human activities, Brecht contends. It is not an accident that
Brecht should be, as a German, so completely concerned with an
analysis of "feeling." Students of German history need not be reminded of the various "crises of feeling" that dot its historical
landscape. From Sturm und Drang to Expressionism, their manifestations are startling and explosive. For Brecht too then, feelings
have their social framework and even their social history. The cry
for "feeling" may in one period of history represent a necessary and
positive social demand; at another—taking the form of the "primal,"
the "instinctual" or the "anti-rational"—it may prove ominous. The
dichotomy, artificial as it may be, of heart and head may run its
gamut from the socially valid call of the English Romantics to the
Walpurgisnacht of Nazism. The true social history of attitudes and
expressions of "feeling" is yet to be written. Brecht only attempted
a sketch.

If he tends to extremes, and he does, in drawing a sharp line of
demarcation between the "rational" and the "emotional," and if he
becomes so thoroughly aroused by Einfühlung, let it be remembered
that he was writing in Germany, where its various manifestations
were already touched with tremendous ambiguities and forebodings.
Brecht confessed that it was fascism,

with its grotesque emphasis on the emotional, and to no smaller extent, the deterioration of the rational momentum of Marxist teachings that prompted me to a more forceful emphasis on the rational.[36]

He had had many occasions, since the early nineteen-twenties, to observe Hitler's mastery of Einfühlung. Hitler's theatricality was deliberate and conscious, and directed toward the streets, not the theatre, and meant to make the "people, or better his public, say that which he was saying, or more accurately, feel that which he is feeling."[37] That, Brecht adds, is "empathy on the part of the public . . . , that being carried along, this transformation of all spectators into a unified mass, that one demands of art."[38]

Rejection of empathy [Brecht insisted], does not arise from a rejection of feeling, and does not point in that direction.[39]

What is needed is to take up the same critical position toward emotions as we take toward ideas. Thoughts are subject to correction. So are feelings.[40] Historically, emotions that accompany progress persist as emotions for a long time; and if today we are able to experience and share them through a work of art, it is because the dead of the past are speaking to us in a language that represents the interests of classes in the van of human progress. Such is not the case with fascism, which conjures up emotions that are certainly not inter-involved with the true interests of those who fall a prey to them.[41] If catharsis and empathy have outlived their historic functions and are no longer viable instruments in the new theatre, what can we offer in their place?

Brecht answers, *Verfremdung—Estrangement.*

4

What is Estrangement?

Estrangement [Brecht wrote] of an incident or character simply means taking from that incident or character that which is self-evident, known, or obvious and arousing about them wonder or curiosity.[42]

Hegel had said, "The known, because it is known, is the un-known."[43] In the same spirit, the Romantic poets had striven to make the familiar unfamiliar. Brecht too asks us to look at ordinary phenomena with an attitude of unfamiliarity. For example, he asks us to take our watch in our hand, and examine it.

Have you ever looked at your watch closely? [he asks]. He who asks the question knows that I've looked at my watch quite frequently, but with this question he withdraws from me that which is habitual, that which has nothing to say to me.[44]

You begin to remark what an extraordinary mechanism you are holding in your hand. Now examine it closely!

Estrangement, then, is the process of setting the object you are examining at a "distance," looking at it anew, finding it "strange," and rediscovering it. It is therefore another aspect of the dialectical process which may be schematized as follows:

I understand (that is, I think I understand, because I take it for granted). I do not understand (it looks strange!). I understand anew. I have made the familiar unfamiliar so as to get to know it truly. I have effected a transition from the "What" to the "How."[45]

Now much confusion has been occasioned, not altogether without reason, by Brecht's theory of Verfremdung and its terminology. Brecht's use of the term Verfremdungseffekt, which is sometimes rendered as "alienation effect," involves an ambiguity because it immediately calls to mind the current philosophical, sociological, and psychological uses of "alienation" (in German Entfremdung) which was introduced into European thought by Hegel and Marx. To avoid confusion we shall in these pages use the term "estrange-ment" for Brecht's Verfremdung; and "alienation" for the tradi-tional Entfremdung.

Actually, as we shall see, Brecht's theory of "estrangement" and its practice were invented to combat traditional "alienation" in our society, to counteract it, particularly as it is evidenced in the theatre. As Herbert Jhering expressed it, Brecht's "estrangement" means not estranged or alienated from human beings, but estranged and removed from that which is shop-worn, sentimental, trashy—from the banal and commonplace.[46]

It is meant, as Proust put it in another connection, to break in on the "anaesthetic effect of custom." One might, without being flippant, call Brecht's Verfremdung an alienation of alienation—that is "positive alienation."

For there *is* positive alienation: that necessary early stage in man's development from a creature and slave of nature to its partial master—that self-division which occurs when man separates himself from nature, as its product, and through consciousness and work makes himself its potential ruler. It is his natural advance from "magic," "myth," and "anthropomorphism"—that is, slavery to the inscrutable forces, into a determinant of those forces. Chance gives way to order and predictability; the gods are at first humanized, then "naturalized," and Prometheus surrenders to the lightning-rod. Man becomes capable of looking objectively not only on Nature but into himself, and of analyzing his own thought processes. This, too, is positive "alienation."

But when we speak of alienation today we speak of a process and a resultant that parallel the historical changes of society from a simple economy to a highly complex one, accompanied by a mounting division of labor, a greater and greater concentration of capital, an ever-increasing dominance of the machine, and an ever-aggravated dismemberment of society and individuals.

Man does not experience himself as the acting agent in his grasp of the world, but that the world (nature, others, and he himself) remain alien to him. They stand above him, and against him as objects, even though they may be the objects of his own creation. Alienation is essentially experiencing the world and oneself passively, receptively, and as subject separated from object.[47]

No more does man experience himself in his own right as "productive power," but the "productive power" itself "appears as an alien force outside" of himself, whose changing manifestations now loom as independent of his will and action, "nay, even being the prime governor of these."[48]

Alienation is the loss of control. Producer and product, in the various senses of these words, have become separated. The "product" has been taken away from him and put to uses alien to himself and to society. As man, he has become "atomized," and just as he has lost relation to the product of his labors, so has he lost relationship to the other atomic units—other men. He stands as a "commodity," a thing, single and alone, without the power of communicating with others, and even with himself. The dichotomy between his "private" world and his "public" world seems unbridgeable. The controlling forces outside of himself become more and more anonymous, the more powerful they grow. But he himself has also become anonymous, a shrunken, nameless entity, ever weaker, and reduced, like Kafka's "heroes" to an initial or a numeral, or as in the story "Metamorphosis," to an insect-being, filled with self-contempt, cynicism, and a need for eventual self-destruction. "Mentally and physically dehumanized," as Marx put it, he has become the "self-conscious and self-acting commodity."[49]

Ideologically, alienated man today, having stripped the directive forces outside of himself of their theological vestments, sees them now as crypto-Satanic—incomprehensible, irrational, immoveable, inexorable. "Absurdity" itself is Mephistopheles turned into a vast computer, gleefully watching man, shaped into a card, being "programmed" into varieties of nonentities. Brecht could scarcely have anticipated this new version of Galy Gay. Will the new Galy Gay gleefully accept his "fate"? Will he wish to remain the "expendable thing"? Will he continue to pronounce funeral orations over his own individuality?

These are the problems that Brecht's epic theatre sets itself to answer. For the epic theatre is a process of "demystification" of these hitherto nameless, anonymous forces: To give them name and place, remove from them their inscrutable "mythology," de-Satanize them and de-mythologize them. The essence of the new theatre is to de-alienate man, restore him to a consciousness of his active power, and to retrieve for him his prize possession, his creative potential, as well as his product—to *provoke* him into seeing that change *is* possible!

How can the theatre, and estrangement do that?

Estrangement [Brecht said] means to *historicize,* that is, consider people and incidents as historically conditioned and transitory . . . The spectator will no longer see the characters on the stage as unalterable, uninfluenceable, helplessly delivered over to their fate. He will see that this man is such and such, because circumstances are such. And circumstances are such, because the man is such. But he in turn is conceivable not only as he is now, but also as he might be—that is, otherwise—and the same holds true for circumstances. Hence, the spectator obtains a new attitude in the theatre, the same attitude that a man of the twentieth century has with respect to Nature. He will be received in the theatre as the great "transformer," who can intervene in the natural processes and the social processes, and who no longer accepts the world but masters it.[50]

Estrangement is the "shock" of recognition and self-recognition. Let us, as an example, take one of Brecht's poems, "Ulm 1592," which is sometimes conspicuously displayed on the Bertolt Brecht Platz in Berlin:

> Bishop, I can fly,
> Said the tailor to the Bishop,
> Just watch how it's done . . .

But the Bishop is contemptuous: "This is nothing but lies," he says, "Man is no bird. No man will ever fly." The tailor tries to fly, but is smashed to bits.

> "Nothing but lies,
> Man is no bird,
> No man will ever fly,"
> Said the Bishop to the people.[51]

That is all there is to the poem. This is *estrangement.* For we, the readers today, know differently. Man does fly. Man *has learned* to fly.

Brecht is crying: "Down with the *Inkubusgewohnheiten!* Down with the incubus habits—or the incubus of habit!"

Let us cite another example of estrangement, this time applying it to a familiar theatrical experience, say the play of *King Lear*:

> Take [says Brecht] . . . Lear's anger at his daughters' ingratitude. By means of the empathy-technique the actors can so display Lear's anger that the spectator accepts it as the most natural thing in the world, so that he cannot imagine how Lear could avoid being angry, and he identifies and aligns himself with Lear, feels along with him, and himself becomes angry. By means of the Estrangement-technique, however, the actor represents Lear's anger in such a way that the spectator can only be amazed; that he can imagine other reactions of Lear than merely that of anger. Lear's attitude is "estranged"—that is, it is represented as peculiar, striking, remarkable, as a social phenomenon that is not self-evident.[52]

Suppose, Brecht says in another place, as Lear is about to divide the kingdom into three parts, he were to tear a map in three, fixing the spectator's attention on the fact not only of his kingdom, but also that he regards it as his private domain. Light is thrown on the entire foundation of feudal society.[53]

Thus we penetrate behind the image of a "universal" father, with "universal" feelings of a father in the face of an apparent ingratitude, into a time-conditioned, socially-conditioned set of feelings, emanating from a particular structure of the feudal society. Instead, therefore, of asking us to be carried along, swept along, instead of "mitzureissen," Brecht wishes to tear us away, to make us see the world as it really is. The "fatality" that hangs over human "destinies" is to be exposed in its mechanism. Brecht had of course already dealt with "alienated" man. Baal, Kragler, Galy Gay, Shlink and Garga: each of them in his own way was an outsider in a disordered universe; their activities had taken the form of fruitless wrestling with circumstances or final surrender to them. The universe they inhabited was immutable as well as inscrutable. Estrangement will now demystify this "fatality." The spectator, lifted from the kingdom of illusion into that of reality, will ask:

Why is this happening? Why should this be so and not otherwise? And what can I do about it?

The term "Verfremdung" did not come into being until 1936, when Brecht was in exile, and in connection with the Danish production of his play, *Die Rundköpfe und die Spitzköpfe*. Speaking of Galy Gay, in 1927, he used the word "befremden," to "astonish." "That which the porter Galy Gay does or does not do might perhaps astonish you."[54] Even as late as 1936, Brecht still speaks of an "Enfremdungsprozess" (process of alienation), using the traditional term of Hegel and Marx. It has been suggested that it was Brecht's visit to the Soviet Union in 1935 that finally fixed both the concept and the term; that Brecht might have derived both from the Russian formalist critic Victor Shklovski, who had written of "Art and Artifice" in 1917 and had stated that the "procedure of art is the procedure of estrangement . . . In Tolstoy's work the process of estrangement consists in his not naming a thing by name, but describing it as if one were seeing it for the first time." Shklovski had also spoken of a "device of making something strange"—an act of "creative deformation" that restores sharpness to our perceptions, freeing them from our habitual torpor. He had asked for an artistic procedure which would "deliberately impede" and provoke the reader to a more strenuous effort and a coming to grips with the world.[55]

Other impulses no doubt also came from Brecht's acquaintance in Moscow in that year with the theatre of China, and one of its foremost actors, Mei Lang-fang,[56] which led Brecht to write an essay on the "Estrangement-effect in Chinese Acting," first published in an English version in 1936. Here Brecht noted that the Chinese theatre had long used estrangement effects, such as "symbols," masks, and formal gesticulation. Props were moved during the performance and the actor behaved as if he knew he was being watched, and appeared as if watching himself in the act of acting. Thus, "depicting a cloud, its unexpected appearance, its soft and quick growth, and its quick, yet gradual transformation, he at the same time looks at the audience as if to say, Isn't that the way it happened? Exactly."[57]

But there can be little doubt that the theory of Estrangement was fully developed before Brecht left Germany in 1933.

It is also likely that Denis Diderot's *Paradox of Acting,* written in the 1770's played a part in Brecht's formulations. One remark of the French *philosophe* must have struck Brecht with particular relevance. Diderot wrote,

Have you ever seen engravings of children's sports? Have you not observed an urchin coming forward under a hideous old man's mask, which hides him from head to foot? Behind the mask he laughs at his little companions, who fly in terror before him. This urchin is the true symbol of the actor; his comrades are the symbol of the audience.[58]

In summary then, may one not be permitted to use an analogy familiar to us today out of the realm of psychiatric procedure? Crudely stated, Estrangement resembles the process in which the patient is moved to stand outside himself and view himself. He is taken out of his solipsistic habits, away from everything he has taken for granted as being "normal" or "usual," and brought to see them as stranger and stranger. He proceeds from an assumed "normality" toward a true one. He has changed. The effectiveness of the change is gauged by his capacity to "function"—to act. He has come closer to reality. The spell of the "familiar" (i. e., the unhealthy) has been broken. From being a passive recipient and "sufferer" at the hands of some force obscure to himself, he has turned into an active determinant of his life's course. He has lifted and thrown off the "incubus of habits."

<h1 style="text-align:center">5</h1>

Let us now accompany our hypothetical spectator of the new theatre, and sitting by his side, follow the procedure of Verfremdung and the epic theatre as it is actually practised.

As he enters the theatre, he observes that the curtain is only half the usual height, and doesn't really hide the stage.

Do not seal off the stage.
Leaning back, let the spectator be aware

Of the busy preparations going on
Cunningly intended for him. He sees
A tin moon floating down, a shingle roof
Brought in. Don't show him too much.
But do show him! And, friends, let him be aware that
You are not conjurers, but workers.[59]

He may be surprised to see that the stage, instead of being darkened, is lit up. For, as Brecht said, "we need spectators who are not only awake but alert."[59]

On the curtain a sign is flashed, a motto, or title, or a brief sentence telling the spectator what the play is about. This is not the theatre of the ordinary "surprise."

The curtains part. At once, our spectator may be struck by the decor and props. In place of an elaborately furnished room (or whatever the scene may be depicting), he sees spare furniture, a chair, a table—mere indications, pointers, so to speak, to the play, but integral parts of it. The properties, however, must be chosen carefully—with the same care, Brecht demands

as the millet farmer chooses the heaviest seed for his experiment, and the poet the appropriate words. Search out things that go with the characters on the stage . . . , everything according to age, purpose and beauty, with the eyes of an expert, and the hands of the connoisseur of reality, such as bakes bread, weaves nets, or cooks a soup.[60]

Now suppose the scene takes place in a factory. Ordinarily our spectator would expect a stage set of a complicated structure, with chimneys, railway tracks and sidings, overhead lines, etc. But such a factory could, in fact, be found anywhere, at any time, in a socialist no less than in a capitalist country. Instead, what does he observe on the epic stage? A placard announcing wage-scales; a photograph of the proprietor; a page from the concern's catalogue depicting typical products; perhaps a photograph of a workers' picnic, some Sunday, in the managerial canteen.[61]

An actor or actress steps forward and addresses the audience. How different from being plunged immediately, as in a play of

Ibsen's (with the fourth wall of the living room removed), into the midst of a family intrigue, where almost everything has happened already, and we are only waiting for the outcome! "I am so and so," the Brechtian performer states, "and this is my son, who . . . , and we shall . . ." The performer sounds as if he were pointing out something, demonstrating. He seems to be standing off and away, and almost at a distance from the role he is portraying, as if looking at it too. At that moment he seems to know more about the character than the character himself. He seems more an intermediary between the actor and the spectator, than the participant in the action.

> This imitator
> Never loses himself in the imitation: he never
> Totally changes into him he is imitating.[62]

How that is to be done Brecht illustrates through the now-famous example of a street accident, a "primitive" instance, as it is witnessed and reported by a bystander. Addressing the actors, Brecht instructs them to watch that sort of man as he is describing what has taken place; how he imitates the driver at the steering wheel and the victim. He shows both of them, but not as if the accident could not have been avoided; he shows how it might have been avoided.

> Nothing superstitious about the eyewitness:
> He does not abandon mortals to the stars,
> Only to their own errors.[63]

But the eye-witness always remains himself, the one who is "showing." "The other one has not taken him into his secret; he does not share his feelings, nor his outlook; he knows little about him."

This "actor" of the streets has in fact "estranged" the action by showing alternate possibilities—suppose the victim had put his right foot forward (and actually shows how he does it). These alternate possibilities the epic theatre can fulfil more thoroughly of course by using documents, choruses, projections, and films, as well as interjected songs.

Perhaps our hypothetical spectator (to come back to him once more) is present at a performance of *Mann ist Mann,* in the revised version of 1931. The actors in this new setting move on stilts, with masks. Everything is exaggerated. Our spectator becomes aware of the fact that Peter Lorre, who is taking the part of Galy Gay, appears in different masks, "representative" of four different situations, and that his speech and manner have correspondingly changed. The four masks mark the changes in Galy Gay in the course of the play (Brecht was directing it): the packer's face up to the time of the trial; the "natural" face up to his awakening after being shot; the "blank page" up to his reassembly after the funeral speech; and finally, "his soldier's face."

In each of these situations Brecht (and Lorre) were establishing another very important element of the new acting: the "Gestus" or the "Grundgestus"—the basic gestus or social gestus. Gestus meant not only the ordinary gesture of the actor, but a composite of "bodily posture, accent, facial expression."[64] In fact, it is gesture, speech, attitude, music—the whole complex that is revealed to the audience not by psychological means, but through behavior and action. It is a summation, one might say, of the expression and behavior of human beings toward one another. Gestus might be called a kind of "quotation"—marking out clearly the particular social relationship of the character at a particular time toward another person or persons. Performance of a piece, Brecht wrote, is not a gestus . . . , "if it does not contain a social relationship, like exploitation or cooperation."[65]

Let us take some examples: Thus, the mere strutting of a fascist does not constitute a social gestus. But his strutting over dead bodies does. The fear of dogs by a man is no social gestus; but in a badly dressed man who is constantly at war with watchdogs, it is a social gestus.[66]

Speech, too, has its gestic character, almost compelling the speaker into an attitude consonant with its structure. Take the sentence, "Pluck out the eye that offends thee," and you see at once that it is less gestic than "If thy eye offend thee, pluck it out."[67]

As for the musicians, the spectator will remark, they are not concealed in the pit, but are visible on the stage. When the actor is to sing, he interrupts the action of the play, steps forward and delivers his song. Once more he has separated himself (as with shears, Brecht would say) from the line of the story. The singer does not have the usual "good" voice of the operatic star. He almost speaks his song singingly. The music too has its independence. It acts not as mere accompaniment, but as commentary, and brings its own gestus.

Then there are the placards, statistics, photographs, films, choral passages that intervene. Brecht suggested that the spectator act as if he were looking at footnotes or turning back the pages of a book. This is what he called the "literalization of the theatre."[68]

Provocation? our spectator may ask. Yes indeed, provocation to thought. Provocation to what Brecht regarded as the most pleasurable of human activities—learning, co-production, and fruitful criticism. This is a high demand to make of an audience, but such an audience there was and such an audience must also be created—an audience of a "scientific age,"—a critical audience, in the best sense of the term—that is, a creative audience.

> The regulating of a river's flow,
> the grafting of a fruit tree,
> the education of a man,
> the reform of a state,
> these are examples of fruitful criticism.
> And they are also
> examples of art.[69]

6

What, one may be inclined to ask, becomes of Tragedy in the light of this new view of theatre as "epic," and the replacement of traditional catharsis and empathy by estrangement? Is tragedy on Brecht's term any longer conceivable or even possible?

That tragedy has been disappearing in modern times has been the chief and sad concern of a number of critics of our century.

From Joseph Wood Krutch to Friedrich Dürrenmatt and George Steiner the problem has been analyzed, dissected, and discussed. Tragedy, according to some, has become an altogether questionable entity in an age so decidedly "unheroic" as ours. This alleged disappearance of heroism in a bourgeois society has also, accordingly, eliminated the high inducements to pity and terror. Tragedy, therefore, disappears not because the sources or causes of it have been eliminated, but because the large heroic enterprises and conflicts of a past age, which made possible the tragic fall from on high, have given way to the puny commercial engagements and the petty issues of dreary squabbles of nonentities. One cannot grow sad or rhapsodically proud of humanity (even in its fall) if the fall happens to concern a million dollars rather than the loss of an empire. Tragic issues have disappeared.

On the subject of heroes and heroism Brecht will have many relevant things to say. Heroism is also where you look for it, and how you look at it.

Yet it must be admitted that from Brecht's point of vantage, the vantage-ground of a dialectical materialist, Tragedy disappears. Tragedy, but not tragic issues. Brecht, who sees the world in process of constant change, and as changeable by man, and that in a constructive social direction, and bases himself on the *rational* potential of man to take part in and direct these changes, cannot see the world as essentially and ultimately tragic. For tragedy sees man as caught up in an ineluctable struggle with transcendent forces. These are sometimes viewed as irrational and unalterable; but ultimately they are destructive of man's efforts and goals—though they may frequently display his grandeur. These forces presumably punish man's *hubris*—his excess of pride in the face of a universe that is just. Or they punish him merely for "existing," existence itself having become an original sin; or for some violation of divine law or order. This being the nature of tragedy, Brecht holds it cannot adequately describe the world as it is today.

We may then redefine Tragedy and its embodiment of the "tragic view of life" as that form of dramatic art that displays the frustrated search for freedom in an unfree world. Since such an "unfree" world is, in the Marxist view, a transitional one, Tragedy too represents transitional forms and attitudes, and corresponds to the limitations of the particular period in which it is produced, or which it expresses. Conflicts being the essence of life, the insights Tragedy offers into the nature and heroism of man are of great and profound value. But as man becomes more and more capable of penetrating into the nature of the powers that allegedly frustrate or are destructive of him and his goals, and as he "naturalizes" the immortal gods into natural forces, and in turn learns to command and control them, Tragedy as such disappears, though tragic situations do not. In an era such as ours, when the old is battling with the new, there are bound to be disenchantments, defeats, and disasters. But even these are not ultimate, so long as the human consciousness penetrates to their causes and learns from them.

The philosopher Ernst Bloch has stated the situation of Tragedy in our age in still another way:

If now the basis of tragic emotion is no longer pity and terror, it is no longer even admiration. It is rather, and as such visible within the tragic personae themselves, *Defiance and Hope.* These are the two primary emotional states within a revolutionary relationship, and they do not capitulate before Fatality.[70]

But Brecht's own epic theatre also reflects many elements of a transitional epoch in the process of radical change. Hence it will partake both of tragedy and comedy, and yet will be neither. It will preserve what Ernst Bloch call "joyfulness," in the discovery of the new, the creative, the socially useful, no matter what the expense. Bloch's "defiance" is fused in Brecht's conceptions with the notion of reason and understanding, pressing forward toward a mastery of nature and circumstance. And "hope," that element that is sometimes derided as "utopianism" and which belongs with the best that man possesses, and is the most essential element in his survival, justifying itself against death and defeat—that "hope" in Brecht becomes the recognition and necessity of change.

If we were challenged to find a more precise term for the Brechtian drama, we would be justified in calling it "serious comedy." Comedy, because in comedy the realm of possibilities is infinite; because comedy ranges within the precincts of obtainable and achievable freedom; and the contradictions within human beings and society can be exposed within these contexts as incongruous, irrational, and resolvable. Serious, because between the possibilities and the ultimate realization there is a profound gulf. Brecht's comedy is also "positive" serious comedy, for it establishes itself on the foundation of a critical rationalism, upon science, and scientific discoveries, and believes in the transformation of man and society by social means.

Brecht once said that he might be inclined to allow pity and terror place in the theatre if only

> by terror were meant terror before human beings, and by pity, pity for human beings, and if the theatre were to cooperate in removing these conditions among human beings that generate mutual fear and necessitate mutual pity. For the Fate of Man is now Man himself.[71]

He undoubtedly would have echoed the thoughts of Bernard Shaw:

> I do not want there to be any more pity in the world, because I do not want there to be anything to pity; and I want there to be no more terror, because I do not want people to have anything to fear.[72]

Thus Brecht formed his epic theatre out of a fusion of the Marxist dialectic and the formal aesthetic elements.

That is not to say that, revolutionary as it is, it pretends to total independence of traditional sources. These Brecht freely acknowledged, whether represented by his idol, Charlie Chaplin and his "gestic way of performing", or the Elizabethan chronicle plays, or the Sturm und Drang and the Romantics with their "Illusionsdurchbrechung" (disruption of theatrical illusion); or such twentieth-century novelists as James Joyce, whose *Ulysses* Brecht had examined under prompting of Alfred Döblin (whose own most ambitious experiment in that style was *Berlin Alexanderplatz*); whether Karl Valentin, or the Chinese or Japanese theatre.

Since the term "epic" theatre is sometimes used to cover a number of disparate styles, it may serve somewhat to clarify Brecht's own contribution, if we examine an example of such style in the hands of one of its most expert practitioners, the Frenchman Paul Claudel. In his *Christophe Colombe,* written in 1927, Claudel, like Brecht, was interested in "dissolving" the older forms of theatre and opera, also through use of radical new stage devices. As a matter of fact, Claudel here goes far beyond Brecht in their multiplicity and complexity, coming closer to Piscator in this respect. Brecht's worship of simplicity did not allow for such aggrandizement. Ideologically, Claudel differs from Brecht in that he was converted to Catholicism in 1886, so that this ideological substratum prevails in his work, as Marxism does in Brecht's.

We do not know whether Brecht saw Claudel's *Christophe Colombe* when it was performed, with music by Darius Milhaud, in Berlin in 1930. Claudel introduced an innovation into his script —the film. What he had composed was a grand "spectacle" in twenty-eight scenes, "like a Mass in which the public takes part." The audience participates in this opera by means of a chorus, which cross-examines the hypothetical reader as well as the actors of the story. The play depicts in ritualistic form the *via crucis* of a "saint" —Christopher Columbus—conceived as a missionary of the true faith, Christ's minister. The leitmotifs of this opera might be called, "martyrdom, death, and transfiguration." Epic style is utilized in the character of the narrator who announces the nature of the play; chorus follows with prayer. Projections depict the symbolism of the Creation, and the dove hovering above a globe, the earth. (Colombe means dove.) The drama proceeds to show Columbus at the end of his career, when, poverty-stricken and dejected, he has returned to Valladolid. Narrator and Chorus invite him to die. "Come to us. We are posterity. Only a small border to cross. This is Death." The two sides of Columbus are physically depicted by two persons, Columbus I and Columbus II. The story retraces his career in a number of scenes.

We need scarcely go farther. As antithetical as they can be, here are two forms of the so-called "epic" theatre, Claudel's and Brecht's. The similarities are only outward, in the technical means used. But even here there are gross differences. However, more central than these are the ideological differences and their consequences. Claudel's is a static drama, whatever its literary virtues. It is a didactic piece, true enough, but as Jhering wrote, "the didactic piece that sets out to activate the spectator, only ends by making him passive once more."[73] Claudel sees his hero transfigured through Death; Brecht sees transfiguration possible only in and through Life.

XII

Individual and Community:
The "Lehrstücke"

Who still recalls
the glory of the giant city New York,
in the decade after the great war? . . .
What a people! Their boxers the strongest,
their inventors the most practical,
their trains the fastest,
and the most crowded.
And all that seemed destined for a thousand
    years . . . .

Then one day came rumors of a strange
    eclipse,
on a famous continent . . . .
What bankruptcy! How quickly
her glory has vanished! What a discovery
that her system of social life
showed more shameful weaknesses
than that of humbler folks!

..BRECHT, "Vanished Glory of the Giant
    City of New York"

The political and social crisis in Germany was nearing a breaking
point. Now a committed writer, Brecht sought the most practical
and practicable ways of utilizing his talents and knowledge. Many
other writers and artists, hitherto removed from the political arena,
now began to take a more active part in politics, and associated

themselves with the efforts to rouse, instruct, and move the population. This was the direction taken by composers Kurt Weill and Paul Hindemith; the painter Georg Grosz; the humorist Kurt Tucholsky.

The richest fields of operation were offered by the schools, the workers' organizations, and the political parties. It was for such groups as these that Gebrauchsmusik and Gemeinschaftsmusik (functional and community music) were specifically prepared and written. Other artists used even more immediate ways of reaching people. Thus Brecht and Hanns Eisler, Helene Weigel and Ernst Busch took their songs to the taverns and even to the larger eating establishments. Eisler recalled how the four of them found no hall too large or too small, no theatre too elegant for them to appear in. Thus, the old Philharmonic Hall in the Bemburgerstrasse witnessed the première of Brecht and Eisler's "Lehrstück" (didactic piece), *Die Massnahme,* "but the very next evening," Eisler recalls, "Ernst Busch sang, with me at the piano, in the tiny tavern near Alexanderplatz—and with the same enthusiasm. . . . We took part in the political struggles of the day. When anything serious occurred, the first one to call me up was Brecht. 'We've got to do something pretty fast.' "[1]

The discussions which took place in those days in the homes of these active writers must have been hot indeed. Serge Tretyakov describes one such occasion in Brecht's room, "heavy-blue with cigar smoke." People were sitting around in a circle. In nearby pubs, Communists and fascists were clashing, and blood was flowing. Unemployment was growing. Not without a certain irony, Tretyakov continues:

Everyone is taking part in the talk. In even tones, without unnecessary movements and intonation, decanted judgments pour from these mental retorts of German intellectuals—economists, critics, political scientists, journalists, philosophers—about the events of the day . . .

Then in a rhetorical question,

Comrade Brecht, get up from your lowly seat, and tell us why all these people are here and not with their party cells, or among the assemblies of the unemployed?

Brecht, too, is participating in the discussions, weaving "a fine network of counter-arguments. . . . His face, with its hooked nose, looks like that of Voltaire or Rameses."[2]

It was out of the crisis, and the need to meet it, that Brecht's "didactic plays," the Lehrstücke took shape. They were composed more with an eye to the participants in them than the audiences, and they mark a highly interesting, though controversial, stage in Brecht's development.

Bourgeois philosophers [he wrote] make a distinction between the active man and the reflective man. The thinking man draws no such distinction.[3]

It was the function of the Lehrstück to make of the participants both active and reflective beings. The principle which underlay these attempts was "the collective practising of art," which would also instruct in certain moral and political ideas. The origins of the Lehrstück go far back, to the Jesuit and humanist drama of instruction. Its contemporary impetus came from the Neue Musik movement of Donaueschingen and Baden-Baden. To build "community sentiment through community performing activities," to arouse "collective feeling" and "collective consciousness," or as Brecht put it, "lernend zu lehren" ("in learning, to teach"), these were the principal goals.

Brecht had recently become interested in the Japanese Nō-drama. His friend Elisabeth Hauptmann translated them for him from the English versions of Arthur Waley. The Nō-drama appealed to Brecht, for they presented the formal and traditional Japanese plays on a bare platform; the actor moved in a stylized fashion, his face masked or expressionless. Props were sparingly used, and always with direct significance; the musicians, few in number, and the chorus were visible and seated on the stage. The voice of the Japanese actor "moved lyrically . . . . between speech and chant, functioning as a musical instrument."[4]

At its simplest, the Nō-play consisted of a dance preceded by a dialogue, explaining the meaning of the dance, or introducing the circumstances that led to the dancing of it.[5]

The Nō actor sometimes addressed the audience directly, was interrupted by the chorus, and the entire action of the play was carried on like a ritual, with a distinct didactic purpose.

It can be readily seen that such drama would appeal strongly to Brecht. One might almost say that Brecht's own didactic plays are Nō-plays moved from their fourteenth-century environment into the present, supplanting the Buddhist ideology with a Marxist dialectic.

For the world in which Brecht's Lehrstück moves is that of modern science. Its moral basis is provided by the credo that "doing" is better than "feeling." Its goal is not to offer "pleasure" but "instruction."[6]

The course of the Lehrstück in Brecht's hand shows the same change and development as the rest of his work. The social and political line becomes sharper with the years, until finally it becomes overtly Communist.

Charles Lindbergh's solo flight across the Atlantic in 1927 had electrified the world. For Brecht it was a revelation of the power of man to overcome nature. The first of Brecht's Lehrstücke was devoted to the American flyer and was written in 1928-1929. Originally it was entitled *Der Flug der Lindberghs* (*The Flight of the Lindberghs*). Subsequently Lindbergh's identification with the political right led Brecht to change the title to *Der Ozeanflug* (*The Ocean Flight*). The principal character was renamed "The Flyer." The essence of the piece remained unchanged, a glorification of one of Brecht's favorite themes—the conquest and transformation of nature and their meaning for man's future. It was written as a radio play for boys and girls. As performed at Baden-Baden it utilized a score by Kurt Weill and Paul Hindemith, a radio orches-

tra and singers, a "listener" who either sang or spoke the part of
Lindbergh, "without," as Brecht insisted, "identifying with the text
—stopping at the end of every verse."[7] In the background of the
stage in large letters appeared the "theory" to be demonstrated.
"This exercise is to subserve discipline, which is the basis of freedom."

This Lehrstück was published as the first in a series of pamphlets
Brecht called *Versuche* (*Experiments*).

The notes that are struck in this Lehrstück, halting and somewhat immature as it may be, will resound again with a deeper and
statelier orchestration in Brecht's *Galileo,* to which this earlier
didactic piece could serve as prologue.

A section of the play entitled "Ideology" proudly proclaims the
central theme:

> Many say the Time is old,
> But I have always known this is a new Time.
> I say to you, not of themselves
> Rise houses like mountains made of steel,
> Multitudes move into cities, as if waiting for something,
>
> And on the laughing continents one hears:
> The vast and terrifying sea is really only
> A tiny pond.

The starkly simple text and music, sometimes deliberately naive,
have a primitive and muscular impressiveness. The Radio (at the
beginning) summons all participants, in the name of the community, to reenact the first solo flight of the Atlantic, and turning to
the Flyer, bids him board his machine, for Europe awaits him. The
Flyer responds simply: "I am boarding the plane." Each of the
seventeen sections carries a title, such as, "The Summons to Everyone," "American Newspapers Laud the Flyer's Daring," etc. Lindbergh (The Flyer) speaks:

> My name is Charles Lindbergh
> I am twenty-five years old.
> My grandfather was Swedish. . . .

> I fly alone.
> In place of a companion I take gasoline
> I fly without a radio. . . .[8]

As the flight proceeds, the poetry becomes more prominent. Various other participants in the play begin to speak through the Radio: New York City, the S.S. *Empress of Scotland* at sea, the Fog, the Snowstorm, Sleep, Water, America.

Lindbergh fights the natural forces, asserting "I am not alone," for seven men helped him in building the *Spirit of St. Louis* in San Diego. (Hence the plural of the title.) There are therefore, he says, eight of us here. He fights snow, ice, and sleep, but he declares, "I am not tired."

The section "Ideology," from which we have already quoted, re-enforces the nature of the Flyer's mission by declaring that this flight is a war against the primitive, "an effort to improve the planet, like to the dialectic of economy, that seeks to change the world from the ground up."[9]

Actually, as the Flyer declares, this is a flight to liquidate the hereafter and banish whatever gods there be, wherever they may come into being.

> When I am flying, I am
> a thoroughgoing atheist.

For God, Lindbergh states, arises where there is ignorance and the disorder of human classes; where there is exploitation. But he vanishes "under the sharper microscopes," and through the "cleansing of cities and the annihilation of misery."[9]

The piece concludes with a "Report Concerning the Unattainable": For one thousand years only the birds were sustained in the air; all else toppled. But toward the end of the second millennium,

> Our steel innocence
> rose up in the air,
> showing the possible,
> without letting us forget
> the *Unattainable*.
> To this we dedicate our report.[10]

There is a certain crude (if fetching) naiveté in the vociferous atheism that takes the edge off the more valid paeans to the mastery of nature, and the transformation of society made possible thereby. No less startling is the admission of the presence of the "unattainable" in nature, so contrary to the tenor of the whole piece, not to mention the Marxist dialectical point of view, which it presumes to convey, if only partially. This is still the Brecht of 1928-1929.

It seems almost as if at this time he is obsessed by the conquest of the air. For the succeeding Lehrstück, the *Badener Lehrstück vom Einverständnis, (The Baden Didactic Play of Acquiescence)*, which was produced at Baden-Baden on July 28, 1929, with a score by Paul Hindemith, treats of the same subject as the Lindbergh play, but in an altogether different and in many respects startling manner. It raises a very touchy problem.

Four airmen have crashed—a pilot, and three mechanics—in trying to cross the Atlantic. They are in need of help. They are in danger of dying. They ask for water. Shall they be helped or not? That is the question the chorus must answer. Actually, there are two choruses to debate this question: a "learned" chorus, and a "mass" chorus.

The problem is enlarged to a debate: Does man help man? The Leader of the Learned Chorus enumerates the various scientific and mechanical advances of which the age could boast: the steam engine made "by one of us," astronomy, physiology, natural history; the fact that "one of us flew over the ocean and discovered a new continent." But to each of these assertions the Learned Chorus replies: "Bread did not thereby grow cheaper," and adds, "But poverty increased in our cities, and now for a long time no one knows what man is."[11] On the screen flashed pictures showing men slaughtering other men. The conclusion reached is: *"Man does not help man."*[12] The arguments take a strange turn, and the "mass chorus" proclaims that violence rules the world, and that to deny help, as well as to obtain help, violence too is required. "Therefore, do not ask for

help, but do away with violence."[13] In other words, change the
world! The chorus then calls on the wrecked airmen to accept
death—to accept the extinction of their individuality. But the pilot,
a famous flyer, refuses to yield to this verdict. He is a strong individualist, who has flown for glory, who has never been praised
enough, and can never get enough praise, and who flies only for
the sake of flying. "I will never die," he says.[14] He must perish. He
has no further social function. He does not belong in the kingdom
of the collective, of those who understand the nature of the world.

The chorus then addresses the three other airmen, who have
accepted the verdict. It directs them, since they "are in accord with
the flow of things," not to sink back into nothingness, but to rise
up, ("dying your death as you have performed you work"), and
rebuild "our plane," "to fly for us," "and to march with us, and
with us to change the world," removing disorder of human classes,
exploitation, and ignorance.[15]

In preparation for the agreement or acquiescence, the flyers must
first be ready to become "nothing," so that they may become something; they must attain to their "smallest greatness" only through
an acknowledgment of their individual nothingness: that "when
they die, no one is dying."

Having improved the world, the chorus continues, having perfected the truth, they must perfect the perfected truth, change the
changed man, and changing the world, they must change themselves.

In one other significant respect, the Badener Lehrstück goes
beyond the *Flight of the Lindberghs*. The flyers, in repeating portions of the earlier "Report concerning the Unattainable," in their
initial chorus, amend it:

> Toward the end of the second millennium
> our steel innocence
> rose up in the air
> showing the possible
> without letting us forget
> *the not yet attained.*[16]

What a long way we have come from the nihilistic individualism of *Baal*! There, extinction of personality was tantamount to achieving a unity with nature—a positive thing. On the negative side, it was a phase of the battle against bourgeois individualism. In Galy Gay it was a means of survival. Now extinction is a prelude to a positive, social resurrection.

If we may use another figure of speech, it is as if Brecht were intent now on slashing through the jungle with his machete, cutting down right and left the tangle of individual nihilism, and in proceeding to make a clearing, were tearing down all the vegetating growth. This uprooting of the individual personality, of the ego, appeared pleasingly to a number of Brecht's former opponents as some sort of secular approximation of the Christian ideal of "renunciation" as well as a "searching of the conscience"—the attainment of the religious "consensus." As such, the piece was welcomed by them. For support, they went to the almost liturgical language of Brecht's text, the language of "acquiescence."

> When the thinking man prevailed over the
> storm, he prevailed because he knew the
> storm, and was in accord with the storm.
> Therefore, if you would prevail over
> dying, you prevail over it if you know
> dying, and are in accord with dying.[17]

That to Brecht this "Einverständnis" meant not merely a passive consenting to what is, but an active consenting through understanding, and coming to an understanding *with* something—people, things, ideas—seemed to have escaped these critics. But Brecht was at fault here. The problem is formulated with such bare stringency, the question is set so abstractly, that the mind is confused. Abstract individuality is enjoined to disappear in an abstract collective. Of course, one needs to understand Brecht's suspicion of bourgeois philanthropy, with its anachronistic morality. "In a system founded on violence, all help is treacherous, self-interested. One must attack cruel reality with even greater cruelty."[18]

The paradigmatic Brecht has taken over. Individuality in our world, he is saying, is a meaningless, useless thing. To learn *that* is essential. But is it also necessary to affirm it to the point where elementary help is denied to one in need, even if he is an individualist? Few human beings, of any persuasion, whether Marxist or not, would be ready to accept such a rigid conclusion.

As if the cantata itself were not provocation enough, Brecht introduced a grotesque and macabre interlude to underscore the theme that man does not help man. Three clowns appear, of whom one, a giant, Herr Schmidt, allows himself to be sawed apart limb by limb by the other two, in illustration of how "man helps man." As was to be expected, there was a scandal. It was not alleviated by the showing of films depicting killings. Gerhart Hauptmann, one of the spectators, is reported to have left in a rage. A critic is said to have fainted. Later, dissensions broke out between Hindemith and Brecht, each desiring changes the other vetoed, so that in the impasse the work could no longer be performed.

In after years Brecht recalled:

At the performance of the *Badener Lehrstück,* the playwright and the composer were visibly present on the stage and intervened constantly. The playwright indicated the spot where the clown should perform, and when the public received the film depicting dead people with noisy disapproval, the playwright directed the speaker to announce at the end: "There will be one more showing of death scenes which have been received with such antagonism." And the film was repeated.[19]

He had, then, reached the point where the pendulum of individuality had swung all the way over. But he was not yet through with the problem. The voluntary and rational acceptance of the extinction of personality—the "agreement"—continues to haunt him. In Arthur Waley's versions of the Nō-plays he found one that was greatly to his taste at this time, and that underscored the theme of "acquiescence." It was called *Taniko,* written by Zenchiku, of the school of Nō-plays established by the great master and theoretician, Seami Motokiyo (1363-1444). Like Brecht, Seami was concerned with adapting traditional materials to the stage of his day. There were other theatrical similarities in their views.

Elisabeth Hauptmann translated *Taniko,* or *The Valley Hurling,* for Brecht. A Teacher announces his intention of undertaking a pilgrimage of ritual mountain-climbing. A pupil of his, whose father is dead and whose mother is sick, begs to go along, so that he might pray for her recovery. It is a difficult and dangerous undertaking. Heedless of the pleas of his mother, the boy insists on going. The arduous journey proves too much for him, and he falls sick. According to the "Great Custom," he must be cast into the valley. The boy accepts his fate stoically. In sorrow the pilgrims fulfill the claims of the "Great Custom":

> Then the pilgrims sighing
> for the sad ways of the world
> and the bitter ordinances of it,
> made ready for the hurling.
> Foot to foot
> They stood together
> heaving blindly,
> none guiltier than his neighbor.
> And clods of earth after
> and flat stones they flung.[20]

In this Japanese play, prayers prove effective, fortunately, and a spirit appears carrying the restored boy in her arms.

Brecht's *Jasager* (*Yes-sayer*) is a replica of the above Nō-play, and was first produced on June 23, 1930, at the Zentralinstitut für Erziehung und Unterricht in Berlin. The score was by Kurt Weill, and the performers were schoolboys and an amateur orchestra. The play opens with the Great Chorus reciting that it is "essential to learn consent." In Brecht's version of the story, the expedition undertaken by the teacher is designed to seek counsel and medical aid to counter a devastating plague. The boy joins in order to obtain medicines for his sick mother. He falls by the wayside, and the "Great Custom" requires that he be asked for his consent to stay behind. The boy consents. "You must not turn back for my sake.

I agree to be left behind. But because I am afraid to be left dying here alone, cast me into the valley." This is done. Three students stand in front of the boy, hiding him from the audience, and the boy (out of sight now) says:

> I well knew that I might lose my life
> on this journey. . . .
> Take my pitcher,
> fill it with medicines
> and bring it to my mother
> when you go back.[21]

Bewailing the sad ways of the world and its bitter laws, they cast him into the valley.

> Foot to foot they stood
> Together
> at the edge of the abyss
> and cast him down with eyes closed,
> none guiltier than his neighbor,
> and threw clods of earth
> and flat stones after.[21]

Once again, the play aroused lively controversy. Since its contents was not overtly political, bourgeois critics, religious and lay, voiced approval. Walter Dirks spoke of the sacrifice of the boy as an acknowledgment that the world was God's, whose voice must be hearkened to, "and in full freedom obeyed."[22] Karl Thieme, who had anathemized *Hauspostille* as the "Devil's Breviary," now spoke with awed reverence: "Acquiescence, consensus, and sacrifice of life for an ailing humanity, not in self-service or heroism, but as the simplest common custom that has been handed down to us—we know no one who has known to preach it in such immediacy as this atheist."[23]

But those who might have been considered closer to Brecht were not so kind. Frank Warschauer, in *Die Weltbühne,* entitled his article, "No! to the Yes-sayer." "All the evil ingredients of reactionary thinking, founded on senseless authority," he wrote, could be read into the play, though effected with great artistry. "This Yes-sayer reminds us strongly of the Yes-sayers during the War."[24]

But the most incisive and perceptive critics and discussants of the Lehrstück were to be found among the pupils of the Karl Marx School in Berlin-Neuköln. They asked relevant questions: Why couldn't the boy's companions have saved the boy by tieing a rope around him? Was the decision really a necessary one? Why didn't the entire company turn back? And take the boy with them? Did the advantage to be gained by the expedition outweigh the boy's death-sacrifice?

Brecht, who was always responsive to cogent criticism, rewrote the play. He turned the Yes-sayer into a No-sayer, the *Jasager* into a *Neinsager*. The constructive amendment involved the conclusion. The boy is not in accord with the "Great Custom." The others ask, Why not? Did he not agree at the outset to do everything that was necessary?

The boy replies:

The answer I gave you was false, but so was the question you asked. He who says A need not necessarily say B. He may even recognize that A is false . . . Your learning is false. . . . And as for the Ancient Custom, I see no sense in it. Furthermore, I need a new Custom, one we must immediately introduce: Namely the Custom of rethinking every situation.[25]

The others are convinced, and the Great Chorus announces:

> And so the friends took their friend
> and established a new custom
> and a new law
> and brought the boy back.
> Side by side they pressed.
> Against ridicule,
> against laughter, with eyes open,
> none more craven than his neighbor.[26]

So far so good. But in reality Brecht had sidestepped the true issue. For he had substituted for the original expedition, undertaken with the high social purpose of aiding the community against a plague, a less pressing and serious one, a journey of "exploration," and thus, in fact, had blunted the moral impact of the solution.

Brecht insisted that henceforth both the *Jasager* and the *Neinsager* be performed together. The philosopher Ernst Bloch, commenting on this dialectical twofold answer to a problem, recalls other instances of such double or antithetical endings, as in Goethe's *Stella,* one version ending in a reconcilement, another tragically; also the parallel instance of Goethe's *Tasso* and the *Ur-Tasso.*[27]

However, we must rest satisfied with Brecht's solution, which, as John Willett says, is humanistic, happy, if not altogether heroic.

From these Lehrstücke one almost obtains the impression that one is looking into a transparent chemical retort, in which the experimenter Brecht was working out questions very close to his heart. Here he mixed and observed the reactions generated by the theoretical and practical problems of the theatre, but also the moral and social problems of the day, as well as his own very profound personal ones. The transition from nihilism to Marxism, like everything else in Brecht, took on the practical but difficult experimental character of a scientific procedure. In everything, it was necessary for him to push to a dialectical extreme, before finding the suitable middle ground. That is why, perhaps, the great Soviet film director Sergei Eisenstein, if correctly reported, saw in him the "persistent professor wielding a political pneumatic drill against the stone wall of conscience, which he could not fire with passion."[28]

He was not yet aware that it is not "extinction of the ego" that is paramount, but the extinction of a certain kind of ego; that the ultimate solution lay in the development and enrichment of the ego to the point where it realizes that these are possible only through a *productive interrelation* with other egos.

But it was the next Lehrstück that was destined to evoke the most heated and most virulent (also, paradoxically, the most gleeful) controversy, drawing in the political right, center, and left. *Die Massnahme* (*The Measure Taken,* or *The Expedient*) is in some ways Brecht's most pointed, direct, and controversial play. It was to be the last of the more abstract treatments of the problem of individual and community claims.

Once more it is in the form of a secular cantata. The background is Chinese. A "control chorus"—an adjudicating Communist body, a sort of Communist "conscience"—addresses Four Agitators who have presumably returned from a mission in Mukden. Praising them for their successful achievement, it expresses approval of what they had done. But the agitators announce the death of one of their comrades, a well-meaning, sincere comrade, whom the three others were forced to kill since he jeopardized the entire movement. And now they ask for a verdict. The "control chorus" requests them to reenact the whole enterprise, before it passes judgment.

In eight scenes we are presented with the story of *The Measure Taken*. Three party workers have arrived from Moscow in Mukden, where they are joined by a fourth one at the frontier, one well acquainted with the country, and capable of serving as guide. Before proceeding on their joint mission, each of them effaces his personality. Each assumes a mask, thus symbolizing the sacrifice of his personal identity. The native comrade is young, passionate, and impatient. While they are carrying on their work among the natives, he gives way to his personal feelings time after time. He is overcome by the misery he sees around him—coolies dragging the rice-barges, unshod, slipping in the mud. He tries to help them by shoving stones underneath their feet, a hopeless undertaking. On another occasion he opens himself to a policeman's attack as he distributes leaflets, and thus alerts the authorities to the presence of the agitators. He frustrates the collaboration of a temporary ally, a capitalist who wishes to aid the natives with arms against a foreign imperialist power, through an outburst of just, but at the moment most impolitic, anger. Finally, he jeopardizes the entire venture by prematurely encouraging an uprising, and then in a fury, he tears off his mask of anonymity and reveals himself to the enemy. Thus he forces his comrades to a most painful decision. Measures must be taken to safeguard the mission. He must disappear without a trace, for the enemy is at hand. He is consulted, and "agrees" to his own death. He is shot and thrown into a chalk-pit.

In each of his acts, the young man has allowed his immediate

personal feelings to master his reason; his own momentary reactions
to outweigh the ultimate purposes and goals of their joint activity.
The "control chorus" had reminded them all that to achieve what
they proposed, it might be necessary for them to submit to all sorts
of humiliations, even "baseness," so that they might be enabled to
extirpate baseness. (How often Brecht will return to this saddening
thought—that force is needed to quell force; unkindness to crush
unkindness!)

> Who are you?
> Sink into the dirt.
> Embrace the butcher.
> Change the world. It needs it![29]

The young comrade who had been listening impatiently to the
singing of coolies at work, thus "masking the pain of their labors,"[30]
and who had risen up enraged against the merchant because he is
revolted by the latter's realistically cynical song about "merchandise,"
in which he includes man:

> What after all is a man?
> Do I know what is a man?
> The Lord knows what's a man!
> I don't know what's a man.
> All I know is his price,[31]

in a final access of rage and disgust as well as impatience, calls upon
the "classics of Communism" for an answer:

Do our great classics then allow misery to wait? And do they not
provide that every wretched human being be helped at once and before
all else? Then the classics are dirt, and I will tear them to shreds![32]

And he does so, and exclaims, "I give up all agreement with the
others. I will do alone what is human." And he reveals himself.

For the others there is no way out. They hesitate, consider other
possibilities, but in vain. For, as they say,

> It is fearful to kill.
> But not only others, ourselves we will kill
> if necessary.

> Since only by force can this murderous world
> be changed,
> as every living creature knows.
> Not yet is it given us not to kill,
> we said.
> And at one with the inflexible will
> to change the world,
> we took the measure.[33]

The "control chorus" judges that what the comrades had done was right. "Not you have given the verdict," they say, "but reality." For how much is needed to change the world: anger, tenacity, knowledge, rebellion, swift action, profound thought, patience, infinite persistence and endurance, "understanding of the one, understanding of the whole." For only by understanding reality, can we alter it.[34]

Hanns Eisler supplied the score for this Lehrstück, their first extensive collaboration. The cantata was to be performed at the music festival in Berlin, in 1930. The directorate of the festival consisted of Hindemith, Heinrich Burkard, and Gerhard Schuenemann. Slatan Dudow was scheduled to direct the performance. But the radical text and Eisler's revolutionary settings met with the opposition of Hindemith and his colleagues. They asked Brecht to submit the text to a committee for a kind of political inspection. Brecht refused, and in turn suggested that Hindemith resign in protest against the implicit censorship. *Die Massnahme* was thereupon rejected because of the "artistic mediocrity of the text."

Whereupon Brecht and Eisler turned to the workers' choral societies, and with the cooperation of the Arbeiterchor of Grossberlin, had the work performed at the Grosses Schauspielhaus, Berlin, on December 10, 1930. Among the actors who participated were Helene Weigel (as the young agitator), Ernst Busch, and Alexander Granach.

Fritz Sternberg was witness to the profound effect of this cantata. *The Measure Taken,* he reported, gave rise to innumerable and heated discussions and controversies. But one thing impressed him.

The working people sang the songs of the Lehrstück, at last having discovered words and music that had a contemporary bearing upon their own problems. This was as true for Social Democrats as for Communists.[35]

Eisler's music had caught the true essence of the words, and the songs became celebrated in their own right. Eisler, who was schooled in the most advanced musical idiom of the day, that of Schoenberg and Anton Webern, now had succeeded in simplifying his musical expression, without cheapening it. Fusing the traditional Lutheran chorale, the popular folksong, and the jazz idiom, he, in his own words, "dissolved conventional musical language" into something fresh and new.

Brecht's language too had acquired an almost classical simplicity —even austerity—and, in many passages, grandeur. For the first time the class-struggle found the poetic voice that corresponded to its mission.

Take, for example, the song "In Praise of Illegal Work":

> Schön ist es
> Das Wort zu ergreifen im Klassenkampf.

> It is lovely
> To seize the word in the class-war.
> And with loud and ringing voice to urge the masses
>   to battle,
> Stamp down the oppressor, and free the oppressed.
> Hard and useful is the daily work
> The patient and secret weaving
> Of the party's net in the face
> Of the exploiter's gun-barrels.
> To speak—
> But to hide the speaker.
> To triumph—
> But to hide the victor.
> To die—
> But to hide his death.

> Who would not do much for glory?
> But who would do it for silence?
> Yet the needy host invites honor to his board,

> From cramped and crumbling huts speaks
> Irresistible greatness.
> And Fame asks in vain
> For the doer of great deeds.
> For one moment only,
> Come forward, you unknown ones,
> With faces hidden,
> And receive
> Our thanks![36]

There is the same simplicity and conviction in the "Song of the Boatmen," "Praise of the Party," and the poetical addresses of the choruses.

The debate over *Die Massnahme* is still with us today, as heated as it was in 1930. Critics of various persuasions and colors have found this piece a useful stick with which to beat whatever "dogma" they wanted, and the most disingenuous have been those who declared themselves as most friendly to the piece and its author. One is tempted to paraphrase a celebrated saying, and apply it in this connection: If you have a critic for a friend, you don't need an enemy. Critics have seen themselves, their Weltanschauung (not to mention their Weltschmerz!) mirrored in this Lehrstück. Thus one critic sees Brecht prophetically foretelling the Moscow "purge trials, and Stalinist Communism."[37] Others, like Herbert Lüthy, perceive Brecht as "a monk—though a false one—rather such for the sake of the style and cassock, than for belief, and perhaps for that reason capable of writing *Die Massnahme*, the most significant, if not the only bolshevist drama."[38]

Another journalist, Willy Haas, writes:

Die Massnahme was the first piece by Brecht which found the most complete party-official Stalinist approbation. . . . Here Brecht unrolls the whole panorama of Jesuitical Machiavellianism (which has scarcely anything in common with the real Jesuit Order).[39]

On the Communist side there were serious reservations. The most forceful argument at the time was advanced by the critic Alfred Kurella in the publication of the International Association of Revolutionary Writers (*Literatur der Weltrevolution*) of Moscow. Kurella had the advantage of having seen the very first version of *Die Massnahme,* which Brecht immediately revised, and which, to our best knowledge, no longer exists. Apparently Brecht modified the incident of the killing, by having the young comrade accede to it of his own free will. More crucial and relevant, though, were Kurella's objections to Brecht's rather rigid severance of "reason" and "emotion," in regarding them as opposed to one another.[40]

It cannot be denied, however, that Kurella is right. At this time Brecht did divorce feeling and reason mechanically, just as he tended to separate "pleasure" and "instruction" in his discussion of the Lehrstück. Both positions he was in time to modify radically. Brecht believed that his medical experiences and studies had "immunized" him strongly against "influences of emotional sort."[41]

O. Biha, in *Die Linkskurve,* reproved the abstract attitude of Brecht, who, he claimed, drew not upon experience but only upon theory for his knowledge of Communism. Why, he asked, was the young comrade entrusted with ever more difficult tasks, when it was obvious he was failing at the less difficut ones? But the writer welcomed Brecht and greeted him on "joining our forces."[42]

Public discussions took place a week after the première of *Die Massnahme.* A not unbiased hearsay report has been recorded by the critic Karl Thieme:

Bert Brecht declared that he would be ready to change a number of passages of his play should the discussion warrant it, and in part he had already done so in response to certain objections, as for example in the death of the young comrade, who would now be made to ask whether there was no other way out, and would himself be compelled to answer in the negative. The discussion concentrated principally on the killing of the young comrade. The Communists would not agree that this was Communist practice. The Communist way was expulsion from the party. . . . The attitude of the Communists [toward the play] was clarified as follows: Everywhere revolutionary theory is taught, it is expressed clearly and classically; for example, in the passage concerning the eyes of the individual, and the eyes of the Party. But where revolutionary practice is taught, Brecht has failed, because he was ignorant of party practice.[43]

To the end of his days, as we shall see, Brecht was troubled by the problem of force and the thought that while force rules it can only be overcome by force, and paradoxically, only eliminated by force. Yet such, he was convinced, was the situation in the world today—a situation that he expressed poignantly while in exile:

> And yet we all know
> Even hatred of baseness
> Distorts the features.
> Even anger at injustice
> Makes the voice grow harsh. Alas, we
> Who wished to lay the foundations of kindness,
> Could not ourselves be kind.[44]

One cannot help wondering, however, if *The Measure Taken* were not a Communist piece, and were considered abstractly, would its ethical conclusions really be deemed exceptionable? Is not self-sacrifice of the individual in the name of the communal good in a great emergency (say on the battlefield) or in the name of some great religious, social, political or ethical ideal, taken for granted in our society, and eulogized as a high "moral" imperative? Are we not all tacit worshippers of saints? Why then should martyrdom in the name of one cause lead to canonization, and in another to obloquy?

Is it possible to lay "the foundations of kindness" in our society without serious risks? That is the question Brecht tries to answer in the next Lehrstück, *Die Ausnahme und die Regel* (*The Exception and the Rule*). In the *Badener Lehrstück* he had stated that "man does not help man." Suppose a man should help another— what happens?

Across an Asian desert, a merchant, eager to reach a newly discovered oil-well well ahead of his competitors, races toward his goal, accompanied by a native guide and a coolie. Suspicious, and always on the defensive, but also arrogant and cruel, especially when they enter upon an unguarded stretch of wilderness, the merchant is left alone with the coolie, having previously dismissed the guide.

He prepares himself for the hardships of the trek by hiding an extra flask of water. The coolie, ignorant of this fact, on one occasion offers his own flask to the merchant, who, mistaking the gesture for an intended attack with a stone, kills the coolie. Arrived at his destination, he is brought to trial by the coolie's widow, but is exonerated by the judge.

For what does the judge hold? Is it not more credible that the coolie approached the merchant to kill him rather than to help him? For did he not belong to a class that could in all good reason feel itself taken advantage of in the distribution of water? And would it not seem reasonable that he would seek to avenge himself? As for the merchant, how could he be led to believe in an act of comradeship at the hands of his exploited coolie? Reason would tell him that he was in mortal danger.

The accused [the judge concludes] has therefore acted in justifiable self-defense, irrespective of whether he was actually threatened or only felt himself threatened. Under the given circumstances, he must have felt himself threatened. The accused is herewith acquitted, the plea of the dead man's wife is herewith rejected.[45]

We live in a world, Brecht says, where violence and terror are taken for granted. That is the rule. Our system of justice takes this for granted too. Exceptions amaze us. We cannot believe them possible. For kindness itself may be a form of treason to the doer. A system built on violence measures all acts in terms of violence. For this is a time of "bloody confusion, of ordered disorder, of planned arbitrariness, of dehumanized humanity."[46] In such a system "humaneness is an exception, and he who shows himself human must pay for it."[47] Once again, the adjuration: Find nothing unalterable!

In this and the preceding Lehrstück, Brecht had brought this genre to artistic perfection. Unfortunately, *The Exception and the Rule* contained more than a touch of prophecy of things to come. It was not produced in Germany. Its first production was not to take place until 1947—in Paris.

XIII

Pity Is Not Enough:
"Saint Joan of the Stockyards"

ST. JOAN. I am for your cause with heart
and soul.
WORKER. Our cause? Well, isn't it your
cause as well?

BRECHT, *St. Joan of the Stockyards*

In 1932 there were six million unemployed in Germany. In the April elections, a run-off after the inconclusive March elections, Hindenburg was chosen president of the Republic with nineteen and a half million votes; Hitler received thirteen million votes. Of Hindenburg, the Socialist Otto Braun said:

[He is] the embodiment of calm and steadiness, of manly loyalty and devotion to duty for the benefit of the entire nation . . . [He] has proved that all those who want to save Germany from chaos can rely on him. . . . That is why I am for Hindenburg.[1]

At the same time, Gregor Strasser, one of Hitler's chief lieutenants, was saying:

The Nazis do not want reaction, but healing; not a systemless revolution, but an organic order. . . . They do not want to persecute the Jews, but they want German leadership without the Jewish spirit, without Jews pulling the strings, and without Jewish capital.[2]

In July, 1932, the Nazis polled fourteen million votes in the Reichstag elections and won 230 mandates; the Social Democrats eight million votes, and the Communists five million. But by November of the same year, the Nazis had lost two million votes, and the Communists had won 101 seats in the Reichstag!

In the midst of this mounting turmoil, Brecht was studying political economy, collecting materials for a new play that would throw light on the gathering crisis. Newspapers, economic journals, reports, materials published by the National City Bank of New York, reviews of agricultural conditions—all these were carefully scanned. He was particularly occupied in studying the wheat market. He underscored items that interested him, such as, "Spring wheat conditions as of June 1, stood at 78.5 per cent, the lowest in 15 years"; "wheat is cheaper"; "prices are falling in America and in Austria."[3] His interest centered on Chicago. He was reading Sherwood Anderson's *Poor White,* the novels of Frank Norris, and noting suitable passages; also Lincoln Steffens' *Autobiography* and Gustavus Myers' *History of American Fortunes.* He was carefully collecting photographs like those of the Wrigley Building, for local color.[4]

He projected a play called *Joe Fleischhacker* (*Joe Butcher*), which was to depict the ruin of a family "coming from the prairies," and the successful manipulation of the wheat market.[5] He was concerned with the economic crisis, and sought ways of showing it so that it could be "demystified"—not seen as something "natural," but man-made. The problem was how to divest capitalism of its "heroic" integument.

He sketched another play (having read a newspaper item about the dispossession of an indigent widow) called *Der Brotladen* (*The Breadshop*). The economic crash, which affects the landlord of a dwelling, brings ruin to one of his poor tenants, Frau Queck. A chorus of the unemployed, drawn by the prospect of some work in chopping firewood, laments, in typical Brechtian fashion, the fall of economic giants. The little man or woman is Brecht's concern.

> Constantly they fall
> Down, through the grating
> In the asphalt—
> All sorts of men—unmarked—

Without character—down below—
Without sound
Quickly
They who were walking by our side
Happy ones
From the midst of the crowd
Chosen at random
Six out of seven, down below
But the seventh goes off
To have his bite of lunch.[6]

You cannot tell who may be the next unpredictable victim of this anarchy.

The country was full of rumors and anxieties. And warnings, too. In December, 1931, Heinrich Mann was saying:

It is possible that now the Germans will fall a prey to National Socialism, and allow it to triumph, because once more they hear the call of the abyss. Germans have heard that call often enough. Victory of National Socialism is made a possibility because in this land democracy was never achieved on the bloody field of battle . . . And now the majority appeal to the State, begging for help. . . . But the State has already deserted the majority. . . . One sees Hitler's private army treated by the government not as its enemy, but as a desirable ally. . . . Granted they succeed in establishing their fatuous autocracy, for whose benefit will they be ruling? For their creditors, a number of people who call themselves the "economy," and who have already twice brought the land to ruin. They spurred the First Reich on to a war; and the Second toward National Socialism. . . . The Reich of the false Germans and the false Socialists will undoubtedly arise after a blood-bath, but that is nothing in comparison to the blood that will flow when it falls.[7]

How many were there to listen to this voice? Here was a nation with a President approaching senility; a Chancellor, Brüning, dreaming of the restoration of the monarchy; an impotent Parliament; a working class, strong in numbers, looking for clearsighted and unified leadership; and a leadership of the working classes disunited and at odds. "Blind mouths!" John Milton would have said.

"The word putsch is in the air," Goebbels noted in his diary prior to the elections of 1932. "Hitler's mines are beginning to go off." The procession toward doom: Brüning is succeeded by Franz von Papen. Papen deposes the legitimate government of Prussia (without even being challenged!) and appoints himself Reich Commissioner for that state. Martial law is proclaimed in Berlin, and arrests follow.

In 1920 a general strike had saved the Republic from being overthrown. Such a measure was now debated among the trade union leaders and the Socialists, and rejected as too dangerous. Thus by deposing the constitutional Prussian government Papen had driven another nail into the coffin of the Weimar Republic. It had taken, as he boasted, only a squad of soldiers to do it.[8]

There was no lack of money for the Nazis, as Goebbels boasted. With Krupp, Bosch, Schnitzler of the IG Farben, Voegler of the United Steel Works, Thyssen, and Freiherr von Schroeder around, Dr. Schacht could proudly report, having, on one occasion, "passed the hat around": "I collected three million marks."[9]

Die heilige Johanna der Schlachthöfe (*St. Joan of the Stockyards*) was written by Brecht before the apex of the crisis, during the years 1929-1930. It was never to be produced in pre-Hitler Germany, except for a partial radio performance on April 11, 1932.

This was a daring play, for many reasons. Brecht was taking a classical theme from history—a traditional "heroic" subject—and marrying it to the contemporary economic struggle, in order thereby to lay bare the operative forces in modern society, at a time of crisis. The scene was to be set in the Chicago stockyards; but once more the locale would be the world at large and Germany in particular. *St. Joan of the Stockyards* constitutes not only an intrepid *tour de force,* but it is probably one of Brecht's most brilliant and successful dramatic efforts.

Joan of Arc was burned at the stake in Rouen in 1431. The 500th anniversary of her martyrdom was approaching, and would no doubt be celebrated with appropriate solemnity. Ever since her death, she had been the object of exaltation and denigration, and had attracted many writers: Shakespeare and Voltaire to scorn and defame her; Friedrich Schiller, Andrew Lang, and Mark Twain to worship her; and, not least, Bernard Shaw, in 1924, to appraise her historic role brilliantly in *St. Joan*. The historical materials of her trial had been available since 1841, and her canonization in 1920 had moved both Shaw and Paul Claudel to write about her.

Brecht, too, was attracted to the figure of the French girl. It was to be a life-long devotion.[10] Whether Brecht was also inspired by Shaw is debatable.[11] But both *St. Joan* and *Major Barbara* were well known in Germany, and both have many points of contact with Brecht's *St. Joan* that are rather striking.

It was a bold notion on the part of Brecht to take the French saint and transform her into a Salvation Army lass (the Black Straw Hats), set her down in Chicago, and involve her in the bitter economic struggles around the stockyards. Upton Sinclair's *The Jungle* helped supply a good part of the background and an incident or two; the economics of the cattle market had been carefully studied (with Elisabeth Hauptmann's help), and there was a Salvation Army in Berlin too.

Joanna Dark (as she is now called), goodness in her heart and the mission of God in her soul, believes she can alleviate the ills attending the workers in the packing industry by an appeal to the finer instinct of the industrial magnate and meat baron, Mauler. She begins a number of "descents" into the lower regions of the industrial hell, each experience bringing her, if not renewed comfort, at least a bitter knowledge of the reality. To instruct her in the "wickedness" of the laboring classes, Mauler sends her down into the stockyards, where she does indeed find that poverty and unemployment bring about moral and spiritual degradation.

Mauler, however, is waging a powerful campaign to obliterate his competitors, and with the skill of a great manipulator, and an expert's knowledge of the mechanics of the meat exchange, he brings them to the verge of bankruptcy and the workers practically to despair. As Joan's education proceeds, she becomes aware of how the meat-packers find the Black Straws useful instruments in pacifying the workers, by giving them God. Now herself brought almost to the point of despair, she drives the "money-changers" from the mission—her temple—and is booted out of her job in consequence. In the meantime, unemployment and starvation have driven the workers to a strike, in which the Communists have a leading role. Joan, though a "neutral," is recruited to convey one of the crucial messages to another factory, but on the way, she is beset by doubts, weakens, and defaults on her urgent mission. The general strike collapses, the leaders are arrested, and the workers are defeated. Mauler has succeeded in cornering the market, and is triumphant. The factories reopen once more. Joan, heartbroken, is dying and is brought back to the mission, where the meat-packers proceed to canonize her, and with their exalted liturgies drown out her last passionate pleas.

Brecht had once asked, Can the modern world of the produce exchange be set in iambics? And he had answered no. In *St. Joan of the Stockyards* he has set the meat industry to iambs, but in parody. He was demystifying the modern heroism of the stock market at the same time as he was demystifying the heroism of classical tragedy. Thus, he was utilizing the process of estrangement —parody, allusion, imitation of classical verse. The immediate literary objects of parody were Schiller and Goethe.

The reader must remember that in pre-Hitler Germany the works of the German classics were well known to audiences, many of whom could recite long passages of the classical drama and poetry by heart. What could be more startling then suddenly to be hearing echoes of the majestic lines, now mouthed by financial moguls?

Schiller's *Die Jungfrau von Orleans* (*The Maid of Orleans*), written in the years 1800 and 1801, was a natural victim. His tragedy opens with heroic pentameters, known to every schoolboy:

> Ja, liebe Nachbarn! Heute sind wir noch
> Franzosen, freie Bürger noch und Herren. . . .

> Yes, my dear neighbors! Today we are still
> Frenchmen, free citizens, and masters still . . .[12]

Into the meat baron Pierpont Mauler's lips Brecht puts similar lofty verses. He has just received advices from New York that the meat market is due for a crisis. In reply to his partner's question, why he is so depressed, he replies:

> Remember, Cridle, how some days ago
> We passed through stockyards—'twas eventide,
> And stood beside our brand-new packing machine.
> Remember, Cridle, the huge blond ox
> That dully gazed up at the sky
> As blows fell on him. It was I was struck down,
> I felt—ah, Cridle—our business is a bloody one.[13]

The parody goes beyond the language into the situations. According to the tradition, followed by Schiller, Joan, in looking for the King, recognizes him at once, though the courtiers test her by trying to deceive her as to his identity.

In Schiller, Charles asks of Joan:

> You've never seen my countenance before,
> Whence comes your knowledge—who I may be?

To which Joan replies:

> I saw thee, where none else but God saw.[14]

Now for Brecht:

JOANNA. You are Mauler.
MAULER. No, he's there. (*Points to Slift*)
JOANNA. You are Mauler . . .
MAULER. How do you know me?
JOANNA. Because you have the bloodiest face of all.[15]

In Schiller's play, DuChatel in an effort to bring about a reconciliation between the Duke of Burgundy and the Dauphin, offers to lay down his life:

> Here is my head. Oft have I ventured it
> For you in battle. And now with joy I lay it
> Here on the headman's block.[16]

Brecht took the cue:

> MAULER. Is this the way, Slift, you carry on the battle I entrust to you?
> SLIFT. Take my head!
> MAULER. What good is your head to me?
>   Your hat—now, that's worth something![17]

Mauler rises to true epic majesty when he delivers his apostrophe to Money. (He had asked Joanna, "Why are you so set against money?)

> What an edifice!
> From days forgotten built up again and again,
> Because ever crumbling—tremendous still;
> Though demanding sacrifice,
> Hard to set up again—and yet with groans
> Again set up—but still inescapably
> Wresting the possible from a malign planet—
> Be that much or little—and so at all time
> Defended by the best. For see, should I
> —Who have much against it, and sleep badly—
> Should I abandon it—it would only be as if a fly
> Had ceased to stem an avalanche. At that very moment,
> I'd turn to nothing—and over me it would sweep.[18]

(Is it possible that Brecht was recalling Bernard Shaw's brilliant apologia for money in the preface to *Major Barbara?*) No, it isn't.

Though estrangement too is used in the case of Joanna's mission, it is not through parody but through revelation of her naiveté. She begins with the simplicity of the well-meaning, and firmly believes that "misfortune, like rain, comes from no one knows where—no one makes it, yet it comes."[19] But a worker tells her, "It comes from Lennox & Co." "I must find out who is responsible," she cries out. Her pleas have a biblical sincerity and intensity, even when directed toward Mauler. She warns him of Judgment Day, when everything will be revealed, and the Lord Savior will ask, "Where are my steers now?"

Then the steers will bellow in back of you, in all your barns, where you have hidden them so that you can raise your prices sky-high, and with their bellowing they will bear witness against you with the Lord.[20]

Instructed by the packers and cattle breeders that the wretched poor have no morality, she asks in anger, Where should they get their morality, if not by stealing? There is also, she says, "a moral purchasing power." Raise that, and you'll have morality. In other words, pay them decent wages.[21]

Finally her eyes have been opened, and she addresses the packers, telling them she sees through them and their uses of religion, that she knows now that their interests and those of the poor are not alike. No, they cannot deal with human beings as if they were animals: "Have you then no reverence for that which wears a human face?"

She drives them from her mission, crying out: "Is it that you want to turn God's house into a stable, or a livestock exchange?" She has finally come to understand the "system," with the few sitting on top, and the many down below—a see-saw. Those on top are there only because there are others on the bottom. Like the other St. Joan, she too has her vision, but it is a vision of the future: herself striding at the head of a procession of the dispossessed, "changing all that my foot touched," and with "words of war-like sound" causing measureless destruction. Toward the end of the play, when she has betrayed the cause of the working people, she sees their leaders being led off by the soldiers, and stands stupefied with admiration at the sacrifice, the sacrifice of the anonymous and gloryless.

Before she dies, she confesses her disenchantment:

> I, for example, have done nothing.
> For count nothing as good—no matter how it seems,
> But that which truly helps.
> And nothing as honorable—except it change
> The world once and for all. That is what I needed.
> As if in answer to their prayers I came to the oppressors.
> O goodness without fruit! Barren intentions!
> I have changed nothing.
> Fast vanishing from this earth without fear:
> I say to you:
> Take heed that when you leave the world,
> You were not only good, but leave
> A good world.[22]

As she lies dying, loudspeakers announce the great world economic crisis. At the command of Mauler, flags are lowered over her body, just as in Schiller, where Joan dies after seeing the heavens open, revealing the Virgin and Child, and is covered with flags at the king's command.

Thus, in Brecht, capitalism canonizes its useful martyrs.

Rarely has Brecht's genius for parody been so brilliantly revealed as in this play. The shades of Schiller and Goethe are invoked to set off the sordid heroics of today. The unsurpassed irony of the death and transfiguration scene owes much to Schiller, but even more to the closing pages of Goethe's *Faust*. Echoes of other portions of that two-part tragedy are sounded throughout Brecht's drama. Lines of Goethe that have become proverbial are placed in the mouths of Mauler and his associates with the terrible impact of "estrangement." Who does not recall Faust's desperate cry about the two souls within him struggling for domination?

> Zwei Seelen wohnen, ach! in meiner Brust!

Could anyone fail to recognize them when Mauler is speaking?

> Alas! In my poor breast
> A knife is plunged unto the hilt
> Plunged, with a double thrust.
> For I am drawn toward the great,
> The selfless, pure, and self-renouncing;
> And I am drawn toward trade and profit—
> All unconscious![23]

With equal adroitness (and *sangfroid*) Brecht lampoons Schiller's celebrated *Song of the Bell*, which that poet had dedicated to labor and to the excoriation of the French Revolution. Its most quoted lines,

> Soll das Werk den Meister loben:
> Doch der Segen kommt von oben—
>
> Let handiwork its master laud:
> But the blessings come from God—

are turned by Brecht into

> Soll der Bau sich hoch erheben
> Muss es Unten und Oben geben . . .
>
> If the building is to grow
> There must be an "up" and a "down below" . . .[24]

a paean to capitalism, naturally, sung by the packers and the cattle breeders.

The duality of a Faust is transported into the soul of the packer Mauler, no less than into that of Joanna. Mauler is the man who cannot stand the bellowing of slaughtered cattle, but considers human beings incorrigible and expendable. Joanna, too, is divided: she exhibits the self-division of the bourgeoisie. Deceived by her feelings, she is led into betrayal and dies before she can put her hard-earned lessons to constructive practices.

St. Joan of the Stockyards reveals two new notable characteristics, in our opinion, profoundly interrelated. Joanna differs markedly from the women Brecht had been portraying heretofore. Until this moment, they had been "outsiders" like their male counterparts, and trailing after them; adventuresses or merely hangers-on; figures like the Jennys, the Widow Begbicks, the Anna Balickes.

Joanna inaugurates a new line of "heroic" women—in the Brechtian sense, of course. From now on we shall meet them as they assert themselves (even if ambiguously): Vlassova, Mother Courage, Señora Carrar, Shen-Te, Grusha—more human, more life-like, and in most of the instances, bearers of positive social and moral values. Like their male partners, they now disappear as nihilists and emerge as active participants in Brecht's changeable, and to be changed, world.

The transformation in Brecht is not, of course, unrelated to the inspiring influence of Helene Weigel, who was to enact most of these roles on the stage. But it could not have taken place, it seems to us, without the ideological change which Brecht himself had un-

dergone, and which for him rescues humanity from being condemned to chaos. The contemporary economic crisis has rarely been
so brilliantly treated by a playwright (only Bernard Shaw comes to
mind as a likely rival). Far from being an oversimplification of
the economic structure of society (as Martin Esslin would have it),
St. Joan is a simplification (in the way in which a work of art
simplifies) of a complex process in which the world of competition,
of markets, of goods cornered, of the classical appropriation by exploitation, of work and poverty is exposed. As a matter of fact, close
observation of the play reveals an unusually astute depiction of
various stages of the economic crisis: the end of prosperity; over-
production; crises; and "normal restoration." In the play each of
these stages is introduced by a letter. The audience is therefore in a
position to "see how ideologies are framed."[25]

Left-wing critics, like Ernst Schumacher, have deplored (others
have rejoiced) that Brecht had not created a proletarian opponent
of Mauler, worthy of him, and commensurate with the dignity and
heroism of the workers' opposition. There is some truth in the
criticism. It was easier for Brecht (as it is for any writer) to express
a dualism within a person than the perfection of unity of character
or purpose. Lucifer has, since the Fall of Adam, always proved a
more viable dramatic subject than either the angels or the Lord
God; and Dante's Inferno is still the grandest and most compelling
part of the Divine Comedy. But Brecht could work out the problem
of the "collective hero" only by implication. His conception of the
heroic and of the proletarian hero involved the grandeur of anonymity, as Joanna realizes, and as Die Massnahme had proclaimed and
as the The Days of the Commune was to declare many years later.
But it cannot also be denied that Brecht puts an unwarranted
burden upon the audience, in making it appear almost as if the
opponents of the brilliantly drawn Pierpont Mauler are not so much
Joanna or the working classes, as Brecht himself, armed with the
linguistic virtuosity of his parody.

But Brecht, let it be remembered, was writing about a self-divided bourgeoisie, and addressing himself to them as well. He wanted to win them over to an understanding of the processes of a capitalist society, the social "truth," and to a recognition of their place in the struggle against the anarchy and chaos around them. This was to be Brecht's function for a long time to come.

Unfortunately, he was not to be given much more chance to appeal to them. The city authorities of Darmstadt refused permission for a performance of *St. Joan of the Stockyards*. Only a partial radio broadcast in April, 1932, involving Carola Neher, Fritz Kortner, Helene Weigel, Ernst Busch, and Peter Lorre, gave pre-Hitler Germans an intimation of this powerful work.

The post-war revival in West Germany of *St. Joan of the Stockyards* in 1964, presented at Frankfurt under the brilliant direction of Harry Buckwitz, brought from the critic of the *Frankfurter Hefte* an emphatic reminder of how timely that play was even in our day. "This is no longer the stock exchange of 1929, but exchanges wherever and whenever they exist." Johanna's dying utterances are such as are "recommended by the [Papal] Encyclicals, only in somewhat different words."[26]

XIV

The Unknown Advance Guard: "Mother"

My task, I considered, to report a great
historical figure
To the advance guard of humanity
For emulation.

BRECHT, "Letter to the Theatre Union"

Brecht's last play to achieve consecutive performances in pre-Hitler Germany was a Lehrstück. An irony of fate—in the persons of the police—was destined to prove that Brecht could write epic theatre for the masses, even such in which they could participate as actors along with the professional artists, and that even under the most unfavorable theatrical circumstances his ideas could come out clear and unequivocal, free of the ambiguities charged to *St. Joan of the Stockyards.* It also proved that proletarian audiences would understand the "positive" proletarian heroine he was presenting and her transformation from an unknowing and ignorant worker's wife into a revolutionary.

Brecht's play *Die Mutter* was based on Maxim Gorki's tender novel of the same name. Gorki's story was completed during his exile from Russia, and published in 1907. Its subject was the upsurge of the Russian workers immediately prior to the Revolution of 1905. In the figure of Pelageya Nilova Vlassova, the abused wife of a brutalized worker, and mother of Pavel Vlassov, her revolutionary son, Gorki created, using actual historical figures and incidents of the day, a novel of "education"—the story of a woman who, through an apprenticeship in the revolutionary activities of her son, gradually elevates herself to a full understanding of and participation in the class struggle. Through a series of touching and illuminating experiences, she comes to replace her son as an active agitator, and is brutally beaten down in the fulfilment of her mission. Vlassova is a devout and simple Christian soul, and she goes through stages of outrage, confusion, and perplexity in the course of her "education." Finally, in her own words, she is "raised from the dead" into the life of an embattled revolutionary and an even more devout and noble Christian.

Wherever published or translated, Gorki's novel stirred and aroused its readers, because of its simplicity and its compassion. Brecht saw possibilities of applying the work to the situation in Germany, and went to work on the adaptation, together with Günther Weisenborn and Slatan Dudow. Hanns Eisler was to set the songs. Brecht did not of course adhere entirely to Gorki's story, but extended it to include the outbreak of the First World War.

The protagonist of the Lehrstück is Pelageya Vlassova, mother of Pavel Vlassov, worker in the Sukhlinov factory. In keeping with the principle of the epic theatre, she addresses the audience directly. As a result of the reduction of wages in the factory in which her son is employed, she is not able to prepare a nourishing soup for her disgruntled son. "There is no way out," she wails. Whereupon the chorus of revolutionary workers replies in a song, really repeating her question: "Brush your coat as long as you will, and then what have you? A rag. Your lack of meat will not be decided in the kitchen."

But what is the way out?

It will be some time before the mother can find the answer. When Pavel, who had recently joined the revolutionary group, brings his comrades home with him to print illegal literature for distribution in the factory, his mother is vexed and mistrustful, as well as frightened for Pavel's job. Masha, one of the comrades, sings the song in answer to the first question, "The Song of the Way Out."

When you have no soup and you have no work, what can you do? Why, turn the state upside down until you have soup, and until you are the one to give work. As in Gorki's novel, so here too, the police invade Vlassova's home in search of the subversive pamphlets and their authors. Even more ruthless than in the original novel, the police are abusive. They slash the furniture, break up the household utensils, and derisively taunt Masha with the news that her brother (who has been imprisoned) sends his greetings. He is now converting bedbugs to the revolution. When Pavel is chosen to distribute the leaflets in the factory, his mother volunteers to replace him; she will come as a food vendor and wrap the victuals in the leaflets. She does not know what is in them, for like so many Russian women of her class, she cannot read.

The factory is in the midst of an upheaval over wages, and the more militant of the workers, including Pavel, have decided on a strike and a demonstration on the first of May.

Vlassova, in the meantime, is learning. In one of the most moving and brilliant scenes of the play, her son and his associates give her her first lesson in political economy, teaching her the difference between such personal property as her table, and the factory and its machines; the relationship of owner to worker, and the dependence of worker on owner. "He does not always need us," they explain, "but we always need him." But what can you do against that? she asks. They answer, *"One* can do nothing; but if all the Vlassovas in Tver, say eight hundred of them, stood up and all spoke the same thing, Mr. Sukhlinov could no longer laugh at them." She is beginning to understand; but as for the strike, she wants none of it. She is against violence. "For forty years I have known nothing but that and could do nothing against it. But when I die, I want to know that I haven't done anything violent."[1]

Yet, in the demonstration of May 1, 1905, when the demonstrators are shot down and beaten by the police, Vlassova seizes the banner fallen from the hands of the worker Smilgin and carries it high. Later, when her son is imprisoned, she takes over the task of agitation in the countryside. She manages to learn to read. "Reading is the class struggle," she tells her companions. The chorus of learners chants the "Praise of Learning."

> Learn to read the simplest things.
> For those whose hour has struck,
> It is never too late.
>
> Learn the ABC; it is not enough;
> But learn it; do not be dismayed.
> Begin! You must know everything.
> You must be ready to be leaders.[2]

She is always *with* her son, though he is far away and in prison. For

> Ever we hear it said, how soon
> Mothers lose their sons, but I
> Kept mine. How did I keep him? Through
> The third thing.
> He and I were two, but the third—
> The thing in common—that which we did together—
> That made us one.[3]

Pavel is killed, and the chorus addresses Vlassova:

> Comrade Vlassova, your son
> has been shot. But
> as he walked toward the wall, to be shot,
> he went toward a wall that had been made by his own kind;
> and the rifles aimed at his breast, and the bullet
> had been made by his kind. Not present then
> perhaps, or scattered elsewhere; but for him,
> they were present there, and present in the work
> of their hands. Not even those who
> shot him were different from him, or for ever unteachable.
> Of course, he went still bound in chains forged
> by his comrades, and laid on by them. Yet
> more frequent grew the factories; he could see from the road
> chimney upon chimney; and since it was early in the day
> for it's in the morning that they're usually taken out—
> they were empty, but he saw them crowded

> with that huge army that grows apace,
> and was still growing.
> But he was led toward the wall by his own kind,
> and he, who understood this, also did not understand it.[4]

In the face of this death, she rejects the well-meaning, traditional, pious condolences of her neighbors. At the outbreak of the First World War, she rises from a sickbed to demonstrate for peace, but is brutally beaten up by the police. Even the workers now refuse to listen to her. Yet she continues to carry on her struggle against the war, trying to enlighten the women who stand on line to deliver up their utensils to be turned into weapons. And finally, in 1917, she is once more among the striking demonstrators of workers and soldiers and sailors, once more with flag in hand encouraging the weary:

> He who is yet alive, let him not say, Never.
> That which is sure is not sure.
> What is today, will not be.
> When the lords have spoken
> Those lorded over will speak.
> Who dares say: Never?
> Whose the responsibility, if oppression stays? Ours.
> Whose the responsibility, if it is crushed? Ours.
> Whoever is struck down, let him arise!
> Whoever is lost, let him fight!
> Whoever knows his lot, how can he be held back?
> For the vanquished of today are the victors of
>   tomorrow.
> And *Never* will yet turn into *Today*.[5]

Die Mutter was written sometime between 1930 and 1931, and performed for the first time in the Theater am Schiffbauerdamm on January 17, 1932—the anniversary of the assassination of Rosa Luxemburg. It was directed by Emil Burri and the scenic designs were by Caspar Neher. Helene Weigel acted the part of Vlassova and Ernst Busch that of Pavel. After some thirty performances at the Schiffbauerdamm, the production was transferred to the Moabiter

Gesellschaftshaus, to be acted before workers. The police intervened and prohibited the performance, alleging a fire hazard, but also stating that "there was no occasion for such a performance."[6]

The actors then went through their parts without costumes or props. When this too was interfered with, they read their parts. The reaction of the audience was amazing. The police had unintentionally heightened the whole tone and effectiveness of the performance and brought it home!

Brecht remarked on the differences in the reactions of the bourgeois and working-class audiences:

While the workers reacted immediately to the subtlest turns of the dialogue, and shared the most complicated presuppositions directly, the bourgeois audience followed the course of action only with difficulty, and the essential elements not at all. . . . The working people reacted at once politically. Those coming from the [fashionable] west side of the city sat bored and grinning . . . , paying attention only to the bare externals. Who, I ask, is primitive, and who is not?[7]

The piece aroused the most violent and, of course, contradictory emotions. Alfred Kerr, in the *Berliner Tageblatt,* in his own caustic way, stated that it was a "euphemism" to say that this was a piece for primitive spectators. "It is a piece by a primitive writer."[8] The ultra-nationalistic *Germania* spoke of Brecht as the "literary interpreter of Bolshevism in Germany," who was no longer to be judged by aesthetic but by political criteria.[9] The Social Democratic *Vorwärts* castigated him for "debauching" the wonderful book by Gorki into the "Stalinism of 1932."[9] The *Linkskurve,* politically left, was also disappointed. The Communist *Rote Fahne* registered a number of complaints, particularly with reference to the Russian workers' reactions to Vlassova's propaganda leaflets at the time of the war. It criticized the call to the sick Vlassova that the "party was in danger" (while, the newspaper claimed, the party was neither in danger at that time nor confused). Serge Tretyakov was much more to the point in stating that Brecht was writing a play about Germany, not Russia. Herbert Jhering was practically the only one to express his unqualified appreciation, particularly of the skilful application of the "epic" practice. But there were no voices that dissented from the praises accorded Helene Weigel as Vlassova. Brecht remarked, on recalling these performances, how humorously Weigel's Vlassova behaved when she chased the revolutionaries from her quarters—a quality that did not desert her even in the most heartrending scenes and situation.[10] One of Brecht's colleagues remembered that the audiences at some of the performances, though mostly petty bourgeois, would weep when the workers refused to take Vlassova's anti-war leaflets. These spectators did not "identify" with Vlassova, but they were outraged at those who "did not know what they were doing."[11]

The sets of Caspar Neher were impressive in their simplicity, and their mere suggestion of furniture. The songs set to Eisler's music became celebrated: "In Praise of Communism," "In Praise of Dialectic," and "In Praise of Learning" were to be repeated in many lands, and became essential components of the working-class song repertory. Among the vivid projections that showed the "Vlassovas of all countries" was also a film of the November Russian Revolution, which was prohibited by the censor. Workers flocked to these performances, especially women. "Some 15,000 Berlin working-class women attended the production of the play," Brecht reported, and thus learned "the methods of illegal revolutionary warfare."[12]

Brecht was delighted by the attitudes of his working-class audiences:

Great was the laughter in the auditorium.
The inexhaustible good humor
of Vlassova, drawn from the confidence
of her young class, roused
happy laughter on the benches of the workers.
Eagerly they utilized the rare occasion,
without pressing danger, to be present at the
       ordinary events,
and thus at leisure to master them and set
their own behavior in readiness.[13]

For while others might not be, Brecht at least was aware of the pressing danger, and the short time in which to meet it.

This was Brecht's first work that fused Marxist doctrine, instruction, and delight in a simple, direct, unpretentious, but highly artistic manner, setting forth ideas in unequivocal terms, so that anyone might understand and act upon them. What Vlassova had done every worker could also do. If the sophisticated bourgeois spectator found the play too "naive," so much the worse for him. No worker would find Vlassova's hard school of education naive.

XV

The Advancing Terror

Gebt mir vier Jahre Zeit, und ihr werdet
Deutschland nicht wiederkennen.

Give me four years' time, and you will not
recognize Germany again.

ADOLF HITLER, 1933

Put out the light, and then put out the light.

SHAKESPEARE, *Othello*

The economic and political crisis reacted drastically on theatrical
life. Most of the theatrical institutions relied on state subsidies for
their existence, which in 1928 had amounted to upward of 15 million dollars. Such subventions fell to nine million in 1931. The
severe cuts affected the employment of personnel critically. Salaries
fell to 50 or 60 percent of normal during the season, and 70 to 80
percent during the summer. To compensate for these losses and to
increase revenues, many of the theatrical groups debased the quality
of their presentations.

Not the least demoralizing factor was the growing hostility of the
rightists. Gloating at the prospect of imminent victory in the political
arena, the Papen regime began crying "Kulturbolschewismus"—
"cultural bolshevism"—at anything that remotely touched on liberal,
progressive, or radical thought. Dr. Goebbels characterized modern
art as that "swamp flower of a democratic asphalt culture," which
stood under "powerful Jewish influence."[1] In August, 1932, the

Völkischer Beobachter published a list of the cultural representatives of a "decadent declining era,"[2] whose works would soon be forbidden. Among those listed were Feuchtwanger, Hofmannsthal, Hasenclever, Klaus Mann, Molnar, Sternheim, Toller, Werfel, Wedekind, Friedrich Wolf, Stefan Zweig, Zuckmayer, Eugene O'Neill, Galsworthy, Pirandello, Rostand, Bernard Shaw, and Strindberg: such "self-proclaimed Germans" as Brecht, Leonhard Frank and Plievier; and such pacifists as Carl Hauptmann and Fritz von Unruh.

That Brecht would now encounter difficulties in his career stood to reason. *St. Joan of the Stockyards* could achieve a partial radio broadcast, but found no theatre. *Mother*, as we have already seen, ran into major difficulties. *Die Massnahme* had come under the watchful eyes of the police, who left their own critical opinion of that play in their archives:

This choral work is outwardly camouflaged. Presumably it takes place in China. But the content shows that all that is needed is to substitute the word "Germany" for the word "China," and the entire choral piece can as readily apply to Germany. . . . Here it is shown how revolutionary ideas are to be introduced into the police and military establishments. . . . All means are utilized to win over and instruct members of the party, in so far as they are not parts of the official apparatus, in the practice of sedition.[3]

A performance of that play in Erfurt was forbidden under Reich law, and "action was instituted against the organizers on a charge of incitement to high treason."

Now additional troubles descended upon Brecht. He had undertaken to do a film in collaboration with Ernst Ottwald and Hanns Eisler. It was *Kuhle Wampe*, and Slatan Dudow was to direct it. Kuhle Wampe was a kind of tent-city—a German "Hooverville"—for workers outside Berlin. The film was begun in 1931. The plot concerned the economic and moral plight of a proletarian family, the Bönickes, at a time of depression and unemployment. Dispossessed of their home, the family moves to these outskirts. Unfortunately, the son of the family succumbs to the hardships and takes his own life. The daughter marries a chauffeur, who, in the class-conscious and militant environment of Kuhle Wampe, becomes a fighting proletarian. Ernst Busch and Hertha Thiele took the principal roles, and workers and sports organizations also parti-cipated. The film pulled no punches. It depicted the suicide of the young worker as having been brought about by the economic meas-ures of the government. It showed the dispossession of the family. It presented sporting contests in which no fewer than three thousand sport enthusiasts participated. It described how the pregnant daugh-ter secured an abortion. And, finally, it showed how Brazilian coffee was being destroyed in order to keep up prices.[4]

In March, 1932, the film fell afoul of the censorship on the grounds that it "endangered the safety of the state." According to the charge,

A number of scenes preach resistance to state authority. . . . The film offends against the vital interests of the state. The system of justice as an institution is held up to ridicule. . . . The frequently repeated sum-mons to solidarity and self-help is nothing but a summons to violence and subversion. This summons to solidarity runs like a thread through-out the film, and culminates in a summons to change the world.[5]

Even President Hindenburg was held to have been insulted by the suggestion that the emergency decrees were in any way subject to question.

Brecht, his collaborators, and a lawyer appeared before the censor, to answer for their "infraction." According to Brecht's later report, the censor proved a perspicacious literary critic. No one, the censor said genially, contested the right of the authors to depict suicides, but there were suicides and suicides. This one, however, "is not sufficiently human." That is, this was not a man of flesh and blood, but a type. Furthermore, the impression was conveyed that the state was somehow "responsible for the suicide of young people" because it denied them work; and the picture even suggested that the work-ers must change things.

No, gentlemen, you have not behaved as artists [the censor continued]. No, not in this case. You were not interested in portraying a deeply moving individual case, the right to which no one would have denied you.

The interview took on the aspect of high comedy, as Brecht declared (tongue in cheek) that his honor as an artist had been impugned; and Dudow called for a physician to testify as an expert. Had anyone ever so clearly seen and understood the theory of "estrangement" as this censor?

You must admit, [he said] that your suicide leaves one with the impression that there was nothing impulsive about it. The spectator is not, in fact, inclined to prevent it, which he would ordinarily feel impelled to do, in an artistic, human, and warm-hearted portrayal. Good Lord, why, the actor behaves as if he were showing one how to peel a cucumber!

Brecht was full of amazement:

We did have a hard time to pull our film through. On leaving, we could not conceal our admiration of the perspicacious censor. He had penetrated more deeply into our artistic intentions than our well-meaning critics. He had held us a brief seminar on realism. Of course, from the standpoint of the policeman.[6]

In the end, the film was passed for presentation. There were some beautiful songs in it, such as "Nature in the Spring" and the "Sporting Song." The "Song of Solidarity" became internationally celebrated, with its call for a united proletariat the world over, and its question: "Whose tomorrow?" "To whom belongs the world?" The "Song of the Homeless" probably also proved troublesome to the censor:

> Think hard, but strain every nerve;
> For things like these cannot go on forever.[7]

If the plays of this period may be said to reflect Brecht's "public" feelings, his "private" reactions and personal feelings are expressed in his poems. He was deeply distressed by the failure of the Socialists and Communists to establish a united front against the fascists. Fritz Sternberg recalled that in 1929, Brecht took him to a mass meeting sponsored by the Socialists, at which a Communist was to present his party's position. They made their way through thousands of men and women who filled the streets outside the meeting hall, but who could not get in. Brecht and Sternberg listened to the discussion carried on by these workers, and they were profoundly moved and impressed by the evidences of strength and confidence they here saw revealed. Not one Nazi had dared show his face! Brecht observed that there was none of that animus that marred the pages of the Communist *Rote Fahne* and the Socialist *Vorwärts.* "He came to the conclusion," Sternberg wrote, "that a united front was necessary."[8]

The intransigence (and blindness) of both sides brought from him a poetic appeal, on the eve of a "united front" congress in July, 1932, to the Social Democrats:

> Comrades, recognize even now, that this lesser evil by which
> Year after year you have been kept apart from battle,
> Will soon enough mean sufferance of the Nazis.

He regrets that heretofore the Socialists have refused to take up the Nazi challenge and fight back alongside the Communists.[9]

He had watched the strength of the working classes as they marched together. Such manifestation had taken place when thousands upon thousands had turned out to protest the slaying of two Social Democratic Reichsbanner members by the Nazis on January 7, 1931.

There are other poems of this time that touch on equally important subjects, tender and moving, dealing with the "heroism of the home"—always so close to Brecht's heart, in contrast to the heroism of war. There is the "Cradle Song," for example, in which a mother is speaking to her baby son, born into an "evil world":

> And I said to myself, You must see to it
> That he at least makes no mistake,
> The boy I'm carrying must see to it,
> That the world is a better place.

Let them boast of military conquests and victories and armies; the battles she is fighting day after day are heroic enough!

> Bread and a little milk are victories,
> A warm home . . . is a battle won!

She is raising another kind of warrior for the future![10]

In another poem, he is watching "Poor Students from the Out-skirts" coming to school in their thin coats, late for their lessons because of the errands and jobs they have to do, being scolded by their teachers who despise them and instruct them how "to lick boots, and look down on their own parents," and prepare them for the "small jobs in government service."

> The small jobs of the indigent pupils from the outskirts
> were underground. Their desks were without seats, and
>   their landscape
> the roots of scrubby plants.
> To what end were they taught
> Greek grammar, and Caesar's campaigns,
> formulas for sulphur and the number *pi*?
> In the mass-graves of Flanders destined for them
> what need had they of anything
> but a bit of lime?[11]

The most powerful and affecting of the poems of this time is "Die drei Soldaten" ("The Three Soldiers"—A Book for Children), which appeared in the *Versuche* of 1932. Georg Grosz supplied the incisive and bitter illustrations. The poem consists of fourteen sections of rhymed couplets, and describes how three soldiers—Hunger, Mishap, and Consumption—desert toward the end of the war, and make their way through various cities. Here they encounter the rich, the poor, children, men of the church. They are witnesses of the destruction of wheat in a time of hunger. They attend the trial of a worker who has been framed. They see mustard gas being manu-factured. They have a private session with God himself; watch the war of the classes, and finally reach Moscow.

They are so outraged by what they saw in Germany, particularly the passivity with which the poor and the stricken accept their plight; the hardened hearts of the well-to-do in the face of misery; the impotence of God; and (most shameful indignity of all!) the fact that they themselves, the soldiers, are taken for granted, that they begin to commit atrocities. When they finally reach Moscow, they discover that the populace there will not stand for them. The three soldiers laugh for the first time. They say: "These people have some sense. None of them takes us for granted. They'll simply put us up against a wall and shoot us." Which is what happens.

Brecht's anger is white-hot—anger at those who tolerate such outrages no less than at those who perpetrate them. Through the three soldiers he voices his affronted conscience. They resolve

> To shoot all
> Who put up with things as they were.
> For there are many who are afraid to grumble,
> Saying Yes and Amen to all.
> And these would have to be shot,
> So that one at last might know what's what.[12]

Among the bitterest passages in the poem is that describing the soldiers' conference with God, which is attended by personages of wealth. The Lord God, seeing that it is "impossible" to change the world agrees to make misery "invisible." So the soldiers become transparent and one can no longer see Hunger, Mishap, and Consumption. One sees only injustice on earth and the people tormented and exploited. One see the results but not the causes! And even God, having lost all authority with His subordinates on earth, and having Himself forgotten the contents of the book He had once written, is found blundering down below. He too has to be stood up against a wall. With the death of God, the invisible becomes visible again. The class war is revealed.

There are also poems written at this time of a topical nature, political and personal—some directed at the errors of the Weimar Republic and its blindness and its betrayal of the people into the hands of ever more dangerous leaders:

> And soon I heard them saying,
> Everything will be all right:
> If only you take the lesser evil,

> The bigger one won't come overnight.
> We swallowed the clerical Brüning,
> So Papen won't come to the top,
> Then we swallowed the Junker Papen,
> So Schleicher wouldn't pop . . .[13]

And then it was Hindenburg's turn, and now the "house-painter!"

There is ballad of the "Weathervane," who manages to trim with the wind, can "take" everything, and find a good reason for doing so. When he sees the "bloody finger," he quickly says, "That's all right." He blesses these "gentlemen" who cannot be bribed at any price to respect law and injustice, hence are really incorruptible! Brecht was carried away by his anger, and sometimes became unjust, as in the case of Thomas Mann, whom he ranges with the righteous "laggards."

> The writer gives us a Magic Mountain to read;
> What he says (for money), that's well said!
> But what he doesn't say (for nothing), would have
>   been the truth.
> I say: This man is blind. But he hasn't been bribed.[14]

(Had Brecht forgotten that it was Mann who in 1930 published the anti-fascist story of *Mario and the Magician?*) Others like him, Brecht consigns to a place among the "good people," who have done and are doing nothing:

> Good, but for what?
> You can't be bribed. But lightning
> Strikes a house, and can't
> Be bribed either.
> You stick by what you once said.
> But what did you say?
> You are honest; you say what you think?
> But what are your thoughts?
> Now listen: We know
> You are our enemy. Which is why
> We'll put you up against a wall.
> But in recognition of your merits,
> And your good qualities,

We'll make it a good wall—and we'll shoot you
With good bullets, good rifles, and we'll bury you
With a good shovel, in the good earth.[15]

Brecht watched a number of those he knew well turning to Hitler (was he thinking of his old friend Arnolt Bronnen?) and he bade them go, find refuge among their comrades in the enemy ranks, "so that we may be left alone, the only people who couldn't go away."[16]

The savagery he had once turned into chorales and liturgies of nihilism, he now turns against Hitler. The traditional hymn, "Nun danket alle Gott,"

Nun danket alle Gott
mit Herzen, Mund und Händen
der grosse Dinge tut
an uns und allen Enden,

with its praise of God, with heart, lips and hand for all benefactions, becomes in Brecht a hymn of praise (ironic, of course) of the Führer:

Now thank we all the Lord
Who sent us Adolf Hitler
Who'll clear away the dirt,
In all our German lands . . .

He maketh pickles sweet
And sugar tasting sour,
And of a fist-wide crack,
He maketh a new wall.[17]

Even Luther's mighty chorale "Ein feste Burg" is transformed into

Ein grosse Hilf' war uns sein Maul . . .

So great a help was his big mouth,
A weapon and a shield . . .

against Communism, of course . . .

Many of these poems could no longer be made public at the time, but they found their way back to Germany when Brecht was in exile, through underground channels. Brecht was also working on an anti-Hitler comedy, *Die Rundköpfe und die Spitzköpfe* (*Round Heads and Peaked Heads*), during the years 1932 and 1933.

What had seemed for a time repressible, and might really have been repressed, now proved irresistible. On February 27, 1933, the journalist Ludwig Marcuse was sitting in a café on the Kurfürstendamm in Berlin in the company of the writers Josef Roth and Ernst Weiss, when—so Marcuse relates:

The waiter approached our table and said, "The Reichstag is on fire." . . . I went to the telephone and called a newspaper editor who was a friend of mine, and then I called out, "The Reichstag is burning." Who had done it? From two tables, between which I was standing, came two sentences: "The Nazis did it." "The Communists did it." Answers generally anticipate the questions. I packed my belongings. The next day Ossietzky, Mühsam, and many others of my friends were apprehended.[18]

Among those who fled on the 28th of February was Bertolt Brecht. On May 10, his books were burned, along with those of many other German and non-German writers.

Part Two

EXILE, 1933-1948

I

The Poet Speaks About Exile

Tu proverai sì come sa di sale
lo pane altrui, e com' è duro calle
lo scender e il salir per l'altrui scale.

You will learn how salty is the savor
Of another's bread. How hard the passage
To descend and climb another's stair.

DANTE, *Paradiso*

In days to come they will not say:
The times were dark.
But: Why were the poets silent?

BRECHT, "In finstern Zeiten"

The history of German liberalism in the nineteenth century is the
history of exile. Heine, Marx, Ludwig Börne, the poet Freiligrath
testify to this, as well as all those who fled Germany after 1848 to
seek freedom in America.

The history of liberalism in the twentieth century is the history of
exile, murder, and suicide.

In the days after February, 1933, those who remained in Germany
under Hitler, whether, like Ossietzky and Mühsam, because they
refused to leave, or whether, like many others, because they could
not leave, fell victims to torture, imprisonment, and finally murder.
Well-known men and women and thousands of little-known men
and women shared in this martyrdom.

Nor were all those who were fortunate enough to escape able to stand the strain of dislocation and exile. Many of them took their own lives. Such were Walter Benjamin, one of Germany's most acute literary critics, Walter Hasenclever, Stefan Zweig, Kurt Tucholsky, Klaus Mann, and Ernst Toller.

For other exiles, it was at first merely a matter of survival. The fast-racing terror pursued them from land to land, from city to city. Sometimes there was no escape. Sometimes the toe of the enemy was hard upon the heel of the refugee. His reception in foreign lands varied. Sometimes he was greeted with suspicion, even hostility, and coldness. Often he was welcomed with warmth. Lack of funds and the barrier of language often proved almost insurmountable obstacles. Separation from those who had been left behind did not make for ease of mind or conscience.

Brecht was in many ways among the fortunates. He had his family with him, his wife Helene Weigel, and his two children Stefan and Barbara, although the latter had to be smuggled out after the others had already left. He was lucky, too, in having friends abroad who were as open-hearted and open-handed with him as they were understanding. Brecht had never been an epicure or sybarite; his demands did not exceed those he had made at home, and he could be satisfied with less.

At first separation from Germany did not seem as something that would or could last very long. To Arnold Zweig, another refugee, Brecht is reported to have said, "Don't go too far away. In five years we shall be back."[1] How was he, or anyone else for that matter, to know that the five years would stretch to fifteen and that for others there would be no return at all?

At the beginning the way of the exile led him to Prague, Vienna, and Zurich. In Zurich Brecht met Anna Seghers, Heinrich Mann, Walter Benjamin, and Kurt Kläber and his wife. Kläber had been the editor of the radical review, *Die Linkskurve*. He invited Brecht and his family to join them in Carona, in the Swiss Ticino. For a time, there was a penumbral idyllic interlude—the reading of newspapers in the morning, the temporary quiet, and most important for Brecht, conversation and discussion, without which he could not live. Those days at Carona he recalled even on his deathbed in 1956, when he wrote to Kläber, "How warmly I think of . . . Carona, and our joint reading of newspapers out in the open."[2]

But Carona was only a stopping place, as was Sanary-sur-Mer in southern France, where he met many German writers and intellectuals who foregathered to consider the future of Germany (and their own too) and its past as well.[3] Many of these were soon to be herded into French concentration camps. But now they pondered: How long would this pestilence last? How long would they have to stay away? What could the writer, the artist, the thinker do to hasten the downfall of Hitler and Nazism?

Brecht went next to Paris. Here, in the summer of 1933, the ballet he had written to music by Weill, *The Seven Deadly Sins of the Petty Bourgeois,* was being staged by "Ballets 1933," with Tilly Losch dancing, Lotte Lenya in the vocal part, and settings by Caspar Neher. (Brecht was not to see Neher again for many years.) The ballet was a failure in Paris, as it proved to be in London and Copenhagen. This was to be the last Brecht-Weill collaboration.

In Paris Brecht looked as disreputable as ever, at least outwardly. His cap was pulled more tightly over his brow; his shoes were a little more scuffed. He behaved as he had before: he would not be tempted by feminine seductions while he was discussing dialectical materialism with his host; in a very fashionable drawing room, faced by a huge mirror, he became starkly aware of his shabby footwear. At least this was what his friend Kläber reported.[4]

How did he really feel? In a longer poem entitled "Time of My Affluence," he described the house he had bought with his earnings in Germany, the garden, the joy with which he entered it, the pleasure of touching his possessions!

For seven weeks of my life I was rich. . . .[5]

He could enjoy the good things when he had them. But now?

The Danish writer Karin Michaelis, offered him a haven in Denmark. He accepted. In Denmark he would be close to Germany, could have his ear to the ground, could meet and converse with refugees pouring across the borders. Here he could wait . . . and hope. . . . (Let it be remembered to her eternal honor that Denmark proved to be one of the most heroic of nations in aiding refugees—housing them and helping them escape in the face of the Nazi advance.)

For a short while Brecht and his family lived in Karin Michaelis' little house on the island of Thurö. Then they moved to the neighboring island of Fünen, near Skovsbostrand and Svendborg. "Brecht's home became the gathering place of literary refugees."[6] Here a stable was whitewashed, a long table set up against a wall and stacked with papers and writing utensils. Brecht set to work.[7]

"I am happy," he wrote to Kläber, "that I am out of Paris. It's not much more amusing here, but there is more time to work, and the radio is on every evening, and contact with the world has been reestablished. But I miss the talks . . ."[8]

He was not altogether free from harassment. The police kept a watchful eye on the immigrants. The director of police forces in Copenhagen was in constant communication with the police president of Berlin.[9] The attempts on the part of the Nazis to force the Danish government to extradite political refugees, and Brecht in particular, were met with a firm refusal. The bulk of the Danish population, and the government as well, sustained anti-fascist sentiments with laudable integrity and courage.

Feuchtwanger once wrote: "If exile grinds a man down, if it makes some miserable and mean, it also hardens others and makes them great."[10]

Though a number of exiles did collapse and some even did away with themselves as a result of their trials, for Brecht, as for Thomas Mann, Heinrich Mann, and many others, the experiences of these years brought a deepening of their understanding and an increase of internal strength. Brecht grew in moral stature, no less than in the mastery of his craft. It was in exile that his most mature and his greatest works came to fruition.

Whatever the inner resources of that steadfastness, he was fortified in his central conviction that victory would come, and that it
would be brought about by the strength of the people's will. His
political training and his thoroughgoing faith (call it "utopianism"),
his humanism, served as sustaining pillars in those years, when it
was all too easy to yield to pessimism, cynicism, and hopelessness.

Not that Brecht was exempt from sadness, occasional doubt, and
bitterness. But he also possessed the saving grace of humor—not the
frivolous, self-blinding humor of the sentimentalist but the sharp,
clear, realistic humor of the far-sighted. It proved a potent antidote
to depression. He recognized the presence of the tragic situation
(such as the world had never witnessed before), but he never yielded
to tragedy as the ultimate destination and bourne of man.

Exile is a bitter thing for anyone. But for the writer, it is a particularly galling experience. Unlike the musician or painter or
dancer, he is bound by the limitations of language. Separated from
his own people—from his readers—he speaks, as it were, in a
vacuum. If he has an international reputation, he may be translated
and thus be saved the nightmare of silence. But if he is a playwright,
he needs a theatre, actors, and directors. As a practising dramatist
Brecht was aware that it might be years before his plays, those he
had written, and those he was about to write, could achieve adequate performances. But for the time being he realized he must make
do with what was available. Not for nothing had he already utilized
lay actors and lay groups for performances. Such working-class units
were also present in Denmark and elsewhere. Helene Weigel and he
would therefore use whatever resources were at hand.

Before him, on the wall of his new home, he had incised the
words, "Truth is concrete." He would now do what he could to
speak that truth to the world at large and also, if possible, to his
countrymen in Germany.

Not that he was unaware of the difficulties that lay in his path.
Nor could he be free of worries for himself and his family. At any
moment he might have to flee once more. Hitler and the Nazis had

not forgotten him, nor his "Legend of the Dead Soldier," nor his other anti-fascist works. As he sat at his table, looking over the peaceful waters of Svendborg, and observed the whitewashed houses in the vicinity, he noted that one of them had "three exits, good for dwellers who are against injustice and can be apprehended by the police."[11]

Not without nostalgia, he recalls the seeming peace of his home town, Augsburg: the quiet of its evening, the sound of the Ursuline bells, the workers sitting in the courtyards or at their windows watching the housewives, neighbors swaddling the peachtrees against the oncoming night-frost.[12]

But he was not one to yield to such moods often. "Teaching without pupils—writing without glory—is difficult," he said. He recalled the pleasure of turning over the fresh-written sheets to the waiting printers, and walking about the marketplaces where things were being bought and sold, and where he too was selling "sentences."[13] Without readers or critics how can one test the truth or falseness of one's beliefs? But he was sure he would never give up his role of learner, learning from his own past errors, and from others. For "only the grave no longer teaches."[14]

These feelings he wrote into his poems of this period, many of them not to see the light until many years later. Despondency occasionally battles with hopefulness:

> My young son asks: Shall I study mathematics?
> What for? I'm inclined to say. That two pieces of bread
> Are more than one—one can see at once.
> My young son asks: Shall I study French?
> What for? I'm inclined to say. This Reich is done for.
> All you need do is to rub your belly with your hand,
> And groan—and people will understand you.
> My young son asks: Shall I study history?
> What for? I'm inclined to say. Learn to bury your
>   head in the ground,
> And then perhaps you'll survive.
>
> Yes, learn mathematics, I say.
> Study French! Study history![15]

At first he thinks,

> Do not drive a nail into the wall!
> Throw your coat over the chair.
> Why provide for four days?
> Tomorrow you'll go back.[16]

For he believes that just like the cracking plaster peeling off the
ceiling, the rotten barriers separating him from his fatherland will
collapse. But, on second thought, he does hammer a nail into the
wall. It will be some time before he can leave. And the work he is
doing, what is it like?

> Look at the tiny chestnut tree in the corner of the yard,
> To which you drag the can full of water.[16]

He has now joined the ranks of the famous exiles of history:
Ovid, Po-Chü-yi, Tu-fu, Villon, Dante, Heine. In one of his poems,
he pays an imaginary visit to these writers of the past, and each of
them gives him appropriate advice, some of it even causing laughter.
But suddenly from a dark corner a voice cries out, "You, do they
know your verses by heart? And those that know them, have they
escaped their persecutors?" In the silence that falls upon all of them,
Dante explains to Brecht that "those are the forgotten ones. They
suffered destruction not only of their bodies, but also of their works."
At which the newcomer turned pale.[17]

Like so many other refugees, he sits close to the frontier, waiting
the day of return, eagerly questioning every arrival, almost hearing,
across the waters, the anguished cries from German prisons and
camps.

> For we are ourselves
> Almost like rumors of misdeeds, escaped beyond the
>   borders. Each of us
> Testifies to the shame that has disfigured our land.[18]

Well, here Brecht had his few possessions: his soldier's trunk,
with his manuscripts; his smoking implements and ashtrays; the
Chinese scroll showing the "Doubter"; the masks; and, not least,
the small radio with its six tubes. He turns on the radio each morn-

ing, and hears the news of "another victory by our enemy." "Do not
go dead, I beg you," he pleads.

There is much beauty around him, but he can see only that which
is deformed. To be lighthearted and frivolous, seems to him a cardinal sin.

> In my songs, a rhyme
> Would almost seem presumptuous.
>
> Within me struggle
> Excitement over the blossoming apple-tree
> And horror at the speeches of the house-painter.
> But only the second
> Drives me to my writing table.[19]

And sometimes there are even nightmares. He dreams he is
in a city, and on the streets he reads inscriptions in German. He
wakes up, bathed in sweat, and sees the dark firs outside his window,
on the island of Lindingö. He knows he is in a foreign country.[20]
Superstitious peasants believe the screech of an owl forebodes death.
He hears such screeching in the spring nights. But he who knows he
has spoken the truth about those in the seats of power, doesn't need
this death-bird to warn him.[21]

He sorrows for the vacillating and for those who have deserted;
he mourns the loss of "a valuable man," "one who went from a good
cause into a worthless one"; he recalls by contrast the episode during
the First World War, when an Italian prisoner scratched on the
prison wall the words, "Long live Lenin!" which no one could
eradicate. "Now," said the soldier, "if you want to get rid of the inscription, you must remove the wall."[22]

To the shaken and despairing who ask, "On whom can we
count?" he replies, "Expect no other answer than your own."

With pride, Brecht acknowledges that there were good reasons for
his banishment. "I grew up the son of well-to-do parents," he wrote,
in one of his most forceful poems. Yes, his family brought up a
traitor in their midst, one who was to reveal their secrets to the
enemy, translate the Latin of their bought priests into the vernacular
of the common people. For this reason, he was driven from his

land. A warrant had it that he was guilty of "low convictions," that
is of the "convictions of the lowly." But those who are dispossessed
know him and give him shelter say, "You have been banished for
good reason."[23]

But he was much less forbearing with those he felt had betrayed
him and his cause. His old admirer, Karl Kraus, the remarkable
Viennese gadfly, who had consistently defended Brecht in *Die
Fackel* and in turn had won Brecht's admiration, had, in the face of
the Nazi terror, given way to silence—an unspoken condemnation of
the regime. Brecht understood, and wrote:

> When the eloquent one excused himself
> That his voice had failed him,
> Silence stepped forward to the judgment seat,
> Removed her veil,
> And revealed herself as a witness.[24]

But even before this poem could reach its destination, Kraus had
spoken up. He spoke up in favor of Chancellor Dollfuss and Prinz
von Starhemberg, and against the defeated and murdered Social
Democrats, victims of the 1934 Vienna putsch. He also denigrated
the Germans who had fled their country.

Brecht wrote again:

> He testified against those whose lips had been sealed,
> And broke his staff over those who had been killed,
> And praised the murderer.

> What an age, we said, shuddering,
> When the man of good will, but no understanding,
> Cannot wait to perform his misdeed,
> Before praise for his good deed has reached him![25]

This must have been a particularly painful wound in Brecht's side,
for Karl Kraus had even in 1933, when fully aware of Brecht's
politics, called the poet a man who put "most of contemporary
German writers in his pocket." Nor had Brecht forgotten the times
Kraus had attended his Berlin rehearsals and had discussed serious
dramatic problems with him and the other participants.[26]

But there is not much sorrow when Brecht turns to Stefan George, who had been invited into the Hitler Academy. Brecht prays for the time when such a "chatterbox" and "fine talker" would be made to perform some useful work at least once in his lifetime, like pushing a wheelbarrow filled with cement.[27]

In even sharper terms he addresses a prose letter to his old associate, the actor Heinrich George, now a renegade, asking him to intercede for another actor, Hans Otto, reportedly arrested and tortured. Actually, Otto was murdered by the Nazis.

We hear that you are under no suspicion of holding anything against the present regime. Quite early you are reported to have recognized the error of your ways in having associated with us Communists for such a long time . . .

Intercede, Brecht asks, for the extraordinary, and absolutely indispensable and incorruptible Hans Otto. Remember, he continues, times change, and you and your like trust too easily in the permanence of barbarism and the invincibility of the butchers.[28]

Brecht was heartsick when he heard that Carl Ossietzky had been done to death in a Nazi prison. Ossietzky had some time before been awarded the Nobel Prize for peace. A deep-felt poetic tribute mourns him:

> He who would not surrender
> Has been slain.
> He who has been slain,
> Did not surrender . . .

The lips of the man who uttered unheeded warnings are now stuffed with earth, and his grave trampled upon by unholy battalions.

> Was the battle then fruitless?
> When he who has not fought alone
> Is slain,
> The enemy
> Has not yet triumphed.[29]

II

Battle Against the Terror

Fled under a thatched Danish roof,
My friends, I follow your struggles.
Here I send you—from time to time—
Verses raked up through bloody visions
Past water-ways and trees.
Use what reaches you with care!
I made them of yellowed books, shreds
    of news.
When we meet again,
I will turn student once more.

BRECHT, "Svendborg 1939."

From the perilous sanctuary on the island of Fünen in Denmark,
Bertolt Brecht watched the civilized world beating retreat before the
thundering footfalls of Nazism. His own life was henceforth, for
many years to come, a kind of historical footnote to that retreat,
marked by his physical flight before the enemy and counterpointed
by his moral and intellectual growth. For a time, like so many
others, he was to become a marginal man, unsure of the morrow,
subsisting and surviving by what he ironically called his "luck."

What he had assumed was only a temporary nightmare, to vanish
with daybreak, unrolled as a long, dark scroll of history. Hitler's
consolidation of power at home and his unparalleled, and often unexpected, successes abroad, seemed for the time being to be writing
an irrepressible *Finis* to a sane world.

In November, 1933, Germany withdrew from the League of

Nations and the disarmament conference. In the same month, a single party slate was elected. The following June, Hitler eliminated the so-called left wing of the Nazi party—Ernst Roehm, General von Schleicher, and Gregor Strasser. President Hindenburg died in the same year. In July, Chancellor Dollfuss of Austria was assassinated. The Nuremberg racial laws were proclaimed; the Saar returned to Germany amidst triumphant rejoicing, and German rearmament was tacitly accepted as a *fait accompli*. In 1936 the Rhineland was occupied; and with the outbreak of the Spanish Civil War, Germany and Italy directly intervened on Franco's side. In March, 1938, Austria was annexed, and the comic tragedy of "appeasement" and "peace in our time" commenced. On September 30, 1938, Neville Chamberlain, Prime Minister of Great Britain, was at Berchtesgaden and signed the Munich agreement; and by March 15, 1939, Czechoslovakia had ceased to exist as an independent state. In August, 1939, came the Nazi-Soviet non-aggression pact, and on September 1, 1939, Poland was invaded. In April, 1939, Brecht fled to Sweden. In April, 1940, he was in Finland. In May of 1941, somewhat ahead of the Nazi divisions, Brecht boarded a train for Vladivostok. He was on his way to the United States.

If in the course of these Odysseys Brecht had not already become immune to ironies, another one of these might have struck him. For on the 19th of April, 1941, *Mother Courage,* his anti-war play, was produced at the Zurich Schauspielhaus by Leopold Lindtberg, with Therese Giehse in the title role. Eight weeks later, the Nazis began their invasion of the Soviet Union, on the 22nd of June, 1941. Brecht was then in mid-ocean. On July 21, 1941, he landed in San Pedro, California.

Brecht, who had fought Hitler and Nazism while he was still on home ground, needed no urgings to go on fighting them when deprived of his country. There was one task before him, and that was the destruction of the enemy. To that task he set himself immediately. He thus kept his eye constantly on the main target, and never allowed himself to be deflected from it. He had always taken the role of the writer seriously. He was now going to use whatever weapons he possessed to attack the main strongholds of the new barbarism.

This is not to say that Brecht was immune to sorrows, doubts, pain, and even depression. But he had the invincible faith in the power of the word to move people to action. Perhaps he over-estimated that power; but it is not recorded that he ever wavered.

There were other difficulties besides the political ones to contend with: the absence of an adequate theatre; the ever-diminishing possibilities of publication. He had brought with him unfinished and finished manuscripts, some of which he was fortunate enough to have published by firms established by refugees in Prague, Amsterdam, and London.

He participated as a contributing editor to anti-fascist publications of journals like *Die Sammlung* issued in Amsterdam; *Das Wort* and *International Literatur,* which appeared in Moscow. He took part actively in writers' congresses and other meetings in various parts of Europe. He read constantly and studied hard. He gathered reports from refugees. Helene Weigel and he worked with local theatrical groups, both professional and amateur.

Like Coriolanus, he might have said of himself:

> While I remain above the ground you shall
> Hear from me still; and never of me aught
> But what is like me formerly.

He did not allow himself to be diverted from work. In 1934 a volume of his poems, *Lieder, Gedichte, Chöre,* with musical settings by Hanns Eisler, appeared in Paris. In the same year, the Amsterdam publisher Allert de Lange issued his *Dreigroschenroman.*

In the summer of 1933 he was in Paris for the production of the ballet *The Seven Deadly Sins of the Petty Bourgeois.*

This ballet was in many ways a postcript to *Mahagonny.* Its anti-bourgeois animus marked it another of those "dances of death" of the bourgeoisie. Once more he went back to America for his setting:

Two sisters (actually two facets of one person) Anna I and Anna II, one representing the self-repression and self-denial necessary for success in modern society; the other representing the natural instincts and healthy needs and responses, set out to earn money to enable their family in Louisiana to build a house. The family prays:

> The Lord enlighten our dear children
> That they may know the way to well-being.
> May He give them strength and joy
> Not to sin against the laws,
> That make men rich and happy.

Anna II is tempted to give way to sins, that is, her natural desires: sloth (she likes to sleep); wrath (she resents injustice); gluttony (she doesn't like to starve herself); pride (she doesn't want to strip-tease); and lust (she falls in love). As an "entertainer" she does succeed in overcoming her good natural impulses, and her venture is crowned with monetary rewards. Again, Brecht treats of the ways nature is throttled in the money-markets, private feelings becoming obstacles in the race for money and success. When this ballet was produced by the Royal Danish Ballet in Copenhagen, the King of Denmark, who was present, was reported so outraged that he left in high dudgeon.[1] Actually, this is not an inspired work, and it is more memorable for Weill's score than for Brecht's lines.

The publication of the novel *Der Dreigroschenroman* (*The Three Penny Novel*) now completed that trilogy which had begun with the *Three Penny Opera,* had run a stormy second variation with the *Three Penny* film, and was now to consummate the theme as a novel. As such it is somewhat disorganized, sometimes slow, but more often than not illuminated by those lightning scenes that show Brecht at his satirical best. In addition to the old and well-known characters, Brecht introduced a new one, a proletarian, George Fewcoombey, a crippled veteran of the Boer Wars, recently returned to London. He is the bearer of Brecht's new social message. We have moved into the world of more complex, higher if not more moral, financial speculation. Macheath in addition to being an underworld crook, is also the owner of a number of stores selling stolen goods. Eventually he becomes a big banker. Peachum, in addition to his old occupation, is also involved in a shady deal of selling rotten ships to the government for the transport of British troops to South Africa.

Brecht's satirical gifts have something of the brilliant savagery and point of Swift. Thus a sermon delivered by the Bishop, in memory of soldiers who had gone down in one of the defective vessels named *The Optimist,* transforms a biblical parable into the cynicism of "from each according to 'talents': from those on high, the governors, the rulers, and the statesmen, wisdom; from those who have gone down, their little services, too." "For we have gained something from the wreck of *The Optimist,* which was destined to go down. It has borne interest upon interest, O Lord. . . . From each according to his ability."[2]

What the narrative lacks in story line or psychology, it makes up in the reflections on life and man, war and peace, "the ways of the world." Thus,

In the ship's hold the rats were scurrying about like sheep in the fields of Wales, big, fat, beasts, who despite their old age, had never seen a human being, and hence did not suspect what a menace he was.[3]

Macheath's reflections on "selling" are not outdated:

To be a seller is to be a teacher. Selling means to make war on ignorance, the shocking ignorance of the public. . . . One must tell them, as if they were children, what they need. . . . They must buy what they can use, not what they need.[4]

Nor, for that matter, Peachum's on "crimes and crimes":

The whole world knows that the crimes of men of substance are protected by nothing so much as by their improbability. Statesmen can take money only because their corruption is considered more refined and cleverer than it really is.[5]

Fewcoombey, who had taken service with Peachum, but is now discharged and homeless, was present at the sermon and listened to the words of the Bishop. Now, alone and destitute, lying under the bridge, he has a dream of the Last Judgment. He, Fewcoombey, is the Judge, and the defendant none other than the author of the parable, Christ himself. For the Bishop had used as text Luke xix, 11-26, concerning the nobleman who "went into a far country," and on parting distributed to his servants ten pounds each, and on returning found that all of them except one had invested their money with profit.

Here is one of the most memorable and moving scenes Brecht ever wrote. Before Fewcoombey stand the witnesses for the accused, those who had propagated the notion that unto each has been given ten pounds to invest, increase, and multiply. But it turns out that these, in addition to their natural gifts of intelligence, human reason, diligence, and skills, also had other more earthly resources. But what of those others, Fewcoombey the Judge inquires of Christ, such as were not endowed with the ten pounds? You are supposed to have said that not only *some* people, but *everybody* receives his or her pound, which then increases to five or even ten pounds. But here they are: the witnesses for the prosecution, the starved, the prematurely old, the crippled and the poor. Did you not see them? The Judge cannot understand all this; he is too ignorant; and in despair summons the *Encyclopedia Britannica* to answer the perplexing question: Why do a few, the least part, multiply their possessions, and out of one pound succeed, as the Bible states and ordains, in making five or even ten? But others, the greater part of mankind, can only multiply not pounds but their misery? What is this pound of the fortunate? But the *Encyclopedia* can only jabber of Capital, Labor Power, Organization, Inventions, and Frugality. Finally, the Judge himself comes upon the truth:

Man is the *Pound*! We are the Pound. And he who has no one else to exploit, exploits himself.

There are hundreds of thousands who have never been paid in full—those who were never given the pound with which to increase their possessions. And Fewcoombey the Judge turns to the accused Christ:

You are the guilty one! All you have described is false! You have spread lies. I convict you of collusion, for you have handed your people this parable, which is also a pound, with which they can accumulate interest. And I also convict all those who transmit it—who dare tell it to others—I sentence them to death! I also sentence whoever lets himself in for that parable, and does not immediately undertake to do something against it. And because I myself have listened to this parable, and because I have kept quiet, I too condemn myself to death.[6]

Actually, a few days later, Fewcoombey is arrested for a murder indirectly committed by Macheath, and is hanged.

Such is Brecht's "heartbreak house," the grief and anger that men in their blindness fail to "see" and "understand" what it is that enslaves them, and that they are often their own slave-drivers.

Brecht had also brought with him from Germany a finished draft of an anti-Nazi play, *Spitzköpfe und Rundköpfe* (*Peaked Heads and Round Heads*), on which he had been working since 1932. Now, in the Danish exile, he began to revise it in view of the gruesome changes that had taken place: the Reichstag Fire and the Nuremberg racial laws, which had also deepened his own understanding of the nature of fascism.

The play had originated as an adaptation of Shakespeare's *Measure for Measure* and had been requested for the Volksbühne by its director Ludwig Berger. As always happened with Brecht, intentions began to take on novel shapes. His imagination immediately transformed an older subject into a contemporary one, and what emerged was something altogether new. He had been attracted to *Measure for Measure* by its philosophical and social content. Aside from being Shakespeare's most "philosophical" play, it was in his eyes "his most progressive one." For it called upon those in power that they be measured as they measure; that they do not demand of their subjects a morality which they themselves do not practice.[7]

The earliest sketches of Brecht's play suggest that he was primarily concerned with exposing the class character of justice, rather than, as in Shakespeare, the problem of mercy and human frailty. The first completed version of the play, now retitled *Die Rundköpfe und die Spitzköpfe* (*Round Heads and Peaked Heads*) was already in print when Hitler took power. The Nazis immediately confiscated it. Brecht had tried to show that an attempt to reconcile class interests by means of some supra-class ideology was futile and deceptive, even if sincerely undertaken. In this version, Shakespeare's Angelo becomes Angelas, an almost tragic character who is anti-capitalist—a sort of Don Quixote—but who hopes to reconcile the conflicts in his society. In the end he is disenchanted. His demagogy is directed against what he believes to be the true enemies of society, the "Peaked Heads." But he soon discovers that the "Round Heads," the purer elements, are motivated by their special interests and think only of money, and are not at all guided by the welfare of the entire state.[8]

After 1933, such an interpretation of fascist ideology could no longer stand up. The transformed Angelo had now to be seen for what he was—a ruthless demagogue, a brutal ruler, a cynic, the willing instrument of the capitalist land-owners. The original setting in a far-distant land was retained, though Lima, Peru, was changed to Luma, in the land of the Yahoos. The country is in a state of collapse, and the vice-king consults with his minister Missena as to the best way out of the economic disaster. The tenant farmers are in rebellion; they have refused to pay their rents, and have joined a revolutionary organization, the "Sickles." The "Big Five," the representatives of wealth, have refused to come to the aid of the government unless the "Sickles" are crushed. There is hope that a middle-of-the-roader, an alleged "neutral," might bring about a reconciliation of the classes. Such a one is Angelo Iberin, who has discovered a new political and social theory, that of the Round Heads and of the Peaked Heads. The latter are an incubus—strangers, intruders, selfish, materialistic—and must be exterminated.

The Round Heads are noble, blue-blooded, unselfish. Iberin can now proceed, for he has the support of the "Big Five."

His stratagem is only too successful, for he manages to split the ranks of the tenant farmers, one of whom, Callas, a Round Head, taking Iberin's demagogy as gospel, possesses himself of two horses belonging to his landlord, a Peaked Head, Guzman, and accuses the latter of having racially defiled his daughter Nanna. But he is very soon undeceived: his honor is restored to him, but he is granted neither remission of rents nor the two horses. In the end, Callas finds himself consigned to the army, for now new enemies have been discovered threatening the country—the "Square Heads."

Into this complicated pattern, Brecht tried to fit another theme, that of *Measure for Measure,* to parallel the Shakespearean Isabella-Angelo motif. But whereas in Shakespeare this theme gives rise to some of the most moving and passionate utterances on the subject of mercy and justice and power, in Brecht, who turns over Guzman's sister to a similar ordeal, it becomes only an added unnecessary burden on an already overburdened plot.

But the master hand of the satirist is revealed in a number of scenes, such as those dealing with the disenchantment of Callas after his first putative successes; and the bitter realism of Nanna, the prostitute, and Frau Cornamontis, the brothel-keeper. The songs, set by Eisler, are among the best Brecht and he wrote; such for example, as the "Song of the Invigorating Effect of Money"—how it changes life and character:

> Your clothes are finer; you eat all you can.
> And now your man is a very different man.[9]

Nanna, prostitute and pessimist, sings the "Song of the Water Wheel," with its theme of the unchangeability of things within change:

> Of the great ones of this earth,
> Ancient tales tell us the story
> How they rose like stars on high,
> And how dimmed at last their glory.

> This sounds soothing: one should heed them.
> But we who serve the great ones, feed them,
> What's it to us? Late or soon,
> Rise or fall—Who pays the tune?
>
> Sure the wheel turns ever faster,
> What's above, soon's down below.
> But to the water what does it matter?
> It's always there to make the wheel go.[10]

Frau Cornamontis, the true realist, has her own song too in reply to the small shop-keepers' blessing of the new times. It is the "Song of the Buttons"—which ever way you toss them, they turn with the hole-side up. For Callas and the shopkeepers there are no heads or tails. Only holes.

The curious reader will also find other sources for Brecht's play. For example, the celebrated affair of Jean Calas in eighteenth-century France, associated with the name of Voltaire. Calas, a French Protestant wrongly accused of bringing about the death of his son to prevent his turning Catholic, was put to the torture, and killed, and posthumously vindicated through the vigorous efforts of Voltaire. Swift supplied Brecht with the name of the Yahoos. Heinrich von Kleist's masterpiece, the story of *Michael Kohlhaas*, the sixteenth-century horse-dealer who, as a result of abuse by a local knight, turns incendiary and rebel, gave Brecht hints for struggle between Guzman and Callas, and may well have suggested the latter's name.

It is not surprising that the play, when produced in Danish in Copenhagen on November 4, 1936, at the Theater "Riddersalen" aroused mixed feelings, and not a little confusion. The enemy press was, of course, savage. But even the friendly audience could not fully understand what it was Brecht had intended. Aside from the strangeness of the "epic" style, the contents itself led to misunderstandings. For Brecht was suggesting collusion between Aryan and non-Aryan capitalists in support of Hitlerism, at a time when the Nuremberg laws already foreshadowed what was in store for the Jews, rich and poor.

Perhaps a more fundamental question that arises at this point is whether the parable forms—and satire and irony—were the most viable instruments for exposing the nature of fascism and opposing its spread; whether, after all, the horror of the historical situation did not, in fact, make it necessary to re-examine the form and objectives of a militant work of art in an era of impending barbarism. That Brecht himself was aware of this problem is evident from the varieties of activities he undertook at this time and his adoption of new forms. His main objective still remained: the elucidation of the nature and sources of Nazism, so as not to render it a transcendent evil, or an aspect of some unavoidable and irrefragable "will," and to make possible its elimination through man's efforts.

In connection with *Rundköpfe und Spitzköpfe* Brecht uses the term "Verfremdung" for the first time. He indicates how the process of estrangement was carried out in the Copenhagen production. When Nanna Callas sings her first song of the prostitute, amid the shopkeepers' signs, she acts out the character of a commodity among commodities. In the scene (which affronted some religious sensibilities) in which Isabella is to be accepted into a convent pending a monetary settlement, a young nun steps from the wings with a gramophone and accompanies parts of the scene with organ music. When Guzman tries to persuade his sister to yield to Iberin, Brecht asked that the acting and speech be "played in all seriousness in the lofty and passionate style of the Elizabethan theatre," thus to set off the sordid commercial dealings of the upper classes.[11]

Brecht did not seem particularly upset by the Copenhagen reception of his play. Some years later, he remarked that he saw some spectators weeping at a scene which others were laughing at. "And I was satisfied with both."[12]

At this time he was completing the last of his Lehrstücke, *Die Horatier und die Kuratier* (*The Horatii and the Curatii*), "a didactic play for children about dialectics." In some respects it is the most compact and the most skilful of his didactic efforts. And it seemed particularly applicable to a time of "retreat." Using a minimal number of characters, in the Chinese tradition, the principal players carry little pennants to indicate their military strength. The Curatii desire the land and possessions of the Horatii, and attack them. At first, because they have the better arms, the Curatii appear to be winning. But the pursued Horatian swordsman succeeds in dividing the enemy, and beats them one by one. This is another example of Einverständnis—acquiescence in a critical situation. Here the need is to utilize whatever weapons one has, in as many ways as possible; to use natural surroundings and nature itself as re-enforcements; to use one's opponents; to know one's enemy and divide him; and not to hesitate to run, to retreat in order later to be able to re-form one's ranks.

Undoubtedly, Brecht's eyes were fixed on the times, when through the lips of the Horatian chorus he adjures the retreating soldier:

> Now begin your retreat!
> You have lost time. Now lose even more!
> You are weakened. Now you must redouble your work.
> Snowstorm and snowfall
> Do not spare the disheartened . . .
>
> Yet the retreat of a staunch fighter
> Is a part of the fresh advance.[13]

This was part of Brecht's unceasing effort to speak to his fellow-men, both those who were abroad and those who still remained in Germany. Among those abroad, divisions which had marked their unquiet life in Germany had not by any means been obliterated. It was necessary to unite them. The popular fronts forged in France in 1935 and in Spain in the following year were favorable omens for the future. But to those who were in Germany, it was harder to speak. The work had to be done by means of the illegal radio, by means of literature smuggled into the country. How difficult it was to convey it, and even more difficult to distribute it! For German underground propaganda, Brecht wrote a series of directives, *Five Difficulties in Writing the Truth,* in which he spoke of "the courage to write the truth although it is everywhere suppressed; the shrewdness to recognize it, although it is concealed; the art of making it available as a weapon; the cunning to disseminate it; and the judgment to choose those in whose hands it will be most effective."[14]

But to convey the truth to others, Brecht recognized, you must first of all be able to convey it to yourself. This was not easy. Brecht proceeds in the same clear-eyed, pitiless way that he was to follow henceforth: to insist that those who were persecuted were persecuted not because they were "good," but also because they were "weak" and had made mistakes. What was needed was not blame and self-pity, but self-examination. Mistakes had been made, but on all sides! After all, one had to face the fact that the vast numbers of working people in Germany had proved powerless to stem the Nazi advance, and had in great part fallen prey to Nazi demagogy. To spread the truth about Nazism in Germany it is necessary to show it not as a "natural catastrophe" but as man- and class-made, and as transitory. This is also the theme of his address to the First Writers Congress for the Defense of Culture, which met in Paris in June, 1935. (That very month Brecht had been officially deprived of his German citizenship.) He opposes mystical talk about the origins of fascism as due to some "miseducation" of the Germans. Writers must understand the economic basis of Nazism, that it is an exploitative movement dominated by big business.[15]

To bring the "truth" to the Germans in Germany he wrote poems particularly adapted to being broadcast by the illegal radio. For this type of poetry, Brecht worked out a new style—a "gestic" language.

The *German Satires* [Brecht explained] were written for the German Freedom Radio. It was a matter of broadcasting individual sentences to a distant, artificially dispersed audience. These sentences had to be cut down to their most concise form, so that interruptions (by jamming) would not do too much harm. Rhyme seemed to me not to be particularly suitable, since it lent the poem the character of something self-enclosed, something that was transitory when heard. Regular rhythms with their even cadences do not etch themselves adequately, and they require circumlocutions; many of the current expressions do not fit into them. What we needed was the tone of direct and immediate speech. Unrhymed verse, with irregular rhythms, seemed to me most suitable.[16]

The cries of street venders, the slogans shouted in demonstrations of workers served him as models for this "gestic" irregular speech. Additional impetus came from the ancient Chinese poets, particularly Po-Chü-yin, whom he admired above all others, and who had used his art to teach peasants, and who would read his poems to them to test them.[17]

Brecht's changes of style or manner were never casual or capricious. They were made in response to both inner and outer necessities. Now he joined a passion for simplicity to succinctness; welded epigrammatic point with dialectics.

The new poems he was now writing are hammered out with precision. Thus he speaks to his fellow-Germans:

> Chalked on the wall:
> "They want war."
> He who wrote it,
> Is already fallen.[18]

Or,

> General, your tank is a powerful vehicle.
> It can break down a forest and crush
>   hundreds of people.
> But it has one fault,
> It needs a driver. . . .
>
> General, man is very usable.
> He can fly and he can kill.
> But he has one fault:
> He can think.[19]

Or, to an immediate point of history:

> The chiefs of state
> Have gathered in a room.
> Man in the street:
> Give up all hope.[20]

The governments
Write non-aggression pacts.
Little man:
Write your testament.[20]

The *German Satires* have their own tinge of bitter humor, as in
the "Dream of a Defeatist," in which a potato speaks to the Germans
at the same time as the Führer is holding forth in the opera house.
The potato warns against the seduction of Hitler's speech. With each
additional word of the Führer, the potato "shrank, and became
smaller, meaner, sicklier."[21]

Though ever anxious to establish himself as a playwright in the
Soviet Union and find acceptance, he never quite succeeded. He was
there in 1935, to see old friends—emigré Germans as well as Russians: Erwin Piscator, Carola Neher, Bernhard Reich, Serge Tretyakov. His motion picture, *Kuhle Wampe,* when shown in Moscow,
met with very cool reception. The Soviet audience could not understand the suicide of a worker who owned a bicycle and a watch.
Nor did Brecht experience much joy from Tairov's production of
the *Three Penny Opera,* which had been performed at Anatole
Lunarcharski's urgent prompting. Tairov had apparently turned
Brecht's bitter satire into something resembling a "musical with
dances." Brecht contended himself with the thought: At least
Tairov has done it; and that's something. Half the audience walked
out; the younger half that remained cheered.

When he revisited Moscow the following year, he could scarcely
have been aware that he was seeing some of his friends for the last
time. Carola Neher was to disappear somewhere in a prison camp
in the next years; Tretyakov was to fall victim to one of Stalin's
purges. But for the moment there was a happy reunion with those
two, as well as with Bernhard Reich, whom he was to see again
in 1941. Tretyakov was translating Brecht' plays; and had actually
interested Nikolai Okhlopov in staging *St. Joan of the Stockyards*
at the latter's "Realistic Theatre." Unfortunately that venture fell
by the wayside, as did the somewhat romantic project of Erwin

Piscator's to establish a Weimar-in-exile in the Soviet Union, that would preserve the best of German humanism. Brecht, too, was to be a part of that undertaking.[21a]

There seemed to be better prospects in America. The New York Theatre Union was to produce *Mother* at the end of 1935, and Brecht left for the United States toward the end of that year. He remained in New York until February, 1936.

The production of *Mother* at the Civic Repertory Theatre in New York, however, proved another bitter disappointment to Brecht. He was very critical of the English version by Paul Peters, and even more so of Victor Wolfson's staging. The sets designed by Mordecai Gorelik pleased him as little. Very few of the participants in the New York production were even vaguely acquainted with the meaning of Brecht's epic theatre. Gorelik confessed that he heard of it for the first time from Brecht's lips. Nor was the acting company, competent as it might prove itself in other plays, capable of establishing the "estrangement" demanded by the author. Brecht, Eisler, and the Epic Theatre were ranged against naturalism and the Stanislavski method of the Theatre Union. Considering the flare-up of tempers on both sides, it was a miracle that *Mother* ever achieved a production at all.[21b] The unfortunate fracas led to some minor scandals, disclosed poor taste on all sides, and was scarcely calculated to promote the cause of the Epic Theatre in America, or on the Left. It resulted in a hybrid that was neither Brechtian fish nor Stanislavski fowl, and, as happens so very often in the theatre, ended by everyone hating everyone else.

This is the way Mordecai Gorelik describes his encounters with Brecht:

[Brecht] declared that someone had turned *Mother* not only into English, but into suspenseful, saccharine trash. And the Gorelik designs were bourgeois, picturesque, and wrong from start to finish.[22]

But Gorelik finally came to understand Brecht's insistence on simplicity of the props, and began to "visualize this Japanese kind of precision." Brecht agreed that Gorelik was catching on. Three years later, when Gorelik visited Brecht in Denmark and witnessed a production of *Round Heads and Peaked Heads,* he had so far advanced in his understanding of Brecht's theatre that he was able to make some valuable suggestions in his own right.

The New York production of *Mother* included such actors as Helen Henry, as Vlassova; John Boruf, as Pavel; and Martin Wolfson, Lee Cobb, and Hester Sondergard. It opened on November 19, 1935, and ran for 36 performances. Its reception on the part of the New York press was as anticipated: The *New Leader* and the *Daily Worker* praised it; the *Herald Tribune,* the *Brooklyn Daily Eagle* and the *Evening Journal* damned it. Brecht was dissatisfied. He objected to a great deal of the textual revision, the Russification of the costumes; the violation of the epic quality of the play by a jazzed-up action; and the practice of having the chorus speak to the characters in the play directly.

In a poem, as serious as it is good-natured, addressed to the Theatre Union, Brecht indicated his points of difference with them:

> Here you add a "Good morning,"
> There a "Hello, young fellow". . . .
>
> The son's death you cleverly place at the end.
> In this way you hope to hold the spectator's interest. . . .
>
> Comrades, the form of this piece
> Is new. But why
> Fear what is new? . . .
>
> For those who are exploited, constantly betrayed,
> Life too is a constant experiment. . . .
>
> But even should your spectator, the worker,
> Hesitate, then you must
> Go in front of him, with broad steps, trusting in
>   his ultimate powers,
> Without reservations.[23]

On July 18, 1936, the Spanish Army Chiefs rebelled against the legally established Republic of Spain; on July 19, General Francisco

Franco joined the rebels, and very soon thereafter German and Italian planes were flying over the country. The Spanish Republic, founded in 1931, and thereafter under constant threat of dismemberment, had as a result of the Popular Front victory of 1936 brought a promise of democracy to the people. Now it had become the skirmishing grounds for Nazis and Italian fascists; and the battlefield for the survival of a democratic state. As never before, nor for a long time after, the best part of the civilized world united in support of the hard-pressed Republic. The embattled Loyalists found reinforcements in large armies of volunteers who joined their colors. "No pasaran!" rang out throughout the world, as it breathlessly watched the uneven struggle. Arms and money flowed into the camp of the rebels, while the forces of the Loyalists were hamstrung by the non-intervention of presumably democratic countries. Blockades and "neutrality" (in which the American government played a major role) were enough to give the *coup-de-grâce* to what was generally acknowledged one of the most heroic efforts in modern history. With the surrender of Madrid in 1939, the war was brought to an end.

But in 1937 the outcome was still undecided. Writers responded, both as participants in the Loyalist brigades and with their pens.

Brecht contributed a short play, *The Rifles of Señora Carrar*, in June, 1937.

The suggestion for this work came from John Millington Synge's tender one-act tragedy, *Riders to the Sea*. Brecht utilized the blockade of Bilbao, as well as the incredible resistance of the Spanish working classes, as the immediate dramatic occasion for his play. The theme of *Señora Carrar* is simple: A fisherwoman, who has already lost her husband in the uprising, is now eager to keep her two sons out of the war against the "Generals." While her older boy, Juan, is out fishing, the younger one, José, is fretting at home, bridling at his enforced inactivity. Señora Carrar is not a pacifist, but she hates violence, and feels guilty because she had two years before supported her husband in his opposition to the fascists. Now she has hidden his cache of arms in her home. When her brother, Pedro Jaqueras, a worker, comes to collect them in defense of the Republic, she refuses to yield them. The local priest, Padre Francisco, though a humanist, is also a pacifist, and supports Señora Carrar. While she is out, uncle and nephew discover the arms. Señora Carrar is outraged; but suddenly the light which marks Juan's fishing boat, and which could be seen from the window, goes out. Has Juan secretly gone off to join the Loyalists? She curses him, if he has. But Juan has actually been wantonly killed by the fascists, and his body is now carried in. Señora Carrar is ready not only to turn over the guns to Pedro, but she will also take up a rifle herself. "For the sake of Juan," she says.

As a polemic against non-intervention, Brecht's brief play also illustrates his flexibility as a writer. For here Brecht has abandoned the epic style and returned to the "Aristotelian" drama. It is a one-character play; its effectiveness rests upon an emotional impact. It is a unified piece, with a climax. It is directed toward producing an immediate reaction and activity. Brecht had already, some years before, spoken of the appropriateness of using Aristotelian "catharsis" when the intention was to produce an immediate and practical effect. This was in connection with Friedrich Wolf's very controversial play, *Cyankali,* written during the Weimar days, and dealing with abortion.

Now Brecht was himself sacrificing an all-important theory in the face of an emergency. He was well aware of the shortcomings of the play, and so were his auditors.

The Danish novelist Martin-Andersen Nexö, author of the masterly epic story, *Pelle the Conqueror,* now another of Brecht's new friends, remarked that the conclusion was not effective on the stage, though it impressed profoundly when read. Brecht was, of course, hampered by his suppression of epic effects, which would have made the canvas much broader and enabled him to clarify the all-important issues behind the Spanish conflict. In a Swedish production of the play, he attempted to correct this shortcoming and wrote a prologue which takes place in a French concentration camp, in which Señora Carrar, her son, and her brother are confined, and which is guarded by Frenchmen. Pedro is skeptically interrogated by one of the French guards as to the usefulness of the Spanish struggle. He points to his sister:

She also asked the question: Why fight? She did not ask it to the end, but for a very long time. And like her, others too asked the question for a long time, almost to the very end. And because they kept on asking the question for so long a time, they were beaten. See? And if some day you keep on asking this question, you'll be beaten too.[24]

There are powerful moments in the play, such as when Señora Carrar heaps curses upon her son; there is a very enlightening discussion between Pedro and the priest about intervention and violence. But the sudden change of heart on the part of Señora Carrar at the end was scarcely adequately motivated, for her complex character had not been sufficiently illuminated—nor, for that matter, had the complex historical moment.

A touching and somewhat amusing instance of how the intensity of a situation might sometimes work havoc with the practice of "epic" acting occurred in the performance of *Señora Carrar* by Helene Weigel, recorded, regretfully, by Brecht himself:

Even Weigel herself on some occasions broke into tears at certain passages, altogether against her own will, and not to the advantage of the performance. . . . Whether it was because the Civil War had taken a bad turn for the oppressed that day, or whether Weigel was upset for some other reason, tears came into her eyes as she delivered her condemnation of her son, who was already murdered. She wept not as a peasant woman, but as a performer over the peasant woman. I see an error here, but I do not see any of my rules violated.[25]

But the novelist Anna Seghers, who witnessed Weigel's performance in Paris, wrote that her voice was worth many newspapers, leaflets, or even a truck full of munitions. "That evening we knew what a German theatre really meant."[26] She adds that the performance was attended by many German-speaking emigrants who ordinarily stayed away from the left-wing theatre.

The Theater am Schiffbauerdamm

Brecht at a Berliner
Ensemble rehearsal

LEFT: *Mann ist Mann* with Theo Lingen, Alexander Granach, and Wolfgang Heinz (19[

FACING PAGE: *Die Dreigroschenoper* with Wolf Kaiser and Felicitas Ritsch; Berliner Ensemble

BELOW: *Das kleine Mahagonny,* Berliner Ensen[

Galileo with Charles Laughton, Hollywood and New York, 1947

But no one who has lived through the Spanish Civil War can be surprised that Weigel found it impossible to control her tears. Weigel must have moved her audience profoundly. Brecht has given us a memorable portrait of her in a poem, as she prepares for such a performance. She bends over her worn stool, and "removing every trace of individuality from her face," she lets her "slight and delicate shoulders droop, like those who work hard." With her patched blouse, she is a true peasant woman, and

> she gets up—a small figure—
> a great warrior
> stepping into her bast shoes ready to enact
> the battle of the Andalusian fisherwoman
> against the generals.[27]

But Germany, too, was at the center of Brecht's thoughts. To bring an understanding of the nature of Nazism to Germans abroad he set to work on thirty sketches entitled *Furcht und Elend im Dritten Reich* (*Fear and Misery in the Third Reich*), which he completed by 1938.

Here too he was ready to sacrifice his non-Aristotelian dramatic principles in favor of achieving an immediate response. He had always been a master of the brief sketch. His quick imagination had worked on newspaper clippings, pictures, and radio reports; and he transformed these into dramatic incidents, etched in "concrete truth," to show how fear and misery within Germany affected all strata of its society—the intelligentsia, the petty bourgeoisie, and the working classes. Perhaps these plays would find their way into Germany, but Brecht was looking primarily to the emigrés. Were not even such brilliant figures as Lion Feuchtwanger, for example, toying with some mumbo-jumbo interpretations of the Nazi phenomenon, treating it like some "natural" accident, bound to disappear of itself in due time?

Foremost in Brecht's mind was the capitulation of the intelligentsia in the face of the terror. They are the subjects of the most brilliant of the sketches, as well as the most terrifying. The accused stand before the judgment seat of Brecht's withering irony: the judge, the teacher, the physicians, the physicist, the priest. One can almost *smell* the terror and the degradation. The perplexed judge, in the sketch called "Justice," is about to enter the courtroom to pass sentence on a rabble of Storm Troopers accused of having assaulted and robbed a Jewish jeweler. How shall he dispense justice? Terrified, he turns first to the criminal inspector, then to the district attorney, finally to the superior judge, feeling more and more helpless after each conversation. His maid is sure he will convict the gangsters, since everyone knows that they are the culprits. In desperation, the judge exclaims to the superior jurist:

Understand, I am ready to do anything. . . . I can decide this way, or I can decide that way, just as they want me to, but I must know what they want. If one doesn't know that, there is no justice any longer.[28]

In a parallel situation, the gymnasium teacher and his wife, troubled by the suspicion that their son might be a Nazi informer, plan to flee. They search their minds and their past for possible misdemeanors. The teacher explodes:

I am ready to teach anything they want me to teach. But what do they want me to teach? How do I know what sort of Bismarck they want me to present?[28]

The physicists in the laboratory dare not discuss science for fear of being overheard naming a foreign scientist—Einstein, for example. The chief surgeon of a hospital, long on ethical mouthings and monitions to his subordinates, is faced with a mutilated victim of the Oranienburg concentration camp and cavalierly passes on to the next patient. The priest at the deathbed of a recalcitrant fisherman is forced to eat the Gospel words about the blessedness of the peacemakers. In "The Jewish Wife," the most moving of all these short plays, the wife of the title is about to leave her Aryan husband, a prominent physician, and addresses her absent husband:

What's come over them? What do they really want? What have I done to them? I never mixed in politics. Was I for Thälmann? . . . .

Her husband appears, hems and haws, but we know he will give way and let her go. Fear and disenchantment everywhere: the petty butcher who voted for Hitler is pilloried because he stocks black-market meats and hangs himself in his own shop window. Nor is the working man spared. He too has fallen for the blandishments of the Führer, turns Storm Trooper, provokes other workers to words of insubordination, and then knows how to pinpoint them later by having marked their backs with chalk. In the concentration camp, among the political prisoners, old squabbles arise again between a Communist and a Social Democrat!

"Wird das Elend die Furcht besiegen?" Brecht asks. "Will misery conquer fear?" He pays tribute to the small contingent of brave, underground fighters, those who face death, and yet dare publish their clandestine literature. A letter from one such is read to an illegal group:

My dear son: Tomorrow I will be no longer. Executions are generally set for six in the morning. I am writing to tell you that my opinions have not changed. I have not asked for a pardon, for I have not committed a crime. . . . You are still very small, but it won't hurt always to remember which side you are on. Stand by your class, and your father will not have suffered in vain. . . .[29]

Various scenes of this group of plays were performed in Paris, London, Stockholm and New York, and proved supremely effective. Eight of them, when staged in Paris in 1938, under the direction of Slatan Dudow, roused the *Deutsche Volkszeitung* of that city to speak of the reception of these plays as a kind of anti-fascist proclamation of a united front. Among the members of the International Brigade these pieces evoked especially warm response.[30] Sometimes the acting groups were of a mixed variety, Helene Weigel appearing alongside an unprofessional actor—very frequently a worker who had never stood on a stage before.

The more professional productions of *Furcht und Elend* must have gained a great deal from Brecht's suggested sets, the principal element of which was an armored tank manned by Nazis. Between the scenes a voice was heard, accompanied by the roar of the rolling tanks. As an example of the effective way in which Brecht visualized these plays, let us take the first of the scenes:

Out of the dark, accompanied by the sounds of a barbarous military band, emerges a huge guidepost with the inscription: "To Poland," and next to it an armored tank. The tank unit, whose faces are painted white, sings the first chorus:

> And when Our Leader himself had created
> Order in Germany with an iron hand,
> He ordered us to create the same order
> With might of arms in every other land.

Furcht und Elend was completed in 1938. During the next three years Brecht was to watch the noose of barbarism being more tightly drawn not only around himself, but also the rest of the world. One by one, Austria, Czechoslovakia, Spain, Poland, the Scandinavian countries, the Lowlands, and France fell prey to the Nazi military might. Nothing but appeasement, collaboration, and even treason!

In the face of all of these, Brecht worked constantly, unintermittently. Numerous sketches of this time indicate his incessant preoccupation with the problem of Hitlerism, and how to overcome it. One of these, *Was kostet das Eisen?* (*What is the Price of Iron?*) outlined in parable form the take-over by Hitler of Austria and Czechoslovakia. The parallelisms are rather obvious: the various victims, who are storekeepers, are called Herr Oesterreicher, the tobacconist; Frau Tscek, owner of a shoe store; Svendson, an iron monger (obviously Sweden); and the Customer, i.e., Hitler. The customer keeps on buying more and more iron with the loot he has squeezed from the others, until finally, when he again approaches Svendson, the latter gives him the iron free. The last scene, "19—?," was to show Svendson in his store, smoking an Austrian cigar, wearing Frau Tscek's shoes. War breaks out, and Svendson immediately raises the price of his wares.[31]

At the same time Brecht was considering an opera around the

subject of David and Goliath, with the same intention of exposing
the machinations of Hitler and the Nazis. Here the Philistines (the
Nazis) are in conflict with the people of Gad (the Germans).[32]

His objective self he set within the plays and the propagandist
poems, his subjective self into published and unpublished personal verse. In both respects a notable change becomes apparent.
His vision has broadened and deepened. A certain aloof, doctrinaire
quality that ran like a leitmotif through his earlier works even
such a one as *Mother*, is now modified by a profound sympathy,
but without a loss of that keen analytic element or of the deep insights of which he was master. In the plays of these years, and in
the poems too, the human and humane element becomes dominant.
Characters in the plays assume dimensions as characters—Galileo,
Mother Courage, Lucullus, Shen-Te, Grusha, Schweyk—without
losing their "typical" essence or their representative qualities as
members of human society or products of social conditions. Brecht
seems to be ever on watch on himself: for a growing "harshness"
within himself; against an atrophy of feelings in the face of the
human cruelty and heartlessness around him.

If we may describe his attitude in this and succeeding periods, we
may call it Marxist humanism. It is reflected in a profounder sense
of responsibility to those who were to read him or listen to his plays.
A teacher needs pupils and a poet readers. But he who elicits the
wisdom of a teacher is no less worthy than he who pronounces it.

This is the theme of an incomparably beautiful poem, "The
Legend of the Birth of the Book Taoteking." Lao-Tse, it tells, the
poet-philosopher, when already ancient and infirm, and despondent
over the presence of so much evil in his country, undertakes a last
journey, accompanied by a young boy. His only possessions are his
learning. With this he confronts the toll-collector at the border. Any
valuables? he is asked. He is a teacher, the boy says. Teacher? And
has he had any profit from that? Yes, is the answer, he has learned
that in due time gentle waters in motion wear down even the
hardest rocks. Hard things always give way. But scarcely have sage

and boy passed the toll-gate, when they are overtaken by the toll-keeper. What was that you said about water? Write it down for me. And the poet remains to write down this piece of wisdom for the man, who was poor, worn, and as the poem puts it, "surely not of the race of conquerors." Let us, says Brecht in conclusion, praise not only the sage. Let us also praise him who has the shrewdness to draw wisdom from the wise.[33] And, in a way, it may be said that Brecht was writing for all the "non-conquerors" of the world.

"Those who have been set on golden seats," he said in another poem, appropriately dedicated to Nexö, and were writers, "will be asked about those who had woven their coats." "In time to come, those will be praised who sat on the bare ground, to write among the lowly; those who sat among the fighters."[34] For it is those (like the tax-collector) who bear the sage's truth to their own kind under their sweat-drenched shirts, and past cordons of police.

Sometimes the personal reserve Brecht had been guarding so carefully drops in these poems, and he reveals his deeper inner feelings. But how could he help feeling deeply when each day might bring news of another friend killed or tortured, another addition to what he called his "personal casualty list"? One by one he counted them off. There was Walter Benjamin, brilliant critic, his intellectual "adversary," "who knew much"—a suicide on the Spanish border. There were even sadder instances—those who had gone over to the enemy not because of principle, but because of "luxuries."[35]

And then there was a casualty that was to touch him most deeply of all—that of Margarete Steffin, who died in a Moscow hospital in 1941. She had been tubercular when she left Germany; she had been with Brecht in exile; had gone to the Spanish front. She had been his teacher and his collaborator; his friend and critic.

> My general has fallen
> My soldier has fallen
>
> My pupil is gone
> My teacher is gone. . . .

In remembrance of this undersized figure, her eyes filled with the fires of anger, he christened the heavenly Orion as the constellation of Steffin.

> Since you are gone, my little teacher,
> I go eyeless, restless, wondering
> In a world that is gray,
> As one without work, as one discharged.[36]

Two years before Margarete Steffin's death he had experienced a poignant, hard blow. His old friend Serge Tretyakov, the Soviet playwright, had been executed in the purges of 1939 as a "Japanese spy."[37] In a poem not published during his lifetime, Brecht mourns Tretyakov's death. The poem is titled, "Are the People Infallible?"

> My teacher
> The great-hearted, the kind-hearted
> Has been shot, condemned by a people's court,
> As a spy. His name is damned.
> His books are destroyed.
> Talk about him is suspect and silenced.
> Supposing now—if he is innocent?[38]

Learn, test, doubt, act—one might say that these became Brecht's own battle cries. Doubt meant testing the truth, so as to enable one to act. Symbolically, two images might be said to have stood before him as embodiments of his beliefs: the scroll of the Chinese sage, "The Doubter," in an attitude of eternal questioning; and the Japanese mask of evil, "swollen veins at the temples, indicating how much effort it takes to be evil."

But doubting did not mean self-pity. To one who had lost heart, he writes:

> Our situation is worse than you think. . . .
> Listen:
> If we cannot do the superhuman
> We are lost. . . .
>
> You say you have fought long. You can fight no more.
> Now hear:

> Whether you are at fault, or no,
> When you can fight no longer, you will perish.[39]

The trap began to close on Brecht. In the anguished year 1939, he inquired of Korsch, who was then already in the U.S.A.,

If I could get the proper immigration papers, Helli [Helene Weigel] and I would come to the States. Would you perhaps know how I might obtain a position as teacher (for only in this way can we avoid the quota, which is hopeless)?[40]

From Denmark he went to Sweden; from Sweden to Finland, where he had friends, and where he found a welcome from the gifted woman novelist Hella Wuolijoki in Tavastland. Her own career had been a heroic one. An Esthonian, she migrated at the beginning of the century to Finland, where she became active in the labor movement. Her early plays were prohibited by the government because they were too radical. She wrote novels of Finnish peasant life, and achieved her greatest success with *The Women of Niskavuori*, a social play of farming life.[41]

Here in Finland Brecht was under no illusions. He knew that country too would soon be drawn into the war. Again he would have to flee:

> Curiously, I examine the map of the continent.
> High above in Lapland
> Toward the polar sea
> I still spy a small door.[42]

If he could only enjoy the splendors of nature! He speaks of the fish-teeming waters, the thick-wooded forests, and savors the fragrance of the birches and the berries.

> Smell, sound, and image, senses merge. . . .
> The fugitive sits underneath the elders and
> Once again takes up the heavy task of hoping.[43]

Hoping meant applying to the U. S. consulate for a visa. Brecht writes an "Ode to a Great Dignitary":

> Exalted vice-consul,
> Deign to accord

> This trembling louse
> The blessed stamp. . . .

Four times he has approached this august presence; he has had his hair cut twice, and carries a hat in his hand (having abandoned his shabby cap):

> The great trapper approaches.
> There's a small door leading
> From the trap into the open. You
> Have the key.
> Will you throw it to me?[44]

Of course, he had not lost his sense of humor. As a matter of fact, one of his most delightful folk-comedies was composed in Finland. This was *Puntila and His Servant Matti*. And yet at the same time he could write:

> This is the year they will speak of.
> This is the year they will not speak of.
>
> The old see the young ones dying.
> The foolish see the wise dying.
>
> Earth no longer bears; she swallows.
> Heaven no longer sends down rain but steel.[45]

And this is also the time when he composed *Galileo, Arturo Ui, The Good Woman of Setzuan, The Trial of Lucullus, Mother Courage,* and numerous poems and essays! At this time, too, he wrote one of his most moving poems, "To Posterity":

> Truly, I live in dark times!
> A guileless word is folly. A smooth forehead
> Betokens insensitiveness. He who laughs
> Has not yet heard
> The terrible news.
>
> What an age is this,
> When to speak of trees is almost a crime,
> For it is silence about innumerable outrages. . . .

You who shall emerge from the flood
Into which we are sinking,
Remember:
When you speak of our weaknesses—
Also the dark time
Which you have escaped.
For we went changing countries more often
        than our shoes,
In the class war, despairing
When there was only injustice and no indignation.

For we know only too well:
Even hatred of baseness
Distorts the features.
Even anger at injustice
Makes the voice harsh. Alas, we
Who wished to lay the cornerstone of kindness
Could not ourselves be kind.

But you, when at last it will come to pass
That man will brother be to man
Remember us
With forbearance.[46]

III

The Responsibility of the Intellectual:
"Galileo"

Ich muss es wissen!

I must know!

BRECHT, *Galileo*

The year 1938 was scarcely one to inspire exhilaration or excessive hopes for the future. It was the year of Munich, of the occupation by the Nazis of Austria and Czechoslovakia, of the approaching expiration of the Spanish Republic—surely not a time in which to celebrate the approach of a new era!

But it was also the fateful year which opened the atomic age.

In his diary, Brecht noted for November 23, 1938: "*The Life of Galileo* completed."[1]

Thus in the midst of darkness Brecht was hailing the new age.

He had been carrying the germs of this play in his mind for some time, and he had already before that epochal event completed a first draft which he called *And Yet It Moves! (Die Erde bewegt sich)*. And now the implications of the new scientific exploits bore in upon him even more fully. With that intensity and scientific curiosity that always characterized his preparatory work, he proceeded to examine the nature and consequences of the new revolution in the physical sciences. In the early part of 1938, he consulted Professor C. Møller, an assistant of Niels Bohr, with whom, among other matters, he discussed Galileo's *Discourses*. Møller recalled that there arose a certain difference of opinion. Since the *Discourses* would never have been composed if Galileo had not many years before submitted to the Catholic Church, I regarded this step as justified. Only in this way could he have finally won a victory over the Inquisition. Brecht, however, was of the opinion that Galileo's recantation of his theory of the motion of the earth in 1633 represented a defeat, which was in years to come to lead to a serious schism between science and human society. I could never understand this point of view, and even today I do not understand it after reading Brecht's *Life of Galileo,* which does not prevent this play from affecting and impressing me deeply.[2]

With his own figurative spy-glass fixed on the historical horizon, it did not take Brecht long to determine the full meaning of eventful changes that would now take place in the world. He recognized that a new era was dawning. What did this discovery portend?

In the midst of a darkness fast enveloping a feverish world, surrounded by bloody deeds and not less bloody thoughts, an expanding barbarism that seems irresistibly leading to perhaps the greatest and most frightful war of all times, it is difficult to adopt an attitude suitable to people standing on the threshold of a new and happy age. Do not all things seem to indicate that night is falling, and nothing that a new age is dawning? Should one not therefore assume an attitude suitable for people who are heading into the night?

How, he continues, can one speak of a new age, when the very terms "new age" and "new order" have been appropriated by enemies of civilization in order to mask a barbarism and exploitation old as the world, but more terrible than ever before? "Shall one therefore try to hold on to old times? Speak of the sunken Atlantis?" As he lies down for the night, Brecht reflects and thinks of the morrow. Would he not rather think of the day just past than of the one that is to come? Is that why he is busying himself with an epoch three hundred years gone, which saw the flowering of the sciences and the arts? "I hope not," he adds.[3]

On every side there was expectation of the deluge. A barbarian, "non-historical" age was in the offing. Western civilization seemed about to collapse. The concepts of "old" and "new" appeared altogether confused, and the teachings of the Socialist classics—Marx, Engels, Lenin—seemed to have forfeited the charm of the "new" and to belong to a worn-out time.[4]

Yet Brecht insists on speaking of a *new* age. A realistic observer of the times, he knew well enough that it was approaching, but not in the garment of light; that its birth-pangs were harsh and bloody, and that birth looked almost like death.

In one of his prose poems, *Visions,* he described the arrival of the Old and the New: how the Old, masquerading as the New, came stumbling on crutches, leading the New in a triumphal procession. The New was in rags and chains, yet her limbs glowed through this defilement. Around them cries arose, "Here comes the New! Hail to the New. Be like us, the New!"—cries that would have been more audible, had they not been drowned out by the roar of cannons.[5] This was fascism, in the mask of the New!

Brecht, as we know, was not one to plunge into history in order to find forgetfulness of the present. Now it seemed important to occupy himself with the historic past. For on the one hand Hitler and the Nazis had gone a long way in rewriting history, distorting it, and successfully promulgating perversions to substantiate their own historic "mission." Nor was it only history they were recasting. All realms of culture were being subjected to revision. The Nobel Prize winner, the brilliant physicist Philipp Lenard, had banished Albert Einstein from the fraternity of scientists, and was composing a four-volume treatise on "German Physics," free of "Jewish" influences.

It was therefore necessary to reconstitute the historical past in its truthfulness; free it from metaphysical, mystical, racist interpretations; relate it to the living present, and thus illuminate the latter. It was essential for man today to rediscover the powerful sources of progressive thought, and thus establish the continuity of a militant democratic tradition. Nor was Brecht the only one to feel such a need. In the French concentration camp of Le Vernet, Friedrich

Wolf was writing a historical play about Beaumarchais and the origins of the French Revolution. Notable novelists like Thomas Mann, Heinrich Mann, and Lion Feuchtwanger were utilizing the bitter experiences of the present to deepen their understanding of history.

It was natural for Brecht to attempt to relate the great scientific revolution of the present to that other revolution that brought modern science into being and is associated with Galileo Galilei and his *Discourses*.

This was to be in some way a lifetime work There were to be three full-fledged versions of the Galileo play, one completed in 1938, another—an English one—in 1946-1947, and last, a German one, upon which he was working up to the time of his death. Preceding the first complete version there were numerous unpublished notes and sketches that suggest a formulation differing from the other three.

Once again be it remarked that Brecht was working under circumstances not particularly favorable to a dramatist with an urgent contemporary theme. Prospects of publication or production were dim. Brecht hoped that his play would find suitable acceptance in New York, but he also sent off a copy to the Schauspielhaus, the theatre in Zurich. Here it lay around for four years before being produced. He was to be somewhat more fortunate with his American experience.

The *Ur-Galileo* (as we may call the first tentative draft of the play) seemed to have been planned as a play for "workers."[6] As a Marxist, he was always aware of the importance of science and scientific discoveries for the fate of the working classes. Thus, in the early 1930's he had attended a meeting of workers which was addressed by Albert Einstein, who was explaining the new physics. A scientific revolution, Brecht recognized, had significance only in so far as it was fruitful of social improvements. Not everything that was labeled "new" necessarily meant new wisdom. Remembering the Nazis, he wrote,

> From the new antennae came ancient folly,
> But wisdom was transmitted from mouth to mouth.[7]

In those very early stages of composition, the play around Galileo was conceived in almost traditional terms. Galileo was seen as a revolutionary scientist, a hero, whose recantation, followed by the whispered (and legendary) "Eppur si muove!" did not in any way detract from the great sum of his achievement or his contribution to the welfare of mankind. In these earliest notes, Galileo is in close touch and sympathy with the life of the people, particularly with mechanics, craftsmen, engineers, no less than the simple people of the streets, market places, and shops. He is not a savant standing above and beyond the common interests of human beings. He is conversant with the workings of the shipyards, kilns, iron foundries; he is surrounded by artisans, glass-grinders, turners, and carpenters. He is happy to stand at the wharfs and shipyards and watch the utilization of a new kind of pulley or some other mechanism to lighten the labor of hands.[8]

But he is above all the scientist who is aware of the distresses and hardships of ordinary life, and he is aroused to fury by injustice and oppression.

Have you heard [he asks] what the House of Nitti says about the Italian people? . . . They command the earth to stand still, lest their possessions be endangered, and their peasants begin to think new thoughts. . . . Never before has a single science like ours been entrusted with such a mission: to forge weapons of reason for an entire people against their oppressors.[9]

He sees in the Church and in the papal authority only another vested interest of a ruling class; and so he becomes a warrior against feudalism with the weapons of science. Cardinals discuss his discoveries exactly like "executives of a chemical trust" faced by a new scientific coup of a rival firm that threatens their monopoly.[10]

As the advance guard of the new thought, Galileo is also intent on spreading the truth abroad, even if (after his recantation) it must be done illegally. Thus he entrusts his friend, a potter, with this mission, which unfortunately cannot be fulfilled.

When he came to writing out his first version of the play, Brecht had already materially changed his conception of both Galileo and his recantation. With immediate historical problems in view, and with greater sharpness, he asks: What is the responsibility of the intellectual in the face of a terror? The answer is, To spread the truth. Agreed. But how is the truth to be disseminated under such conditions? Illegally. Brecht had already described the five principal difficulties in such an effort. *Galileo,* in the finished Danish version of 1938, is the dramatic reply to the same questions.

> Like the burglar
> in a moon-less night, who peers all around,
> for fear of the police,
> so is he who is after truth.
>
> And like something stolen,
> his shoulder ever atingle
> that a hand may be laid on it,
> he carries off the truth.[11]

That is the way, Brecht remarked, Confucius, Lenin, Sir Thomas More, and others had been able to smuggle truth into enemy territory.

The play was written also for his fellow emigrés, disunited as they were, and only too prone to despair. It was meant to make them aware of their responsibilities not only to their callings and professions, but also to the millions of people who would ultimately determine both their own and the intellectuals' survival. Brecht realized how bourgeois society all too often, and with success, tended to isolate the scientist by luring him on to an "autarchic island," where he could carry on his researches unhampered. How it attached him gradually to its politics, economy, and ideology.[12] How it created for him the comfortable and comforting myth of a "pure" vocation, of a "pure" science, and left it to others to manipulate it to less pure ends. How it used flattery, money, offices—and in default of these, force, proscription, and other forms of compulsion to effect its ends.[13]

The Galileo who emerges now in the first complete version of 1938 is no longer quite the socially conscious hero of the preliminary notes and sketches. Traces of heroism still cling to him, but his connection with the people has been materially reduced. What emerges is a complex, contradictory, ambiguous "hero" of science, who damages both his health and his resources in continuing his researches, even after his recantation. He is still engaged in disseminating his ideas abroad with the help of a potter. He employs the means prescribed by Brecht for the dissemination of the truth under conditions of terror: to have the wisdom to recognize it; to make it usable; properly to choose the true recipients; and possess the cunning to disseminate it. He even preaches the wisdom of patient silence, so as ultimately to outlive the lords of terror. He is, however, suspected of somehow getting his manuscript smuggled across the borders piecemeal and surreptitiously. In a memorable scene toward the end of the play, the potter, who has been the intermediary between Galileo and the outside world, reappears on the pretext of repairing one of the fireplaces, but actually to return one of Galileo's manuscripts. He whispers to the half-blind scientist:

> They are on our trail. Villagio has been arrested. . . . This is the third time I'm compelled to return this book to you. . . .
>
> GALILEO (*agitated*). Where shall I put it?
> POTTER. Open, on the table.[14]

But the crucial problem is, of course, the recantation. How to explain that? Brecht thought at first of making the recantation a subterfuge to permit Galileo to continue his work and his propaganda. A brief note suggests that Galileo yielded to the Inquisition solely because he felt both his life and the survival of his work were being threatened. Had it been only his life that was at stake (he says to his pupil Andrea Sarti), his repudiation would indeed have been contemptible.[15]

But on second thought Brecht rejected this notion. He did not want to give the impression that the recantation was a wily, premeditated act, intended to safeguard Galileo's discoveries. In the finished version, therefore, Galileo confesses to Andrea that it was only the fear of death that prompted the recantation.

Shortly after my trial [Galileo says], a number of people who had known me before, treated me with a certain degree of indulgence, in that they attributed to me all sorts of high-minded intentions. I rejected all of them. . . . After a careful consideration of all the circumstances, the extenuating ones as well as the others, one cannot but conclude that a man would find no other ground for such submission but in the fear of death. . . . No less than a threat of death is generally needed to deflect a man from that to which his intellect has led him—this most dangerous of all the gifts of the Almighty.[16]

When Andrea remonstrates, citing Galileo's courageous defiance of the plague, the latter retorts, "Oh no, the plague is not so deadly."

Science [Galileo continues] is in the same boat as humanity. Science cannot say, What is it to me, if the boat runs a leak at one end? The same is true of reason . . . which is a concern in which all men have a share. . . . Science cannot use men who hesitate to stand up for reason. . . . When the hand, which she feeds, at some time or other and without warning seizes her by the throat, man must cut it off. That is why Science cannot suffer a man like me to remain in her ranks.[17]

Yet, he confesses to Andrea, he has remained active as a scientist, for "his flesh is weak." He has written another book, the *Discourses Concerning the Two New Sciences*. And the sly fox of a Galileo suggests to Andrea that he runs the danger of having the pages of his manuscript fall into the wrong hands; that readers ignorant of the arguments of the Inquisition might draw false conclusions from it. Andrea understands. He slips the manuscript into his pocket.

Galileo concludes:

I remain convinced that this is a new time. Should she appear like a blood-stained whore—then the new time may very well look like that. The break of day occurs in the deepest darkness. While in some places the greatest discoveries are being made, which immeasurably increase the well-being of mankind, a very large part of the world lives in deep darkness. The darkness may in fact have grown thicker there! Take care when you cross Germany and carry the truth under your cloak![18]

Already, even before the completion of the first version, Brecht was filled with misgivings about the play. On the one hand, he felt that the play violated his own aesthetic principles, those of the epic theatre, and therefore appeared as "opportunistic." On the other hand he also felt doubts about the interpretations of the recantation, and the need to clarify the role of the scientist in an age of crisis, in view of the epoch-making discoveries.

Before the war [he wrote] I experienced in front of my radio a truly historical scene. The Physics Institute of Niels Bohr in Copenhagen was interviewed concerning a world-shaking discovery in the field of atom fission. The physicists reported that a vast new source of energy had been discovered. When the interviewer inquired whether there was a possibility of practically utilizing these experiments, he was told, "No, not yet." In a tone of the profoundest relief the interviewer said, "Thank God! I truly believe that mankind is not yet ready to take possession of this source of energy."

It was obvious, Brecht adds, that what immediately came to mind was the war industry. The great inventions and discoveries of the day had only come to represent an ever more direful threat to mankind, so that "practically every new invention is greeted with a shout of triumph, which immediately turns into a cry of horror."[19]

With approval Brecht quotes Albert Einstein's statement on the occasion of the 1939 World's Fair Exposition in New York, to the effect that man's scientific and technical achievements have far outrun his ability to plan equally well in the fields of the "production and distribution of goods," so that he lives in constant terror of an economic collapse, no less than of ever-present war.[20]

In creating his figure of Galileo, Brecht had imposed upon the play and the character a touchy moral issue: How did the problem of survival not also involve the question of moral cowardice?

Brecht had himself struggled with the problem. It involved not only himself, as a survivor, but also hundreds and thousands of his countrymen who had remained in Germany and had been forced either to go underground and wait for a "better day" or to simply retreat into what was to be called "psychic emigration."

More than once Brecht returned to this question. In one of those aphoristic anecdotes in which a man named Keuner is Brecht's philosophical alter ego, Brecht considers the attitudes to be taken toward violence and force. Keuner, so the story goes, was once addressing an audience, and was attacking violence, when he suddenly saw that his audience was drawing back and then vanished. Looking around, he saw Violence standing behind him. "What did you say?" Violence asks. "I was speaking out in favor of Violence," Keuner answers. Later his pupils ask Keuner about his "backbone." "I have no backbone that I'd like to see broken. I must live longer than Violence." This is followed by an anecdote which is quoted by Galileo, when he is defending his silence.

Such observations have led many of Brecht's commentators to a variety of interpretations of Brecht's moral attitudes. Was Brecht advocating opportunism? Was Galileo only another configuration of Brecht himself, who had escaped the terror?

The biographer of Leon Trotsky, Isaac Deutscher, believes that Brecht was writing the play under the impact of the great Soviet trials of 1936-1938.

He [Brecht] had been in some sympathy with Trotskyism and was shaken by the purges; but he could not bring himself to break with Stalinism. He surrendered to it with a load of doubt on his mind, as the capitulators in Russia had done; and he expressed artistically his and their predicament in *Galileo Galilei*. It was through the prism of the Bolshevik experience that he saw Galileo going down on his knees before the Inquisition and doing this from an 'historic necessity,' because of the people's spiritual and political immaturity. The Galileo of his drama is Zinoviev, or Bukharin or Rakovsky dressed up in historical costume. . . .[21]

There is little fact to support Deutscher's conjectures. There is no basis that we know of for supposing that Brecht had been in "sympathy with Trotskyism." But Brecht did follow the trials with profound interest; he annotated and underscored the published proceedings. Walter Benjamin, who saw a great deal of Brecht in 1938, remarked on his interest in the statements of Trotsky, but noted that he believed that there were "criminal cliques" in the Soviet Union at work undermining the regime. He recognized that the regime constituted, as he put it, a dictatorship *over* the proletariat, which he felt was necessary to bring about a reconciliation of proletarian and peasant interests. But he still believed Stalin's achievements significant and worthy of a poetic tribute. There can be no question that he saw drama in the trials. It may even be surmised that he found analogies between the recantations of the accused and that of Galileo. Thus, Nikolai Bukharin's confession of his crimes, his confession of his innner self-division, now "writing in glorification of Socialist construction, and the next day refuting it through practical acts of a criminal character," might strike one as having affinities with Galileo's final self-castigation, and the quality of his self-analysis. So far as "ideas" are concerned, Brecht's analysis and Bukharin's are poles apart. Bukharin is ready to surrender his former beliefs (those of the "Right"); Galileo, however, wishes his former stand to become universal. Galileo condemns his own capitulation.[22]

Just as the 1938 version had taken on new meaning under the impact of the splitting of the atom, so many years later, in 1945, the American version was affected by the full realization of the consequences of atomic power in war. Brecht was then already in Hollywood, and had begun the new English version in collaboration with Charles Laughton, the actor, toward the end of 1944.

In order to round out the story of the *Galileo* versions, it is necessary here to break into the strict chronological sequence we have been following.

On August 6, 1945, an American atomic bomb attack destroyed the Japanese city of Hiroshima, and killed thousands of people.

The "atomic age" [Brecht wrote] made its debut in Hiroshima in the middle of our work. Overnight the biography of the founder of modern physics had to be read differently. The infernal effect of the huge bomb projected the conflict between Galileo with the authorities of his day into a new, sharper light. We merely had to make a few changes, none in the structure of the play.[23]

It is not of importance to enter into every detail of difference between the first and the second versions. The most significant change took place in the matter of the recantation. Brecht himself summarized the change:

In the first version of the piece, the last scene was different. Galilei had written his *Discorsi* in the greatest secrecy. When his favorite pupil Andrea visits him, he arranges to have the book smuggled abroad across the frontier. His recantation offered him the possibility of creating a crucial work. He was wise.

In the California version Galilei interrupts the pupil's encomium and proves to him that the recantation was a crime, and not to be balanced by the work, no matter how important.

Should it interest anyone, this too is the opinion of the playwright.[24]

In this, and in the final German version, the ambiguities are removed. Galileo is the voracious scientist and inquirer, to whom the pursuit of the secrets of nature is as much a passion as his love of good food and good things around him. He is unscrupulous when the matter of research is involved. He is not above palming off a Dutch spy-glass as his own invention merely in order to eke out his mean income as a teacher. But he is a magnificent teacher, as the first scene of the play proves, when he introduces his very young pupil Andrea Sarti to the new astronomy. His is a giant intellect, insatiable and greedy—he is as greedy in the flesh as in the mind— deeply concerned to bring his knowledge to the vast thousands of superstition-ridden men and women. That is why he will write his *Discorsi* in Italian and not in Latin. He stands on the borderline of two ages, and knows it.

And one of his noblest utterances (and Brecht's too) is his apostrophe to the new era:

For two thousand years mankind believed that the sun and all the stars of heaven revolved around them. The pope, the cardinals, the princes, the scholars, captains, merchants, fishwives, and school-children believed that they sat motionless on this crystal globe. But now we are off—on a vast journey, Andrea. For the old time is gone, and this is a new time. For a hundred years, it seems, people have been waiting for something. . . .

There is a great hunger abroad to explore the cause of all things: Why a stone falls when released, and how it rises when thrown into the air. Every day something is being discovered. Even those who are a hundred years old let young ones shout novelties into their ears. . . .

For where belief has ruled for a thousand years, now doubt prevails. The whole world says, "Yes, it's written in the books; but let us see for ourselves." . . .

I predict that even in our own lifetime astronomy will be talked in the market places. Even the sons of fishwives will be running to school. . . . It has always been held that the stars are fixed in crystalline spheres to keep them from falling down. But now we have plucked up courage to let them soar through space, unbound, and they are now on their great courses, like our ships, unbound and in full career. And the earth rolls happily around the suns, and the fishwives, merchants, princes and cardinals, yes, even the pope, roll along with them.[25]

The play carries us from 1609 to 1637 in fifteen scenes. We follow Galileo almost step by step in his revolutionary discoveries. On January 10, 1610, he boasts to Sagredo, his friend: "Mankind will write in its journal: The heavens abolished." He has discovered that the moon is like the earth. It has no light of its own. Both receive their light from the sun.

He is passionate in his belief in man and in reason. "Without this belief," he says, "I would not have the strength to get up in the morning." The "gentle sway" of reason is for him one of the irresistible impulses in man. It is also among the greatest pleasures accorded humanity. A lover of good food, a contemner of those who cannot make their heads yield them a comfortable living, Galileo, against the advice of his friend, entrusts himself to the good graces of the Duke of Florence, hopeful of making his new theories acceptable there. But though the principal astronomer of the Vatican confirms Galileo's theories, the vested interests of the Church soon recognize the dangerous implications of the new discoveries. Not even the pestilence raging in the city can move Galileo to flight. Or away from his researches. The Inquisition, however, has in the meantime put the Copernican theories on the Index and Galileo too is silenced. In the years of retirement in Florence he devotes himself to physics and, stealthily, to astronomy.

The accession to the Papacy of Cardinal Barberini, a friend and a mathematician, revives Galileo's hopes. But he is soon undeceived. The Inquisition is stronger even than the Pope. And Galileo, whose investigations have now become known and talked about, must be made to recant, confess his errors, even be threatened with torture. The Pope reluctantly agrees. On June 22, 1633, Galileo recants, while his pupils—Andrea Sarti, the little monk, Federzoni the lens-grinder —wait in disbelief. The sound of the bell proclaims the evil news, and as Galileo emerges, Andrea exclaims in anguish, "Pity the land that has no heroes," to which Galileo replies, "Pity the land that needs heroes." With the passing years, Galileo, half-blind already, but feigning even greater blindness, a prisoner of the Inquisition, kept under the watchful eyes of his pious daughter Virginia, manages to keep on writing his *Discorsi* in secret, hiding them in a globe. His pupil, Andrea Sarti now a mature scientist, returns to visit the old man, and hearing of the existence of the *Discorsi,* is filled with remorse; for now he says he understands the recantation. It was a pretext! Galileo rejects this notion. No, he says, I am a criminal, who could have spoken out at that time without fear of reprisal. But I have betrayed both science and humanity. And he hands the *Discorsi* to Andrea to carry across the border.

In the eyes of many critics, including this one, *The Life of Galileo* represents the peak of Brecht's achievement. Brecht himself had many reservations about the play. He felt that like *The Rifles of Señora Carrar* it represented a culpable deflection from the epic style and was "opportunistic," that is, written for a special occasion. He had sacrificed the crucial element of "Verfremdung." The use of factual historical material made such a transformation as, for example, occurred in *St. Joan of the Stockyards* impossible. *Galileo* does not, Brecht believed, lend itself to such devices as direct addresses to the audience or songs out of the central context. And, what probably disturbed Brecht most, it tended to provoke more empathy than the playwright could possibly desire.[26]

It is, however, scarcely conceivable that a man of Brecht's theatrical and poetical imagination could not have solved these problems in purely epic terms if he had so desired. Actually, it seems that the material shaped itself in Brecht's imagination in the only possible way. That it at times ran counter to the theory was one of those fortunate misfortunes, just as the fact that the theory could be magnificently realized, as in *St. Joan of the Stockyards,* was a fortunate fortune. Each of these works has its own artistic integrity and greatness, and each is undeniably Brecht!

In fact, the play of *Galileo* does preserve much of the epic character: the scenes are independent, autarchic, though subtly related. Each could stand by itself as an episode. But there is a dramatic structure throughout of an architectonic impressiveness. Thus, the hymn to the new age at the beginning is balanced by the sad confessional at the end. At the midpoint we find two outstanding scenes: the conversation with the "little monk" and the robing of the Pope. The first of these again is counterbalanced by Galileo's dictation to his daughter of a letter repudiating his noble words to the "little monk," in which he had castigated oppression and injustice. It has not often been remarked how brilliantly most of the scenes end with a statement or verbal fillip that works with startling effect on the intelligence.

It is futile to attempt to charge Brecht with a violation of historical accuracy in his depiction of Galileo, as it would be to do so in the cases of Shakespeare or Schiller. It is equally naive to use the play as a gateway entitling one to enter into the innards of Brecht's unconscious "ambivalences." One reads or views the play not to obtain an apprehension of a historic past, but as a reinterpretation of such a past, and a historical figure, in the light of the present. Brecht was no more "objective" than Shakespeare; but he was no more "objective" than historians are in their treatment of history, if "objective" means the fatuous conception of absence of presuppositions or points of view. Brecht was speaking to the present, and was concerned with indicating the irreversible damage committed by an intellectual when he betrays his responsibilities to science and to the world.

But would the *Discorsi* have been written if Galileo had not recanted? Would the world have gained anything if he had been martyred? Futile questions. Brecht believed that the *Discorsi* would have been written—if not by Galileo, then by some other great scientist. Perhaps later. But what Brecht is affirming is that the recantation of a man of Galileo's stature and influence cannot but deal a serious blow to the interests of free inquiry, and, most important, the interests of the people as a whole. And in that thought Brecht was undoubtedly right.

This is not a tragedy, Brecht insisted. Nor is it the tragedy of a man. If anything, it is a study of the dire consequences of a man's actions on the better part of humanity. To that part, Galileo was intimately related: it consists of such people as Federzoni, the lens-grinder, who cannot read Latin (hence Galileo will write his works in Italian), but who understands well what Galileo is driving at; the "little monk," who is intimidated by the decree of the Church, but who cannot resist the lure of knowledge; the hard-headed iron-founder Vanni,[26a] who warns Galileo against the impending disaster; and the brilliant student Andrea Sarti; not to mention, Sarti's mother, the courageous and faithful housekeeper. They are the "people" whom Galileo betrays in betraying his science, no less than the scientists themselves who, in the wake of the recantation, shut up their writings in their desks.

For sheer brilliance there are few scenes in Brecht to match that in which Cardinal Barberini, now Pope, is being attired. The relentless and terrifying Inquisitor presses upon him the need to bring Galileo to his knees. With each garment, the Pope yields a little, until he is persuaded that a show of instruments of torture would suffice. Outside is heard the shuffling of innumerable feet, symbolic, as one writer remarked, of the numberless generations that were to judge the actions of the Pope in the future.[27]

So Galileo's preoccupation with his *Discorsi* at the end of his career must be viewed as evidence not of courage (as in the first version) but of a self-indulgent vice. He cannot help it any more than he can help savoring a well-cooked goose. He knows better than he does. He knows, as he says to Andrea in that last scorching confessional, that it is the responsibility of the scientist to disperse the clouds of superstition and ignorance and to "lighten the drudgery of mankind." He has no use for scientists who, intimidated by authority, content themselves with "heaping up knowledge for the sake of knowledge" and so turn science into a cripple and their inventions into fresh means of oppression.

In time [he says] you may come to discover everything that is to be discovered, and yet your progress will only be a progress away from humanity. The gulf between you and humanity can in time become so great that your triumphal cries over some new achievement could be answered by a universal scream of horror.

For himself, he continues, he had the rare opportunity—for astronomy was already reaching into the "market places." All that was needed was the "firmness, the steadfastness of one man," and these would have brought about world-shaking results. As it was, he himself stood in no immediate danger. He was strong enough at the time to have won.

I delivered my knowledge to those in power, to use it, not to use it, to misuse it as suited their purposes.

He has betrayed his vocation, and no longer deserves to be counted in the ranks of science. Yes, a new age is coming, he admits to Andrea.

Take good care of yourself as you pass through Germany, with the truth under your cloak.[28]

Brecht is, in fact, echoing Andrea's bitter words, at the time preceding the recantation:

So much is already won when only one man stands up and says, No![29]

In order to satisfy this passion for knowledge, Galileo has sacrificed a great deal, even his daughter's happiness. This passion, which he had epitomized in the words, *Ich muss es wissen,* he surrendered at the biddings of the flesh. He signs his own moral demise when he abandons people to exploitation by their superiors, and dictates to his daughter a letter approving the suppression of the rope-makers: "Give them more soup, but no more wages."

And this is the man who once said to the "little monk":

I see the divine patience of your people; but where is their divine anger?[29]

and who added,

Only so much of truth prevails, as we make prevail. The victory of reason can only be the victory of those who possess reason.

This is the man who told the "little monk," son of poor peasants:

This is not a question of planets, but of the peasants of the Campagna. . . . Do you know how the oyster Margaritifera produces its pearls? At the risk of its life and sickness it encloses an insupportable foreign body—a grain of sand—within a ball of slime. . . . I say, To the devil with the pearl! I prefer the healthy oyster![30]

IV

Of Heroes and War:
"Lucullus" and "Mother Courage"

Who built the seven-gated Thebes?
In the books are inscribed the names of Kings.
Did the Kings haul the blocks of stone? . . .
Young Alexander conquered India.
By himself alone?
Caesar beat the Gauls.
Didn't he even have a cook along with
    him? . . .
Philip of Spain wept, when the fleet
Went under. Did no one else weep? . . .
Each page a victory.
Who cooked the victory feast?
Every ten years a great man.
Who paid the piper?

So many reports.
So many questions.

> BRECHT, "Questions of a Working Man
> Who Reads."

While there was still hope of speaking out against war, even though
hope was diminishing, Brecht spoke out. As history had served him
in the case of Galileo to underscore the responsibility of the intellectual to his age, so now history supplied him with the raw and
bloody material out of which to shape his warnings against the
impending war. He composed the radio play, *The Trial of Lucullus*,
and *Mother Courage and Her Children*.

The Trial of Lucullus was written in 1939 and broadcast by the Swiss Berne Radio in 1940. For hundreds of years the image of Rome had been that of imperial glory and warlike heroism. Schoolbooks interminably celebrated the triumphs of Roman generals and emperors. Brecht himself had always been attracted by Roman history. He was, in fact, at this time planning a play about Julius Caesar, for which he saw a prospective production in Paris. The play never materialized, but years later gave way to a chronicle novel, *The Affairs of Mr. Julius Caesar.* Now Brecht was reading the histories of Suetonius and Dio Cassius, as well as the moderns.

For his radio play, Brecht chose the Roman general Lucullus, of the first century B.C., a highly successful military commander (according to the traditional point of view, once one forgets the thousands of slaughtered legionaries), but also a sybarite and *bonvivant,* celebrated in history for his culinary artistry. According to a tradition he also introduced the cherry tree into Europe from Asia.

Brecht's radio play is a majestic and masterly piece, marked by a simplicity and economy which by now had become proverbial. It depicts the trial of the dead general Lucullus at the portals of the nether regions to determine whether he is to be sent to Hades or allowed into the Elysian fields. In partly rhymed, mostly unrhymed, conversational verse, chorus, criers, heralds, and other characters: accusers, defendants, and judge and jury, as well as the populace at large, set forth for us the "achievements" and the "crimes" of the soldier.

The question to be decided is: Has he done more harm than good? Has his life been useful to mankind?

We follow the funeral procession as it accompanies Lucullus to his last resting place. Slaves carry a heavy frieze on which are portrayed his accomplishments and which will serve as his memorial. At the burial place a hollow voice suddenly orders a halt. The general must appear in his own person, go alone through the gateway of his tomb, and with others await his turn to be tried. Outraged by this unaccustomed treatment, he is assured by an old woman, waiting her turn ahead of him, that within each candidate is being examined as to his qualifications for admission to the Fields of the Blessed. After the woman, it is Lucullus' turn.

He is now on trial before the highest tribunal of the Realm of Shadows, presided over by the Judge of the Dead, and a jury consisting of shadows, formerly a farmer, a slave-teacher, a fishwife, a baker, and a courtesan. Lucullus is instructed to call for an advocate, but when he proposes Alexander of Macedon as most fit to testify to his worth, it is discovered that neither Alexander nor any like him is to be found in the Elysian Fields. In desperation, Lucullus suggests that the figures on his triumphal frieze be called to testify to his achievements and good works. In turn they come forward—the Asian king whom he has conquered, the queen, girls bearing tablets inscribed with the names of fifty-three cities which the Roman had razed, slaves hauling the god of gold captured along with prisoners. Each is interrogated by the jurors. Then the fishwife on the jury asks to speak. There was talk of gold, she heard. Yet she never saw any of the gold at the fishstalls. "Though you brought nothing to our fishmarket," she continues, "yet you took our sons."

Lucullus protests: How can any one like that judge of wars, who does not understand? To which the fishwife replies:

> I understand it. My son
> fell in the war.

She proceeds to tell how having heard that the ships from Asia were disembarking in the harbor, she ran and waited, but no son appeared; and how having caught cold in the windy surroundings, she fell into a fever and died and came down below into the Realm of Shadows; how she roamed the Realm calling for Faber, her son; but there was no answer. A gatekeeper assured her that the Fabers were numerous and nameless down there; they had had names only when they responded to a roll-call up in the world. But down here they would not even speak with their mothers "since they let them go off to bloody wars." Is she not then qualified to speak of war as one who knows? The Judge of the Dead announces: "The court recognizes that the mother of the fallen soldier understands war."

Lucullus is in trouble. The Court adjures him to call upon some weakness of his which might stand for him. The baker on the jury calls attention to the figure of the cook on the frieze. That man has a happy face. Yes, the cook is ready to testify for Lucullus. The general, he reports, who is a connoisseur of food, gave him a free hand to use his talents. On the frieze he allowed him to stand right beside the king. "That is why I call him human," he says.

Lucullus has one other good deed which he can call upon. The farmer on the jury points to the frieze, with its bearer of a tree. That is the cherry tree that was brought in triumph from Asia and planted on the slopes of the Apennines! The farmer is overjoyed, and he engages Lucullus in a delightfully intimate conversation:

THE FARMER. It needs little soil.
LUCULLUS. But it cannot stand the wind.
THE FARMER. The red cherries have more meat.
LUCULLUS. But the black ones are sweeter.[1]

The farmer then addresses judge and jury:

My friends, of all the detestable memorials
Conquered in bloody wars,
I call this the best. For this sapling lives.
New and friendly, it joins the vine
And the fruitful berry bush
And growing with growing generations
Bears fruit for them. And I felicitate you
Who brought it to us. When all the spoils of war
From both the Asias have long since moldered,
This loveliest of your trophies will
Flutter in the wind from the hillsides,
Each spring renewed, with branches white with flowers.[2]

But that is not enough to vindicate Lucullus. For the conquest of the cherry tree one man would have sufficed. Did he have to send eighty thousand down to the Realm of Shadows? The judge and the jury retire, and the play ends. But we are aware of the impending verdict.

The criterion of "heroism" is usefulness to the community. In

Galileo with Anthony Quayle at the Repertory
Theatre of Lincoln Center, New York, 1967

Die Tragödie des Coriolan with Ekkehard Schall,
Wolf Kaiser, and Manja Behrens; Berliner Ensemble

that Lucullus had failed. Again, as in *The Life of Galileo,* the eloquent accusers are not this world's potentates, or those of the hereafter, but the little people—the fishwife and the farmer.

The fishwife learns too late to understand the nature of war. When, Brecht asks horrified, oh, when will human beings become wise to their own best interests? Such is the question he asked but did not answer in *Mother Courage and Her Children.*

In this play, we are no longer in the so-called "heroic" period of Imperial Rome, nor the "heroic" Renaissance, but in the dark hour of German history that is known as the Thirty Years War. This was a conflict that lasted from 1618 to 1648, and set the country back for centuries to come. Culturally, morally, and economically it represented the low-water mark of German history, a time when predatory monarchs, Catholic and Protestant, harried the land, plundered and looted it, laid it in ruins. The period had only one salutary consequence: It produced one of the very greatest of German narrative works of all times: *Simplicissimus* by Hans Jakob Christian Grimmelshausen. This work appeared in 1669, five years before the author's death, and is the most valuable, as it is the most vivid, document of those terrible times. Through the eyes of the "vagabond," after whom the book is named, it gives us a picture of the devastations and horrors of the time, where "everything was full of war, fire, robbery, looting, raping of women and girls." "War," Grimmelshausen wrote, "makes people worse rather than better." Grimmelshausen followed this work with a counterpart narrative entitled *The Arch-Cozener and Vagabond Courashe,* which was the immediate source of Brecht's play. Brecht drew on both works for background and reflections. Grimmelshausen was a notably advanced writer for his times: his books are commentaries not only upon the bestialities and cruelties committed in wars, but also upon the nature of man and his beliefs, on tolerance and bigotry, on goodness and evil. In some portions he comes close to heresy; for example in his unqualified admiration of the Anabaptists and the Hutterites. Grimmelshausen was deeply troubled by

the way of this world, and no less by the government of it by the
Supreme Ruler on High. He is filled with a truly liberal Christianity. His language, too, is of a kind that would attract Brecht: homely,
earthy, vivid, simple, direct; brutal and effective in its more
elevated no less than in its obscene chapters.

Grimmelshausen's Courashe is the vagabond counterpart to Simplicissimus (whom she indeed meets and unfortunately infects)—
a German Moll Flanders. The illegitimate daughter of a count,
she finds her way into the wars, experiences innumerable adventures,
amatory as well as picaresque, steals, cheats, fights as a soldier,
whores, becomes a sutler, and finally turns gypsy.

It was for the atmosphere, the times, and the background that
Brecht was indebted to Grimmelshausen, rather than for specific
events or incidents. Brecht's play, *Mother Courage and Her Children,* unrolls the chronicle of a sutler woman and her canteen wagon
during the years of war 1624 to 1636. The Thirty Years War has
been in progress for some time already when Anna Fierling, called
Courage, makes her appearance with her three children, variously
fathered: Eilif, Swiss Cheese, and the dumb Kattrin. The two sons
draw the sutler wagon. In the course of the twelve scenes of the
play, disparate as they are according to the "chronicle" style, there
are three connecting elements which appear throughout, from the
beginning to the end: the War (chief protagonist), the wagon, and
Mother Courage. Mother Courage is first of all a business woman,
and she lives off the war. Against this bleak, unruly background
of destruction of life and property, her fortunes vary. They sag
when there is promise of peace, they rise when there is war. In the
course of her many vivid adventures she is joined by various characters: a prostitute, Yvette Pottier, for whom the war proves a
godsend; the chaplain and the cook of the Swedish commander.
But in the end, she is left altogether alone, having lost her three
children as well as her companion, the cook. The desolation of the
last scenes are symbolic of the only profiteers of war, War itself and
those on top who wage it for their own interests. Symbolic of the

little people who make it possible for others to wage wars, Mother Courage harnesses herself to her wagon, as depleted as the desolate landscape around her, and proceeds anew, to recoup her "fortunes."

The characters are crushed by the historical circumstances they do not understand or fathom. Mother Courage herself is the prime example of that blindness. In such an uneven struggle the virtues people possess often prove their undoing. Thus, her son Eilif is brave; he willingly joins the army, is honored by the Swedish commander for an unscrupulous "heroic" act of looting cattle. But when he perpetrates a similar "heroic" act in time of temporary truce or peace, he is court-martialled. Swiss Cheese, the other son, perishes because he is too honest (though not too bright). He refuses to surrender the company's strongbox to the enemy, and is executed. The dumb girl Kattrin, a pathetic victim of soldiers' violence, falls a prey to her love of children. And Mother Courage herself is as much a victim of her business acumen as of her unshakable intrepidity.

But once more, as in *Galileo*, this is not a play about character, but about a historic situation and its impact on human beings. Once more a historical event is being presented to illuminate the contemporary scene. The "heroism" of war is unmasked, but not through the figures of its great men. None of the commanders (with one exception) appears on the scene—neither Count Tilly, of the Catholic side, nor Gustavus of Sweden, on the Protestant side. The "heroism" of the great and small and the nature of the war are revealed to the audience by means of the little man.

The mercenary character of war is brought out in the pathetic and hopeless activities of Mother Courage. She loses Eilif to the recruiting officer while she is haggling with his companion soldier over the price of a buckle. She loses Swiss Cheese while she is haggling over the price of his release. She loses Kattrin in the end because she is off on one of her trading expeditions to the city. To save her wagon and her skin, she is forced to feign ignorance as to the identity of Swiss Cheese when he is brought dead before her.

Yet, it may seem almost paradoxical to insist that despite this background of carnage, rape, ruin, it is comic irony that dominates the play and forms something of a counterblast to the tragedy that pervades it.

Rarely has Brecht used "Verfremdung" with such telling effect, to make the audience see what the participants in action on the stage do not. Thus, at the very outset of the play the sergeant expresses himself on the nature of war:

> You can see at once there's been no war here for a long while. Now tell me, where should they get morality from? Peace, why that's a slovenly thing. Only war brings order. . . . Only where there's war do you find regular lists and registrations; shoes are stacked up neatly; corn is piled in sacks; men and cattle are counted the way they should be and taken off; because everyone knows: without organization, no war![3]

This produces an immediate shock. The audience thinks: This is true. Then they ask, but why should it be like this?

The remarks of the sergeant and the recruiting officer are followed by the appearance of Mother Courage, who sings her raucous and ironic song, adjuring (in good chorale style) all good Christians, but particularly Christian officers, to see to it that their soldiers are well equipped with sausages and shoes, so that they may go to their "hell-pit" courageously! "Cannons on empty stomachs—why, that isn't healthy at all . . . So rise up, you Christians: Spring is here. The dead are at rest. Get going!"

What is good for Mother Courage is good for the army!

No less ironic are the conversations of the chaplain and the cook, who have joined Mother Courage's wagon, seeking both physical and alcoholic warmth from her presence. The chaplain proclaims the continuity of wars. This one will go on forever. But really it isn't so very bad: there is peace even in war. One can ease oneself just as well in one as the other; one loses a leg, cries, but then hops around just as one did before; one can take one's pleasure with a wench behind a barn and bring future generations into the world to feed other wars. So why should wars have to stop?[4]

As a matter of fact, it is a blessing to fall in a war that is waged for religion's sake, for that's a special kind of war, pleasing to the Lord. To which the cook rejoins:

That's right. Now in one sense it is war: you levy on the population, you murder, you plunder and you do a little raping on the side; but on the other hand, it's different from all other wars, because it is a war of religion—that's clear. All the same, it gives you a thirst.[5]

But even the chaplain has second thoughts when he looks at the disfigured Kattrin:

I reproach them with nothing. At home they never did shameful things like this. Those who start the war are responsible for all of this. They bring out the worst in people.[6]

Which echoes Grimmelshausen's sentiments.

It is left to Mother Courage really to expose the nature of war and heroism, though she little realizes that to make a profit from war, one has, in Brecht's words, "to shear with big shears." She is in fact a "blind" realist. She sees and she does not see. She takes nothing for granted, not even the regularity of the seasons—except, unfortunately, war. Her occasional moments of lucidity are amazing.

To hear the big shots talk, they wage war from fear of God and for all that is good and beautiful. But if you just look a little more closely, they're not so dumb. They wage war for gain. Otherwise little folk like me wouldn't go along with them.[7]

Once and once only she gives full vent to her fury, and curses out the war. Kattrin, who already as a child had been outraged by a soldier so that she has lost her powers of speech, now has come back from an errand beaten up and badly disfigured. Yet Mother Courage accepts even this calamity realistically as a blessing. It will spare her daughter further exposure to violence. But in the very next scene she says:

I will not let any of you spoil my war for me. They say it wipes out the weaklings. But they're done for even in time of peace. War feeds people better.[8]

She is without doubt an authority on the subject of heroism. General Tilly has fallen in battle, and is being given a hero's funeral. Mother Courage is thereupon led to remark: "That must be a very bad commander." The cook asks, "Why a bad commander?"

Because he needs brave soldiers, that's why. If he could plan a good campaign, what would he need brave soldiers for? Ordinary ones would do just as well. As a matter of fact, where there are great virtues around, it shows that there's something rotten . . . A good country doesn't need virtues. All the people can be run-of-the-mill, middling smart, and, so far as I'm concerned, even cowards.[9]

The chaplain is beside himself with admiration of Mother Courage: "The way you manage your business and always come through," he says. "I understand why they call you Mother Courage." But she replies:

Poor people need courage. Otherwise they're lost. That's why. Merely getting up in the morning is something in their situation. Or plowing up a field in the midst of war! Even bringing children into the world shows that they have courage, for what do they have to look forward to? They've got to cut each other up, butcher each other—and look at each other—and that also takes courage. And then they've got to put up with an Emperor or a Pope, and that takes an extraordinary amount of courage, for they pay for it with their lives.

But immediately after that, she is her humorous old self again, as she turns to the chaplain: "You might chop up some firewood for me." The chaplain objects: "I am a keeper of souls, not a wood-cutter." And she: "But I have no soul, and I need firewood."[10]

Thus sixteen years pass. Villages and towns have been razed, the land is desolate, and Mother Courage, the Cook, and Kattrin, bedraggled and beggared, are forced to ask for bread. The Cook remarks, "Die Welt stirbt aus." "The world is dying out." And indeed it seems so. Of what use are talent, courage, wisdom, sainthood, happiness? This is the song the Cook now sings before the parsonage, as he begs for food. He urges Mother Courage to leave with him for Utrecht, where he has inherited an inn. But she must abandon

Kattrin, for the inn will feed two, but not three mouths. One moment of great-heartedness lights up the dismal scene: Mother Courage refuses, and dismisses the Cook. Once more she is off with her wagon, Kattrin now in harness. Soon she will lose her too. Before the city of Halle, which is being besieged by Catholic troops, Kattrin will give way to her love of children, which will prove her undoing. In her desire to warn the besieged city of a night-time assault by the enemy, Kattrin climbs to a loft and beats the drum. She is shot down.

Ignorant of the fact that her son Eilif is dead too, and still hopeful of meeting him again, Courage sets off, now alone, harnesses herself to the wagon—a worn, old woman who has learned nothing, once more to start all over again.

If virtues are dangerous in society today, then venality may be a blessing. This is one of Brecht's favorite themes. Thus, Mother Courage reflects, as she is about to bribe the enemy to spare her son's life:

Thank God they can be bribed. After all, they're men, not wolves. They're after money, that's what. Bribery is to man what mercy is to the Lord. It is our only hope. So long as it's here, judges' verdicts will be mild, so that even the innocent may get by.[11]

Such bitter paradoxes pervade the entire play. And they constitute its subversive humor. They are intended to give "pleasure" to an audience, while also delivering their subtle, intellectual buffets. Brecht avoids the over-didactic element of direct address. Instruction—if one may use the term—filters in through the live dialogue. The songs, though as always independent in character, are also directly related to the action: so Mother Courage's sales-chorale; Eilif's song in the Swedish Commander's tent—"The Woman and the Soldier"—or the cook's song of the "Inadequacy of Virtue" (these two Brecht repeats from earlier texts); or the "Song of Capitulation" sung by Courage to dissuade the emotionally overcharged young soldier from venting his justified but hopeless anger at the commander.

The dialogue and exchanges are full of gusto and verve; the language itself is direct, homely, and adjusted to the characters. All flows so simply but so deceptively; it is so full of meaning, that an audience can hardly be blamed for not always grasping the full sense of what is being said at the moment of its utterance. The paradoxes and deliberate ambiguities can only be enjoyed through repeated hearing.

Brecht was fearful of being misunderstood. *Mother Courage* was produced in Zurich in April, 1941, with that extraordinary actress Therese Giehse in the leading role. Coming as it did at a particularly dark moment in history, it created an unforgettable impression. But to Brecht's horror, the reviews stressed the emotional impact of the play, extolling it as a "Niobe-tragedy," and spoke with warmth about the "overwhelming vital force of the mother animal."[12] This took place, Brecht said, "despite the anti-fascist and pacifistic attitude of the Zurich playhouse, staffed in greater part by German emigrés."[12] "Duly warned," Brecht altered a few brief portions of three scenes for the postwar Berlin productions, subduing some of the more debatable emotional parts, but actually altering very little of the main effect.

But a much more crucial objection was raised after the war in the East German press upon the presentation of *Mother Courage*. The notable East German playwright Friedrich Wolf engaged Brecht in a friendly dialogue on this subject in 1952. Like other critics, but from his particular point of view too, Wolf called attention to the fact that for the spectators of this piece, in which, he admitted, the "epic" style is most consistently realized, the high-water mark of the performance was reached in scenes which were emotionally charged: the death of the older son, Eilif; the scene between mother and daughter upon Kattrin's disfigurement, when Courage exclaims, "Cursed be the war!"; and the scene in which Kattrin signals the inhabitants of Halle with her drum-beat. In addition, Wolf asked:

Would not Mother Courage (history being the possible) after seeing that the war didn't pay, after having lost not only her possessions but her children too, have to become an altogether different person at the end from what she was at the beginning?

Since they are both, Wolf and Brecht, concerned with the same goal—that is "to change people"—though from differing dramatic points of view, was it not important to show Courage changed? "How," Wolf asks, "can our German theatre show our people that which is needed? . . . How can we activate them against another war, and away from their fatalism?" Would not *Mother Courage* have been even more effective if at the end her curses against the war had shown concrete results in her behavior and deeds?[13]

Brecht replied:

This piece was written in 1938, when the playwright foresaw a great war. He was not convinced that people, abstractly, learn from the misfortunes, which, in his eyes, had to befall them. Dear Friedrich Wolf, you yourself will agree that the playwright was the realist here. If, however, Mother Courage herself learns nothing further—it is my opinion that the public, viewing her, can learn something.[14]

For, as he says in another connection, ill fortune is a bad teacher. Her pupils learn hunger and thirst, but not too often hunger for knowledge, or thirst for truth . . . Sufferings do not necessarily make for skill in medicine.[15] Even after 1945, he was to wonder how many of the spectators of his piece actually understood its warnings.[16] Had he succeeded in showing the relationship of war to a social system?

The Thirty Years War is one of the first gigantic wars waged by capitalism over Europe. But under and within capitalism it is extremely difficult for the individual to see that war is not necessary; for it is necessary within capitalism, namely for capitalism. This economic system is based upon a war of all against all, the great ones against the great ones, the little ones against the little ones, the great ones against the little ones. One would already have had to recognize that capitalism itself is a misfortune, in order to recognize that war and the misfortunes it brings are bad—that is, unnecessary.[17]

V

This Side of Good and Evil: "The Good Woman of Setzuan" and "Puntila"

I don't know: Isn't too much asked of human
beings?

BRECHT, *Die Judith von Shimoda*

It may already have been remarked that in the poetry, drama, and theoretical works of the period of exile a certain new note enters Brecht's world-view. On the purely formal side, there is a greater simplification, if not austerity, of tone, without loss of humor; on the emotional side a deepening of his sense of human beings as human beings. Both sides are interdependent and fused within his Marxist world-outlook. The tragic historic present, while it does not undo him, has made him more flexible, less doctrinaire. A more humane, less categorical, outlook on human relations becomes evident. Without abandoning the dialectical principle, which for him represents the central truth, and the guiding principle in judging history, he begins to look differently at individuals, and their feelings and reactions. For one, it becomes apparent that women play a more and more important part in his theatrical creations. The trend that had begun with *St. Joan of the Stockyards,* and continued with *Mother* in the pre-Hitler days, is now fortified in *Mother Courage* and *The Good Woman of Setzuan,* products of his European exile, and will be extended with *The Caucasian Chalk Circle, The Visions of Simone Machard,* and other variants of the St. Joan theme in the following years.

Other, unpublished, material testifies to the same preoccupation. Thus, the sketches for a play intended to demystify myth—in this case the myth of the heroic Judith of the Bible—center around the Japanese geisha girl Okichi, who, like another Judith, is sent to foil, with her own particular devices, the evil intentions of the American ambassador to Japan, Townsend Harris, who threatens the welfare and peace of the Oriental country. The girl's lover, a carpenter, is bribed to consent to her "heroic sacrifice." Thus, love itself has become a commodity to be bartered away like any other piece of goods, to create a spurious heroic myth.[1]

It is perhaps equally interesting to observe that for the first time the love relationship is treated in other than purely physical terms. Even in *Mother Courage* a certain element of tenderness enters into the attachment between the cook and Courage; nor is it entirely absent in *Galileo*. But it is with *The Good Woman of Setzuan* that a love relationship, at least on the woman's part, is avowed passionately and freely. That it is, as we shall see, debased by a corrupted suitor, is beside the question.

The aggressive, overtly didactic quality disappears; the issues are more subtly, but no less clearly, stated. In the poems there is a greater terseness, without sacrifice of the aesthetic. It may be that here Brecht was helped considerably by his interest in Oriental, predominantly Chinese, poetry, in the translations of Arthur Waley. His own adaptations of these testify to the forceful way he had of shaping other poets' work to his own interests and ends.

Brecht had a way of sharpening his models, pinpointing, so to speak, their social meaning. One example may suffice:

Arthur Waley translated the poem "The Big Rug" by the eighth-century Chinese poet Po-Chü-yi as follows:

> That so many of the poor should suffer from cold, what can
>   we do to prevent?
> To bring warmth to a single body is not much use.
> I wish I had a big rug ten thousand feet long
> Which at one time could cover up every inch of the city.

Now Brecht:

> Der Gouverneur, von mir befragt, was nötig wäre
> Den Frierenden in unsrer Stadt zu helfen
> Antwortete: Eine Decke, zehntausend Fuss lang
> Die die ganzen Vorstädte einfach zudeckt.

> The Governor, when I asked what would suffice
> To help the numb with cold in our city
> Replied: A rug ten thousand feet long
> Simply to cover all the slums at one time.[2]

This is the theme of the parable play of *The Good Woman of Setzuan.* (Actually the English title should read *The Good Soul of Setzuan.*)

Goodness, Brecht has been saying, is natural to man. Cruelty needs intense effort. But the price of goodness in a world like ours too often runs high! In this play, three gods visit our earth in search of a "good person"—something that is very scarce. A poor water-carrier, whom they accost, tries to find lodgings for them, but is everywhere turned away by the well-to-do inhabitants of the town. Only one person, the prostitute Shen-Te, is ready to shelter them. As a reward, they bestow enough money on her to enable her to open a tobacco shop. Immediately, she is beset by petitioners of all sorts —deserving as well as parasitic ones—so that in desperation and self-defense she is forced to assume another face. She personates a "cousin," Shui-Ta, by means of a mask. She becomes a hard-hearted, cruel, efficient counterpart to the good Shen-Te. In love, too, Shen-Te finds herself exploited. Having saved an unemployed flyer, Yang-Sun, from suicide, and having fallen in love with him, she finds that he too uses her to advance his own ends (obtaining a pilot's post by bribery), in the pursuit of which he is ready to bring Shen-Te to financial ruin. Pregnant now by her lover, Shen-Te vows to turn into a tiger in defense of her young one. It is left to her alter-ego, Shui-Ta, to restore her fortunes by means of a tobacco factory which exploits its workers ruthlessly and uses the ambitious and unscrupulous Yang-Sun as a slave-driving foreman. The disappearance of Shen-Te arouses the suspicions of the simple and honest water-carrier (with whom the gods are in constant communication), so that finally Shui-Ta is brought to trial for having done away with her. Instead of the judges, the gods themselves preside at the trial. Shen-Te reveals herself. The good woman is still there to the smug satisfaction of the foolish gods and they leave her and the world to get along as best they can, while they make off to their restful heavens.

What a world is this, where goodness must pay an exorbitant price to be good and do good, and where survival presupposes cruelty, ruthlessness, and exploitation!

The poor water-carrier Wang would like to be good, but even he is forced to cheat. His water mug has a false bottom!

Shen-Te pleads with the gods:

Oh, Illustrious Ones, I am not at all sure that I am good. I would like to be good, but how shall I pay my rent? . . . Even when I break a few of the commandments, I can't make ends meet.[3]

How can she be good when everything is so dear? To which the gods reply:

That's something we know nothing about. You know, we don't meddle in economics.[4]

And they will go off. It will remain for the Wangs and the Shen-Tes to plead the cause of humanity and to act. They stand for the decencies and goodness in life. "There is a saying," says Shen-Te, "to speak without hope, is to speak without goodness."[5] And that is what is left her—hope. If man were only given the chance to be good! "When someone sings a song, builds a machine, or plants rice, that is really kindliness."[6]

"Too much is asked of human nature," Brecht wrote elsewhere.[7] Shen-Te, the "angel of the slums," as she is called, cannot do much by herself. And Wang in a similar appeal to the gods, pleads, "Don't ask for too much at the beginning!"[8] But Shen-Te herself finally is outraged by injustice and the quietism with which the oppressed face it. When Wang is maltreated by a wealthy and cruel barber, she exclaims in horror at the general indifference:

> What a city is this! and what sort of men! . . .
> Your brother is outraged before you, and you shut your eyes. . . .
> When an injustice is done in a city, there must be an uproar,
> And where there is no uproar, it is better the city perish
> In flames, before nightfall.[9]

And,

> Why do not the gods above say out loud
> That they owe the good ones a good world?
> And why do they not stand by the good ones with tank and
>   cannon
> And shout: "Fire!" and call a halt to human forbearance?[10]

There is a scene of tenderness, almost unprecedented in Brecht's work, when Shen-Te contemplates her pregnant body:

SHEN-TE (*softly*). O joy! A small man is coming to life within me. Nothing to be seen as yet. But he is here already. The world awaits him in secret. In the cities it is already rumored: There's someone coming with whom we must reckon. (*She presents her small son to the audience.*) A flyer!

> Salute a new conqueror
> Of unknown mountains, inaccessible regions,
>   One
> Carrying letters from man to man
> Across pathless untrodden wastes![11]

She proceeds to take a stroll with her unborn son, meeting strangers, greeting them, asking her child to do likewise; stealing a few cherries from the rich man's orchard; avoiding the police. . . .

But her love also extends to children not hers. Or, as she puts it incomparably, when offering shelter to a homeless child:

> A thing of Tomorrow is asking for a touch of Today![12]

She cannot resist "the temptation to give." How pleasant it is to be kind! "A good word escapes like a contented sigh."[13]

How can a human being, living in a world like ours, fulfill all prescriptions for the good life? There is something wrong and false in this world of yours, Shen-Te says to the departing gods. She will need her cousin now and then, she pleads. To which the gods reply: Once a month will be enough! And they disappear.

If you cannot rely on the gods, on whom can you rely? So, once more, Brecht turns the problem over to the audience. There are no prescriptions for the future in this play of Brecht's. An actor steps forward at the end with his epilogue: What is the solution? What ending can we give this play? We, he says, haven't been able to find any. Shall it be another kind of human being? Another kind of world? Perhaps other gods? Or none? There is only one way out of this quandary: It is for you, the spectator, to think up a good ending: How can the good man be helped?

> Honored public: find the conclusion yourself:
> There must be a good one around: There must, must, must![14]

There is no false sentimentality, no vapid utopianism in Brecht. He had never shut his eyes to the inadequacies of the lower orders. He had seen them for what they were in *St. Joan of the Stockyards;* and he sees them now in *The Good Woman.* He sees them in their pettiness; he sees them in their courage and their grandeur. They are what they are because the world made them so. In their littleness, in their meanness, they are not spokesmen for Brecht, or for the world. Brecht's spokesmen are to be found in the captured worker of *St. Joan,* in Shen-Te, and in Wang, the water-carrier. And, it must be added, in the spectators of the plays themselves, once they have begun to answer the questions raised in them.

Nor need one look to the three well-meaning gods for an answer. They are the embodiments of the bourgeois mentality—muddled, meddlesome, fussy—trying to solve crucial problems with moderate outlays of money. That is the way the gods salve their conscience. The evil inherent in capitalist society they leave only for man to cope with.[15] To be good means to be oneself, and vice-versa. Evil is alienation, the "not-being oneself," the "not-being-human." *A fortiori,*

Nazism is the extension and the foulest manifestation of that alienation. As the French critic Bernard Dort puts it:

Brecht's dramatic critique culminates in this pathetic, anguished appeal
to the public. The world is engaged in a second world war. Nazism is
contaminating all of Europe, or almost all of it. It is urgent to find a
resolution to this drama—a resolution different from that of Shen-Te.
It is not man who has to be changed, by himself. It is the world. It is
necessary to create, recreate a world in which it is possible for man to
be himself, to be that fully, along with other men, and not against them.[16]

Brecht once said, "Life is somewhat undramatic. It does not know
Yes or No; White or Black; All or Nothing."[17] Both may be contained within one person. In *The Good Woman* he had exhibited
that dualism as Shen-Te and Shui-Ta. Now, in hilarious, comic
form he was to exhibit it in the folk-comedy *Puntila and His Servant Matti*. This work was based on a story written by his Finnish
hostess, the writer Hella Wuolijiki, and once more exhibits the
capacity of Brecht to laugh even in the most disheartening circumstances.

The well-to-do landowner Puntila loves to drink. When he is
under the influence of alcohol, he is generous, high-minded, selfless,
and humane. In that state of humanitarian intoxication he is a good
friend to his chauffeur Matti, a proletarian gifted with good common sense and of radical leanings. Drunk, Herr Puntila gets himself
engaged to four different girls of the lower classes. Sober, he disowns them and drives them away. Drunk, he is candid with the
priggish and vacuous suitor of his daughter, a diplomatic attaché,
insults him, and offers Eva as a wife to Matti. Sober, he is harsh,
overbearing, exploiting, and calculating. Drunk, Puntila is in his
right senses. Sober, he is alienated! He is blood-brother to a character
in Charlie Chaplin's *City Lights*.

At least two hilarious scenes highlight the absurdity. At the
betrothal feast in honor of the attaché and Eva, Puntila's insults
drive the future bridegroom from the house. Puntila settles down
to a joyous celebration, seating himself among his servants and the

remaining guests, and proposes Matti as a substitute and far more agreeable future son-in-law. Matti is clearheaded enough to suggest that before he marries Eva she submit to a series of rigorous tests which will qualify her for the life of a proletarian's wife and the daughter-in-law of a deprived proletarian woman.

Does she know the kind of food a proletarian is forced to eat? So they enact a little play. Eva brings in a herring. Matti proceeds to apostrophize the fish of the poor:

MATTI. Yes, there he is. I recognize him. (*He takes the plate.*) I only saw his brother yesterday, and another member of his family the day before, and so on—all members of his family, ever since I ever laid hold of a dish. How often will you be eating herring during the week?

EVE. Three times, Matti, if I have to. . . .

MATTI. You still have to learn a great deal. My mother, cook on an estate, gave him to us five times during the week, and Laina, here, gives him to us eight times. (*He takes hold of the herring by the tail.*) Welcome, herring, thou banquet of the poor! Thou appeaser of hunger in all hours, and salty stomachache! Out of the ocean thou hast come, and to dust thou returnest. By thy virtue pine-forests are hewed down and fields sown; by thy virtue those machines, called servants, are set in motion. . . . Oh herring, thou dog, if thou didst not exist, we might begin to ask for a good slice of ham—and then what would become of Finland?[18]

Of course, Eva cannot pass the examination!

Puntila, the master, who has rarely tasted herring, likes it. But, he adds, that's an inequity that must no longer exist. If he had his way, he would put all his income into a common hoard and let everyone of his employees take whatever he needed, for without them, he wouldn't exist. . . . He insists that he is "almost a Communist"; and that if he were a servant, he would make Puntila's life one long hell.[19]

In another scene, equally delightful, Puntila has decided to destroy his whole stock of intoxicants. He orders them brought into his library and begins, in the presence of Matti, an excoriation of the latter, then, forgetting himself, starts drinking until the inevitable happens: Puntila changes. He offers Matti a rise in wages, and invites him to climb the Hatelma mountain—that is, by means of the billiard table. They proceed to demolish the furniture to build the mountain ascent, from whose heights they survey the beauties of Finland, to ecstatic panegyrics from Puntila's poetically besotten lips: Where, he asks his companion Matti, will you find such a sky as in Tavastland? And the wild swans? And the smells of Tavastland! "Oh blessed Tavastland," he cries out to the amazed servants who have now come into the library, "with her skies, her seas, her people and her forests! Tell me, Matti, does not your heart melt, when you look at them?" To which Matti agrees.

Unable to adjust to this double life, Matti leaves Puntila's service:

> You are not the worst [he concludes] of those I've met; you are almost a human being, when you are in your cups. This amicable union could not last: the drunken transport passes. . . . Servants will only find a good master, when they themselves become their own masters.[20]

Students of the "theatre of absurdity" have tended to point to Brecht's earlier works, like *Man is Man,* as possible sources for this kind of theatre. How much more relevant is the present play! Few dramas of "absurdity" have so absurdly—and joyously—unmasked a social system in which it is necessary to be drunk to be human, and in which sobriety is tantamount to cruelty and selfishness!

Critics have remarked one undeniable truth: the "villain" Puntila is a much more interesting character than the "hero" Matti. But they have overlooked the fact that he and the other characters, particularly the peasant women of the play, have a dignity and directness that set off Puntila's dualism in a glaring way. Nor have they sufficiently taken note of the fact that Brecht was once more dealing with the problem of good and evil in our bourgeois world —how mixed up and startling! For it is Puntila himself that becomes the judge not only of himself but of the whole system of which he is a part. Only in the drunken state can he be brother to Matti and see clearly. In the sober state, he is the embodiment of crude exploitation. Then, he is no sentimentalist. In a drunken state he can woo the women of lowly estate. In a sober state he treats them like dirt. So far as the character of Matti is concerned, Brecht has already discovered what he was to state some time later, that a contradictory character is much more interesting and "dramatic" than one without contradictions. The fate of angels, no less than of "positive heroes" is to be less attractive than devils.

VI

The Fertile Womb: "Arturo Ui"

> Let none of us exult too soon,
> The womb is fruitful still, from which
> this one crawled.
>
> BRECHT, *Arturo Ui*

Contemporary history was ever-present in Brecht's mind. On April 29, 1941, a few short weeks before he himself had to leave Finland, he completed *The Resistible Rise of Arturo Ui,* a play he was never destined to see produced in his lifetime. It was written in hopes of being performed that year.

The idea of composing a "gangster" play, with Hitler as "hero," came to Brecht while he was in New York during the winter of 1935-1936, on the occasion of the performance of *Mother.* On March 10, 1941, he notes in his diary: "I am sketching a plan for 11 to 12 scenes. Naturally it must be written in the grand manner."[1] Margarete Steffin's "knowledge of the interrelation of the gangster-world and its administration" proved very helpful to him.

He was aware that time was against him, as well as against his work.

The world once more is holding its breath. The German army is rolling toward Saloniki in exactly the same tempo as autos are capable of . . . It is as if only this army is capable of movement—it alone creates and dominates the dice of war, which have now displaced the battle-field. The obsolete armies compete here like the spinning wheel against the jenny. Valor loses to the driver's skill, tirelessness to punctuality, patience to diligence. Strategy has turned into surgery: an enemy territory is "opened up," after it has been anaesthetized, then it is "plugged" up, disinfected, sewed up, etc.—all done with perfect calm.[2]

Perhaps, if luck was with him, the play would be performed in English. In this atmosphere, he manipulates, corrects, alters the blank verse which is to underscore Verfremdung: or as he calls it, "double estrangement," i.e., that effected through the use of the "gangster" theme and the elevated poetical style. Already he is thinking of a sequel, something he is sure will never be produced, called *Ui, Part Two: Spain, Munich, Poland, France.*

The completed play, *Der aufhaltsame Aufstieg des Arturo Ui* carries forward the line begun with *St. Joan of the Stockyards, Round Heads and Peaked Heads,* and the innumerable sketches, like *Was kostet das Eisen?* and *Goliath.* Parody, elevated verse, and reminiscences of Goethe's *Faust* and Shakespeare's *Richard III,* are now used to expose the vacuity and moral and spiritual mediocrity of a "gangster-hero"—Hitler—to denude him of that aura of heroism and greatness which attach in the popular imagination to murderers and criminals who commit acts of epic proportions.

Arturo Ui, a petty gangster leader from the Bronx, succeeds through terror in making himself the "protector" of the cauliflower trust of Chicago. He manages to undo and displace the corrupted political boss Dogborough (Hindenburg); and, with his lieutenants Giri (Goering) and Givola (Goebbels), to exterminate his other henchman, Roma (Roehm). He eliminates the head of the neighboring vegetable trust, Dullfeet (Dollfuss) of Cicero (Austria), and wins the latter's widow. In the end he obtains the overwhelming vote of approval of both Chicago and Cicero. The Reichstag Fire Trial is parodied in a similar vein.

In subsequent discussions of this play, after 1945, Brecht showed that he was sensitive to the criticism that might be directed against it on the score of its humor. "The great political criminals," he stated, "must be exposed—and particularly exposed to laughter. For they are by no means great political criminals, but the perpetrators of great political crimes, which is something altogether different."[3] The play, as he saw it, must avoid the spirit of travesty, and even in the grotesqueness of its many scenes the element of horror must never be forgotten. The important thing is to effect a total dissolution of "respect for killers."

It is doubtful, however, if even in 1941 *Arturo Ui* could have carried conviction. In 1945 and thereafter, when the full increment of Nazi barbarism and savagery had come to light, the play was bound to fail of its anticipated terrifying impact. To an audience dominated by memories of a horror unprecedented in civilized or uncivilized history, perpetrated by a nation once allegedly dedicated to humanism, Arturo Ui could only appear as a distorted parodistic puppet, and the analogy with American gangsterism as trivial. Under no circumstances could one equate the latter with Hitlerism, particularly in view of the fact that gangsterism is an accepted phenomenon in modern life, a part of the structure of modern society, not likely to rouse more than a genteel gesture of protest. Not even such exciting performances of the play as those of the Berliner Ensemble could make (at least for this spectator) the analogy convincing.

Brilliant episodes, however, do occur. The parodistic virtuosity of the master is evident in such scenes as that between Ui, Dullfeet, Givola and Betty Dullfeet—which, of course, immediately brings to mind the garden scene of Goethe's *Faust,* where Mephistopheles softens up Martha, while Faust is preparing the ground for Gretchen's ruin. The scene takes place in Givola's flower shop, and the couples, Givola and Dullfeet and Betty and Ui, appear alternately, as their prototypes do in Goethe's tragedy. Gretchen's celebrated questioning of Faust:

> Nun sag', wie hast du's mit der Religion?
> Now tell me, how do you feel about religion?

becomes in Brecht an interchange between Betty Dullfeet and Ui:

BETTY. Herr Ui, what are your thoughts on religion?
UI. I am a Christian, that's enough—
BETTY. But the Ten Commandments, in which we believe . . .
UI. They mustn't get mixed up in our daily lives.

BETTY. Forgive me, Herr Ui, if I trouble you further: How do you feel about the social question?

UI. I'm social. That's what everyone can see. Now and then I even attract the rich ones too.

The gangster flower merchant entertains Dullfeet:

DULLFEET. Flowers too have their life's experience.

GIVOLA. And how! Interments, too—interments!

DULLFEET. Oh, I'm forgetting—flowers are your bread.

GIVOLA. Quite right. My best customer is Death.

DULLFEET. I hope you're not dependent on him alone.

GIVOLA. No. Not with people who can take a hint.[4]

A number of the burlesque effects attain a horrifying grimness. Like Shakespeare's Richard III, Arturo Ui woos and wins the widow of the man he has murdered; and like his British prototype, he has a nightmare vision in which he sees another of his recent victims, Roma.

The broad comedy scenes are the most successful—such for example as that in which Ui takes acting lessons from a somewhat shopworn Thespian. He studies walking, standing, and reciting (this is actual history), and the Actor instructs him in Shakespeare:

Shakespeare. Nothing but Shakespeare. Caesar. Ancient hero . . . What do you think of Antony's oration? At Caesar's funeral. Against Brutus. Leader of the assassins. A model of popular appeal, very famous indeed. I played Antony in Zenith, in 1908. Just what you need, Herr Ui.[5]

But the other gory incidents scarcely lend themselves to this kind of treatment. Brecht had miscalculated. Neither "epic" theatre, nor the "Verfremdung" device could be just to so weighty a historic subject. Gangsterism is scarcely a phenomenon that could adequately describe Nazism and its atrocities. Nor does control of the "cauliflower trust" adequately parallel the economic manipulations that made Nazism possible. The weight of its innumerable victims lies too heavily upon the spectator's mind, to allow for that "distancing" necessary for a proper enjoyment of the exposure.

But that Brecht was able to laugh at this time reflects his unquenchable hope and confidence in the future.

VII

Reflections of One in Flight: "The Refugee Dialogues"

Emigration is the best school of dialectics. Refugees are the keenest dialecticians. They are refugees as a result of changes, and their sole object of study is change. They are able to deduce the greatest events from the smallest hints—that is, if they have intelligence. When their opponents are winning, they calculate how much their victory has cost them; and they have the sharpest eyes for contradictions. Long live dialectics!

BRECHT, *Flüchtlingsgespräche*

There are few places where Brecht's bright mind and keen spirit shine forth more luminously and engagingly than in the dialogues written in Finland in 1941 and published posthumously—the *Flüchtlingsgespräche* (*The Refugee Dialogues*). Setting aside a number of his poems, it is here that we come as close as we ever can to the more personal Brecht. Though in a measure autobiographic, the chief delight of the book lies in the way it reveals Brecht's pleasure in experimental thinking.

Two strangers, refugees from Nazi Germany, meet by chance in a railway depot in Helsinki, Finland. One, "large, heavy, and with white hands," is Ziffel, a physicist. The other calls himself Kalle. He is thickset, short, and has the hands of a metal worker. They enter into conversation. Though superficially it is Ziffel who stands for Brecht (he supplies brief autobiographic notes), both of them are spokesmen for the writer. In the interplay of their conversation, which ranges over a wide variety of matters—personal, political, social, and historical—is revealed that unique capacity which Brecht possessed for transmuting profound ideas into everyday common sense.

Kalle has been in a concentration camp, and can bring some of his own experiences there to throw light on both captors and captives. Ziffel is an intellectual out of work, unwanted in a foreign land. The sword of Damocles hangs over both, as Ziffel puts it, "with two motorized German divisions in the country, and no visa in sight."

But such serious times deserve to be treated with humor. "A good thing can always be expressed vivaciously."[1]

Take, for example, the philoshopher Hegel. Along with Socrates, Ziffel remarks, he had the stuff of one of the great humorists. His *Logic,* which Ziffel read during one of his severe attacks of rheumatism, is incomparably entertaining:

It treats of the habits of ideas, those slippery, unstable, irresponsible entities; how they abuse each other, and fight with knives; and then sit down to dinner together, as if nothing had happened. They even appear in pairs, married, every one of them with his antithesis; and they carry on their activities as a pair . . . , that is, a couple that has wrangled with a vengeance, and is at odds on every subject! If Order affirms one thing, Disorder, her inseparable companion, immediately affirms the opposite. They cannot live with each other or without each other.[2]

This "wit" in an object Hegel called dialectics. It takes humor to understand Hegel, Ziffel adds.

It is this sort of dialectical "wit" that Brecht brings to bear upon serious subjects through his two interlocutors. Germany is, of course, in the forefront of their discussion. Autobiography, too, plays a considerable part in it, as, for example, in connection with German education, of which we have already spoken above. The speakers consider the term "German." What does it mean? "German means being thorough—in agriculture as well as in the extermination of Jews. . . . 'The German has a natural bent for a professorship of philosophy,' it is often asserted. And this is said with a soulful, bloodthirsty expressiveness."[3]

Or take the matter of orderliness. Actually, Ziffel contends, humanity today could not survive without a good measure of disorderliness and corruptibility. Orderliness is dangerous; mankind is not yet up to it. He recalls having had a laboratory assistant when he was still in Germany, whose passion for order was so great he was always clearing away—no matter what—and throwing things into a wastebasket. Laboratory tables and desks were always spick and span, cleared while you were engaged in a telephone conversation. One couldn't imagine, looking into those eyes in which there was not a speck of intelligence, that this assistant, Herr Zeisig, had a private life of his own. But

when Hitler came to power, it transpired that Herr Zeisig had all the time been a staunch adherent of his. That morning, when Hitler became Chancellor, he said to me, while he carefully hung my coat on the rack, "Herr Doctor, now there will be order in Germany." Well, Herr Zeisig kept his word.[4]

Now take this question of "materialism." Ziffel expresses amazement that writers on the political left have been so much concerned with bringing philosophy and morality to the lower classes that they tended to overlook the greater cogency of "eating and other such pleasures." "A simple description of varieties of cheeses, presented clearly and vividly, or an artistic depiction of a true omelette would undoubtedly also have a cultural effect." "A good beef stew comports well with humanism."[5]

As for war, it is becoming obvious that populations, that is civilians, are getting more and more in the way of an effective conduct of total warfare. Only a thoroughgoing evacuation of the population makes possible the full utilization of modern weapons. "And the evacuation must take place the world over, for wars are spreading like mad, and one doesn't know what's going to be attacked next. . . . The question really boils down to the following," Ziffel says, "either the population is liquidated, or war simply becomes impossible."[6]

And so, in turn, favorite subjects are brought forth, tossed in the air with the skill of an expert juggler, who, however, is not at all concerned with hiding his technique: Heroism, the necessity of egoism, the unconscionable demands made upon ordinary human beings to become "superhuman." "Kalle, fellow, friend: I have had enough of all virtues. I am reluctant to turn into a hero."[7]

If only human beings practised the "egoism" of tanks, Stukas, motors. "These alone are unwilling to suffer hunger or thirst and are deaf to all arguments; deaf to the cry that their country is lost if they do not come through; deaf to the glories of a national past; they are without faith in the Führer or fear of the police. . . . If they are neglected, they show neither anger, nor understanding; only rust. These creatures find it easiest to preserve their dignity."[8]

Not so our fellow Germans, Kalle adds. They are so obedient they can be changed into heroes and into a "master race." With slogans of blood and soil, "they have been convinced that only a German is worthy of shedding his blood for the Führer; that only a German may have his soil taken away from him by another German."

Such and other weighty matters occupy our two refugees. And now they come to the end of their dialogues.

You have given me to understand [Kalle says to Ziffel] that you are looking for a country in which such exhausting virtues as patriotism, thirst for freedom, goodness, unselfishness, are as little needed as abuse of one's country, servility, brutality, and egoism. Such a condition is represented by socialism. . . . I ask you now to rise and toast socialism, but in such a way as not to attract attention in this place. At the same time I must apprise you that to attain this goal all sorts of things are necessary: extraordinary courage, the deepest thirst for freedom, the greatest unselfishness, and the greatest egoism.[9]

And as they are speaking, "That-There-Thing attacked Greece, Roosevelt was campaigning in America, Churchill and the fish waited for the invasion, What's-His-Name was sending troops into Rumania, and the Soviet Union was still keeping quiet."[10]

VIII

The Poet on the Gold Coast, 1941-1947

Fleeing from the housepainter toward the
States,
Suddenly we noticed our little ship lay
becalmed.
A whole night through and a whole day
She lay in the Chinese Ocean in the latitude
of Luzon.
Some said it was because of the hurricane
raging in the north.
Others feared onslaught of German pirate
boats.
All
Chose the hurricane rather than the Germans.

BRECHT, "Der Taifun"

On May 3, 1941 Brecht received an American visa from the resident
vice-consul in Helsinki. He had hoped that Margarete Steffin would
also obtain one, and he waited. There was none forthcoming, but
ten days later she received a visitor's permit. The Brecht family,
accompanied by Margarete Steffin and Ruth Berlau, another of
Brecht's assistants, left for the Soviet Union. It was none too soon.
Brecht had to leave a considerable portion of valuable manuscript
material, gathered by Helene Weigel, in the hands of friends, who
kept it until after the war, when it was deposited as the first collection in the Brecht Archives.[1]

In Moscow, Margarete Steffin collapsed and was hospitalized. The
Brechts and Ruth Berlau left on the 30th of May. While they were

on the Trans-Siberian Express bound for Vladivostok, they received the news that Margarete Steffin had died.

Brecht was shocked and grieved, and expressed his feelings in the memorial verses we have already quoted. He had also written a number of poems describing their mutual devotion, which he was to include in his unpublished *Book of Changes*. At Vladivostok they boarded the *Anni Johnson,* a Swedish vessel. While they were still on the high seas, news came of the Nazi invasion of the Soviet Union.

It must all have seemed like some long, drawn-out nightmare. Once more he was in flight. "The messenger of misfortune," as he called himself, on the last boat out, was now watching with some joy the rosy dawn in the rigging of the ship and the vaulting of the dolphins in the Japanese Ocean; the horse-drawn carts of Manila —"doomed Manila"—and the matrons walking down the streets. And then what exhilaration when they came in sight of the "oil derricks" of Los Angeles! At last, on July 21, they landed in San Pedro, California.

At that moment Hitler's drive toward Leningrad, Moscow, and the Caucasus seemed irresistible.

Fritz Kortner, the actor, records that it was through his and Dorothy Thompson's efforts that the Brechts were enabled to come to the United States.[2] He was only one of many friends who were now in Hollywood, to welcome and assist him. The Brechts settled in a modest house in Santa Monica. Once more began the battle to survive.

Here in Hollywood, in Los Angeles and its vicinity, were to be found the foremost representatives of Germany's "culture in exile": Lion Feuchtwanger (himself escaped from a French concentration camp); Hanns Eisler, Peter Lorre, Oskar Homolka, Paul Dessau, Fritz Lang, Leopold Jessner, Albert Bassermann, Leonhard Frank, Ferdinand Bruckner, Berthold Viertel, and not least, Heinrich and Thomas Mann. Friends rallied around him, and returned that generosity of which he himself had been in better days, no mean dispenser. New friendships and associations were formed, with Vladimir Pozner, the French writer; W. H. Auden, Christopher Isherwood, Aldous Huxley, Charlie Chaplin, and, somewhat later, with Charles Laughton.

With other German and Austrian refugees he could now meet in a sort of "reading club," to discuss, argue, quarrel. When Brecht was around there would be no lack of fiery disagreement.

Brecht was no voluptuary. He continued living the way he had always done—what Kortner described as "an almost Gandhi-like ascetic existence, occasionally seasoned with small pleasures." An open-handed host, Brecht had numerous guests and visitors, who sat on hard chairs, and ate Helene Weigel's Viennese apple-strudel.

The cigars he smoked were now of a different nationality, but the fumes continued as thick as ever. The newspaper clippings and photographs were as numerous as before. Brecht's curiosity, sharp wit, and of course his contentiousness (rarely marked by discourtesy) had remained unaltered.

Brecht was not happy here. Not as happy, strange as it may seem, as he had been in Denmark or in Finland. One reason was that Germany was far, far away. The prospect of an internal collapse within that country seemed more fanciful than ever. Her armies were steadily advancing into Russia. The America that he had so preposterously and wildly (and almost affectionately) caricatured and hymned in his earlier works had lost her dubious glamor. The fraudulent glitter of Hollywood repelled him. Though he soon found employment, he saw himself only as so much marketable ware, a commodity such as he had been describing for years. No doubt, a part of the disappointment was personal. His works did not find that acceptance he had hoped for. There seemed to be no rush here to put on his plays, those he had brought from the Scandinavian countries: *Mother Courage, The Good Woman of Setzuan,* or *Arturo Ui.* What was produced was in driblets and fragments: scenes from *Fear and Misery of the Third Reich,* and this mostly through the fervent ministry of a new-found admirer and translator, Eric Bentley. True, the *Three Penny Opera* had been produced in 1933 in New York, but had lasted only for twelve performances. And the 1935 production of *The Mother* had not had much greater success.

But Brecht never spoke exclusively from a personal resentment. Rank commercialization seemed to him to pervade the atmosphere in this showplace of the easy-going. Americans seemed to him to be nomads, always on the march. He was horrified by the commercial theatre here, in contrast to that in the Scandinavian countries. He could not adjust himself to the "nice fellow" atmosphere. What if he were to speak out frankly and say what he thought!

As a guest of this country, he refrained from political activity— a difficult thing for him; but he was abetted by the fact that he could never quite master the English language. (Did he ever really try?) As an unreconstructed, unreformed, and unregenerate Marxist, how could he tell his California hosts to look around at their own world and note the contrast between the wealth and luxury on the one hand, and the poverty so close by? Always he heard the cry: Deliver the goods! We've got the dough. Tell us something that will inspire us! Guess our secret wishes! Rule over us, while you serve us.[3]

> Every morning, to earn my bread,
> I go to the market, where lies are bought.
> Hopefully
> I join the ranks of the sellers.[4]

Into his poems, the few letters he wrote, and his journals he poured his disaffection; many of these were not to be made public until after his death, and many are still in manuscript.

He is practically unknown here, he laments. "Spell your name," he is asked, when everyone should know this "name" "belonged with the great ones!"[5] But he must be happy too that he is unknown, for like someone for whom a warrant is out, he would scarcely find employment.

> In the face of the situation prevailing in this city,
> This is the way I behave:
> When I enter, I give my name and show

The papers, verifying it, with the stamps
That cannot be counterfeited.
When I say something, I adduce witnesses whose
    credibility
I document.
When I am silent, I give my face
An expression of emptiness, so that they can see:
I am not reflecting. . . .[6]

"Hell is a city much like London," Shelley had written. Los Angeles, Brecht imagined, must be like Hell. For even Hell must have luxuriant gardens with flowers, and fruit markets with tasty fruit, and autos skimming by like shadows, with rosy-cheeked men and women in them, going nowhere and coming from nowhere, and homes built for *"happy"* people, therefore looking empty though occupied.

Even the houses in Hell are not all ugly.
But the apprehension of being thrown on the streets
Consumes the occupants of the villas no less than
The occupants of the shacks.[7]

It is unfortunate that Brecht's notions of America were to be limited to his experiences in Hollywood, and even there narrowed down to a wholly negative attitude. That he did not in the course of his six years' stay deepen his knowledge of the profounder currents of American thought, and of the major literary figures of the past and the present century, and that he remained almost wholly indifferent to the literary upsurge of the twenties and the thirties, many of whose representatives were even then in Hollywood or nearby, reflects the limitations of his mind. That mind, otherwise so alert and so given to ready assimilation, would undoubtedly itself have been deepened by a more positive contact with such movements. He never really discovered Hemingway, Dos Passos, Dreiser, Farrell, Steinbeck, Lillian Hellman; nor for that matter any of the poets of that era. Where, as in the case of Clifford Odets, there was an acquaintance, it was one of rejection on the score of ideological blindness.[8] *Paradise Lost* of that playwright Brecht scored for its too great sympathy with the plight of the petty bourgeois family. In this instance, at least, and in the light of Odets' moral collapse before a Congressional investigating committee, Brecht did not prove a poor psychologist.

But he was no less hard on his own compatriots. Despite the fact that they had been driven into exile by a common enemy, they still preserved many of their old-time hostilities, grudges, prejudices, and failings, not to mention illusions and nostalgias. Brecht, who if anything at all, looked history in the face, could not stand their irresolution, their fantasies, their rigidities.

> Driven out of seven countries
> —I see them playing the same foolish game,
> I praise those who can change,
> And yet in changing remain the same.[9]

For many years now he had been planning a novel dealing with "intellectuals" and their role in contemporary society. He had coined a term "Tui" for them out of "tellekt-uell-in." Such a "Tui" novel he now found almost ready at hand in his Hollywood environment. To his old friend Karl Korsch he complained about the aridity of his associations with such personalities as Herbert Marcuse and Leonhard Frank. "The intellectual isolation here is monstrous. In comparison with Hollywood, Svendborg was a world-center."[10] Thomas Mann, whom he met only occasionally, and towards whom his lack of sympathy had not changed with the years, impressed him as if "three thousand years were looking down upon" him. "Alfred Döblin constantly speaks of home, and means France. Leonhard Frank now sees the 'man who is good' making a second world war, and is writing a Boy-Meets-Girl romance."[11]

Nor was he particularly impressed by the neo-Catholic atmosphere that appeared to be hovering around a number of his associates in Hollywood. He was thinking of Franz Werfel and the "Lourdes film," *The Song of Bernadette,* which was being prepared. "I am not susceptible to the Catholic infection," he wrote to Korsch.

To earn his bread and butter he set to work on a number of

movie scenarios, one, *Pagliacci,* for Richard Tauber, the great Austrian tenor. More timely and more powerful was the film *Hangmen Also Die,* on which he collaborated with Fritz Lang, who also directed it. Although much altered in its final form, it proved to be an effective story of the Czech resistance to the Nazi butcher Heydrich. Hanns Eisler composed the score. The cast included Walter Browning, Gene Lockhart, Brian Donlevy, Anna Lee and Alexander Granach. Other plans and even completed scripts fell by the wayside.

Aside from that, Hollywood life was not without its great compensations. He met and became friendly with Charlie Chaplin, whom he had admired since his boyhood, and who inspired so many of his own ways of thinking. Now a closer association only served to strengthen that admiration.[12]

Another personality proved of even greater importance to him— Charles Laughton. The British actor had an almost intuitive grasp of what Brecht was aiming at. Brecht recognized in Laughton a special gift and insight for interpreting his work. Each understood the genius in the other. In Laughton Brecht saw his ideal Galileo.

A plan to produce Brecht's *Galileo* with Charles Laughton had been broached by Orson Welles and Mike Todd in 1943, but nothing came of it. Joseph Losey, who was to co-direct the production, recalls a typical Brechtian scene, when all of the participants met in the offices of Mike Todd, and Todd began talking of how he would "dress" the production in "Renaissance furniture" drawn from Hollywood warehouses. Brecht only listened and giggled. From that moment, Losey states, there was no chance that Todd would do the play.[13]

In 1945, Laughton asked Brainerd Duffield and Emerson Crocker to prepare an acting version of the play. But in the meantime, as we have seen, Brecht had begun reconsidering the whole concept of *Galileo.* And now took place one of the strangest collaborations in literary history. Brecht knew very little English; Laughton knew no German. Yet playwright and actor understood each other across these seemingly insurmountable barriers. In a poetical letter addressed to Laughton, Brecht describes the experiences of those days. While the nations were dismembering each other in war, Brecht says, and while the walls of cities were tumbling, their own walls, those of language were also crumbling: The playwright turned actor, showing through accents and *gestus* what he wanted; and the actor turned writer, turning Brecht's German into English; yet each remained rooted in his own profession.[14]

Laughton recognized the urgency of the ideas in *Galileo*.

An atom bomb had been exploded over Hiroshima. Though, as Brecht noted, Laughton was politically on the reserved side, he yet insisted on sharpening certain elements of the play to underline the current political crisis. Brecht's spirits rose. They worked in Laughton's palatial villa overlooking the Pacific. Armed with large dictionaries and thesauruses of similes, they set about translating the play. Laughton illustrated with his rich repertory of Shakespeare and the English poets; Brecht tapped out the rhythms of Walt Whitman. Brecht looked forward to those meetings: Laughton coming toward him in the garden, barefoot, carelessly attired, eagerly discoursing on the plants and flowers, all without pedantry or pretension; then in the study hungrily examining books and designs with that care and intensity which Brecht admired and which he had always demanded. In Laughton Brecht had found the artist who "had eyes not only to give light with, but also to see; hands for work, not only to gesticulate with." "Enchanting," Brecht exclaimed, "how Laughton drinks down a glass of milk," while instructing little Sarti's mother that a great new age is dawning![15] And how brilliantly he apprehended the ambiguity of Galileo—that incomprehensibility, the combination of fortitude and servility, aggressiveness and vulnerability, sensuality and intellect!

Rarely had Brecht been so happy. Here was an artist, who at great cost to himself, was willing to undertake a work that he recognized to be a *contribution* both artistically and ideologically, and spared neither time nor energy in its realization. And here was

Brecht with a chance to say what he wanted to say, and working
with an artist who was capable of saying it!

It is important to know [Brecht wrote at that time] that our production
took place at a moment and in the country where the atom bomb had
just been created and used militarily, and when atomic physics was
surrounded by a thick veil of secrecy. The day of the dropping of the
bomb will scarcely ever be forgotten by any one who experienced it in
the United States."[15]

Though America had suffered severe losses in the war with Japan,
Brecht noted that

the great city of Los Angeles was filled with a deep sense of mourning.
This playwright heard from the lips of bus drivers and fruit venders
expressions of horror.[16]

Brecht, as we have seen, was revising Galileo's ultimate declaration to re-emphasize the heavy responsibility of the scientist to
speak out against this new war-monster, and to battle for the freedom to do so: to stand up against repressive authorities that threatened to stifle science, so that "it had become shameful to make
discoveries."[17]

Brecht's and Laughton's Galileo did not reach the stage until
the summer of 1947, on the eve of Brecht's departure from America.
By that time many changes had taken place in Brecht's life as well
as on the American scene. "Cold war" and "iron curtain" had replaced the honeymoon of the Grand Atlantic Alliance of 1941-1945.
On October 20, 1947, the House Committee on Un-American Activities opened its hearings on "subversive" elements in Hollywood.
But of all that later.

For Brecht these years had been years of steady work—hack work
by which to survive—and serious work having in mind the "unsolved, but not unsolvable problems of mankind."[18]

He writes in praise of a "discontent" that is active:

> He should be our teacher, the discontented,
> At the rebuilding of the commonwealth,[19]

at one with the saying of the great Irish labor leader, James Larkin, about the "divine mission of discontent."

His own "active discontent" had kept him from falling into depression or inertia. He was hoping for some signs of that discontent within the ranks of the German soldiers. To those caught in the Russian vastnesses, he had said, "There is no return."

> Brothers, were I with you,
> With you stamping through the icy deserts,
> I would ask, like you: Why
> Have I come here? When
> There is no way home. . . .

He thought he heard them say:

> And I will never see
> The land from which I came.
> Not the Bavarian woods, nor the southern hills,
> Nor the sea, nor the Brandenburg marches,
> Neither pine, nor the Frankish vineyards.
> Not the gray of morning, nor the noon of day,
> Nor the sinking sun of evening.[20]

He recalled for them their military "victories" as they advanced on Prague, on the Vistula, on Oslo, and Paris, and asked, "What did the soldier's wife receive" from those places—recounting the rich loot.

> And what did the soldier's wife receive
> From the wide Russian lands?
> From Russia she got her widow's veil
> For the funeral rite, the widow's mite
> She received from the Russian lands.[21]

As the Soviet armies encircled Paulus's Stalingrad regiments, and as news of the surrender of that General came, soon followed by an over-all retreat of the Nazis; as the last hopes of Hitler, based on the "secret weapons" crashed with the Allied invasion of the Continent, Brecht's thoughts and those of his fellow Germans in exile turned more and more to the question: What of the German morrow?

What did Brecht think of the Germans in Germany? Were there, as some urged, two Germanies: a "good" one (Goethe's) and a "bad" one (Hitler's)?

Alfred Kantorowicz recalled a meeting with Brecht in New York, toward the end of 1946, in which, he reports,

the skeptic Brecht is much . . . more confident about the future of Germany than I. He believes that there had arisen sufficient forces in the country even under the occupation, to be equal to the new historical tasks. That, coming from him, surprised me. He did not succeed in convincing me.[22]

Fritz Kortner, on the other hand, mentions a disagreement between Brecht and himself on the same subject:

Once Brecht complained about the incapacity of Germans to revolt, and called them "lackey-souled." I disagreed and we quarreled. I was then filled with a somewhat excessive enthusiasm for a so-called "other, good Germany." Years later, after my return to Germany, I learned to modify my enthusiasm.[23]

The question of "Whither Germany?" was not a frivolous one. It concerned the Germans in and out of Germany, as well as the Allies. There had been talk since early in the war of the formation of a "Free Germany Committee" in the U.S.A. Thomas Mann, whose political development and importance Brecht tended to underrate, had become the spokesmen for the more liberal elements of Germans in exile. In November, 1943, when it was already apparent that the Nazis faced ultimate defeat, Mann delivered an address at Columbia University on the subject of "The New Humanism." The report of the address distressed Brecht, and he entered into an exchange with the German novelist.

In his letter to Mann, Brecht expressed his "pained astonishment" that Mann reputedly had given voice to strong doubts concerning the contrast between the Hitler regime and its followers, and the democratic forces in Germany. He stated that he was not, of course, unaware of the extent of the crimes committed by German Nazism. But he added that despite the terror, there were some 300,000 men and women in Germany who had laid down their lives in "for the most part invisible battles against the regime," and that even today the underground opposition was tying up fifty of Hitler's élite S. S. divisions.[24]

Thomas Mann replied courteously. He said he was irked that among the thousand auditors of his speech there was not one German present with whom he had been discussing the unification of the anti-Hitler forces in exile. Mann explained that he had spoken of a "universal" guilt of all Germans in the crime of the Nazis, but that he had not equated German with Nazi. On the contrary, he had counseled "wisdom in the treatment of the beaten enemy," particularly in view of the share the democracies had had in the rise and growth of the fascist dictatorship. Not Germany or the German people were to be destroyed, but the combined power of the Junkers, the military and large-scale industry, which were responsible for two world wars. Mann concluded with the hope that Brecht and his friends would not imagine that he was using his influence in America to aggravate doubts about the existence of strong democratic forces in Germany. He was, however, hesitant about the feasibility of forming a movement of "Free Germans" abroad, lest it be taken as an attempt to protect Germany from the consequences of her crimes. He counseled waiting until Germany's defeat and the time when Germany had purged herself, was free, and proved that she deserved to live. The controversy rankled in Brecht's mind for some time, and he gave vent to his dissatisfaction in a poem attacking Mann's attitude.[24]

In the light of subsequent revelations of Nazi extermination camps, and the apathy of the great majority of Germans in the face of their past guilt, it is no longer easy to say that Mann was wrong and Brecht right. Despite the heroism of those who remained in Germany and resisted Hitler, their forces were too limited appreciably to influence the outcome of the war or the immediate future of Germany.

Many other projects occupied Brecht at this time aside from

Galileo. Among those that fascinated him particularly, was that of writing a modern parallel to the greatest philosophical poem of antiquity Lucretius' *De Rerum Natura.* Brecht's was to be a poem on the Nature of Man. A significant portion of the work was to be devoted to a poetic restatement of the *Communist Manifesto* of Marx and Engels. Only fragments came into being—enough, however, to justify the feeling that Brecht could have created a poetic masterpiece. *The Communist Manifesto,* Brecht wrote,

is as a pamphlet itself a work of art. But it seems to me that it is possible to renew its propaganda effect today, a hundred years later, supporting it with recent authority, and curtailing its pamphleteering character.[25]

The idea for the poem came to him in his Danish exile, when he received a copy of Karl Korsch's book on Marx. In the succeeding correspondence with this scholar, Brecht took occasion to obtain further counsel, as well as to express some of his own ideas on the *Manifesto,* and also as on other conclusions of Korsch's, with which he frequently took friendly issue.

Korsch's bias was strongly anti-Soviet, and he did not conceal it from Brecht. But Brecht was independent enough and open-minded, and he enjoyed the dialectical arguments with one of his former teachers.

We differ [Brecht wrote to Korsch from Santa Monica] for a long time now in our evaluation of the USSR, but I believe that your position toward the Soviet Union is not the only application one can make of your scholarly researches.[26]

Brecht holds fast to "the good old dialectic." For him it has not yet been transcended, and is far from antediluvian. Dialectic will still have to take over the leadership and the battle of the working classes, though presently obscured by the momentary weakening of the proletarian movement.[27]

He applies his own dialectic in questioning Korsch's position toward the USSR as having betrayed Marxism. Brecht points out that the Soviet Union "is not only a workers' *state,* but also a *workers'* state";—that is, that a specific historical situation, the Five Year Plan, collectivization and industrialization, as well as the strengthening of the defensive apparatus were responsible for the specific form of state—the Stalinist; but that it too was subject to change, and that by the working classes themselves.[28] This is an argument which is constantly in Brecht's mind: the separation of the *mechanics* of state, from its fundamental class character. Social- ism, in his eyes being founded upon reason and science, is therefore a self-corrective phenomenon, in that way distinguished from any other system founded, say, on a mystical, instinctual, anti-rational premise.

Actually Brecht set to work on this "Lehrgedicht" (didactic poem), as he called his *Manifest,* in February, 1945. He continued it, intermittently, on his return to Germany. The original plan in- cluded four cantos, of which the introductory first was to depict the difficulty of living in our "unnatural" society; the two middle ones were to be a poetic restatement of the *Manifesto;* and the fourth a description of the brutalization and barbarization of mod- ern society. Feuchtwanger was sceptical of this venture, especially as to its poetic rendering, but Brecht went ahead and proceeded to set the hexameters. That was a paradoxical choice, indeed, for Brecht was employing the classical metre of the ancients, as well as that of Goethe and Schiller.

While working on this poem, he kept his ears tuned to world events, and in March, 1945, he noted "the frightful newspaper re- ports from Germany—ruins, and not a sign from the working classes there."[29] He submitted portions of his own *Manifest* to be tested aloud in readings by Helene Weigel and Fritz Kortner, and for critical examination by friends in the East. Karl Korsch encour- aged him through the years, and urged him to complete it in time for the centennial celebration of the *Communist Manifesto* in 1948.[30]

Sparse as the extant fragments are, they give one a sense of the epic sweep that characterized the work. As one academic critic remarked: "The poem . . . . belies the frequently held notion that political literature must of necessity be bad; in the hands of a poet such as Brecht, political conviction and true artistry can combine to produce literature that is both political and good."[31]

Marx and Engels wrote: "A specter is haunting Europe."

And Brecht:

> Kriege zertrümmern die Welt und im Trümmerfeld geht ein Gespenst um.
> Nicht geboren im Krieg, auch in Frieden gesichtet, seit lange Schrecklich den Herrschenden, aber den Kindern der Vorstädte freundlich.

> Wars lay the world in ruins; amidst its ravages stalks a specter.
> Not born in the war; also sighted in peace.
> Long since terror to rulers, kindly to children in slums,
> Watchful in wretched kitchens, misprising the scanty table. . . .

The triumph of the bourgeoisie is depicted as follows:

> Niemals zuvor ward entfesselt ein solcher Rausch der
> Erzeugung . . .
> Wie ihn die Bourgeoisie in der Zeit ihrer Herrschaft entfacht hat. . . .

> Never before had been seen such frenzy of production,
> Such as in time of her triumph the bourgeoisie unleashed:
> Subjugating all Nature; releasing power electric,
> Mastering unsailable streams; clearing gigantic wastes.
> Never before had man dreamt that slumbering in his loins,
> Dwelt such potent freedoms, dwelt such fruitful powers.[32]

And the proletariat:

> Seine ist die Bewegung der Mehrzahl. . . .

> His the movement of numbers; and were he to rule,
> His rule would not be ruling, but making slave of rule.
> Only oppression oppressed; for the proletariat must,
> Lowest in social scale, if he wills to rise,
> Shatter the social structure, with all its layers on high,
> For only in freeing all
> Can he free himself.[33]

Sometimes, Brecht's imagery attains an overpowering effect, as when, describing the misguided "machine wreckers" of the early Industrial Revolution, he sees them smashing machines,

> thus to shake off the new
> and lowlier enslavement, recapture the feudal and old,
> and thoughtless, weary and desperate to hold up
> the iron hand of the world-clock that they themselves
> had forged.[34]

The poem was intended for the future. But the present also made irresistible claims. During his American sojourn Brecht completed, in addition to *Galileo*, three other plays: *Die Gesichte der Simone Machard* (*The Visions of Simone Machard*), *Schweyk im zweiten Weltkrieg* (*Schweyk in the Second World War*), *Der Kaukasische Kreidekreis* (*The Caucasian Chalk Circle*), as well as a number of adaptations, among them John Webster's *The Duchess of Malfi*.

IX

A St. Joan of the Resistance:
"The Visions of Simone Machard"

Not for nothing
Is every day's dawn
Heralded by cock's crow
Proclaiming from times immemorial
Another betrayal,

BRECHT, "Tagesanbruch"

It is June, 1940. The German armies are advancing toward the
south of France. The French front is broken. Hundreds of refugees
are streaming southward, blocking the roads, desperate, hungry.
The French army is demoralized, and many of its officers are
deserting. Betrayal and collusion are around everywhere.

This is the background of *The Visions of Simone Machard,* upon
which Brecht and Lion Feuchtwanger collaborated. Brecht had
been deeply moved by Feuchtwanger's autobiographical description
of his internment in a French concentration camp. Out of that experience Feuchtwanger had also created a novel, *Simone,* that served
as the source of the new play. Together, Brecht and Feuchtwanger
set to work between October, 1942, and February, 1943.

Feuchtwanger's *Simone* is a swift, bare story about an orphan
girl, Simone Planchard, daughter of a deceased radical. She is the
ward of his brother, Prosper Planchard, owner of a freight and
trucking establishment. To keep a store of gasoline owned by her
uncle from falling into the hands of the advancing Nazis, the girl

sets fire to it, and is consequently committed to a "reformatory." She had been an avid reader of lives of St. Joan, and imagines herself another such heroine.

The Visions of Simone Machard of Brecht and Feuchtwanger adheres in general to the central theme of the novel. Simone Machard is a deformed and very young slavey in the hostelry "Du Relais," owned by M. Henri Soupeau, and his mother, Mme. Soupeau. Simone's brother, André, is seventeen, and is the only one who has volunteered for the French army in his entire town of Saint-Martin. The Soupeaus are more concerned for their properties than for the fate of France. But M. Soupeau has given Simone a book about St. Joan, because, as he says sanctimoniously, "the Lord knows, we could use a Maid of Orleans." He has accumulated a stock of black-market gasoline and is busy trying to keep his vans from being taken over to transport refugees. He remains deaf to the urging of the Mayor of the town and pleads his duty to Captain Fétain, whose wine he has promised to transport to Bordeaux. Simone overhears the quarrel between Soupeau and the Mayor, especially the latter's last words: "Only a miracle can save France. She is rotten to the core."

Simone is filled with her reading of the life of St. Joan and has a vision: Her brother André, in the guise of an angel, appears to her on the roof of the garage, and urges her to take the small drum he is carrying and awaken the country. Other characters around the inn also appear transformed, some as her bodyguard, the Mayor as King Charles. She beats the drum. France is awakened. She crowns the King.

The Germans are advancing. Mme. Soupeau closes the inn for a time, while M. Soupeau transports their valuables to safety. Simone has another vision, and the angel appears:

SIMONE (*to the Angel*). Shall we still fight on when the enemy has already won?
ANGEL. Will the wind blow in the night?
SIMONE. Yes.

ANGEL. Is there a tree in the yard?
SIMONE. Yes. A poplar.
ANGEL. Do the leaves rustle in the wind?
SIMONE. Yes, distinctly.
ANGEL. Then one must fight on, even if the enemy has won.[1]

But how fight? Simone asks. The answer is: Scorch the earth; give the enemy neither food nor lodging. "Go forth and destroy!"

With the Germans in town, Madame Soupeau welcomes the invading Captain with open arms and offers to sell him the gasoline. The French fascist, Captain Fétain, is no less hospitable; and even the Mayor is now acquiescent. But no sooner have they emerged from the inn, than the sky is lit up, and there is an explosion.

THE GERMAN CAPTAIN. What is that?
THE FRENCH CAPTAIN. That's the brickyard.[2]

Simone has set fire to the gasoline. She refuses to lie. She has done the deed. In the final vision she sees herself condemned to death in a trial, even without a hearing. One by one the accusers appear, in medieval garb of bishop, knight, judge, king, or queen. But when they unmask, they are all people she knows: Frenchmen. Each pronounces her death sentence:

His Eminence, the Bishop of Beauvais, because she liberated the city of Orleans—Death.[3]

In the Bishop, Simone recognizes the French Colonel; and thus successively, in the Captain her employer; and even the Mayor. In amazed horror she exclaims: "It is the Mayor himself, Monsieur Chavez! But they are all Frenchmen! It must be a mistake!"[4]

She demands and is granted a hearing, in which she is taunted about the vision of the angel she has been seeing, and is urged to implore him to appear once more. But no angel comes. On the 22nd of June the flags of the town are flown at half-mast. Maréchal Pétain has proclaimed the truce, which, in his words, "does not at all touch the honor of France." Simone is apprehended and committed to an institution for the feebleminded. Everything appears

to have returned to normal. Suddenly the master of the inn rushes
out:

> THE MASTER. Maurice! Robert! Find out immediately what's burning.
> PÈRE GUSTAVE. It must be the town gymnasium. That's where the
> refugees are. They seem to have learned something . . .
> GEORGES. The carriage with Simone cannot have reached Saint-Ursula's
> as yet. It is possible Simone saw the fire from the carriage.[5]

The Visions of Simone Machard is an unusual play for Brecht
to have written. It has a unified and single plot, uninterrupted by
"epic" elements. It also has something unprecedented in Brecht,
"visionary" scenes, with an angel.

Simone and a number of other characters are treated with tenderness, and there is no attempt to avoid "Einfühlung." We identify
with the deformed child Simone, whose heroism, naive and direct
as it is, is devoid of sentimentality. She acts upon simple impulses,
and those are the impulses of the best that is in France. In that way
she is the surrogate of her brother in the army, and the general
population for whom her heart beats and bleeds. The complex
involutions that prompt her superiors to collaboration and treachery
she can barely understand, but she grasps their essence. There are
two matters she is sure of: the refugees are hungry and they must
be fed, (and she does the latter despite her superiors); and that the
supplies must not fall into the hands of the Nazis.

If we look for Brecht's hand in the play, it is undoubtedly to be
found in the clarification of the social issues that played a part in
the history of this episode. The poetic portions are also undeniably
Brecht's. It was Brecht too, probably, who was responsible for including a second fire at the conclusion of the play, an incident
which is absent from Feuchtwanger's novel. Thus, Simone's own
action is not without heirs.

The fact that Simone's brother appears as the inspiring angel is
itself significant, for her brother is shabby and poor, like herself,
and like millions of other French soldiers. Simone's "heroism" therefore has concrete and cogent reality and reason. She does what she
does for his sake, and for the sake of thousands like him. She is,

in fact, the people; she is like the wind, the poplar, and the leaves —permanently there, ineradicable.

It would not have been Brecht's play had he not also laid bare the economic divisions that played such an important role in the betrayal and fall of France. When the disabled soldier Georges calls attention to the fact that every part of his gear and outfit undoubtedly enriched some French industrialist, he speaks with Brecht's voice. So also when he says:

Yes, there are one thousand war planes in two hundred hangars, paid for, manned, tested; but in the hour of France's danger, they don't even get off the ground. Our fortifications have cost ten billion francs, they are of concrete and steel, they are one thousand kilometers long, seven stories deep, and stand out in the open. But when the battle began, our Colonel stepped into his car, drove to the rear, and behind him were two trucks full of wine and provisions. Two million men waited for the word of command, ready to die, but the lady-friend of the minister of war was at odds with the lady-friend of the minister-president. And so there was no word of command. Yes, *our* fortifications sit immovable; but *theirs* ride on wheels and roll over us.[6]

We may contrast Simone with her counterpart in *St. Joan of the Stockyards,* and we are struck by Simone's almost instinctive understanding of what to *do*. So too, in contrast with Kattrin of *Mother Courage,* who is a crippled figure, and acts almost completely from a primitive sort of maternal feeling, almost a reflex action, Simone is an *active* personality; she reads, she tries to understand the vital issues that are at stake—the life and death of her country, the welfare of her brother and millions like him, and the treason of those on top.

The miracles she is led to perform are earthly ones, and their realization within the scope of human beings. Such miracles were performed daily by members of the French Resistance.

So far as Brecht was concerned, once again in those years 1941 to 1943 he was reaffirming his refusal to accept defeat as the ultimate destiny of man and the end of human struggles.

X

The Unheroic Hero:
"Schweyk in the Second World War"

BULLINGER (*distraught*). Are you an idiot?

SCHWEYK. I beg to report: Yes, sir. I can't
help it . . . I have been officially declared
an idiot by a military commission.

BRECHT, *Schweyk in the Second World War*

Now, once more, Brecht turned back to a theme that had been with
him for almost two decades, that of the Good Soldier Schweik. And
like Charlie Chaplin in *The Great Dictator,* Brecht succeeded in
turning the Nazi adventure into a subject for broad laughter.

In 1928, he had collaborated with Erwin Piscator on the latter's
production of *Schweik.* This had been one of the landmarks in the
theatre of that era. But even as he was working with Piscator, he
was projecting his own version of a political Schweik.

Fritz Sternberg recalled that in 1927 Brecht came to him and
immediately described his idea for Schweyk. He thought of representing General Ludendorff, standing before gigantic maps in a
room extraordinarily high—almost two stories. Ludendorff was to
be shown directing the movements of vast armies in various regions,
but the armies never seem to arrive at the right time, nor in the
right place, nor in the right numbers. Why isn't it all working out?
Because underneath Ludendorff's giant room there is a cellar filled
with soldiers, all of them looking like Schweyk. All these Schweyks,
when they are set in motion, do not seem to resist.

They follow all instructions, they respect their superiors, they move when commanded; but they never arrive at their destination in time, and never in their full complement.[1]

So once more, between 1941 and 1944, particularly as the Nazi reverses on the Eastern front and before Stalingrad made the heart lighter, Brecht turned to Jaroslav Hašek's hilarious satire about the little soldier of the First World War. Hašek died in 1923, and he never completed his *Good Soldier Schweik*, but what he left behind constituted one of the most devastating gibes at the Austrian army command, as well as at armies and wars in general. The Czech writer's book soon acquired international acclaim, and Josef Schweik became an international "hero."

Schweik is Hašek's "little man" who discomfits the Austro-Hungarian army in the First World War by his almost diabolical imbecilities, half-innocent, half intentional, and drives his superior officers to distraction. His double-edged idiocy assumes almost epic contours. Thus (and Brecht was to use this and other episodes in his own way) on hearing of the assassination of the Austrian Archduke Francis Ferdinand at Sarajevo, he asks, "Which Ferdinand"? For he knows two Ferdinands, one who does odd jobs for Prusa the chemist, and the other who collects manure.[2]

His favorite resort is the tavern, The Flagon, to which also come the undercover police in search of subversives—and Policeman Brettschneider in particular. The effusive Schweik is drawn by Brettschneider into a compromising discussion, in which Schweik remarks that it was a pity Ferdinand was done away with "for you can't replace him with just any sort of idiot." Arrested, he even befuddles the examining police chief, to whom he admits that he had been "officially declared an idiot" by the army medical board. In his enthusiasm for the war, Schweik eventually finds his way into the army, being wheeled there in a chair, along with his crutches. Among his many crazy adventures, he is traded in a game of cards to a Lieutenant Lukasch; is lost in a railroad station; has to make his way by way of an Anabasis toward his master's regiment; is arrested as a Russian spy and obtains a good meal because of it; finally reaches the Galician front, where, coming upon a Russian soldier who is taking a swim, he gets into the Russian uniform and is promptly captured by the Austrian army, and sent back to work in a prison camp.

Thus far Hašek. Now Brecht. Like his predecessor, Brecht's Schweyk is a Czech dog-dealer, not averse to stealing an animal to satisfy a customer. But, in addition, he is endowed with the gift of finding distinguished pedigrees for the animals he is trading. On which occasion he can deliver himself of some very penetrating remarks.

Bullied into agreeing to find for the Nazi platoon leader Bullinger a Pomeranian "spitz" belonging to the Czech Quisling Vojta, Schweyk describes the dog as being so aristocratic that he doesn't eat unless begged on bended knee, and only a special cut of beef. That, says Schweyk, shows that "he is of a pure race. The unpure ones are smarter, but the pure ones are finer and are much more eagerly stolen. They are mostly so stupid that they need two or three servants to tell them when to shit, and when to open their mouths to eat. Just the same as with refined people."[3]

He resorts to a tavern, The Goblet, owned by the patriotic and handsome widow Kopecka, and visited regularly by these guests: Baloun, the Czech who is so hungry he is almost ready to volunteer for the Nazi army; Prochazka, young son of a butcher, who is in love with Kopecka; and, of course, many Nazis, including the Gestapo agent, Brettschneider—all ears. The attempt on Hitler's life in the Munich Rathskeller leads (like Hašek's discussion of Ferdinand's assassination) to an interesting conversation between Schweyk and the Gestapo agent:

BRETTSCHNEIDER. They've made an attempt on the Führer's life in a Munich Bräuhaus. What do you say to that?

SCHWEYK. Did he have to suffer long?

BRETTSCHNEIDER. He wasn't hurt. The bomb exploded too late.

SCHWEYK. Obviously a cheap one. Today everything is mass-produced;

and then they're surprised that there's no quality any more. You see, such an article is not made with love, like those they used to make by hand. Am I right? But that they shouldn't have used a better bomb for such an occasion shows a sloppiness on their part. . . .[4]

It is such ambiguous statements as these that land Schweyk in the Gestapo interrogation chamber, where his "servility," "readiness to agree," and his deadpan replies baffle, fascinate, and amaze the platoon leader. As an "officially declared idiot" Schweyk has another naive thrust or two. He is about to leave, when he adds to Bullinger:

Before I go, I'd like to put in a word for a gentleman who is waiting outside with the arrested. He shouldn't sit with them. It would be unpleasant for him if he should be suspected because he is sitting on the same bench with the politicals. He is here only because he robbed and murdered a peasant from Holitz.[5]

With the help of Baloun, Schweyk succeeds in stealing the dog, by tricking the maid who is leading him; but both he and Baloun are themselves soon picked up and put to forced labor. They are assigned to a freightyard where railroad cars with military and other supplies are being dispatched. They are guarded by a soldier, whom Schweyk so confuses that he forgets the right number of the car to be dispatched. Hopefully, Schweyk remarks that the car carrying munitions might land in Munich and the one carrying farm equipment in Stalingrad. Kopecka brings them food, but whispers to Schweyk that the stolen dog she is housing for him has become a political issue in the city and must be gotten rid of. And he is. Comes Sunday, and we're back again at The Goblet, and in walks Schweyk with a package under his arm. To Baloun he says, "I'm here with the goulash meat." But Kopecka suspects the worst, and she is right. I had to do it, Schweyk whispers, because the shame that would befall The Goblet if one of her regular guests were to join the Germans would be unbearable. The place is raided. The search is on for the dog, who of course can't be found. But the package is discovered and black market trading is suspected. Once again Schweyk is marched off. From the military prison he is sent on to the front. The last scene takes place somewhere "fifty kilometers from Stalingrad," in a blinding snowstorm. Schweyk has lost his way, wanders round and round, but always comes back to the same guidepost. In his dreams he sees The Goblet and his old friends there. Baloun has remained faithful to his promise, and is now engaged to the servant girl Anna (from whom Schweyk had stolen the dog); Mrs. Kopecka is celebrating her wedding feast with her new husband Prochazka; and Schweyk is still looking for Stalingrad.

Suddenly . . . he bends down and snaps his fingers. From a scrub wood heavy with snow a starving dog emerges.

SCHWEYK. I knew it. Crawling around in that bush, wondering whether to come out. Eh? You're a cross between a terrier and a sheep-dog, with a bit of mastiff too. I'll call you Ajax. Don't cringe, and stop shaking like that. I can't stand it. (*He marches on, followed by the dog.*) We're off to Stalingrad. There'll be other dogs there; and there'll be lots of doings . . . The war won't last forever, and peace neither. Then I'll take you along with me to the Goblet, and we'll have to be careful of this fellow Baloun, so he doesn't bolt you down, Ajax, my boy. Then there'll be people again, who'll want dogs, and pedigrees will again be counterfeited, because they all want the pure breed—it's all nonsense of course, but that's what they want. Don't run between my legs, or I'll—On to Stalingrad!

(*The snowdrift grows thicker, and hides them.*)[6]

Along with the main plot, Brecht interwove brief scenes, in which Hitler, Goering, Himmler, raised to monster size, and Goebbels, reduced to pygmy stature, discuss the role of the "little man" in the war, assured that he is with them heart and soul. In another of these scenes, doubts begin to creep in. General von Bock is unsure that they will be able to take Stalingrad, but is urged on by Hitler, And finally, in the very last scene of the play, an epilogue, Schweyk lost in the snow, meets Hitler, and both wander about helplessly, as Hitler desperately turns from one direction to another: to the north there is the snow; to the south mountains of corpses; to the east the Reds; and home? The German people are there and Hitler doesn't care to go back.

Such is Brecht's "little man" Schweyk. The German critic Walter
Benjamin coined a term for such "heroes." He called them the
"caned heroes"—"geprügelte Helden." Candidates for survival, they
are beaten one day, only to live on to another. Like Mother Courage,
Schweyk reiterates the theme that merely being alive and keeping
body and soul together constitute heroism enough. If he must
achieve that through a temporary servility, well, he will be servile.
He is the embodiment of folk-wisdom from immemorial times; he
is also the comic converse of the more dramatic and mythical "idiot-
saint" like Parsifal or Prince Myshkin, whose innocence or "idiocy"
both baffles and amazes. Typically for Brecht, his soldier Schweyk
is also endowed with political insight, which he knows how to
mask. He is the great embodiment of the untranslatable "Schlam-
perei"—that slovenliness, incompetence, and carelessness that con-
found the most far-reaching plans of his higher-ups.

In *Schweyk in the Second World War* Brecht found that right
fusion of "Einfühlung" and "Verfremdung" that makes it possible
for the audience at once to identify with the plight of the characters
like Frau Kopecka, the ever-hungry Baloun, and, of course, Schweyk,
and at the same time savor the "Verfremdung" of seeing the reality
behind their actions and speech. Not less successful is Brecht's in-
clusion of some of the best songs he and Eisler had ever written
such as the "Und was bekam des Soldaten Weib" which we already
know, and the beautiful "Song of the Moldau," both sung by
Kopecka, (the second one after she and the others had been beaten
up by the Gestapo agents) with its haunting folk idiom:

Am Grunde der Moldau wandern die Steine.
Es liegen drei Kaiser begraben in Prag.
Das Grosse bleibt gross nicht, und klein nicht das Kleine.
Die Nacht hat zwölf Stunden, dann kommt schon der Tag.

On Moldau's bottom, the stones still are rolling,
Three Emperors lie buried in tombs in Prague.
For the great don't stay great; nor the little ones little.
The night has twelve hours and then comes the day.[7]

Brecht and Hanns Eisler wrote the "Song of the Moldau" at a moment when Hitler's armies were only some sixty kilometers from Moscow!

The widow Kopecka is the steady anchor, rooting all of the others to the significant certainty that there will be a change. And she caps the "Song of the Moldau" with another one, which she sings in celebration of her marriage. It is the song of the Goblet, an invitation to the "little man"—a man without the world's credentials of honors or posts—but with the more honorable credentials of being human, to come and join in the festivities.[8]

The last song of the play is a "German Miserere"—sung by the snowbound German soldiers. It has an ominous refrain: "May the Lord preserve us and bring us home."

> And one fine day our leaders will command us
> To conquer the deeps of the ocean and the heights of the moon,
> And it is hard for us here in the land of the Russians,
> For the foe is strong, the winter cold and the way home unknown.
> May the Lord preserve us and bring us safely home![9]

Schweyk is Brecht's unchangeable hero, who changes the world.[10] His dignity (to use a phrase of Henry James's) is never "aggressive." "It never sits in state; but if you push it far enough, you can find it."

"Under no circumstance," Brecht wrote in one of his notebooks, "must Schweyk be conceived as a sly, underhanded saboteur. He is simply the opportunist of the few opportunities offered him. . . . His wisdom is subversive. His indestructibility makes him the inexhaustible object of abuse, and at the same time the fruitful soil of liberation."[11]

The income from the film script *Hangmen Also Die* and other hack-work had provided Brecht with the leisure to complete at least three plays close to his heart. And now, after the conclusion of *Schweyk*, he reflected somewhat sadly:

Whenever we are through with a piece of work these days, there is a desolating pause that follows—of an unnatural non-utilization—that must be overcome. The fugitive stonemason, once again following his habit, like some vice, has transformed one of his stoneblocks into a statue, and now sits near it, resting (so he claims); but actually waiting (as he does not admit). So long as no one reaches out for it, he can stand anything. It is when they pass by, yes, when they suddenly look up—then it's really bad. And these works of art are only with difficulty transportable—for they are made of stone blocks—that have been worked over.

He recalls the ten plays he had written in the ten years following his exile, and concludes: "Not a bad repertory for a thoroughly beaten class!"[12]

XI

Justice in Utopia:
"The Caucasian Chalk Circle"

Terrible is the temptation of goodness!
BRECHT, *The Caucasian Chalk Circle*

The Orient continued to fascinate Brecht. Among the many unfinished projects of this time he was considering a rather extensive play on the subject of Confucius, inspired by a reading of Carl Crow's *Master Kung.* Part of this play was to be acted by children, and only one full scene, called *The Ginger Jar,* has been preserved. But from the elaborate outline it appears that this was to be a kind of socio-historical study of changes within Chinese society, and the supplantation of a primitive Utopian community by the "Chou dynasty of large property owners." "Ancient kings," Brecht wrote in his notes, "recognized that it is hard to be hardhearted to one's fellowman; today no one understands this." This statement is put into the mouth of Kung. In the "golden age" of the Kings Yao, Shun and Yu "there were no police, because there was no crime; very few laws; no conception of private property; no thieves; no taxes; no soldiers, hence no wars; no poverty, because there were no riches; not even kings!"[1]

At the instigation of an actress, presumably Luise Rainer, he set to work on another play built around an Oriental theme, *The Caucasian Chalk Circle.* Once again he turned to already available material, this time to an old Chinese play, *The Chalk Circle.* When Brecht was working alongside Max Reinhardt in Berlin, the latter produced in

1925 a beautiful version of this play by Klabund, the husband of one of Brecht's favorite actresses, Carola Neher. The theme stayed with Brecht, for he wrote a short story *The Augsburg Chalk Circle,* which was published in the Moscow edition of *International Literatur* in 1941.[2]

Klabund's version is worthy to stand beside Brecht's, for its rare beauty and sensitiveness, though utterly different in general outlook. Klabund's *Der Kreidekreis (The Chalk Circle)* tells the story of the penniless and beautiful young girl Haitang, who is forced to enter a house of prostitution because her family has been ruined by the mandarin tax-farmer Ma, and her father has in consequence committed suicide at the door of the malefactor. In the brothel, Haitang is seen by the prince Pao, traveling incognito, who falls in love with her, but is too poor to outbid Ma, who also succumbs to her charms. Married to Ma, she bears him a son, and thus arouses the hatred of his barren first wife, who succeeds in poisoning her husband and throwing suspicion on beautiful Haitang. The wicked woman claims the child as her own, for in that way she will be assured of her property rights. Haitang is brought before a corrupt judge, who decides in favor of the first wife and orders the execution of the girl. Fortunately, a courier arrives, announcing the death of the old Emperor and the accession of the new one, as well as bringing a command that all judgments be suspended and the litigants brought to Peking. The young Emperor decides the case by means of a chalk circle, in the center of which he places the boy, asking each of the claimant mothers to pull him out. The true mother hesitates to handle the child roughly and is declared the victor. The Prince (now Emperor) and Haitang have recognized each other and, to cap the story, the Prince discloses to her that it was he who came to her lone bedside the night of the wedding, and it is he who is the father of the child. What could be better? He will wed Haitang, who has already endowed him with an heir to the throne!

But the *Kreidekreis* is actually more than a fairy tale. Sharp social satire is directed against the oppression by the rich, the corruption of the courts, the violence of the rulers.

Thus, the "supreme court judge" Tshu (having received a little something from the Ma widow):

Gold—gold—no more lovely music than when you hear the sound of gold rolling across a hard table. It sounds like the pagoda bells. When I hear the ringing of gold I turn downright religious.[3]

Haitang's brother expresses himself boldly:

Emperor and Judges—you're all cut from the same cloth! The new Emperor will be no better than the old one. We poor wretches will be croaking by the wayside even under his dragon-banner.[4]

He is the spokesman for the underdog, and the accuser of the times. But his sister, Haitang, speaks for human justice and mercy, when she declines to pass judgment on her accusers:

> I hold above you the staff of judgment,
> But break it, for I cannot act the judge.
> No man is worthy to wear the judge's robe,
> Who thinks unjustly, and unjustly acts.[5]

These are all themes that attracted Brecht. The framework and prologue of his *Caucasian Chalk Circle* is a quarrel between two Soviet collective farms, one of sheep breeders, and the other of fruit growers. Both had been driven from their settlements by the war, but are now returning. The fruit growers have developed an irrigation scheme which will require the land of the sheep breeders. The discussion is lively, but peaceful. The sheep breeders become convinced that their rivals' scheme is bound to be more useful to the community than their own, and in honor of the agreement, the fruit growers present a play. Reason and good common sense and social utility have won the day. Communal good has triumphed.

The principal play itself fuses many elements in typical Brechtian fashion. It is a "piece with songs" and has a narrating and singing minstrel in the familiar Nō-style. It is a fast-paced series of incidents;

it also includes burlesque elements. As a play it falls into two distinct but not completely separated parts: the flight of Grusha and the judgment of Azdak.

The scene takes place in a city in the ancient Caucasus, at a time of political turmoil and upheaval. The reigning governor is overthrown and executed. In her hurry to escape, the governor's wife leaves her little child, a boy, behind. Grusha, a kitchen wench, after a few moments' hesitation, saves the child from the approaching assassins and flees with it. She suffers hardships because of the child. In an effort to give the child status, she marries a peasant who feigns mortal illness to escape the military. However, before her flight, she and a soldier had plighted their troth. When the disturbances are over, the soldier returns, finds her with the boy, and, misunderstanding the situation, leaves her. The returning governor's wife claims the child.

The second major episode deals with the tramp Azdak, who at the outbreak of the upheavals had hidden an escaping Grand Duke, and in the midst of the hurly-burly is appointed local judge. His fantastic decisions and verdicts are all topsy-turvy. He takes from the rich and gives to the poor. The return of the status quo threatens him with death; but the Grand Duke rewards him for the past favor, and it is Azdak who sits in judgment on Grusha, the Governor's wife and the child. Availing himself of the device of the chalk circle, he allots the child to Grusha, and through another trick, he divorces her from her husband, and enables her to retain her fiancé, Chachava, as well as the child.

Humaneness in time of upheaval—how contemporary that theme was for the years 1943 to 1945! Had Brecht not written

> Always in the time of carnage
> There is a man tearing his shirt
> Into strips, to staunch a fellowman's wounds.[6]

And about himself:

> The Finnish workers
> Gave him a bed and a writing table,
> The Soviet writers brought him to the boat,

> A Jewish laundryman in Los Angeles
> Sent him a suit of clothes:
> The enemy of the butchers
> Found friends.[7]

The Caucasian Chalk Circle defines morality in terms of social "use." The biological mother has abandoned her child. Grusha brings her social morality into play and makes the child her own through her own privations and sacrifices. Each act of benefit to the child jeopardizes her own chances of escape or survival. She brings order into the disorder of the times, just as the disorderly tramp Azdak, spokesman for the "insulted and injured," cynically does the same. But through his actions traditional order is revealed as oppression and tyranny, and his disorderliness as humaneness. Yet, as Brecht puts it, "in evil times humanity and humaneness themselves become dangerous." Grusha is a "sucker" (Brecht uses the American term). She illegally appropriates the child. All her acts are self-contradictory and suicidal. Her transformation is into a "productive" personality. She produces motherhood within herself.[8] The final test, in the court scene, is utterly paradoxical according to traditional standards: When Azdak asks Grusha why, as a good mother, she would not return the child to his princely comforts and luxuries, she looks around at the biological mother, at the servants, at the armed warriors, at the mother's counsel. She remains silent, and it is the minstrel who speaks for her:

> If he walked in golden shoes,
> He would crush the weak.
> Evil he would have to do,
> And laugh in doing it.[9]

She will turn the child into a human being. The minstrel summarizes the "moral" of the story after the judgment has been given: "That what there is should belong to those who are good for it; so, the children to the motherly, that they may thrive; the carts to good drivers, that they may be well driven; and the valley to these who water it, so that it may bring forth fruit."[10]

It may not be amiss to pause for a moment at an extraordinary scene: the wooing of Chachava and Grusha at the opening of the play, with its humorous indirection, sly tenderness, touching simplicity. He has been commanded to accompany the Governor's wife; she is being left behind.

SIMON CHACHAVA. May it be permitted to ask if the lady still has parents?
GRUSHA. No. Only a brother.
SIMON. As the time is short, the second question might be: Is the young lady as healthy as a fish in water?
GRUSHA. Maybe once or twice a stitch, in the right shoulder; otherwise strong enough for any job. No one has yet complained. . . .
SIMON. Question three: Is the young lady inclined to be impatient? Does she ask for apples in winter?
GRUSHA. Impatient—no. But if a man goes to war without rhyme or reason and there's no news of him, that's bad.
SIMON. A message will come. Finally, the principal question—
GRUSHA. Simon Chachava, because I must hurry to the third court, the answer is Yes. . . .[11]

Once more the small heroism of the small hero projects a new world. As the minstrel recites:

> O blindness of the great! They wander like gods
> Great upon bent backs, sure
> Of their hired fists, trusting
> In force, which has lasted so long.
> But long is not forever.
> O change of times! Thou hope of the people![12]

XII

The Trial of Bertolt Brecht

> I have the honor to expose myself as a hostile witness. . . . I testify, moreover, that to my mind the ignorant and superstitious persecution of the believers in a political and economic doctrine, which is, after all, the creation of great minds and great thinkers—I testify that this persecution is not only degrading for the persecutors themselves, but also very harmful to the cultural reputation of this country.
>
> THOMAS MANN, "Spoken on behalf of the Committee for the First Amendment."

If dialectical irony was Brecht's forte and delight, he could not but have been particularly struck by that which now, in the year 1947, befell him. On September 19 of that year he was cited before the House Committee on Un-American Activities. Had this situation, which marked one of the blackest pages in the history of American democracy, not been so serious and fraught with so much tragedy for so many victims, it might almost have appeared as a subject for one of his own plays.

For it was in July of 1947 that Brecht's play, *The Life of Galileo,* with its indictment of the capitulation of the intellectual, and its declaration of the responsibilities of the scientist to the community was produced in Los Angeles, with Charles Laughton in the role of Galileo. In December of that year it was being readied for pro-

duction in New York. And here was one of the leading playwrights
of the world, exiled because of his anti-Nazi activities and works,
being hauled in to answer for his political opinions.

Nor did this paradox complete the full "scenario" of the drama.
Had Brecht been gifted with a fortune-teller's prescience, he would
undoubtedly have enjoyed another aspect of the gruesome situation.
For seated as chairman of the committee was Representative J.
Parnell Thomas of New Jersey, who, some time after Brecht had
already returned to Berlin, was indicted, prosecuted, convicted, and
sentenced to jail for conspiracy to defraud his own government.
Subsequently he was pardoned by President Truman.

Could the master of "estrangement" have invented a more powerful example of what he had been aiming for all his life long?

The long succession of these investigations stretched from the
1930's, the years of Depression and the New Deal, when the ante-
cedents of such committees were chaired by Hamilton Fish. The
particular committee before which Brecht was cited was established
in 1938, under Representative Martin Dies of Texas. Its example
was to be followed by other committees, lesser and greater, such
as the Senate Internal Security Subcommittee, and those in various
states, notably the Rapp-Coudert Committee in New York. Sub-
siding momentarily during the great coalition of World War II,
they assumed more formidable and terrifying forms with the
emergence of the "Cold War" and the evocation of the "Iron
Curtain," to reach their apogees in the witch-hunts under the direction of Senator Joseph J. McCarthy in the early 1950's.

The immediate objective of these hearings of 1947 was "subversion" in Hollywood. Joining Representative J. Parnell Thomas on
the committee were John McDowell of Pennsylvania, Richard B.
Vail of Illinois, and Richard M. Nixon of California.

In this instance some of the most distinguished and talented
members of the film colony were called, questioned, exposed to the
light of a publicity which could not but react unfavorably on their
careers should they fail to "cooperate." Ten, who invoked the First

Amendment of the Constitution, were indicted for contempt in refusing to answer critical questions, and sent to jail.

Among those caught in the dragnet was Bertolt Brecht, who appeared before the Committee on October 30. He was represented by Robert W. Kenny and Bartley C. Crum.

Apparently, before the investigations friends and acquaintances of Brecht had been interrogated in private as to his associations, activities, and opinions. This is what Fritz Kortner reports:

[Dorothy Thompson] too, was made to answer for having assisted in bringing Brecht to America. Those of us who had financed Brecht's escape from Finland were investigated. With a clear conscience I could declare that Brecht was no political agent, but a revolutionary poet. In the files of the FBI, the political police, were to be found several of his poems. They were shown to me. Well, I hinted, a political agent does not write poems in which he expresses his political convictions. An agent conceals them. When I was pressed to reveal something about our political discussions, I recounted a conversation which had taken place shortly before, between Brecht and myself. I was then at work on a film about Garibaldi, which was in the making. The reading I had to do in connection with this film opened my eyes to the backward conditions of Italy. I learned about the brothels in the seaports of Italy, frequented by sailors and seamen in such great numbers that it was not unusual for a girl to service over a hundred clients a day. I expressed my horror to Brecht. Brecht opined: "You liberals say that more than a hundred is inhuman? No more than eighty!" More radical sentiments I never heard from Brecht's lips. The American official was amused.[1]

The interrogation of Brecht by Robert E. Stripling, the Committee's investigator, took on some of the grotesque semblances of the trial scenes in *Mann ist Mann* or *Mahagonny*. Brecht understood little English and spoke less. The Committee members, of course, knew no German. An official translator had frequently to intervene. Brecht, who to the very end of his life savored a dialectical sparring with opponents, apparently enjoyed this confrontation, though it was difficult to determine whether one or two ambiguous statements he made were due to misunderstanding of the language or sheer perverseness. He was not permitted to read his dignified statement of his history and beliefs. Since he was not a member of the Communist Party, and so declared, he was handled gingerly, even with some (almost deliberate?) maladroitness. He had not engaged in political activity in this country; he had actually written only one major film scenario; he had not been mixed up with American subversives, etc., etc. Anyway, the Committee was interested in larger and more local game, and where it did not shoot it down, lured it to its humble knees by threatening its livelihood. Here was proof positive that if the Committee had not heard, it instinctively understood, Brecht's celebrated, and much excoriated, dictum, "Erst kommt das Fressen, dann die Moral." ("First comes the belly; then morality.")[2]

The Committee was not interested in Brecht's activities against Hitler and Nazism, nor in his conception of the function of a writer, and sought to pin him down to speaking about works which had been translated into English and had appeared in the United States. The report by Tretyakov had been published in English in *International Literature* in 1937,[3] with its comments on Brecht's politics as revealed in his plays. Brecht claimed he could not recall the interview. He seemed especially confused or confusing in discussing *Die Massnahme*. An extended commentary on the idea of "Einverständis"—the acquiescence of the Communist agitator in his own liquidation—would have required time. So we get the ambiguous exchange:

THE CHAIRMAN. I gather from your remarks, from your answer, that he was just killed, he was not murdered?

MR. BRECHT. He wanted to die.

THE CHAIRMAN. So they killed him?

MR. BRECHT. No; they did not kill him—not in this story. He killed himself. They supported him, but of course they told him it were better he disappeared, for him and them and the cause he also believed in.

Upon which Mr. Stripling shifted to Brecht's visits to Moscow and the Tretyakov interview, in which a different account is given of *Die Massnahme*. Further questions were concerned with whether Brecht had based a number of his writings on Marx and Lenin.

MR. BRECHT. No; I don't think that is quite correct but, of course, I studied, had to study as a playwright who wrote historical plays. I, of course, had to study Marx's ideas about history. I do not think intelligent plays today can be written without such study. Also, history now written is vitally influenced by the studies of Marx about history.

Had Brecht been approached to join the Communist Party? Yes, Brecht replied, by some readers of his poems or members of his audiences, but "then I found out that it was not my business." Obviously Brecht was not the setter hound they were looking for. After the reading of one or two translated poems, which Brecht rightly claimed were "very different" in the original, he was released with some words of approbation from the Chairman.

Having had long experience as a refugee, and sensing the ever-thickening atmosphere in the United States, Brecht did not remain here very long. Not even waiting for the pending production of *Galileo* in New York, he bade this country adieu, and once more set out, this time in the direction of a very uncertain, and much changed, "home." The fact that there were now two potential "homes" did not make the return easier. As a matter of fact, prevented by the American authorities from entering the West German Zone, Brecht's first stopping place was Switzerland. It was a good place from which to reconnoiter the surrounding territory. After fourteen years' absence he was once more on the periphery of his native land.

When he drew up a hypothetical balance sheet of his experiences and creativeness of those exile years, what could he really show? Externally, a series of works certainly among the best he was ever to produce: from *Mother Courage* and *Puntila* to *Galileo* and the *Caucasian Chalk Circle*. On the theoretical side, a clarification of his dramatic ideas, culminating in the *Brief Organon*. Personally, a radical deepening of his understanding both of himself and the world around him, which led to a full ripening of what may be called his "Marxist humanism." And, finally, a substantial conviction that his political and social credo had been the right one, and that history, in exhibiting the victory over Hitler and Nazism, had more than corroborated his profound faith in the "people." Ever a realist, he was not blind to the problems that now lay in front of him, or the German people, or the world in general. Having, as he himself was fond of putting it, overcome the difficulties of the mountains, he was now ready to encounter the even greater hardships of the plains.

As for his impact on America and the American public, it could not be called very extensive or profound. True, he was better known, but considering his importance and gifts, scarcely sufficiently. But was he better understood? Hardly. His plays were familiar to few, and here mostly through the efforts of the university and college theatres and the zeal of Eric Bentley. His poems were being translated, notably by H. R. Hays. His songs—the more radical and revolutionary ones, those set by Eisler—were by far the most popular of his works. Only one of his serious film ventures had come to fruition. Perhaps the most disappointing experience of all must have been the reception of *Galileo.*

He had worked with Laughton for almost two years. On July 30, 1947, the play opened at the Coronet Theatre in Hollywood. Brecht had every reason to hope that in the light of the historic dropping of the atom bomb, the play would be understood for what it was. Charles Laughton's magnificence fell upon almost indifferent ears and eyes. *Variety* found the script dull. Gladwin Hill, reporting to *The New York Times* from California, reflected the general reaction. "The production . . . somehow lacks the impact implicit in the story. It seems barren of climaxes and even sparse in stirring moments. . . . Hardly a sigh of sympathy is inspired when Galileo's scientific determination cuts off his daughter's romance. His recantation comes off cut-and-dried." And then there was the "overzealous underplaying" of Laughton, as well as the rest of the cast. And, finally, and most crucially, "it seems questionable whether the episodic technique is as facile a vehicle for a theme that is less expository than emotional. The ebb and flow of a human conflict is hard to present in small compasses."[4]

A few words of praise for some of the other actors were scarcely enough to outweigh the preponderant condemnation of the whole work. Hugo Haas took the part of Cardinal Barberini, and Frances Heflin that of Virginia. Brecht had participated in the direction, of which Joseph Losey had charge.

When the production of *Galileo* reached New York's Maxine Elliot Theatre on December 7 of that year, Brecht was already in Europe. He would scarcely have been heartened by its reception. The reviews were almost uniformly unfavorable. Brooks Atkinson, who was to go overboard with Arthur Miller's *All My Sons*, found Brecht's work "loose and episodic"; the performance "pretentious," especially on the part of Laughton, who "throws away his part"; the acting "full of awe in design, but trifling and casual in texture as though everyone were ashamed to be earnest about serious matters. . . . Although his Galileo is good Laughton, it is not Galileo."[5]

Though there may be some truth in the criticism of the production (actually, Joseph Losey, who directed, thought it was better than that in California), there is no inkling in Atkinson's review that here was a radically new style of writing, or that deep and important ideas had been brought to dramatic realization. An otherwise well-meaning and perceptive critic had missed a historic moment.

Part Three

HOMECOMING

I

Within Sight of Home

Say, house, that stands between the pear tree
    and the sound,
Have those old words a fugitive once scratched
On walls—*Truth always is concrete*—
Outlived the ruin of bombers and of war?

    BRECHT, "An die dänische Zufluchtsstätte"

Switzerland was not home, but it was closer to home than America.
Here he settled in a modest house overlooking the Zurich Lake,
at Herrliberg, and in typical Brechtian fashion set to work at once.
He was used to waiting—waiting for permission to enter the western
part of Germany; waiting for a passport (no matter from where);
waiting to see where he might best settle and begin reconstructing
his life, and establish a theatre. Once again, he was fortunate in his
friendships. At the Zurich Schauspielhaus he could greet a great
many of the German artists who had been performing his plays
during the dark days of Hitlerism. It was here that *Mother Courage,
Galileo,* and *The Good Woman of Setzuan* had been produced.
Caspar Neher, an old associate, came up from limbo to join him—
alive, active, and eager to work with him once more. There were
new friends: the brilliant younger Swiss playwrights, Max Frisch
and Friedrich Dürrenmatt. There was that very gifted actress
Therese Giehse, celebrated interpreter of Mother Courage.

    Max Frisch has given us an unforgettable picture of Brecht and
Helene Weigel, at this time. Frisch, a very talented writer himself,

and a skilled architect too, was deeply impressed by the unpretentiousness of Brecht, so modest yet always so curious, always asking
questions, loving contradiction, but "fascinating. . . . because here,"
as Frisch put it, was "a life that derives from thought and thinking."
Brecht loved talk—about architecture, about politics, and of course
about theatre. Brecht loved to read aloud:

> "I came into the cities in times of disorder. . . .
> When hunger reigned."

He reads [this is how Frisch sees him] almost timidly, but without stiff-
ness, no different from the Brecht before or after. His voice is soft, without change of native speech . . . , almost without emphasis . . . with
the bearing of a man who is reading a letter—informative.

He is unperturbed when interrupted by an unexpected visitor, and
continues. The effect of the reading is profound, but not church-
like, for, as Frisch adds, "The real world is here and in the poem as
well."

Frisch and Brecht discuss the theatre. Brecht is completing his
Brief Organon, the definitive statement of his dramatic theory.
Frisch is puzzled, impressed. He speculates on whether Brecht's
"Verfremdung" theory might not be applied to story-telling. Sub-
sequent works of Frisch will show how deep a mark Brecht had
made on him.

"And then," Frisch notes, "it is time to go home."

Brecht takes his cap, and the milk-jug, which must be set at the doorstep
. . . When I don't have my bicycle with me, he accompanies me to the
railroad station . . . He leaves the platform with fast, not long, rather
light steps, his arms conspicuously immobile, his head at an angle, his
cap drawn down over his forehead, as if to hide his face, half-conspira-
torial, half timid. He gives the impression of an inconspicuous workingman, a metal worker, yet somewhat too slight, too slim for one . . . ,
secretive, and attentive . . . , a fugitive who has left many a railway
station, too timid for a man of the world, too experienced for a scholar,
too well-informed not to be anxious, a stateless man, a man with a
short-term sojourn, a passer-by of our day, a man named Brecht, a
physicist, a poet without incense . . .[1]

Brecht was stateless, "paper-less," a citizen of no land, but he was on German-speaking soil, a land with theatres, good actors, a land in which he was respected. The Zurich Schauspielhaus was preparing a revival of *Mother Courage*; and on June 5, 1948, under the direction of Kurt Hirschfeld and Brecht it presented, for the first time, *Puntila*.

But an event of even greater importance had occurred in February of that year. The Municipal Theatre at Chur, the capital of Grisons, had invited Brecht to produce his adaptation of the *Antigone* of Sophocles, in the translation of Friedrich Hölderlin. Helene Weigel was to take the part of the heroine and Caspar Neher had arrived to do the designs. In all respects this was an impressive production, and was received as such. It was the first Greek play (not to say subject) that Brecht had taken up for adaptation; he had always found himself closer to Rome than to Greece. But the theme attracted him: It was political and dealt with resistance to tyranny. Brecht was greatly concerned for the future of the theatre, and particularly interested in restoring and reviving for the new age a dramatic repertory that had been fearfully distorted and mangled by the Nazis. Such, indeed, had been the case with Hölderlin's version of the *Antigone,* which had been utilized, especially in Viennese productions, to exhibit Nazi doctrine, by setting off "feminine sensibility" (Antigone) against "masculine reason." (Creon), underscoring the text with its Bacchic and mystical frenzies.

Brecht's version opens with a contemporary prologue that sets the scene in Berlin, in April, 1945. The war is coming to an end. At daybreak two sisters emerge from an air-raid shelter on their way home. Outside their door they discover their brother, who had apparently deserted the retreating army, hanging. He may still be alive. Will one of the sisters dare to cut him down in the face of the S.S. man?

Then the play of *Antigone* commences. Nominally it was an adaptation of the translation made by Friedrich Hölderlin more than a hundred years before. This version has long stood as one of those great classical translations which succeed in conveying the majesty and grandeur of the original. But a close examination of Brecht's and Hölderlin's texts reveals departures which at once show that the play is neither Hölderlin nor Sophocles, though containing many elements of both. For, as Brecht remarked in a note, the point of his play was not the representation of resistance (in this instance the German internal resistance to Nazism), as much as the study of a collapsing tyranny. After the First World War, Walter Hasenclever had written a powerful *Antigone,* in which the heroine stands as the embodiment of a passionate pacifism. For Brecht, too, the play becomes the vehicle of conveying his sentiments about war. The center of attention is shifted from Antigone to Creon. The play opens with the traditional and beautiful plaint of Antigone about the curse resting on her family, but Brecht has replaced Hölderlin's liturgically lofty and magnificent, but archaic, lines with briefer, though no less noble, verses.

Thus Hölderlin:

> Gemeinsamschwesterliches! o Ismenes Haupt!
> Weisst du etwas, das nicht der Erde Vater
> Erfuhr, mit uns, die wir bis hieher leben,
> Ein Nennbares, seit Ödipus gehascht ward?[2]

> Sister mine, my own dear sister, Ismene!
> Know'st thou one ill that Zeus, earth's father
> Has not brought on us while still we live
> Since Oedipus has been snatched from us?

And Brecht:

> Schwester, Ismene, Zwillingsreis
> Aus des Ödipus Stamm, weisst du etwas
> Irrsal, traurige Arbeit, Schändliches
> Das der Erde Vater noch nicht verhängt hat
> Über uns, die bis hieher lebten?[3]

> Sister Ismene, twin scion
> Of the race of Oedipus, knowest thou any
> Baseness, painful labor, ruinous shame
> That our earth's father, Zeus, has failed
> To bring upon us while we still live?

Brecht's verses are terse, less lumbering, and more easily comprehensible to the ears of an audience than Hölderlin's. But immediately we become aware of a radical transformation of the original: Creon's defense of Thebes against the assaults of the Argives led by Polyneices, one of the two sons of Oedipus, is turned by Brecht into a predatory war by Creon and the Thebans against Argos, with the objective of winning the iron deposits of the latter city. Antigone's brothers, Eteocles and Polyneices, instead of being ranged on opposite sides, as in the original drama, are now both fighting in the ranks of Creon. Appalled by the death of Eteocles, Polyneices breaks ranks, and is slain by Creon, who refuses him ritual burial because of his cowardice. The play then proceeds in the traditional manner: Antigone's attempt to cover the body of her brother with earth, and the discovery of her act by the guarding soldiers.

The play would not be Brecht's if the class element had been omitted. It is here introduced in the speeches of the guard who reports the violation of Creon's edict before he has discovered the culprit. Accused by Creon of being bribed, he replies,

What I more fear is to receive something made of hemp, for in the hands of the lofty ones, there is more of hemp than gold for the likes of us. As you can well understand.[4]

Sophocles' unforgettable Hymn to Man is beautifully rendered by Brecht, but with a characteristic addendum. Man is endowed with infinite capacities, Sophocles chants, "Wonders are many, but none is more wonderful than Man...." He recites the many great achievements of which he is capable, but also his impotence in the face of death; and his duty to honor the laws of the gods and of the city. Brecht expands the latter parts:

> He bends his fellow-man's neck like an ox's
> While his fellow-man tears at his entrails. . . .
> Scarcely his own maw can he fill,
> But he must enclose with a wall what he owns. . . .
> That which is human he esteems not,
> And so, becomes monster even to himself.[5]

Antigone is changed from being the scourge of Creon's ir-
religiousness and inhumanity, into an accuser of his imperialism
and war-mindedness, as well as a prophetess foreseeing the tyrant
he will become. Creon's son, Haemon, betrothed of Antigone, and
Antigone both go to their deaths, but not before the Argives,
roused to fury in the final battle, turn on the Thebans and defeat
them, also killing Creon's other son. "Now Thebes has fallen,"
Creon laments, as he returns from his vain mission to forestall
Haemon's death, and brings with him Haemon's bloody garment.

The production of Brecht's *Antigone* at Chur was notable for a
number of circumstances: Brecht was directing once more; Helene
Weigel was acting, after a decade of near-silence, and Caspar
Neher had rejoined the two to design the sets.

For the audience it must also have been an extraordinary experience. For gone were the old classical props customary in the
production of Greek plays. Instead

In front of a semicircle of screens, covered with reddish matting stand
long benches, on which the actors remain, while awaiting their cues.
In the center of the screen there is an opening, in which the record
turntable stands and is operated in full view, and which also serves as
exit for the actors when they are through with their parts. The acting
area is framed by four posts, on which are mounted horses' skulls. . . .
The reason the actors sit openly on the stage, and only adopt their
proper attitudes as actors when they enter the acting area (which is
brightly lit up) is that the audience might not imagine that it has
been transported to the scene of the story, but is being invited to take
part in the delivery of an ancient poem, no matter in what manner it
has been restored. . . . The men's costumes were made of undyed
sacking, that of the women of cotton. . . . Particular care was taken
with the props; they were turned over to good craftsmen. This was
done not so that the audience or the actors should imagine them to be
real, but to provide the audience and the actors with beautiful objects.[6]

It is certainly characteristic of Brecht and Helene Weigel, no
less than of Caspar Neher, that they should have spent such great
care on a production addressed to a provincial audience, in a small

theatre also used as a movie house, and with a core of inexperienced actors. But such primitivism really suited Brecht. He directed sitting in his valued folding chair (later used as Creon's throne) and guiding the performers, not always, of course, without some tension on all sides. Hans Curjel, the artistic director of the theatre, reported that the work made a profound impression on a number of spectators, but that the generality of Chur "intellectuals" reacted unfavorably to this unconventional and "hard" presentation. The theatre, he added, remained half-empty throughout the few performances. The younger generation of local and neighboring students, however, fully appreciated Brecht's contribution.[7]

Yet, it is questionable whether Brecht had succeeded in his objective of actually forming a new play by dismembering the tragedy of Sophocles. The magnificent inexorable force of Creon's seemingly sacrilegious treatment of the dead Polyneices, in Sophocles, because he is an enemy, seems vitiated in Brecht's attenuation of the offense by turning it into cowardice. Nor is the war between the Argives and the Thebans made as convincing through the economic interpretation as it is in the original, as the affirmation of power.

With this production of *Antigone* Brecht initiated a series of "Model" books. These consist of detailed and numerous photographs by Ruth Berlau (who had begun the experiment with Brecht in Denmark), accompanied by documentary notations, discussions of every step taken in preparation of a play for production. They were to prove invaluable not only for the light they throw on Brecht's own way of working but also to other theatrical groups interested in producing his works.

But neither his prestige nor his activities saved him from annoyances by the Swiss governmental authorities. He was after all still "stateless." Though in the course of years he had become somewhat hardened by bureaucratic pressures, they were never too pleasant. Something would have to be done.

Prospects of relief opened when Caspar Neher introduced him to the composer Gottfried von Einem, the musical director of the

Salzburg Festivals. Von Einem was eager to revitalize that institution. In Brecht, he saw a potential new theatrical spirit that would
bring the festivals out of their staid and anachronistic debility.
Brecht was interested, and von Einem directed his efforts to securing the necessary papers for him. Brecht and his family journeyed
to Salzburg, and here ambitious plans were set afoot for productions
in Salzburg, as well as Vienna, of *Mother Courage, Antigone, The
Caucasian Chalk Circle,* and in anticipation of a Goethe centennial,
of the entire *Faust.* Unfortunately, all these plans were to come to
nothing.

Von Einem had secured the cooperation of the Salzburg Landes-
hauptmann, Dr. Rehrl, and though it took two years, Brecht
was able to obtain Austrian citizenship in 1950. The scandal
aroused in Austria by the publication of this action effectively
brought to an end the Salzburg enterprise. It also, even more unfortunately, doomed an original work intended for the festivals,
which might have done much to resuscitate them. This was the
uncompleted *Salzburger Totentanz* (*The Salzburg Dance of Death*)
on which Brecht worked until the summer of 1951.

Much has been made of Brecht's vigorous efforts to find a home
in Austria and various ambiguous motives have been imputed to
him by critics provided with passports into a man's unconscious.
Suffice it here to quote one letter written by Brecht to von Einem in
April, 1949:

. . . . I know what would be more helpful to me than the advance
royalty [on the Salzburg project], i.e., a passport. If this is possible it
should be done without publicity. The best way would be as follows:
H. W. [Weigel] is Austrian by birth (Viennese). Since 1933 I have
been stateless. There is no German government existing at present.
Could she obtain an Austrian passport? And I as her husband. . . . I
cannot settle in one part of Germany and thus become dead to the
other part. . . . The Swiss are making difficulties for me again.[8]

He had been refused entry into the Western sector of Germany by
the Allied governments. There were two Germanies now, but

without autonomous governments. The DDR (the German Democratic Republic), it must be remembered, did not come into being as an independent state until October 7, 1949.

Since the *Salzburg Dance of Death* actually originated on Swiss soil, it may well be considered in this place, although Brecht was sketching it until 1951.

Brecht's play was to be a modern counterpart of the time-honored and celebrated old English morality play, *Everyman,* which Hugo von Hofmannsthal had modernized, and which was the inescapable "war-horse" at the Salzburg festivals in pre-Hitler days. Those programs had begun to suffer from a natural senescence and the heaviness of Max Reinhardt's scenic megalomania. It was to be hoped that after the Second World War—this was von Einem's dream—a new Salzburg Festival would come into being, with new life and new matter. For Brecht, who was looking for a place in which to be active, this too appeared the fulfilment of an old ambition. Temperamentally, he was close to the folk element of the medieval drama, if not to its religious content; and now he saw the possibility of giving it a contemporary tone. What could be more attractive than a "dance of death," particularly since a prodigious one had just taken place? In the possibilities opening up after a war, was it not likely that even staid Salzburg and conservative Austria would be eager for a change?

The *Salzburg Dance of Death* was planned as a two-part morality play, one part dealing with the Emperor and Death, in which Death would enter into a contract with the Emperor to devote himself to the poor and lowly and spare the mighty—a silly arrangement, since Death cannot be trusted! The other portion was to deal with the Plague and its impact on the well-to-do middle class family of Frau Frühwirt, who with a typical Brechtian touch, would meet her doom in hurrying to profit from the plague by buying up cattle cheap. There was also to be a macabre carnival dance against the background of the raging plague.

The extant fragments[9] lead one to believe that the completed play would have been a very powerful morality. Brecht was used to working in similar mediums, and the scenes, such as that between Death and the carpenters who are building a bridge for the Emperor, in which Death attempts to persuade them to skimp on the materials, only to be refused, and then goes off in a huff to build ramshackle dwellings for the poor; or that in which Death and the Emperor discourse, and Death (figuring as Capitalism) complains that he is being maligned, and the Emperor assures him that he is too; or the more homely exchanges that take place in Frau Frühwirt's household, with their utterly medieval folk quality—all these could have served as elements of a highly successful drama. And Salzburg would truly have been reborn!

Even while he was eagerly looking around for a place in which to anchor his career, Brecht did not allow himself to be diverted from work. While he was still in his Scandinavian exile, his late collaborator Margarete Steffin had translated a play by the Norwegian playwright, Nordahl Grieg, *The Defeat: A Play about the Paris Commune*.

Nordahl Grieg was a gifted poet and dramatist who took part in the anti-Nazi resistance movement and was shot down in an air raid over Berlin in 1943. His play about the Paris Commune was occasioned by the heartbreaking conclusion of the Spanish Civil War and the triumph of Franco and his allies. He paralleled and conjoined the events of 1936-1939 and those of the bitter Paris days between March 18, 1871, and the gory days in May when the Commune was brought to an end, though not to its knees.

Grieg's *Defeat* opens at the moment when the war between France and Prussia is ended. The humiliating conditions have been accepted by Thiers, who now proceeds, with Bismarck's assistance, to crush the proletarian Commune of Paris and the National Guard, who had opposed the national surrender and the attempted restoration of the *status quo*. The workers of Paris refuse to give up the weapons which they had bought with their own savings to be used against the Prussians. Thiers calls upon Bismarck to release some

40,000 French soldiers captured by the Germans, and doubling that number, begins the assault on Paris. Against that force and its superior weapons the Commune is helpless. The two months of agonizing hope and bitter struggle Grieg depicts with moving force. The conflicts within the Communard camp itself revolve around the use of terror; the treatment of internal treason and collaboration; the question of whether the practice of "goodness" might not in the end be a betrayal of the cause; and the failure to resolve the internal dissensions. All these point to the ultimate defeat of the Commune. How, indeed, could the words of the Communard, the noble Delescluze: "Man shall no longer be used; he shall be!" be realized? How could "goodness" armed with an archaic rifle win over the machine guns of Thiers?

Grieg's play is a tragedy of unresolved questions. In the final scene of the play, the last of the Communards, including the children, have retreated to a churchyard where they await the advancing counter-revolutionary force. Old Delescluze is with them.

DELESCLUZE. Thus ends the Commune. More than anyone else I have the responsibility for terror and death. Do you hate me? . . .

PIERRE. Don't you understand, Delescluze? At home, in the streets we did nothing but slave and worry, worry about tomorrow, and then again slave—and then death came, what a useless and miserable thing that was! But now it is different. Life has become something grand, which it is a pity to leave.

DELESCLUZE. . . . Yes, those over there can scorch this grass with their grenades, but they can never kill the earth's power to turn green again.

LUCIEN. But those, who come after us, must have better weapons! Next time we must win! Win! Win!

Then comes Delescluze's bitter confessional: Goodness can only triumph through force. "Our avengers, our children must become a generation of inhuman strength. . . . Generations coming after us will have to fight through horrible times. Shall they be mangled? Yes. Shall they be blinded? Yes. Shall they die? Yes, rather than lose the will to become free men." To which young Gabrielle replies that if that is the law, then man must transcend it—must transcend it with

only one intransigence—toward injustice. And as their executioners near, she urges the little ones to meet them with their "ir-
reconcilable belief, their future," mirrored in their smiles.[10]

Neither Grieg nor his translator, Margarete Steffin, was to live
long enough to see the end of Hitler. In 1947 an East German publishing house issued the Steffin translation, and it may have been
this event that occasioned Brecht's renewed interest in the Paris
Commune. Libraries at Zurich supplied additional historical materials, and Brecht worked on his own version between 1948 and
1949. With justice, Brecht regarded his own play less as an adaptation and more as a "counter-statement" to Grieg's. Though he uses
a number of situations and characters of the Norwegian's drama, the
over-all atmosphere, though not less shadowed by death and defeat,
is more nearly concerned with subduing and mitigating the more
overtly pathetic scenes and situations of Grieg and underscoring the
political and social elements. Brecht also attenuates the very vivid,
but somewhat hair-raising, horrors of the Paris citizenry under the
siege, when starvation reigned, working men were forced to sell
their tools merely to buy bread for their families, and young boys
fished in the waters of the river for rats, which they sold as food.
He also shifts the center of gravity away from the Bakuninite an-
archo-syndicalist terrorism of Rigault and the atrocities committed by both sides, to a clarification, at least attempted, of the
tragic errors committed by the Commune.

Brecht never completed the final revisions of this play, and never
saw it staged. One must witness it in the incomparable production
of the Berliner Ensemble to appreciate its true grandeur. Even in its
incomplete form it is moving in a way which does not detract from
its central ideological analysis, of which Brecht was master. Humor
alternates with tenderness, irony with sharp anger. This might be
termed a serious folk-drama, if the issues were not so world-shaking.
As in other of Brecht's plays, wisdom speaks not so much through
the leaders of the people (in this they are play working men and
women), as much as through the people themselves.

The play opens on January 22, 1871, eight days before the French government surrendered Paris to the foe. The fighters of the National Guard are still fighting and dying for the sake of France, though it is apparent that betrayal is going on against them at the same time. The simple people of Paris have bought the guns with their own wages, and on hearing of the capitulation and the demand to disarm, they are rising up. Such simple people we see here in the Montmartre, "Papa," the stonemason; Madame Cabet and her son Jean; Coco the watchmaker; Geneviève, the school-teacher; Langevin, Madame Cabet's brother-in-law and later delegate to the Paris Commune. These are all people on whom the burden of the war and starvation has fallen and on whom again the major portion of the burden of the peace and reparations will fall. They are the makers of the Paris Commune, which will set itself against Thiers and his Versailles soldiery.

It may seem strange to speak of "tenderness" in connection with a Brecht play, but it is there in *The Days of the Commune*. Perhaps more: a kind of decent respect of person for person (Brecht called it "Freundlichkeit") most clearly embodied in "Papa" as he offers Madame Cabet the casserole of chicken abandoned by the fat profiteer in haste; or, as later, he and his aides present her with a cannon saved from confiscation, which Madame Cabet and the other women will soon, without the use of force, defend from the depredation of the regular soldiers. There is humor in both these situations; as well as in the lampoon, when "Papa" and the others on the Montmartre, celebrating the organization of the Paris Commune, rejoice and toast freedom; and "Papa" and Jean Cabet enact an imaginary conversation between Bismarck and Thiers. But the serious undercurrent of anxiety is always there—in the deliberations of the newly-formed Commune, with its new Charter of Rights, in the conflicts within the delegations, and particularly in the worries of "Papa" as he conveys them to Langevin, now a delegate, with prophetic, almost instinctive, political sense urging an immediate attack on Versailles, before Thiers' armies attack Paris.

There is a simple beauty in "Papa's" rejoicing at the Commune's beginnings:

This is the first night in history, friends, in which Paris will have no murder, no robbery, no shameless swindling, and no rape. For the first time her streets are secure, and she needs no police. For the bankers and the petty thieves, the tax-collectors and the manufacturers, the ministers, the cocottes, and the priests have all emigrated to Versailles: the city is now inhabitable.[11]

Already, Langevin is having reservations about all-embracing "freedom," and as they toast, Langevin says: "I drink to partial freedom." Asked why by Geneviève, he adds, "Because she leads to total freedom."[12] For he, too, is convinced that they should have taken the offensive against Versailles on the 18th of March. It is the people who instruct their teachers. Langevin has occasion to inform Geneviève: "Lerne, Lehrerin" ("Learn, Teacher"). As in Grieg's play, so here too the simple, honest Beslay is double-crossed by the Governor of the Bank of France, who has all the time been conspiring with Thiers.

Langevin's cry is also Brecht's:

What mistakes we make; what mistakes we have made! Naturally, we should have marched on Versailles, at once, on March 18. If we only had had time! But the people never have more than one hour. Woe to them if they do not stand there, fully armed, ready to strike![13]

And why, asks Geneviève, hadn't they taken the money in the vaults of the Bank of France, which rightfully belonged to the people, and with which they could also have bribed Bismarck's gentlemen and politicians, and their own too?

For the sake of Freedom, which no one understands. We were not yet ready, like every member of an army fighting a life and death struggle, to forego personal freedom until the freedom of all had been won.

When Geneviève asks, "But wasn't it because we were unwilling to soil our hands with blood?" Langevin replies, "Yes, but in this war there are only bloodstained hands or amputated ones."[13]

In the uneven struggle against the overpowering forces of Thiers and MacMahon, his commanding general, the inadequate arms and numbers of the Communards are of no avail.

They are well armed [says François Faure] with machine guns. Why is it that the new times always give their weapons first to the hyenas of the old?[14]

And as the Commune goes down in flames and blood, from the heights of Versailles, the upper bourgeoisie watches with lorgnettes and opera glasses:

AN ARISTOCRATIC LADY. Monsieur Thiers, this means immortality for you. You have returned Paris to her true mistress, France.
THIERS. France, that is—You, Mesdames et Messieurs.[15]

In *The Days of the Commune,* Brecht had written his first tragedy. It was not altogether in the traditional form, but close enough to it to raise interesting questions. Why had Brecht turned to this theme at this time? It is only possible to suggest the answers. Was the play intended as a warning? The historic period was one in which the cleavages between East and West had become dangerously sharpened. International tensions had been heightened by the "Truman Doctrine" and the "cold war." Actual war was not outside the range of possibilities. In America the right-wing forces had become more blatant and arrogant, investigations of so-called "subversives" by Congressional and other committees more frequent and savage. The American intellectual élite was becoming more and more demoralized, driven into capitulation, or entirely silenced. Was Brecht's play also intended as a warning to the Socialist states, particularly that in East Germany?

For the drama of the Paris Commune tries to lay bare a historical process, the movement by which a social class, the working class, takes power for a time, establishes a new form of proletarian state, but fails to keep it alive. The tragedy follows from two sorts of conflicts: one between the workers and the bourgeoisie, that will soon be storming at the gates of Paris; the other from the internal struggles and mistakes of the new Commune. It is from the second primarily, rather than from the first, that the inevitable defeat must flow. What is the "tragic flaw," to use the conventional term, that brings about the destruction of the protagonists? It is a composite of the "inadequate capabilities of an immature, unschooled, unled class" in conflict with the necessity to build a new society.[16] Its "errors," if so they may be called, consist in its "good nature"[17] (its failure to march on Versailles at the right moment) as well as in its other scruples born of inexperience, and its almost forgetting "the cannibals that waited at the gates." In Brecht's play, as well as in historic reality, Beslay's weakness in the face of the Governor of the Bank of France, as well as that of the others *vis-à-vis* internal treachery, are brought out forcefully in "Papa's" distress at the release of one of Thiers' spies at the behest of Madame Cabet and the children.

Was the French playwright Arthur Adamov (one of Brecht's fervent admirers) right in holding that Brecht's play fails because it falls between the two stools of character and historical situation, and brings neither of these off adequately?[18]

In part, Adamov was no doubt right. For Brecht was deliberately refusing to give his principal characters a "pre-history" and thus establish them as *individual* characters, rather than members of a mass movement. What interested him most was the historical element as evidenced in the proceedings of the delegates to the Commune and the activities of the almost nameless workers on the barricades or in their normal pursuits. But how was one to represent these "nameless heroes"? It was they who in the fateful seventy-three days of the Commune legislated, decreed, and changed the entire aspect of the city of Paris. It was then that the hitherto "dishonest face of the rabble" achieved a legendary self-respect. They proved to be the teachers of their teachers and leaders.

Since Brecht left the play in its incompleted form, it is hard to tell what he might have done to solve this difficult problem.

From Brecht's point of view, *The Days of the Commune* would not of course constitute a "tragedy." It is a tragedy for the members of the Commune, at a particular historic moment. But the failure that brought it about was not due to invariant or transcendent forces. Though insight and wisdom came too late to many of the characters of the play, they need not come too late to the spectator of today. He, at any rate, may be able to act as a result of such insight. This was Brecht's hope and objective.

II

Return to Berlin

When I came back
My hair was not yet gray
And I was happy.

The hardships of the mountains are behind
us,
Before us lie the hardships of the plains.

BRECHT, "Wahrnehmung"

On October 22, 1948, Bertolt Brecht finally returned to Berlin. True, it was now a sharply divided Berlin, East against West, but it was Berlin, the city where he had made his reputation more than a quarter of a century before. In January of that year, Wolfgang Langhoff had reintroduced Brecht to German audiences at the Deutsches Theater with *Fear and Misery of the Third Reich*. It had made a profound impression, and aroused in the Communist press the hope that Brecht's work had taken the realistic direction that was needed in the new Germany.

Now, in October, he was welcomed back at a banquet by the Cultural League in East Berlin, attended by the German Communist leader Wilhelm Pieck, and the Soviet political chief, Colonel Serge Tulpanov. The Stadttheater was placed at his disposal, and he set to work on a production of *Mother Courage*. Months of rehearsal followed, and when the play opened on January 11, 1949, with Helene Weigel and Ernst Busch (among other notable actors) and under the direction of another old friend, Erich Engel, it was received triumphantly. There was no question now where he would settle, nor where his theatrical future lay.

After a brief sojourn in Switzerland, he returned in the autumn of 1949. He was given a house in the Weissensee district of Berlin. In November the Ministry of Popular Education authorized Brecht and Helene Weigel to found the Berliner Ensemble. Its first production at the Stadttheater was *Herr Puntila.*

On October 7, 1949, the German Democratic Republic came into being. Wilhelm Pieck was chosen President, and Otto Grotewohl Premier.

For Brecht, the decision to throw in his fortunes with the East German state was not a frivolous one. He had hoped, at one time, to be able to speak to all of Germany, to be *the* German poet and dramatist. But he was realist enough to see, not too long after 1945, that the cleavages between East and West might for a time at least, be unbridgeable. He saw Western Germany being reconstructed with millions of American dollars; he saw rising once more a "bulwark" against Eastern Communism, a capitalist Germany come into being, with many of the Nazi liegemen more or less prominently restored to offices, high and low. And West Berlin was soon to be made a "showplace" of democracy, and the Kurfürstendamm garishly rebuilt, neon lights and all, and the coffee-houses ostentatiously displaying whipped cream to crowding clienteles.

But there were plenty of ruins on both sides of the dividing line to remind one of the gory tragedy that was just over.

Brecht could not but have been horrified by what he saw. It seemed to him that no matter "how fast he would have walked, he could never escape these ruins."[1] There was the Reichstag building, just beyond the Brandenburg Gate—a skeleton above a pile of rubble. And, nearby, the mound under which Hitler and his cronies found their end. Endless nightmare monuments to monumental enormity. With his friend the French writer Vladimir Pozner he walked the city, watching the women piling up bricks in neat arrangements, polishing them, and sorting them. They looked into the innards of destroyed homes, struck by their grotesqueness. They peered into shop windows with their cheap array of state-made goods testifying to the hunger for luxuries of a class newly come to power, now ravenous for petty-bourgeois fineries.[2]

With another writer friend, Günther Weisenborn, he visited the cellar of the Gestapo where Weisenborn had spent seven months' imprisonment.[3] Other survivors dived up from the nether regions —miraculous ghosts!

And the ghosts of memories! How often he had wandered through Berlin with his friend Caspar Neher in the good old days! Well, Neher was alive and had rejoined him in Switzerland. Now Brecht was seeing Berlin again, but through Neher's eyes. That piece of wash, for example, hanging there—with its blue color—"my friend would have placed differently." Gone, all gone . . . those places they had known so well!

He was under no illusions about the problems that confronted him as well as the new state. It was not mere whim that induced him to present *Mother Courage* as his first effort when he arrived in 1948. The incubus of the past, he knew, lay heavy upon the population, a great section of which, he remarked, had "participated in Hitler's predatory wars as collaborators and co-profiteers, and learned as little as Mother Courage."[4] He was not one to underestimate the difficulty that lay in the path of Socialism. He knew that Communism was the "simple that was difficult to make,"[5] but he also knew that it was here and nowhere else that he belonged. He would have to battle prejudices both high and low. But the first job was to rebuild—rebuild the physical as well as the cultural life of the country, in both respects an overwhelming prospect.

On the physical side destruction was everywhere. Soviet reparation claims had exacted a heavy toll of industry and machinery. The partition of Germany into two had left the Eastern sector without such natural resources as coal and oil. The task of re-educating the population was immense, and vast funds were allotted to this effort. Not the least beneficiaries were the theatres, the opera houses, the schools and universities. The blessing lay in the fact that of the exiled writers and intellectuals, many of them returned to the Eastern rather than the Western sector. Those, like Thomas Mann, reluctant to come back to Germany at all, settled in Switzerland. The overlay of the old ideas was strongest of course in the vast farming areas, in which socialization was to find its most formidable opposition for a time.

But what a joy to have a theatre of his own, and such associates! Helene Weigel, Caspar Neher, Hanns Eisler, Paul Dessau, Erich Engel, Elisabeth Hauptmann, Ruth Berlau, Ernst Busch, Friedrich Gnass, Gerhart Bienert, Erwin Geschonnek; Teo Otto, the stage designer; and guest artists like Therese Giehse, and Leonhard Steckel. In addition, a corps of younger people, whom Weigel and he could train.

What mattered that the rehearsal hall was a battered huge shed, opposite the Deutsches Theater, in the Max Reinhardt Strasse? The door of the rehearsal hall was always open and anyone could enter. Visitor after visitor has testified to Brecht's unconventionality. You came in, Brecht nodded recognition, and then went on with his work. Thus Erwin Leiser, the Swedish director:

The director Brecht is seldom alone in the auditorium. His place is on an old chair, his cap hangs deep over his brow, and the cigar often goes out between his lips. His quick reactions, his spontaneous exclamations, and his broad laughter inspire the actors.[6]

and Pozner:

Never have I seen a director who guarded his secret less jealously than Brecht. Anyone who wanted could come in.[7]

For him and Helene Weigel the task was a double one: to reconstitute a repertory that had been perverted and corrupted by the Nazi regime; to build a new repertory that would correspond to the needs of a new society. Yet both efforts were meant to illuminate the work of the past, not as archaeology or museum pieces but in the full light of their historical meaning—to free them, as Brecht put it, "from the dross of a class society."[8] His clear eye saw that both the public and many of the artists had lived in the

Third Reich, in the Weimar Republic, and some even within the Empire under some form of capitalism, and had been subjected to the perversion of their emotional life in one way or another.

The cleansing process of revolution was not granted Germany. The great upheaval, which otherwise comes from a revolution, came without one.[9]

Conflict in general and class conflicts in particular were therefore to be the subjects of the plays. Unsolved problems were all around, and there were many of them. "Everywhere," he said, "we must uncover the elements of crisis, of that which is problematical, rich in conflicts within this new life, else how can we ever show that which is creative in it?"[10] Everywhere, he contended, where we show solutions, we must indicate the problem; where we show victories we must show the threat of failure and defeat. For victories are not easy to win.

Within the theatre, and outside, he was to fight continually for truthfulness in the face of unsolved problems. And he had no use, and would have no use for what he called "bureaus with windows of rosy glass, through which officials gaze and see a wonderful world, and the world, looking in, sees wonderful officials."[11]

But he never lost sight of two major objectives: the interests of the people and the interests of peace.

The sight of the horrible devastations fills me with one wish: in my way to do my share so that the world may finally have peace. Without peace, she will not be habitable.[12]

Despite its depleted economy, the government had placed at his disposal extensive manpower and capital, to enable him to develop his theatre. He recognized his responsibility there, and in the course of the next few years he could boast that the German Democratic Republic had if not the greatest, certainly one of the very greatest theatrical companies in the world. That this was achieved in very difficult years for the state should be noted to its credit. Much has been made of the pressures brought upon Brecht by a bureaucratic officialdom to bend him to its purposes and many tears (some slightly crocodile) have been shed for the plight of "poor B.B.," facing if not the hostility, certainly the pointed reservations of the official Communist Party. That there were such pressures and much criticism need not, and cannot, be denied.

But, as will become evident in the following pages, Brecht did not need the "pity" of his friends. He could stand his own ground pretty well, and he did. The fact remains that he forged the Berliner Ensemble and its repertory in the light of his own purposes and goals, which, by the way, he never regarded as hostile to the interests of the people at large, or to the Marxist ideal. He, who was a keen dialectician, did not avoid a dialectical encounter in the matter of art. And his colleagues, even those who later defected from the East German state, testify at first hand to his consistent and persistent steadfastness in opposing what he believed to be narrow-minded and bureaucratic resolutions or procedures. But neither in his theory nor in his practice was he always right. Nor, for that matter, was the other side. Brecht was never averse to discussion, criticism, or open opposition. When convinced, he changed his mind or his work; when unconvinced, he did not. When in doubt, he published the old and the new version. But whatever form his opposition might take, it was always within the context and framework of the Socialist objective, and in the firm belief in change and in the self-corrective nature of Socialism.

The struggle then between Brecht and officialdom was not a struggle as to objectives as much as to how those were to be attained. As a matter of fact, the general agreement between the two sides was much greater than is realized. Both wanted an art that would enable the East German population to understand and enter upon a Socialist form of society. Both agreed that the art, the only art, that could do this was a "realistic" one. It is in their definition of the nature of realism that the sharp difference arose. Brecht always regarded himself as a "realist." The functionaries of the Socialist Unity Party questioned this. Thus, at the fifth Plenum of the Central Committee of the Party, Fred Oelssner stated, in speaking of the production of *The Mother* in January, 1951:

No one will contest the skill, the effectiveness of some scenes in *The Mother*, that actually thrill the masses. But I ask: Is this truly Realism? Are typical figures presented in typical surroundings? . . . In my opinion this is not theatre; this is something of a cross or synthesis of Meyerhold and Proletkult.[13]

The year before, Brecht's adaptation of the Sturm und Drang play by Lenz, *Der Hofmeister* (*The Tutor*), was attacked by some East Berlin critics as "negative." To which criticism Brecht replied.[14]

The *cause célèbre*, however, was the opera *The Trial of Lucullus* by Brecht and Paul Dessau. Long-awaited and preceded by rumors of all kinds, the episode around the opening performance did not disappoint the curiosity hunters. After its première on March 17, 1951, it was removed from the repertory of the Berlin State Opera, at the behest of the authorities. The attack in *Neues Deutschland* was both political and aesthetic, directed against the text as well as Dessau's music. On the one hand, the play was a pacifist play and appeared to condemn all wars. On the other hand, formally, because it set the scene in the kingdom of the dead, the whole conception was thought to give the central theme an unreal air, and brought it dangerously close to symbolism. *Neues Deutschland* said:

A highly gifted playwright and a talented composer whose progressive intentions are unquestionable, have strayed into an experiment which had to and did fail because of ideological as well as artistic reasons . . . The world peace camp with its more than eight hundred millions under the leadership of the Soviet Union is not merely not a court of shades, but has the real power to subject all war criminals to a very terrestrial court of justice.[15]

Dessau's music was condemned for its dissonances and its intellectuality, and also because as such it was not capable of arousing the masses against a new war of aggression. The absence of violins in the score was also noted and the preponderating presence of percussive instruments and effects.

In the West, the controversy was of course watched with mixed feelings of awe and "Schadenfreude." It was almost as if a crowd were gathered watching an Alpine climber dangling from a rope, which was giving way, commiserating with him, and at the same time hoping he would fall once and for all. If Brecht was dangling on a rope, he enjoyed the adventure. The conferences and discussions that took place between writer, composer, audience and collaborators on the one hand, and the Council of Ministers on the other, testified, as Brecht was reported to have humorously remarked, to the concern of the State for the arts. Locked in a full day's discussion with the officials, we may be sure that Brecht both took and gave. The episode of the *Ja-* and *Neinsager* controversy was repeated, but on a much more significant and publicized level. Brecht and Dessau agreed to certain revisions. There is no reason not to believe that they may have been convinced in the course of the discussions that there were just wars in self-defense in the light of the contemporary political situations in which war-mongering had assumed frightening proportions. The changes introduced were minor: One of the defeated kings, whom Lucullus had humiliated, is brought forward as a patriot who defended his land and people, and receives the praise of the Romans; and the legionaries now, in sending Lucullus into "nothingness," add, "If only we had refused to serve the aggressor; if only we had joined the defenders."[16] The title of the opera was changed to *The Condemnation of Lucullus,* and the new version was produced on October 12, 1951.

So much has been made of this incident and the views of critics hostile to the East German government have been given so much prominence that it may not be altogether useless to consider what one or two other West European writers might have to say about the case. In Mr. Martin Esslin's view the attack on *Lucullus,* particularly its musical score, was "reminiscent of the Nazis' campaign against 'decadent' music."[17] For Jürgen Rühle the original play represented a dangerous exposure of Soviet policies.[18]

On the other hand, Ernest Bornemann, who had known Brecht for many years, writes of this incident:

The western critics who have sighed for poor Brecht's ordeal completely misunderstood the man's character. He never felt himself restricted in the freedom of expression. He felt, on the contrary, that it was not only the right but the *duty* of the Party to correct him. And he felt that he was constantly improving the political effectiveness and the artistic clarity of his work in the process of correcting it under party guidance. But, of course, the more changes he made, the more Brechtian became his prose, his logic, his dramatic technique. . . . Brecht took to the discussions like a duck to water. . . . He made his changes, publishing a new version, and had the old one printed side by side, explaining exactly why he had made the change.[19]

Nor did the distinguished veteran West German critic Walter Dirks share the horror of the others. Writing in the *Frankfurter Neue Presse* apropos of *The Good Woman of Setzuan,* he came to speak also of *Lucullus*:

In the West Brecht has been adversely criticized above all for altering the tendentious *Lucullus*. He has corrected the pacifist first version and made another that takes account of war in a just cause. This alteration may have been commanded, at any rate it corresponds at least also to the changed situation in the West and its new awareness that had in the meantime arisen after the collapse of the postwar expectations in the West as well as in the East . . . It did not speak well for the honesty of the West, which had in the meantime, for a long time now, decided on the bitter possibility of a war against aggression, to give preference to a version in whose pacifist morality no one now believes.[20]

Brecht's theatre, though still provisionally housed pending the reconstruction of one to be given over to him entirely, was winning fame abroad as well. In the year of the *Lucullus* controversy, the Théâtre Nationale Populaire of Paris produced a highly impressive version of *Mère Courage.* The following year, the Berliner Ensemble traveled abroad. In Warsaw its impact was so great that one Polish critic credited the company and its performances and repertory with completely revolutionizing and liberating the theatrical life of Poland.[21] Brecht's plays became part of the standard repertory in West Germany as well, occupying a high place after Shakespeare, Goethe, and Schiller. The German Democratic Republic conferred upon him the National Prize First Class in October, 1951.

He loved the life at the Ensemble. He was at his best when working collectively, giving and taking, arguing, directing, questioning.

At any rate, when I get up in the morning, [he noted], who is there? I. When I drink my tea, who sits there? I. When I take a short walk in the street, who walks? I. I go upstairs again, and who is there? I again. Again, I. Well, then I'd rather go to the Berliner Ensemble.[22]

But he never lost his awareness of what was outside the theatre, in the streets. As he wanders through the still ruined city, he reflects that he has received a new house, that he has hung up his Chinese scroll depicting the "Doubter"; and that he enjoys unusual privileges.

> Ich hoffe
> Es macht mich nicht geduldig mit den Löchern
> In denen so viele Tausende sitzen.

> I hope it does not make me patient with the holes
> In which so many thousands are living.

Still, even here, life seemed provisional (did not everything in the world seem so too?). Though he has his own house now, his manuscripts are still piled in the trunk.[23]

His unpublished poems and notes at the time reflect the discontents with governmental plans that rest upon merely physical rebuilding, or constructions based upon statistics. More important, he thought, than building cities is "the wisdom of the people."[24] He suspected rosy promises, or rosy visions; and he pleaded for truth, even if it hurt. "Truth unites," he said. And addressing those who governed, he added, "Friends, I wish you knew the truth and said it. Not like fleeing, tired Caesars: 'Tomorrow you will have flour.' But like Lenin, 'Tomorrow night we are lost unless. . .'" He pleads for "forceful admissions and a forceful UNLESS!"[25]

Then came the turmoils of 1953. In January, Brecht addressed a plea to Albert Einstein, Arthur Miller, and Ernest Hemingway on behalf of Ethel and Julius Rosenberg, two Americans accused and convicted of espionage. In May, he introduced at the Berliner Ensemble the new playwright, Erwin Strittmatter, with the social play *Katzgraben,* dealing with the struggle between the old and the newer farming population. On March 5, 1953, Stalin died. Brecht had never been a worshipper of heroes, and the personality cult had never been a part of his character. But he paid tribute to Stalin for his leadership of a people that had turned the tide against Nazism, thus saving the rest of the world at the price of incomparable sacrifice of human lives and territory.

On June 17, 1953, occurred the uprising of workers in Berlin, soon followed by similar incidents in other parts of the republic. Partisan interpretations once again colored the picture according to taste. In the East the uprising was condemned by the authorities as the work of fascist and other imperialist provocateurs. In the West it was taken as a revolutionary upsurge against a repressive regime. There can be no doubt that justified grievances sparked the outbreak—untimely and ill-considered raising of working norms by ten percent; over-hasty collectivization of the farms—no less than a failure of the officialdom to gauge correctly the temper of the people. On the other hand, there can be little doubt that counter-revolutionary and Nazi elements played a considerable part in provoking the disturbances, particularly in the socially more backward farming communities. The lure of the Kurfürstendamm with its whipped cream and its displays of commodities also played its part. It was no secret that there was a plan to undermine the East German currency, and that black-market activities enabled West Berlin housewives to buy up East German goods with East German marks they obtained at the rate of four or even five to one. But the errors and shortsightedness of the government officials were equally inexcusable. It was too easy to lay the blame for their own mistakes on the shoulders of provocateurs and fascists. The workers' protest was directed against measures undertaken by the government, but not against socialization. Significantly, too, there was no clamor for the removal of the Soviet forces. The latter, called in to suppress the uprising, behaved with creditable restraint.

The repercussions of the uprising and its suppression were of course far-reaching. For one, they shocked the officials and functionaries into a realization that Socialism cannot be brought about by decrees and pronouncements, and that clichés were poor substitutes for very much needed consumers' goods and comestibles. Corrective measures, soon taken, could not at once calm the stormy seas. Through all sectors of the republic there was a growing awareness of the implications of the breach between government and the people. Brecht, no less than others, was severely troubled by the events. He recognized that anti-social elements might have been involved; but he also recognized the just claims of the workers.

According to now verified reports, Brecht immediately dispatched a long letter to Walter Ulbricht, the Party Secretary, expressing his criticism as well as making constructive suggestions. He is supposed to have concluded his letter with a reiteration of his loyalty to and agreement with the Party. It was this complimentary close that was published with his signature.[26]

I feel it necessary to write to you and express to you at this moment my attachment to the Socialist Unity Party. Yours, Bertolt Brecht.[27]

The alleged first portion of the letter went as follows:

History will pay due respect to the revolutionary impatience of the Socialist Unity Party of Germany. The great discussion with the masses concerning the tempo of Socialist construction will lead to a sifting and securing of Socialist achievements. I feel it necessary, etc.

He is also reported to have sent the following telegram to Ulbricht:

On the day after June 17, when it became clear that the demonstrations of the workers were being misused for warlike purposes, I expressed my agreement with the Socialist Unity Party of Germany. I now hope that the provocateurs will be isolated, and their networks destroyed; but that the workers who demonstrated in justifiable dissatisfaction will not be placed on the same footing as the provocateurs, so that the very much needed discussion of the errors committed on all sides may not be disturbed beforehand.[27]

A number of poems written at about this time reveal his state of mind. Though not published during his lifetime, they appear in the authorized edition of his works. One such is directed at the uprising of the 17th of June and the attitude of the officials towards it:

> After the uprising of the 17th of June
> The secretary of the Writers Union
> Had leaflets distributed in the Stalinallee
> In which one could read that the People
> Had forfeited the confidence of the Government
> Which it could only retrieve
> By a redoubled effort.
> Would it then not really be simpler
> If the Government dissolved the people
> And elected another?[28]

Another poem, forceful and deeply impassioned, speaks of "Justice as the Bread of the People," the indispensable nourishment. But who should bake it? Who bakes the other kind of bread?

> Just as that other bread
> So too must the bread of justice
> Be baked by the people—
>
> Copious, wholesome, daily.[29]

Is poem entitled "Bad Morning" also of this period? The silver poplar and the lake seem drained of all beauty, and revolting. A dream of the night before showed him a finger pointing at him, work-roughened and broken.

> "Oh you who do not know!" I cried,
> Guilt-stricken.[30]

In both the Academy of Arts, of which Brecht was a member, and in the Writers Union, stormy sessions took place, at which demands were set forth urging the greater responsibility for the artist in determining government art policies. Brecht led the way, joined by such figures as Eisler, Arnold Zweig, and Friedrich Wolf, in framing a resolution in the name of the Academy of Arts, and specifically directed at the party figures of Kuba (Kurt Barthel) and Alexander Abusch. According to Kantorowicz, when there was talk of the suppression of this declaration, a good many members threatened to resign, and it was only through Premier Otto Grotewohl's intervention that the resolution was published. According to another account, Brecht openly called for the removal of bureaucratic government functionaries from the domain of the arts. The resolution demanded freedom for the directors of the theatres in the choice of their repertoires, freedom of a like kind for publishers and artists, as well as a cessation of direct interference by the state organs.[31]

In *Neues Deutschland* of August 12, Brecht spoke out again, even more forcefully, criticizing the "unfortunate practice of the commissions," "their dictatorial proposals, inartistic administrative measures, their vulgar-Marxist language which repelled the artists (even the Marxist ones)."[32] He opposed the tendency to meet the requirements of the people by giving them "Kitsch." The level of art appreciation must be raised, but it cannot be done by a schematized series of proposals worked out by a commission.[32]

On another occasion he wrote: "No painter can paint when his hand trembles before the judgment of the functionary who may perhaps be politically well-informed and conscious of his political responsibility, but who is aesthetically badly trained and not fully aware of his responsibility to the artist." "How can an intimidated art move the masses to great and bold deeds? And we *do* need bold deeds!"[33]

In the same spirit, and with the same vigor, Brecht intervened in support of a memorial exhibition of the work of Ernst Barlach, upon which East German officialdom looked with jaundiced eye as running counter to the demands of their interpretation of Socialist Realism. Barlach, in addition to being an outstanding sculptor, was also a remarkable poet and playwright. Though he remained in Germany, he had been disowned by the Nazis, and spent the last years of his life in desperate seclusion. The exhibition was held notwithstanding, and Brecht wrote, "I consider Barlach one of the greater sculptors we Germans ever had." In one of the bronze figures of an old woman, he saw the "nobility" with which Helene Weigel had portrayed Vlassova.[33a]

The fact that a number of these statements found place in the official publications of the Party and the government speaks for the changed atmosphere in the country. As a consequence, the State Commission for the Arts was dissolved at the beginning of 1954, and a Ministry of Culture organized under the chairmanship of Johannes Becher, who had also joined in criticism of past artistic and cultural policies.

Once again, be it remarked, Brecht's animadversions and activities were all undertaken within the framework of the Socialist state in which he was participating, and for which he was working. He was not to be taken in by the jubilant outcries from the Western camp that greeted all the convulsions, discussions, and disagreements in East Berlin. He was not ready to join in what they imagined were the imminent obsequies of the German Democratic Republic.

> Easy [he wrote] my pretty ones.
> Close upon the Judas kiss for the workers,
> Follows the Judas kiss for the artists.
> The firebug carrying a gasoline can
> Is approaching
> The Academy of Arts with a broad grin. . .
>
> Even the most straitened foreheads
> Where dwell thoughts of peace
> Are more welcome to the arts than that friend
>   of the arts
> Who is also a friend of the arts of war.[34]

That the "thaw" had entered did not mean the end of sharp controversies and differences in the cultural fields. But the discussions were more open, and Brecht was in the midst of them. The prestige of the Berliner Ensemble continued to grow. In March, 1954, the company moved into its own theatre on the Schiffbauer-damm, where more than a quarter of a century before Brecht had scored his first international triumph with the *Dreigroschenoper*. Restored to its original shape, except that now it was equipped with the most modern machinery and stage devices, it became the theatrical center to which the world looked. A brilliant company of actors, old and young, a technical staff of exceptional efficiency, with younger men and women as future directors—a theatrical city in fact—it afforded Brecht and Helene Weigel opportunities rarely offered a theatrical enterprise. State subventions were generous, and the audiences grew. Young people and workers began attending in ever-increasing numbers. Marianne Kesting, Brecht's West German biographer, reports overhearing frequent remarks to the effect that "so wie bei Brecht ist es nirgends auf dem Theater" ("the kind of thing Brecht gives us you can't get anywhere else in the theatre")—a tribute, since it came from the lips of non-professional audiences.[35]

But the activities of the Berliner Ensemble and its directors were not confined to the Schiffbauerdamm theatre. They extended to training lay groups of actors, particularly in the various industries throughout the country; broadcasting their performances and preparing special programs for workers; in other words, fulfilling Brecht's intentions of creating a responsive audience and raising the cultural level as well as the political understanding throughout the country. Not least, their efforts were bent on encouraging developing new talents, such as those (to mention only very few) of Regine Lutz and Ekkehard Schall; and directors Manfred Wekwerth, Joachim Tenschert, and Werner Hecht.

Internationally, the Berliner Ensemble celebrated triumphs at the Festival de Paris, where it won first prize with *Mother Courage,* in July of 1954.

The preceding June 15, it had opened its doors at the Schiffbauerdamtheater with *The Caucasian Chalk Circle,* with Angelika Hurwicz as Grusha, Helene Weigel as the Governor's wife, Ernst Busch as Azdak, and the settings of Karl von Appen. This was a brilliant production, though the official press disregarded it. Brecht celebrated the opening with a brief poem:

> You've acted theatre in ruins here,
> Now act in this lovely house, not as a pastime.
> From you and us let arise the peaceful WE,
> So that this house and others too may stand.[36]

"Welch reicher Himmel!" "What a rich heaven!" he could have exclaimed with Goethe's minstrel, looking around him: a company of more than sixty actors and actresses; all in all more than two hundred fifty associates . . . almost unlimited time for rehearsals . . . and an *esprit de corps* such as few organizations could boast of.

He had also received a new home in the city, in addition to the country house in Buckow. In the Chausseestrasse, a few minutes' walk from the theatre, two stories were allotted him and his family. Through his windows he could look out on the peaceful Protestant cemetery next door, where rested Hegel, one of his philosophical demi-gods.

He had his harmonium, his portable typewriter, cigars, Chinese etchings, masks, photos of Marx and Engels as young men, and, of course, papers, manuscripts, newspaper clippings, and books.

In the spring of 1955 he went to Moscow to accept the international Stalin Peace Prize.

He no longer regarded himself or his theatre as a "bridge" between East and West. "It isn't true," he told a Swedish colleague, "that I have set myself down between two chairs. I am already sitting on one. And that one stands in the East."[37]

Helene Weigel, his principal collaborator, brought to the theatre the authority, the experience, and the genius of a great actress and director. Brecht had more than once paid tribute to her remarkable art. She had been associated in one way or another with his principal plays since the late twenties, but it was in the thirties and thereafter that she assumed the prime role in his works, so that many of his outstanding theatrical figures are identified with her impersonations of them. He had made a glowing portrait of her as Señora Carrar while they were in exile.[38] In a poem, he praised her as "the same yet the changing one," who was not undone

> When suddenly the ground she stood on was another;
> And when the winds proved hostile, and roughly seized her hair,
> She merely said: That is the hair of many of my fellow men.[39]

He had taken motion pictures of her as she was putting on make-up, and then cut them up into small segments. "Each of these individual pictures showed a finished expression, complete in itself and with its own significance."[40] Her devotion to social causes, and her adherence to the political left in the thirties had brought about what Brecht called her "descent to glory." In her he saw an artist who did not transport or overwhelm her audiences, as others did, but one who caused them to see more than they were seeing and hear more. "She showed not only one art, but many arts: How, for example goodness and wisdom were also arts that could be learned and must be learned."[41]

Brecht admired the care with which Helene Weigel sought out the props for her scenes, comparing her procedure to that of the meticulous farmer seeking out the heaviest seeds for his trial plot of land, or the poet's search for the right word. Everything she chose, pewter spoon, fishing net, straps and belts, all were with an eye to "age, purpose and beauty," with the eye of the knowing and the hands of the "connoisseur of reality who cooks soup, weaves nets, and bakes bread."[42]

And what dramatic roles she had filled! Vlassova, Courage, Carrar, Antigone; and now there were fresh roles for her in the new plays and adaptations.

Sitting alongside Erich Engel, Ernst Busch, Hanns Eisler, Frau Hauptmann, and Caspar Neher, it must have seemed to Brecht and Weigel as if they were back in the early thirties.

Brecht had grown stouter with the years; he moved around little. Even to the theatre, only a few blocks away from his home, he would drive in the disreputable old car he had (he disdained a new one) to the amusement and perhaps also astonishment of the mechanics, who couldn't understand why the "old man" wouldn't indulge himself. That which was old, that which he could tinker with, that which was "usable"—"brauchbar" is a word he loves— is what appealed to him. So, too, after his death, soldiers visiting the Brecht home to inspect the relics of a famous man could not get over their surprise at the simplicity and unpretentiousness of his cramped quarters, when "he could have had anything he wanted." In the early part of 1954 he lists his satisfactions: no

serious illness, no serious enmities; work—enough; his share of
potatoes, cucumbers, asparagus, strawberries; and the pleasures of
seeing lilacs in Buckow; visiting various European cities, and
of course, the production of *The Caucasian Chalk Circle*.[43]

Being human, Brecht, unlike his critics, also had his moods, heart-
aches, and disappointments. In difficult times, he sometimes sees
himself back in Augsburg as a boy, and the elderbushes near his
home. He is still impatient with the survival of so much of the old
in the new state. He hopes for the time when all weapons will be
laid aside and turn rusty, and he himself will witness "the beautiful
day, when he becomes useless." Like Shelley, he regards the good
things in life as consisting in the homely decencies—food, meat,
cheese, beer, as much as in art and books. Again and again, he
returns to his favorite exhortation: Teachers, learn from your pupils!
Leaders, learn from the people! Do not strain the truth too greatly,
and listen while you are speaking.[45] Addressing his comrades, he
pleads: Let us not constantly say "I," even though it is constantly
heard around us. Let us fight the conditions in which these sentences
with the "I's" prevail. So he had adjured his Ensemble to change
the "I" into "We."

The presupposition on which the Berliner Ensemble was built
was of course political, the kind of theatre Brecht had been hoping
for since the twenties. The study of Marxist-Leninist classics was
a part of the Ensemble's training, and two-hour discussions took
place once every week. The "dramaturgs" and the directorial staffs
also studied at the Humbolt University of Berlin, devoting themselves to a more thorough understanding of dialectical materialism.
New plays as well as old plays were approached with a socio-
historical analysis.

The subsidy by the state that amounted to over three million
marks a year enabled Brecht and Weigel to devote long periods to
rehearsals; and, on the average, only one new production was
mounted each year.

To watch Brecht directing during a rehearsal was accounted by many a visitor a rare experience. Surrounded by students, he sat in the middle of the auditorium, the eternal cigar in his mouth (a sketch of him smoking in the theatre was shown to the Berlin fire-department). His directions were inconspicuous; he was always seeking the actors' point of view and ideas, working along with them, rather than for them. He assumed an attitude of "ignorance" toward both his own and others' plays, always asking questions as if he didn't know the answers, working with suggestions, rather than with final dicta. It was remarked that there were very few discussions of a psychological nature during these rehearsals. Things had to be tested and proved, but not overly discussed. "Why give me reasons?" he would say to the actors. "Show me."[46]

When a suggestion seemed valuable, he was ready to accept it no matter where it came from.

The text of a play was as always a provisional thing. It had to prove itself in the process of production. He was ready to alter it when necessary.

"Why do you always stop work on a scene before you are finished with it?" he was asked. He replied: "Because when you are boring through a thick board, you must look to see if your drill isn't over-heating. In art you must also do the difficult thing so that it becomes easy. . . . I find it necessary to cook the scenes at the same time, so that one is not done before the other. Otherwise I lose the impact of one scene upon another."[47]

But each scene or segment was analyzed separately and thoroughly. Very often the actors saw the text of a play for the first time when they gathered on the stage for the first rehearsal. They did not know what was in the rest of the play. Brecht believed in the creative impulse of "surprise." The actor was to make discoveries in the process of reading the script.

Then the first act was discussed in a typical Brechtian fashion—question and answer. Suppose the play was a new one, Erwin Stritt-matter's *Katzgraben,* for example.

What happens in the first scene? Brecht asks. A street is being
built, leading to the town. At whose behest? At the behest of the
Socialist Unity Party. Brecht says no. Silence . . . Brecht then adds,
"That is revealed only in the third scene." Etc., etc.[48]

The discussions surrounding the other plays were fascinating,
Brecht probing, asking, always testing. This "dialectical" process he
applied with particular effectiveness in such a play as his adaptation
of Shakespeare's *Coriolanus*.

To train the actors in the practice of estrangement he composed
original scenes for *Romeo and Juliet* and *Hamlet*. A favorite device
of his was to transpose the dialogue of a play he was rehearsing
from the direct discourse to the indirect. The actors would then
speak as follows (this is a transposed scene from *Der Hofmeister*):

LISE. During a stormy night in November, while Läuffer was correcting copy-books, Lise came into his chamber. But he did not greet
her. She must have startled him, she began. She only wanted to ask
him if he needed something else, if he needed something else.

LÄUFFER. If he needed something else! Läuffer replied. Never, he
exclaimed. What should a wretch like him need? He had everything,
and he was about to go to bed.

Brecht's note added that these texts were handed to the actors,
who were asked to read them in their natural inflections, supply
the principal movements, and suggest the gestures. The general
tone was to be that of an eye witness report. In this way they achieved
"distance."[49]

In rehearsal, Brecht was concerned for the well-being of his actors.
He asked for bright lights so that they might be able to read their
parts more easily and for comfortable chairs so that the older actors
might rest, waiting for their cues. And he was always alert for
suggestions from any member of the staff. A member of his technical crew once called his attention to an error in *Die Mutter*,
indicating to him that a policeman earned less than a worker.
Brecht immediately corrected the oversight. Upon the reopening
of the Schiffbauerdamm Theatre, he had written the technicians

a note: "Please remind me when I scold you again," which they did, when the occasion arose, by lowering a canvas with his inscription on it.[50]

Caspar Neher, his stage designer, shared Brecht's and Weigel's scrupulousness and meticulousness when it came to such details as stage props and scenery. Simple and unpretentious as they very often had to be, they always had to be well and beautifully made. This applied to the printed programs, which are one of the delights at the performances of the Berliner Ensemble, and could well serve as models for all other theatres of the world. The illustrative material, whether pictorial or explanatory, the format, the opinions, notes and information are presented so as to satisfy both the eye and the brain. Thus, the program for *The Days of the Commune* not only illustrated the Paris of 1870, but also reproduced historical prints of important figures and incidents, taken from contemporary sources, and included a highly informative history of the uprising, as well as an interpretation and photographs of the current production.

No one observing the rehearsals and the performances of the Ensemble would be inclined to fall into the mistaken notion that Brecht desired above all schematization, dehumanization, lifelessness and abstraction of his actors and his plays. In reply to an actor's query as to whether his technique did not lead to a purely "artistic" (perhaps "arty") and inhuman kind of theatre, Brecht said:

It must have been my way of writing that took too much for granted and that has created such an impression. The devil take it! Naturally we must have on the stage of a realistic theatre, live, rounded, contradictory people, with all their passions, their direct expressions, and actions. The stage is no herbarium or a zoological museum with stuffed animals. The actor must know how to create such people (and if you could see our productions, you would really see such people, and they *are* people not despite, but thanks to our principles)![51]

III

The Last Works

There is no more difficult advance than that
back to reason.

BRECHT, "Der Messingkauf"

The most arduous task was to restock the repertory. As can be easily understood, for Brecht it could not mean merely a return to the old theatre as such, or merely a revival of old plays for the sake of old plays. Once again, it was not a question of restoring them to show continuity or the "universal" in them, but, as Brecht put it, "to play them historically, that is to set them off in powerful contrast to our own times."[1] That meant to bring the mechanism of contemporary insights and knowledge to play upon them, to lay bare the ideology behind them, so as both to delight and instruct the new audiences that were now available.

He was too much of the dialectician not to observe contradictions when they hovered around him. If "truth is concrete," as he always insisted, the "concrete truth" showed him, as it did others, that the new society that was in the process of formation with its "new" man had much of the overlay of the old; the new metal wasn't all steel, or all pure. Old habits persisted. What he called, in one of his poems, the "Prussian eagle" still seemed to shout out his commands, if only at meals, and to youngsters.[2] Since he was now a world figure, and his works were available both in East and West Germany, he was speaking, more forcefully to his fellow Germans across the border, where, if anything the work of "purging" off the immediate past went on with a "Gemütlichkeit" that took the form of a gentle guilt and an expectation of proximate but full forgiveness.

If with *Antigone* he initiated his "recovery" of the Greek past and set it in contrast to the present, he turned with a similar plan to the German Sturm und Drang, to rehabilitate, and adapt, *Der Hofmeister* (*The Tutor*) by that typically unhappy Storm and Stresser and near-genius, Jakob Michael Reinhold Lenz, whose life was as hectic as his plays, and who poured tumult and anger into his poems and dramas. He died in 1792, in Moscow, for many years mildly insane.

Two of his plays have survived the centuries, *Die Soldaten* (*The Soldiers*) and *The Tutor*, both the fruits of Lenz's actual personal experiences. The horrors of the retainer of the petty aristocratic family, his degradation and servitude, are well known. One need merely recall the humiliations exacted of Mozart and Haydn and Hölderlin not to be amazed that the fate of an obscure household tutor at the hands of a petty nobleman might have been even worse. Such is the theme of this terrifying "comedy" of which Läuffer is the protagonist in *The Tutor*.

Brecht preserved the general line and in part the language of the original. What he did in his adaptation was to sharpen, in his customary way, the central theme of the play, reduce and simplify it, yet without altering its own historic character.

This play, as the Tutor announces in Brecht's prologue, is a lesson in the "German Misere"—a term difficult to define in English, denoting the degradation and demoralization of the Germans under the ravages of absolutism from the time of the Thirty Years War. Once more Brecht is presenting a critique of Germany. The story is that of a tutor Läuffer, son of a pastor, who is hired out to a petty aristocratic family, the von Bergs, whose numbskull son he is to instruct. He is subjected to innumerable scurrilities by the tight-fisted family. Hemmed in, though well-fed; restricted in his movements (being denied the freedom to give vent to his feelings), he seduces the not unwilling daughter of the family, with the usual biological consequences. Escaping the anticipated threats, he finds shelter with a pedantic village schoolmaster, where he is discovered by his pursuers, and wounded slightly. But overcome by his attractions for the gentle ward of his host, he castrates himself, rather than once more commit a shameful act. In that state he is accepted by the ward.

While for Lenz, the plea of the play rested on a liberalization of education, and an exposure of the abasements of tutorship, Brecht lifts the play to the level of a critique of society, both in its feudal aspects (he notes that the "beautiful" feelings of Frau von Berg for music could be paralleled by the Nazi executioner Heydrich's love of Bach), as well as in its general manifestations in the bourgeoisie. Just as the feudal relations exploit Läuffer, so he exploits himself. His self-emasculation is also a spiritual one, for it is the self-castration of the German intellectuals of the bourgoisie, who "experience not only the revolutions of other peoples, but also their own private lives solely 'in the spirit.'"[3] It is in the state of his eunuchism that Läuffer finds satisfactory employment (as his village schoolmaster joyfully exclaims), and he will even obtain laudatory references from the family he has injured (though here too the matter is brought to a satisfactory conclusion). This mutilation, then, is the mutilation of the German spirit, its teachers, and its pupils. It does not matter that Läuffer escapes the feudal world; he falls into the clutches of the petty bourgeois one. His self-mutilation is a "deed to end all deeds."

Thus the schoolmaster Wenzeslaus congratulates his new assistant, Läuffer, after the act of unmanning:

Let me embrace you, young man, you dear, chosen instrument of instruction! This is the road on which you can become the shining light of the schools, a star of the first magnitude in pedagogy. . . . Who should be a teacher, if not you? For you have the highest qualifications of all. Have you not forever crushed within you the spirit of rebellion? Subordinated all to duty? No private life can now withhold you from forming human beings in your own image . . . Every teaching post in our district is now open to you.[4]

Has the combination of barbarism and "spirituality" ever been so clearly delineated and so frightfully exposed? The performance of the play by the Berliner Ensemble accentuated its cruelly "comic" aspects, in the behavior of Läuffer at the beginning, who moved like one of those wound-up figures on a music-box. An epilogue by Brecht warned the new generation of Germans:

> That German schoolmaster, mark him well!
> Creator and creature of monstrousness.
> You pupils and teachers of the new age,
> Observe his servility,
> That you may free yourselves from it![5]

The Ensemble gave this play a most brilliant performance in April of 1950. But the official East German press did not receive it with unqualified approval. The play was considered too "negative." Brecht replied to this criticism with a note of his own:

The production could serve as a contribution to the major educational reforms which are now being carried out in the Republic. Satire in general dispenses—as do works of the type of *Tartuffe, Don Quixote, The Inspector General, Candide*—with counterposing the type that is being satirized with an exemplary type. In the concave mirror which is set up in order to work out in an exaggerated manner that which is to be attacked, positive characters could not escape distortion. In *The Tutor* the positive element consists in the fierce anger at a condition unworthy of man exposed to unjustified privileges and twisted thinking.[6]

In the matter of his depiction and presentation of the "German Misere," Brecht and his associates came into frequent conflict with the official critics. The issues reached a controversial boiling point in connection with the interpretation of the *Faust* figure, long considered a sacred heritage of the German intellect. At the same time, the Ensemble's production of Heinrich von Kleist's classic comedy, *Der zerbrochene Krug* (*The Broken Jug*) came under similar attack. In the case of Faust, both Brecht and Hanns

Eisler underwent scrutiny and criticism, this time not as collaborators, but as individual artists.

Hanns Eisler had composed a new Faust drama entitled *Johann Faustus,* in which he had set the figure of Faust unfavorably as a representative of the bourgeois order against the militant Ur-communist, Thomas Münzer, the Anabaptist reformer and martyr. A lengthy discussion, conducted principally by the Communist party leader Alexander Abusch, Ernst Fischer, and *Neues Deutschland,* condemned the work as "anti-national" and "anti-social," and as a serious derogation of the classical German figure. Eisler intended to set his book to music as an opera. Abusch's criticism stated that "a Faust opera can only become a German national opera, if, even when connected with the age of the great German Peasant Wars, it understands how to represent Faust as the spiritual heroic figure of the passionate war *against* the German Misere, at the same time as *for* an all-sided understanding of the world."[7]

Brecht participated in the discussion, which, coming not very long after the reception of the Ensemble's *Urfaust* of Goethe, gave him an opportunity to reply in a less personal form. Eisler, he held, had the right, like every other poet, to reframe the figure of Faust; he simply set him off as the humanist, who, though the son of peasants, abandons the cause of the peasants and identifies himself with their oppressors, in pursuit of that knowledge and experience which will best develop his personality. Far from disparaging German history, Eisler had, in the persons of the militant peasants (though incompletely) and in Thomas Münzer, their leader, done honor to the best part of German history. This, Brecht continued, is a piece for our times, when the (West) German bourgeoisie is again calling upon the intelligence to perform its work of treason toward the people. "This is a significant literary work."[8]

Of course, much more was involved in this discussion than the "caricature" of a great national figure, to wit, Faust; or a distortion of a great literary work, Goethe's *Faust.* The incubus of the Faustian legend over the German mind need scarcely be enlarged upon here.

Thomas Mann had come to terms with him in his novel *Doctor Faustus*; but he had already in the *Magic Mountain* indirectly suggested (even though not himself then fully aware of all the implications) the meaning of German "self-development," which had become assimilated to the figure of Faust and of Goethe too. The horrible ends to which "self-enrichment" might be used could not even in 1924 have been fully clear. Of course, in Goethe's version, Faust, toward the end of his life, comes to realize his social function, his responsibility to mankind. But in the first part of the tragedy he makes his way to his satisfactions as a kind of Brechtian Baal endowed with supreme intellect, doctoral degrees, and a helpful assistant, Mephistopheles. Alas, poor Gretchen! what chance did she have against all these—and a Faust transformed from an old, doddering scholar into a fully virile, strongly sexed, handsome young man!

Brecht had entrusted his disciple Egon Monk with the staging of Goethe's *Urfaust,* which opened on April 23, 1952. The conception was Brecht's, who advanced to the classical first version of the tragedy without the "intimidation", as he called it, of classical works. Enough of the orotund, bombastic treatment of Goethe's works! This version at least was to exhibit Goethe's "humor". Two scenes particularly aroused the dissatisfaction of the critics: the broad and almost rowdy treatment of the student gathering in Auerbach's Cellar and the scene in which Mephistopheles plays the professor vis-à-vis the student Wagner. Brecht took advantage of his knowledge of German students and German professors, as well as German universities. No less heretical was Brecht's conception of Faust himself. Faust was seen as an "exploitative" figure (which he is), able to cash in because he has the unlimited forces of Mephisto at his call. The depravity (and Brecht calls it such in his notes) that makes it possible for Faust to enter and heroically seduce Gretchen, and bring destruction to the simple girl, her brother, and her mother[9] is scarcely compensated for by his final conversion to what Brecht calls "productivity" at the end of a long career.

It was this conception of the German past, and Brecht's insistence on keeping it before the eyes of the audience, that provoked official opposition, and the criticism that Brecht's Ensemble had employed a "marionette style," that did not arouse "deep human feelings." He was also accused of a deliberate primitivism designed to give a "symbolic picture of the German Misere." Thus the German Misere became "the only hero," and Brecht was really taking sides against the German national cultural heritage.[10]

With the same vigor with which he attempted to lay bare the predatory parasitism and exploitativeness of Faust, he unmasks in *Don Juan,* the more joyful, rollicking, but no less serious amatory "Lebenskünstler" ("life-artist") Don Juan. The adaptation of Molière's incomparable satirical portrait Brecht uses to expose the "splendor of the parasite," which, in his words, must become the "parasitism of Don Juan's splendor." Molière seems to Brecht to have voted for Don Juan and for his "epicureanism"—and to have "mocked heaven" as a somewhat ambiguous institution for the extermination of joy in life. Much as one may disagree with this interpretation of Molière's intentions, the original remains unharmed; and the concluding cry of Don Juan's faithful and critical servant, Sganarelle, after Don Juan has been dragged down into Hell by the Commandatore—"My wages, my wages!"—only serves to underline both Molière's and Brecht's independent, though here overlapping, intentions.

The same vivid critical joyousness pervades Brecht's adaptation of the early eighteenth-century English comedy by George Farquhar, *The Recruiting Officer,* renamed *Mit Pauken und Trommeln (With Trumpets and Drums).* By a brilliant stroke, Brecht shifted the time from the early to the late eighteenth century, to the period of the American Revolution, and so was enabled to introduce references to British imperialism, and the American War of Independence. Altogether in keeping with the mood of the piece are the interpolated songs, which in their way capture the eighteenth-century style and spirit. The anti-war purposes of the play are expressed

in the difficulties the British recruiting officers find in pressing
recruits, at a time when leaflets are being discovered in the recruiting station, containing preliminary drafts of the American Declaration of Independence, as well as incendiary statements by Benjamin Franklin.

For the third, and last time, Brecht came back to the theme of
Joan of Arc. *Der Prozess der Jeanne d'Arc zu Rouen, 1431,* a recasting of a radio script by Anna Seghers, is a simple but moving
dramatic retelling of the trial scenes. The "voices" that guide St.
Joan are, in this version, the voices of the people. After her execution,
two peasant farmers, Grandfather Breuil and a younger man,
Jacques Legrain, speak of her:

LEGRAIN. I saw her burned, Pierre.
BREUIL. She guided France.
LEGRAIN. But France guided her too.
BREUIL. I thought it was the voices that guided her.
LEGRAIN. Yes, ours.
BREUIL. What do you mean?
LEGRAIN. This is the way it was: At first she rushed against the enemy
far ahead of the people—so she was captured. And when she was imprisoned in the tower in Rouen, she heard nothing of us, and she
became weak—just like you and me. In fact, she recanted. But when
she did recant, the simple people of Rouen were so angered, that they
smote the Englishmen in that sea-port with might and main. She found
out about it—the Lord knows how—and regained her courage. She
saw that the Tribunal was no worse a battlefield than the communica-
tions trench of Orléans. And so she turned her greatest defeat into our
greatest victory. When her lips were silenced, her voice was heard.
BREUIL. Yes, the war isn't over yet.

And from the vineyards come the singing voices of the girl
vintners, joyously chanting Christine de Pisan's beautiful lines about
Jeanne d'Arc.[11]

Who is the leader? And who the follower? Who the teacher? And
who the pupil? He had always been concerned with these questions.
And he had always come back to the same answer: The people
are the teachers; the leaders, the pupils, the followers.

Since 1952 Brecht had been working on an adaptation of Shakespeare's *Coriolanus,* a tragedy with which he had been taken as far back as the twenties, when Erich Engel produced it with magnificent éclat in Berlin. Coming back to it now, after these many years, he saw its renewed possibilities. Though he was not to complete it in his lifetime, he left enough to make it possible for the Berliner Ensemble to mount it and make of it one of its most successful and overpowering productions—after his death.

Though, in general, Brecht's version remains faithful to the Shakespearean original, there are a number of significant major changes that indicate a shift from the central Shakespearean theme. Brecht's interest in the tragedy was undoubtedly based on two factors: the conflict between plebeians and patricians, and the crisis of leadership. For Brecht, the tragedy of Coriolanus is no longer merely that of a proud leader offended by the people he despises, seeking retribution, and finally deflected from his purposes by a pleading mother. It is the problem rather of the indispensability of the leader. Brecht's Coriolanus believes himself indispensable and irreplaceable. His contempt for the mass of his own Romans draws him closer to his age-old enemy Aufidius than to his own people. The justified disaffection of the plebeians at the inequitable distribution of the corn supplies that almost sparks a revolt is for the time being allayed by the threat of invasion by an enemy. But the unity established is only a temporary one and breaks down in the face of the arrogance and intransigence of Coriolanus. Does Rome need him? Brecht answers no. In his interpolations Brecht indicates that the Romans can do well without Coriolanus; and if he does threaten them with an assault, they brace themselves to resist him. That sentiment is placed on the lips not only of the plebeians themselves, but even on those of Coriolanus' mother Volumnia.

When the patricians appear to be deserting Rome in the face of Coriolanus' threat to the city, one of the tribunes remarks:

If those who live off Rome, do not want to defend her, then we, off whom Rome has lived hitherto, will defend her. . . . It seems Rome is worth defending now, for the first time since her foundation.[12]

We have seen that Brecht never adapted plays for his theatre *ad hoc*. They represented long periods of arduous work, and we may be sure that in this "tragedy" too he was pointing a contemporary "moral." As he remarked in an explanatory note:

So far as the hero is concerned, society is also interested in another aspect, which affects it directly: namely, the firm belief of the hero in his own indispensability. It cannot bow to this belief, without risking destruction. So it sets itself into an irrevocable opposition to this hero.

So far as Coriolanus' pride is concerned,

It is society, it is Rome that pays for it, almost to the point of destruction.[13]

With typical irony, Brecht concludes the play with a brief scene, in which, having received news of the death of the "hero" Coriolanus, the senate proceeds to its everyday business in the name of the people of Rome, and for its benefit. Thus, once more, as in the earlier *Edward II*, Brecht has dissolved the tragic issue in irony.

While still in his Danish exile, he had planned a drama around Julius Caesar. He had written a short story, "Caesar and his Legionnaire," and was thinking of a film on the same subject. In the course of the years, all these projects culminated in a chronicle-novel, *The Affairs of Mr. Julius Caesar,* which was left unfinished at the time of his death.

Brecht was always best when he could use the pointed aphoristic style. A long, tightly-knit narrative found him ill at ease. In narrative, he found himself at his best in the short apologue, in the tale, in the anecdote. They came closest to the epic style of his theatre and to his own psychological and aesthetic needs. Thus the parable, too, served him best. The need for compression, for conciseness, for brevity—and for objectivity—became more insistent with him during the years of exile and world crisis. But even before that he had projected in the brief aphorisms and apologues around Herr Keuner, his alter ego, the very special dialectical wit of which he was master. So too in the *Calendar Tales* which came into being during the exile years, and among which are to be found the germs of some of his later plays, as well as the striking stories of "The Shameless Old

Lady" (in reality a depiction of Brecht's grandmother), "The Heretic's Cloak" (Giordano Bruno), and "Caesar and His Legionnaire."

Now, in *The Affairs of Mr. Julius Caesar* he was actually following the same narrative, chronicle procedure.

In the depiction of the way in which a dictator comes into being, he could play all the keys of his instrument—satire, irony, estrangement. This is allegedly the diary of Caesar's slave-secretary Rarus, who notes the occurrences in his master's household. Here is the valet looking at the master, not at the hero. Occasionally other sidelights on Julius Caesar are also thrown by the remarks of the bailiff, Mummlius Spicer, a frequent caller on Caesar, since the latter is often in debt. The greatness of Rome and its leaders is laid bare in the sordid manipulations that involve the vast Asian conquests and booty, the three hundred families of Rome, the generals; Cicero, Catiline—and Caesar himself, seen first at the age of thirty-eight—and finally as he is about to be elected Consul, after his "triumphal" return from Spain. In the eyes of Rarus, who notes the transactions taking place with meticulous care, the grandeur of Caesar consists in his being a model entrepreneur, one who knows the value of money and uses it with unapproachable skill. We are in a time of crisis. The Asiatic triumphs have brought wealth to the few but also innumerable slaves who compete with Roman free labor to the detriment of the latter. The threat of an uprising by Catiline and the disaffected plebeians is suppressed by a highly skilled demagogue, Cicero. The sordid manipulations of the self-styled "democrats" fix the elections neatly. Caesar's skill consists in playing off opponents against each other; he speculates, like all the others, in real estate. Of the statesmen and politicians it could be said, as it was of generals, "No piece of clothing has so many pockets as the general's cloak." In the bedlam of competitive shouts and clamors, one cry begins to be heard: We need a strong man! The unheroic Caesar will rise to the occasion. Returned from his province, Spain, he will be honored in an engineered triumph. To celebrate it, it is necessary to exhibit Spanish booty—precious articles collected by the conqueror. But Caesar has really brought back something much more valuable, coveted concessions in the Spanish lead mines. So the articles have to be manufactured in Rome. Sensing the temper of the moment, Caesar dispenses with a triumph (allegedly celebrating a victory in a war), and begins campaigning on a platform of "Democracy is Freedom" and "Peace."

Never before had Roman history been written or seen this way. Never before had Roman heroism and its conquests been analyzed quite so radically. As the bailiff Spicer says to the hypothetical editor of Rarus' notes:

[Caesar] always took money wherever he could get it. A glance at the diaries of his secretary will show you how things stood with him. . . . Do not expect to find heroic deeds in them, in the ancient style, but if you read them with an open mind, you will discover certain hints in them as to how dictatorships are built, and empires founded.[14]

IV

The Credo of a Realist

How shall the linden tree enter into a discussion with someone who reproaches him for not being an oak?

BRECHT

"I do not believe in the separability of art and instruction," Brecht wrote. Yet, he had never been misled into sacrificing the idea of the autonomy of the artist and art itself. Attacked from all sides practically all his life long—by the realists for being a formalist, by the formalists for being doctrinaire and "committed"—he always conceived of himself as a realist, and a "socialist realist" in particular.

So perceptive and profound a critic as Georg Lukács took a long time before coming to the conclusion that Brecht was, in his later works at least, or had become, the "greatest realist playwright of his time."[1] He had previously, and in no uncertain terms, rejected Brecht's dramatic theories as mostly concerned with the form of the drama and hence formalistic. He had contrasted, unfavorably for Brecht, his and Tolstoy's critiques of art, though both made their point of departure its corruption in the present society. Tolstoy, Lukács said, went to the very root of the evil—the content of modern art. Not so Brecht.[2]

Perhaps Lukács saw better than Brecht. But it is a delightful exemplification of the dialectical principle that he should have come to accept not only *Mother Courage,* but *The Good Woman of Setzuan* and *The Caucasian Chalk Circle* as well, as those works

476

which revealed Brecht's "realistic" mastery at its best, on the score that Brecht here had abandoned the "abstract" the "schematic," and was creating live human beings, with a more complex dialectic of good and evil.[3]

Brecht was never frightened of words, and the word "formalism" did not shake him. He was as much as any socialist realist opposed to "formalism," as we have seen, since it represented to him not only the separation of form from content but also the utilization of technical devices, auditory as well as visual, to conceal both the poverty and paucity of the material (he called these devices "montage") as well as the true nature of the real world. But he also said, "We see specters when we see Formalism everywhere."[4] For the worst formalists are themeslves those who shriek accusingly, "Formalism!" while they worship the old forms of art at any price and pay attention only to them. The frantic retention of old forms for new themes and tasks, isn't that also Formalism?[5]

So Brecht attacks on the one hand the clichés of the critics, as well as their tendency to adhere slavishly to old, though undeniably great, models as legislative and decisive.

The controversy was not a new one—it went back to the late thirties, when Lukács, Ernst Bloch, Alfred Kurella, and others argued the question of realism in the pages of the anti-fascist periodicals Das Wort and International Literature, which were published in Moscow.

It may be of some use to touch briefly on this and the related, but prior, controversy over "formalism" and "realism" which had such wide repercussions not only in the Socialist world, but in other parts as well. To simplify matters, let us define, for our present discussion, formalism as that procedure in art that sets the "how" a work is being done above the "what" the particular work means or has to say. In art and literature, its best known exemplars are to be found in the work of the so-called "aesthetic school." Actually, in the discussions which took place after 1934, associated with A. A. Zhdanov, the term was applied to departures

from the traditional artistic methods employed by the great writers
and artists of the nineteenth century, preponderantly Balzac and
Tolstoy. Even so brilliant and scholarly a Marxist critic as Lukács
himself, whose acquaintance with literature and philosophy was wide
indeed, insisted on regarding these realists as prescriptive criteria
for writers of the present. In that sense, he had rejected Brecht's
Massnahme and *Mother*; but had accepted *Furcht und Elend,* and
Señora Carrar—not in the least deterred by the fact that Brecht,
ironically enough, had regarded these works as well as *Galileo* as
"opportunistic" departures from his own aesthetic principles, and
almost betrayals of them.

In a beautiful essay, written in 1938, in the midst of the realistic
controversy, entitled *Weite und Vielfalt der realistischen Schreibweise (Extent and Diversity of Literary Realism),* Brecht centers
his argument on opposing the notion that a work is realistic only
in so far as it "is written in the manner of the bourgeois realistic
novel of the past century."[6] With vigor he proceeds to show that
Shelley (he quotes extensively from "The Mask of Anarchy" in
English) must be called a realist, though he utilizes symbols; yet for
all that could be most concrete in speaking of Freedom. Shelley is
superior to Balzac as a realist, for he enables one to abstract more
easily than the other; and, in addition, he was a friend and not an
enemy of the lower classes.[7] In the same way, Cervantes, Swift,
Grimmelshausen, and Voltaire are realists, each in his own way. It
is dangerous to chain the great concept of Realism to a few names,
no matter how celebrated, and to a few forms, even useful ones.
"Concerning literary forms, one must ask Reality, not Aesthetics,
even that of Realism. Truth can be concealed in many ways, and
uttered in many ways. We base our aesthetics, as we do our morality,
on the necessities of our struggles."[8]

Nor was he gentle with an altogether too vulgar interpretation
of "popular." All his life he had striven for a language, a style, and
forms that would reach the people. But he was always aware that
the "people" were not a homogeneous, monolithic mass. Different

in background, training, class influences, they required a differentiated appeal. His opposition, during the last years, to the official edicts and regulations of the state commissions had this particular element in view too.

What was it to be "popular"?

Popular means to be intelligible to the broad masses of people, taking up their forms of expression, and enriching them—adopting and strengthening their point of view—representing the most progressive section of the people in such a way that it can take over leadership—and thus also intelligible to other sections of the people—linking up with traditions, and also advancing them—and transmitting the achievements of the section now in leadership to the sections striving for leadership.[9]

And Realism?

Realistic means to uncover the causal complex in society—to unmask the dominant viewpoint as the viewpoint of the rulers—to write from the standpoint of the class which already holds the broadest solutions for the most pressing problems humanity has ever faced, emphasizing the dynamics of development—concretely—but making abstractions possible. These are gigantic assignments. . . . and we will allow the artist to apply all his imagination, all his originality, all his humor, all his inventiveness toward its fulfilment.[10]

The essence of Realism and its principal task are the depiction of reality in such a way that it is not merely seen but understood; not merely mirrored but penetrated. If art reflects life, he said elsewhere, it does so with special mirrors. "Art does not become unrealistic when it alters the proportions, but only when it alters them in such a way that the public, in applying the representations as practical guides to insights and impulses, would come to grief as a result."[11]

The end of art then is the "mastery of reality." Reality must be made perspicuous and the laws that govern the life-processes must be made visible. That is socialist realism: The truthful rendering of the social life of man from the standpoint of socialism, by means of art. A great part of the pleasure in such art lies in the recognition of the possibility of mastering human destiny through social means. Socialist realism shows characters and historical events as changeable, therefore contradictory.

What is its relation to the works of the past? How will it reproduce them? It will rest upon the assumption that such "classic" works of art have been preserved that artistically represent humanity's course toward a more kindly, more powerful, and bolder realization of its aims.

Art then is a special and original potential of man, which is neither solely veiled morality nor prettified knowledge but an independent discipline, representing in contradictory form the various other disciplines.[12]

Art must give pleasure and joy. "A theatre," Brecht said toward the end of his life, "in which one should not laugh is a theatre over which one should laugh. Humorless people are ridiculous."[13]

"There are many roads to Athens."[14] Brecht's way was only one of these, as he insisted time and again. He gradually modified his early rigidity and intolerance in the face of other dramatic ways and forms, as he also changed his attitudes toward other dramatists. Nor did he remain fixed in his insistence on the dichotomy between reason and feeling. As Lukács might have, but did not, remark, what he was looking at in the latter-day Brecht was the dialectical synthesis that had ranged from the early nihilism to the middle-period schematicism of the "Lehrstücke," to the late plays that richly combined the theory of estrangement, the dialectical principles of Marxism, and the deepened sense of individual humanity.

Though he tended to speak more kindly, in the last years, of the theatrical principles of Stanislavski, there could actually be no fundamental reconciliation between Brecht's epic theatre and Stanislavski's insistence that "in our art you must live the part every moment that you are playing it,"[15] or you "must creep into the skin and body" of the character to be portrayed or, one must employ "conscious means to the subconscious." These were two different ways of doing theatre, and each had its particular function. In so far as every theatre is theatre, it in one way or another directly or indirectly uses Stanislavski.

Brecht admitted that much could be learned from the Russian director: the sense of the poetic, responsibility toward society, ensemble acting, the "grand line," obligation to truthfulness, and to a reality depicted in its contradictions, and the recognition of importance of human beings.[16] While an official Stanislavski Conference called by the Art Commission tried hard to bring the two theatres together, a note of Brecht's shows he did not regard such a reconciliation as possible:

The Stanislavski methods of concentration remind me always of the methods of the psychoanalyst: In both instances the problem was to combat a social illness; but this was not effected through social means. The result was that the effects of the illness were attacked, but not its causes.[17]

This is no doubt one-sided and unfair. Can it be truly said that the Moscow Art Theatre's presentation of Chekhov's *The Cherry Orchard* does not unveil the social scene? Or fails to depict a society in the course of transition and change?

And can it, furthermore, be said that a spectator's "empathy" with one of Chekhov's characters effected through the actor's art necessarily means an acceptance of that character's point of view or ethical or moral standards, rather than a recognition of the complexity involved in his attitude?

Is not the crucial question really one of a *degree* of empathy which Brecht is concerned with—that point where *empathy* merges with *identification,* and the spectator takes on emotionally and psychically the attitudes and role of the character enacted on the stage, to the detriment of his over-all understanding of the forces at work within the character's world? The point, in other words, where emotional identification blurs or stultifies the intelligence and reason?

Are we not, in Stanislavski and Brecht actually dealing with two different procedures of seeing the world in a period of hectic transition: one entirely encased in a bourgeois world view—though, of course, critical of the bourgeois world; the other, no less transitional, but already advanced beyond the first, in more clearly demarcating the forces at work—those that make for the old world, and those making for the newer one? Two dramatic and theatrical procedures, not necessarily contradictory, except in themselves reflecting the contradictions of the world in which they manifest themselves? Both giving "pleasure" in their own special way?

Of his own theatre, Brecht wrote:

It is not enough to demand of our theatre that it offer understanding, and instructive reflections of reality. Our theatre must arouse delight in knowledge, and organize pleasurable convivial feelings at the changing of reality. Our spectators must not only hear how Prometheus is liberated, but must also school themselves in the joys of liberating him. Our theatres must teach all the joys and pleasures of the inventors and discoverers, the triumphant feelings of the liberators.[18]

V

The End

I, Bertolt Brecht, come from the Black Forests.

"VOM ARMEN B. B."

In 1955 Brecht's health began to give way, but his activities continued undiminished. In January, he produced a new play by Johannes Becher, *Winterschlacht,* which did not meet with a favorable reception. In May he was in Moscow to accept the Stalin Prize. He moved around a great deal, now to Dresden, for a peace congress; now to Hamburg, for a meeting of the PEN club. His duties at the Ensemble claimed his energies, particularly as it was preparing for another engagement in Paris. And on his table there were unfinished manuscripts and plans for new works.

One of these, which he almost brought to completion, was *Turandot, or the Congress of the Whitewashers,* a playful, but also sharp, variant of the comedy by Carlo Gozzi, written in 1762, which Friedrich Schiller had translated in 1801. The charming story told of the wilful daughter of the Emperor of China, whose beauty was only matched by her unwillingness to marry, and who finally agreed to test her suitors with three riddles. If they solved them, they would win her; if they failed, they would lose their heads. For Brecht this became the incentive to flay his favorite sacrificial goats, the "intellectuals" (here called *Tuis*)—those who sell their persons, their consciences, and their opinions, and whitewash authority. Here they are called in to justify the monopoly of cotton

483

in the hands of the Emperor of China and his brother, which is arousing grave disaffection in the country. The most successful Tui Whitewasher will win the Emperor's daughter. The revolutionary Kai Ho is leader of the opposition. Various complications follow, too intricate to bear retelling, but Kai Ho presumably triumphs in the end.[1] In its present unfinished form it scarcely strikes one as one of Brecht's better works.

He had also since 1940 been hatching another plan, for an opera, with music by Paul Dessau. Only a few songs were completed, but the outline, which Brecht wrote, is extremely revealing. *Die Reisen des Glückgotts (The Journeys of the God of Fortune)* was to be a sort of counterpiece to *Baal* and deal with the happiness of man. Brecht was actuated to write the piece by a "little fat figure of the Chinese god of fortune," whose pronounced embonpoint suggested ease and comfort and satisfaction.

The god is reported to have come from the East, after a great war, into the destroyed cities, and desiring to make people fight for their personal happiness and well-being. He gathers disciples of all kinds, and brings down upon himself persecutors, when some of them begin to teach that the peasants must have land, the workers must take over the factories and the workers' and peasants' children must take possession of the schools. He is convicted and condemned to death. The hangmen try their arts on the little god of fortune, but the poison they administer tastes good; his head, which they cut off, grows back again immediately; and on the gallows he executes a dance which infects with its joviality. . . . *It is impossible to kill man's yearning for happiness.*[2]

To a Darmstadt Conference on the Theatre in 1955, at which Friedrich Dürrenmatt had raised the question of whether the theatre of today was capable of representing the world today, Brecht contributed a brief essay. Yes, he said, "the world today is describable to man today only when it is described as a changeable world." In an age, he continued, in which science has done wonders to change nature, so that the world seems almost habitable, man can no longer be described as a victim, the object of an unknown, but fixed universe. From the standpoint of a football, the laws of motions are scarcely conceivable. It is because the nature of human society has been kept in the dark, in contrast to Nature in general, that we today stand, as the shocked scientists are assuring us, before the total destructibility of the scarcely habitable planet. He called attention to his Ensemble in Berlin, where theatrical attempts were being made to make the theatre responsive to the world situations; as well as the state in which he was working, where efforts were being made to change the world and the social life of man.[3]

Max Frisch, more than ever a profound admirer, saw him in 1955, and found him weak, though fully alert, but less inclined to argue. Gracious as ever, he did not, as was his custom, accompany his guest out. Brecht had asked about the feasibility of buying a house on Lake Geneva.[4]

He came into conflict with the authorities once more when toward the end of 1955 he was refused publication of his *Kriegsfibel (The ABC of War)* a series of short poems, illustrated with photographs, and dealing with various aspects of the Second World War. Brecht called these "photograms." Grimly epigrammatic, filled with a mordant pacifism, and bitter against war and warmongers, these are among the best satirical quatrains Brecht ever wrote. Brecht insisted on publication and threatened to offer the book to the World Peace Council. He won out and the book appeared at the end of 1955, with the Eulenspiegel Verlag, Berlin.

On his last birthday, February 10, 1956, he was in Milan to attend the performances of *The Three Penny Opera,* which Giorgio Strehler was staging for the Piccolo Teatro. It was there that the Swedish director Erwin Leiser spoke with him for the last time.

The snowstorm rattles against the window panes of the Hotel Manin. We joke somewhat hesitatingly about our common—my own only slight—heart ailments. Suddenly his voice becomes muffled, and he says, "At any rate, one can be sure that it will be an easy death—a gentle knocking on the window panes."[5]

They joked about the "chairs" again. Brecht had said he was sitting not between two chairs, but firmly on one, that was in the East.

Brecht humorously remarked at another time that the chair was shaky; it probably stood on only three legs.

During the last conversation I had with him, [Leiser reported] he said: "The chair stands firmly. Only there are some who think one shouldn't sit on it the way I do."[6]

Apropos of the new Italian production of *The Three Penny Opera* (generally acknowledged a brilliant one), Brecht stated:

Ten years after the First World War came my *Three Penny Opera*. Ten years after the Second World War it lives again in a new witches' cauldron. If it comes back again after a third world war, the whole world won't be worth three pennies.[7]

The year promised, as always, to be a busy one. There was the staging of *Galileo,* which had begun the year before; there was *The Days of the Commune* which was awaiting production in the Karl-Marx Stadt under the direction of Manfred Wekwerth. There was the first visit of the Ensemble to England in August.

On his desk lay innumerable plans, projects, sketches, folders full of notes, aphorisms, collections,—some almost complete save for revisions. He had finished an acting version that blended two of Gerhart Hauptmann's plays, *The Beaver Coat* and *The Red Rooster*. His unquenchable interest in science and the scientist had not been sated with Galileo. He was projecting a play about Prometheus, with the atom bomb in mind. Prometheus was to be turned topsy-turvy: it was not those up above that had chained Prometheus, but those below on earth, because he had dared surrender fire to the gods, with which they could destroy the world.[8]

More even than Prometheus, it was Albert Einstein who fascinated him and in whose life he saw a possible source for a sequel to *Galileo,* especially after the great scientist's death on April 18, 1955. There are reasons to believe that Brecht conceived of Einstein as a "tragic" character in delivering his knowledge over to an aggressive imperialism represented by the U.S.A. In preparation, Brecht had read an enormous number of books about Einstein, and had en-

gaged in scientific conversations about him and his theories with
one of Einstein's former colleagues, Leopold Infeld.[9]

Brecht's annotations to Samuel Beckett's *Waiting for Godot*
indicate more than a passing interest—perhaps an intention to write
a counter-play.[10]

Not least important of his unrevised writings was *Me-Ti: Buch
der Wendungen (The Book of Changes)* modeled on the great
Chinese classic of the same name. This is Brecht's philosophical,
political and ethical "breviary"—or as he loved to call it a "little
book of instructions in social attitudes." It had been begun in the
early years of exile and continued thereafter intermittently. It was
issued ten years after his death, and then only in part, and is a
personal journal of sorts. Pseudo-Chinese anagrams in abbreviated
form stand for proper names: Min-en-leh for Lenin, Ni-en for
Stalin, Meister Hü-Jeh for Hegel, Ka-meh for Karl Marx, Eh-Fu for
Engels, and Kin-jeh for Brecht himself (it is our old friend Keuner
again). Here he argues once more with Karl Korsch on the subject
of freedom in the USSR and with himself about the Stalin-Trot-
sky rift. On that subject he is, as we have already seen, divided. He
has reservations about the cult of personality; the sacrifices demanded in the haste to industrialize and collectivize agriculture; the
procedures in the trials; though he seems to have little doubt about
the criminality of some of those accused. But he gives credit to
Stalin for his achievements in building the Soviet state. The more
personal note is not absent, though in the published volume sparse:
his deep attachment to Steffin. But the general tone of these notes,
though not free of a typical Brechtian skepticism, is one of strength,
optimism, and confidence in the future. Here he identifies himself
with the "classics"—Marx, Engels, and Lenin—who worked under
similar conditions of upheaval and confusion, but who never
abandoned hopes for the future, though, as he put it, they lived
"in the darkest and bloodiest of times." He admires their "serenity
and confidence."[11]

Up to the very end of his life he was involved with the new staging of *Galileo*. He was full of fresh ideas, and was studying the paint-ings of Breughel for color, arrangements, and costumes. He was extemporizing and improvising. Already more than half a hundred rehearsals! Ernst Busch, the prospective Galileo, and Ekkard Schall, the Andrea Sarti, teased him about the length of prepara-tions. Would it take six years or seven? Busch asked. Brecht said, "If it doesn't work, we'll need seven. You are an impatient fellow, Busch, and you want to do it in six."[12]

He attended rehearsals until March, when he was ill again. He returned to the theatre four days before his death, bringing with him a new "proclamation" of the "new age," of which Galileo had been both prophet and betrayer.

In the spring of 1956 he was confined to the Charité Hospital with a serious virus attack. In August, in his country home in Buckow, he was visited by Manfred Wekwerth, who came to dis-cuss the production of *The Days of the Commune*. Wekwerth found him as lively, original, and brilliant as ever. For the antici-pated London visit of the Berliner Ensemble Brecht had prepared a brief directive to the company, urging them to remember that the English audience would not understand German, and therefore to make their playing "quick, light, and strong," but always the result of "quick thinking." The English, he thought, had a way of imagining that Germans and German drama were heavy. The memorandum is dated August 5.

The West Berlin Dramaturg Claus Hubalek visited him toward the middle of 1956 at Brecht's Chausseestrasse home, and asked him how he felt at being so close to the Dorotheen Cemetery. "One gets used to it," Brecht said. "You don't have to get used to it, Herr Brecht. You won't get there, you know. It's no longer in use." Brecht reassured him. "You've got to have connections," he said.[13]

On August 10, he was at his theatre for the last time. Three days later he fell critically ill. He died of a coronary thrombosis on August 14, 1956. His friend of Augsburg days, Dr. H. O. Münsterer, signed the death certificate.

A year before, in anticipation of his death, he had addressed a memorandum to the Academy of Arts:

In the event of my death, I would not like to lie in state anywhere, or be publicly exhibited. At my grave, let there be no speeches. I would like to be buried in the cemetery close to my home, in the Chaussee-strasse.

In accordance with his wishes, his stone bears the simple inscription: *Brecht.* Nothing else. It stands in the Dorotheen Cemetery, and faces the grave of his philosopher-idol, Hegel. Nearby lies his companion and collaborator of many years, Hanns Eisler.

Before his death, Brecht had written:

> I need no tombstone, but
> If you must make one for me,
> I would wish it inscribed:
> "He made proposals. We
> Followed them."
> Through such an inscription
> All would be honored.

Epilogue

Mensch sein ist eine grosse Sache. Das Leben
wird für zu kurz gelten.

To be a man is a great thing. Life will be
deemed too brief.

BRECHT

M'inhumaniser est ma tendance profonde.

My profound tendency is to dehumanize
myself.

JEAN GENÊT

Bertolt Brecht has been dead since 1956, yet today the world is
more aware of him than it was during his lifetime. His plays appear
in the repertories of hundreds of theatres, from Tokyo to Milan,
from San Francisco to Moscow. In German-speaking lands (whether
East or West) he ranks immediately after Shakespeare, Goethe, and
Schiller in the number of representations, exceeding a thousand
each season. In the Socialist countries he has served as a powerful
fermenting agent, and more recently, in the Soviet Union, he has
helped break down an atrophied and narrow aesthetic and reinvig-
orate the theatres there, once noted for their pre-eminence.

But he remains a subject of debate and controversy, and the object of encomia and objurgation. Wherever he is today, he must be
looking with that amused smile of his on the contradictions which

490

he has loosed. For he was himself a fervent believer in contradictions, and he never concealed them whether they appeared within himself, or within that world he was subjecting to his dialectical analysis.

Had he not shown in his own history how a nihilistic individualism could turn into social responsibility? Had he not in himself exhibited the confirmation of his unshaken belief that "in contradictions lies our hope"? And in change?

Yet he was himself unchangeable in many respects: In his friendliness and friendships. If, as we believe, the test of the true man is the attachment to and of friends, Brecht emerges as such. Few artists had the power to bind and keep friends, such as Brecht possessed. They remained with him from his earliest days in Augsburg to the moment of his death. There is no better criterion of character.

Of course, he made many enemies. How could he have helped that? He believed strongly and made no secret of those beliefs. He affronted by his directness—he who was, according to report, the most courteous of men.

Often he was not pleasant to be with. He was not always fastidious about his appearance. And he smoked incessantly. Cigars. But there was scarcely a moment when he was not provocative.

About himself and his own life and feelings, he was reserved. Perhaps too much so. Perhaps he drew too sharp a line between feeling and thought—between heart and head, to the disadvantage of the former.

But there is no doubt he left enough contradiction and ambiguity to batten the purses and intellects of a whole generation of critics and playwrights. Günther Grass has recently "canonized" him— left-handedly—as the failed and "lost" leader of the uprising of 1953. Friedrich Dürrenmatt has set him alongside of Friedrich Schiller as a sort of conscience and tribunal of modern man. An Evangelical Congress at Dortmund devoted a whole session to a discussion of "Brecht and Christianity" in 1963. Max Frisch already speaks of him as a "classic"—a fate Brecht always dreaded. Reviewing the first volume containing Brecht's early plays, Frisch is led to remark with wonder and admiration on the numerous germinal and revolutionary innovations to be found in them. Where, he asks, would Thornton Wilder have been without Brecht? Had not Brecht, long before T. S. Eliot, drastically transformed the language and the very nature of the modern poetic drama? Had he not already in the twenties of this century anticipated and pointed to the crisis of modern opera?

Brecht has an honorable list of debtors: W. H. Auden, Stephen Spender, Marc Blitzstein, Tennessee Williams, Robert Bolt, John Osborne, Max Frisch, Dürrenmatt, Peter Weiss, Arthur Adamov, Jean-Paul Sartre.

His relevance to our time is more than confirmed by the conscious opposition he arouses. Arrayed against him there is a formidable army of very gifted writers and thinkers, united in one major respect: They are laureates of doom. The landscape they see stretching before them from their little corners is the bleak landscape of despair and disaster. Their festooned poetry and prose cannot hide the emptiness within them.

What can Brecht offer against them or to them? Can his ethos of "Freundlichkeit"—"Kindliness"—win over, say, Atonin Artaud's "alchemical" and plague-inspired theatre of "cruelty"? Can Brecht's advocacy of reason and intelligence counterpoise the liturgies of the brothel and the litanies of self-castration and illusion promulgated by Jean Genêt? Or Eugene Ionesco's "existential vacuum" and his pyrotechnic and necrophilic world of absurdity? Or bring relief to the heartbreak of Samuel Beckett and his last sacraments administered to a crippled and blinded humanity? A humanity living in figurative dustbins and refuse heaps, hopeless relicts of our aborted civilization?

Brecht is not of their company. A realist and a humanist Socialist, he ranges himself on the side of those who see "possibilities" within humanity, rather than only their impotence.

To the generation of today, rousing itself from the torpor and inertia born of the intellectual repressions of recent years, facing threats of extinction made the more vivid through Brecht's *Galileo* and *Mother Courage*—aware of unprecedented terrors as well as unprecedented possibilities that lie within their reach; aware also with *Mann ist Mann* of how man may be made into an automaton that slays and butchers; aware, however, with Shen-Te and Grusha, of capacities for goodness and change—it is to a generation like this that Brecht addresses himself most forcefully. Not to the grave-diggers of mankind.

It is to this generation that Brecht is speaking of a vision—to paraphrase Hegel—that must be translated from a night of possibility into the day of reality.

APPENDIX

APPENDIX

MR. STRIPLING. Mr. Brecht, will you please state your full name and present address for the record, please? Speak into the microphone.

MR. BRECHT. My name is Berthold Brecht. I am living at 34 West Seventy-third Street, New York. I was born in Augsburg, Germany, February 10, 1898.

MR. STRIPLING. Mr. Brecht, the committee has a—

THE CHAIRMAN. What was that date again?

MR. STRIPLING. Would you give the date again?

MR. BRECHT. Tenth of February 1898.

MR. MCDOWELL. 1898?

MR. BRECHT. 1898.

MR. STRIPLING. Mr. Chairman, the committee has here an interpreter, if you desire the use of an interpreter.

MR. CRUM. Would you like an interpreter?

THE CHAIRMAN. Do you desire an interpreter?

MR. BRECHT. Yes.

THE CHAIRMAN. Mr. Interpreter, will you stand and raise your right hand, please?

Mr. Interpreter, do you solemnly swear you will diligently and correctly translate from English into German all questions which may be propounded to this witness and as diligently and correctly translate from German into English all answers made by him, so help you God?

MR. BAUMGARDT. I do.

THE CHAIRMAN. Sit down.

(Mr. David Baumgardt was seated beside the witness as interpreter.)

MR. STRIPLING. Now, Mr. Brecht, will you state to the committee whether or not you are a citizen of the United States?

MR. BRECHT. I am not a citizen of the United States; I have only my first papers.

MR. STRIPLING. When did you acquire your first papers?

MR. BRECHT. In 1941 when I came to the country.

MR. STRIPLING. When did you arrive in the United States?

MR. BRECHT. May I find out exactly? I arrived July 21 at San Pedro.

MR. STRIPLING. July 21, 1941?

MR. BRECHT. That is right.

MR. STRIPLING. At San Pedro, California?

MR. BRECHT. Yes.

MR. STRIPLING. You were born in Augsburg, Bavaria, Germany, on February 10, 1888; is that correct?

MR. BRECHT. Yes.

MR. STRIPLING. I am reading from the immigration records——

MR. CRUM. I think, Mr. Stripling, it was 1898.

MR. BRECHT. 1898.

MR. STRIPLING. I beg your pardon.

MR. CRUM. I think the witness tried to say 1898.

MR. STRIPLING. I want to know whether the immigration records are correct on that. Is it '88 or '98?

MR. BRECHT. '98.

MR. STRIPLING. Were you issued a quota immigration visa by the American vice consul on May 3, 1941, at Helsinki, Finland?

MR. BRECHT. That is correct.

MR. STRIPLING. And you entered this country on that visa?

MR. BRECHT. Yes.

MR. STRIPLING. Where had you resided prior to going to Helsinki, Finland?

MR. BRECHT. May I read my statement? In that statement——

THE CHAIRMAN. First, Mr. Brecht, we are trying to identify you. The identification won't be very long.

MR. BRECHT. I had to leave Germany in 1933, in February, when Hitler took power. Then I went to Denmark but when war seemed imminent in '39 I had to leave for Sweden, Stockholm. I remained there for one year and then Hitler invaded Norway and Denmark and I had to leave Sweden and I went to Finland, there to wait for my visa for the United States.

MR. STRIPLING. Now, Mr. Brecht, what is your occupation?

MR. BRECHT. I am a playwright and a poet.

MR. STRIPLING. A playwright and a poet?

MR. BRECHT. Yes.

MR. STRIPLING. Where are you presently employed?

MR. BRECHT. I am not employed.

MR. STRIPLING. Were you ever employed in the motion-picture industry?

MR. BRECHT. Yes; I—yes. I sold a story to a Hollywood firm, "Hangmen Also Die," but I did not write the screenplay myself. I am not a professional screenplay writer. I wrote another story for a Hollywood firm but that story was not produced.

MR. STRIPLING. "Hangmen Also Die"—whom did you sell to, what studio?

MR. BRECHT. That was to, I think, an independent firm, Pressburger at United Artists.

MR. STRIPLING. United Artists?

MR. BRECHT. Yes.

MR. STRIPLING. When did you sell the play to United Artists?

MR. BRECHT. The story—I don't remember exactly, maybe around '43 or '44; I don't remember, quite.

MR. STRIPLING. And what other studios have you sold material to?

MR. BRECHT. No other studio. Besides the last story I spoke of I wrote for Enterprise Studios.

MR. STRIPLING. Are you familiar with Hanns Eisler? Do you know Johannes Eisler?

MR. BRECHT. Yes.

MR. STRIPLING. How long have you known Johannes Eisler?

MR. BRECHT. I think since the middle of the Twenties, twenty years or so.

MR. STRIPLING. Have you collaborated with him on a number of works?

MR. BRECHT. Yes.

MR. STRIPLING. Mr. Brecht, are you a member of the Communist Party or have you ever been a member of the Communist Party?

MR. BRECHT. May I read my statement? I will answer this question but may I read my statement?

MR. STRIPLING. Would you submit your statement to the chairman?

MR. BRECHT. Yes.

THE CHAIRMAN. All right, let's see the statement.

(Mr. Brecht hands the statement to the chairman.)

THE CHAIRMAN. Mr. Brecht, the committee has carefully gone over the statement. It is a very interesting story of German life but it is not at all pertinent to this inquiry. Therefore, we do not care to have you read the statement.

Mr. Stripling.

MR. STRIPLING. Mr. Brecht, before we go on with the questions, I would like to put into the record the subpoena which was served upon you on September 19, calling for your appearance before the committee. You are here in response to a subpoena, are you not?

MR. BRECHT. Yes.

MR. STRIPLING. Now, I will repeat the original question. Are you now or have you ever been a member of the Communist Party of any country?

MR. BRECHT. Mr. Chairman, I have heard my colleagues when they considered this question not as proper, but I am a guest in this country and do not want to enter into any legal arguments, so I will answer your question fully as well I can.

I was not a member or am not a member of any Communist Party.

THE CHAIRMAN. Your answer is, then, that you have never been a member of the Communist Party?

MR. BRECHT. That is correct.

MR. STRIPLING. You were not a member of the Communist Party in Germany?

MR. BRECHT. No; I was not.

MR. STRIPLING. Mr. Brecht, is it true that you have written a number of very revolutionary poems, plays, and other writings?

MR. BRECHT. I have written a number of poems and songs and plays in the fight against Hitler and, of course, they can be considered, therefore, as revolutionary because I, of course, was for the overthrow of that government.

THE CHAIRMAN. Mr. Stripling, we are not interested in any works that he might have written advocating the overthrow of Germany or the government there.

MR. STRIPLING. Yes; I understand.

Well, from an examination of the works which Mr. Brecht has written, particularly in collaboration with Mr. Hanns Eisler, he seems to be a person of international importance to the Communist revolutionary movement.

Now, Mr. Brecht, is it true or do you know whether or not you have written articles which have appeared in publications in the Soviet zone of Germany within the past few months?

MR. BRECHT. No; I do not remember to have written such articles. I have not seen any of them printed. I have not written any such articles just now. I write very few articles, if any.

MR. STRIPLING. I have here, Mr. Chairman, a document which I will hand to the translator and ask him to identify it for the committee and to refer to an article which refers on page 72.

MR. BRECHT. May I speak to that publication?

MR. STRIPLING. I beg your pardon?

MR. BRECHT. May I explain this publication?

MR. STRIPLING. Yes. Will you identify the publication?

MR. BRECHT. Oh, yes. That is not an article, that is a scene out of a play I wrote in, I think, 1937 or 1938 in Denmark. The play is called *The Private Life of the Master Race,* and this scene is one of the scenes out of this play about a Jewish woman in Berlin in the year of '36 or '37. It was, I see, printed in this magazine *Ost und West,* July 1946.

MR. STRIPLING. Mr. Translator, would you translate the frontispiece of the magazine, please?

MR. BAUMGARDT. "East and West, Contributions to Cultural and Political Questions of the Time, edited by Alfred Kantorowicz, Berlin, July 1947, first year of publication enterprise."

MR. STRIPLING. Mr. Brecht, do you know the gentleman who is the editor of the publication whose name was just read?

MR. BRECHT. Yes; I know him from Berlin and I met him in New York again.

MR. STRIPLING. Do you know him to be a member of the Communist Party of Germany?

MR. BRECHT. When I met him in Germany I think he was a journalist on the Ullstein Press. That is not a Communist—was not a Communist —there were no Communist Party papers so I do not know exactly whether he was a member of the Communist Party of Germany.

MR. STRIPLING. You don't know whether he was a member of the Communist Party or not?

MR. BRECHT. I don't know, no; I don't know.

MR. STRIPLING. In 1930 did you, with Hanns Eisler, write a play entitled, *Die Massnahme* [*The Measures Taken*]?

MR. BRECHT. *Die Massnahme.*

MR. STRIPLING. Did you write such a play?

MR. BRECHT. Yes; yes.

MR. STRIPLING. Would you explain to the committee the theme of that play—what is dealt with?

MR. BRECHT. Yes; I will try to.

MR. STRIPLING. First, explain what the title means.

MR. BRECHT. "Die Massnahme" means [speaking in German].

MR. BAUMGARDT. Measures to be taken, or steps to be taken—measures.

MR. STRIPLING. Could it mean disciplinary measures?

MR. BAUMGARDT. No; not disciplinary measures; no. It means measures to be taken.

MR. MCDOWELL. Speak into the microphone.

MR. BAUMGARDT. It means only measures or steps to be taken.

MR. STRIPLING. All right.

You tell the committee now, Mr. Brecht—

MR. BRECHT. Yes.

MR. STRIPLING (continuing). What this play dealt with.

MR. BRECHT. Yes. This play is the adaptation of an old religious Japanese play and is called No Play, and follows quite closely this old story which shows the devotion for an ideal until death.

MR. STRIPLING. What was that ideal, Mr. Breecht?

MR. BRECHT. The idea in the old play was a religious idea. This young people——

MR. STRIPLING. Didn't it have to do with the Communist Party?

MR. BRECHT. Yes.

MR. STRIPLING. And discipline within the Communist Party?

MR. BRECHT. Yes, yes; it is a new play, an adaptation. It had as a background the Russia-China of the years 1918 or 1919, or so. There some Communist agitators went to a sort of no man's land between the Russia which then was not a state and had no real——

MR. STRIPLING. Mr. Brecht, may I interrupt you? Would you consider the play to be pro-Communist or anti-Communist, or would it take a neutral position regarding Communists?

MR. BRECHT. No; I would say—you see, literature has the right and the duty to give to the public the ideas of the time. Now, in this play— of course, I wrote about twenty plays, but in this play I tried to express the feelings and the ideas of the German workers who then fought against Hitler. I also formulated in an artistic——

MR. STRIPLING. Fighting against Hitler, did you say?

MR. BRECHT. Yes.

MR. STRIPLING. Written in 1930?

MR. BRECHT. Yes, yes; oh, yes. That fight started in 1923.

MR. STRIPLING. You say it is about China, though; it has nothing to do with Germany?

MR. BRECHT. No, it had nothing to do about it.

MR. STRIPLING. Let me read this to you.

MR. BRECHT. Yes.

MR. STRIPLING. Throughout the play reference is made to the theories and teachings of Lenin, the A, B, C of communism and other Communist classics, and the activities of the Chinese Communist Party in general. The following are excerpts from the play:

The Four Agitators: We came from Moscow as agitators; we were to travel to the city of Mukden to start propaganda and to create, in the factories, the Chinese Party. We were to report to party headquarters closest to the border and to requisition a guide. There, in the anteroom, a young comrade came toward us and spoke of the nature of our mission. We are repeating the conversation.

The Young Comrade: I am the secretary of the party headquarters which is the last toward the border. My heart is beating for the revolution. The witnessing of wrongdoing drove me into the lines of the fighters. Man must help man. I am for freedom. I believe in mankind. And I am for the rules of the Communist Party which fights for the classless society against exploitation and ignorance. . . .

Now, Mr. Brecht, will you tell the committee whether or not one of the characters in this play was murdered by his comrade because it was in the best interest of the party, of the Communist Party; is that true?

MR. BRECHT. No, it is not quite according to the story.

MR. STRIPLING. Because he would not bow to discipline he was murdered by his comrades, isn't that true?

MR. BRECHT. No; it is not really in it. You will find when you read it carefully, like in the old Japanese play where other ideas were at stake, this young man who died was convinced that he had done damage to the mission he believed in and he agreed to that and he was about ready to die in order not to make greater such damage. So, he asks his comrades to help him, and all of them together help him to die. He jumps into an abyss and they lead him tenderly to that abyss, and that is the story.

THE CHAIRMAN. I gather from your remarks, from your answer, that he was just killed, he was not murdered?

MR. BRECHT. He wanted to die.

THE CHAIRMAN. So they killed him?

MR. BRECHT. No; they did not kill him—not in this story. He killed himself. They supported him, but of course they had told him it were better when he disappeared, for him and them and the cause he also believed in.

MR. STRIPLING. Mr. Brecht, could you tell the committee how many times you have been to Moscow?

MR. BRECHT. Yes. I was invited to Moscow two times.

MR. STRIPLING. Who invited you?

MR. BRECHT. The first time I was invited by the Voks Organization for Cultural Exchange. I was invited to show a picture, a documentary picture I had helped to make in Berlin.

MR. STRIPLING. What was the name of that picture?

MR. BRECHT. The name—it is the name of a suburb of Berlin, Kuhle Wampe.

MR. STRIPLING. While you were in Moscow, did you meet Sergi Tretyakov—S-e-r-g-i T-r-e-t-y-a-k-o-v; Tretyakov?

MR. BRECHT. Tretyakov; yes. That is a Russian playwright.

MR. STRIPLING. A writer?

MR. BRECHT. Yes. He translated some of my poems and, I think one
play.

MR. STRIPLING. Mr. Chairman, *International Literature,* No. 5, 1937,
published by the State Literary Art Publishing House in Moscow had an
article by Sergi Tretyakov, leading Soviet writer, on an interview he had
with Mr. Brecht. On page 60, it states—he is quoting Mr. Brecht—

"I was a member of the Augsburg Revolutionary Committee," Brecht continued. "Nearby, in Munich, Leviné raised the banner of Soviet power.
Augsburg lived in the reflected glow of Munich. The hospital was the only
military unit in the town. It elected me to the revolutionary committee. I
still remember Georg Brem and the Polish Bolshevik Olshevsky. We did not
boast a single Red guardsman. We didn't have time to issue a single decree
or nationalize a single bank or close a church. In two days General Epp's
troops came to town on their way to Munich. One of the members of the
revolutionary committee hid at my house until he managed to escape."

He wrote *Drums in the Night.* This work contained echoes of the revolution. The drums of revolt persistently summon the man who has gone home.
But the man prefers [the] quiet peace of his hearthside.

The work was a scathing satire on those who had deserted the revolution
and toasted themselves at their fireplaces. One should recall that Kapp
launched his drive on Christmas Eve, calculating that many Red guardsmen
would have left their detachments for the family Christmas trees.

His play *Die Massnahme,* the first of Brecht's plays on a Communist theme,
is arranged like a court where the characters try to justify themselves for
having killed a comrade, and judges, who at the same time represent the
audience, summarize the events, and reach a verdict.

When he visited in Moscow in 1932, Brecht told me his plan to organize a
theater in Berlin which would re-enact the most interesting court trials in the
history of mankind.

Brecht conceived the idea of writing a play about the terrorist tricks resorted
to by the landowners in order to peg the price of grain. But this requires a
knowledge of economics. The study of economics brought Brecht to Marx
and Lenin, whose works became an invaluable part of his library.

Brecht studies and quotes Lenin as a great thinker and as a great master
of prose.

The traditional drama portrays the struggle of class instincts. Brecht demands
that the struggle of class instincts be replaced by the struggle of social consciousness, of social convictions. He maintains that the situation must not only

be felt, but explained—crystallized into the idea which will overturn the world.

Do you recall that interview, Mr. Brecht?

MR. BRECHT. No. [Laughter.] It must have been written twenty years ago or so.

MR. STRIPLING. I will show you the magazine, Mr. Brecht.

MR. BRECHT. Yes. I do not recall there was an interview. [Book handed to the witness.] I do not recall—Mr. Stripling, I do not recall the interview in exact. I think it is a more or less journalistic summary of talks or discussions about many things.

MR. STRIPLING. Yes. Have many of your writings been based upon the philosophy of Lenin and Marx?

MR. BRECHT. No; I don't think that is quite correct but, of course, I studied, had to study as a playwright who wrote historical plays. I, of course, had to study Marx's ideas about history. I do not think intelligent plays today can be written without such study. Also, history now written now is vitally influenced by the studies of Marx about history.

• • •

MR. STRIPLING. Are you familiar with the magazine *New Masses*?

MR. BRECHT. No.

MR. STRIPLING. You never heard of it?

MR. BRECHT. Yes; of course.

MR. STRIPLING. Did you ever contribute anything to it?

MR. BRECHT. No.

MR. STRIPLING. Did they ever publish any of your work?

MR. BRECHT. That I do not know. They might have published some translation of a poem, but I had no direct connection with it, nor did I send them anything.

MR. STRIPLING. Did you collaborate with Hanns Eisler on the song "In Praise of Learning"?

MR. BRECHT. Yes; I collaborated. I wrote that song and he only wrote the music.

MR. STRIPLING. You wrote the song?

MR. BRECHT. I wrote the song.

MR. STRIPLING. Would you recite to the committee the words of that song?

MR. BRECHT. Yes; I would. May I point out that song comes from another adaptation I made of Gorky's play, *Mother.* In this song a Russian worker woman addresses all the poor people.

MR. STRIPLING. It was produced in this country, wasn't it?

MR. BRECHT. Yes. '35, New York.

MR. STRIPLING. Now, I will read the words and ask you if this is the one.

MR. BRECHT. Please.

MR. STRIPLING. (reading):

Learn now the simple truth, you for whom the time has come at last; it is not too late.

Learn now the ABC. It is not enough but learn it still.

Fear not, be not downhearted. Again you must learn the lesson, you must be ready to take over—

MR. BRECHT. No, excuse me, that is the wrong translation. That is not right. [Laughter.] Just one second, and I will give you the correct text.

MR. STRIPLING. That is not a correct translation?

MR. BRECHT. That is not correct, no; that is not the meaning. It is not very beautiful, but I am not speaking about that.

MR. STRIPLING. What does it mean? I have here a portion of *The People,* which was issued by the Communist Party of the United States, published by the Workers' Library Publishers. Page 24 says:

In praise of learning, by Bert Brecht; music by Hanns Èisler.

It says here:

You must be ready to take over; learn it.

Men on the dole, learn it; men in the prisons, learn it; women in the kitchen, learn it; men of sixty-five, learn it. You must be ready to take over—

and goes right on through. That is the core of it—

You must be ready to take over.

MR. BRECHT. Mr. Stripling, maybe his translation——

MR. BAUMGARDT. The correct translation would be, "You must take the lead."

THE CHAIRMAN. "You must take the lead"?

MR. BAUMGARDT. "The lead." It definitely says, "The lead." It is not "You must take over." The translation is not a literal translation of the German.

MR. STRIPLING. Well, Mr. Brecht, as it has been published in these publications of the Communist Party, then, if that is incorrect, what did you mean?

MR. BRECHT. I don't remember never—I never got that book myself. I must not have been in the country when it was published. I think it was published as a song, one of the songs Eisler had written the music to. I did not give any permission to publish it. I don't see—I think I never saw the translation.

MR. STRIPLING. Do you have the words there before you?

MR. BRECHT. In German, yes.

MR. STRIPLING. Of the song?

MR. BRECHT. Oh, yes; in the book.

MR. STRIPLING. Not in the original.

MR. BRECHT. In the German book.

MR. STRIPLING. It goes on:

You must be ready to take over; you must be ready to take over. Don't hesitate to ask questions, stay in there. Don't hesitate to ask questions, comrade—

MR. BRECHT. Why not let him translate from the German, word for word?

MR. BAUMGARDT. I think you are mainly interested in this translation which comes from——

THE CHAIRMAN. I cannot understand the interpreter any more than I can the witness.

MR. BAUMGARDT. Mr. Chairman, I apologize. I shall make use of this.

THE CHAIRMAN. Just speak in that microphone and maybe we can make out.

MR. BAUMGARDT. The last line of all three verses is correctly to be translated: "You must take over the lead," and not "You must take over." "You must take the lead," would be the best, most correct, most accurate translation.

MR. STRIPLING. Mr. Brecht, did you ever make application to join the Communist Party?

MR. BRECHT. I do not understand the question. Did I make——

MR. STRIPLING. Have you ever made application to join the Communist Party?

MR. BRECHT. No, no, no, no, no, never.

MR. STRIPLING. Mr. Chairman, we have here——

MR. BRECHT. I was an independent writer and wanted to be an independent writer and I point that out and also theoretically, I think, it was the best for me not to join any party whatever. And all these things you read here were not only written for the German Communists, but they were also written for workers of any other kind; Social Democrat workers were in these performances; so were Catholic workers from Catholic unions, so were workers which never had been in a party or didn't want to go into a party.

THE CHAIRMAN. Mr. Brecht, did Gerhart Eisler ever ask you to join the Communist Party?

MR. BRECHT. No, no.

THE CHAIRMAN. Did Hanns Eisler ever ask you to join the Communist Party?

MR. BRECHT. No; he did not. I think they considered me just as a writer who wanted to write and do as he saw it, but not as a political figure.

THE CHAIRMAN. Do you recall anyone ever having asked you to join the Communist Party?

MR. BRECHT. Some people might have suggested it to me, but then I found out that it was not my business.

THE CHAIRMAN. Who were those people who asked you to join the Communist Party?

MR. BRECHT. Oh, readers.

THE CHAIRMAN. Who?

MR. BRECHT. Readers of my poems or people from the audiences. You mean—there was never an official approach to me to publish——

THE CHAIRMAN. Some people did ask you to join the Communist Party.

MR. KENNY. In Germany. [Aside to witness.]

MR. BRECHT. In Germany, you mean in Germany?

THE CHAIRMAN. No; I mean in the United States.

MR. BRECHT. No, no, no.

THE CHAIRMAN. He is doing all right. He is doing much better than many other witnesses you have brought here.

Do you recall whether anyone in the United States ever asked you to join the Communist Party?

MR. BRECHT. No; I don't.

THE CHAIRMAN. Mr. McDowell, do you have any questions?

MR. MCDOWELL. No; no questions.

THE CHAIRMAN. Mr Vail?

MR. VAIL. No questions.

THE CHAIRMAN. Mr. Stripling, do you have any more questions?

MR. STRIPLING. I would like to ask Mr. Brecht whether or not he wrote a poem, a song, rather, entitled, "Forward, We've Not Forgotten."

MR. MCDOWELL. "Forward," what?

MR. STRIPLING. "Forward, We've Not Forgotten."

MR. BRECHT. I can't think of that. The English title may be the reason.

MR. STRIPLING. Would you translate it for him into German?

(Mr. Baumgardt translates into German.)

MR. BRECHT. Oh, now I know; yes.

MR. STRIPLING. You are familiar with the words to that?

MR. BRECHT. Yes.

MR. STRIPLING. Would the committee like me to read that?

THE CHAIRMAN. Yes; without objection, go ahead.

MR. STRIPLING (reading):

Forward, we've not forgotten our strength in the fights we've won;
No matter what may threaten, forward, not forgotten how strong we are
as one;
Only these our hands now acting, built the road, the walls, the towers.
All the world is of our making.
What of it can we call ours?

The refrain:

Forward. March on to the tower, through the city, by land the world;
Forward. Advance it on. Just whose city is the city? Just whose world is
the world?
Forward, we've not forgotten our union in hunger and pain, no matter what
may threaten, forward, we've not forgotten.
We have a world to gain. We shall free the world of shadow; every shop
and every room, every road and every meadow.
All the world will be our own.

Did you write that, Mr. Brecht?

MR. BRECHT. No. I wrote a German poem, but that is very different
from this. [Laughter.]

MR. STRIPLING. That is all the questions I have, Mr. Chairman.

THE CHAIRMAN. Thank you very much, Mr. Brecht. You are a good
example to the witnesses of Mr. Kenny and Mr. Crum.

We will recess until two o'clock this afternoon.

(Whereupon, at 12:15 P.M., a recess was taken until 2 P.M. of the
same day.)

NOTES

NOTES

Notes

LIST OF ABBREVIATIONS

Archiv Mappe
Portfolios or Files of materials in the Brecht Archives. Thus, Archiv Mappe 132/16 means File 132, page or sheet 16.

Gedichte
Brecht's Poems, 9 volumes.

Prosa
Brecht's Miscellaneous Prose Works, 6 volumes.

Stücke
Brecht's Dramatic Works, 13 volumes.

Schriften
Brecht's Writings on the Theatre, 7 volumes.

Versuche
Brecht's Writings published in pamphlet form, 15 issues or Hefte.

Esslin
Martin Esslin, *Brecht: The Man and His Work.*

Kesting
Marianne Kesting, *Bertolt Brecht in Selbstzeugnissen und Bilddokumenten.*

Mittenzwei
Werner Mittenzwei, *Bertolt Brecht: Von der Massnahme zu Leben des Galileo.*

Pinson
Koppel S. Pinson, *Modern Germany: Its History and Civilization.*

Schumacher
Ernst Schumacher, *Die dramatischen Versuche Brechts, 1918-1933.*

Prologue—Chapter I

1. Karl Marx, *Kritik der Hegelschen Rechtsphilophie,* in *Der historische Materialismus,* I, 265.

Prologue 1—Chapter II

2. Gerhart Hauptmann, *Das Abenteuer meiner Jugend*, II, 432-433.
3. Thomas Mann, "Nietzsche in the Light of Recent History," in *Last Essays*, 142.
4. Heinrich Mann, "Nietzsche," in *Mass und Wert* II (1939), 297.
5. Gottfried Benn, "Gesänge," in *Gedichte*, 25.
6. Rainer Maria Rilke, *Gesammelte Gedichte: Das Stundenbuch*, 71.
7. *Ibid.*, 31.
8. Letter to Lisa Heise, *Briefe aus den Jahren 1914-1921*, 86.
9. Erich Heller, *The Disinherited Mind*, 165.
10. *Stundenbuch, Gesammelte Gedichte*, 103.
11. *Tagebücher aus der Frühzeit* (1898), 38-39.
12. Heinrich Mann, *Der Untertan*, 501.
13. Heinrich Mann, "Voltaire und Goethe," in *Essays*, 10-20.
14. Thomas Mann, "Der Künstler und der Literat," in *Gesammelte Werke*, X, 62-70.
15. Thomas Mann, *Betrachtungen eines Unpolitischen*, xxxi-xxxii.
16. Thomas Mann, *Buddenbrooks*, II, Book IX, chap. 15, 344.
17. *Ibid.*, 346.
18. Cited by Friedrich Wolf, *Aufsätze über Theater*, 62.
19. Julius Bab, *Wesen und Weg der Berliner Volksbühnenbewegung*, 6-7.
20. Walther Rathenau, *Gesammelte Schriften* I, 206-207.
21. Frank Wedekind, "Silvester," *Prosa, Dramen, etc.*, 67-68.

Prologue 1—Chapter III

1. *Manchester Guardian*, January 15, 1919.

Part 1—Chapter I

1. "Verjagt mit gutem Grund," *Gedichte* IV, 141.
2. "Auslassungen eines Märtyrers," *Gedichte* II, 25.
3. "Lied von meiner Mutter," *ibid.*, 84.
4. "Meiner Mutter," *ibid.*, 85.
5. "Bei Durchsicht meiner ersten Stücke," *Stücke* I, 12-13.
6. "Briefe des jungen Brecht an Herbert Jhering, *Sinn und Form*, X, Heft 1, 1958, 31.
7. As is hinted in the *Flüchtlingsgespräche. Prosa* II, 180, in a cryptic mention of Hasengasse 11.
8. "Bei Durchsicht . . .", *loc. cit.*, 12.
9. *Flüchtlingsgespräche*, 171-172.
10. *Ibid.*, 173.
11. *Ibid.*, 172-173.

12. Wilhelm Brüstle, "Wie ich Bertolt Brecht entdeckte," *Neue Zeitung,* Munich, November 27, 1948. Quoted in Ernst Schumacher, *Die dramatischen Versuche* . . . , 26-27.

13. These poems, for the most part, have not been reprinted. Archiv Mappe 1866/04.

14. Archiv Mappe 1866/09. Republished *Gedichte* II, 8.

15. Archiv Mappe 1866/10.

16. *Ibid.,* 1866/12.

17. *Ibid.,* 1866/14.

18. "Der brennende Baum," *Gedichte* II, 7.

19. "Das Lied von der Eisenbahntruppe von Fort Donald," *Gedichte* II, 9-11.

20. Max Högel, *Bertolt Brecht,* 17.

21. Serge Tretyakov, "Bert Brecht," *International Literature,* May 1937. Reprinted in *Erinnerungen an Brecht,* 73.

22. "Die Legende vom toten Soldaten," *Gedichte* I, 136-140.

23. "Rede anlässlich der Verleihung des Lenin-Preises," *Versuche* 15, 146.

24. Quoted in Hans Mayer, *Bertolt Brecht und die Tradition,* 24-25.

25. Tretyakov, *loc. cit.,* 74.

26. "Karl Valentin," in *Schriften* I, 161.

27. Lion Feuchtwanger, *Success,* 215.

28. *Ibid.,* 211.

29. "Frank Wedekind," *Schriften* I, 7-8.

30. Frank Wedekind, *Der Marquis von Keith,* Act II.

31. Wedekind, *Franziska.*

32. "François Villon," *Gedichte* II, 51-52.

33. Letter of April 5, 1833. Georg Büchner, *Sämtliche Werke,* 382.

34. The hold *Wozzeck* exercised on the German imagination in the postwar era was strengthened by its transformation into an opera by Alban Berg in 1925, surely one of the most remarkable musical works of the century.

Part 1—Chapter II

1. Hugo Ball, *Die Flucht aus der Zeit,* 163.

2. *Ibid.,* 99.

3. *Ibid.,* 107.

4. Walter Muschg, *Von Trakl zu Brecht,* 91.

5. *Ibid.,* 87.

6. Kasimir Edschmid, quoted in Michael Hamburger, *Modern German Poetry,* xxxix.

7. Franz Werfel, "An den Leser" (1911), *Gesänge aus den drei Reichen,* 4-5.

8. Walter Hasenclever, *Der Sohn,* 15, 56, 98-99.

9. Ludwig Rubiner, *Der Mensch in der Mitte,* 148, 5.

10. Ludwig Rubiner, *Die Gewaltlosen,* (1919), 122, 126.

11. Fritz von Unruh, *Vor der Entscheidung*, (1914), 57.
12. Ernst Toller, *Wandlung*, in *Prosa, Briefe, Dramen*, 285.
13. Ernst Toller, *Massemensch*, loc. cit., 328-330.

Part 1—Chapter III

1. John Willett, *The Theatre of Bertolt Brecht*, 67.
2. "Vom armen B. B." *Hauspostille, Gedichte* I, 147-149.
3. "Über die Städte," *ibid.*, 71.
4. "Lied am schwarzen Samstag," *Gedichte* II, 36-38.
5. "Das Lied vom Geierbaum," *ibid.*, 39.
6. "Hymne an Gott," *ibid.*, 39.
7. "Anna redet schlecht von Bidi," *ibid.*, 28.
8. "Letzte Hoffnung," *ibid.*, 138.
9. "Gesang von einer Geliebten," *ibid.*, 79.
10. "Sentimentale Erinnerungen," *ibid.*, 29-30.
11. "Bidi im Herbst," *ibid.*, 27.
12. Arnold Bronnen, *Tage mit Bertolt Brecht*, 92.
13. Arthur Rimbaud, "Le Bateau ivre."
14. Brecht, "Das Schiff," *Hauspostille, Gedichte* I, 23-24.
15. "Vom Schwimmen in Seen und Flüssen," *ibid.*, 65-66.
16. "Ballade von den vielen Schiffen," *ibid.*, 83.
17. "Weihnachtsgedichte—Maria," *Gedichte* II, 104.
18. "Weihnachtslegende," *ibid.*, 105-106.
19. Peter Suhrkamp, Preface to *Bertolt Brecht: Gedichte und Lieder*, 5.
20. "Von der Kindermörderin Marie Farrar," *Hauspostille, Gedichte* I, 18-19.
21. "Grosser Dankchoral," *Hauspostille, Gedichte* I, 74.
22. "Liturgie vom Hauch," *ibid.*, 25-31.
23. "Ballade vom Weib und dem Soldaten," *ibid.*, 106-107. Brecht later included this poem in *Mother Courage*.
24. 1927 edition of *Hauspostille*, 15 ff.
25. Julius Bab in the *Hannoverscher Kurier*, May 20, 1927, reprinted in *Über den Tag Hinaus*, 114.
26. Kurt Tucholsky, *Gesammelte Werke* II, 1065.
27. Muschg, *op. cit.*, 340.
28. Alfred Kantorowicz, *Deutsches Tagebuch*, I, 628.
29. Lion Feuchtwanger, "Bertolt Brecht dargestellt für Engländer," *Weltbühne* XXIV, September 4, 1928, 372-376.
30. Lion Feuchtwanger, *Success*, translated by Willa and Edwin Muir, 135-136.
31. *Ibid.*, 143.
32. *Ibid.*, 235.
33. According to Högel, *op. cit.*, the boy died in the Second World War.

34. H. O. Münsterer, *Bert Brecht: Erinnerungen*, 116.
35. *Ibid.*, 117.
36. *Schriften*, I, 30-31.
37. *Ibid.*, 15-17.
38. *Ibid.*, 35.
39. *Ibid.*, 48-49.
40. *Ibid.*, 57.
41. Herbert Jhering, "Zwischen Reinhardt und Jessner," *Sinn und Form* II (1950), Heft 2, 61.
42. Quoted by Hans Mayer, *Brecht und die Tradition*, 23.
43. Not republished. Archiv Mappe 1278/08.
44. Münsterer, *op. cit.*, 90-91.
45. Brecht, "Bei Durchsicht meiner ersten Stücke," *Stücke* I, 13.
46. Muschg, *op. cit.*, 337.
47. *Baal*, in *Stücke* I, 90.
48. *Ibid.*, 91.
49. *Ibid.*, 95.
50. *Ibid.*, 19-22.
51. *Ibid.*, 38.
52. *Ibid.*, 99.
53. "Bei Durchsicht . . . . ," *Stücke* I, 8.

Part I—Chapter IV

1. Arnolt Bronnen, *Tage mit Bertolt Brecht*, 13-15.
2. Lotte Eisner, "Sur le procès de l'opéra de quat'sous," *Europe* XXXV (1957), 112.
3 Willy Haas, *Bert Brecht*, 5.
4. "Briefe des jungen Brecht an Herbert Jhering," *Sinn und Form* X, (1958), No. 1, 31.
5. *Arnolt Bronnen gibt zu Protokoll*, 98-99.
6. Arnolt Bronnen, *Vatermord*, 185-186.
7. "Briefe des jungen Brecht . . . ," *loc. cit.* 28-29.
8. Münsterer, *op. cit.*, 178-179.
9. Herbert Jhering, October 5, 1922; reprinted in *Sinn und Form*, Brecht Sonderheft II, 230-232.
10. *Idem*, October 2, 1922, reprinted in *Von Reinhardt zu Brecht*, I, 272.
11. Julius Bab, in *Hannoversches Tageblatt*, December 23, 1922; reprinted in *Über den Tage Hinaus*, 213.
12. Alfred Kerr, *Die Welt im Drama*, 164-166.
13. Herbert Jhering, "Begegnungen," *Sinn und Form* XIII (1961), Heft 3, 477.
14. Brecht, *Trommeln in der Nacht*, Stücke I, 159.
15. *Ibid.*, 167.

16. *Ibid.,* 165.
17. *Ibid.,* 162.
18. *Ibid.,* 175.
19. *Trommeln* . . . , ed. of 1923, Act IV.
20. *Trommeln* . . . , *Stücke* I, 204-205.
21. Alfred Kantorowicz, *Deutsches Tagebuch,* II, 301.
22. Georg Büchner, *Wozzeck* (Woyzeck), *Sämtliche Werke,* 183.
23. "Briefe des jungen Brecht . . . ," *loc. cit.,* 32.
24. "Bei Durchsicht . . . ," *Stücke* I, 7.
25. *Ibid.,* 6-7.
26. Lion Feuchtwanger, "Bertolt Brecht dargestellt . . . ," *Weltbühne* XXIV (August 28, 1928), 373.

Part I—Chapter V

1. Unpublished. Archiv Mappe 520/11-48.
2. Bronnen, *Tage mit Brecht,* 126.
3. *Ibid.,* 130. Bronnen gives the date as May 8.
4. Brecht, "Sang der Maschinen," *Gedichte* II, 158.
5. As in the late Victorian poetry of W. E. Henley and Arthur Symons.
6. Brecht, "Zum Lesebuch für Städtebewohner gehörige Gedichte," *Gedichte* I, 186.
7. "Verschollener Ruhm der Riesenstadt New York," *Gedichte* III, 85.
8. Brecht, *Im Dickicht der Städte, Stücke* I, 209.
9. Brecht, "Bargan lässt es sein," published in *Der neue Merkur* in September 1921; reprinted in *Geschichten,* 8-25.
10. *Im Dickicht* . . . , 242-243.
11. Arthur Rimbaud, *Une saison en enfer,* Penguin Poets Edition, 305.
12. *Im Dickicht* . . . , 310.
13. *Une saison* . . . , 346.
14. *Ibid.,* 312.
15. H. V. Jensen, *Das Rad,* 107-108.
16. Bronnen, *op. cit.,* 131.
17. *Ibid.,* 107.
18. Herbert Jhering, December 11, 1923; reprinted in *Von Reinhardt zu Brecht,* 360.
19. *Ibid.,* 313-314.
20. *Ibid.,* 313.
21. Julius Bab, *Die Chronik des deutschen Dramas,* V, 211-212.
22. Fritz Kortner, *Aller Tage Abend,* 373-377.
23. Jhering, Dec. 9, 1923, *loc. cit.,* 356.
24. Egbert Delpy in the *Neue Leipziger Nachrichten,* December 10, 1923.
25. Hanns Henny Jahn, "Vom armen B. B.," in *Sinn und Form,* Brecht Sonderheft II, 424-425.

26. Hugo von Hofmannsthal, "Das Theater des Neuen," *Lustspiele* IV, 403-426. Egon Friedell was the well-known historian and actor, who committed suicide when the Nazis occupied Vienna.

27. Brecht, *Kleinbürgerhochzeit,* Archiv Mappe 218.

Part I—Chapter VI

1. Lion Feuchtwanger in *Die Weltbühne* XX (1924), Part II, 673.
2. Brecht, *Leben Eduard des Zweiten von England, Stücke* II, 20-21.
3. *Ibid.,* 37.
4. *Ibid.,* 95-96.
5. *Ibid.,* 101.
6. *Ibid.,* 130-131.
7. *Ibid.,* 158.
8. *Ibid.,* 45.
9. Bernhard Reich, "Erinnerungen an den jungen Brecht," *Sinn und Form,* Brecht Sonderheft II, 431-434. There is a later, and fuller, account in the Supplement to *Theater der Zeit,* XXI (1966), Heft 14.
10. Marieluise Fleisser, in the *Süddeutsche Zeitung,* Munich, June 8, 1951, quoted in Schumacher, 91-92.
11. Julius Bab, quoted *ibid.,* 92.
12. Herbert Jhering, *Die zwanziger Jahre,* 166.
13. Bronnen, *op. cit.,* 143-144.
14. *Ibid.,* 140, 141.
15. Bernhard Reich, *loc. cit.,* 434.
16. Archiv Mappe 218.
17. Unpublished to date. Archiv Mappe 218.
18. Bernhard Reich, *"Erinnerungen an Brecht," Theater der Zeit* XXI (1966), Heft 14, Supplement, p. 10.
19. *Idem, Sinn und Form:* Brecht Sonderheft II, 434-435.

Part I—Chapter VII

1. Notebooks (May 1921), *Schriften* II, 25-26.
2. Martin Esslin, *Brecht,* 284.
3. Brecht, *Mann ist Mann, Stücke* II, 229-230.
4. Heraclitus, Fragment 41, in John Burnet, *Early Greek Philosophy,* 136.
5. *Mann ist Mann, loc. cit.,* 204.
6. *Ibid.,* 232.
7. *Ibid.,* 268.
8. *Ibid.,* 282.
9. *Ibid.,* 289.
10. *Ibid.,* 218.

11. *Ibid.*, 235-236.
12. *Ibid.*, 247, 269.
13. Alfred Döblin, *Die drei Sprünge des Wang-lun*, 28.
14. *Mann ist Mann*, 286.
15. John Willett, *The Theatre of Brecht*, 113.
16. Martin Esslin, *Brecht*, 284.
17. Brecht, *Das Elephantenkalb, Stücke* II, 313.
18. Quoted by Schumacher, 122.
19. Lion Feuchtwanger, in *Die Weltbühne*, XXIV (1928), 375.
20. Herbert Jhering, *Von Reinhardt bis Brecht* II, 231-232.
21. Schumacher, 119.

Part I—Chapter VIII

1. T. R. Clark, *The Fall of the German Republic*, 94.
2. Pinson, 447.
3. Quoted in Schumacher, 143.
4. Schumacher, 145 ff., gives an excellent review of these "Zeitstücke."
5. From Vakhtangov's *Diary*, quoted in Willett, *The Theatre of Brecht*, 112.
6. Jürgen Rühle, *Das gefesselte Theater*, 88, 89.
7. Quoted *ibid.*, 89.
8. Quoted in Schumacher, 523.
9. Erwin Piscator, in "Supplement au Théâtre politique, 1930-1960," *Théâtre Populaire*, No. 47 (1962), 4.
10. Erwin Piscator, *Das politische Theater*, 9.
11. *Ibid.*, 34.
12. *Ibid.*, 36.
13. *Ibid.*, 58-59.
14. Willett, *Theatre of Brecht*, 110.
15. Piscator, *op. cit.*, 131-132.
16. Report by Jacob Altmeier, quoted in Piscator, *op. cit.*, 61.
17. *Frankfurter Zeitung*, April 1, 1926, quoted in Piscator, *loc. cit.*, 69.
18. *Ibid.*, 113.
19 *Ibid.*, 212.
20. *Ibid.*, 82-83.
21. Brecht, *Schriften* III, 86-87.
22. "Gedenktafel für 9 Weltmeister," *Gedichte* II, 132-135.
23. The poem is reprinted in *Brecht über Lyrik*, 10.
24. *Ibid.*, 8-9.
25. Rudolf Borchardt, "Baccalaureus über Faust," August 24, 1928, reprinted in *Prosa* I, 495.
26. Hans Mayer, "Gelegenheitsdichtung des jungen Brecht," in *Sinn und Form* X (1958), 276-290.
27. *Ibid.*, 287-288.

28. Lotte Eisner, "Sur le procès de quat'sous," *Europe* XXXV (Jan.-Feb. 1957), 113, 114.

29. As told by Rudolf Frank, *Spielzeit meines Lebens*, 238-239.

30. Recorded by Elisabeth Hauptmann, "Notizen über Brechts Arbeit 1926," *Sinn und Form*, Brecht Sonderheft II (1957), 243.

31. *Ibid.*, 243.

32. "Mehr guten Sport," *Schriften* I, 61-62.

33. "Unser Publikum," (Fragment), *Schriften* I, 168.

34. "Mehr guten Sport," *ibid.*, 61.

35. "Weniger Gips," *ibid.*, 84.

36. "Über das Theatre der grossen Städte," *ibid.*, 165-166.

37. "Sollten wir nicht die Ästhetik liquidieren?" *Schriften* I, 98-99.

38. *Ibid.*, 96.

39. "Vorrede zu *Macbeth*," *Schriften* I, 104-106.

40. Fragment, *Schriften* I, 108-109.

41. Cologne Radio Broadcast, incompletely preserved, *Schriften* I, 117-121.

42. *Ibid.*, 122-126.

43. "Ovation für Shaw," *Schriften* I, 176 (July 25, 1926).

44. "Betrachtungen über die Schwierigkeiten des epischen Theaters," *ibid.*, 185 (1927).

45. Fragment, *Schriften* I, 181 (1927?).

46. "Vorrede zu *Mann ist Mann*," *Schriften* II, 84.

47. *Ibid.*, 84-85.

48. "Über eine neue Dramatik," *Schriften* I, 196-204 (1928).

Part I—Chapter IX

1. "Das waren Zeiten," in *Bertolt Brechts Dreigroschenbuch*, 220-225.

2. John Gay, *The Beggar's Opera*, Act I, sc. 4.

3. *Ibid.*, Act II, sc. 1.

4. *Ibid.*, Act III, scenes 2, 1.

5. *Ibid.*, Act III, sc. 16.

6. Brecht, *Die Dreigroschenoper*, *Stücke* III, 10.

7. *Ibid.*, 59-62.

8. *Ibid.*, 135-136.

9. *Ibid.*, 140.

10. *Ibid.*, 99-101.

11. *Ibid.*, 111.

12. "Anmerkungen zur *Dreigroschenoper*," *Stücke* III, 146-150.

13. Alfred Kerr, *"Die Dreigroschenoper*," reprinted in *Brechts Dreigroschenbuch*, 199-201.

14. Reprinted *ibid.*, 204.

15. Published posthumously, *ibid.*, 204-205.

16. "Sonet zur Neuausgabe des François Villon," *Gedichte* III, 158.

17. "Kerrs Enthüllung," *Die Fackel* XXXI (August 1929), Nos. 811-819, 129-132. Reprinted in *Erinnerungen*, 64-68.

18. Kurt Tucholsky, *Gesammelte Werke*, II, 126.

19. *Rudyard Kipling's Verse*, 349.

20. Wieland Herzfelde, "Über Bertolt Brecht," *Erinnerungen an Brecht*, 130-131.

21. Kurt Weill in *Die Szene* (1929), reprinted in Schumacher, 250.

22. Kurt Weill, "Zur Komposition der *Dreigroschenoper*," *Die Szene* (1929), quoted in *Dreigroschenbuch*, 219-220.

23. Brecht, "Über die Verwendung von Musik für ein episches Theater," *Schriften* III, 268-269.

Part I—Chapter X

1. Quoted in Erich Eyck, *A History of the Weimar Republic*, II, 47.

2. W. M. Knight-Patterson, *Germany from Defeat to Conquest*, 423.

3. *Ibid.*, 424.

4. *Ibid.*, 434.

5. *Ibid.*, 462.

6. *Ibid.*, 483.

7. Fritz Sternberg, *Der Dichter und die Ratio*, 30-31.

8. *Ibid.*, 25-26.

9. In a conversation with this author.

10. Brecht, *Gedichte* II, 247.

11. *Ibid.*, 242-243.

12. *Ibid.*, 244-246.

13. Portions in *Versuche*, Heft I, 20-21; in *Gedichte* II, 194-199; some unpublished fragments in Archiv Mappe 109-112.

14. Piscator, *op. cit.*, 251 n.

15. Unpublished fragment, Archiv Mappe 109/90.

16. *Versuche* I, 40-41; *Gedichte* II, 194-196; 199.

17. "*Die Beule*," in *Dreigroschenbuch*, 76-77.

18. Ludwig Marcuse, *Mein zwangzigstes Jahrhundert*, 131-132. The controversy was further heightened by an acrimonious exchange between Balázs and Herbert Jhering in *Die Weltbühne* in February and March 1931.

19. Esslin, 41.

20. "Der Dreigroschenprozess . . . ," *Versuche*, Heft 3, 258.

21. *Ibid.*, 257, 268.

22. Alfred Polgar, "Theater Skandal," *Handbuch des Kritikers*, 32-34.

23. Knight-Patterson, *op. cit.*, 428-429; 453-454.

24. *Aufstieg und Fall der Stadt Mahagonny*, *Stücke* III, 172.

25. *Ibid.*, 202-203.

26. *Ibid.*, 212.

27. *Ibid.*, 216-218.

28. *Ibid.*, 246.
29. *Ibid.*, 254 ff.
30. *Ibid.*, 256.
31. Schumacher, 275.
32. "Bei Durchsicht . . . ," *Stücke* I, 15.

Part I—Chapter XI

1. See above, pp. 148 ff. and Index.
2. Rudolf Frank, *Spielzeit meines Lebens*, 266.
3. "Anmerkungen zu der Oper *Mahagonny*," *Schriften* II, 120.
4. Brecht, *Kleines Organon für das Theater*, section 26, *Schriften* VII, 23-24.
5. Richard Wagner, *Tristan und Isolde*, Act II.
6. Carl Zuckmayer, quoted in Melchinger, *Drama zwischen Shaw und Brecht*, 63.
7. Richard Wagner, quoted in Mordecai Gorelik, *New Theatres for Old*, 288-289.
8. "Anmerkungen zu . . . . *Mahagonny*," *loc. cit.*, 122.
9. Sigmund Freud, *Civilization and Its Discontents. The Standard Edition*, vol. XXI, 75.
10. *Ibid.*, 78.
11. Brecht, *Kleines Organon*, *Schriften* VII, 25.
12. "Anmerkungen zu . . . *Mahagonny*," *loc. cit.*, 55.
13. "Vergnügungstheater oder Lehrtheater?", *Schriften* III, 55.
14. "Das Theater, Stätte der Träume," *Gedichte aus dem Messingkauf*, *Schriften* V, 271-272.
15. "Dialoge über die Schauspielkunst," *Schriften* I, 211.
16. "Was arbeiten Sie?" (Interview with Guillemin), *Schriften* I, 268.
17. "Die dialektische Dramatik," *ibid.*, 258.
18. Kurt Muno, in *Die neue Zeit*, discussing Brecht. Quoted by Werner Hecht, *Brechts Weg* . . . , 49.
19. "Vergnügungstheater oder Lehrtheater?", *Schriften* III, 55.
20. "Der Messingkauf: Bruchstücke zur vierten Nacht," *Schriften* V, 231-232.
21. "Vergnügungstheater oder Lehrtheater?", *Schriften* III, 56.
22. G. W. Hegel, *Vorlesungen über Aesthetik*, quoted in Schumacher, 169.
23. "Notes to the *Dreigroschenoper*," *Schriften* II, 104.
24. "Über Stoffe und Form," *Schriften* I, 225.
25. Karl Marx, *Critique of Political Economy*, Introduction, 310-311.
26. "Über Stoffe und Form," *Schriften* I, 225-226.
27. "*Kritik der Einfühlung*," *Schriften* III, 22-23.
28. Aristotle, *Poetics*. Translated by W. D. Ross, section 1449b.
29. Aristotle, *Politics*. Translated by W D. Ross, 1341b-1342a.

30. *Poetics.* Translated by Gilbert, chap. xvii.

31. Horace, *The Art of Poetry.* Translated by E. H. Blakeney.

32. Goethe, "Supplement to Aristotle's *Poetics.* Translated by R. S. Bourne, quoted in Lieder and Withington, *The Art of Literary Criticism,* 331.

33. Schopenhauer, *The World as Will and Idea,* section 51, in Allen and Clark, *Literary Criticism from Pope to Croce,* 252-253.

34. *Hegel on Tragedy,* edited by Anne and Henry Paolucci, 49, 50, 71, 72.

35. Norman N. Holland, "Shakespearean Tragedy and the Three Ways of Psychoanalytic Criticism," in *The Hudson Review* XV, No. 2 (Summer 1962), 225-226.

35a. See Herbert Weisinger, *Tragedy and the Paradox of the Fortunate Fall,* p. 26.

36. Über rationellen und emotionellen Standpunkt," *Schriften* III, 27.

37. "Über die Theatralik des Faschismus," *Der Messingkauf, Schriften* V, 94.

38. *Ibid.,* 92.

39. "Über rationellen und emotionellen Standpunkt," *Schriften* III, 25.

40. "Die Sprache des Dramatikers," *ibid.,* 130.

41. "Über rationellen . . . ," *ibid.,* 25-27.

42. "Über experimentelles Theater," *ibid.,* 101.

43. Quoted by Reinhold Grimm, in *Ärgernis Brecht,* 60.

44. "Anhang zur kurzen Beschreibung . . . ," *Schriften* III, 174.

45. Brecht, "Dialektik und Verfremdung," *Schriften* III, 180.

46. Herbert Jhering, "Der Volksdramatiker," *Sinn und Form,* Brecht Sonderheft I, (1949), 9.

47. Erich Fromm, *Marx's Concept of Man,* 43-44.

48. Karl Marx, *Deutsche Ideologie,* in *Der historische Materialismus,* ed. S. Landshut and J. P. Mayer, 25-26.

49. Quoted by Fromm, *op. cit.,* 56.

50. "Über experimentelles Theater," *Schriften* III, 101-102.

51. "Ulm 1592," *Gedichte* IV, 28.

52. "Über experimentelles Theater," *loc. cit.,* 101.

53. "Anhang zur kurzen Beschreibung einer neuen Technik," *Schriften* III, 172.

54. "Vorrede zu *Mann ist Mann,*" *Schriften* II, 84.

55. Quoted in Paul Böckmann, *Provokation und Dialektik,* 32, and Victor Erlich, *Russian Formalism,* 176-177.

56. Willett, *Brecht on Theatre,* 99.

57. In an English translation by Eric Walter White, in *Life and Letters Today,* No. 6, 1936-1937. The German text, "Verfremdungseffekt in der chinesischen Schauspielkunst," is reprinted in *Schriften* V, 166-182.

58. Denis Diderot, *The Paradox of Acting,* 67-68.

59. "Die Vorhänge," and "Die Beleuchtung," *Schriften* V, 264-265.

60. "Die Requisiten der Weigel," *ibid.*, 267.
61. "Zeichen und Symbole," *Schriften* III, 243.
62. "Über alltägliches Theater," *Gedichte aus dem Messingkauf, Schriften* V, 253.
63. "Die Strassenszene," *ibid.*, 69-86.
64. *Kleines Organon, Schriften* VII, 44.
65. "Gestik," *Schriften* VI, 213.
66. "Über gestische Musik," *Schriften* III, 281-284.
67. *Ibid.*, 281.
68. *Ibid.*, 90-91.
69. "Über die kritische Haltung," *Gedichte aus dem Messingkauf, Schriften* V, 270.
70. Ernst Bloch, *Das Prinzip Hoffnung* I, 499.
71. "Die Einfühlung," in *Der Messingkauf, Schriften* V, 41.
72. Bernard Shaw, "An Address before the Royal Academy of Dramatic Arts, December 7, 1928." Reprinted in *Shaw on Theatre*, 197.
73. Herbert Jhering, *Die zwanziger Jahre*, 212.

Part I—Chapter XII

1. Hanns Eisler, "Das Lied im Kampf geboren," *Reden und Aufsätze*, 129-130.
2. Serge Tretyakov, "Bert Brecht," reprinted in *Erinnerungen an Brecht*, 69-71.
3. "Zu den Lehrstücken—Theorie der Pädagogien," *Schriften* II, 129.
4. Earle Ernst, *Three Japanese Plays from the Traditional Theatre*, 4-14.
5. Arthur Waley, *The No-Plays of Japan*, 17 ff.
6. "Erläuterungen zu *Der Ozeanflug*," *Versuche* I, 23.
7. *Ibid.*, 24.
8. Brecht, *Der Ozeanflug*," *Versuche* I, 7-8.
9. *Ibid.*, 14-15.
10. *Ibid.*, 22.
11. *Das Badener Lehrstück* . . . , *Stücke* III, 283-284.
12. *Ibid.*, 284.
13. *Ibid.*, 297.
14. *Ibid.*, 307-308.
15. *Ibid.*, 313-314.
16. *Ibid.*, 280.
17. *Ibid.*, 301.
18. Walter Weideli, *Bertolt Brecht*, 56-57.
19. "Zu den Lehrstücken: Theorie des Lehrstückes," *Schriften* VI, 80.
20. *Taniko*, from *The No-Plays of Japan*, by Arthur Waley, 194-195.
21. Brecht, *Der Jasager, Stücke* IV, 232.

22. In the *Rhein-Mainische Volkszeitung,* December 20, 1930, quoted in Schumacher, 337.

23. In *Hochland,* February 1932, 411; quoted in Schumacher, 337.

24. "Nein, dem Jasager!" in *Die Weltbühne,* July 8, 1930; quoted in Schumacher, 338.

25. Brecht, *Der Neinsager, Stücke* IV, 245.

26. *Ibid.,* 246-247.

27. Ernst Bloch, *Das Prinzip Hoffnung* I, 483.

28. Marie Seton, *Sergei M. Eisenstein,* 132.

29. Brecht, *Die Massnahme, Stücke* IV, 290.

30. *Ibid.,* 269.

31. *Ibid.,* 288-289.

32. *Ibid.,* 295.

33. *Ibid.,* 304.

34. *Ibid.,* 307.

35. Fritz Sternberg, *op. cit.,* 28.

36. *Die Massnahme, loc. cit.,* 266-267.

37. Esslin, 294.

38. Herbert Lüthy, "Vom armen Bert Brecht," in *Der Monat* No. 44, May 1952, 127.

39. Willy Haas, *Bert Brecht,* 62, 70.

40. Alfred Kurella, "Ein Versuch mit nicht ganz tauglichen Mitteln," quoted in Schumacher, 365-366.

41. Unpublished autobiographical fragment, in Archiv Mappe 348/23-24.

42. *Die Linkskurve* III (January 1931), 12-14.

43. Quoted in Schumacher, 366-367.

44. "An die Nachgeborenen," *Gedichte* IV, 145.

45. Brecht, *Die Ausnahme und die Regel, Stücke* V, 228.

46. *Ibid.,* 187.

47. *Ibid.,* 226.

Part I—Chapter XIII

1. Knight-Patterson, *op. cit.,* 541.

2. *Ibid.,* 525.

3. Materials in the Brecht Archiv Mappe 675/9-55.

4. Archiv Mappe 524/13-90.

5. Archiv Mappe 678/02-09.

6. Brecht, *Der Brotladen, Sinn und Form* X (1958), Heft I, 6.

7. Heinrich Mann, "Die deutsche Entscheidung," in the *Luxemburger Zeitung,* December 13, 1931; reprinted in *Essays,* 603-608.

8. William Shirer, *The Rise and Fall of the Third Reich,* 165.

9. At the Nuremberg Trials. Quoted in Shirer, 190.

10. See below, pp. 396 ff., 471.

11. Frau Elisabeth Hauptmann assured the present writer that this was not the case.

12. Friedrich Schiller, *Die Jungfrau von Orleans,* Prolog.

13. Brecht, *Die heilige Johanna, Stücke* IV, 7-8.

14. *Die Jungfrau von Orleans,* Act I, sc. 9.

15. *Die heilige Johanna, loc. cit.,* 37.

16. *Die Jungfrau . . . ,* Act I, sc. 6.

17. *Die heilige Johanna, loc. cit.,* 181-182

18. *Ibid.,* 119-120.

19. *Ibid.,* 18.

20. *Ibid.,* 69-70.

21. *Ibid.,* 73.

22. *Ibid.,* 202.

23. *Ibid.,* 210-211.

24. *Ibid.,* 203.

25. Käthe Rülicke, "Die heilige Johanna," in *Sinn und Form* X (1959), Heft 3, 429-444.

26. W. M. Guggenheim, in *Frankfurter Hefte* XIX (1964), 126-128.

Part I—Chapter XIV

1. *Die Mutter, Stücke* V, 40.

2. *Ibid.,* 57.

3. *Ibid.,* 89.

4. *Ibid.,* 90-91.

5. *Ibid.,* 116-117.

6. Schumacher, 418.

7. "Eine kleine Bemerkung," *Schriften* II, 213.

8. January 18, 1932, reprinted in *Stücke* V, 166.

9. *Ibid.,* 174, 165.

10. Brecht, "Anmerkungen zur *Mutter,*" *Schriften* II, 156-157.

11. Brecht, "Einige Irrtümer über die Spielweise . . . ," *Schriften* VII, 268.

12. Brecht, "Das Stück *Die Mutter,*" *Schriften* II, 207.

13. Brecht, "Brief an das Arbeitertheater," *Stücke* V, 160-161.

Part I—Chapter XV

1. Quoted in Schumacher, 490.

2. *Ibid.,* 491.

3. Quoted in Werner Mittenzwei, *Bertolt Brecht,* 62, 71.

4. Brecht, "Tonfilm *Kuhle Wampe,*" *Schriften* II, 223-227.

5. Quoted in Werner Hecht, *Brechts Weg . . . ,* 154.

6. Brecht, "Ein kleiner Beitrag zum Thema Realismus," *Schriften* II, 227-231.

7. The poems are reprinted in *Gedichte* III, 220-223, 167.
8. Sternberg, *op. cit.,* 26-27.
9. "Als der Faschismus immer stärker wurde," *Gedichte* III, 189.
10. "Wiegenlieder," *Gedichte* III, 21-22.
11. "Die ärmeren Mitschüler aus den Vorstädten," *ibid.,* 155-156.
12. Brecht, "Die drei Soldaten," *ibid.,* 106.
13. "Das Lied vom Klassenfeind," *Gedichte* III, 29.
14. "Ballade von der Billigung der Welt," *Gedichte* III, 80.
15. "Einige Fragen an einen guten Mann," *Gedichte* III, 164.
16. "Die da wegkonnen," *ibid.,* 192.
17. "Hitler Choräle," *ibid.,* 37-39, 47.
18. Ludwig Marcuse, *Mein zwanzigstes Jahrhundert,* 157.

Part 2—Chapter 1

1. Quoted by Hans Bunge, "Brecht im zweiten Weltkrieg," *Neue deutsche Literatur* X (1962), No. 3, 37.
2. Marianne Kesting, *Brecht,* 70.
3. There is a vivid description of that period in Sanary in Ludwig Marcuse's *Mein zwanzigstes Jahrhundert.*
4. Kesting, *op. cit.,* 70-71.
5. "Zeit meines Reichtums," *Gedichte* III, 196-197.
6. Karin Michaelis, *Der kleine Kobold,* 257.
7. Hanns Henrik Jacobsen, "Bert Brecht in Denmark, 1933-1939," *Orbis Litterarum* XV (1960), 247-249.
8. Kesting, 74.
9. Mittenzwei, 138 ff.
10. Lion Feuchtwanger, "Die Arbeitsprobleme des Schriftstellers im Exil," *Sinn und Form* VI (1954), Heft 3, 352.
11. "Naturgedichte-Svendborg," *Gedichte* V, 86.
12. "Augsburg," *ibid.,* 87.
13. "Über das Lehren ohne Schüler," *ibid.,* 65.
14. "Der Lernende," *ibid.,* 66.
15. "1940," *Gedichte* IV, 221-222.
16. "Gedanken über die Dauer des Exils," *ibid.,* 138-139.
17. "Besuch bei den verbannten Dichtern," *Gedichte* IV, 55-56.
18. "Über die Bezeichnung Emigranten," *ibid.,* 137.
19. "Schlechte Zeit für Lyrik," *Gedichte* V, 105.
20. "1940," *Gedichte* IV, 221.
21. "Frühling 1938," *ibid.,* 218.
22. "Die unbesiegliche Inschrift," *ibid.,* 62.
23. "Verjagt mit gutem Grund," *ibid.,* 141-142.
24. "Über die Bedeutung des zehnzeiligen Gedichtes in der Fackel," *Gedichte* V, 19-20.

25. Über den schnellen Fall des guten Unwissenden," *ibid.*, 21-22.

26. Caroline Kohn, "Bert Brecht, Karl Kraus, et le 'Kraus Archiv,' " *Études Germaniques*, XI (1956), 342-348, where the author, it seems from personal knowledge, reports that upon his return to Germany after the war, Brecht was planning a commemoration of Kraus, on the 20th anniversary of his death, apparently having forgiven him.

27. "Einmal eine nützliche Handlung verrichten," *Gedichte* V, 26.

28. "Offener Brief an den Schauspieler Heinrich George," *Schriften* III, 7-13, (1933).

29. "Auf den Tod eines Kämpfers für Frieden," *Gedichte* IV, 79.

Part 2—Chapter II

1. Kesting, 72.

2. *Der Dreigroschenroman*, in *Brechts Dreigroschenbuch*, 451-453.

3. *Ibid.*, 249.

4. *Ibid.*, 305.

5. *Ibid.*, 347-348.

6. *Ibid.*, 461-463.

7. Quoted by Mittenzwei, 162, from Archiv Mappe 268/81.

8. *Rundköpfe und Spitzköpfe, Versuche*, Heft 8, 348.

9. *Rundköpfe und Spitzköpfe, Stücke* VI, 121-122.

10. *Ibid.*, 162-163.

11. "Anmerkung zu *Rundköpfe* . . . ," *Stücke* VI, 226-228.

12. "Über die Verwendung von Prinzipien," *Schriften* III, 118.

13. *Die Horatier und die Kuratier, Stücke* V, 257-258.

14. *Fünf Schwierigkeiten beim Schreiben der Wahrheit, Versuche*, Heft 9, 87.

15. "Rede auf dem 1. Internationalen Schriftstellerkongress," *Versuche*, Heft 15, 137-141.

16. "Über reimlose Lyrik mit unregelmässigen Rhythmen," *Versuche*, Heft 12, (1939), 141-147.

17. "Chinesische Gedichte: Anmerkungen," *Gedichte* IV, 157-158.

18. "Svendborger Gedichte," *Gedichte*, IV, 13.

19. *Ibid.*, 15.

20. *Ibid.*, 12.

21. "Traum einer grossen Miesmacherin," *Gedichte* IV, 100-101.

21a. Bernhard Reich, "Erinnerungen . . .," *Theater der Zeit* XXI (1966), Heft 14, Supplement, 14-16.

21b. For a vivid account of this episode, see Lee Baxendall, "Brecht in America," *Tulane Drama Review* XII (1967), No. 1.

22. Mordecai Gorelik, "Brecht: I am the Einstein of the New Stage Form," *Theatre Arts Monthly*, March 1957, 72-73.

23. "Brief an . . . Theater Union," *Stücke* V. 161-163.
24. Quoted by Mittenzwei, 227, from Archiv Mappe 167/27.
25. "Der Messingkauf," *Schriften* V, 142-143.
26. Anna Seghers, "Helene Weigel spielt in Paris," *Internationale Literatur,* 1938, Heft 4, 126-127.
27. "Die Schauspielerin im Exil," *Schriften* V, 280.
28. *Furcht und Elend . . .,* "Rechtsfindung," *Stücke* VI, 307.
28. "Der Spitzel," *ibid.,* 347-348.
29. "Volksbefragung," *ibid.,* 405-408.
30. Mittenzwei, 202, and Walter Benjamin, *Briefe* II, 818.
31. *"John Kent—Was kostet das Eisen",* Archiv Mappe 919/01-21.
32. "Goliath—Oper," Archiv Mappe 519/01-42.
33. "Legende von der Entstehung des Buches Taoteking," *Gedichte* IV, 51-54.
34. "Die Literatur wird durchforscht werden," *Gedichte* VI, 15-16.
35. "Die Verlustliste," *ibid.,* 51.
36. "Die gute Genossin, M. S.," *Gedichte* V, 81; "Nach dem Tode meiner Mitarbeiterin, M. S.," *Gedichte* VI, 46-47, 48.
37. Unpublished note in the correspondence with Karl Korsch, Archiv Mappe 2098/13.
38. "Ist das Volk unfehlbar?," *Gedichte* V, 139-141.
39. "Wir hören: Du willst nicht mehr mit uns arbeiten," *Gedichte* V, 8-9.
40. Archiv Mappe 2098/01.
41. Friedrich Ege, "Hella Wuolijoki," *Theater der Zeit* IX (1954), No. 9, 32-33.
42. "1940," *Gedichte* IV, 222.
43. "Finnische Gutsspeisekammer," and "Finnische Landschaft," *ibid.,* 224; 228.
44. "Ode an einen hohen Würdenträger," *Gedichte* VI, 17-18.
45. "Finland 1940," *Gedichte* V, 144.
46. "An die Nachgeborenen," *Gedichte* IV, 143-145.

Part 2—Chapter III

1. Archiv Mappe, "Tagebücher," quoted by Mittenzwei, 255.
2. Quoted in Ernst Schumacher, *Bertolt Brechts "Leben des Galilei,"* 113.
3. "Zu Leben Galilei," *Schriften* VIII, 199-200.
4. *Schriften* IV, 209.
5. "Visionen—Parade des alten Neuen," *Gedichte* V, 112.
6. Schumacher, *op. cit.,* 77-78.
7. "Die neuen Zeiten," *Gedichte* VI, 69.
8. Archiv Mappe 426/01; 366/09; quoted by Mittenzwei, 270.
9. Archiv Mappe 609/25, Mittenzwei, 273.

10. Archiv Mappe 648/53, Mittenzwei, 274.
11. "Wie der Einbrecher," *Gedichte* V, 78.
12. *Schriften* IV, 210.
13. Archiv Mappe 426/48; Mittenzwei, 267.
14. "Galileo Galilei, Manuscript," Brecht Archiv, p. 110, Mittenzwei, 276-277; and Schumacher, *Brechts "Galilei,"* 29.
15. Archiv Mappe 426/34; Mittenzwei, 278.
16. Mittenzwei, 280-281; Schumacher, *Brechts "Galilei,"* 32-33.
17. Schumacher, *op. cit.*, 34-35.
18. Mittenzwei, 282; Schumacher, *op. cit.*, 37.
19. Über experimentelles Theater," (1939), *Schriften* III, 93.
20. Quoted, *ibid.*, 93-94.
21. Isaac Deutscher, *The Prophet Outcast: Trotsky, 1929-1940*, London, Oxford University Press, 1963, 370.
22. Cf. Schumacher, *op. cit.*, 107-111. Walter Benjamin, *Versuche über Brecht*, 131-135; Benjamin, *Briefe* II, 771-772.
23. Brecht, *Stücke* VIII, 201.
24. *Schriften* IV, 224.
25. *Leben des Galilei, Stücke* VIII, 9-12.
26. Quoted by Ernst Schumacher, "Form und Einfühlung," *Materialen zu Galileo*, 153.
26a. He is called Matti in the Laughton version.
27. Serreau, *Bertolt Brecht*, 98-99.
28. *Leben des Galilei*, 184-188.
29. *Ibid.*, 166.
30. *Ibid.*, 113-116.

Part 2—Chapter IV

1. *Das Verhör des Lukullus, Stücke* VII, 261.
2. *Ibid.*, 261-262.
3. *Mutter Courage und ihre Kinder, Stücke* VII, 63-64.
4. *Ibid.*, 147-148.
5. *Ibid.*, 100.
6. *Ibid.*, 155.
7. *Ibid.*, 103.
8. *Ibid.*, 158.
9. *Ibid.*, 89.
10. *Ibid.*, 149-150.
11. *Ibid.*, 124-125.
12. "Anmerkung zu Mutter Courage," *Stücke* VII, 205.
13. "Formprobleme des Theaters," *Materialen zu Mutter Courage*, 86-90.
14. *Ibid.*, 90.
15. *Ibid.*, 91.

16. *Ibid.*, 92.
17. "Gespräch mit einen junge Zuschauer," *ibid.*, 92-93.

Part 2—Chapter V

1. *Die Judith von Shimoda*, Archiv Mappe 518/01-93.
2. Patrick Bridgwater, "Arthur Waley and Brecht," *German Life and Letters* XVII (1964), No. 3, 216-232.
3. *Der gute Mensch von Sezuan*, *Stücke* VIII, 230.
4. *Ibid.*, 231.
5. *Ibid.*, 275.
6. *Ibid.*, 275-276.
7. *Die Judith von Shimoda* (unpublished) Archiv Mappe 518/45.
8. *Der gute Mensch*, 283.
9. *Ibid.*, 292.
10. *Ibid.*, 298.
11. *Ibid.*, 344-345.
12. *Ibid.*, 347.
13. *Ibid.*, 349.
14. *Ibid.*, 407-408.
15. Volker Klotz, *Bertolt Brecht*, 18.
16. Bernard Dort, *Lecture de Brecht*, 161.
17. *Die Judith von Shimoda* (unpublished), Archiv Mappe 518/19.
18. *Herr Puntila und sein Knecht Matti*, *Stücke* IX, 129-130.
19. *Ibid.*, 130-131.
20. *Ibid.*, 164-165.

Part 2—Chapter VI

1. "Aus dem Arbeitsbuch: Der aufhaltsame Aufstieg . . . ," *Sinn und Form*, Brecht Sonderheft II, 100.
2. *Ibid.*, 101 (April 9, 1941).
3. "Zu der *Aufhaltsame Aufstieg* . . . ," *Stücke* IX, 369.
4. *Der aufhaltsame Aufstieg* . . . , *Stücke* IX, 336-337
5. *Ibid.*, 263.

Part 2—Chapter VII

1. Brecht, *Flüchtlingsgespräche*, *Prosa* II, 215.
2. *Ibid.*, 235.
3. *Ibid.*, 208.
4. *Ibid.*, 159.
5. *Ibid.*, 161.
6. *Ibid.*, 199.
7. *Ibid.*, 276.

8. *Ibid.,* 273.
9. *Ibid.,* 277-278.
10. *Ibid.,* p. 117 of the Aufbau edition.

Part 2—Chapter VIII

1. Helene Weigel's account to the present author.
2. Fritz Kortner, *Aller Tage Abend,* 499-501.
3. "Liefere die Ware," *Gedichte* VI, 56-57.
4. "Hollywood," *Gedichte* VI, 7.
5. "Sonett in der Emigration," *ibid.,* 53.
6. "Angesichts der Zustände in dieser Stadt," *ibid.,* VI, 54.
7. "Nachdenkend über die Hölle," *ibid.,* 52.
8. "Brief an den Stückeschreiber Odets," *ibid.,* 95.
9. "Sah verjagt aus sieben Ländern," *ibid.,* 61.
10. Quoted in Wolfdietrich Rasch, "Brechts marxistischer Lehrer," *Merkur* XVII (1963), No. 10, 991, 992.
11. Leonhard Frank's most famous work was a series of stories about the First World War entitled, *Der Mensch ist gut (Man is Good).*
12. Chaplin's *Autobiography* mentions Brecht only once, and that very cursorily, on page 434.
13. Joseph Losey, "The Individual Eye," *Encore,* March 1961; reprinted in *The Encore Reader,* 200.
14. "Brief an den Schauspieler Charles Laughton," *Gedichte* VI, 114.
15. "Der Galilei des Laughton," *Schriften* IV, 239, 243.
16. *Ibid.,* 272-273.
17. *Ibid.,* 272-273.
18. "Das Fischgerät," *Gedichte* VI, 73.
19. "Die handelnd Unzufriedenen," *Gedichte* VI, 77.
20. "An die deutschen Soldaten im Osten," *ibid.,* 29-34.
21. "Und was bekam des Soldaten Weib?" *ibid.,* 35-36.
22. Kantorowicz, *op. cit.,* I, 188.
23. Kortner, *op. cit.,* 501.
24. Brecht, "Bertolt Brecht an Thomas Mann," *Sinn und Form* XVI (1964), Heft 5, 691-692; Thomas Mann, *Briefe: 1937-1947:* 339-341; Brecht, "An den Nobelpreisträger Thomas Mann," *Gedichte* VIII, 195-196.
25. Note to *Gedichte* VI, 210.
26. Rasch, *loc. cit.,* 999.
27. *Ibid.,* 994.
28. *Ibid.,* 999.
29. H. J. Bunge, "Das Manifest von Bertolt Brecht, *Sinn und Form* XV (1963), Heft 2-3, 200.
30. Robert Spaethling, "Bertolt Brecht and *The Communist Manifesto,*" *Germanic Review* XXXVII (1962), 282-291.

31. *Ibid.*, 91.
32. "Das Manifest," *Gedichte* VI, 133; 141.
33. *Ibid.*, 154.
34. *Ibid.*, 148.

Part 2—Chapter IX

1. *Die Gesichte der Simone Machard, Stücke* IX, 436.
2. *Ibid.*, 452.
3. *Ibid.*, 462.
4. *Ibid.*, 464.
5. *Ibid.*, 486.
6. *Ibid.*, 379-380.

Part 2—Chapter X

1. Sternberg, *op. cit.*, 13-14.
2. Jaroslav Hašek, *The Good Soldier Schweik*, 9-10.
3. *Schweyk im zweiten Weltkrieg, Stücke* X, 34-35.
4. *Ibid.*, 23.
5. *Ibid.*, 38.
6. *Ibid.*, 124-125.
7. *Ibid.*, 91.
8. *Ibid.*, 121-122.
9. *Ibid.*, 123-124.
10. Herbert Jhering, *Berliner Dramaturgie*, 91.
11. *Notebooks,* quoted in Pavel Petr, *Hašeks Schweyk in Deutschland*, 143.
12. *Ibid.*, 144.

Part 2—Chapter XI

1. Unpublished notes in Archiv Mappe 440 and 191. *The Ginger Jar (Der Ingvertopf)* republished in *Neue deutsche Literatur* VI (1958), Heft 2, 10-13; and in an English translation by H. E. Rank, in the *Kenyon Review* XX (1958), 393-398.
2. Republished in the *Kalendergeschichten* and *Geschichten*. Translated as "The Augsburg Chalk Circle" in *Tales from the Calendar.*
3. Klabund, *Der Kreidekreis*, 145.
4. *Ibid.*, 161.
5. *Ibid.*, 189.
6. "Immer wieder," *Gedichte* VI, 72.
7. "Über Freunde," *ibid.*, 60.
8. "Die Dialektik auf dem Theater," *Schriften* VII, 249; 269; VI, 365.
9. *Der kaukasische Kreidekreis, Stücke* X, 295-296.
10. *Ibid.*, 301.

11. *Ibid.*, 162.
12. *Ibid.*, 157-158.

Part 2—Chapter XII

1. Fritz Kortner, *op. cit.*, 547-548.
2. For the story of the "Hollywood Ten," see Gordon Kahn, *Hollywood on Trial*. We reproduce a condensed version of the Brecht interrogation in the Appendix.
3. See above, pp. 61, 63.
4. Gladwin Hill, in the *New York Times*, August 1, 1947.
5. Brooks Atkinson, in *The New York Times*, December 8, 1947. An incredible travesty of the relationship between Brecht and Laughton is offered in Kurt Singer's "official" *The Laughton Story*, pp. 249-250. Laughton, intimidated by the "witch-hunts," cut off all contact with Brecht.

Part 3—Chapter I

1. Max Frisch, *Tagebuch*, 225-227, 286, 292-294.
2. Friedrich Hölderlin, *Antigonä, Sämtliche Werke* V, 187.
3. Brecht, *Die Antigone des Sophokles, Stücke* XI, 19.
4. *Ibid.*, 33.
5. *Ibid.*, 35-36.
6. "Antigonemodell, 1948," *Schriften* VI, 14-16.
7. Hans Curjel, "Brechts Antigone-Inszenierungen in Chur 1948," in *Bertolt Brecht: Gespräche auf der Probe*, 9-19.
8. Quoted in Siegfried Melchinger, "Bertolt Brechts *Salzburger Totentanz*," *Stuttgarter Zeitung*, January 5, 1963.
9. Contained in Archiv Mappe 921/03-43, and in part reproduced in Melchinger, *loc. cit.* The latter translated by Eric Bentley, *The Jewish Wife, etc.*, The Grove Press, New York, 1965.
10. Nordahl Grieg, *Die Niederlage*, Act IV, sc. 3, pp. 116-119.
11. Brecht, *Die Tage der Commune, Stücke* X, 369.
12. *Ibid.*, 367.
13. *Ibid.*, 406-408.
14. *Ibid.*, 431.
15. *Ibid.*, 437.
16. Hans Kaufmann, *Bertolt Brecht: Geschichtsdrama und Parabelstück*, 88.
17. Karl Marx, "Adresse des Generalrats über den deutsch-französischen Krieg," quoted in Kaufmann, *op. cit.*, 62.
18. Arthur Adamov, in *La Nouvelle Critique*, No. 123, February 1961, 9-10.

Part 3—Chapter II

1. Brecht, "Als ich in die Heimat," *Gedichte* VII, 36.
2. Vladimir Pozner, "bb," *Sinn und Form*, Brecht Sonderheft II, 450.

3. Günther Weisenborn, *Der gespaltene Horizont,* 160-162.

4. Brecht, "Konflikt," *Schriften* VII, 296.

5. "Einige Irrtümer. . . .," *Schriften* VII, 283.

6. Erwin Leiser, "Der freundliche Frager," in *B. Brecht: Gespräche auf der Probe,* 44.

7. Pozner, *loc. cit.,* 451.

8. Brecht, "Einige Irrtümer. . . ," *Schriften* VII, 272.

9. *Ibid.,* 271.

10. "Krisen," *Schriften* VII, 118.

11. Brecht, "Soll man denn nicht die Wahrheit sagen?" *Schriften* VII, 296.

12. *Schriften* VI, 48.

13. Quoted in Rühle, *Das gefesselte Theater,* 238-239.

14. For a discussion of *Der Hofmeister* and the controversy, see pp. 448, 467.

15. *Neues Deutschland,* March 21, 1951.

16. Brecht, *Die Verurteilung des Lukullus, Stücke* VII, 271-274.

17. Esslin, 173.

18. Rühle, *op. cit.,* 241.

19. Ernest Bornemann, "Credo Quia Absurdum," *Kenyon Review* XXI (1959), 195-196.

20. Walter Dirks, "Der gute Mensch und die Christen," *Frankfurter Neue Presse,* November 18, 1952.

21. Jerzy Pomianowski, "Un Théâtre du renouveau en Pologne," *Les Temps Modernes* XIV (July 1957), 27.

22. Quoted in Heinz Kächele, *Bertolt Brecht,* 48.

23. "Ein neues Haus," *Gedichte* VII, 38.

24. "Grosse Zeit, Vertan," *ibid.,* 10.

25. "Die Wahrheit einigt," *ibid.,* 14.

26. Kesting, 139; Esslin, 181; Willett, *The Theatre of Brecht,* 201. The West German journalist Wolfgang Paul conjectures that the above declaration is taken from another letter of Brecht's altogether: "Aus Bertolt Brechts späteren Jahren," *Neue deutsche Hefte* V (1958), 710-723.

27. Quoted in Kesting, 139.

28. "Die Lösung," *Gedichte* VII, 9.

29. "Das Brot der Gerechtigkeit," *ibid.,* 103-104.

30. "Böser Morgen," *Gedichte* VII, 11.

31. Kantorowicz, *op. cit.,* II, 400-401; 406-407. "Mitteilungen der deutschen Akademie der Künste," *Sinn und Form* V (1953), Heft 3-4, 255-256.

32. "Kulturpolitik und Akademie der Künste," *Neues Deutschland,* August 12, 1953.

33. Archiv Mappe 49/08; 09.

33a. "Notizen zur Barlach-Ausstellung," *Sinn und Form* IV, Heft 1 (1952), 182-186.

34. "Nicht so gemeint," *Gedichte* VII, 99.

35. Kesting, 132.

36. "Zum Einzug des Berliner Ensemble," *Gedichte* VII, 107.
37. Reported by Erwin Leiser, in *Brecht: Gespräche auf der Probe,* 43.
38. "Die Schauspielerin in Exil," *Gedichte* IV, 209; and see p. 321.
39. "Die Schauspielerin," *Gedichte* V, 16.
40. "Der Messingkauf," *Schriften* V, 149.
41. "Abstieg der Weigel in den Ruhm," *ibid.,* 151-152.
42. "Die Requisiten der Weigel," *Gedichte aus dem Messingkauf, ibid.,* V, 267.
43. "1954: Erste Hälfte," *Gedichte* VII, 111.
44. Brecht, "Fröhlich vom Fleisch zu essen," *Gedichte* VII, 121, and P. B. Shelley, "The Mask of Anarchy," stanzas xxxix ff.
45. "Lehre, Lerne!", *Gedichte* VII, 101.
46. "Die Regie Bertolt Brechts," *Theaterarbeit,* 130-132.
47. "Katzgraben Notate," *Schriften* VII, 151.
48. *Ibid.,* 88.
49. "Beispiel der Episierung," *Theaterarbeit,* 94.
50. "Dreizehn Bühnentechniker erzählen," *Sinn und Form,* Brecht Sonderheft II, 465, 471.
51. "Aus einem Brief an einen Schauspieler," *Schriften* VI, 185-186.

Part 3—Chapter III

1. Brecht, *Der Messingkauf, Schriften* V, 129.
2. "Gewohnheiten, noch immer," *Gedichte* VII, 12.
3. "Anmerkung" to *Der Hofmeister, Versuche* Heft 11, 61.
4. Brecht, *Der Hofmeister, Stücke* XI, 193-195.
5. *Ibid.,* 213.
6. Brecht, "Ist der *Hofmeister* ein negatives Stück?," *Theaterarbeit,* 120.
7. Alexander Abusch, "Zu Hanns Eislers *Johann Faustus," Sinn und Form* V (1953), Heft 3, 194.
8. Brecht, "Thesen zur Faustus-Diskussion," *ibid.,* 194-197.
9. Brecht, "Zu *Urfaust* von Goethe," *Schriften* VI, 321-332.
10. Quoted in Rühle, *Das gefesselte Theater,* 244-245.
11. Brecht, *Der Prozess der Jeanne d'Arc, Stücke* XII, 81-83.
12. Brecht, *Coriolan, Stücke,* XI, 343, 365, 368.
13. "Zu Coriolan," *Schriften* VI, 315.
14. Brecht, *Die Geschäfte des Herrn Julius Caesar, Prosa* IV, 48.

Part 3—Chapter IV

1. Georg Lukács, Preface to the new edition of *Skizze einer Geschichte der neueren deutschen Literatur,* (1963), 10.
2. *Ibid.,* 207-209.
3. Lukács, *Realism in Our Time,* 87-89.

4. "Dessaus Lukullus Musik," *Schriften* VI, 311.

5. "Die grossen Gegenstände," and "Zur Formalismusdebatte," *Schriften* III, 125; and "Formalismus—Realismus," *Schriften* VII, 304-307.

6. "Weite und Vielfalt der realistischen Schreibweise," *Versuche*, Heft 13, 99.

7. *Ibid.*, 106.

8. *Ibid.*, 107.

9. "Volkstümlichkeit und Realismus," (1938) *Schriften* IV, 153.

10. *Ibid.*, 154-155.

11. *Kleines Organon*, section 73, *Schriften* VII, 55.

12. "Definition der Kunst," *Messingkauf, Schriften* V, 236.

13. "Formalismus," *Schriften* VII, 305.

14. *Ibid.*, 234.

15. Quoted in Mordecai Gorelik, *New Theatres for Old*, 136.

16. "Was unter anderem vom Theater Stanislawskis gelernt werden kann," *Schriften* VII, 210-212.

17. "Methoden der Konzentration," *ibid.*, 196.

18. "Politik auf dem Theater," *Schriften* VII, 70.

Part 3—Chapter V

1. *Turandot oder der Kongress der Weisswäscher*. As yet unpublished. Frau Hauptmann, who is editing the manuscript for publication, was kind enough to show it to the author.

2. "Bei Durchsicht meiner ersten Stücke," *Stücke*, I, 8-9.

3. "Kann die heutige Welt durch Theater wiedergegeben werden?" *Schriften* VII, 300-302.

4. Max Frisch, "Brecht ist tot," *Weltwoche*, August 24, 1956.

5. Erwin Leiser, "Der freundliche Frager," in *Brecht: Gespräche auf der Probe*, 47.

6. *Ibid.*, 43.

7. *Ibid.*, 48.

8. Ernst Schumacher, *Brechts Galilei*, 317.

9. *Ibid.*, 320-326.

10. Werner Hecht, *Theater der Zeit* XXI (1966), No. 14, 28-30.

11. *Me-Ti: Buch der Wendungen, Prosa* V, 176, and *passim*.

12. Transcript of Tape, edited by Käthe Rülicke, in the Brecht-Archiv.

13. *Der Spiegel*, 1956. No. 49, p. 65.

BIBLIOGRAPHY

Bibliography

I

BRECHT'S WORKS IN GERMAN

Gedichte. 9 volumes. Frankfurt-am-Main: Suhrkamp Verlag, 1960-1965.
Prosa. 5 volumes. Suhrkamp Verlag, 1965.
Schriften zum Theater. 7 volumes. Suhrkamp Verlag, 1963-1964.
Schriften zur Literatur und Kunst. 3 volumes. Suhrkamp Verlag, 1967.
Stücke. 13 volumes. Suhrkamp Verlag, 1957-1967.
Versuche. 15 issues. Suhrkamp Verlag, 1957-1959.
Theaterarbeit. Sechs Aufführungen des Berliner Ensemble. Edited by
    Ruth Berlau, Bertolt Brecht, Helene Weigel, and others. Dresden:
    VVV Dresdner Verlag (n.d.).
Brechts Dreigroschenbuch. Suhrkamp Verlag, 1960.
Flüchtlingsgespräche. Suhrkamp Verlag, 1962.
Gespräche auf der Probe. Zürich: Sanssouci Verlag, 1961.
Materialen zu Brechts "Leben des Galilei." Suhrkamp Verlag, 1963.
Materialen zu Brechts "Mutter Courage." Suhrkamp Verlag, 1964.
Bertolt Brecht über Lyrik. Suhrkamp Verlag, 1964.
Gedichte und Lieder. Auswahl Peter Suhrkamp. Suhrkamp Verlag
    (n.d.).
"Briefe des jungen Brecht und Herbert Jhering." *Sinn und Form* X,
    Heft 1 (1958), 30-32.
Trommeln in der Nacht. Munich: Drei Masken Verlag, 1923.
Baal: Drei Fassungen. Suhrkamp Verlag, 1966.
Der Jasager und der Neinsager: Vorlagen, Fassungen und Materialen.
    Suhrkamp Verlag, 1966.

II

BRECHT'S WORKS IN TRANSLATION

Plays. (Various translators). 2 vols. London: Methuen & Co., 1961. (Other
    volumes in preparation.)

Seven Plays by Bertolt Brecht. Edited and with an Introduction by Eric Bentley. New York: Grove Press, 1961.
Works of Bertolt Brecht. The Grove Press Edition. General Editor: Eric Bentley. Grove Press, Inc., 1964- . (In progress.)
Tales from the Calendar. Tr. by Yvonne Kapp and Michael Hamburger. London: Methuen & Co., 1961.
Brecht on Theatre. The Development of an Aesthetic. Edited and tr. by John Willett. New York, Hill & Wang, 1964.
The Messingkauf Dialogues. Tr. by John Willett. Methuen & Co., 1965.
The Threepenny Novel. Tr. by Desmond L. Vesey and Christopher Isherwood. New York: Grove Press, 1956.
————. *Die Hauspostille; Manual of Piety.* A Bi-Lingual Edition with English Text by Eric Bentley and Notes by Hugo Schmidt. New York: The Grove Press, 1966.

III

BIBLIOGRAPHY

Nubel, Walter. *Bertolt Brecht Bibliographie. Sinn und Form.* Special Brecht Number II. Berlin: Rütten & Loening (n.d.).
Grimm, Reinhold. *Bertolt Brecht.* Realienbücher für Germanisten. 2 ed. Stuttgart: J. B. Metzlersche Verlagsbuchhandlung, 1963.
(*Revue d'histoire du Théatre* [Paris] 1948-to date runs a current bibliography.)
Arbeitskreis Bertolt Brecht. Düsseldorf. (Irregular reports on Brecht literature and productions.)

IV

SECONDARY LITERATURE

Abel, Lionel. *Metatheatre.* New York: Hill and Wang, 1963.
Adamov, Arthur. "Le Printemps 71." *La Nouvelle Critique,* No. 123 (1961), 9-10.
Das Ärgernis Brecht. Mit Beiträgen von Siegfried Melchinger, Rudolf Frank, Reinhold Grimm, Erich Franzen, und Otto Mann. Basel: Basilius Presse, 1961.
Anders, Günther. *Bert Brecht: Gespräche und Erinnerungen.* Zürich: Verlag der Arche, 1962.
Angress, Werner T. *Stillborn Revolution.* The Communist Bid for Power in Germany, 1921-1923. Princeton: Princeton University Press, 1963.

Arbeitskreis Bertolt Brecht: Mitteilungen und Diskussion. Wiesbaden: 1960-to date.

Bab, Julius. *Die Chronik des deutschen Dramas.* Fünfter Teil: 1919-1926. Berlin: Oesterheld & Co., 1926.

————. *Wesen und Weg der Berliner Volksbühnenbewegung.* Berlin: Verlag Ernst Wasmuth (n.d.).

Ball, Hugo. *Die Flucht aus der Zeit.* Luzern: Josef Stocker Verlag, 1946.

Balluseck, Lothar von. *Dichter im Dienst.* Der sozialistische Realismus in der deutschen Literatur. 2 ed. Wiesbaden: Limes Verlag, 1963.

Benjamin, Walter. *Schriften.* 2 vols. Frankfurt-am-Main: Suhrkamp Verlag, 1955.

————. *Briefe.* 2 vols. Frankfurt-am-Main: Suhrkamp, 1966.

————. *Versuche über Brecht.* Suhrkamp, 1966.

Benn, Gottfried. *Gesammelte Werke.* 3 vols. Wiesbaden: Limes Verlag, 1958-1960.

Bentley, Eric. *In Search of Theater.* New York: Alfred A. Knopf, 1953.

————. *The Life of the Drama.* New York: Athenaeum, 1965.

————. *The Playwright as Thinker.* New York: Meridian Books, 1955.

Berendsohn, Walter A. *Die humanistische Front.* Einführung in die deutsche Emigranten-Literatur. Part I, 1933-1939. Zürich: Europa Verlag, 1946.

Berliner Ensemble. *Bertolt Brecht and the Berlin Ensemble.* Berlin: Society for Cultural Relations with Foreign Countries, 1958.

Bithell, Jethro. *Modern German Literature, 1880-1950.* 3d edition. London: Methuen & Co., 1959.

Blau, Herbert. *The Impossible Theater—A Manifesto.* New York: The Macmillan Company, 1964.

Bloch, Ernst. "Aufsätze über Brecht." *Aufbau* XII (August 1956), 809-814.

————. *Das Prinzip Hoffnung.* 2 vols. Frankfurt-am-Main: Suhrkamp, Verlag, 1959.

Böckmann, Paul. *Provokation und Dialektik in der Dramatik Bert Brechts.* Krefeld: Scherpe Verlag, 1961.

Borchardt, Rudolf. *Prosa I.* Stuttgart: Ernst Klett Verlag, 1957.

Bornemann, Ernst. "Credo Quia Absurdum: Epitaph for Bertolt Brecht." *Kenyon Review* XXI (1959), 169-198.

————. "Two Brechtians." *Kenyon Review* XXII (1960), 465-492.

Brandt, Thomas O. "Die Sprachführung Bertolt Brechts." *Neue deutsche Hefte* No. 108 (Nov.-Dec. 1965), 55-69.

Bridgewater, Patrick. "Arthur Waley and Brecht." *German Life and Letters* XVII (1964), 216-232.

Bronnen, Arnolt. *Arnolt Bronnen gibt zu Protokoll*. Hamburg: Rowohlt Verlag, 1954.
————. *Tage mit Bertolt Brecht*. Geschichte einer unvollendeten Freundschaft. Wien, München: Kurt Desch Verlag, 1960.
————. *Vatermord*. Emsdetten: Verlag Lechte, 1954.
Brustein, Robert. *The Theatre of Revolt*. Boston: Little, Brown, 1964.
Büchner, Georg. *Sämtliche Werke*. Gütersloh: Sigbert Mohn Verlag, 1963.
Butler, E. M. *Paper Boats*. London: Collins, 1959.
Butler, Rohan D'O. *The Roots of National Socialism*. New York: E. P. Dutton, 1942.
Cahiers du Cinéma. Special Brecht Number. XIX, No. 114 (1956).
Chiarini, Paolo. *Bertolt Brecht*. Bari: Editori Laterza, 1959.
Clark, R. T. *The Fall of the German Republic*. A Political Study. London: George Allen & Unwin, 1935.
Claudel, Paul. *Le Livre de Christophe Colomb. Théatre de Paul Claudel*, vol. 2. Bibliothèque de la Pleiade. Paris: Librairie Gallimard, 1956.
Clurman, Harold. "The Achievement of Bertolt Brecht." *Partisan Review* XXVI (1959), 624-628.
Coper, Rudolf. *Failure of a Revolution*: Germany in 1918-1919. Cambridge (England): Cambridge University Press, 1935.
Demetz, Peter (editor). *Brecht: A Collection of Critical Essays*. Englewood Cliffs: Prentice-Hall, 1962.
De Quinto, Jose Maria. *La Tragedia y el Hombre*. Barcelona: Editorial Seix Barral, 1962.
Desuché, Jacques. *Bertolt Brecht*. Paris: Presses Universitaires de France, 1963.
Diderot, Denis. *The Paradox of Acting*. New York: Hill and Wang, 1957.
Dietrich, Margarete. "Episches Theater?" *Maske und Kothurn* II (1956), 97-124; 301-334.
Döblin, Alfred. *Die drei Sprünge des Wang-lun*. Berlin: S. Fischer Verlag, 1918.
Donner, Jörn. *Report from Berlin*. Tr. Albin T. Anderson. Bloomington, Indiana University Press, 1961.
Dort, Bernard. "Cariolan-Pièce fasciste?" *Théatre Populaire* No. 28 (1958), 9-24.
————. *Lecture de Brecht*. Paris: Edition de Seuil, 1960.
Dürrenmatt, Friedrich. "Schiller. Eine Rede." *Veröffentlichungen der deutschen Schiller Gesellschaft, Band 24*. Stuttgart: Ernst Klett Verlag, 1961.

Duwe, Wilhelm. *Deutsche Dichtung des 20. Jahrhunderts.* 2 vols. Zürich: Orell Füssli Verlag, 1962.

Eisler, Hanns. *Reden und Aufsätze.* Herausgegeben von Winfried Höntsch. Leipzig: Philip Reclam jun. (n.d.).

Eisner, Lotte H. "Sur le procès de Quat'Sous." *Europe.* Special Brecht Number, XXXV (1957), 111-118.

The Encore Reader. A Chronicle of the New Drama. Ed. Charles Marowitz and Owen Hale. London: Methuen & Co., 1965.

Erinnerungen an Brecht. Zusammengestellt von Hubert Witt. Leipzig: Philip Reclam jun., 1964.

Erlich, Victor. *Russian Formalism: History. Doctrine.* The Hague: Mouton & Co., 1965.

Ernst, Earle (ed.). *Three Japanese Plays from the Traditional Theatre.* London: Oxford University Press, 1959.

Esslin, Martin. *Brecht—The Man and His Work.* Anchor Books. Garden City: Doubleday and Company, 1961.

Europe. Special Brecht Number, XXXV (Jan.-Feb. 1957).

Eyck, Erich. *A History of the Weimar Republic.* Tr. Harlan P. Hanson and G. L. Waite. 2 vols. Cambridge, Mass: Harvard University Press, 1962-1963.

Fassmann, Kurt. *Brecht: Eine Bildbiographie.* München: Kindler Verlag, 1958.

Fergusson, Francis. "Three Allegorists: Brecht, Wilder, and Eliot." *Sewanee Review* LXIV (1956), 544-573.

Feuchtwanger, Lion. "Die Arbeitsprobleme des Schriftstellers im Exil." *Sinn und Form* VI, Heft 3 (1954), 348-353.

———. "Bertolt Brecht dargestellt für Engländer." *Weltbühne* XXIV (August 28, 1928), 372-376.

———. *Simone.* Stockholm: Neuer Verlag (n.d.).

———. *Erfolg.* 2 vols. Berlin: Gustav Kiepenheuer, 1930.

———. *Success.* Tr. Willa and Edwin Muir. New York: Viking Press, 1930.

———. "Zur Entstehungsgeschichte des Stückes Simone." *Neue deutsche Literatur* V (1957), 56-58.

Fischer, Ernst. *The Necessity of Art.* Hammersmith: Penguin Books, 1963.

Fleisser, Marieluise. *Avantgarde. Erzählungen.* Munich: Carl Hanser Verlag, 1963.

Frank, Rudolf. *Spielzeit meines Lebens.* Heidelberg: Verlag Lambert Schneider, 1960.

Freud, Sigmund. *Civilization and Its Discontents.* The Standard Edition translated from the German under the General Editorship of James Strachey, vol. XXI. London: The Hogarth Press, 1961.

Frisch, Max. "Brecht als Klassiker." *Die Weltwoche* (Zurich), July 1, 1955.

————. *Tagebuch*: 1946-1949. Frankfurt-am-Main: Suhrkamp Verlag, 1950.

Fromm, Erich. *Marx's Concept of Man.* New York: Ungar Publishing Company, 1961.

Gansel, Mireille and Philip Ivernel. "L'Antigone de Brecht." *Théatre Populaire,* No. 54 (1964) 130-140.

Garten, H. F. *Modern German Drama.* London: Methuen & Co., 1959.

Gay, John. *The Beggar's Opera.* Boston and New York: Houghton Mifflin, 1939.

Geissler, Rolf. "Versuch über Brechts Kaukasischer Kreidekreis." *Wirkendes Wort* IX (1959), 93-99.

Goedhart, Gerda. *Bertolt Brecht Porträts* (Photographs). Zürich: Verlag Die Arche, 1964.

Gorelik, Mordecai. *New Theatres for Old.* New York: Samuel French, 1940.

Graf, Roland. *Augsburg: Die Geschichte einer 2000 jährigen Stadt.* Augsburg: Victor-Georg Hohmann Verlag, 1954.

Grass, Günter. *Die Plebejer proben den Aufstand.* Neuwied am Rhein: Leuchterhand Verlag, 1966.

————. "Vor und Nachgeschichte des Coriolanus von Livius und Plutarch, über Shakespeare bis zu Brecht und mir." *Akzente* XI (1964), 194-221.

Gray, Ronald. *Brecht.* Edinburgh: Oliver and Boyd, 1961.

Grieg, Nordahl. *Die Niederlage.* Tr. into German by Margarete Steffin. Berlin: Verlag Bruno Henschel & Sohn, 1947.

Grimm, Reinhold. "Brecht, Ionesco und das moderne Theater." *German Life and Letters* XIII (1960), 220-225.

————. "Ideologische Tragödie und Tragödie der Ideologie." *Zeitschrift für deutsche Philologie* LXXVIII-IX (1959-1960), 394-424.

————. *Bertolt Brecht: Die Struktur seines Werkes.* Nürnberg: Verlag Hans Carl, 1959.

————. *Brecht und die Weltliteratur.* Verlag Hans Carl, 1961.

Grimmelshausen, Hans Jacob Christoffel von. *Courage: The Adventuress and the False Messiah.* Tr. Hans Speier. Princeton: Princeton University Press, 1964.

———. *Der abenteuerliche Simplicissimus.* Berlin: Propyläen Verlag (n.d.).
Grossvogel, David I. *Four Playwrights and a Postscript.* Ithaca: Cornell University Press, 1962.
Haas, Willy. *Bert Brecht.* Berlin: Colloquium Verlag, 1958.
———. (ed.). *Zeitgemässes aus der "Literarischen Welt" von 1925-1932.* Stuttgart: Cotta'sche Buchhandlung, 1963.
Hašek, Jaroslav. *The Good Soldier Schweik.* Tr. Paul Selver. New York: Penguin Books, 1942.
Hasenclever, Walter. *Der Sohn.* Leipzig: Kurt Wolff Verlag, 1917.
Hauptmann, Carl. *Krieg: Ein Te Deum.* Leipzig: Kurt Wolff Verlag, 1914.
Hauptmann, Elisabeth. "Notizen über Brechts Arbeit 1926." *Sinn und Form,* Special Brecht Number II, 1956, 241-243.
Hauptmann, Gerhart. *Das Abenteuer meines Lebens.* 2 vols. Berlin: S. Fischer Verlag, 1937.
Hecht, Werner. *Brechts Weg zum epischen Theater.* Berlin: Henschelverlag, 1962.
———. "The Development of Brecht's Theory of the Epic Theatre, 1918-1933." *Tulane Drama Review* VI (1961) 40-97.
Hayman, Ronald. "A Last Interview with Brecht." *New London Magazine* III (1956), 47-52.
Henneberg, Fritz. *Dessau-Brecht musikalische Arbeiten.* Berlin: Henschelverlag, 1963.
Hinck, Walter. *Die Dramaturgie des späten Brecht.* Göttingen: Vandenhoeck & Ruprecht, 1959.
Hoffmann, Ludwig and Daniel Hoffmann-Ostwald. *Deutsches Arbeitertheater* 1918-1933. Berlin: Henschelverlag, 1961.
Hofmannsthal, Hugo von. "Das Theater des Neuen." *Lustspiele* IV. Frankfurt-am-Main: S. Fischer Verlag, 1956.
Högel, Max. *Bertolt Brecht: Ein Porträt.* Augsburg: Verlag der schwäbischen Forschungsgemeinschaft, 1962.
Hölderlin, Friedrich. *Sämtliche Werke,* V. Ed Ludwig V. Pigenot and Friedrich Seebass. Berlin: Propyläen Verlag, 1923.
Holland, Norman N. "Shakespearean Tragedy and the Three Ways of Psychoanalytic Criticism." *Hudson Review* XV, No. 2 (1962), 217-227.
Hultberg, Helge. *Die aesthetischen Anschauungen Bertolt Brechts.* Copenhagen: Munksgaard, 1962.
Hurwicz, Angelica. *Brecht inszeniert Der kaukasische Kreidekreis.* Fotos von Gerda Goedhart. Velber: Erhard Friedrich, 1964.

Ionesco, Eugene. *Notes and Counternotes.* Tr. Donald Watson. New York: Grove Press, 1964.

Jacobsen, Hans Henrik. "Bert Brecht in Dänemark 1933-1939." *Orbis Litterarum* XV (1960), 247-249.

Jens, Walter. *Statt einer Literaturgeschichte.* Pfullingen: Verlag Neske, 1957.

Jensen, Johannes V. *Das. Rad.* Berlin: S. Fischer Verlag, 1921.

Jhering, Herbert. "Begegnungen." *Sinn und Form* XIII (1961) 475-485.

——. *Begegnungen mit Zeit und Menschen.* Berlin: Aufbau Verlag, 1963.

——. *Berliner Dramaturgie.* Aufbau Verlag, 1947.

——. *Von Reinhardt bis Brecht.* 3 vols. Aufbau Verlag, 1958-1961.

——. *Die zwanziger Jahre.* Aufbau Verlag, 1948.

Johst, Hanns, *Der Einsame.* Munich: Delphin Verlag, 1917.

Kahn, Gordon. *Hollywood on Trial.* Foreword by Thomas Mann. New York: Boni & Gaer, 1948.

Kantorowicz, Alfred. *Deutsches Tagebuch.* 2 vols. Munich: Kindler Verlag, 1961.

Kaufmann, Hans. *Bertolt Brechts Geschichtsdrama und Parabelstück.* Berlin: Rütten & Loening, 1962.

Kerr, Alfred. *Die Welt im Drama.* Köln-Berlin: Kiepenheuer & Witsch, 1954.

Kesting, Marianne. *Bertolt Brecht in Selbaszeugnissen und Bilddokumenten.* Hamburg: Rowohlt Verlag, 1959.

——. *Das epische Theater.* Stuttgart:Kohlhammer Verlag, 1959.

Klabund. (Alfred Henschke). *Der Kreidekreis. Gesammelte Nachdichtungen.* Wien: Phaidon Verlag, 1930.

Klotz, Volker. *Bertolt Brecht: Versuch über das Werk.* Darmstadt: Hermann Gentner Verlag, 1957.

Knight-Patterson, W. M. *Germany: From Defeat to Conquest. 1913-1933.* London: George Allen and Unwin, 1945.

Kohn, Caroline. "Bert Brecht, Karl Kraus, et le 'Kraus Archiv.'" *Études Germaniques* XI (1956) 342-348.

Kortner, Fritz. *Aller Tage Abend.* Munich: Kindler Verlag, 1959.

Krolop, Kurt. "Bertolt Brecht und Karl Kraus." *Philologica Pragensia* IV, No. 2 (1961), 95-112; IV, No. 4 (1961), 203-230.

Kutscher, Arthur. *Frank Wedekind.* 3 vols. Munich: Georg Müller, 1922-1931.

Leibowitz, René. "Brecht et la musique." *Théatre Populaire,* No. 11 (1955), 43-49.

Lenz, Jakob Michael Reinhold. *Der Hofmeister*. (1774) *Sturm und Drang*. ed. Karl Freye. Berlin: Bong & Co. (n.d.).

Losey, Joseph. "The Individual Eye." *The Encore Reader*, 195-209.

Lukács, Georg. *Aesthetik*. 2 vols. Neuwied am Rhein: Luchterhand Verlag, 1963.

———. *Skizze einer Geschichte der neueren deutschen Literatur*. Luchterhand Verlag, 1963.

———. *Realism in Our Time*. Tr. by J. and N. Mander. New York: Harper and Row, 1964.

Lüthy, Herbert. "Vom arment B. B." *Der Monat*, No. 44 (1952), 115-144.

Mann, Heinrich. *Essays*. Hamburg: Claassen Verlag, 1960.

———. *Der Untertan*. Leipzig: Kurt Wolff Verlag, 1918.

Mann, Otto. *B. B. Mass oder Mythos?* Heidelberg: Wolfgang Rothe Verlag, 1958.

Mann, Thomas. *Betrachtungen eines Unpolitischen*. Berlin: S. Fischer Verlag, 1919.

———. *Briefe*. Ed. Erika Mann. 2 vols. Frankfurt-am-Main, S. Fischer Verlag, 1961-1965.

———. *Buddenbrooks*. 2 vols. Berlin: S. Fischer Verlag, 1920.

———. "Der Künstler und der Literat." *Gesammelte Werke* X. S. Fischer Verlag, 1960.

———. *Last Essays*. Tr. R. and C. Winston and T. and J. Stern. New York: Alfred A. Knopf, 1959.

Marcuse, Ludwig. *Mein zwanzigstes Jahrhundert*. Munich: P. List, 1960.

Mayer, Hans. *Bertolt Brecht und die Tradition*. Pfullingen: Neske Verlag, 1961.

———. "Brecht und die plebeische Tradition." *Sinn und Form*, Special Brecht Number I, 1949, 5-10.

———. "Gelegenheitsdichtung des jungen Brechts." *Sinn und Form* X (1958), 276-290.

———. *Georg Büchner und seine Zeit*. Wiesbaden: Limes Verlag, 1946.

———. *Anmerkungen zu Brecht*. Frankfurt-am-Main: Suhrkamp Verlag, 1965.

Mehring, Walter. *Berlin Dada*. Zürich: Verlag der Arche, 1959.

Melchinger, Siegfried. "Bertolt Brechts Salzburger Totentanz." *Stuttgarter Zeitung*, Jan. 5, 1963.

———. *Drama zwischen Shaw und Brecht*. Bremen: Carl Schünemann Verlag, 1957.

Mellinger, Michael. "Good-bye to East Berlin." *Encore* VII, No. 5 (1960), 11-18.

Michaelis, Karin. *Der kleine Kobold.* Wien: Humboldt Verlag, 1948.

Mittenzwei, Johannes. *Das musikalische in der Literatur*: Eine Uberblick von Gottfried von Strassburg bis Brecht. Halle: VEB Verlag, 1962.

Mittenzwei, Werner. *Bertolt Brecht: Von der Massnahme zu Leben des Galilei.* Berlin: Aufbau Verlag, 1962.

———. *Gestaltung und Gestalten im modernen Drama.* Berlin: Aufbau Verlag, 1965.

Münsterer, Hans Otto. *Bert Brecht: Erinnerungen aus den Jahren 1917-1922.* Zürich: Verlag der Arche, 1963.

Muschg, Walter. *Von Trakl zu Brecht.* Dichter des Expressionismus. Munich: Piper Verlag, 1961.

Nexö, Martin-Andersen. "Die Gewehre der Frau Carrar." *Das Wort* III (1938), 139-142.

Nellhaus, Gerhard. *Bertolt Brecht: The Development of a Dialectical Poet-Dramatist.* (Thesis) Harvard University, 1946.

Niessen, Carl. *Brecht auf der Bühne.* Köln: Institut für Theaterwissenschaft, 1959.

Nietzsche, Friedrich. *The Philosophy of Nietzsche.* New York: The Modern Library, (n.d.).

Orbis Litterarum (Copenhagen). Special Brecht Issue, XX (1965), No. 1.

Paul, Wolfgang. "Aus Bertolt Brechts späteren Jahren." *Neue deutsche Hefte* V (1958), 710-723.

Petr, Pavel. *Hašeks Schwejk in Deutschland.* Berlin: Rütten & Loening, 1963.

Pinson, Koppel S. *Modern Germany: Its History and Civilization.* New York: Macmillan, 1954.

Piscator, Erwin. *Das politische Theater.* Berlin: Adalbert Schultz Verlag, 1929.

———. "Supplement au Théatre politique, 1930-1960." *Théatre Populaire*, No. 47 (1962), 1-22.

Polgar, Alfred. *Handbuch des Kritikers.* Zürich: Verlag Oprecht, 1938.

Rasch, Wolfdietrich. "Brechts marxistischer Lehrer." *Merkur* XVII (1963), 989-1003.

Rathenau, Walther. *Gesammelte Schriften.* Berlin: S. Fischer Verlag, 1918.

Reich, Bernhard. "Bemühungen um Brecht im Sowjettheater." *Theater der Zeit* XX (1965), 28-30.

———. "Erinnerungen an den jungen Brecht." *Sinn und Form* Special Brecht Number II, 431-436.

———. "Erinnerungen an Brecht." *Theater der Zeit* XXI (1966), Heft 14, Supplement.

Rilke, Rainer Maria. *Briefe aus Muzot: 1921 bis 1926*. Leipzig: Insel Verlag, 1936.
——. *Gesammelte Gedichte*. Frankfurt-am-Main: Insel Verlag, 1962.
——. *Tagebücher aus der Frühzeit*. Leipzig: Insel Verlag, 1942.
Rimbaud, Arthur. *Rimbaud*. Introduced and ed. by Oliver Bernard. Baltimore: Penguin Books, 1962.
Rosenberg, Arthur. *Entstehung und Geschichte der Weimarer Republik*. Frankfurt-am-Main: Europäische Verlagsanstalt, 1955.
Rubiner, Ludwig. *Die Gewaltlosen*. Potsdam: Gustav Kiepenheuer, 1919.
——. *Der Mensch in der Mitte*. Kiepenheuer, 1920.
Rühle, Jürgen. *Das gefesselte Theater*. Köln-Wien: Kiepenheuer & Witsch, 1957.
——. *Literatur und Revolution*. Kiepenheuer & Witsch, 1960.
Rülicke, Käthe. "Die heilige Johanna der Schlachthöfe." *Sinn und Form* XI (1959), 429-444.
——. "Zur Theorie des epischen Theaters." *Theater der Zeit* XVI (Sept. 1961), 64-72; (Oct. 1961), 64-72.
Rülicke-Weiler, Käthe. *Die Dramaturgie Brechts: Drama als Mittel der Veränderung*. Berlin: Henschelverlag, 1966.
Schuhmann, Klaus. *Der Lyriker Bertolt Brecht: 1913-1933*. Berlin: Rütten & Loening, 1964.
Sartre, Jean-Paul. "Brecht et les classiques." *World Theatre* VII (1958), 11-19.
Schrimpf, Hans Joachim. *Lessing und Brecht*. Pfullingen: Neske, 1965.
Schmidt, Dieter. *"Baal" und der junge Brecht*. Stuttgart: J. B. Metzler, 1966.
Schumacher, Ernst. *Die dramatischen Versuche Bertolt Brechts 1918-1933*. Berlin: Rütten & Loening, 1955.
——. *Bertolt Brechts "Leber des Galilei."* Berlin: Henschelverlag, 1965.
Seghers, Anna. "Helene Weigel spielt in Paris." *Internationale Literatur* 1938, Heft 4, 126-127.
Serreau, Geneviève. *Bertolt Brecht: Dramaturge*. Paris: L'Arche, 1955.
Schevill, James. "Bertolt Brecht in New York." *Tulane Drama Review* VI (1961), 98-107.
Sinclair, Upton. *The Jungle*. New York: Harper and Brothers, 1951.
Singer, Kurt. *The Laughton Story*. Philadelphia: John C. Winston, 1954.
Sinn und Form. Beiträge zur Literatur. Special Brecht Number I (1949).
Sinn und Form Special Brecht Number II (1957). (Erstes und zweites Sonderheft Bertolt Brecht). Berlin: Rütten & Loening.
Snyder, Louis L. *From Bismarck to Hitler*. Williamsport, 1935.

Sokel, Walter H. *The Writer in Extremis*: Expressionism in Twentieth-Century German Literature. Stanford: Stanford University Press, 1959.

Sorge, Reinhard. *Der Bettler*. Berlin: S. Fischer Verlag, 1912.

Spaethling, Robert H. "Bertolt Brecht and the Communist Manifesto." *Germanic Review* XXXVII (1962), 282-291.

————. "Zu Bertolt Brechts Cäsar-Fragment." *Neophilologus* XLV (1961), 213-217.

Sternberg, Fritz. *Der Dichter und die Ratio*: Erinnerungen an Bertolt Brecht. Göttingen: Sachse & Pohl, 1963.

Szondi, Peter. *Theorie des modernen Dramas*. Frankfurt-am-Main: Suhrkamp Verlag, 1963.

Théatre Populaire. Special Brecht Number, Jan.-Feb. 1955, No. 11.

Thieme, Karl. "Des Teufels Gebetbuch." *Hochland* XXXIX (1932), 397-413.

The Third Reich: A Study published under the Auspices of the International Council for Philosophy. Ed. by Maurice Baumont, John H. Fried, and Edmond Vermeil. New York: Frederick A. Praeger, 1955.

Toller, Ernst. *Prosa, Briefe, Dramen, Gedichte*. Hamburg: Rowohlt Verlag, 1961.

Tretyakov, Sergei. "Bert Brecht." *International Literature*, May 1937, No. 5, 60-70.

Tucholsky, Kurt. *Gesammelte Werke*. 3 vols. Hamburg: Rowohlt Verlag, 1960-1961.

Tulane Drama Review. Special Brecht Number, vol. VI, No. 1 (1961).

Tynan, Kenneth. *Curtains*. New York: Athenaeum, 1961.

Valentin, Karl. *Gesammelte Werke*. Munich: Piper Verlag, 1962.

Vinaver, Michel. "Stanislavski et Brecht." *Théatre Populaire*, No. 32 (1958), 17-28.

Waley, Arthur. *The No-Plays of Japan*. New York: Alfred A. Knopf, 1922.

————. *Translations from the Chinese*. Knopf, 1941.

Wedekind, Frank. *Prosa-Dramen-Verse*. Munich: Albert Langen (n.d.).

Weideli, Walter. *Bertolt Brecht*. Paris: Pierre Seghers, 1954.

Weigel, Helene. *Helene Weigel, Actress*. Texts by Bertolt Brecht, Photos by Gerda Goedhart. Tr. by John Berger and Anna Bostock. Leipzig: VEB Edition, 1961.

Weill, Kurt. "Gestus in Music." *Tulane Drama Review* VI (1961), No. 1, 28-32.

Werfel, Franz. *Gesänge aus den drei Reichen*. Leipzig: Kurt Wolff Verlag, 1917.

Willett, John. *The Theatre of Bertolt Brecht*: A Study from Eight Aspects. Norfolk, Conn.: New Directions, 1959.

Wintzen, René. *Bertolt Brecht*. Paris: Pierre Seghers, 1954.

Wolf, Friedrich. *Aufsätze über Theater*. Berlin: Aufbau Verlag, 1952.

Zimmermann, Werner. *Brechts "Leben des Galilei."* Düsseldorf: Verlag Schwann, 1965.

[In addition, numerous articles on Brecht have appeared in the *Tulane Drama Review* and *Modern Drama* (U.S.A.); *Encore* (Gt. Britain); *Théatre Populaire* (France); *Theater Heute* (West Germany); *Theater der Zeit* (East Germany); *Sipario* and *Il Dramma* (Italy).]

Index

555

THIS BOOK has been set in Linotype Granjon, a face named in honor of Robert Granjon, a sixteenth-century French type founder and printer, but based chiefly on designs by the great Claude Garamond. It is thought by many to resemble Garamond's types more closely than do any of the widely-used faces which bear his name today.

Format by Arthur Smith